The Short Story in Louisiana, 1880-1990

The Short Story in Louisiana, 1880-1990

edited by
Mary Dell Fletcher

Published by The Center for Louisiana Studies
University of Southwestern Louisiana
Lafayette, Louisiana

Second Edition
Library of Congress Catalog Number: 93-72884
ISBN Number: 0-940984-84-9

Copyright © 1993
University of Southwestern Louisiana

Published by The Center for Louisiana Studies
P.O. Box 40831
University of Southwestern Louisiana
Lafayette, LA 70504-0831

CONTENTS

POST LOCAL COLORISTS   (1930-1980)

ANOTHER DECADE   (1980-1990)

PREFACE

Selection of stories for this second edition builds on the first. It includes most of same stories, yet it broadens the scope of the work by including two older stories—a novelette and a short story—and three new stories, written after the first edition was published. As in the first preparation, I read many stories and with great difficulty chose only a few. Since my purpose was and is to depict Louisiana in short fiction, I did not consider stories by native writers set in other areas of the country. At the same time, I have not confined my selection of writers to native Louisianians. Most of the twenty-six stories are by native writers; others are by writers who spent a good portion of their lives here.

This edition has other new features. Following each story is a critical commentary. It is not meant to be an exhaustive study, but rather an attempt to place the story in the context of Louisiana short fiction as well as point out its significant literary features. While these commentaries will not take the place of the teachers' lectures, they might prove useful to students when teachers require reading without class discussion. In addition to the commentaries, I have added "Short Fiction for Further Reading." Although it is not a comprehensive bibliography, this feature should prove helpful in student research. In preparing this list, I used Lizzie Carter McVoy's *A Bibliography of Fiction by Louisianians and on Louisiana* Subjects (LSU Press, 1940), Dorothy Brown and Barbara Ewell's "Louisiana Women Writers: a Bibliography" in *Louisiana Women Writers* (LSU Press, 1992), and several bibliographies of Southern and American authors. For biographical material, I relied on *Southern Writers: a Biographical Dictionary.*

INTRODUCTION

Much of the way of life in Louisiana in the last century is revealed in these few selected short stories. The short story as a literary form was just coming into its own a hundred years ago; and although its very shortness precludes depiction of the kind of sweeping historical changes often found in the novel, it does offer brief glimpses of life in a particular time and place, thus reflecting segments of history. The segments in these stories give pictures of Louisiana from antebellum plantation days to the present as it has been portrayed by writers of short fiction.

It is an accepted fact that no period can be properly understood or assessed without a critical examination of its literature. Because the historian's account is objective, it often lacks life. And while creative writers add life and then search for its meaning, it is left to the critic to examine in retrospect—to flesh out and interpret both the historical and literary account—by bringing to light ideas, images, and attitudes that lie buried in literature. In view of the recent national emphasis on the contribution of minority groups to the cultural shaping of this country, it is essential to look to literature, the pages of history being conspicuously empty. Of particular value is local color literature, which is by its very nature concerned with minority groups. It may be too early to grasp larger patterns of meaning in twentieth-century literature in general; and to search for such patterns in one literary genre, in one geographical area, will surely produce no startling revelations. However, a chronological reading of these stories should provide some insight into the past as well as an understanding of the value of local literature in revealing fundamental attitudes.

The best in American fiction has always had a strong provincial flavor. From Nathaniel Hawthorne in the East to Mark Twain in the West to William Faulkner in the South, life has been interpreted in terms of the writer's particular culture, the local quality often being more immediately perceptible than the universal. Flannery O' Connor, who drew her material from her native Georgia, yet gave it universal appeal, was especially proud of the regional quality in her writing:

ix

> To call yourself a Georgia writer is certainly to declare a limitation, but one which, like all other limitations, is a gateway to reality. It is a great blessing, perhaps the greatest blessing a writer can have, to find at home what others have to go elsewhere seeking.[1]

Although from the beginning, local peculiarities of life and landscape have assumed large proportions in American literature, local color writing—the kind of fiction that exploits surface peculiarities—geographical and cultural eccentricities—was not dominant until after the Civil War. The beginning of the local color movement in short fiction is usually associated with Bret Harte and his colorful stories of mining camps, robust characters, and picturesque mountainous settings which captivated Eastern audiences. The main rush of local color fiction came in the four decades between 1890 and 1930 with the popularization of magazines and the consequent development of a mass literary taste that craved a brief glimpse into an alien way of life. Just as Harte won popular success with his stories of miners and outlaws of the West, Sarah Orne Jewett and Mary Wilkins Freeman delighted readers with accounts of rural New England life, and Joel Chandler Harris and George Washington Cable recorded life in their particular areas of the South. Local color writing departed to some extent from the romantic fiction of the antebellum period in its attempt to achieve realism through concrete details and dialect; but local color by its very nature is romantic, for it selects whatever is unusual or different, seldom concerning itself, as does realistic writing, with the average, ordinary, or typical.

It is possible for local color literature to emerge from any region, but the most appealing subject matter has always been found in remote or exotic areas where both culture and landscape depart furthest from the norm, particularly the Anglo-American norm and its environs. Thus Louisiana, unusual in its combination of large Latin, as well as African, population and semi-tropical landscape provides abundant material for local colorists and regional writers. Lewis P. Simpson described it as "the most special place [in the

---

[1]The Regional Writer," in *Mystery and Manners*, ed. Sally and Robert Fitzgerald (New York: Farrar Strauss and Giroux, 1957), p. 54.

South] in the sense of local color,"[2] and Merrill M. Skaggs, as "the only state with [literary] stereotypes based not only on class and geography, but also on national origins."[3]

The state is diverse, of course, in both culture and terrain and indeed is often referred to as North and South Louisiana, these directional designations having far more to do with life style than with geography. The low-lying bayou country of the South was settled early by French and Spanish Roman Catholics who brought with them their Latin culture and who readily adapted to the hot humid climate. The northern part was settled later, largely by Scotch-Irish Protestants to whom the red clay hills were as unyielding as their Calvinistic God. In topography and national origins, as well as in religious persuasion, this portion of the state is far closer to William Faulkner's Yoknapatawpha country than to its southern half. Struck by the dichotomous nature of the state, A. J. Liebling in *The Earl of Louisiana* compares its political balance of southern Catholics and northern Protestants to that of Moslems and Christians in Lebanon.[4] Although an assimilation of population has occurred over the years, the difference in lifestyle is still noticeable and is often characterized in contrasting stereotypes— the happy-go-lucky Creole or Cajun who can frolic on Saturday night and have his sins absolved on Sunday morning as opposed to the uptight Protestant who may well frolic but whose theology denies him this access to God.

Local color fiction relies heavily on such stereotypes;[5] that is, it generally presents a character or scene in terms of outstanding features already established in literature. A character, for example, is given qualities previously associated with not only his religion but also his race or nationality: in Louisiana, the proud Creole, the big-hearted Cajun, the comic Black, the tragic mulatto. And since colorful characters usually suggest a colorful background, a picturesque awe-inspiring landscape is present in many stories.

[2]Preface to *The Collected Works of Ada Jack Carver*, ed. and with an introduction by Mary Dell Fletcher (Natchitoches, La.: N. S. U. Press, 1980), xiv.

[3]*The Folk of Southern Fiction* (Athens: University of Georgia Press, 1972), p. 146.

[4](Louisiana State University Press, 1970), p. 18.

[5]George Washington Cable's "Posson Jone" is structured around such a contrast.

Like characters it unfolds in terms of the reader's previous association and expectations: raging tidal waves of the gulf, unleashed fury of the flooding Mississippi, sluggish bayous and rivers, salty marshlands, and spreading moss-filled oaks. Often the landscape, rendered in highly poetic language, functions only to create atmosphere and exists more figuratively than functionally.

The best of these early local colorists managed to subdue the exotic, to transcend local concerns for universal themes, but most succumbed to the temptation of exploiting the strange and colorful. The heterogeneous population was naturally appealing: Negroes, Creoles, Acadians, Indians, and various other mixtures speaking colorful patois and dwelling in quaint communities provide the subject matter for these stories. Strictly speaking, the literary image of Louisiana produced by these local colorists relates more closely to the southern than to the northern part of the state, particularly to New Orleans, which was attractive because of its large foreign element. The French Quarter with its unusual old-world atmosphere, its historic buildings, flop-houses, internationally famous restaurants, antique shops, and motley assortment of inhabitants has always been interesting to the artist; in fact, during the twenties it became a sort of Greenwich Village or Left Bank, counting among its population Sherwood Anderson, Roark Bradford, and William Faulkner; later it attracted such literary personalities as Tennessee Williams, Katherine Ann Porter, Eudora Welty, and Walker Percy. Predominately Anglo-American North Louisiana lacked the exotic qualities to stir the literary imagination, an understandable fact considering that most early local colorists were themselves Anglo-Americans and did not regard their own people as either unusual or artistically stimulating.[6]

The stories in this collection all have the flavor of Louisiana and are representative in both subject matter and style of short fiction in Louisiana for the last century. They begin in 1879 with the depiction of antebellum Creole society by George Washington

---

[6]Natchitoches, in northwest Louisiana, is the exception. Founded as an outpost in 1714 by Louis Juchereau de St. Denis and settled by French, and later Spanish colonists, it is more closely related in culture to southern Louisiana and hence appears often in local color stories.

Cable, the first Louisiana short story writer to achieve national prominence, and end with the probing of the values of modern technological society, with one concern constant—racial relations. If we use as a dividing line the early 1930s, the date associated with both the final phases of the local color period and the beginning of the Southern Renaissance, we note a decrease in the tendency to set off and analyze quaint features of a group or culture and more interest in the development of a character as a product of his environment. For example, the rendering of dialect through accurate painstaking transcription, characteristic of most early writers, gave way to the sprinkling of a few dialectal features to convey both local and individual character. The newer writers, influenced by naturalism, searched for wider and deeper meanings in the local picture, using landscape, local customs, and speech to probe into both psychological and moral issues. Nevertheless, the break was neither sharp nor sudden: the tradition of local color fiction was strong and its roots deep, and most of the short fiction produced since the 1930s has precedence in the earlier literature. Viewing the stories according to subject matter—racial and national groups and conventions associated with them—will best point up continuity with and divergence from the local color tradition. If from the vantage point of the present, the picture of minority groups seems less than accurate and contradicts our present assessment of them, we must place it in historical context and derive from it the sensibility of the age.

LOCAL COLORISTS (1880-1930)

The cultural eccentricities of the Latin groups, both Creoles and Acadians, provided material for the early local colorists, particularly George Washington Cable, Grace King, and Kate Chopin. Cable's fiction established the stereotype for both the Creole and the Acadian. Although King and Chopin criticized Cable's unfavorable depiction of the Creoles, they did little to correct it. In *Creoles of Louisiana* Cable defines *Creole* rather loosely as "any native of French or Spanish by either parent, whose non-alliance with the slave race entitled him to social rank," a definition which offended many Creoles since they claimed aristocratic descent. Although Cable endows his fictional Creoles with grace and *gaiété de coeur*, he attributes to them as a "race" such negative features as wastefulness, contempt for honest labor, and excessive pride in lineage and family name. His lengthy description of the protagonist DeCharleu in "Belles Demoiselles Plantation" fits most of his Creoles:

> He had had his vices,—all his life; but had borne them, as his race do, with a serenity of conscience and a cleanness of mouth that left no outward blemish on the surface of the gentleman. He had gambled in Royal Street, drank hard in Orleans Street, run his adversary through in the duelling-ground at Slaughterhouse Point, and danced and quarrelled at the St. Philippe-street-theatre quadroon balls. Even now, with all his courtesy and bounty, and a hospitality which seemed to be entertaining angels, he was bitter-proud and penurious, and deep down in his hard-finished heart loved nothing but himself, his name, and his motherless children.

DeCharleu's excessive vanity leads him to try to outwit DeCarlos (Injun Charlie), his half-breed cousin, in a property exchange; but cheating a blood kinsman is impossible for him just as it would be for any other Creole. According to Cable's fiction, all Creoles are alike: they allow family ties to triumph over morality.

The Creoles of neither King nor Chopin differ markedly from those of Cable; however they, as well as other local colorists, soften the features attributed to those people and avoid such sweeping statements about them as a "race." King's stories, like Cable's, deal largely with Creoles in New Orleans and present a stereotyped picture of what she referred to as "the brilliant little world of New Orleans"—"the ease, idleness, extravagance, self-indulgence, pomp, pride, arrogance, in short the whole enumeration, the moral *sine qua non* of the wealthy slaveholder of aristocratic descents and tastes" (*Balcony Stories*). Idalia of "La Grande Demoiselle" is a typical Creole according to the stereotype—arrogant, undisciplined, wasteful, contemptuous, the darling of antebellum society. King does allow her to change, however, but is ambiguous about what causes the change.

Although Chopin sets some of her stories in New Orleans, a large number are set in the Natchitoches area and deal with both plantation aristocracy and the lower classes who tenant the land. The general stereotype she accepts and uses, especially in her earlier stories, but she often pictures the Creole woman as an individual seeking self-identity. In "The Story of an Hour" Mrs. Mallard dreams of personal freedom but never achieves it; in *The Awakening* Edna Pontellier, an Anglo-American living in a Creole society, defies all Creole conventions but is defeated not by the society but by herself.

Acadians (Cajuns) are to be distinguished from Creoles, who claim aristocratic connections. A group of French peasants originally from northern France who were exiled from Nova Scotia during the French and Indian War, the Acadians eventually settled in the Bayou Teche area of southwestern Louisiana. Looked down upon by the haughty Creoles, Cajuns are usually depicted far more positively in literature: they are proud but not arrogant, their pride stemming from their own resources rather than their lineage. As portrayed by Cable, King, and Chopin, they are hardworking but respectable, uneducated but big-hearted people who love group merriment—dances, shrimp festivals, and jambalayas. Cable's picture of Acadian life in "Bonaventure" is idyllic: Cajuns, a rustic people with strong family ties who graze their herds in the marshlands, are oblivious to and independent of the outside world. Weddings are rude but colorful, occasions for great excitement: "loud calls and outcries, children . . . shouting and running, women's heads thrust out[doors], horsemen . . . dashing into the village."

Chopin's "A Night in Acadie" is a typical picture of hardworking Cajuns taking pleasure at a Saturday night dance; it stands in sharp contrast to the picture of the brilliant Creole soirees in New Orleans. Attended by the entire family, the dance is held in Foche's big bulky weather-beaten house. Outside are ponies, wagons, and carts, along with a mammoth pot of gumbo that bubbles and steams as chickens, ham, onions, sage, and garlic are tossed into it. Inside the guests assemble for the all-night festivity.

Love (particularly unrequited) is very much a part of the literature of the Acadians, perhaps because of the tragic love story of Evangeline and Gabriel, which epitomizes their wanderings and hardships. Cable's love story "Bonaventure" is a variation of the unrequited love theme; so is King's "The Story of a Day." Charles Tenney Jackson's story, set in the "lily-filled" bayous of Acadian country, does not concern Cajuns except in a peripheral way. Like

Cable's "Bonaventure," his story is romantic; his one Cajun character, a girl for whom the Texan is searching, is highly idealized.

Early local color writers with their inherent interest in the exotic rather than in the ordinary were naturally attracted to the Negro[7] as a subject. Seen through the eyes of a white middle-class narrator, the Negro is quaint and curious, not altogether understandable but nevertheless fascinating. As in depicting the Latin groups. the local colorist nearly always stands at a distance, the distance in this case being much greater. This method of presentation, which actually involves no more than taking long-established conventions in American literature and building a plot around them, allows the Negro no individuality. He is treated humorously as a comic figure or sentimentally as a long-suffering servant, but in either case entirely loyal and obedient to the white man, thus indicating his master's goodness. As a source of entertainment, he is naturally endowed with qualities that amuse white people, the humor often being based on condescension. Sometimes the writer's attitude is one of benevolent or tender amusement at Negro customs and beliefs, as in Ruth McEnery Stuart's stories of the romantic affairs of plantation Negroes or Roark Bradford's plantation hands who narrate Old Testament stories in an amusing childlike manner. Somewhat less patronizing in their depiction of variation from the norm are writers who are fascinated by the mystique of the culture on which they base their stories. Lyle Saxon's "Cane River" reveals seething, teeming sexuality and primal emotions unrepressed by white man's mores; and stories by Mollie Moore Davis, Ada Jack Carver, and several others, concern the mysteries surrounding the blue-gum Negro whose bite, according to local lore, is fatal. The well-known contention in anti-stereotype criticism that the Negro has met with as great

[7]Conscious of the connotations of *Negro* and *Black*, I use the terms cautiously, as well as purposefully. In discussing early literature, I use Negro. It seems more fitting, not only because it is used in the literature but also because it suggests the economic and social servitude that is a part of the history of the region; its associations convey not only the white man's attitude toward the Negro but also the Negro's self-concept. In discussing modern stories, those written after the rise of Black consciousness (overt expressions of racial pride and social equality), I prefer the term *Black*. It suggests dignity.

injustice in American literature as he has in American life is surely borne out in the Louisiana short story.

A very compelling theme in local color literature is the tragic results of miscegenation; therefore a totally different stereotype developed for the part-Negro, particularly the female, who is usually depicted as a sad, tragic figure with no identity. She is highly idealized—good, sweet, and beautiful; she dreams of a miracle that will reveal she is really white; and she is associated with illicit love. In nearly all of the stories, the young woman of mixed blood discovers at the end that she is actually white; thus the stories end happily.

Through his portrayal of mulattoes, quadroons, and octoroons and the way of life forced on them by New Orleans Creole society, Cable's stories speak out against the injustice of a system that condoned such inhumanity. Since his feelings on racial inequality were strong, his portraits are usually highly romantic, his heroines often catalogs of virtue. Madam John in "'Tite Poulette" is a lady of the quadroon balls whose sweet smile suggests sorrow; she is an unselfish, devoted hardworking protective mother, as well as the "best yellow-fever nurse around." Cable never hints of moral judgment: Madam John's only shame is the shame she feels: "Sin made me, yes." The position of the quadroon woman is not quite so clear cut in King's writings. Most are treated as prostitutes living outside the moral code in splendid New Orleans brothels; however, in "Monsieur Motte" King idealizes the loyalty of a quadroon woman to the daughter of her former mistress, and in "Little Convent" she presents the pathetic story of a child who cannot bear to live with the stigma of mixed blood.

Chopin, Lyle Saxon, and Ada Jack Carver treat the plight of the Cane River free-mulatto, a very special case since their ancestors once owned large plantations on Isle Brevelle in the Natchitoches area. (Most trace their lineage back to Thomas Metoyer, a French planter and Coin Coin, his slave and mistress, in the early 1700s). These people of mixed racial stock, who were rejected by whites and who themselves rejected Negroes, occupied an indeterminate position in the complex cast system of Cane River country. In Chopin's "Little Free Mulatto," little Aurelia "was not permitted to play with the white children up at the big house . . .

neither was she allowed in any way to associate with the little darkies"; in "Désirée's Baby" the husband drives both Désirée and her baby from their home when he suspects that Désirée has mixed blood. The title of Lyle Saxon's novel *Children of Strangers* points up the pathos in their lack of identity. The displacement in modern society of the proud people of Isle Brevelle who "once lived in clover and even owned slaves" but who are now scorned even by Negroes is the subject of Carver's "The Old One." Her much-anthologized "Redbone" deals with a people "forever beyond the pale," a mixture composed of "Spanish, French, and Indian, and God knows what besides." Carver once explained in an interview that "God knows what besides" indicates Negro blood, that Redbones had been classed as Negroes by the federal courts.

POST LOCAL COLORISTS (1930-1980s)

Most modern Louisiana writers are now aware of the problems involved in depicting Louisiana in fiction. They recognize that fascination with the colorful or exotic inevitably diminishes the artistic imagination. Modern interest in psychological development of character has shifted the emphasis from the external—cultural peculiarities—to the internal—workings of the mind, and in doing so has revealed not differences but similarities. Thus their characters, however colorful in speech and mannerisms, experience the same loneliness, doubt, fear, frustration, love, ambition of people everywhere. Although traces of cultural and geographical stereotypes are still discernible, they rarely serve as the focus. Most of the post-local-color writers, for example, when using a colorful setting or depicting unusual speech or manners, use these features as a backdrop against which they unfold their narratives.

The French groups—Creole and Cajun—still appear, since southern Louisiana is still predominately French. But their national heritage is rarely taken into account, except in a peripheral way—names, idioms of speech, details of setting that establish a strong sense of place. Writers do not depend upon local material for effect, as did the early local colorists.

John Hazard Wildman's "A House in Arabia," set in South Louisiana French culture at a time when traditional family ties and obligations are disappearing, treats the universal problem of old age in the modern context of institutionalization. The dichotomous landscape—sugarcane fields and commerce-laden river—conveys a strong sense of place, but the focus is not on landscape or Cajun ways; in fact the old man seems scarcely related to the industrious fun-loving people of early local color.[8] Also set in Acadian country is John William Corrington's "Every Act Whatever of Man," a story that utilizes both landscape and sensibility of this Roman Catholic culture to explore moral and ethical problems involving euthansia. Although multiple viewpoints point up the complexity of the problem, the major voice is that of an aging attorney who is deeply grieved by modern-day attitudes toward life and death.

Throughout the 1920s and 1930s most white writers portrayed black characters chiefly as sources of humor or specimens of genuine interest. However, during the 1930's Negro writer Arna Bontemps, determined to correct the stereotype of his people, revealed the thoughts and emotions of his Negro characters, thus giving them individuality and universality. Except for his designation of the family as "black" in "A Summer Tragedy" the story could just as well be the tragedy of any poor family, for nothing in the fear and despair of the old couple is unique to their race. Bontemps' stories notwithstanding, the literary portrait of the Negro continued to be simplistic, without depth or complexity, and to have either a sentimental or condescending tone.

The partial assimilation of the Black into white society, brought about largely by civil rights legislation, has made him a less frequently treated subject, either because much of his native culture has been lost or the strangeness, the remoteness, depicted by earlier writers, has diminished on close contact. The focus is no longer on his quaintness: the tone is no longer condescending or sentimental. A frequently used framework is the white narrator who, while focusing on civil rights problems, reveals his own burden of guilt. Thus new stereotypes have been created—the

[8]Although Moreau is a Creole name, the old man seems to be of peasant stock, probably a mixture of Cajun and Creole. The surnames of his grandsons—Landry and Boudreaux (both Cajun)—denote the intermarriage of the groups.

Black activist and his sympathetic white liberal brother. Many of the newer stories are ideological and the tone polemical, showing less concern with the Black as an individual than with social and political issues. Junius Edwards' story, for example, depicts a Black ex-soldier's test of endurance in trying to register to vote. There are numerous variations, however, each writer bringing his own vision and creativity into his work.

The best fictional treatment of Blacks comes from Ernest Gaines. Although he understands and sympathizes with the problems of his people, he maintains aesthetic distance when treating them. "Just Like a Tree" tells the poignant story of family bonds and closeness through a series of ten interior monologues, eight of which are given to family members. Although a racial problem is the pivot on which the entire story turns, it remains in the background; in the forefront is the strength of Aunt Fe, who is "just like a tree." This story, like others by Gaines, deals most directly with the Black as a human being, with universals such as love and hate, pride and fear, old age and death. Although his stories are rooted firmly in the bayou country where Blacks are still economically deprived, they present inequality not in doctrinal but in cosmic terms.

Most white writers, realizing the inherent difficulties in portraying the consciousness of the Black, continue to rely on the external viewpoint. Shirley Ann Grau, for example, uses this viewpoint to great advantage in developing her Black characters as individuals without regard to race. By recording the simple physical responses and almost mechanical actions of her characters in "The Way of a Man," she suggests their emptiness, loneliness, and inability to feel; and by restricting the action to a few Black characters who have no interaction with the white community, she develops them as human beings sharing a common human condition—spiritual alienation in a meaningless world. The exotic landscape, though functional, is subdued: the lonely stretches of coastal marshes are tied firmly to plot and theme, and the impenetrable fog suggests the impermeable membrane of the young man's estrangement.

With realism firmly entrenched in American literature by the 1930s, a few Louisiana writers, searching for the typical, looked to Anglo-American groups. The stories included here are eclectic and have no common denominator other than treatment of middle-class whites, which has been rare in the short fiction of Louisiana; but they complete the cross section of the state and its population. The plight of the white sharecropper during the depression is revealed in Elma Godchaux's protrayal of a sensitive farm wife whose daily physical and mental struggles convey an overwhelming sense of futility. Louisiana politics—its powerful machine, its capacity to corrupt—is the subject of James Aswell's "The Shadow of Evil" in which a young gubernatorial aspirant experiences moral degradation.

Generally speaking these Louisiana writers, like other Southern writers, care little for the typical or commonplace of the realist or for surface peculiarities of the local colorist, preferring instead psychologically unusual characters, those who behave unconventionally or compulsively. "A Christmas Memory" shows Truman Capote's attraction to the unusual, and while the setting is not definitely Louisiana, the Southern flavor of life—attitudes, customs, idioms—are typical of rural North Louisiana. A shocking view of a modern New Orleans family emerges in Ellen Gilchrist's "Rich"; and her portrayal of New Orleans Uptown society suggests that members of it are normal only on the surface.

ANOTHER DECADE (1980-1990)

Three newer stories have been added to this second edition, and the fact that all three are set in South Louisiana suggests that the area continues to be most artistically stimulating to the writer. In David Madden's "The New Orleans of Possibilities" the protagonist, bored with the standard tourist attractions, spends his morning in a sleazy flea market; and while the romance of the city is present, it is kept in the background. Andre Dubus dramatizes the story of a boy's growing awareness of racial inequality and his empathy with Blacks in a southern Louisiana city. In the style of Eudora Welty, Martha Lacy Hall brings a bit of humor to the Louisiana scene. Blending the serious with the comic, she recounts a woman's journey to a funeral with a brother too fat to fit into her car.

Although varied in subject matter and technique, the stories in this collection reveal much of Louisiana's social and literary history in the last century. Moving from a relatively simple agrarian society (urban New Orleans notwithstanding) to a complex technological one with problems relating to depersonalization, these stories begin and end with a consciousness of social inequality. Changes in the way of life are reflected in literary techniques, for with emphasis on social and cultural integration came also an emphasis on integration of fictional elements. With a more unified view of their culture around them, the best of these contemporary writers, unlike early local colorists, are able to see wider and deeper meanings in the landscape and customs and hence to transcend, while at the same time use, local elements. But whatever the influence of intellectual or literary currents, these short story writers, like creative writers of any age, had their own originality to draw on. They combined tradional material and contemporary ideas in a fresh way, each with a distinct style. The stories in this collection are intended to illustrate not only the change in literary and social trends but also to illustrate individual talent of these writers. Neither the selection of the stories nor my comments are intended to suggest the superiority in either form or matter of one literary period over another; for although fiction changes to reflect the tastes and concerns of its age, change in the world of art signifies neither improvement nor decline.

The Short Story in Louisiana, 1880-1990

George Washington Cable

(1844-1925)

The first Louisiana short story writer to gain national recognition, Cable was born in New Orleans on October 12, 1844. After service in the Civil War and employment with the New Orleans *Picayune*, Cable began writing short fiction about New Orleans. In 1879 he published *Old Creole Days*, followed shortly by *The Grandissimes* and *Madame Delphine*, stories dealing with Creole insensitivity and racial injustice. He continued to explore these topics in both fiction and non-fiction even after his unpopularity caused him to move to the North. In spite of their local color surface and such shortcomings as sentimentality and open bias, his stories transcend the purely topical and offer insight into the human condition. He ranks in the forefront of American local colorists. The stories printed below first appeared in *Scribner's Monthly* in 1874 and became a part of his first collection *Old Creole Days* in 1879.

Belles Demoiselles Plantation

George Washington Cable

The original grantee was Count _____, assume the name to be
De Charleu; the old Creoles never forgive a public mention. He was
the French king's commissary. One day, called to France to explain
the lucky accident of the commissariat having burned down with
his account-books inside, he left his wife, a Choctaw Comptesse,
behind.

Arrived at court, his excuses were accepted, and that tract
granted him where afterwards stood Belles Demoiselles
Plantation. A man cannot remember every thing! In a fit of forgetfulness he married a French gentlewoman, rich and beautiful, and
"brought her out." However, "All's well that ends well;" a famine
had been in the colony, and the Choctaw Comptesse had starved,
leaving nought but a half-caste orphan family lurking on the edge
of the settlement, bearing our French gentlewoman's own new name,
and being mentioned in Monsieur's will.

And the new Comptesse—she tarried but a twelve-month, left
Monsieur a lovely son, and departed, led out of this vain world by
the swamp-fever.

From this son sprang the proud Creole family of De Charleu. It
rose straight up, up, up, generation after generation, tall,
branchless, slender, palmlike; and finally, in the time of which I
am to tell, flowered with all the rare beauty of a century-plant, in
Artemise, Innocente, Felicité, the twins Marie and Martha,
Leontine and little Septima; the seven beautiful daughters for
whom their home had been fitly named Belles Demoiselles.

The Count's grant had once been a long Pointe, round which the
Mississippi used to whirl, and seethe, and foam, that it was horrid
to behold. Big whirlpools would open and wheel about in the
savage eddies under the low bank, and close up again, and others
open, and spin, and disappear. Great circles of muddy surface
would boil up from hundreds of feet below, and gloss over, and seem
to float away,—sink, come back again under water, and with only a
soft hiss surge up again, and again drift off, and vanish. Every few
minutes the loamy bank would tip down a great load of earth upon
its besieger, and fall back a foot,—sometimes a yard,—and the

3

writhing river would press after, until at last the Pointe was quite swallowed up, and the great river glided by in a majestic curve, and asked no more; the bank stood fast, the "caving" became a forgotten misfortune, and the diminished grant was a long, sweeping, willowy bend, rustling with miles of sugar-cane.

Coming up the Mississippi in the sailing craft of those early days, about the time one first could descry the white spires of the old St. Louis Cathedral, you would be pretty sure to spy, just over to your right under the levee, Belles Demoiselles Mansion, with its broad veranda and red painted cypress roof, peering over the embankment, like a bird in the nest, half hid by the avenue of willows which one of the departed De Charleus,—he that married a Marot,—had planted on the levee's crown.

The house stood unusually near the river, facing eastward, and standing four-square, with an immense veranda about its sides, and a flight of steps in front spreading broadly downward, as we open arms to a child. From the veranda nine miles of river were seen; and in their compass, near at hand, the shady garden full of rare and beautiful flowers; farther away broad fields of cane and rice, and the distant quarters of the slaves, and on the horizon everywhere a dark belt of cypress forest.

The master was old Colonel De Charleu,—Jean Albert Henri Joseph De Charleu-Marot, and "Colonel" by the grace of the first American governor. Monsieur,—he would not speak to any one who called him "Colonel,"—was a hoary-headed patriarch. His step was firm, his form erect, his intellect strong and clear, his countenance classic, serene, dignified, commanding, his manners courtly, his voice musical,—fascinating. He had had his vices,— all his life; but had borne them, as his race do, with a serenity of conscience and a cleanness of mouth that left no outward blemish on the surface of the gentleman. He had gambled in Royal Street, drank hard in Orleans Street, run his adversary through in the duelling-ground at Slaughter-house Point, and danced and quarrelled at the St. Philippe-street-theatre quadroon balls. Even now, with all his courtesy and bounty, and a hospitality which seemed to be entertaining angels, he was bitter-proud and penurious, and deep down in his hard-finished heart loved nothing but himself, his name, and his motherless children. But these!— their ravishing beauty was all but excuse enough for the unbounded idolatry of their father. Against these seven goddesses he never rebelled. Had they even required him to defraud Old De Carlos—

I can hardly say.

Old De Carlos was his extremely distant relative on the Choctaw side. With this single exception, the narrow thread-like line of descent from the Indian wife, diminished to a mere strand by injudicious alliances, and deaths in the gutters of old New Orleans, was extinct. The name, by Spanish contact, had become De Carlos; but this one surviving bearer of it was known to all, and known only, as Injin Charlie.

One thing I never knew a Creole to do. He will not utterly go back on the ties of blood, no matter what sort of knots those ties may be. For one reason, he is never ashamed of his or his father's sins; and for another,—he will tell you—he is "all heart!"

So the different heirs of the De Charleu estate had always strictly regarded the rights and interests of the De Carloses, especially their ownership of a block of dilapidated buildings in a part of the city, which had once been very poor property, but was beginning to be valuable. This block had much more than maintained the last De Carlos through a long and lazy lifetime, and, as his household consisted only of himself, and an aged and crippled negress, the inference was irresistible that he "had money." Old Charlie, though by *alias* an "Injin," was plainly a dark white man, about as old as Colonel De Charleu, sunk in the bliss of deep ignorance, shrewd, deaf, and, by repute at least, unmerciful.

The Colonel and he always conversed in English. This rare accomplishment, which the former had learned from his Scotch wife, —the latter from upriver traders, —they found an admirable medium of communication, answering, better than French could, a similar purpose to that of the stick which we fasten to the bit of one horse and breast-gear of another, whereby each keeps his distance. Once in a while, too, by way *of* jest, English found its way among the ladies of Belles Demoiselles, always signifying that their sire was about to have business with old Charlie.

Now a long-standing wish to buy out Charlie troubled the Colonel. He had no desire to oust him unfairly; he was proud of being always fair; yet he did long to engross the whole estate under one title. Out of his luxurious idleness he had conceived this desire, and thought little of so slight an obstacle as being already somewhat in debt to old Charlie for money borrowed, and for which Belles Demoiselles was, of course, good, ten times over. Lots, buildings, rents, all, might as well be his, he thought, to give, keep, or destroy. "Had he but the old man's heritage. Ah! he might bring that into existence which his *belles demoiselles* had been begging for, 'since many years;' a home, —and such a home,—in the gay city. Here he should tear down this row of cottages, and make his garden wall; there that long rope-walk should give place to vine-covered arbors; the bakery yonder should make way for a costly conservatory; that wine warehouse should come down, and the mansion go up. It should be the finest in the State. Men should never pass it, but they should say—'the palace of the De Charleus; a family of grant descent, a people of elegance and bounty, a line as old as France, a fine old man, and seven daughters as beautiful as happy; whoever dare attempt to marry there must leave his own name behind him!'"

The house should be of stones fitly set, brought down in ships from the land of 'les Yankees,' and it should have an airy belvedere, with a gilded image tiptœing and shining on its peak, and from it you should see, far across the gleaming folds of the river, the red roof of Belles Demoiselles, the countryseat. At the big stone gate there should be a porter's lodge, and it should be a privilege even to see the ground."

Truly they were a family fine enough, and fancy-free enough to have fine wishes, yet happy enough where they were, to have had no wish but to live there always.

To those, who, by whatever fortune, wandered into the garden of Belles Demoiselles some summer afternoon as the sky was reddening towards evening, it was lovely to see the family gathered out upon the tiled pavement at the foot of the broad front steps, gayly chatting and jesting, with that ripple of laughter that comes so pleasingly from a bevy of girls. The father would be found seated in their midst, the centre of attention and compliment, witness, arbiter, umpire, critic, by his beautiful children's unanimous appointment, but the single vassal, too, of seven absolute sovereigns.

Now they would draw their chairs near together in eager discussion of some new step in the dance, or the adjustment of some rich adornment. Now they would start about him with excited comments to see the eldest fix a bunch of violets in his button hole. Now the twins would move down a walk after some unusual flower, and be greeted on their return with the high pitched notes of delighted feminine surprise.

As evening came on they would draw more quietly about their paternal centre. Often their chairs were forsaken, and they grouped themselves on the lower steps, one above another, and surrendered themselves to the tender influences of the approaching night. At such an hour the passer on the river, already attracted by the dark figures of the broad roofed mansion, and its woody garden standing against the glowing sunset, would hear the voices of the hidden group rise from the spot in the soft harmonies of an evening song; swelling clearer and clearer as the thrill of music warmed them into feeling, and presently joined by the deeper tones of the father's voice; then, as the daylight passed quite away, all would be still, and he would know that the beautiful home had gathered its nestlings under its wings.

And yet, for mere vagary, it pleased them not to be pleased.

"Arti!" called one sister to another in the broad hall, one morning,—mock amazement in her distended eyes, —"something is goin' to took place !"

"*Comme-n-t?*"—long-drawn perplexity. "Papa is goin' to town!"

The news passed up stairs.

"Inno!" —one to another meeting in a doorway, —"something is goin' to took place!"

"*Qu'est-ce que c'est!*"—vain attempt at gruffness.

"Papa is goin' to town !"

The unusual tidings were true. It was afternoon of the same day that the Colonel tossed his horse's bridle to his groom, and stepped up to old Charlie, who was sitting on his bench under a China-tree, his head, as was his fashion, bound in a Madras handkerchief. The "old man" was plainly under the effect of spirits, and smiled a deferential salutation without trusting himself to his feet.

"Eh, well Charlie!"—the Colonel raised his voice to suit his kinsman's deafness,—"how is those times with my friend Charlie?"

"Eh?" said Charlie, distractedly.

"Is that goin' well with my friend Charlie?"

"In de house,—call her,"—making a pretence of rising.

"*Non, non!* I don't want,"—the speaker paused to breathe—"ow is collection?"

"Oh!" said Charlie, "every day he make me more poorer!"

"What do you hask for it?" asked the planter indifferently, designating the house by a wave of his whip.

"Ask for w'at?" said Injin Charlie.

"De *house!* What you ask for it?"

"I don't believe," said Charlie.

"What you would *take* for it!" cried the planter.

"Wait for w'at?"

"What you would *take* for the whole block?"

"I don't want to sell him!"

"I'll give you *ten thousand dollah* for it."

"Ten t'ousand dollah for dis house? On, no, dat is no price. He is blame good old house,—dat old house." (Old Charlie and the Colonel never swore in presence of each other.) "Forty years dat old house didn't had to be paint! I easy can get fifty t'ousand dollah for dat old house."

"Fifty thousand picayunes; yes," said the Colonel.

"She's a good house. Can make plenty money," pursued the deaf man.

"That's what make you so rich, eh, Charlie?"

"*Non,* I don't make nothing. Too blame clever, me, dat's de troub'. She's a good house,—make money fast like a steamboat,—make a barrel full in a week! Me, I lose money all the days. Too blame clever."

"Charlie!"

"Eh?"

"Tell me what you'll take."

"Make? I don't make *nothing. Too* blame clever."

"What will *you take?*"

"Oh! I got enough already,—half drunk now."

"What will you take for the 'ouse?"

"You want to buy her?"

"I don't know,"—(shrug),—"maybe,—if you sell it cheap."

"She's a bully old house."

There was a long silence. By and by old Charlie commenced—

"Old Injin Charlie is a low-down dog."

"*C'est vrai, oui!*" retorted the Colonel in an undertone. "He's got Injin blood in him."

The Colonel nodded assent.

"But he's got some blame good blood, too, ain't it?"

The Colonel nodded impatiently.

"*Bien!* Old Charlie's Injin blood says, 'sell de house, Charlie, you blame old fool!' *Mais,* old Charlie's good blood says, 'Charlie! if you sell dat old house, Charlie, you low-down old dog, Charlie, what de Compte De Charleu make for you grace-gran-muzzer, de dev' can eat you, Charlie, I don't care.'"

"But you'll sell it anyhow, won't you, old man?"

"No!" And the no rumbled off in muttered oaths like thunder out on the Gulf. The incensed old Colonel wheeled and started off.

"Curl!" (Colonel) said Charlie, standing up unsteadily.

The planter turned with an inquiring frown.

"I'll trade with you!" said Charlie.

The Colonel was tempted. "Ow'l you trade?" he asked.

"My house for yours!"

The old Colonel turned pale with anger. He walked very quickly back, and came close up to his kinsman.

"Charlie!" he said.

"Injin Charlie,"—with a tipsy nod.

But by this time self-control was returning. "Sell Belles Demoiselles to you?" he said in a high key, and then laughed "Ho, ho, ho!" and rode away.

A cloud, but not a dark one, overshadowed the spirits of Belles Demoiselles' plantation. The old master, whose beaming presence had always made him a shining Saturn, spinning and sparkling with the bright circle of his daughters, fell into musing fits, started out of frowning reveries, walked often by himself, and heard business from his overseer fretfully. No wonder. The daughters knew his closeness in trade, and attributed to it his failure to negotiate for the Old Charlie buildings,—so to call them.

They began to depreciate Belles Demoiselles. If a north wind blew, it was too cold to ride. If a shower had fallen, it was too muddy to drive. In the morning the garden was wet. In the evening the grasshopper was a burden. *Ennui* was turned into capital; every headache was interpreted a premonition of ague; and when the native exuberance of a flock of ladies without a want or a care burst out in laughter in the father's face, they spread their French eyes, rolled up their little hands, and with rigid wrists and mock vehemence vowed and vowed again that they only laughed at their misery, and should pine to death unless they could move to the sweet city. "Oh! the theatre!   Oh! Orleans Street! Oh! the masquerade! the Place d'Armes! the ball!" and they would call upon Heaven with French irreverence, and fall into each other's arms, and whirl down the hall singing a waltz, end with a grand collision and fall, and, their eyes streaming merriment, lay the blame on the slippery floor, that would some day be the death of the whole seven.

Three times more the fond father, thus goaded, managed, by accident,—business accident,—to see old Charlie and increase his offer; but in vain. He finally went to him formally.

"Eh?" said the deaf and distant relative. "For what you want him, eh? Why you don't stay where you halways be 'appy? Dis is a blame old rat-hole,—good for old Injin Charlie,—da's all. Why you don't stay where you be halways 'appy? Why you don't buy somewhere else?

"That's none of your business," snapped the planter. Truth was, his reasons were unsatisfactory even to himself.

A sullen silence followed.

Then Charlie spoke:

"Well, now, look here; I sell you old Charlie's house."

"*Bien!* and the whole block," said the Colonel.

"Hold on," said Charlie. "I sell you de 'ouse and de block. Den I go and git drunk, and go to sleep; de dev' comes along and says, 'Charlie! old Charlie, you blame low-down old dog, wake up! What you doin' here? Where's de 'ouse what Monsieur le Compte give your grace-gran-muzzer? Don't you see dat fine gentyman, De Charleu, done gone and tore him down and make him over new, you blame old fool, Charlie you low-down old Injin dog!"

"I'll give you forty thousand dollars," said the Colonel.

"For de 'ouse?"

"For all."

The deaf man shook his head.

"Forty-five!" said the Colonel.

"What a lie? For what you tell me 'What a lie?' I don't tell you no lie."

"Non, non ! I give *you forty-five !"* shouted the Colonel.

Charlie shook his head again. "Fifty!" He shook it again. The figures rose and rose.

"Seventy-five!"

The answer was an invitation to go away and let the owner alone, as he was, in certain specified respects, the vilest of living creatures, and no company for a fine gentyman.

The "fine gentyman" longed to blaspheme,—but before old Charlie!—in the name of pride, how could he? He mounted and started away."

Tell you what I'll make wid you," said Charlie.

The other, guessing aright, turned back without dismouting, smiling.

"How much Belles Demoiselles hoes me now?" asked the deaf one.

"One hundred and eighty thousand dollars," said the Colonel, firmly.

"Yass," said Charlie. "I don't want Belles Demoiselles."

The old Colonel's quiet laugh intimated it made no difference either way.

"But me," continued Charlie, "me,—I'm got le Compte De Charleu's blood in me, any'ow,—a litt' bit, any'ow, ain't it?"

The Colonel nodded that it was.

"Bien! If I got out of dis place and don't go to Belles Demoiselles, de peoples will say,—dey will say, 'Old Charlie he been all doze time tell a blame *lie!* He ain't no kin to his old grace-gran-muzzer, not a blame bit! He don't got nary drop of De Charleu blood to save his blame low-down old Injin soul! No, sare! What I want wid money, den? No sare! My place for yours!"

He turned to go into the house, just too soon to see the Colonel make an ugly whisk at him with his riding-whip. Then the Colonel, too, moved off.

Two of three times over, as he ambled homeward, laughter broke through his annoyance, as he recalled old Charlie's family pride and the presumption of his offer. Yet each time he could but think better of—not the offer to swap, but the preposterous ancestral loyalty. It was so much better than he could have expected from his "low-down" relative, and not unlike his own whim withal—the proposition which went with it was forgiven.

This last defeat bore so harshly on the master of Belles Demoiselles, that the daughters, reading chagrin in his face, began to repent. They loved their father as daughters can, and when they saw their pretended dejection harassing him seriously they restrained their complaints, displayed more than ordinary tenderness, and heroically and ostentatiously concluded there was no place like Belles Demoiselles. But the new mood touched him more than the old, and only refined his discontent. Here was a man, rich without the care of riches, free from any real-trouble, happiness as native to his house as perfume to his garden, deliberately, as it were with premeditated malice, taking joy by the shoulder and bidding her be gone to town, whither he might easily have followed, only that the very same ancestral nonsense that kept Injin Charlie from selling the old place for twice its value prevented him from choosing any other spot for a city home.

But by and by the charm of nature and the merry hearts around him prevailed; the fit of exalted sulks passed off, and after a while the year flared up at Christmas, flickered, and went out.

New Year came and passed; the beautiful garden of Belles Demoiselles put on its spring attire; the seven fair sisters moved from rose to rose; the cloud of discontent had warmed into invisible vapor in the rich sunlight of family affection, and on the common memory the only scar of last year's wound was old Charlie's sheer impertinence in crossing the caprice of the De Charleus. The cup of gladness seemed to fill with the filling of the river.

How high that river was! Its tremendous current rolled and tumbled and spun along, hustling the long funeral flotillas of drift,—and how near shore it came! Men were out day and night, watching the levee. On windy nights even the old Colonel took part, and grew light-hearted with occupation and excitement, as every minute the river threw a white arm over the levee's top, as though it would vault over. But all held fast, and, as the summer drifted in, the water sunk down into its banks and looked quite incapable of harm.

On a summer afternoon of uncommon mildness, old Colonel Jean Albert Henri Joseph De Charleu-Marot, being in a mood for revery, slipped the custody of his feminine rulers and sought the crown of the levee, where it was his wont to promenade. Presently he sat upon a stone bench,—a favorite seat. Before him lay his broad-spread fields; near by, his lordly mansion; and being still,—perhaps by female contact,—somewhat sentimental, he fell to musing on his past. It was hardly worthy to be proud of. All its morning was reddened with mad frolic, and far toward the meridian it was marred with elegant rioting. Pride had kept him well-nigh useless, and despised the honors won by valor; gaming had dimmed prosperity; death had taken his heavenly wife; voluptuous ease had mortgaged his lands; and yet his house still stood, his sweet-smelling fields were still fruitful, his name was fame enough; and yonder and yonder, among the trees and flowers, like angels walking in Eden, were the seven goddesses of his only worship.

Just then a slight sound behind him brought him to his feet. He cast his eyes anxiously to the outer edge of the little strip of bank between the levee's base and the river. There was nothing visible. He paused, with his ear toward the water, his face full of frightened expectation. Ha! There came a single plashing sound, like some great beast slipping into the river, and little waves in a wide semi-circle came out from under the bank and spread over the water!

"My God!"

He plunged down the levee and bounded through the low weeds to the edge of the bank. It was sheer, and the water about four feet below. He did not stand quite on the edge, but fell upon his knees a couple of yards away, wringing his hands, moaning and weeping, and staring through his watery eyes at a fine, long crevice just discernible under the matted grass, and curving outward on either hand toward the river.

"My God!" he sobbed aloud; "my God!" and even while he called, his God answered: the tough Bermuda grass stretched and snapped, the crevice slowly became a gape, and softly, gradually, with no sound but the closing of the water at last, a ton or more of earth settled into the boiling eddy and disappeared.

At the same instant a pulse of the breeze brought from the garden behind, the joyous, thoughtless laughter of the fair mistresses of Belles Demoiselles.

The old Colonel sprang up and clambered over the levee. Then forcing himself to a more composed movement, he hastened into the house and ordered his horse.

"Tell my children to make merry while I am gone," he left word. "I shall be back to-night," and the horse's hoofs clattered down a by-road leading to the city.

"Charlie," said the planter, riding up to a window, from which the old man's nightcap was thrust out, "what you say, Charlie,— my house for yours, eh, Charlie—what you say?"

"'Ello!" said Charlie; "from where you come from dis time of to-night?"

"I come from the Exchange in St. Louis Street." (A small fraction of the truth.)

"What you want?" said matter-of-fact Charlie.

"I come to trade."

The low-down relative drew the worsted off his ears. "Oh! yass," he said with an uncertain air.

"Well, old man Charlie, what you say: my house for yours,— like you said,—eh, Charlie?"

"I dunno," said Charlie; "it's nearly mine now. Why you don't stay dare you se'f?"

"Because I don't want!" said the Colonel savagely. "Is dat reason enough for you? You better take me in de notion, old man, I tell you,—yes!"

Charlie never winced; but how his answer delighted the Colonel! Quoth Charlie:

"I don't care—I take him!—*mais,* possession give right off."

"Not the whole plantation, Charlie; only"—

"I don't care," said Charlie; we easy can fix dat. *Mais,* what for you don't want to keep him? I don't want him. You better keep him."

"Don't you try to make no fool of me, old man," cried the planter.

"Oh, no!" said the other. "Oh, no! but you make a fool of yourself, ain't it?"

The dumbfounded Colonel stared; Charlie went on:

"Yass! Belles Demoiselles is more wort' dan tree block like dis one. I pass by dare since two weeks. Oh, pritty Belles Demoiselles! De cane was wave in de wind, de garden smell like a bouquet, de white-cap was jump up and down on de river; seven *belles demoiselles* was ridin' on horses. 'Pritty, pritty, pritty!' says old Charlie. Ah! *Monsieur le pere, 'ow* 'appy, 'appy, 'appy!"

"Yass!" he continued—the Colonel still staring—"le Compte De Charleu have two familie. One was low-down Choctaw, one was high up *noblesse*. He gave the low-down Choctaw dis old rat-hole; he give Belles Demoiselles to you gran-fozzer; and now you don't be *satisfait*. What I'll do wid Belles Demoiselles? She'll break me in two years, yass. And what you'll do wid old Charlie's house, eh? You'll tear her down and make you'se'f a blame old fool. I rather wouldn't trade!"

The planter caught a big breathful of anger, but Charlie went straight on:

"I rather wouldn't, *mais* I will do it for you,—just the same, like Monsieur le Compte would say, 'Charlie, you old fool, I want to shange houses wid you.'"

So long as the Colonel suspected irony he was angry, but as Charlie seemed, after all, to be certainly in earnest, he began to feel conscience-stricken. He was by no means a tender man, but his lately-discovered misfortune had unhinged him, and this strange, undeserved, disinterested family fealty on the part of Charlie touched his heart. And should he still try to lead him into the pitfall he had dug? He hesitated; no, he would show him the place by broad daylight, and if he chose to overlook the "caving bank," it would be his own fault,—a trade's a trade.

"Come," said the planter, "come at my house tonight; to-morrow we look at the place before breakfast, and finish the trade."

"For what?" said Charlie.

"Oh, because I got to come in town in the morning."

"I don't want," said Charlie. "How I'm goin' to come dere?"

"I git you a horse at the liberty stable."

"Well—anyhow—I don't care—I'll go." And they went.

When they had ridden a long time, and were on the road darkened by hedges of Cherokee rose, the Colonel called behind him to the "low-down" scion:

"Keep the road, old man."

"Eh?"

"Keep the road."

"Oh, yes; all right; I keep my word; we don't goin' to play no tricks, eh?"

But the Colonel seemed not to hear. His ungenerous design was beginning to be hateful to him. Not only old Charlie's unprovoked goodness was prevailing; the eulogy on Belles Demoiselles had stirred the depths of an intense love for his beautiful home. True, if he held to it, the caving of the bank, at its present fearful speed, would let the house into the river within three months; but were it not better to lose it so, than sell his birthright? Again,—coming back to the first thought,—to betray his own blood! It was only Injin Charlie; but had not the De Charleu blood just spoken out in him? Unconsciously he groaned.

After a time they struck a path approaching the plantation in the rear, and a little after, passing from behind a clump of live-oaks, they came in sight of the villa. It looked so like a gem, shining through its dark grove, so like a great glow-worm in the dense foliage, so significant of luxury and gayety, that the poor master, from an overflowing heart, groaned again.

"What?" asked Charlie.

The Colonel only drew his rein, and, dismounting mechanically, contemplated the sight before him. The high, arched doors and windows were thrown wide to the summer air; from every opening the bright light of numerous candelabra darted out upon the sparkling foliage of magnolia and bay, and here and there in the spacious verandas a colored lantern swayed in the gentle breeze. A sound of revel fell on the ear, the music of harps; and across one window, brighter than the rest, flitted, once or twice, the shadows of dancers. But oh! the shadows flitting across the heart of the fair mansion's master!

"Old Charlie," said he, gazing fondly at his house, "You and me is both old, eh?"

"Yaas," said the stolid Charlie.

"And we has both been bad enough in our time, eh, Charlie?"

Charlie, surprised at the tender tone, repeated "Yaas."

"And you and me is mighty close?"

"Blame close, yaas."

"But you never know me to cheat, old man!"

"No,"—impassively.

"And do you think I would cheat you now?"

"I dunno," said Charlie. "I don't believe."

"Well, old man, old man,"—his voice began to quiver,—"I sha'n't cheat you now. My God!—old man, I tell you—you better not make the trade!"

"Because for what?" asked Charlie in plain anger; but both looked quickly toward the house! The Colonel tossed his hands wildly in the air, rushed forward a step or two, and giving one fearful scream of agony and fright, fell forward on his face in the path. Old Charlie stood transfixed with horror. Belles Demoiselles, the realm of maiden beauty, the home of merriment, the house of dancing, all in the tremor and glow of pleasure, suddenly sunk, with one short, wild wail of terror—sunk, sunk, down, down, down, into the merciless, unfathomable flood of the Mississippi.

Twelve long months were midnight to the mind of the childless father; when they were only half gone he took his bed; and every day, and every night, old Charlie, the "low-down," the "fool," watched him tenderly, tended him lovingly, for the sake of his name, his misfortunes, and his broken heart. No woman's step crossed the floor of the sick-chamber, whose western dormer-windows overpeered the dingy architecture of old Charlie's block; Charlie and a skilled physician, the one all interest, the other all gentleness, hope, and patience—these only entered by the door; but by the window came in a sweet-scented evergreen vine, transplanted from the caving bank of Belles Demoiselles. It caught the rays of sunset in its flowery net and let them softly in upon the sick man's bed; gathered the glancing beams of the moon at midnight, and often wakened the sleeper to look, with his mindless eyes, upon their pretty silver fragments strewn upon the floor.

By and by there seemed—there was—a twinkling dawn of returning reason. Slowly, peacefully, with an increase unseen from day to day, the light of reason came into the eyes, and speech became coherent; but withal there came a failing of the wrecked body, and the doctor said that monsieur was both better and worse.

One evening, as Charlie sat by the vine-clad window with his fireless pipe in his hand, the old Colonel's eyes fell full upon his own, and rested there.

"Charl—," he said with an effort, and his delighted nurse hastened to the bedside and bowed his best ear. There was an unsuccessful effort or two, and then he whispered, smiling with sweet sadness,—

"We didn't trade."

The truth, in this case, was a secondary matter to Charlie; the main point was to give a pleasing answer. So he nodded his head decidedly, as who should say—"Oh yes, we did, it was a bonafide swap!" but when he saw the smile vanish, he tried the other expedient and shook his head with still more vigor, to signify that they had not so much as approached a bargain; and the smile returned.

Charlie wanted to see the vine recognized. He stepped backward to the window with a broad smile, shook the foliage, nodded and looked smart.

"I know," said the Colonel, with beaming eyes, "—many weeks."

The next day—

"Charl—"

The best ear went down. "Send for a priest."

The priest came, and was alone with him a whole afternoon. When he left, the patient was very haggard and exhausted, but smiled and would not suffer the crucifix to be removed from his breast.

One more morning came. Just before dawn Charlie, lying on a pallet in the room, thought he was called, and came to the bedside.

"Old man," whispered the failing invalid, "is it caving yet?"

Charlie nodded.

"It won't pay you out."

"Oh, dat makes not'ing," said Charlie. Two big tears rolled down his brown face. "Dat makes not'in."

The Colonel whispered once more:

"*Mes belles demoiselles!* in paradise;—in the garden—I shall be with them at sunrise," and so it was.

BELLES DEMOISELLES PLANTATION

Discursive and almost plotless, this story exhibits much of the antebellum tendency to romanticize plantation society. It is an idyllic picture of early French plantation aristocracy, a scene of domestic bliss on the bank of the river: the "shady garden is full of rare and beautiful flowers; . . . [it] put on its spring attire: the seven fair sisters moved from rose to rose."

Set in counterpoint is the picture of the plantation's adversary: "Big whirlpools would open and whirl about in the savage eddies under the low bank, and close up again, and others open, and spin and disappear. Great circles of muddy surface would boil up hundreds of feet below. . . . Every few minutes the loamy bank would tip down a great load of dirt upon its besieger. . . ." Later the river's imagery is personified: it "throw[s] a great arm over the levee's top as though it would vault over."

Two parallel conflicts are recognizable: the river's threat to swallow up the land and De Charleu's dilemma on whether to swallow up De Carlos in an unfair ancestral land trade. Knowing that the plantation is doomed, he negotiates a trade for De Carlos's town property to satisfy his seven daughters. At the heart of his moral dilemma are the racial features that Cable attributes to Creoles—arrogance, contempt for honest labor, and excessive pride in family lineage.

Although the characters are one-dimensional and serve to exemplify Cable's general statements about Creoles, they emerge as interesting individuals. Cable uses De Carlos (Injin Charlie) as a foil to De Charleu; that is, he pits the pure Creole who exhibits all the negative features of the "race" against the mixed breed whose Indian blood has apparently stripped away the arrogance and diluted the ancestral pride. There is also a humorous contrast between Injin Charlie's high self-deprecation (he calls himself a "low down dog") and De Charleu's high self-esteem. Thus Cable illuminates the character of each.

The omniscient point of view exposes De Charleu's conniving mind, his plan to trick his naive mixed-breed relative, as well as his Creole inability to cheat a kinsman. De Carlos, on the other hand, is not only naive but also good at heart (De Charleu speaks of his "unprovoked goodness"). These traits allow him to agree to the trade at the crucial point in the story.

The seven daughters, who remain in the background, function like a Greek chorus. At first, they chatter gaily to evince the happiness and harmony of the home; then they begin to complain of weather, insects, and boredom and to clamor for a move to the city. Thus they provide the motivation for the action.

Stereotypical landscape is often used in local color stories solely for atmosphere; in this story the mighty Mississippi, twisting and rushing past the broad verandas and shady gardens of Belles Demoiselles, is both atmospheric and functional. It contributes to the edenic atmosphere and ties landscape firmly to plot. The story reaches its climax when in a Poe-like scene Charleu's beautiful house and daughters are swallowed up by the river.

Grace King

(1852-1932)

Born in New Orleans on November 29, 1852, Grace King, although Protestant, was educated in private Creole schools and was always strongly allied with Creole society. The title story of her first book *Monsieur Motte* (1888) dramatizes the love of a former slave for her dead Creole mistress's daughter and was written to suggest that goodness begets loyalty and therefore to correct the impression, conveyed by Cable, that Creoles are insensitive. Both Charles Dudley Warner, her close friend and literary advisor, and William Dean Howells had high praise for the book. Howells compared her representation of Creole life with Hawthorne's representation of Puritan life. By 1893 she was established as a leading Southern local colorist. In addition to fiction, she wrote biography. The story printed below was included in *Balcony Stories* in 1892.

La Grande Demoiselle

Grace King

That was what she was called by everybody as soon as she was seen or described. Her name, besides baptismal titles, was Idalie Sainte Foy Mortemart des Islets. When she came into society, in the brilliant little world of New Orleans, it was the event of the season, and after she came in, whatever she did became also events. Whether she went, or did not go; what she said, or did not say; what she wore, and did not wear—all these became important matters of discussion, quoted as much or more than what the president said, or the governor thought. And in those days, the days of '59, New Orleans was not, as it is now, a one-heiress place, but it may be said that one could find heiresses then as one finds type-writing girls now.

Mademoiselle Idalie received her birth, and what education she had, on her parents' plantation, the famed old Reine Sainte Foy place, and it is no secret that, like the ancient kings of France, her birth exceeded her education.

It was a plantation, the Reine Sainte Foy, the richness and luxury of which are really well described in those perfervid pictures of tropical life, at one time the passion of philanthropic imaginations, excited and exciting over the horrors of slavery. Although these pictures were then often accused of being purposely exaggerated, they seem now to fall short of, instead of surpassing, the truth. Stately walls, acres of roses, miles of oranges, unmeasured fields of cane, colossal sugar-house—they were all there, and all the rest of it, with the slaves, slaves, slaves everywhere, whole villages of negro cabins. And there were also, most noticeable to the natural, as well as to the visionary, eye— there were the ease, idleness, extravagance, self-indulgence, pomp, pride, arrogance, in short the whole enumeration, the moral *sine qua non*, as some people considered it, of the wealthy slaveholder of aristocratic descent and tastes.

What Mademoiselle Idalie cared to learn she studied, what she did not she ignored; and she followed the same simple rule untrammeled in her eating, drinking, dressing, and comportment generally; and whatever discipline may have been exercised on the

23

place, either in fact or fiction, most assuredly none of it, even so much as in a threat, ever attainted her sacred person. When she was just turned sixteen, Mademoiselle Idalie made up her mind to go into society. Whether she was beautiful or not, it is hard to say. It is almost impossible to appreciate properly the beauty of the rich, the very rich. The unfettered development, the limitless choice of accessories, the confidence, the selfesteem, the sureness of expression, the simplicity of purpose, the ease of execution—all these produce a certain effect of beauty behind which one really cannot get to measure length of nose, or brilliance of eye. This much can be said: there was nothing in her that positively contradicted an assumption of beauty on her part, or credit of it on the part of others. She was very tall and very thin with small head, long neck, black eyes, and abundant straight black hair,—for which her hair-dresser deserved more praise than she,—good teeth, of course, and a mouth that, even in prayer, talked nothing but commands; that is about all she had *en fait d'ornements*, as the modistes say. It may be added that she walked as if the Reine Sainte Foy plantation extended over the whole earth, and the soil of it were too vile for her tread. Of course she did not buy her toilets in New Orleans. Everything was ordered from Paris, and came as regularly through the custom-house as the modes and robes to the milliners. She was furnished by a certain house there, just as one of a royal family would be at the present day. As this had lasted from her layette up to her sixteenth year, it may be imagined what took place when she determined to make her debut. Then it was literally, not metaphorically, *carte blanche*, at least so it got to the ears of society. She took a sheet of notepaper, wrote the date at the top, added, "I make my debut in November," signed her name at the extreme end of the sheet, addressed it to her dressmaker in Paris, and sent it.

It was said that in her dresses the very handsomest silks were used for linings, and that real lace was used where others put imitation,—around the bottoms of the skirts, for instance,—and silk ribbons of the best quality served the purposes of ordinary tapes; and sometimes the buttons were of real gold and silver, sometimes set with precious stones. Not that she ordered these particulars, but the dressmakers, when given *carte blanche* by those who do not condescend to details, so soon exhaust the outside limits of garments that perforce they take to plastering them inside with gold, so to speak, and, when the bill goes in, they depend upon the furnishings to carry out a certain amount of the contract in justifying the price. And it was said that these costly dresses, after being worn once or twice, were cast aside, thrown upon the floor, given to the negroes—anything to get them out of sight. Not an inch of real lace, not one of the jeweled buttons, not a scrap of ribbon, was ripped off to save. And it was said that if she wanted to romp with her dogs in all her finery, she did it; she was known to have ridden horseback, one moonlight night, all around the plantation in a white silk dinner-dress flounced with Alencon. And at night, when she came from the balls, tired, tired to death as only balls can render one, she would throw herself down upon her bed in her tulle skirts,—on top, or not, of the exquisite flowers, she did not care,— and make her maid undress her in that position; often having her bodices cut off her, because she was too tired to turn over and have them unlaced.

That she was admired, raved about, loved even, goes without saying. After the first month she held the refusal of half the beaux of New Orleans. Men did absurd, undignified, preposterous things for her; and she? Love? Marry? The idea never occurred to her. She treated the most exquisite of her pretenders no better than she treated her Paris gowns, for the matter of that. She could not even bring herself to listen to a proposal patiently; whistling to her dogs, in the middle *of* the most ardent protestations, or jumping up and walking away with a shrug of the shoulders, and a "Bah!"

Well! Every one knows what happened after '59. There is no need to repeat. The history of one is the history of all. But there was this difference—for there is every shade of difference in misfortune, as there is every shade of resemblance in happiness. Mortemart des Islets went off to fight. That was natural; his family had been doing that, he thought, or said, ever since Charlemagne. Just as naturally, he was killed in the first engagement. They, his family, were always among the just killed; so much so that it began to be considered assassination to fight a duel with any of them. All that was in the ordinary course of events. One difference in their misfortunes lay in that after the city was captured, their plantation, so near, convenient, and rich in all kinds of provisions, was selected to receive a contingent of troops—

a colored company. If it had been a colored company raised in Louisiana it might have been different; and these negroes mixed with the negroes in the neighborhood,—and negroes are no better than whites, for the proportion of good and bad among them,—and the officers were always off duty when they should have been on, and on when they should have been off.

One night the dwelling caught fire. There was an immediate rush to save the ladies. Oh, there was no hesitation about that! They were seized in their beds, and carried out in the very arms of their enemies; carried away off to the sugar-house, and deposited there. No danger of their doing anything but keep very quiet and still in their *chemises de nuit,* and their one sheet apiece, which was about all that was saved from the conflagration—that is, for them. But it must be remembered that this is all hearsay. When one has not been present, one knows nothing of one's own knowledge; one can only repeat. It has been repeated, however, that although the house was burned to the ground, and everything in it destroyed, wherever, for a year afterward, a man of that company or of that neighborhood was found, there could have been found also, without search-warrant, property that had belonged to the Des Islets. That is the story; and it is believed or not, exactly according to prejudice.

How the ladies ever got out of the sugar-house, history does not relate; nor what they did. It was not a time for sociability, either personal or epistolary. At one offensive word your letter, and you, very likely, examined; and Ship Island for a hotel, with soldiers for hostesses! Madame Des Islets died very soon after the accident—of rage, they say; and that was about all the public knew.

Indeed, at that time the society of New Orleans had other things to think about than the fate of the Des Islets. As for *la grande demoiselle,* she had prepared for her own oblivion in the hearts of her female friends. And the gentlemen,—her *preux chevaliers,*—they were burning with other passions than those which had driven them to her knees, encountering a little more serious response than "bahs" and shrugs. And, after all, a woman seems the quickest thing forgotten when once the important affairs of life come to men for consideration.

It might have been ten years according to some calculations, or ten eternities,—the heart and the almanac never agree about time,—but one morning old Champigny (they used to call him Champignon) was walking along his levee front, calculating how soon the water would come over, and drown him out, as the Louisianians say. It was before a seven-o'clock breakfast, cold, wet, rainy, and discouraging. The road was knee-deep in mud, and so broken up with hauling, that it was like walking upon waves to get over it. A shower poured down. Old Champigny was hurrying in when he saw a figure approaching. He had to stop to look at it, for it was worth while. The head was hidden by a green barege veil, which the showers had plentifully besprinkled with dew; a tall, thin figure. Figure! No; not even could it be called a figure: straight up and down, like a finger or a post; high shouldered, and a step—a step like a plowman's. No umbrella; no—nothing more, in fact. It does not sound so peculiar as when first related—something must be forgotten. The feet—oh, yes, the feet—they were like waffle-irons, or frying pans, or anything of that shape.

Old Champigny did not care for women—he never had; they simply did not exist for him in the order of nature. He had been married once, it is true, about a half century before; but that was not reckoned against the existence of his prejudice, because he was *célibataire* to his finger-tips, as any one could see a mile away. But that woman *intrigué'd* him.

He had no servant to inquire from. He performed all of his own domestic work in the wretched little cabin that replaced his old home. For Champigny also belonged to the great majority of the *nouveaux pauvres*. He went out into the rice-field, where were one or two hands that worked on shares with him, and he asked them. They knew immediately; there is nothing connected with the parish that a field-hand does not know at once. She was the teacher of the colored public school some three or four miles away. "Ah," thought Champigny, "some Northern lady on a mission." He watched to see her return in the evening, which she did, of course; in a blinding rain. Imagine the green barege veil then; for it remained always down over her face.

Old Champigny could not get over it that he had never seen her before. But he must have seen her, and, with his abstraction and old age, not have noticed her, for he found out from the negroes that she had been teaching four or five years there. And he found out also—how, is not important—that she was Idalie Sainte Foy

Mortemart des Islets. *La grande demoiselle!* He had never known her in the old days, owing to his uncomplimentary attitude toward women, but he knew her, of course, and of her family. It should have been said that his plantation was about fifty miles higher up the river, and on the opposite bank to Reine Sainte Foy. It seemed terrible. The old gentleman had had reverses of his own, which would bear the telling, but nothing was more shocking to him than this—that Idalie Sainte Foy Mortemart des Islets should be teaching a public colored school for—it makes one blush to name it—seven dollars and a half a month. For seven dollars and a half a month to teach a set of—well! He found out where she lived, a little cabin—not so much worse than his own, for that matter—in the corner of a field; no companion, no servant, nothing but food and shelter. Her clothes have been described.

Only the good God himself knows what passed in Champigny's mind on the subject. We know only the results. He went and married *la grande demoiselle.* How? Only the good God knows that too. Every first of the month, when he goes to the city to buy provisions, he takes her with him—in fact, he takes her everywhere with him.

Passengers on the railroad know them well, and they always have a chance to see her face. When she passes her old plantation *la grande demoiselle* always lifts her veil for one instant—the inevitable green barege veil. What a face! Thin, long, sallow, petrified! And the neck! If she would only tie something around the neck! And her plain coarse cottonade gown! The negro women about her were better dressed than she.

Poor old Champignon! It was not an act of charity to himself, no doubt cross and disagreeable, besides being ugly. And as for love, gratitude!

Like Cable's story, King's story focuses on character, but it does not utilize the exotic New Orleans landscape. The pampered daughter of a wealthy Creole slaveholder, Idalie is initially described as extravagant, self-indulgent, pompous, prideful, and arrogant; in short, she possesses the same negative features that Cable attributes to his Creoles. The difference is that he treats these traits as innate Creole character flaws, whereas King, in allowing Idalie to change, suggests that slothful living of the idle rich has shaped her.

The story is told by an objective narrator whose vision is limited to externals only; she is not privy to what goes on in Idalie's mind. Furthermore, she doesn't claim any personal knowledge of the character, but rather relies on secondhand information provided by gossipers. This narrative device is an old convention used to gain plausibility.

The change in Idalie's life style is brought about by the ravages of the Civil War. The great plantation, as a part of the old order, is destroyed; and in the bitter Reconstruction period, the public loses sight of and forgets "la grande demoiselle." When years later she reappears, through the eyes of an old man, she has undergone a remarkable outward change. Her figure is like a "finger or post" and her feet are "like waffle irons or frying pans." Having joined the ranks of the *nouveaux pauvres*, she dresses in cottonade (slave clothing) and teaches in a public colored school—a double comedown.

Because of the limited point of view, the reader does not experience the change and therefore cannot fully understand it. Was Idalie's confrontation with reality so powerful that she is not quite the same person; has she undergone a metamorphosis? If the change is deep and elemental, it would necessarily alter her view of self in relation to the universe. Does she no longer see herself as special, but rather as a part of the struggling human race? Is her teaching former slaves a part of a commitment to humanity? Her attire suggests such an interpretation. The veil which hides her head, mentioned three times in the last paragraphs, is a traditional symbol suggesting separation from the material world, and the coarse cotton dress is associated with religious vows of poverty. These carefully selected physical details reveal a very different Idalie—not just economically impoverished—but spiritually chastened.

Kate Chopin

(1851 -1904)

Born Katherine O'Flaherty in St. Louis on February 8, 1851, Kate Chopin moved to Louisiana as the bride of Oscar Chopin, a wealthy Creole planter. After his death in 1883 she managed the family plantation at Natchitoches for a brief period but returned to St. Louis in 1884 where she began her writing career based on her memories of and feelings about life in Louisiana. An early advocate of women's rights, Chopin expressed ideas that were shocking and distasteful to Victorian society, ideas relating to women's entrapment and lack of fulfillment in marriage. Although local landscape and customs are prominent in her Creole and Cajun stories, the theme that pervades most of her fiction—need for freedom and self-expression—is universal. Because her works were censured by society for their frankness, they were unappreciated except for their local color element until recent decades. "The Awakening," printed below was first published in 1897 and later included in *The Complete Works of Kate Chopin*, ed. Per Seyersted, 1969. "A Night in Acadie," also printed below was first published in *A Night in Acadie* in 1897.

The Awakening

Kate Chopin

A green and yellow parrot, which hung in a cage outside the door, kept repeating over and over:

"*Allez vous-en! Allez vous-en! Sapristi!*" That's all right!"

He could speak a little Spanish, and also a language which nobody understood, unless it was the mocking-bird that hung on the other side of the door, whistling his fluty notes out upon the breeze with maddening persistence.

Mr. Pontellier, unable to read his newspaper with any degree of comfort, arose with an expression and an exclamation of disgust. He walked down the gallery and across the narrow "bridges" which connected the Lebrun cottages one with the other. He had been seated before the door of the main house. The parrot and the mocking-bird were the property of Madame Lebrun, and they had the right to make all the noise they wished. Mr. Pontellier had the privilege of quitting their society when they ceased to be entertaining.

He stopped before the door of his own cottage, which was the fourth one from the main building and next to the last. Seating himself in a wicker rocker which was there, he once more applied himself to the task of reading the newspaper. The day was Sunday; the paper was a day old. The Sunday papers had not yet reached Grand Isle. He was already acquainted with the market reports, and he glanced restlessly over the editorials and bits of news which he had not had time to read before quitting New Orleans the day before.

Mr. Pontellier wore eye-glasses. He was a man of forty, of medium height and rather slender build; he stooped a little. His hair was brown and straight, parted on one side. His beard was neatly and closely trimmed.

Once in a while he withdrew his glance from the newspaper and looked about him. There was more noise than ever over at the house. The main building was called "the house," to distinguish it from the cottages. The chattering and whistling birds were still at it. Two young girls, the Farival twins, were playing a duet from "Zampa" upon the piano. Madame Lebrun was bustling in and out,

33

giving orders in a high key to a yard-boy whenever she got inside
the house, and directions in an equally high voice to a dining-room
servant whenever she got outside. She was a fresh, pretty woman,
clad always in white with elbow sleeves. Her starched skirts
crinkled as she came and went. Farther down, before one of the
cottages, a lady in black was walking demurely up and down,
telling her beads. A good many persons of the *pension* had gone over
to the *Chênière* Caminada in Beaudelet's lugger to hear mass. Some
young people were out under the water-oaks playing croquet. Mr.
Pontellier's two children were there—sturdy little fellows of four
and five. A quadroon nurse followed them about with a far-away,
meditative air.

Mr. Pontellier finally lit a cigar and began to smoke, letting the
paper drag idly from his hand. He fixed his gaze upon a white
sunshade that was advancing at snail's pace from the beach. He
could see it plainly between the gaunt trunks of the water-oaks and
across the stretch of yellow camomile. The gulf looked far away,
melting hazily into the blue of the horizon. The sunshade continued
to approach slowly. Beneath its pink-lined shelter were his wife,
Mrs. Pontellier, and young Robert Lebrun. When they reached the
cottage, the two seated themselves with some appearance of
fatigue upon the upper step of the porch, facing each other, each
leaning against a supporting post.

"What folly! to bathe at such an hour in such heat!" exclaimed
Mr. Pontellier. He himself had taken a plunge at daylight. That
was why the morning seemed long to him.

"You are burnt beyond recognition," he added, looking at his
wife as one looks at a valuable piece of personal property which
has suffered some damage. She held up her hands, strong, shapely
hands, and surveyed them critically, drawing up her lawn sleeves
above the wrists. Looking at them reminded her of her rings, which
she had given to her husband before leaving for the beach. She
silently reached out to him, and he, understanding, took the rings
from his vest pocket and dropped them into her open palm. She
slipped them upon her fingers; then clasping her knees, she looked
across at Robert and began to laugh. The rings sparkled upon her
fingers. He sent back an answering smile.

"What is it?" asked Pontellier, looking lazily and amused from
one to the other. It was some utter nonsense; some adventure out

there in the water, and they both tried to relate it at once. It did not seem half so amusing when told. They realized this, and so did Mr. Pontellier. He yawned and stretched himself. Then he got up, saying he had half a mind to go over to Klein's hotel and play a game of billiards.

"Come go along, Lebrun," he proposed to Robert. But Robert admitted quite frankly that he preferred to stay where he was and talk to Mrs. Pontellier.

"Well, send him about his business when he bores you, Edna," instructed her husband as he prepared to leave.

"Here, take the umbrella," she exclaimed, holding it out to him. He accepted the sunshade, and lifting it over his head descended the step and walked away.

"Coming back to dinner?" his wife called after him. He halted a moment and shrugged his shoulders. He felt in his vest pocket; there was a ten-dollar bill there. He did not know; perhaps he would return for the early dinner and perhaps he would not. It all depended upon the company which he found over at Klein's and the size of "the game." He did not say this, but she understood it, and laughed, nodding good-by to him.

Both children wanted to follow their father when they saw him starting out. He kissed them and promised to bring them back bonbons and peanuts.

II

Mrs. Pontellier's eyes were quick and bright; they were a yellowish brown, about the color of her hair. She had a way of turning them swiftly upon an object and holding them there as if lost in some inward maze of contemplation or thought.

Her eyebrows were a shade darker than her hair. They were thick and almost horizontal, emphasizing the depth of her eyes. She was rather handsome than beautiful. Her face was captivating by reason of a certain frankness of expression and a contradictory subtle play of features. Her manner was engaging.

Robert rolled a cigarette. He smoked cigarettes because he could not afford cigars, he said. He had a cigar in his pocket which Mr. Pontellier had presented him with, and he was saving it for his after-dinner smoke.

This seemed quite proper and natural on his part. In coloring he was not unlike his companion. A clean-shaved face made the resemblance more pronounced than it would otherwise have been. There rested no shadow of care upon his open countenance. His eyes gathered in and reflected the light and languor of the summer day.

Mrs. Pontellier reached over for a palm-leaf fan that lay on the porch and began to fan herself, while Robert sent between his lips light puffs from his cigarette. They chatted incessantly: about the things around them; their amusing adventure out in the water— it had again assumed its entertaining aspect; about the wind, the trees, the people who had gone to the *Chênière;* about the children playing croquet under the oaks, and the Farival twins, who were now performing the overture to "The Poet and the Peasant."

Robert talked a good deal about himself. He was very young, and did not know any better. Mrs. Pontellier talked a little about herself for the same reason. Each was interested in what the other said. Robert spoke of his intention to go to Mexico in the autumn, where fortune awaited him. He was always intending to go to Mexico, but some way never got there. Meanwhile he held on to his modest position in a mercantile house in New Orleans, where an equal familiarity with English, French and Spanish gave him no small value as a clerk and correspondent. He was spending his summer vacation, as he always did, with his mother at Grand Isle. In former times, before Robert could remember, "the house" had been a summer luxury of the Lebruns. Now, flanked by its dozen or more cottages, which were always filled with exclusive visitors from the *"Quartier Français,"* it enabled Madame Lebrun to maintain the easy and comfortable existence which appeared to be her birthright.

Mrs. Pontellier talked about her father's Mississippi plantation and her girlhood home in the old Kentucky blue-grass country. She was an American woman, with a small infusion of French which seemed to have been lost in dilution. She read a letter from her sister, who was away in the East, and who had engaged herself to be married. Robert was interested, and wanted to know what manner of girls the sisters were, what the father was like, and how long the mother had been dead.

When Mrs. Pontellier folded the letter it was time for her to dress for the early dinner.

"I see Léonce isn't coming back," she said, with a glance in the direction whence her husband had disappeared. Robert supposed he was not, as there were a good many New Orleans club men over at Klein's.

When Mrs. Pontellier left him to enter her room, the young man descended the steps and strolled over toward the croquet players, where, during the half-hour before dinner, he amused himself with the little Pontellier children, who were very fond of him.

III

It was eleven o'clock that night when Mr. Pontellier returned from Klein's hotel. He was in an excellent humor, in high spirits, and very talkative. His entrance awoke his wife, who was in bed and fast asleep when he came in. He talked to her while he undressed, telling her anecdotes and bits of news and gossip that he had gathered during the day. From his trousers pockets he took a fistful of crumpled bank notes and a good deal of silver coin, which he piled on the bureau indiscriminately with keys, knife, handkerchief, and whatever else happened to be in his pockets. She was overcome with sleep, and answered him with little half utterances.

He thought it very discouraging that his wife, who was the sole object of his existence, evinced so little interest in things which concerned him, and valued so little his conversation.

Mr. Pontellier had forgotten the bonbons and peanuts for the boys. Notwithstanding he loved them very much, and went into the adjoining room where they slept to take a look at them and make sure that they were resting comfortably. The result of his investigation was far from satisfactory. He turned and shifted the youngsters about in bed. One of them began to kick and talk about a basket full of crabs.

Mr. Pontellier returned to his wife with the information that Raoul had a high fever and needed looking after. Then he lit a cigar and went and sat near the open door to smoke it.

Mrs. Pontellier was quite sure Raoul had no fever. He had gone to bed perfectly well, she said, and nothing had ailed him all day. Mr. Pontellier was too well acquainted with fever symptoms to be mistaken. He assured her the child was consuming at that moment in the next room.

He reproached his wife with her inattention, her habitual neglect of the children. If it was not a mother's place to look after children, whose on earth was it? He himself had his hands full with his brokerage business. He could not be in two places at once; making a living for his family on the street, and staying at home to see that no harm befell them. He talked in a monotonous, insistent way.

Mrs. Pontellier sprang out of bed and went into the next room. She soon came back and sat on the edge of the bed, leaning her head down on the pillow. She said nothing, and refused to answer her husband when he questioned her. When his cigar was smoked out he went to bed, and in half a minute he was fast asleep.

Mrs. Pontellier was by that time thoroughly awake. She began to cry a little, and wiped her eyes on the sleeve of her *peignoir*. Blowing out the candle, which her husband had left burning, she slipped her bare feet into a pair of satin mules at the foot of the bed and went out on the porch, where she sat down in the wicker chair and began to rock gently to and fro.

It was then past midnight. The cottages were all dark. A single faint light gleamed out from the hallway of the house. There was no sound abroad except the hooting of an old owl in the top of a water-oak, and the everlasting voice of the sea, that was not uplifted at that soft hour. It broke like a mournful lullaby upon the night.

The tears came so fast to Mrs. Pontellier's eyes that the damp sleeve of her *peignoir* no longer served to dry them. She was holding the back of her chair with one hand; her loose sleeve had slipped almost to the shoulder of her uplifted arm. Turning, she thrust her face, steaming and wet, into the bend of her arm, and she went on crying there, not caring any longer to dry her face, her eyes, her arms. She could not have told why she was crying. Such experiences as the foregoing were not uncommon in her married life. They seemed never before to have weighed much against the abundance of her husband's kindness and a uniform devotion which had come to be tacit and self-understood.

An indescribable oppression, which seemed to generate in some unfamiliar part of her consciousness, filled her whole being with a vague anguish. It was like a shadow, like a mist passing across her soul's summer day. It was strange and unfamiliar; it was a mood. She did not sit there inwardly upbraiding her husband, lamenting at Fate, which had directed her footsteps to the path which they had taken. She was just having a good cry all to herself. The mosquitoes made merry over her, biting her firm, round arms and nipping at her bare insteps.

The little stinging, buzzing imps succeeded in dispelling a mood which might have held her there in the darkness half a night longer.

The following morning Mr. Pontellier was up in good time to take the rockaway which was to convey him to the steamer at the wharf. He was returning to the city to his business, and they would not see him again at the Island till the coming Saturday. He had regained his composure, which seemed to have been somewhat impaired the night before. He was eager to be gone, as he looked forward to a lively week in Carondelet Street.

Mr. Pontellier gave his wife half of the money which he had brought away from Klein's hotel the evening before. She liked money as well as most women, and accepted it with no little satisfaction.

"It will buy a handsome wedding present for Sister Janet!" she exclaimed, smoothing out the bills as she counted them one by one.

"Oh! we'll treat Sister Janet better than that, my dear," he laughed, as he prepared to kiss her good-by.

The boys were tumbling about, clinging to his legs, imploring that numerous things be brought back to them. Mr. Pontellier was a great favorite, and ladies, men, children, even nurses, were always on hand to say good-by to him. His wife stood smiling and waving, the boys shouting, as he disappeared in the old rockaway down the sandy road.

A few days later a box arrived for Mrs. Pontellier from New Orleans. It was from her husband. It was filled with *friandises*, with luscious and toothsome bits—the finest of fruits, *patés*, a rare bottle or two, delicious syrups, and bonbons in abundance.

Mrs. Pontellier was always very generous with the contents of such a box; she was quite used to receiving them when away from home. The *patés* and fruit were brought to the dining-room; the bonbons were passed around. And the ladies, selecting with dainty

and discriminating fingers and a little greedily, all declared that
Mr. Pontellier was the best husband in the world. Mrs. Pontellier
was forced to admit that she knew of none better.

IV

It would have been a difficult matter for Mr. Pontellier to
define to his own satisfaction or any one else's wherein his wife
failed in her duty toward their children. It was something which
he felt rather than perceived, and he never voiced the feeling
without subsequent regret and ample atonement.

If one of the little Pontellier boys took a tumble whilst at play,
he was not apt to rush crying to his mother's arms for comfort; he
would more likely pick himself up, wipe the water out of his eyes
and the sand out of his mouth, and go on playing. Tots as they were,
they pulled together and stood their ground in childish battles
with doubled fists and uplifted voices, which usually prevailed
against the other mother-tots. The quadroon nurse was looked upon
as a huge encumbrance, only good to button up waists and panties
and to brush and part hair; since it seemed to be a law of society
that hair must be parted and brushed.

In short, Mrs. Pontellier was not a mother-woman. The mother-
women seemed to prevail that summer at Grand Isle. It was easy to
know them, fluttering about with extended, protecting wings when
any harm, real or imaginary, threatened their precious brood. They
were women who idolized their children, worshiped their
husbands, and esteemed it a holy privilege to efface themselves as
individuals and grow wings as ministering angels.

Many of them were delicious in the rôle; one of them was the
embodiment of every womanly grace and charm. If her husband did
not adore her, he was a brute, deserving of death by slow torture.
Her name was Adèle Ratignolle. There are no words to describe her
save the old ones that have served so often to picture the bygone
heroine of romance and the fair lady of our dreams. There was
nothing subtle or hidden about her charms; her beauty was all
there, flaming and apparent: the spun gold hair that comb nor
confining pin could restrain; the blue eyes that were like nothing
but sapphires; two lips that pouted, that were so red one could only
think of cherries or some other delicious crimson fruit in looking at

them. She was growing a little stout, but it did not seem to detract an iota from the grace of every step, pose, gesture. One would not have wanted her white neck a mite less full or her beautiful arms more slender. Never were hands more exquisite than hers, and it was a joy to look at them when she threaded her needle or adjusted her gold thimble to her taper middle finger as she sewed away on the little night-drawers or fashioned a bodice or a bib.

Madame Ratignolle was very fond of Mrs. Pontellier, and often she took her sewing and went over to sit with her in the afternoons. She was sitting there the afternoon of the day the box arrived from New Orleans. She had possession of the rocker, and she was busily engaged in sewing upon a diminutive pair of night-drawers.

She had brought the pattern of the drawers for Mrs. Pontellier to cut out—a marvel of construction, fashioned to enclose a baby's body so effectually that only two small eyes might look out from the garment, like an Eskimo's. They were designed for winter wear, when treacherous drafts came down chimneys and insidious currents of deadly cold found their way through key-holes.

Mrs. Pontellier's mind was quite at rest concerning the present material needs of her children, and she could not see the use of anticipating and making winter night garments the subject of her summer meditations. But she did not want to appear unamiable and uninterested, so she had brought forth newspaper, which she spread upon the floor of the gallery, and under Madame Ratignolle's directions she had cut a pattern of the impervious garment.

Robert was there, seated as he had been the Sunday before, and Mrs. Pontellier also occupied her former position on the upper step, leaning listlessly against the post. Beside her was a box of bonbons, which she held out at intervals to Madame Ratignolle.

That lady seemed at a loss to make a selection, but finally settled upon a stick of nougat, wondering if it were not too rich; whether it could possibly hurt her. Madame Ratignolle had been married seven years. About every two years she had a baby. At that time she had three babies, and was beginning to think of a fourth one. She was always talking about her "condition." Her "condition" was in no way apparent, and no one would have known a thing about it but for her persistence in making it the subject of conversation.

Robert started to reassure her, asserting that he had known a lady who had subsisted upon nougat during the entire—but seeing the color mount into Mrs. Pontellier's face he checked himself and changed the subject.

Mrs. Pontellier, though she had married a Creole, was not thoroughly at home in the society of Creoles; never before had she been thrown so intimately among them. There were only Creoles that summer at Lebrun's. They all knew each other, and felt like one large family, among whom existed the most amicable relations. A characteristic which distinguished them and which impressed Mrs. Pontellier most forcibly was their entire absence of prudery. Their freedom of expression was at first incomprehensible to her, though she had no difficulty in reconciling it with a lofty chastity which in the Creole woman seems to be inborn and unmistakable.

Never would Edna Pontellier forget the shock with which she heard Madame Ratignolle relating to old Monsieur Farival the harrowing story of one of her *accouchements*, withholding no intimate detail. She was growing accustomed to like shocks, but she could not keep the mounting color back from her cheeks. Oftener than once her coming had interrupted the droll story with which Robert was entertaining some amused group of married women.

A book had gone the rounds of the *pension*. When it came her turn to read it, she did so with profound astonishment. She felt moved to read the book in secret and solitude, though none of the others had done so—to hide it from view at the sound of approaching footsteps. It was openly criticized and freely discussed at table. Mrs. Pontellier gave over being astonished, and concluded that wonders would never cease.

V

They formed a congenial group sitting there that summer afternoon—Madame Ratignolle sewing away, often stopping to relate a story or incident with much expressive gesture of her perfect hands; Robert and Mrs. Pontellier sitting idle, exchanging occasional words, glances or smiles which indicated a certain advanced stage of intimacy and *camaraderie*.

He had lived in her shadow during the past month. No one thought anything of it. Many had predicted that Robert would devote himself to Mrs. Pontellier when he arrived. Since the age of fifteen, which was eleven years before, Robert each summer at Grand Isle had constituted himself the devoted attendant of some fair dame or damsel. Sometimes it was a young girl, again a widow; but as often as not it was some interesting married woman.

For two consecutive seasons he lived in the sunlight of Mademoiselle Duvigné's presence. But she died between summers; then Robert posed as an inconsolable, prostrating himself at the feet of Madame Ratignolle for whatever crumbs of sympathy and comfort she might be pleased to vouchsafe.

Mrs. Pontellier liked to sit and gaze at her fair companion as she might look upon a faultless Madonna.

"Could any one fathom the cruelty beneath that fair exterior?" murmured Robert. "She knew that I adored her once, and she let me adore her. It was 'Robert, come; go; stand up; sit down; do this; do that; see if the baby sleeps; my thimble, please, that I left God knows where. Come and read Daudet to me while I sew.' "

"*Par example!* I never had to ask. You were always there under my feet, like a troublesome cat."

"You mean like an adoring dog. And just as soon as Ratignolle appeared on the scene, then it *was* like a dog. '*Passez! Adieu! Allez vous-en!*' "

"Perhaps I feared to make Alphonse jealous," she interjoined, with excessive naïveté. That made them all laugh. The right hand jealous of the left! The heart jealous of the soul! But for that matter, the Creole husband is never jealous; with him the gangrene passion is one which has become dwarfed by disuse.

Meanwhile Robert, addressing Mrs. Pontellier, continued to tell of his one time hopeless passion for Madame Ratignolle; of sleepless nights, of consuming flames till the very sea sizzled when he took his daily plunge. While the lady at the needle kept up a little running, contemptuous comment:

"*Blageur—farceur—gros bête, va!*"

He never assumed this serio-comic tone when alone with Mrs. Pontellier. She never knew precisely what to make of it; at that moment it was impossible for her to guess how much of it was jest and what proportion was earnest. It was understood that he had often spoken words of love to Madame Ratignolle, without any thought of being taken seriously. Mrs. Pontellier was glad he had not assumed a similar rôle toward herself. It would have been unacceptable and annoying.

Mrs. Pontellier had brought her sketching materials, which she sometimes dabbled with in an unprofessional way. She liked the dabbling. She felt in it satisfaction of a kind which no other employment afforded her.

She had long wished to try herself on Madame Ratignolle. Never had that lady seemed a more tempting subject than at that moment, seated there like some sensuous Madonna, with the gleam of the fading day enriching her splendid color.

Robert crossed over and seated himself upon the step below Mrs. Pontellier, that he might watch her work. She handled her brushes with a certain ease and freedom which came, not from long and close acquaintance with them, but from a natural aptitude. Robert followed her work with close attention, giving forth little ejaculatory expressions of appreciation in French, which he addressed to Madame Ratignolle.

"Mais ce n'est pas mal! Elle s'y connait, elle a de la force, oui."

During his oblivious attention he once quietly rested his head against Mrs. Pontellier's arm. As gently she repulsed him. Once again he repeated the offense. She could not but believe it to be thoughtlessness on his part; yet that was no reason she should submit to it. She did not remonstrate, except again to repulse him quietly but firmly. He offered no apology.

The picture completed bore no resemblance to Madame Ratignolle. She was greatly disappointed to find that it did not look like her. But it was a fair enough piece of work, and in many respects satisfying.

Mrs. Pontellier evidently did not think so. After surveying the sketch critically she drew a broad smudge of paint across its surface, and crumpled the paper between her hands.

The youngsters came tumbling up the steps, the quadroon following at the respectful distance which they required her to observe. Mrs. Pontellier made them carry her paints and things into the house. She sought to detain them for a little talk and some pleasantry. But they were greatly in earnest. They had only come to investigate the contents of the bonbon box. They accepted without murmuring what she chose to give them, each holding out two chubby hands scoop-like, in the vain hope that they might be filled; and then away they went.

The sun was low in the west, and the breeze soft and languorous that came up from the south, charged with the seductive odor of the sea. Children, freshly befurbelowed, were gathering for their games under the oaks. Their voices were high and penetrating.

Madame Ratignolle folded her sewing, placing thimble, scissors and thread all neatly together in the roll, which she pinned securely. She complained of faintness. Mr. Pontellier flew for the cologne water and a fan. She bathed Madame Ratignolle's face with cologne, while Robert plied the fan with unnecessary vigor.

The spell was soon over, and Mrs. Pontellier could not help wondering if there were not a little imagination responsible for its origin, for the rose tint had never faded from her friend's face.

She stood watching the fair woman walk down the long line of galleries with the grace and majesty which queens are sometimes supposed to possess. Her little ones ran to meet her. Two of them clung about her white skirts, the third she took from its nurse and with a thousand endearments bore it along in her own fond, encircling arms. Though, as everybody well knew, the doctor had forbidden her to lift so much as a pin!

"Are you going bathing?" asked Robert of Mrs. Pontellier. It was not so much a question as a reminder.

"Oh, no," she answered, with a tone of indecision. "I'm tired; I think not." Her glance wandered from his face away toward the Gulf, whose sonorous murmur reached her like a loving but imperative entreaty.

"Oh, come!" he insisted. "You mustn't miss your bath. Come on. The water must be delicious; it will not hurt you. Come."

He reached up for her big, rough straw hat that hung on a peg outside the door, and put it on her head. They descended the steps, and walked away together toward the beach. The sun was low in the west and the breeze was soft and warm.

VI

Edna Pontellier could not have told why, wishing to go to the beach with Robert, she should in the first place have declined, and in the second place have followed in obedience to one of the two contradictory impulses which impelled her.

A certain light was beginning to dawn dimly within her,—the light which, showing the way, forbids it.

At that early period it served but to bewilder her. It moved her to dreams, to thoughtfulness, to the shadowy anguish which had overcome her the midnight when she had abandoned herself to tears.

In short, Mrs. Pontellier was beginning to realize her position in the universe as a human being, and to recognize her relations as an individual to the world within and about her. This may seem like a ponderous weight of wisdom to descend upon the soul of a young woman of twenty-eight—perhaps more wisdom than the Holy Ghost is usually pleased to vouchsafe to any woman.

But the beginning of things, of a world especially, is necessarily vague, tangled, chaotic, and exceedingly disturbing. How few of us ever emerge from such beginning! How many souls perish in its tumult!

The voice of the sea is seductive; never ceasing, whispering, clamoring, murmuring, inviting the soul to wander for a spell in abysses of solitude; to lose itself in mazes of inward contemplation. The voice of the sea speaks to the soul. The touch of the sea is sensuous, enfolding the body in its soft, close embrace.

VII

Mrs. Pontellier was not a woman given to confidences, a characteristic hitherto contrary to her nature. Even as a child she had lived her own small life all within herself. At a very early period she had apprehended instinctively the dual life—that outward existence which conforms, the inward life which questions.

That summer at Grand Isle she began to loosen a little the mantle of reserve that had always enveloped her. There may have been—there must have been—influences, both subtle and apparent, working in their several ways to induce her to do this; but the most obvious was the influence of Adèle Ratignolle. The excessive physical charm of the Creole had first attracted her, for Edna had a sensuous susceptibility to beauty. Then the candor of the woman's whole existence, which every one might read, and which formed so striking a contrast to her own habitual reserve—this might have furnished a link. Who can tell what metals the gods use in forging the subtle bond which we call sympathy, which we might as well call love.

The two women went away one morning to the beach together, arm in arm, under the huge white sunshade. Edna had prevailed upon Madame Ratignolle to leave the children behind, though she could not induce her to relinquish a diminutive roll of needlework, which Adèle begged to be allowed to slip into the depths of her pocket. In some unaccountable way they had escaped from Robert.

The walk to the beach was no inconsiderable one, consisting as it did of a long, sandy path, upon which a sporadic and tangled growth that bordered it on either side made frequent and unexpected inroads. There were acres of yellow camomile reaching out on either hand. Further away still, vegetable gardens abounded, with frequent small plantations of orange or lemon trees intervening. The dark green clusters glistened from afar in the sun.

The women were both of goodly height, Madame Ratignolle possessing the more feminine and matronly figure. The charm of Edna Pontellier's physique stole insensibly upon you. The lines of her body were long, clean and symmetrical; it was a body which occasionally fell into splendid poses; there was no suggestion of the trim, stereotyped fashion-plate about it. A casual and indiscriminating observer, in passing, might not cast a second glance upon the figure. But with more feeling and discernment he would have recognized the noble beauty of its modeling, and the graceful severity of poise and movement, which made Edna Pontellier different from the crowd.

She wore a cool muslin that morning—white, with a waving vertical line of brown running through it; also a white linen collar and the big straw hat which she had taken from the peg outside the door. The hat rested any way on her yellow-brown hair, that waved a little, was heavy, and clung close to her head.

Madame Ratignolle, more careful of her complexion, had twined a gauze veil about her head. She wore dogskin gloves, with gauntlets that protected her wrists. She was dressed in pure white, with a fluffiness of ruffles that became her. The draperies and fluttering things which she wore suited her rich, luxuriant beauty as a greater severity of line could not have done.

There were a number of bath-houses along the beach, of rough but solid construction, built with small, protecting galleries facing the water. Each house consisted of two compartments, and each family at Lebrun's possessed a compartment for itself, fitted out with all the essential paraphernalia of the bath and whatever other conveniences the owners might desire. The two women had no intention of bathing; they had just strolled down to the beach for a walk and to be alone and near the water. The Pontellier and Ratignolle compartments adjoined one another under the same roof.

Mrs. Pontellier had brought down her key through force of habit. Unlocking the door of her bathroom she went inside, and soon emerged, bringing a rug, which she spread upon the floor of the gallery, and two huge hair pillows covered with crash, which she placed against the front of the building.

The two seated themselves there in the shade of the porch, side by side, with their backs against the pillows and their feet extended. Madame Ratignolle removed her veil, wiped her face with a rather delicate handkerchief, and fanned herself with the fan which she always carried suspended somewhere about her person by a long, narrow ribbon. Edna removed her collar and opened her dress at the throat. She took the fan from Madame Ratignolle and began to fan both herself and her companion. It was very warm, and for a while they did nothing but exchange remarks about the heat, the sun, the glare. But there was a breeze blowing, a choppy, stiff wind that whipped the water into froth. It fluttered the skirts of the two women and kept them for a while engaged in adjusting, readjusting, tucking in, securing hair-pins and hat-pins. A few persons were sporting some distance away in the water. The beach was very still of human sound at that hour. The lady in black was reading her morning devotions on the porch of a neighboring bath-house. Two young lovers were exchanging their hearts' yearnings beneath the children's tent, which they had found unoccupied.

Edna Pontellier, casting her eyes about, had finally kept them at rest upon the sea. The day was clear and carried the gaze out as far as the blue sky went; there were a few white clouds suspended idly over the horizon. A lateen sail was visible in the direction of

Cat Island, and others to the south seemed almost motionless in the far distance.

"Of whom—of what are you thinking?" asked Adèle of her companion, whose countenance she had been watching with a little amused attention, arrested by the absorbed expression which seemed to have seized and fixed every feature into a statuesque repose.

"Nothing," returned Mrs. Pontellier, with a start, adding at once: "How stupid! But it seems to me it is the reply we make instinctively to such a question. Let me see," she went on, throwing back her head and narrowing her fine eyes till they shone like two vivid points of light. "Let me see. I was really not conscious of thinking of anything; but perhaps I can retrace my thoughts."

"Oh! never mind!" laughed Madame Ratignolle. "I am not quite so exacting. I will let you off this time. It is really too hot to think, especially to think about thinking."

"But for the fun of it," persisted Edna. "First of all, the sight of the water stretching so far away, those motionless sails against the blue sky, made a delicious picture that I just wanted to sit and look at. The hot wind beating in my face made me think—without any connection that I can trace—of a summer day in Kentucky, of a meadow that seemed as big as the ocean to the very little girl walking through the grass, which was higher than her waist. She threw out her arms as if swimming when she walked, beating the tall grass as one strikes out in the water. Oh, I see the connection now!"

"Where were you going that day in Kentucky, walking through the grass?"

"I don't remember now. I was just walking diagonally across a big field. My sun-bonnet obstructed the view. I could see only the stretch of green before me, and I felt as if I must walk on forever, without coming to the end of it. I don't remember whether I was frightened or pleased. I must have been entertained.

"Likely as not it was Sunday," she laughed; "and I was running away from prayers, from the Presbyterian service, read in a spirit of gloom by my father that chills me yet to think of."

"And have you been running away from prayers ever since, *ma chère?*" asked Madame Ratignolle, amused.

"No! oh, no!" Edna hastened to say. "I was a little unthinking child in those days, just following a misleading impulse without question. On the contrary, during one period of my life religion took a firm hold upon me; after I was twelve and until—until—why, I suppose until now, though I never thought much about it—just driven along by habit. But do you know," she broke off, turning her quick eyes upon Madame Ratignolle and leaning forward a little so as to bring her face quite close to that of her companion, "sometimes I feel this summer as if I were walking through the green meadow again; idly, aimlessly, unthinking and unguided."

Madame Ratignolle laid her hand over that of Mrs. Pontellier, which was near her. Seeing that the hand was not withdrawn, she clasped it firmly and warmly. She even stroked it a little, fondly, with the other hand, murmuring in an undertone, *"Pauvre chérie."*

The action was at first a little confusing to Edna, but she soon lent herself readily to the Creole's gentle caress. She was not accustomed to an outward and spoken expression of affection, either in herself or in others. She and her younger sister, Janet, had quarreled a good deal through force of unfortunate habit. Her older sister, Margaret, was matronly and dignified, probably from having assumed matronly and housewifely responsibilities too early in life, their mother having died when they were quite young. Margaret was not effusive; she was practical.

Edna had had an occasional girl friend, but whether accidentally or not, they seemed to have been all of one type—the self-contained. She never realized that the reserve of her own character had much, perhaps everything, to do with this. Her most intimate friend at school had been one of rather exceptional intellectual gifts, who wrote fine-sounding essays, which Edna admired and strove to imitate; and with her she talked and glowed over the English classics, and sometimes held religious and political controversies.

Edna often wondered at one propensity which sometimes had inwardly disturbed her without causing any outward show or manifestation on her part. At a very early age—perhaps it was when she traversed the ocean of waving grass—she remembered that she had been passionately enamored of a dignified and sad-eyed cavalry officer who visited her father in Kentucky. She could not leave his presence when he was there, nor remove her eyes from his face, which was something like Napoleon's, with a lock of black hair falling across the forehead. But the cavalry officer melted imperceptibly out of her existence.

At another time her affections were deeply engaged by a young gentleman who visited a lady on a neighboring plantation. It was after they went to Mississippi to live. The young man was engaged to be married to the young lady, and they sometimes called upon Margaret, driving over of afternoons in a buggy. Edna was a little miss, just merging into her teens; and the realization that she herself was nothing, nothing, nothing to the engaged young man was a bitter affliction to her. But he, too, went the way of dreams.

She was a grown young woman when she was overtaken by what she supposed to be the climax of her fate. It was when the face and figure of a great tragedian began to haunt her imagination and stir her senses.

The persistence of the infatuation lent it an aspect of genuineness. The hopelessness of it colored it with the lofty tones of a great passion. The picture of the tragedian stood enframed upon her desk. Any one may possess the portrait of a tragedian without exciting suspicion or comment. (This was a sinister reflection which she cherished.) In the presence of others she expressed admiration for his exalted gifts, as she handed the photograph around and dwelt upon the fidelity of the likeness. When alone she sometimes picked it up and kissed the cold glass passionately.

Her marriage to Léonce Pontellier was purely an accident, in this respect resembling many other marriages which masquerade as the decrees of Fate. It was in the midst of her secret great passion that she met him. He fell in love, as men are in the habit of doing, and pressed his suit with an earnestness and an ardor which left nothing to be desired. He pleased her; his absolute devotion flattered her. She fancied there was a sympathy of thought and taste between them, in which fancy she was mistaken. Add to this the violent opposition of her father and her sister Margaret to her marriage with a Catholic, and we need seek no further for the motives which led her to accept Monsieur Pontellier for her husband.

The acme of bliss, which would have been a marriage with the tragedian, was not for her in this world. As the devoted wife of a man who worshiped her, she felt she would take her place with a certain dignity in the world of reality, closing the portals forever behind her upon the realm of romance and dreams.

But it was not long before the tragedian had gone to join the cavalry officer and the engaged young man and a few others; and Edna found herself face to face with the realities. She grew fond of her husband, realizing with some unaccountable satisfaction that no trace of passion or excessive and fictitious warmth colored her affection, thereby threatening its dissolution.

She was fond of her children in an uneven, impulsive way. She would sometimes gather them passionately to her heart; she would sometimes forget them. The year before they had spent part of the summer with their grandmother Pontellier in Iberville. Feeling secure regarding their happiness and welfare, she did not miss them except with an occasional intense longing. Their absence was a sort of relief, though she did not admit this, even to herself. It seemed to free her of a responsibility which she had blindly assumed and for which Fate had not fitted her.

Edna did not reveal so much as all this to Madame Ratignolle that summer day when they sat with faces turned to the sea. But a good part of it escaped her. She had put her head down on Madame Ratignolle's shoulder. She was flushed and felt intoxicated with the sound of her own voice and the unaccustomed taste of candor. It muddled her like wine, or like a first breath of freedom.

There was the sound of approaching voices. It was Robert, surrounded by a troop of children, searching for them. The two little Pontelliers were with him, and he carried Madame Ratignolle's little girl in his arms. There were other children beside, and two nurse-maids followed, looking disagreeable and resigned.

The women at once rose and began to shake out their draperies and relax their muscles. Mrs. Pontellier threw the cushions and rug into the bath-house. The children all scampered off to the awning, and they stood there in a line, gazing upon the intruding lovers, still exchanging their vows and sighs. The lovers got up, with only a silent protest, and walked slowly away somewhere else.

The children possessed themselves of the tent, and Mrs. Pontellier went over to join them.

Madame Ratignolle begged Robert to accompany her to the house; she complained of cramp in her limbs and stiffness of the joints. She leaned draggingly upon his arm as they walked.

VIII

"Do me a favor, Robert," spoke the pretty woman at his side, almost as soon as she and Robert had started on their slow, homeward way. She looked up in his face, leaning on his arm beneath the encircling shadow of the umbrella which he had lifted.

"Granted; as many as you like," he returned, glancing down into her eyes that were full of thoughtfulness and some speculation.

"I only ask for one; let Mrs. Pontellier alone."

"*Tiens!*" he exclaimed, with a sudden, boyish laugh. "*Voilà que Madame Ratignolle est jalouse!*"

"Nonsense! I'm in earnest; I mean what I say. Let Mrs. Pontellier alone."

"Why?" he asked; himself growing serious at his companion's solicitation.

"She is not one of us; she is not like us. She might make the unfortunate blunder of taking you seriously."

His face flushed with annoyance, and taking off his soft hat he began to beat it impatiently against his leg as he walked. "Why shouldn't she take me seriously?" he demanded sharply. "Am I a comedian, a clown, a jack-in-the-box? Why shouldn't she? You Creoles! I have no patience with you! Am I always to be regarded as a feature of an amusing programme? I hope Mrs. Pontellier does take me seriously. I hope she has discernment enough to find in me something besides the *blagueur.* If I thought there was any doubt—"

"Oh, enough, Robert!" she broke into his heated outburst. "You are not thinking of what you are saying. You speak with about as little reflection as we might expect from one of those children down there playing in the sand. If your attentions to any married women here were ever offered with any intention of being convincing, you would not be the gentleman we all know you to be, and you would be unfit to associate with the wives and daughters of the people who trust you."

Madame Ratignolle had spoken what she believed to be the law and the gospel. The young man shrugged his shoulders impatiently.

"Oh! well! That isn't it," slamming his hat down vehemently upon his head. "You ought to feel that such things are not flattering to say to a fellow."

"Should our whole intercourse consist of an exchange of compliments? *Ma foi!*"

"It isn't pleasant to have a woman tell you—" he went on, unheedingly, but breaking off suddenly: "Now if I were like Arobin—you remember Alcée Arobin and that story of the consul's wife at Biloxi?" And he related the story of Alcée Arobin and the consul's wife; and another about the tenor of the French Opera, who received letters which should never have been written; and still other stories, grave and gay, till Mrs. Pontellier and her possible propensity for taking young men seriously was apparently forgotten.

Madame Ratignolle, when they had regained her cottage, went in to take the hour's rest which she considered helpful. Before leaving her, Robert begged her pardon for the impatience—he called it rudeness—with which he had received her well-meant caution.

"You made one mistake, Adèle," he said, with a light smile; "there is no earthly possibility of Mrs. Pontellier ever taking me seriously. You should have warned me against taking myself seriously. Your advice might then have carried some weight and given me subject for some reflection. *Au revoir.* But you look tired," he added, solicitously. "Would you like a cup of bouillon? Shall I stir you a toddy? Let me mix you a toddy with a drop of Angostura."

She acceded to the suggestion of bouillon, which was grateful and acceptable. He went himself to the kitchen, which was a building apart from the cottages and lying to the rear of the house. And he himself brought her the golden-brown bouillon, in a dainty Sèvres cup, with a flaky cracker or two on the saucer.

She thrust a bare, white arm from the curtain which shielded her open door, and received the cup from his hands. She told him he was a *bon garçon,* and she meant it. Robert thanked her and turned away toward "the house."

The lovers were just entering the grounds of the *pension*. They were leaning toward each other as the water-oaks bent from the sea. There was not a particle of earth beneath their feet. Their heads might have been turned upside-down, so absolutely did they tread upon blue ether. The lady in black, creeping behind them, looked a trifle paler and more jaded than usual. There was no sign of Mrs. Pontellier and the children. Robert scanned the distance for any such apparition. They would doubtless remain away till the dinner hour. The young man ascended to his mother's room. It was situated at the top of the house, made up of odd angles and a queer, sloping ceiling. Two broad dormer windows looked out toward the Gulf, and as far across it as a man's eye might reach. The furnishings of the room were light, cool, and practical

Madame Lebrun was busily engaged at the sewing-machine. A little black girl sat on the floor, and with her hands worked the treadle of the machine. The Creole woman does not take any chances which may be avoided of imperiling her health.

Robert went over and seated himself on the broad sill of one of the dormer windows. He took a book from his pocket and began energetically to read it, judging by the precision and frequency with which he turned the leaves. The sewing-machine made a resounding clatter in the room; it was of a ponderous, by-gone make. In the lulls, Robert and his mother exchanged bits of desultory conversation.

"Where is Mrs. Pontellier?"

"Down at the beach with the children."

"I promised to lend her the Goncourt. Don't forget to take it down when you go; it's there on the bookshelf over the small table." Clatter, clatter, clatter, bang! for the next five or eight minutes.

"Where is Victor going with the rockaway?"

"The rockaway? Victor?"

"Yes; down there in front. He seems to be getting ready to drive away somewhere."

"Call him." Clatter, clatter!

Robert uttered a shrill, piercing whistle which might have been heard back at the wharf.

"He won't look up."

Madame Lebrun flew to the window. She called "Victor!" She waved a handkerchief and called again. The young fellow below got into the vehicle and started the horse off at a gallop. Madame Lebrun went back to the machine, crimson with annoyance.

Victor was the younger son and brother—a *tête montée*, with a temper which invited violence and a will which no ax could break.

"Whenever you say the word I'm ready to thrash any amount of reason into him that he's able to hold."

"If your father had only lived!" Clatter, clatter, clatter, clatter, bang! It was a fixed belief with Madame Lebrun that the conduct of the universe and all things pertaining thereto would have been manifestly of a more intelligent and higher order had not Monsieur Lebrun been removed to other spheres during the early years of their married life.

"What do you hear from Montel?" Montel was a middle-aged gentleman whose vain ambition and desire for the past twenty years had been to fill the void which Monsieur Lebrun's taking off had left in the Lebrun household. Clatter, clatter, bang, clatter!

"I have a letter somewhere," looking in the machine drawer and finding the letter in the bottom of the work-basket. "He says to tell you he will be in Vera Cruz the beginning of next month"—clatter, clatter!—"and if you still have the intention of joining him"—bang! clatter, clatter, bang!

"Why didn't you tell me so before, mother? You know I wanted—" Clatter, clatter, clatter!

"Do you see Mrs. Pontellier starting back with the children? She will be in late to luncheon again. She never starts to get ready for luncheon till the last minute." Clatter, clatter!

"Where are you going?" "Where did you say the Goncourt was?"

IX

Every light in the hall was ablaze; every lamp turned as high as it could be without smoking the chimney or threatening explosion. The lamps were fixed at intervals against the wall, encircling the whole room. Some one had gathered orange and lemon branches, and with these fashioned graceful festoons between. The dark green of the branches stood out and glistened against the white muslin curtains which draped the windows, and which puffed, floated, and flapped at the capricious will of a stiff breeze that swept up from the Gulf.

It was Saturday night a few weeks after the intimate conversation held between Robert and Madame Ratignolle on their way from the beach. An unusual number of husbands, fathers, and friends had come down to stay over Sunday; and they were being suitably entertained by their families, with the material help of Madame Lebrun. The dining tables had all been removed to one end of the hall, and the chairs ranged about in rows and in clusters. Each little family group had had its say and exchanged its domestic gossip earlier in the evening. There was now an apparent disposition to relax; to widen the circle of confidences and give a more general tone to the conversation.

Many of the children had been permitted to sit up beyond their usual bedtime. A small band of them were lying on their stomachs on the floor looking at the colored sheets of the comic papers which Mr. Pontellier had brought down. The little Pontellier boys were permitting them to do so, and making their authority felt.

Music, dancing, and a recitation or two were the entertainments furnished, or rather, offered. But there was nothing systematic about the programme, no appearance of prearrangement nor even premeditation.

At an early hour in the evening the Farival twins were prevailed upon to play the piano. They were girls of fourteen, always clad in the Virgin's colors, blue and white, having been dedicated to the Blessed Virgin at their baptism. They played a duet from "Zampa," and at the earnest solicitation of every one present followed it with the overture to "The Poet and the Peasant."

"*Allez vous-en! Sapristi!*" shrieked the parrot outside the door. He was the only being present who possessed sufficient candor to admit that he was not listening to these gracious performances for the first time that summer. Old Monsieur Farival, grandfather of the twins, grew indignant over the interruption, and insisted upon having the bird removed and consigned to regions of darkness. Victor Lebrun objected; and his decrees were as immutable as those of Fate. The parrot fortunately offered no further interruption to the entertainment, the whole venom of his nature apparently having been cherished up and hurled against the twins in that one impetuous outburst.

Later a young brother and sister gave recitations, which every one present had heard many times at winter evening entertainments in the city.

A little girl performed a skirt dance in the center of the floor. The mother played her accompaniments and at the same time watched her daughter with greedy admiration and nervous apprehension. She need have had no apprehension. The child was mistress of the situation. She had been properly dressed for the occasion in black tulle and black silk tights. Her little neck and arms were bare, and her hair, artificially crimped, stood out like fluffy black plumes over her head. Her poses were full of grace, and her little black-shod toes twinkled as they shot out and upward with a rapidity and suddenness which were bewildering.

But there was no reason why every one should not dance. Madame Ratignolle could not, so it was she who gaily consented to play for the others. She played very well, keeping excellent waltz time and infusing an expression into the strains which was indeed inspiring. She was keeping up her music on account of the children, she said; because she and her husband both considered it a means of brightening the home and making it attractive.

Almost every one danced but the twins, who could not be induced to separate during the brief period when one or the other should be whirling around the room in the arms of a man. They might have danced together, but they did not think of it.

The children were sent to bed. Some went submissively; others with shrieks and protests as they were dragged away. They had been permitted to sit up till after the ice-cream, which naturally marked the limit of human indulgence.

The ice-cream was passed around with cake—gold and silver cake arranged on platters in alternate slices; it had been made and frozen during the afternoon back of the kitchen by two black women, under the supervision of Victor. It was pronounced a great success—excellent if it had only contained a little less vanilla or a little more sugar, if it had been frozen a degree harder, and if the salt might have been kept out of portions of it. Victor was proud of his achievement, and went about recommending it and urging every one to partake of it to excess.

After Mrs. Pontellier had danced twice with her husband, once with Robert, and once with Monsieur Ratignolle, who was thin and tall and swayed like a reed in the wind when he danced, she went out on the gallery and seated herself on the low window-sill, where she commanded a view of all that went on in the hall and could look out toward the Gulf. There was a soft effulgence in the east. The moon was coming up, and its mystic shimmer was casting a million lights across the distant, restless water.

"Would you like to hear Mademoiselle Reisz play?" asked Robert, coming out on the porch where she was. Of course Edna would like to hear Mademoiselle Reisz play; but she feared it would be useless to entreat her.

"I'll ask her," he said. "I'll tell her that you want to hear her. She likes you. She will come." He turned and hurried away to one of the far cottages, where Mademoiselle Reisz was shuffling away. She was dragging a chair in and out of her room, and at intervals objecting to the crying of a baby, which a nurse in the adjoining cottage was endeavoring to put to sleep. She was a disagreeable little woman, no longer young, who had quarreled with almost every one, owing to a temper which was self-assertive and a disposition to trample upon the rights of others. Robert prevailed upon her without any too great difficulty.

She entered the hall with him during a lull in the dance. She made an awkward, imperious little bow as she went in. She was a homely woman, with a small weazened face and body and eyes that glowed. She had absolutely no taste in dress, and wore a batch of rusty black lace with a bunch of artificial violets pinned to the side of her hair.

"Ask Mrs. Pontellier what she would like to hear me play," she requested of Robert. She sat perfectly still before the piano, not touching the keys, while Robert carried her message to Edna at the window. A general air of surprise and genuine satisfaction fell upon every one as they saw the pianist enter. There was a settling down, and a prevailing air of expectancy everywhere. Edna was a trifle embarrassed at being thus signaled out for the imperious little woman's favor. She would not dare to choose, and begged that Mademoiselle Reisz would please herself in her selections.

Edna was what she herself called very fond of music. Musical strains, well rendered, had a way of evoking pictures in her mind.

She sometimes liked to sit in the room of mornings when Madame Ratignolle played or practiced. One piece which that lady played Edna had entitled "Solitude." It was a short, plaintive, minor strain. The name of the piece was something else, but she called it "Solitude." When she heard it there came before her imagination the figure of a man standing beside a desolate rock on the seashore. He was naked. His attitude was one of hopeless resignation as he looked toward a distant bird winging its flight away from him.

Another piece called to her mind a dainty young woman clad in an Empire gown, taking mincing dancing steps as she came down a long avenue between tall hedges. Again, another reminded her of children at play, and still another of nothing on earth but a demure lady stroking a cat.

The very first chords which Mademoiselle Reisz struck upon the piano sent a keen tremor down Mrs. Pontellier's spinal column. It was not the first time she had heard an artist at the piano. Perhaps it was the first time she was ready, perhaps the first time her being was tempered to take an impress of the abiding truth.

She waited for the material pictures which she thought would gather and blaze before her imagination. She waited in vain. She saw no pictures of solitude, of hope, of longing, or of despair. But the very passions themselves were aroused within her soul, swaying it, lashing it, as the waves daily beat upon her splendid body. She trembled, she was choking, and the tears blinded her.

Mademoiselle had finished. She arose, and bowing her stiff, lofty bow, she went away, stopping for neither thanks nor applause. As she passed along the gallery she patted Edna upon the shoulder.

"Well, how did you like my music?" she asked. The young woman was unable to answer; she pressed the hand of the pianist convulsively.

Mademoiselle Reisz perceived her agitation and even her tears. She patted her again upon the shoulder as she said:

"You are the only one worth playing for. Those others? Bah!" and she went shuffling and sidling on down the gallery toward her room.

But she was mistaken about "those others." Her playing had aroused a fever of enthusiasm. "What passion!" "What an artist!"

"I have always said no one could play Chopin like Mademoiselle Reisz!" "That last prelude! Bon Dieu! It shakes a man!"

It was growing late, and there was a general disposition to disband. But some one, perhaps it was Robert, thought of a bath at that mystic hour and under that mystic moon.

X

At all events Robert proposed it, and there was not a dissenting voice. There was not one but was ready to follow when he led the way. He did not lead the way, however, he directed the way; and he himself loitered behind with the lovers, who had betrayed a disposition to linger and hold themselves apart. He walked between them, whether with malicious or mischievous intent was not wholly clear, even to himself.

The Pontelliers and Ratignolles walked ahead; the women leaning upon the arms of their husbands. Edna could hear Robert's voice behind them, and could sometimes hear what he said. She wondered why he did not join them. It was unlike him not to. Of late he had sometimes held away from her for an entire day, redoubling his devotion upon the next and the next, as though to make up for hours that had been lost. She missed him the days when some pretext served to take him away from her, just as one misses the sun on a cloudy day without having thought much about the sun when it was shining.

The people walked in little groups toward the beach. They talked and laughed; some of them sang. There was a band playing down at Klein's hotel, and the strains reached them faintly, tempered by the distance. There were strange, rare odors abroad—a tangle of the sea-smell and of weeds and damp, new-plowed earth, mingled with the heavy perfume of a field of white blossoms somewhere near. But the night sat lightly upon the sea and the land. There was no weight of darkness; there were no shadows. The white light of the moon had fallen upon the world like the mystery and the softness of sleep.

Most of them walked into the water as though into a native element. The sea was quiet now, and swelled lazily in broad billows that melted into one another and did not break except upon the beach in little foamy crests that coiled back like slow, white serpents.

Edna had attempted all summer to learn to swim. She had received instructions from both the men and women; in some instances from the children. Robert had pursued a system of lessons almost daily; and he was nearly at the point of discouragement in realizing the futility of his efforts. A certain ungovernable dread hung about her when in the water, unless there was a hand near by that might reach out and reassure her.

But that night she was like the little tottering, stumbling, clutching child, who of a sudden realizes its powers, and walks for the first time alone, boldly and with over-confidence. She could have shouted for joy. She did shout for joy, as with a sweeping stroke or two she lifted her body to the surface of the water.

A feeling of exultation overtook her, as if some power of significant import had been given her to control the working of her body and her soul. She grew daring and reckless, overestimating her strength. She wanted to swim far out, where no woman had swum before.

Her unlooked-for achievement was the subject of wonder, applause, and admiration. Each one congratulated himself that his special teachings had accomplished this desired end.

"How easy it is!" she thought. "It is nothing," she said aloud; "why did I not discover before that it was nothing. Think of the time I have lost splashing about like a baby!" She would not join the groups in their sports and bouts, but intoxicated with her newly conquered power, she swam out alone.

She turned her face seaward to gather in an impression of space and solitude, which the vast expanse of water, meeting and melting with the moonlit sky, conveyed to her excited fancy. As she swam she seemed to be reaching out for the unlimited in which to lose herself.

Once she turned and looked toward the shore, toward the people she had left there. She had not gone any great distance— that is, what would have been a great distance for an experienced swimmer. But to her unaccustomed vision the stretch of water behind her assumed the aspect of a barrier which her unaided strength would never be able to overcome.

A quick vision of death smote her soul, and for a second of time appalled and enfeebled her senses. But by an effort she rallied her staggering faculties and managed to regain the land.

She made no mention of her encounter with death and her flash of terror, except to say to her husband, "I thought I should have perished out there alone."

"You were not so very far, my dear; I was watching you," he told her.

Edna went at once to the bath-house, and she had put on her dry clothes and was ready to return home before the others had left the water. She started to walk away alone. They all called to her and shouted to her. She waved a dissenting hand, and went on, paying no further heed to their renewed cries which sought to detain her.

"Sometimes I am tempted to think that Mrs. Pontellier is capricious," said Madame Lebrun, who was amusing herself immensely and feared that Edna's abrupt departure might put an end to the pleasure.

"I know she is," assented Mr. Pontellier; "sometimes, not often."

Edna had not traversed a quarter of the distance on her way home before she was overtaken by Robert.

"Did you think I was afraid?" she asked him, without a shade of annoyance.

"No; I knew you weren't afraid."

"Then why did you come? Why didn't you stay out there with the others?"

"I never thought of it."

"Thought of what?"

"Of anything. What difference does it make?"

"I'm very tired," she uttered, complainingly.

"I know you are."

"You don't know anything about it. Why should you know? I never was so exhausted in my life. But it isn't unpleasant. A thousand emotions have swept through me to-night. I don't comprehend half of them. Don't mind what I'm saying; I am just thinking aloud. I wonder if I shall ever be stirred again as Mademoiselle Reisz's playing moved me to-night. I wonder if any night on earth will ever again be like this one. It is like a night in a dream. The people about me are like some uncanny, half-human beings. There must be spirits abroad to-night."

"There are," whispered Robert. "Didn't you know this was the twenty-eighth of August?"

"The twenty-eighth of August?"

"Yes. On the twenty-eighth of August, at the hour of midnight, and if the moon is shining—the moon must be shining—a spirit that has haunted these shores for ages rises up from the Gulf. With its own penetrating vision the spirit seeks some one mortal worthy to hold him company, worthy of being exalted for a few hours into realms of the semi-celestials. His search has always hitherto been fruitless, and he has sunk back, disheartened, into the sea. But to-night he found Mrs. Pontellier. Perhaps he will never wholly release her from the spell. Perhaps she will never again suffer a poor, unworthy earthling to walk in the shadow of her divine presence."

"Don't banter me," she said, wounded at what appeared to be his flippancy. He did not mind the entreaty, but the tone with its delicate note of pathos was like a reproach. He could not explain; he could not tell her that he had penetrated her mood and understood. He said nothing except to offer her his arm, for, by her own admission, she was exhausted. She had been walking alone with her arms hanging limp, letting her white skirts trail along the dewy path. She took his arm, but she did not lean upon it. She let her hand lie listlessly, as though her thoughts were elsewhere—somewhere in advance of her body, and she was striving to overtake them.

Robert assisted her into the hammock which swung from the post before her door out to the trunk of a tree.

"Will you stay out here and wait for Mr. Pontellier?" he asked.

"I'll stay out here. Good-night."

"Shall I get you a pillow?"

"There's one here," she said, feeling about, for they were in the shadow.

"It must be soiled; the children have been tumbling it about."

"No matter." And having discovered the pillow, she adjusted it beneath her head. She extended herself in the hammock with a deep breath of relief. She was not a supercilious or an over-dainty woman. She was not much given to reclining in the hammock, and when she did so it was with no cat-like suggestion of voluptuous ease, but with a beneficent repose which seemed to invade her whole body.

"Shall I stay with you till Mr. Pontellier comes?" asked Robert, seating himself on the outer edge of one of the steps and taking hold of the hammock rope which was fastened to the post.

"If you wish. Don't swing the hammock. Will you get my white shawl which I left on the window-sill over at the house?"

"Are you chilly?"

"No; but I shall be presently."

"Presently?" he laughed. "Do you know what time it is? How long are you going to stay out here?"

"I don't know. Will you get the shawl?"

"Of course I will," he said, rising. He went over to the house, walking along the grass. She watched his figure pass in and out of the strips of moonlight. It was past midnight. It was very quiet.

When he returned with the shawl she took it and kept it in her hand. She did not put it around her.

"Did you say I should stay till Mr. Pontellier came back?"

"I said you might if you wished to."

He seated himself again and rolled a cigarette, which he smoked in silence. Neither did Mrs. Pontellier speak. No multitude of words could have been more significant than those moments of silence, or more pregnant with the first-felt throbbings of desire.

When the voices of the bathers were heard approaching, Robert said good-night. She did not answer him. He thought she was asleep. Again she watched his figure pass in and out of the strips of moonlight as he walked away.

XI

"What are you doing out here, Edna? I thought I should find you in bed," said her husband, when he discovered her lying there. He had walked up with Madame Lebrun and left her at the house. His wife did not reply.

"Are you asleep?" he asked, bending down close to look at her.

"No." Her eyes gleamed bright and intense, with no sleepy shadows, as they looked into his.

"Do you know it is past one o'clock? Come on," and he mounted the steps and went into their room.

"Edna!" called Mr. Pontellier from within, after a few moments had gone by.

"Don't wait for me," she answered. He thrust his head through the door.

"You will take cold out there," he said, irritably. "What folly is this? Why don't you come in?"

"It isn't cold; I have my shawl."

"The mosquitoes will devour you."

"There are no mosquitoes."

She heard him moving about the room; every sound indicating impatience and irritation. Another time she would have gone in at his request. She would, through habit, have yielded to his desire; not with any sense of submission or obedience to his compelling wishes, but unthinkingly, as we walk, move, sit, stand, go through the daily treadmill of the life which has been portioned out to us.

"Edna, dear, are you not coming in soon?" he asked again, this time fondly, with a note of entreaty.

"No; I am going to stay out here."

"This is more than folly," he blurted out. "I can't permit you to stay out there all night. You must come in the house instantly."

With a writhing motion she settled herself more securely in the hammock. She perceived that her will had blazed up, stubborn and resistant. She could not at that moment have done other than denied and resisted. She wondered if her husband had ever spoken to her like that before, and if she had submitted to his command. Of course she had; she remembered that she had. But she could not realize why or how she should have yielded, feeling as she then did.

"Léonce, go to bed," she said. "I mean to stay out here. I don't wish to go in, and I don't intend to. Don't speak to me like that again; I shall not answer you."

Mr. Pontellier had prepared for bed, but he slipped on an extra garment. He opened a bottle of wine, of which he kept a small and select supply in a buffet of his own. He drank a glass of the wine and went out on the gallery and offered a glass to his wife. She did not wish any. He drew up the rocker, hoisted his slippered feet on the rail, and proceeded to smoke a cigar. He smoked two cigars;

then he went inside and drank another glass of wine. Mrs. Pontellier again declined to accept a glass when it was offered to her. Mr. Pontellier once more seated himself with elevated feet, and after a reasonable interval of time smoked some more cigars.

Edna began to feel like one who awakens gradually out of a dream, a delicious, grotesque, impossible dream, to feel again the realities pressing into her soul. The physical need for sleep began to overtake her; the exuberance which had sustained and exalted her spirit left her helpless and yielding to the conditions which crowded her in.

The stillest hour of the night had come, the hour before dawn, when the world seems to hold its breath. The moon hung low, and had turned from silver to copper in the sleeping sky. The old owl no longer hooted, and the water-oaks had ceased to moan as they bent their heads.

Edna arose, cramped from lying so long and still in the hammock. She tottered up the steps, clutching feebly at the post before passing into the house.

"Are you coming in, Léonce?" she asked, turning her face toward her husband.

"Yes, dear," he answered, with a glance following a misty puff of smoke. "Just as soon as I have finished my cigar."

XII

She slept but a few hours. They were troubled and feverish hours, disturbed with dreams that were intangible, that eluded her, leaving only an impression upon her half-awakened senses of something unattainable. She was up and dressed in the cool of the early morning. The air was invigorating and steadied somewhat her faculties. However, she was not seeking refreshment or help from any source, either external or from within. She was blindly following whatever impulse moved her, as if she had placed herself in alien hands for direction, and freed her soul of responsibility.

Most of the people at that early hour were still in bed and asleep. A few, who intended to go over to the *Chênière* for mass, were moving about. The lovers, who had laid their plans the night before, were already strolling toward the wharf. The lady in

black, with her Sunday prayerbook, velvet and gold-clasped, and
her Sunday silver beads, was following them at no great distance.
Old Monsieur Farival was up, and was more than half inclined to
do anything that suggested itself. He put on his big straw hat, and
taking his umbrella from the stand in the hall, followed the lady
in black, never overtaking her.

The little negro girl who worked Madame Lebrun's sewing-
machine was sweeping the galleries with long, absent-minded
strokes of the broom. Edna sent her up into the house to awaken
Robert.

"Tell him I am going to the *Chênière*. The boat is ready; tell
him to hurry."

He had soon joined her. She had never sent for him before. She
had never asked for him. She had never seemed to want him
before. She did not appear conscious that she had done anything
unusual in commanding his presence. He was apparently equally
unconscious of anything extraordinary in the situation. But his face
was suffused with a quiet glow when he met her.

They went together back to the kitchen to drink coffee. There
was no time to wait for any nicety of service. They stood outside the
window and the cook passed them their coffee and a roll, which
they drank and ate from the window-sill. Edna said it tasted good.
She had not thought of coffee nor of anything. He told her he had
often noticed that she lacked forethought.

"Wasn't it enough to think of going to the *Chênière* and waking
you up?" she laughed. "Do I have to think of everything?—as
Léonce says when he's in a bad humor. I don't blame him; he'd
never be in a bad humor if it weren't for me."

They took a short cut across the sands. At a distance they could
see the curious procession moving toward the wharf—the lovers,
shoulder to shoulder, creeping; the lady in black, gaining steadily
on them; old Monsieur Farival, losing ground inch by inch, and a
young barefooted Spanish girl, with a red kerchief on her head and
a basket on her arm, bringing up the rear.

Robert knew the girl, and he talked to her a little in the boat.
No one present understood what they said. Her name was
Mariequita. She had a round, sly, piquant face and pretty black
eyes. Her hands were small, and she kept them folded over the
handle of her basket. Her feet were broad and coarse. She did not

strive to hide them. Edna looked at her feet, and noticed the sand and slime between her brown toes.

Beaudelet grumbled because Mariequita was there, taking up so much room. In reality he was annoyed at having old Monsieur Farival, who considered himself the better sailor of the two. But he would not quarrel with so old a man as Monsieur Farival, so he quarreled with Mariequita. The girl was deprecatory at one moment, appealing to Robert. She was saucy the next, moving her head up and down, making "eyes" at Robert and making "mouths" at Beaudelet.

The lovers were all alone. They saw nothing, they heard nothing. The lady in black was counting her beads for the third time. Old Monsieur Farival talked incessantly of what he knew about handling a boat, and of what Beaudelet did not know on the same subject.

Edna liked it all. She looked Mariequita up and down, from her ugly brown toes to her pretty black eyes, and back again.

"Why does she look at me like that?" inquired the girl of Robert.

"Maybe she thinks you are pretty. Shall I ask her?"

"No. Is she your sweetheart?"

"She's a married lady, and has two children."

"Oh! well! Francisco ran away with Sylvano's wife, who had four children. They took all his money and one of the children and stole his boat."

"Shut up!"

"Does she understand?"

"Oh, hush!" "Are those two married over there—leaning on each other?"

"Of course not," laughed Robert.

"Of course not," echoed Mariequita, with a serious, confirmatory bob of the head.

The sun was high up and beginning to bite. The swift breeze seemed to Edna to bury the sting of it into the pores of her face and hands. Robert held his umbrella over her.

As they went cutting sidewise through the water, the sails bellied taut, with the wind filling and overflowing them. Old Monsieur Farival laughed sardonically at something as he looked at the sails, and Beaudelet swore at the old man under his breath.

Sailing across the bay to the *Chênière Caminada*, Edna felt as if she were being borne away from some anchorage which had held her fast, whose chains had been loosening—had snapped the night before when the mystic spirit was abroad, leaving her free to drift whithersoever she chose to set her sails. Robert spoke to her incessantly; he no longer noticed Mariequita. The girl had shrimps in her bamboo basket. They were covered with Spanish moss. She beat the moss down impatiently, and muttered to herself sullenly.

"Let us go to Grande Terre to-morrow?" said Robert in a low voice.

"What shall we do there?"

"Climb up the hill to the old fort and look at the little wriggling gold snakes, and watch the lizards sun themselves."

She gazed away toward Grande Terre and thought she would like to be alone there with Robert, in the sun, listening to the ocean's roar and watching the slimy lizards writhe in and out among the ruins of the old fort.

"And the next day or the next we can sail to the Bayou Brulow," he went on.

"What shall we do there?"

"Anything—cast bait for fish."

"No; we'll go back to Grande Terre. Let the fish alone."

"We'll go wherever you like," he said. "I'll have Tonie come over and help me patch and trim my boat. We shall not need Beaudelet nor any one. Are you afraid of the pirogue?"

"Oh, no."

"Then I'll take you some night in the pirogue when the moon shines. Maybe your Gulf spirit will whisper to you in which of these islands the treasures are hidden—direct you to the very spot, perhaps."

"And in a day we should be rich!" she laughed. "I'd give it all to you, the pirate gold and every bit of treasure we could dig up. I think you would know how to spend it. Pirate gold isn't a thing to be hoarded or utilized. It is something to squander and throw to the four winds, for the fun of seeing the golden specks fly."

"We'd share it, and scatter it together," he said. His face flushed.

They all went together up to the quaint little Gothic church of Our Lady of Lourdes, gleaming all brown and yellow with paint in the sun's glare.

Only Beaudelet remained behind, tinkering at his boat, and Mariequita walked away with her basket of shrimps, casting a look of childish ill-humor and reproach at Robert from the corner of her eye.

XIII

A feeling of oppression and drowsiness overcame Edna during the service. Her head began to ache, and the lights on the altar swayed before her eyes. Another time she might have made an effort to regain her composure; but her one thought was to quit the stifling atmosphere of the church and reach the open air. She arose, climbing over Robert's feet with a muttered apology. Old Monsieur Farival, flurried, curious, stood up, but upon seeing that Robert had followed Mrs. Pontellier, he sank back into his seat. He whispered an anxious inquiry of the lady in black, who did not notice him or reply, but kept her eyes fastened upon the pages of her velvet prayer-book.

"I felt giddy and almost overcome," Edna said, lifting her hands instinctively to her head and pushing her straw hat up from her forehead. "I couldn't have stayed through the service." They were outside in the shadow of the church. Robert was full of solicitude.

"It was folly to have thought of going in the first place, let alone staying. Come over to Madame Antoine's; you can rest there." He took her arm and led her away, looking anxiously and continuously down into her face.

How still it was, with only the voice of the sea whispering through the reeds that grew in the salt-water pools! The long line of little gray, weather-beaten houses nestled peacefully among the orange trees. It must always have been God's day on that low, drowsy island, Edna thought. They stopped, leaning over a jagged fence made of sea-drift, to ask for water. A youth, a mild-faced Acadian, was drawing water from the cistern, which was nothing more than a rusty buoy, with an opening on one side, sunk in the ground. The water which the youth handed to them in a tin pail was not cold to taste, but it was cool to her heated face, and it greatly revived and refreshed her.

Madame Antoine's cot was at the far end of the village. She welcomed them with all the native hospitality, as she would have opened her door to let the sunlight in. She was fat, and walked heavily and clumsily across the floor. She could speak no English, but when Robert made her understand that the lady who accompanied him was ill and desired to rest, she was all eagerness to make Edna feel at home and to dispose of her comfortably.

The whole place was immaculately clean, and the big, four-posted bed, snow-white, invited one to repose. It stood in a small side room which looked out across a narrow grass plot toward the shed, where there was a disabled boat lying keel upward.

Madame Antoine had not gone to mass. Her son Tonie had, but she supposed he would soon be back, and she invited Robert to be seated and wait for him. But he went and sat outside the door and smoked. Madame Antoine busied herself in the large front room preparing dinner. She was boiling mullets over a few red coals in the huge fireplace.

Edna, left alone in the little side room, loosened her clothes, removing the greater part of them. She bathed her face, her neck and arms in the basin that stood between the windows. She took off her shoes and stockings and stretched herself in the very center of the high, white bed. How luxurious it felt to rest thus in a strange, quaint bed, with its sweet country odor of laurel lingering about the sheets and mattress! She stretched her strong limbs that ached a little. She ran her fingers through her loosened hair for a while. She looked at her round arms as she held them straight up and rubbed them one after the other, observing closely, as if it were something she saw for the first time, the fine, firm quality and texture of her flesh. She clasped her hands easily above her head, and it was thus she fell asleep.

She slept lightly at first, half awake and drowsily attentive to the things about her. She could hear Madame Antoine's heavy, scraping tread as she walked back and forth on the sanded floor. Some chickens were clucking outside the windows, scratching for bits of gravel in the grass. Later she half heard the voices of Robert and Tonie talking under the shed. She did not stir. Even her eyelids rested numb and heavily over her sleepy eyes. The voices went on—

Tonie's slow, Acadian drawl, Robert's quick, soft, smooth French. She understood French imperfectly unless directly addressed, and the voices were only part of the other drowsy, muffled sounds lulling her senses.

When Edna awoke it was with the conviction that she had slept long and soundly. The voices were hushed under the shed. Madame Antoine's step was no longer to be heard in the adjoining room. Even the chickens had gone elsewhere to scratch and cluck. The mosquito bar was drawn over her; the old woman had come in while she slept and let down the bar. Edna arose quietly from the bed, and looking between the curtains of the window, she saw by the slanting rays of the sun that the afternoon was far advanced. Robert was out there under the shed, reclining in the shade against the sloping keel of the overturned boat. He was reading from a book. Tonie was no longer with him. She wondered what had become of the rest of the party. She peeped out at him two or three times as she stood washing herself in the little basin between the windows.

Madame Antoine had laid some coarse, clean towels upon a chair, and had placed a box of *poudre de riz* within easy reach. Edna dabbed the powder upon her nose and cheeks as she looked at herself closely in the little distorted mirror which hung on the wall above the basin. Her eyes were bright and wide awake and her face glowed.

When she had completed her toilet she walked into the adjoining room. She was very hungry. No one was there. But there was a cloth spread upon the table that stood against the wall, and a cover was laid for one, with a crusty brown loaf and a bottle of wine beside the plate. Edna bit a piece from the brown loaf, tearing it with her strong, white teeth. She poured some of the wine into the glass and drank it down. Then she went softly out of doors, and plucking an orange from the low-hanging bough of a tree, threw it at Robert, who did not know she was awake and up.

An illumination broke over his whole face when he saw her and joined her under the orange tree.

"How many years have I slept?" she inquired. "The whole island seems changed. A new race of beings must have sprung up, leaving only you and me as past relics. How many ages ago did

Madame Antoine and Tonie die? and when did our people from
Grand Isle disappear from the earth?"

He familiarly adjusted a ruffle upon her shoulder.

"You have slept precisely one hundred years. I was left here to
guard your slumbers; and for one hundred years I have been out
under the shed reading a book. The only evil I couldn't prevent was
to keep a broiled fowl from drying up."

"If it has turned to stone, still will I eat it," said Edna, moving
with him into the house. "But really, what has become of Monsieur
Farival and the others?"

"Gone hours ago. When they found that you were sleeping they
thought it best not to awake you. Any way, I wouldn't have let
them. What was I here for?"

"I wonder if Léonce will be uneasy!" she speculated, as she
seated herself at table.

"Of course not; he knows you are with me," Robert replied, as
he busied himself among sundry pans and covered dishes which
had been left standing on the hearth.

"Where are Madame Antoine and her son?" asked Edna.

"Gone to Vespers, and to visit some friends, I believe. I am to
take you back in Tonie's boat whenever you are ready to go."

He stirred the smoldering ashes till the broiled fowl began to
sizzle afresh. He served her with no mean repast, dripping the
coffee anew and sharing it with her. Madame Antoine had cooked
little else than the mullets, but while Edna slept Robert had
foraged the island. He was childishly gratified to discover her
appetite, and to see the relish with which she ate the food which
he had procured for her.

"Shall we go right away?" she asked, after draining her glass
and brushing together the crumbs of the crusty loaf.

"The sun isn't as low as it will be in two hours," he answered.

"The sun will be gone in two hours."

"Well, let it go; who cares!"

They waited a good while under the orange trees, till Madame
Antoine came back, panting, waddling, with a thousand apologies
to explain her absence. Tonie did not dare to return. He was shy,
and would not willingly face any woman except his mother.

It was very pleasant to stay there under the orange trees, while
the sun dipped lower and lower, turning the western sky to flaming

copper and gold. The shadows lengthened and crept out like stealthy, grotesque monsters across the grass.

Edna and Robert both sat upon the ground—that is, he lay upon the ground beside her, occasionally picking at the hem of her muslin gown.

Madame Antoine seated her fat body, broad and squat, upon a bench beside the door. She had been talking all the afternoon, and had wound herself up to the story-telling pitch.

And what stories she told them! But twice in her life she had left the *Chênière Caminada,* and then for the briefest span. All her years she had squatted and waddled there upon the island, gathering legends of the Baratarians and the sea. The night came on, with the moon to lighten it. Edna could hear the whispering voices of dead men and the click of muffled gold.

When she and Robert stepped into Tonie's boat, with the red lateen sail, misty spirit forms were prowling in the shadows and among the reeds, and upon the water were phantom ships, speeding to cover.

XIV

The youngest boy, Etienne, had been very naughty, Madame Ratignolle said, as she delivered him into the hands of his mother. He had been unwilling to go to bed and had made a scene; whereupon she had taken charge of him and pacified him as well as she could. Raoul had been in bed and asleep for two hours.

The youngster was in his long white nightgown, that kept tripping him up as Madame Ratignolle led him along by the hand. With the other chubby fist he rubbed his eyes, which were heavy with sleep and ill humor. Edna took him in her arms, and seating herself in the rocker, began to coddle and caress him, calling him all manner of tender names, soothing him to sleep.

It was not more than nine o'clock. No one had yet gone to bed but the children.

Léonce had been very uneasy at first, Madame Ratignolle said, and had wanted to start at once for the *Chênière.* But Monsieur Farival had assured him that his wife was only overcome with sleep and fatigue, that Tonie would bring her safely back later in the day; and he had thus been dissuaded from crossing the bay. He had gone over to Klein's, looking up some cotton broker whom he wished to see in regard to securities, exchanges, stocks, bonds, or something of the sort, Madame Ratignolle did not remember what. He said he would not remain away late. She herself was suffering from heat and oppression, she said. She carried a bottle of salts and a large fan. She would not consent to remain with Edna, for Monsieur Ratignolle was alone, and he detested above all things to be left alone.

When Etienne had fallen asleep Edna bore him into the back room, and Robert went and lifted the mosquito bar that she might lay the child comfortably in his bed. The quadroon had vanished. When they emerged from the cottage Robert bade Edna good-night.

"Do you know we have been together the whole livelong day, Robert—since early this morning?" she said at parting.

"All but the hundred years when you were sleeping. Good-night."

He pressed her hand and went away in the direction of the beach. He did not join any of the others, but walked alone toward the Gulf.

Edna stayed outside, awaiting her husband's return. She had no desire to sleep or to retire; nor did she feel like going over to sit with the Ratignolles, or to join Madame Lebrun and a group whose animated voices reached her as they sat in conversation before the house. She let her mind wander back over her stay at Grand Isle; and she tried to discover wherein this summer had been different from any and every other summer of her life. She could only realize that she herself—her present self—was in some way different from the other self. That she was seeing with different eyes and making the acquaintance of new conditions in herself that colored and changed her environment, she did not yet suspect.

She wondered why Robert had gone away and left her. It did not occur to her to think he might have grown tired of being with her the livelong day. She was not tired, and she felt that he was not. She regretted that he had gone. It was so much more natural to have him stay when he was not absolutely required to leave her.

As Edna waited for her husband she sang low a little song that Robert had sung as they crossed the bay. It began with "Ah! *Si tu savais*," and every verse ended with *"si tu savais."*

Robert's voice was not pretentious. It was musical and true. The voice, the notes, the whole refrain haunted her memory.

XV

When Edna entered the dining-room one evening a little late, as was her habit, an unusually animated conversation seemed to be going on. Several persons were talking at once, and Victor's voice was predominating, even over that of his mother. Edna had returned late from her bath, had dressed in some haste, and her face was flushed. Her head, set off by her dainty white gown, suggested a rich, rare blossom. She took her seat at table between old Monsieur Farival and Madame Ratignolle.

As she seated herself and was about to begin to eat her soup, which had been served when she entered the room, several persons informed her simultaneously that Robert was going to Mexico. She laid her spoon down and looked about her bewildered. He had been with her, reading to her all the morning, and had never even mentioned such a place as Mexico. She had not seen him during the afternoon; she had heard some one say he was at the house, upstairs with his mother. This she had thought nothing of, though she was surprised when he did not join her later in the afternoon, when she went down to the beach.

She looked across at him, where he sat beside Madame Lebrun, who presided. Edna's face was a blank picture of bewilderment, which she never thought of disguising. He lifted his eyebrows with the pretext of a smile as he returned her glance. He looked embarrassed and uneasy.

"When is he going?" she asked of everybody in general, as if Robert were not there to answer for himself.

"To-night!" "This very evening!" "Did you ever!" "What possesses him!" were some of the replies she gathered, uttered simultaneously in French and English.

"Impossible!" she exclaimed. "How can a person start off from Grand Isle to Mexico at a moment's notice, as if he were going over to Klein's or to the wharf or down to the beach?"

"I said all along I was going to Mexico; I've been saying so for years!" cried Robert, in an excited and irritable tone, with the air of a man defending himself against a swarm of stinging insects.

Madame Lebrun knocked on the table with her knife handle.

"Please let Robert explain why he is going, and why he is going tonight," she called out. "Really, this table is getting to be more and more like Bedlam every day, with everybody talking at once. Sometimes—I hope God will forgive me—but positively, sometimes I wish Victor would lose the power of speech."

Victor laughed sardonically as he thanked his mother for her holy wish, of which he failed to see the benefit to anybody, except that it might afford her a more ample opportunity and license to talk herself.

Monsieur Farival thought that Victor should have been taken out in mid-ocean in his earliest youth and drowned. Victor thought there would be more logic in thus disposing of old people with an established claim for making themselves universally obnoxious. Madame Lebrun grew a trifle hysterical; Robert called his brother some sharp, hard names.

"There's nothing much to explain, mother," he said; though he explained, nevertheless—looking chiefly at Edna—that he could only meet the gentleman whom he intended to join at Vera Cruz by taking such and such a steamer, which left New Orleans on such a day; that Beaudelet was going out with his lugger-load of vegetables that night, which gave him an opportunity of reaching the city and making his vessel in time.

"But when did you make up your mind to all this?" demanded Monsieur Farival.

"This afternoon," returned Robert, with a shade of annoyance.

"At what time this afternoon?" persisted the old gentleman, with nagging determination, as if he were cross-questioning a criminal in a court of justice.

"At four o'clock this afternoon, Monsieur Farival," Robert replied, in a high voice and with a lofty air, which reminded Edna of some gentleman on the stage.

She had forced herself to eat most of her soup, and now she was picking the flaky bits of a *court bouillon* with her fork.

The lovers were profiting by the general conversation on Mexico to speak in whispers of matters which they rightly considered were interesting to no one but themselves. The lady in black had once received a pair of prayer-beads of curious workmanship from Mexico, with very special indulgence attached to them, but she had never been able to ascertain whether the indulgence extended outside the Mexican border. Father Fochel of the Cathedral had attempted to explain it; but he had not done so to her satisfaction. And she begged that Robert would interest himself, and discover, if possible, whether she was entitled to the indulgence accompanying the remarkably curious Mexican prayer-beads.

Madame Ratignolle hoped that Robert would exercise extreme caution in dealing with the Mexicans, who, she considered, were a treacherous people, unscrupulous and revengeful. She trusted she did them no injustice in thus condemning them as a race. She had known personally but one Mexican, who made and sold excellent tamales, and whom she would have trusted implicitly, so soft-spoken was he. One day he was arrested for stabbing his wife. She never knew whether he had been hanged or not.

Victor had grown hilarious, and was attempting to tell an anecdote about a Mexican girl who served chocolate one winter in a restaurant in Dauphine Street. No one would listen to him but old Monsieur Farival, who went into convulsions over the droll story.

Edna wondered if they had all gone mad, to be talking and clamoring at that rate. She herself could think of nothing to say about Mexico or the Mexicans.

"At what time do you leave?" she asked Robert.

"At ten," he told her. "Beaudelet wants to wait for the moon."

"Are you all ready to go?"

"Quite ready. I shall only take a hand-bag, and shall pack my trunk in the city."

He turned to answer some question put to him by his mother, and Edna, having finished her black coffee, left the table.

She went directly to her room. The little cottage was close and stuffy after leaving the outer air. But she did not mind; there appeared to be a hundred different things demanding her attention indoors. She began to set the toilet-stand to rights, grumbling at the negligence of the quadroon, who was in the adjoining room putting the children to bed. She gathered together stray garments that were hanging on the backs of chairs, and put each where it belonged in closet or bureau drawer. She changed her gown for a more comfortable and commodious wrapper. She rearranged her hair, combing and brushing it with unusual energy. Then she went in and assisted the quadroon in getting the boys to bed.

They were very playful and inclined to talk—to do anything but lie quiet and go to sleep. Edna sent the quadroon away to her supper and told her she need not return. Then she sat and told the children a story. Instead of soothing it excited them, and added to their wakefulness. She left them in heated argument, speculating about the conclusion of the tale which their mother promised to finish the following night.

The little black girl came in to say that Madame Lebrun would like to have Mrs. Pontellier go and sit with them over at the house till Mr. Robert went away. Edna returned answer that she had already undressed, that she did not feel quite well, but perhaps she would go over to the house later. She started to dress again, and got as far advanced as to remove her *peignoir*. But changing her mind once more she resumed the *peignoir*, and went outside and sat down before her door. She was overheated and irritable, and fanned herself energetically for a while. Madame Ratignolle came down to discover what was the matter.

"All that noise and confusion at the table must have upset me," replied Edna, "and moreover, I hate shocks and surprises. The idea of Robert starting off in such a ridiculously sudden and dramatic way! As if it were a matter of life and death! Never saying a word about it all morning when he was with me."

"Yes," agreed Madame Ratignolle. "I think it was showing us all—you especially—very little consideration. It wouldn't have surprised me in any of the others; those Lebruns are all given to heroics. But I must say I should never have expected such a thing from Robert. Are you not coming down? Come on, dear; it doesn't look friendly."

"No," said Edna, a little sullenly. "I can't go to the trouble of dressing again; I don't feel like it."

"You needn't dress; you look all right; fasten a belt around your waist. Just look at me!"

"No," persisted Edna; "but you go on. Madame Lebrun might be offended if we both stayed away."

Madame Ratignolle kissed Edna good-night, and went away, being in truth rather desirous of joining in the general and animated conversation which was still in progress concerning Mexico and the Mexicans.

Somewhat later Robert came up, carrying his hand-bag.

"Aren't you feeling well?" he asked.

"Oh, well enough. Are you going right away?"

He lit a match and looked at his watch. "In twenty minutes," he said. The sudden and brief flare of the match emphasized the darkness for a while. He sat down upon a stool which the children had left out on the porch.

"Get a chair," said Edna.

"This will do," he replied. He put on his soft hat and nervously took it off again, and wiping his face with his handkerchief, complained of the heat.

"Take the fan," said Edna, offering it to him.

"Oh, no! Thank you. It does no good; you have to stop fanning some time, and feel all the more uncomfortable afterward."

"That's one of the ridiculous things which men always say. I have never known one to speak otherwise of fanning. How long will you be gone?"

"Forever, perhaps. I don't know. It depends upon a good many things."

"Well, in case it shouldn't be forever, how long will it be?"

"I don't know."

"This seems to me perfectly preposterous and uncalled for. I don't like it. I don't understand your motive for silence and mystery, never saying a word to me about it this morning." He remained silent, not offering to defend himself. He only said, after a moment:

"Don't part from me in an ill-humor. I never knew you to be out of patience with me before."

"I don't want to part in any ill-humor," she said. "But can't you understand? I've grown used to seeing you, to having you with me all the time, and your action seems unfriendly, even unkind. You don't even offer an excuse for it. Why, I was planning to be together, thinking of how pleasant it would be to see you in the city next winter."

"So was I," he blurted. "Perhaps that's the—" He stood up suddenly and held out his hand. "Good-by, my dear Mrs. Pontellier; good-by. You won't—I hope you won't completely forget me." She clung to his hand, striving to detain him.

"Write to me when you get there, won't you, Robert?" she entreated.

"I will, thank you. Good-by."

How unlike Robert! The merest acquaintance would have said something more emphatic than "I will, thank you; good-by," to such a request.

He had evidently already taken leave of the people over at the house, for he descended the steps and went to join Beaudelet, who was out there with an oar across his shoulder waiting for Robert. They walked away in the darkness. She could only hear Beaudelet's voice; Robert had apparently not even spoken a word of greeting to his companion.

Edna bit her handkerchief convulsively, striving to hold back and to hide, even from herself as she would have hidden from another, the emotion which was troubling—tearing—her. Her eyes were brimming with tears.

For the first time she recognized anew the symptoms of infatuation which she had felt incipiently as a child, as a girl in her earliest teens, and later as a young woman. The recognition did not lessen the reality, the poignancy of the revelation by any suggestion or promise of instability. The past was nothing to her; offered no lesson which she was willing to heed. The future was a mystery which she never attempted to penetrate. The present alone was significant; was hers, to torture her as it was doing then with the biting conviction that she had lost that which she had held, that she had been denied that which her impassioned, newly awakened being demanded.

XVI

"Do you miss your friend greatly?" asked Mademoiselle Reisz one morning as she came creeping up behind Edna, who had just left her cottage on her way to the beach. She spent much of her time in the water since she had acquired finally the art of swimming. As their stay at Grand Isle drew near its close, she felt that she could not give too much time to a diversion which afforded her the only real pleasurable moments that she knew. When Mademoiselle Reisz came and touched her upon the shoulder and spoke to her, the woman seemed to echo the thought which was ever in Edna's mind; or, better, the feeling which constantly possessed her.

Robert's going had some way taken the brightness, the color, the meaning out of everything. The conditions of her life were in no way changed, but her whole existence was dulled, like a faded garment which seems to be no longer worth wearing. She sought him everywhere—in others whom she induced to talk about him. She went up in the mornings to Madame Lebrun's room, braving the clatter of the old sewing-machine. She sat there and chatted at intervals as Robert had done. She gazed around the room at the pictures and photographs hanging upon the wall, and discovered in some corner an old family album, which she examined with the keenest interest, appealing to Madame Lebrun for enlightenment concerning the many figures and faces which she discovered between its pages.

There was a picture of Madame Lebrun with Robert as a baby, seated in her lap, a round-faced infant with a fist in his mouth. The eyes alone in the baby suggested the man. And that was he also in kilts, at the age of five, wearing long curls and holding a whip in his hand. It made Edna laugh, and she laughed, too, at the portrait in his first long trousers; while another interested her, taken when he left for college, looking thin, long-faced, with eyes full of fire, ambition and great intentions. But there was no recent picture, none which suggested the Robert who had gone away five days ago, leaving a void and wilderness behind him.

"Oh, Robert stopped having his pictures taken when he had to pay for them himself! He found wiser use for his money, he says," explained Madame Lebrun. She had a letter from him, written before he left New Orleans. Edna wished to see the letter, and Madame Lebrun told her to look for it either on the table or the dresser, or perhaps it was on the mantelpiece.

The letter was on the bookshelf. It possessed the greatest interest and attraction for Edna; the envelope, its size and shape, the post-mark, the handwriting. She examined every detail of the outside before opening it. There were only a few lines, setting forth that he would leave the city that afternoon, that he had packed his trunk in good shape, that he was well, and sent her his love and begged to be affectionately remembered to all. There was no special message to Edna except a postscript saying that if Mrs. Pontellier desired to finish the book which he had been reading to her, his mother would find it in his room, among other books there on the table. Edna experienced a pang of jealousy because he had written to his mother rather than to her.

Every one seemed to take for granted that she missed him. Even her husband, when he came down the Saturday following Robert's departure, expressed regret that he had gone.

"How do you get on without him, Edna?" he asked.

"It's very dull without him," she admitted. Mr. Pontellier had seen Robert in the city, and Edna asked him a dozen questions or more. Where had they met? On Carondelet Street, in the morning. They had gone "in" and had a drink and a cigar together. What had they talked about? Chiefly about his prospects in Mexico, which Mr. Pontellier thought were promising. How did he look? How did he seem—grave, or gay, or how? Quite cheerful, and wholly taken up with the idea of his trip, which Mr. Pontellier found altogether natural in a young fellow about to seek fortune and adventure in a strange, queer country.

Edna tapped her foot impatiently, and wondered why the children persisted in playing in the sun when they might be under the trees. She went down and led them out of the sun, scolding the quadroon for not being more attentive.

It did not strike her as in the least grotesque that she should be making of Robert the object of conversation and leading her husband to speak of him. The sentiment which she entertained for Robert in no way resembled that which she felt for her husband, or had ever felt, or ever expected to feel. She had all her life long been accustomed to harbor thoughts and emotions which never voiced themselves. They had never taken the form of struggles. They belonged to her and were her own, and she entertained the conviction that she had a right to them and that they concerned no one but herself. Edna had once told Madame Ratignolle that she would never sacrifice herself for her children, or for any one. Then had followed a rather heated argument; the two women did not appear to understand each other or to be talking the same language. Edna tried to appease her friend, to explain.

"I would give up the unessential; I would give my money, I would give my life for my children; but I wouldn't give myself. I can't make it more clear; it's only something which I am beginning to comprehend, which is revealing itself to me."

"I don't know what you would call the essential, or what you mean by the unessential," said Madame Ratignolle, cheerfully; "but a woman who would give her life for her children could do no more than that—your Bible tells you so. I'm sure I couldn't do more than that."

"Oh, yes you could!" laughed Edna.

She was not surprised at Mademoiselle Reisz's question the morning that lady, following her to the beach, tapped her on the shoulder and asked if she did not greatly miss her young friend.

"Oh, good morning, Mademoiselle; is it you? Why, of course I miss Robert. Are you going down to bathe?"

"Why should I go down to bathe at the very end of the season when I haven't been in the surf all summer," replied the woman, disagreeably.

"I beg your pardon," offered Edna, in some embarrassment, for she should have remembered that Mademoiselle Reisz's avoidance of the water had furnished a theme for much pleasantry. Some among them thought it was on account of her false hair, or the dread of getting the violets wet, while others attributed it to the natural aversion for water sometimes believed to accompany the artistic temperament. Mademoiselle offered Edna some chocolates in a paper bag, which she took from her pocket, by way of showing that she bore no ill feeling. She habitually ate chocolates for their sustaining quality; they contained much nutriment in small compass, she said. They saved her from starvation, as Madame Lebrun's table was utterly impossible; and no one save so impertinent a woman as Madame Lebrun could think of offering such food to people and requiring them to pay for it.

"She must feel very lonely without her son," said Edna, desiring to change the subject. "Her favorite son, too. It must have been quite hard to let him go."

Mademoiselle laughed maliciously.

"Her favorite son! Oh, dear! Who could have been imposing such a tale upon you? Aline Lebrun lives for Victor, and for Victor alone. She has spoiled him into the worthless creature he is. She worships him and the ground he walks on. Robert is very well in a way, to give up all the money he can earn to the family, and keep the barest pittance for himself. Favorite son, indeed! I miss the poor fellow myself, my dear. I liked to see him and to hear him about the place—the only Lebrun who is worth a pinch of salt. He comes to see me often in the city. I like to play to him. That Victor!

hanging would be too good for him. It's a wonder Robert hasn't beaten him to death long ago."

"I thought he had great patience with his brother," offered Edna, glad to be talking about Robert, no matter what was said.

"Oh! he thrashed him well enough a year or two ago," said Mademoiselle. "It was about a Spanish girl, whom Victor considered that he had some sort of claim upon. He met Robert one day talking to the girl, or walking with her, or bathing with her, or carrying her basket—I don't remember what;—and he became so insulting and abusive that Robert gave him a thrashing on the spot that has kept him comparatively in order for a good while. It's about time he was getting another."

"Was her name Mariequita?" asked Edna.

"Mariequita—yes, that was it; Mariequita. I had forgotten. Oh, she's a sly one, and a bad one, that Mariequita!"

Edna looked down at Mademoiselle Reisz and wondered how she could have listened to her venom so long. For some reason she felt depressed, almost unhappy. She had not intended to go into the water; but she donned her bathing suit, and left Mademoiselle alone, seated under the shade of the children's tent. The water was growing cooler as the season advanced. Edna plunged and swam about with an abandon that thrilled and invigorated her. She remained a long time in the water, half hoping that Mademoiselle Reisz would not wait for her.

But Mademoiselle waited. She was very amiable during the walk back, and raved much over Edna's appearance in her bathing suit. She talked about music. She hoped that Edna would go to see her in the city, and wrote her address with the stub of a pencil on a piece of card which she found in her pocket.

"When do you leave?" asked Edna.

"Next Monday; and you?"

"The following week," answered Edna, adding, "It has been a pleasant summer, hasn't it, Mademoiselle?"

"Well," agreed Mademoiselle Reisz, with a shrug, "rather pleasant, if it hadn't been for the mosquitoes and the Farival twins."

XVII

The Pontelliers possessed a very charming home on Esplanade Street in New Orleans. It was a large, double cottage, with a broad front veranda, whose round, fluted columns supported the sloping roof. The house was painted a dazzling white; the outside shutters, or jalousies, were green. In the yard, which was kept scrupulously neat, were flowers and plants of every description which flourishes in South Louisiana. Within doors the appointments were perfect after the conventional type. The softest carpets and rugs covered the floors; rich and tasteful draperies hung at doors and windows. There were paintings, selected with judgment and discrimination, upon the walls. The cut glass, the silver, the heavy damask which daily appeared upon the table were the envy of many women whose husbands were less generous than Mr. Pontellier.

Mr. Pontellier was very fond of walking about his house examining its various appointments and details, to see that nothing was amiss. He greatly valued his possessions, chiefly because they were his, and derived genuine pleasure from contemplating a painting, a statuette, a rare lace curtain—no matter what—after he had bought it and placed it among his household gods.

On Tuesday afternoons—Tuesday being Mrs. Pontellier's reception day—there was a constant stream of callers—women who came in carriages or in the street cars, or walked when the air was soft and distance permitted. A light-colored mulatto boy, in dress coat and bearing a diminutive silver tray for the reception of cards, admitted them. A maid, in white fluted cap, offered the callers liqueur, coffee, or chocolate, as they might desire. Mrs. Pontellier, attired in a handsome reception gown, remained in the drawing-room the entire afternoon receiving her visitors. Men sometimes called in the evening with their wives.

This had been the programme which Mrs. Pontellier had religiously followed since her marriage, six years before. Certain evenings during the week she and her husband attended the opera or sometimes the play.

Mr. Pontellier left his home in the mornings between nine and ten o'clock, and rarely returned before half-past six or seven in the evening—dinner being served at half-past seven.

He and his wife seated themselves at table one Tuesday evening, a few weeks after their return from Grand Isle. They were alone together. The boys were being put to bed; the patter of their bare, escaping feet could be heard occasionally, as well as the pursuing voice of the quadroon, lifted in mild protest and entreaty. Mrs. Pontellier did not wear her usual Tuesday reception gown; she was in ordinary house dress. Mr. Pontellier, who was observant about such things, noticed it, as he served the soup and handed it to the boy in waiting.

"Tired out, Edna? Whom did you have? Many callers?" he asked. He tasted his soup and began to season it with pepper, salt, vinegar, mustard—everything within reach.

"There were a good many," replied Edna, who was eating her soup with evident satisfaction." I found their cards when I got home; I was out."

"Out!" exclaimed her husband, with something like genuine consternation in his voice as he laid down the vinegar cruet and looked at her through his glasses. "Why, what could have taken you out on Tuesday? What did you have to do?"

"Nothing. I simply felt like going out, and I went out."

"Well, I hope you left some suitable excuse," said her husband, somewhat appeased, as he added a dash of cayenne pepper to the soup.

"No, I left no excuse. I told Joe to say I was out, that was all."

"Why, my dear, I should think you'd understand by this time that people don't do such things; we've got to observe *les convenances* if we ever expect to get on and keep up with the procession. If you felt that you had to leave home this afternoon, you should have left some suitable explanation for your absence.

"This soup is really impossible; it's strange that woman hasn't learned yet to make a decent soup. Any free-lunch stand in town serves a better one. Was Mrs. Belthrop here?"

"Bring the tray with the cards, Joe. I don't remember who was here."

The boy retired and returned after a moment, bringing the tiny silver tray, which was covered with ladies' visiting cards. He handed it to Mrs. Pontellier.

"Give it to Mr. Pontellier," she said.

Joe offered the tray to Mr. Pontellier, and removed the soup.

Mr. Pontellier scanned the names of his wife's callers, reading some of them aloud, with comments as he read.

"'The Misses Delasidas.' I worked a big deal in futures for their father this morning; nice girls; it's time they were getting married. 'Mrs. Belthrop.' I tell you what it is, Edna; you can't afford to snub Mrs. Belthrop. Why, Belthrop could buy and sell us ten times over. His business is worth a good, round sum to me. You'd better write her a note. 'Mrs. James Highcamp.' Hugh! the less you have to do with Mrs. Highcamp, the better. 'Madame Laforcé.' Came all the way from Carrolton, too, poor old soul. 'Miss Wiggs,' 'Mrs. Eleanor Boltons.'" He pushed the cards aside.

"Mercy!" exclaimed Edna, who had been fuming. "Why are you taking the thing so seriously and making such a fuss over it?"

"I'm not making any fuss over it. But it's just such seeming trifles that we've got to take seriously; such things count."

The fish was scorched. Mr. Pontellier would not touch it. Edna said she did not mind a little scorched taste. The roast was in some way not to his fancy, and he did not like the manner in which the vegetables were served.

"It seems to me," he said, "we spend money enough in this house to procure at least one meal a day which a man could eat and retain his self-respect."

"You used to think the cook was a treasure," returned Edna, indifferently.

"Perhaps she was when she first came; but cooks are only human. They need looking after, like any other class of persons that you employ. Suppose I didn't look after the clerks in my office, just let them run things their own way; they'd soon make a nice mess of me and my business."

"Where are you going?" asked Edna, seeing that her husband arose from table without having eaten a morsel except a taste of the highly seasoned soup.

"I'm going to get my dinner at the club. Good night." He went into the hall, took his hat and stick from the stand, and left the house.

She was somewhat familiar with such scenes. They had often made her very unhappy. On a few previous occasions she had been completely deprived of any desire to finish her dinner. Sometimes she had gone into the kitchen to administer a tardy rebuke to the cook. Once she went to her room and studied the cookbook during an entire evening, finally writing out a menu for the week, which left her harassed with a feeling that, after all, she had accomplished no good that was worth the name.

But that evening Edna finished her dinner alone, with forced deliberation. Her face was flushed and her eyes flamed with some inward fire that lighted them. After finishing her dinner she went to her room, having instructed the boy to tell any other callers that she was indisposed.

It was a large, beautiful room, rich and picturesque in the soft, dim light which the maid had turned low. She went and stood at an open window and looked out upon the deep tangle of the garden below. All the mystery and witchery of the night seemed to have gathered there amid the perfumes and the dusky and tortuous outlines of flowers and foliage. She was seeking herself and finding herself in just such sweet, half-darkness which met her moods. But the voices were not soothing that came to her from the darkness and the sky above and the stars. They jeered and sounded mournful notes without promise, devoid even of hope. She turned back into the room and began to walk to and fro down its whole length, without stopping, without resting. She carried in her hands a thin handkerchief, which she tore into ribbons, rolled into a ball, and flung from her. Once she stopped, and taking off her wedding ring, flung it upon the carpet. When she saw it lying there, she stamped her heel upon it, striving to crush it. But her small boot heel did not make an indenture, not a mark upon the little glittering circlet.

In a sweeping passion she seized a glass vase from the table and flung it upon the tiles of the hearth. She wanted to destroy something. The crash and clatter were what she wanted to hear.

A maid, alarmed at the din of breaking glass, entered the room to discover what was the matter.

"A vase fell upon the hearth," said Edna. "Never mind; leave it till morning. "

"Oh! you might get some of the glass in your feet, ma'am," insisted the young woman, picking up bits of the broken vase that were scattered upon the carpet. "And here's your ring, ma'am, under the chair."

Edna held out her hand, and taking the ring, slipped it upon her finger.

XVIII

The following morning Mr. Pontellier, upon leaving for his office, asked Edna if she would not meet him in town in order to look at some new fixtures for the library.

"I hardly think we need new fixtures, Léonce. Don't let us get anything new; you are too extravagant. I don't believe you ever think of saving or putting by."

"The way to become rich is to make money, my dear Edna, not to save it," he said. He regretted that she did not feel inclined to go with him and select new fixtures. He kissed her good-by, and told her she was not looking well and must take care of herself. She was unusually pale and very quiet.

She stood on the front veranda as he quitted the house, and absently picked a few sprays of jessamine that grew upon a trellis near by. She inhaled the odor of the blossoms and thrust them into the bosom of her white morning gown. The boys were dragging along the banquette a small "express wagon," which they had filled with blocks and sticks. The quadroon was following them with little quick steps, having assumed a fictitious animation and alacrity for the occasion. A fruit vender was crying his wares in the street.

Edna looked straight before her with a self-absorbed expression upon her face. She felt no interest in anything about her. The street, the children, the fruit vender, the flowers growing there under her eyes, were all part and parcel of an alien world which had suddenly become antagonistic.

She went back into the house. She had thought of speaking to the cook concerning her blunders of the previous night; but Mr. Pontellier had saved her that disagreeable mission, for which she was so poorly fitted. Mr. Pontellier's arguments were usually convincing with those whom he employed. He left home feeling quite sure that he and Edna would sit down that evening, and possibly a few subsequent evenings, to a dinner deserving of the name.

Edna spent an hour or two in looking over some of her old sketches. She could see their shortcomings and defects, which were glaring in her eyes. She tried to work a little, but found she was not in the humor. Finally she gathered together a few of the sketches—those which she considered the least discreditable; and she carried them with her when, a little later, she dressed and left the house. She looked handsome and distinguished in her street gown. The tan of the seashore had left her face, and her forehead was smooth, white, and polished beneath her heavy, yellow-brown hair. There were a few freckles on her face, and a small, dark mole near the under lip and one on the temple, half-hidden in her hair.

As Edna walked along the street she was thinking of Robert. She was still under the spell of her infatuation. She had tried to forget him, realizing the inutility of remembering. But the thought of him was like an obsession, ever pressing itself upon her. It was not that she dwelt upon details of their acquaintance, or recalled in any special or peculiar way his personality; it was his being, his existence, which dominated her thought, fading sometimes as if it would melt into the mist of the forgotten, reviving again with an intensity which filled her with an incomprehensible longing.

Edna was on her way to Madame Ratignolle's. Their intimacy, begun at Grand Isle, had not declined, and they had seen each other with some frequency since their return to the city. The Ratignolles lived at no great distance from Edna's home, on the corner of a side street, where Monsieur Ratignolle owned and conducted a drug store which enjoyed a steady and prosperous trade. His father had been in the business before him, and Monsieur Ratignolle stood well in the community and bore an enviable reputation for integrity and clear-headedness. His family lived in commodious apartments over the store, having an entrance on the side within the *porte cochère.* There was something which Edna thought very French, very foreign, about their whole manner of living. In the large and pleasant salon which extended across the width of the house, the Ratignolles entertained their friends once a fortnight with a *soirée musicale*, sometimes diversified by card-playing. There was a friend who played upon the 'cello. One brought his flute and another his violin, while there were some who sang and a number who performed upon the piano with various degrees of taste and agility. The Ratignolles' *soirées musicales* were widely known, and it was considered a privilege to be invited to them.

Edna found her friend engaged in assorting the clothes which had returned that morning from the laundry. She at once abandoned her occupation upon seeing Edna, who had been ushered without ceremony into her presence.

"'Cité can do it as well as I; it is really her business," she explained to Edna, who apologized for interrupting her. And she summoned a young black woman, whom she instructed, in French, to be very careful in checking off the list which she handed her. She told her to notice particularly if a fine linen handkerchief of Monsieur Ratignolle's, which was missing last week, had been returned; and to be sure to set to one side such pieces as required mending and darning.

Then placing an arm around Edna's waist, she led her to the front of the house, to the salon, where it was cool and sweet with the odor of great roses that stood upon the hearth in jars.

Madame Ratignolle looked more beautiful than ever there at home, in a negligé which left her arms almost wholly bare and exposed the white, melting curves of her white throat.

"Perhaps I shall be able to paint your picture some day," said Edna with a smile when they were seated. She produced the roll of sketches and started to unfold them. "I believe I ought to work again. I feel as if I wanted to be doing something. What do you think of them? Do you think it worth while to take it up again and study some more? I might study for a while with Laidpore."

She knew that Madame Ratignolle's opinion in such a matter would be next to valueless, that she herself had not alone decided, but determined; but she sought the words of praise and encouragement that would help her to put heart into her venture.

"Your talent is immense, dear!"

"Nonsense!" protested Edna, well pleased.

"Immense, I tell you," persisted Madame Ratignolle, surveying the sketches one by one, at close range, then holding them at arm's length, narrowing her eyes, and dropping her head on one side. "Surely, this Bavarian peasant is worthy of framing; and this basket of apples! never have I seen anything more lifelike. One might almost be tempted to reach out a hand and take one."

Edna could not control a feeling which bordered upon complacency at her friend's praise, even realizing, as she did, its true worth. She retained a few of the sketches, and gave all the rest to Madame Ratignolle, who appreciated the gift far beyond its value and proudly exhibited the pictures to her husband when he came up from the store a little later for his midday dinner.

Mr. Ratignolle was one of those men who are called the salt of the earth. His cheerfulness was unbounded, and it was matched by his goodness of heart, his broad charity, and common sense. He and his wife spoke English with an accent which was only discernible through its unEnglish emphasis and a certain carefulness and deliberation. Edna's husband spoke English with no accent whatever. The Ratignolles understood each other perfectly. If ever the fusion of two human beings into one has been accomplished on this sphere it was surely in their union.

As Edna seated herself at table with them she thought, "Better a dinner of herbs," though it did not take her long to discover that it was no dinner of herbs, but a delicious repast, simple, choice, and in every way satisfying.

Monsieur Ratignolle was delighted to see her, though he found her looking not so well as at Grand Isle, and he advised a tonic. He talked a good deal on various topics, a little politics, some city news and neighborhood gossip. He spoke with an animation and earnestness that gave an exaggerated importance to every syllable he uttered. His wife was keenly interested in everything he said, laying down her fork the better to listen, chiming in, taking the words out of his mouth.

Edna felt depressed rather than soothed after leaving them. The little glimpse of domestic harmony which had been offered her, gave her no regret, no longing. It was not a condition of life which fitted her, and she could see in it but an appalling and hopeless ennui. She was moved by a kind of commiseration for Madame Ratignolle,—a pity for that colorless existence which never uplifted its possessor beyond the region of blind contentment, in which no moment of anguish ever visited her soul, in which she would never have the taste of life's delirium. Edna vaguely wondered what she meant by "life's delirium." It had crossed her thought like some unsought, extraneous impression.

XIX

Edna could not help but think that it was very foolish, very childish, to have stamped upon her wedding ring and smashed the crystal vase upon the tiles. She was visited by no more outbursts, moving her to such futile expedients. She began to do as she liked and to feel as she liked. She completely abandoned her Tuesdays at home, and did not return the visits of those who had called upon her. She made no ineffectual efforts to conduct her household *en bonne ménagère,* going and coming as it suited her fancy, and, so far as she was able, lending herself to any passing caprice.

Mr. Pontellier had been a rather courteous husband so long as he met a certain tacit submissiveness in his wife. But her new and unexpected line of conduct completely bewildered him. It shocked him. Then her absolute disregard for her duties as a wife angered him. When Mr. Pontellier became rude, Edna grew insolent. She had resolved never to take another step backward.

"It seems to me the utmost folly for a woman at the head of a household, and the mother of children, to spend in an atelier days which would be better employed contriving for the comfort of her family." "I feel like painting," answered Edna. "Perhaps I shan't always feel like it."

"Then in God's name paint! but don't let the family go to the devil. There's Madame Ratignolle; because she keeps up her music, she doesn't let everything else go to chaos. And she's more of a musician than you are a painter."

"She isn't a musician, and I'm not a painter. It isn't on account of painting that I let things go."

"On account of what, then?"

"Oh! I don't know. Let me alone; you bother me."

It sometimes entered Mr. Pontellier's mind to wonder if his wife were not growing a little unbalanced mentally. He could see plainly that she was not herself. That is, he could not see that she was becoming herself and daily casting aside that fictitious self which we assume like a garment with which to appear before the world.

Her husband let her alone as she requested, and went away to his office. Edna went up to her atelier—a bright room in the top of the house. She was working with great energy and interest, without accomplishing anything, however, which satisfied her even in the smallest degree. For a time she had the whole household enrolled in the service of art. The boys posed for her. They thought it amusing at first, but the occupation soon lost its attractiveness when they discovered that it was not a game arranged especially for their entertainment. The quadroon sat for hours before Edna's palette, patient as a savage, while the house-maid took charge of the children, and the drawing-room went undusted. But the house-maid, too, served her term as model when Edna perceived that the young woman's back and shoulders were molded on classic lines, and that her hair, loosened from its confining cap, became an inspiration. While Edna worked she sometimes sang low the little air, "*Ah! si tu savais!*"

It moved her with recollections. She could hear again the ripple of the water, the flapping sail. She could see the glint of the moon upon the bay, and could feel the soft, gusty beating of the hot south wind. A subtle current of desire passed through her body, weakening her hold upon the brushes and making her eyes burn.

There were days when she was very happy without knowing why. She was happy to be alive and breathing, when her whole being seemed to be one with the sunlight, the color, the odors, the luxuriant warmth of some perfect Southern day. She liked then to wander alone into strange and unfamiliar places. She discovered many a sunny, sleepy corner, fashioned to dream in. And she found it good to dream and to be alone and unmolested.

There were days when she was unhappy, she did not know why,—when it did not seem worth while to be glad or sorry, to be alive or dead; when life appeared to her like a grotesque Pandemonium and humanity like worms struggling blindly toward inevitable annihilation. She could not work on such a day, nor weave fancies to stir her pulses and warm her blood.

XX

It was during such a mood that Edna hunted up Mademoiselle Reisz. She had not forgotten the rather disagreeable impression left upon her by their last interview; but she nevertheless felt a desire to see her—above all, to listen while she played upon the piano. Quite early in the afternoon she started upon her quest for the pianist. Unfortunately she had mislaid or lost Mademoiselle Reisz's card, and looking up her address in the city directory, she found that the woman lived on Bienville Street, some distance away. The directory which fell into her hands was a year or more old, however, and upon reaching the number indicated, Edna discovered that the house was occupied by a respectable family of mulattoes who had *chambres garnies* to let. They had been living there for six months, and knew absolutely nothing of a Mademoiselle Reisz. In fact, they knew nothing of any of their neighbors; their lodgers were all people of the highest distinction, they assured Edna. She did not linger to discuss class distinctions with Madame Pouponne, but hastened to a neighboring grocery store, feeling sure that Mademoiselle would have left her address with the proprietor.

He knew Mademoiselle Reisz a good deal better than he wanted to know her, he informed his questioner. In truth, he did not want to know her at all, or anything concerning her—the most disagreeable and unpopular woman who ever lived in Bienville Street. He thanked heaven she had left the neighborhood, and was equally thankful that he did not know where she had gone.

Edna's desire to see Mademoiselle Reisz had increased tenfold since these unlooked-for obstacles had arisen to thwart it. She was wondering who could give her the information she sought, when it suddenly occurred to her that Madame Lebrun would be the one most likely to do so. She knew it was useless to ask Madame Ratignolle, who was on the most distant terms with the musician, and preferred to know nothing concerning her. She had once been almost as emphatic in expressing herself upon the subject as the corner grocer.

Edna knew that Madame Lebrun had returned to the city, for it was the middle of November. And she also knew where the Lebruns lived, on Chartres Street.

Their home from the outside looked like a prison, with iron bars before the door and lower windows. The iron bars were a relic of the old *régime,* and no one had ever thought of dislodging them. At the side was a high fence enclosing the garden. A gate or door opening upon the street was locked. Edna rang the bell at this side garden gate, and stood upon the banquette, waiting to be admitted.

It was Victor who opened the gate for her. A black woman, wiping her hands upon her apron, was close at his heels. Before she saw them Edna could hear them in altercation, the woman—plainly an anomaly—claiming the right to be allowed to perform her duties, one of which was to answer the bell.

Victor was surprised and delighted to see Mrs. Pontellier, and he made no attempt to conceal either his astonishment or his delight. He was a dark-browed, good-looking youngster of nineteen, greatly resembling his mother, but with ten times her impetuosity. He instructed the black woman to go at once and inform Madame Lebrun that Mrs. Pontellier desired to see her. The woman grumbled a refusal to do part of her duty when she had not been permitted to do it all, and started back to her interrupted task of weeding the garden. Whereupon Victor administered a rebuke in the form of a volley of abuse, which, owing to its rapidity and incoherence, was all but incomprehensible to Edna. Whatever it was, the rebuke was convincing, for the woman dropped her hoe and went mumbling into the house.

Edna did not wish to enter. It was very pleasant there on the side porch, where there were chairs, a wicker lounge, and a small table. She seated herself, for she was tired from her long tramp; and she began to rock gently and smooth out the folds of her silk parasol. Victor drew up his chair beside her. He at once explained that the black woman's offensive conduct was all due to imperfect training, as he was not there to take her in hand. He had only come up from the island the morning before, and expected to return next day. He stayed all winter at the island; he lived there, and kept the place in order and got things ready for the summer visitors.

But a man needed occasional relaxation, he informed Mrs. Pontellier, and every now and again he drummed up a pretext to bring him to the city. My! but he had had a time of it the evening before! He wouldn't want his mother to know, and he began to talk in a whisper. He was scintillant with recollections. Of course, he couldn't think of telling Mrs. Pontellier all about it, she being a woman and not comprehending such things. But it all began with a girl peeping and smiling at him through the shutters as he passed by. Oh! but she was a beauty! Certainly he smiled back, and went up and talked to her. Mrs. Pontellier did not know him if she supposed he was one to let an opportunity like that escape him. Despite herself, the youngster amused her. She must have betrayed in her look some degree of interest or entertainment. The boy grew more daring, and Mrs. Pontellier might have found herself, in a little while, listening to a highly colored story but for the timely appearance of Madame Lebrun.

That lady was still clad in white, according to her custom of the summer. Her eyes beamed an effusive welcome. Would not Mrs. Pontellier go inside? Would she partake of some refreshment? Why had she not been there before? How was that dear Mr. Pontellier and how were those sweet children? Had Mrs. Pontellier ever known such a warm November?

Victor went and reclined on the wicker lounge behind his mother's chair, where he commanded a view of Edna's face. He had taken her parasol from her hands while he spoke to her, and he now lifted it and twirled it above him as he lay on his back. When Madame Lebrun complained that it was *so* dull coming back to the city; that she saw *so* few people now; that even Victor, when he came up from the island for a day or two, had *so* much to occupy him and engage his time; then it was that the youth went into contortions on the lounge and winked mischievously at Edna. She somehow felt like a confederate in crime, and tried to look severe and disapproving.

There had been but two letters from Robert, with little in them, they told her. Victor said it was really not worth while to go inside for the letters, when his mother entreated him to go in search of them. He remembered the contents, which in truth he rattled off very glibly when put to the test.

One letter was written from Vera Cruz and the other from the City of Mexico. He had met Montel, who was doing everything toward his advancement. So far, the financial situation was no improvement over the one he had left in New Orleans, but of course the prospects were vastly better. He wrote of the City of Mexico, the buildings, the people and their habits, the conditions of life which he found there. He sent his love to the family. He inclosed a check to his mother, and hoped she would affectionately remember him to all his friends. That was about the substance of the two letters. Edna felt that if there had been a message for her, she would have received it. The despondent frame of mind in which she had left home began again to overtake her, and she remembered that she wished to find Mademoiselle Reisz.

Madame Lebrun knew where Mademoiselle Reisz lived. She gave Edna the address, regretting that she would not consent to stay and spend the remainder of the afternoon, and pay a visit to

Mademoiselle Reisz some other day. The afternoon was already well advanced.

Victor escorted her out upon the banquette, lifted her parasol, and held it over her while he walked to the car with her. He entreated her to bear in mind that the disclosures of the afternoon were strictly confidential. She laughed and bantered him a little, remembering too late that she should have been dignified and reserved.

"How handsome Mrs. Pontellier looked!" said Madame Lebrun to her son.

"Ravishing!" he admitted. "The city atmosphere has improved her. Some way she doesn't seem like the same woman."

XXI

Some people contended that the reason Mademoiselle Reisz always chose apartments up under the roof was to discourage the approach of beggars, peddlers and callers. There were plenty of windows in her little front room. They were for the most part dingy, but as they were nearly always open it did not make so much difference. They often admitted into the room a good deal of smoke and soot; but at the same time all the light and air that there was came through them. From her windows could be seen the crescent of the river, the masts of ships and the big chimneys of the Mississippi steamers. A magnificent piano crowded the apartment. In the next room she slept, and in the third and last she harbored a gasoline stove on which she cooked her meals when disinclined to descend to the neighboring restaurant. It was there also that she ate, keeping her belongings in a rare old buffet, dingy and battered from a hundred years of use.

When Edna knocked at Mademoiselle Reisz's front room door and entered, she discovered that person standing beside the window, engaged in mending or patching an old prunella gaiter. The little musician laughed all over when she saw Edna. Her laugh consisted of a contortion of the face and all the muscles of the body. She seemed strikingly homely, standing there in the afternoon light. She still wore the shabby lace and the artificial bunch of violets on the side of her head.

"So you remembered me at last," said Mademoiselle. "I had said to myself, 'Ah, bah! she will never come.'"

"Did you want me to come?" asked Edna with a smile.

"I had not thought much about it," answered Mademoiselle. The two had seated themselves on a little bumpy sofa which stood against the wall. "I am glad, however, that you came. I have the water boiling back there, and was just about to make some coffee. You will drink a cup with me. And how is *la belle dame?* Always handsome! always healthy! always contented!" She took Edna's hand between her strong wiry fingers, holding it loosely without warmth, and executing a sort of double theme upon the back and palm.

"Yes," she went on; "I sometimes thought: 'She will never come. She promised as those women in society always do, without meaning it. She will not come.' For I really don't believe you like me, Mrs. Pontellier."

"I don't know whether I like you or not," replied Edna, gazing down at the little woman with a quizzical look.

The candor of Mrs. Pontellier's admission greatly pleased Mademoiselle Reisz. She expressed her gratification by repairing forthwith to the region of the gasoline stove and rewarding her guest with the promised cup of coffee. The coffee and the biscuit accompanying it proved very acceptable to Edna, who had declined refreshment at Madame Lebrun's and was now beginning to feel hungry. Mademoiselle set the tray which she brought in upon a small table near at hand, and seated herself once again on the lumpy sofa.

"I have had a letter from your friend," she remarked, as she poured a little cream into Edna's cup and handed it to her.

"My friend?"

"Yes, your friend Robert. He wrote to me from the City of Mexico."

"Wrote to *you?*" repeated Edna in amazement, stirring her coffee absently.

"Yes, to me. Why not? Don't stir all the warmth out of your coffee; drink it. Though the letter might as well have been sent to you; it was nothing but Mrs. Pontellier from beginning to end."

"Let me see it," requested the young woman, entreatingly.

"No; a letter concerns no one but the person who writes it and the one to whom it is written."

"Haven't you just said it concerned me from beginning to end?"

"It was written about you, not to you. 'Have you seen Mrs. Pontellier? How is she looking?' he asks. 'As Mrs. Pontellier says,' or 'as Mrs. Pontellier once said.' 'If Mrs. Pontellier should call upon you, play for her that Impromptu of Chopin's, my favorite. I heard it here a day or two ago, but not as you play it. I should like to know how it affects her,' and so on, as if he supposed we were constantly in each other's society."

"Let me see the letter."

"Oh, no."

"Have you answered it?"

"No."

"Let me see the letter."

"No, and again, no."

"Then play the Impromptu for me."

"It is growing late; what time do you have to be home?"

"Time doesn't concern me. Your question seems a little rude. Play the Impromptu."

"But you have told me nothing of yourself. What are you doing?"

"Painting!" laughed Edna. "I am becoming an artist. Think of it!"

"Ah! an artist! You have pretensions, Madame."

"Why pretensions? Do you think I could not become an artist?"

"I do not know you well enough to say. I do not know your talent or your temperament. To be an artist includes much; one must possess many gifts—absolute gifts—which have not been acquired by one's own effort. And, moreover, to succeed, the artist must possess the courageous soul."

"What do you mean by the courageous soul?"

"Courageous, *ma foi!* The brave soul. The soul that dares and defies."

"Show me the letter and play for me the Impromptu. You see that I have persistence. Does that quality count for anything in art?"

"It counts with a foolish old woman whom you have captivated," replied Mademoiselle, with her wriggling laugh.

The letter was right there at hand in the drawer of the little table upon which Edna had just placed her coffee cup. Mademoiselle opened the drawer and drew forth the letter, the topmost one. She placed it in Edna's hands, and without further comment arose and went to the piano.

Mademoiselle played a soft interlude. It was an improvisation. She sat low at the instrument, and the lines of her body settled into ungraceful curves and angles that gave it an appearance of deformity. Gradually and imperceptibly the interlude melted into the soft opening minor chords of the Chopin Impromptu.

Edna did not know when the Impromptu began or ended. She sat in the sofa corner reading Robert's letter by the fading light. Mademoiselle had glided from the Chopin into the quivering love-notes of Isolde's song, and back again to the Impromptu with its soulful and poignant longing.

The shadows deepened in the little room. The music grew strange and fantastic—turbulent, insistent, plaintive and soft with entreaty. The shadows grew deeper. The music filled the room. It floated out upon the night, over the housetops, the crescent of the river, losing itself in the silence of the upper air.

Edna was sobbing, just as she had wept one midnight at Grand Isle when strange, new voices awoke in her. She arose in some agitation to take her departure. "May I come again, Mademoiselle?" she asked at the threshold.

"Come whenever you feel like it. Be careful; the stairs and landings are dark; don't stumble."

Mademoiselle reentered and lit a candle. Robert's letter was on the floor. She stooped and picked it up. It was crumpled and damp with tears. Mademoiselle smoothed the letter out, restored it to the envelope, and replaced it in the table drawer.

XXII

One morning on his way into town Mr. Pontellier stopped at the house of his old friend and family physician, Doctor Mandelet. The Doctor was a semi-retired physician, resting, as the saying is, upon his laurels. He bore a reputation for wisdom rather than skill— leaving the active practice of medicine to his assistants and younger contemporaries—and was much sought for in matters of consultation. A few families, united to him by bonds of friendship, he still attended when they required the services of a physician. The Pontelliers were among these.

Mr. Pontellier found the Doctor reading at the open window of his study. His house stood rather far back from the street, in the center of a delightful garden, so that it was quiet and peaceful at the old gentleman study window. He was a great reader. He stared up disapprovingly over his eye-glasses as Mr. Pontellier entered, wondering who had the temerity to disturb him at that hour of the morning.

"Ah, Pontellier! Not sick, I hope. Come and have a seat. What news do you bring this morning?" He was quite portly, with a profusion of gray hair, and small blue eyes which age had robbed of much of their brightness but none of their penetration.

"Oh! I'm never sick, Doctor. You know that I come of tough fiber—of that old Creole race of Pontelliers that dry up and finally blow away. I came to consult—no, not precisely to consult—to talk to you about Edna. I don't know what ails her."

"Madame Pontellier not well?" marveled the Doctor. "Why, I saw her—I think it was a week ago—walking along Canal Street, the picture of health, it seemed to me."

"Yes, yes; she seems quite well," said Mr. Pontellier, leaning forward and whirling his stick between his two hands; "but she doesn't act well. She's odd, she's not like herself. I can't make her out, and I thought perhaps you'd help me."

"How does she act?" inquired the doctor.

"Well, it isn't easy to explain," said Mr. Pontellier, throwing himself back in his chair. "She lets the housekeeping go to the dickens."

"Well, well; women are not all alike, my dear Pontellier. We've got to consider—"

"I know that; I told you I couldn't explain. Her whole attitude—toward me and everybody and everything—has changed. You know I have a quick temper, but I don't want to quarrel or be rude to a woman, especially my wife; yet I'm driven to it, and feel like ten thousand devils after I've made a fool of myself. She's making it devilishly uncomfortable for me," he went on nervously. "She's got some sort of notion in her head concerning the eternal rights of women; and—you understand—we meet in the morning at the breakfast table."

The old gentleman lifted his shaggy eyebrows, protruded his thick nether lip, and tapped the arms of his chair with his cushioned fingertips.

"What have you been doing to her, Pontellier?"

"Doing! *Parbleu!*"

"Has she," asked the Doctor, with a smile, "has she been associating of late with a circle of pseudo-intellectual women— super-spiritual superior beings? My wife has been telling me about them."

"That's the trouble," broke in Mr. Pontellier, "she hasn't been associating with any one. She has abandoned her Tuesdays at home, has thrown over all her acquaintances, and goes tramping about by herself, moping in the street-cars, getting in after dark. I tell you she's peculiar. I don't like it; I feel a little worried over it."

This was a new aspect for the Doctor. "Nothing hereditary?" he asked, seriously. "Nothing peculiar about her family antecedents, is there?"

"Oh, no, indeed! She comes of sound old Presbyterian Kentucky stock. The old gentleman, her father, I have heard, used to atone for his weekday sins with his Sunday devotions. I know for a fact, that his race horses literally ran away with the prettiest bit of Kentucky farming land I ever laid eyes upon. Margaret—you know Margaret—she has all the Presbyterianism undiluted. And the youngest is something of a vixen. By the way, she gets married in a couple of weeks from now."

"Send your wife up to the wedding," exclaimed the Doctor, foreseeing a happy solution. "Let her stay among her own people for a while; it will do her good."

"That's what I want her to do. She won't go to the marriage. She says a wedding is one of the most lamentable spectacles on earth. Nice thing for a woman to say to her husband!" exclaimed Mr. Pontellier, fuming anew at the recollection.

"Pontellier," said the Doctor, after a moment's reflection, "let your wife alone for a while. Don't bother her, and don't let her bother you. Woman, my dear friend, is a very peculiar and delicate organism—a sensitive and highly organized woman, such as I know

Mrs. Pontellier to be, is especially peculiar. It would require an inspired psychologist to deal successfully with them. And when ordinary fellows like you and me attempt to cope with their idiosyncrasies the result is bungling. Most women are moody and whimsical. This is some passing whim of your wife, due to some cause or causes which you and I needn't try to fathom. But it will pass happily over, especially if you let her alone. Send her around to see me."

"Oh! I couldn't do that; there'd be no reason for it," objected Mr. Pontellier.

"Then I'll go around and see her," said the Doctor. "I'll drop in to dinner some evening *en bon ami*."

"Do! by all means," urged Mr. Pontellier. "What evening will you come? Say Thursday. Will you come Thursday?" he asked, rising to take his leave.

"Very well; Thursday. My wife may possibly have some engagement for me Thursday. In case she has, I shall let you know. Otherwise, you may expect me."

Mr. Pontellier turned before leaving to say:

"I am going to New York on business very soon. I have a big scheme on hand, and want to be on the field proper to pull the ropes and handle the ribbons. We'll let you in on the inside if you say so, Doctor," he laughed.

"No, I thank you, my dear sir," returned the Doctor. "I leave such ventures to you younger men with the fever of life still in your blood."

"What I wanted to say," continued Mr. Pontellier, with his hand on the knob; "I may have to be absent a good while. Would you advise me to take Edna along?"

"By all means, if she wishes to go. If not, leave her here. Don't contradict her. The mood will pass, I assure you. It may take a month, two, three months—possibly longer, but it will pass; have patience."

"Well, good-by, *à jeudi*," said Mr. Pontellier, as he let himself out.

The Doctor would have liked during the course of conversation to ask, "Is there any man in the case?" but he knew his Creole too well to make such a blunder as that.

He did not resume his book immediately, but sat for a while meditatively looking out into the garden.

XXIII

Edna's father was in the city, and had been with them several days. She was not very warmly or deeply attached to him, but they had certain tastes in common, and when together they were companionable. His coming was in the nature of a welcome disturbance; it seemed to furnish a new direction for her emotions.

He had come to purchase a wedding gift for his daughter, Janet, and an outfit for himself in which he might make a creditable appearance at her marriage. Mr. Pontellier had selected the bridal gift, as every one immediately connected with him always deferred to his taste in such matters. And his suggestions on the question of dress—which too often assumes the nature of a problem—were of inestimable value to his father-in-law. But for the past few days the old gentleman had been upon Edna's hands, and in his society she was becoming acquainted with a new set of sensations. He had been a colonel in the Confederate army, and still maintained, with the title, the military bearing which had always accompanied it. His hair and mustache were white and silky, emphasizing the rugged bronze of his face. He was tall and thin, and wore his coats padded, which gave a fictitious breadth and depth to his shoulders and chest. Edna and her father looked very distinguished together, and excited a good deal of notice during their perambulations. Upon his arrival she began by introducing him to her atelier and making a sketch of him. He took the whole matter very seriously. If her talent had been ten-fold greater than it was, it would not have surprised him, convinced as he was that he had bequeathed to all of his daughters the germs of a masterful capability, which only depended upon their own efforts to be directed toward successful achievement.

Before her pencil he sat rigid and unflinching, as he had faced the cannon's mouth in days gone by. He resented the intrusion of the children, who gaped with wondering eyes at him, sitting so stiff up there in their mother's bright atelier. When they drew near he motioned them away with an expressive action of the foot, loath to disturb the fixed lines of his countenance, his arms, or his rigid shoulders.

Edna, anxious to entertain him, invited Mademoiselle Reisz to meet him, having promised him a treat in her piano playing; but Mademoiselle declined the invitation. So together they attended a *soirée musicale* at the Ratignolle's. Monsieur and Madame Ratignolle made much of the Colonel, installing him as the guest of honor and engaging him at once to dine with them the following Sunday, or any day which he might select. Madame coquetted with him in the most captivating and naïve manner, with eyes, gestures, and a profusion of compliments, till the Colonel's old head felt thirty years younger on his padded shoulders. Edna marveled, not comprehending. She herself was almost devoid of coquetry.

There were one or two men whom she observed at the *soirée musicale;* but she would never have felt moved to any kittenish display to attract their notice—to any feline or feminine wiles to express herself toward them. Their personality attracted her in an agreeable way. Her fancy selected them, and she was glad when a lull in the music gave them an opportunity to meet her and talk with her. Often on the street the glance of strange eyes had lingered in her memory, and sometimes had disturbed her.

Mr. Pontellier did not attend these *soirées musicales.* H e considered them *bourgeois*, and found more diversion at the club. To Madame Ratignolle he said the music dispensed at her *soirées* was too "heavy," too far beyond his untrained comprehension. His excuse flattered her. But she disapproved of Mr. Pontellier's club, and she was frank enough to tell Edna so.

"It's a pity Mr. Pontellier doesn't stay home more in the evenings. I think you would be more—well, if you don't mind my saying it—more united, if he did."

"Oh! dear no!" said Edna, with a blank look in her eyes. "What should I do if he stayed home? We wouldn't have anything to say to each other."

She had not much of anything to say to her father, for that matter; but he did not antagonize her. She discovered that he interested her, though she realized that he might not interest her long; and for the first time in her life she felt as if she were thoroughly acquainted with him. He kept her busy serving him and ministering to his wants. It amused her to do so. She would not permit a servant or one of the children to do anything for him which she might do herself. Her husband noticed, and thought it was the expression of a deep filial attachment which he had never suspected.

The Colonel drank numerous "toddies" during the course of the day, which left him, however, imperturbed. He was an expert at concocting strong drinks. He had even invented some, to which he had given fantastic names, and for whose manufacture he required diverse ingredients that it devolved upon Edna to procure for him.

When Doctor Mandelet dined with the Pontelliers on Thursday he could discern in Mrs. Pontellier no trace of that morbid condition which her husband had reported to him. She was excited and in a manner radiant. She and her father had been to the race course, and their thoughts when they seated themselves at table were still occupied with the events of the afternoon, and their talk was still of the track. The Doctor had not kept pace with turf affairs. He had certain recollections of racing in what he called "the good old times" when the Lecompte stables flourished, and he drew upon this fund of memories so that he might not be left out and seem wholly devoid of the modern spirit. But he failed to impose upon the Colonel, and was even far from impressing him with this trumped-up knowledge of bygone days. Edna had staked her father on his last venture, with the most gratifying results to both of them. Besides, they had met some very charming people, according to the Colonel's impressions. Mrs. Mortimer Merriman and Mrs. James Highcamp, who were there with Alcée Arobin, had joined them and had enlivened the hours in a fashion that warmed him to think of.

Mr. Pontellier himself had no particular leaning toward horse-racing, and was even rather inclined to discourage it as a pastime, especially when he considered the fate of that blue-grass farm in Kentucky. He endeavored, in a general way, to express a particular disapproval, and only succeeded in arousing the ire and opposition of his father-in-law. A pretty dispute followed, in which Edna warmly espoused her father's cause and the Doctor remained neutral.

He observed his hostess attentively from under his shaggy brows, and noted a subtle change which had transformed her from the listless woman he had known into a being who, for the moment, seemed palpitant with the forces of life. Her speech was warm and energetic. There was no repression in her glance or gesture. She reminded him of some beautiful, sleek animal waking up in the sun.

The dinner was excellent. The claret was warm and the champagne was cold, and under their beneficent influence the threatened unpleasantness melted and vanished with the fumes of the wine.

Mr. Pontellier warmed up and grew reminiscent. He told some amusing plantation experiences, recollections of old Iberville and his youth, when he hunted 'possum in company with some friendly darky; thrashed the pecan trees, shot the grosbec, and roamed the woods and fields in mischievous idleness.

The Colonel, with little sense of humor and of the fitness of things, related a somber episode of those dark and bitter days, in which he had acted a conspicuous part and always formed a central figure. Nor was the Doctor happier in his selection, when he told the old, ever new and curious story of the waning of a woman's love, seeking strange, new channels, only to return to its legitimate source after days of fierce unrest. It was one of the many little human documents which had been unfolded to him during his long career as a physician. The story did not seem especially to impress Edna. She had one of her own to tell, of a woman who paddled away with her lover one night in a pirogue and never came back. They were lost amid the Baratarian Islands, and no one ever heard of them or found trace of them from that day to this. It was a pure invention. She said that Madame Antoine had related it to her. That, also, was an invention. Perhaps it was a dream she had had. But every glowing word seemed real to those who listened. They could feel the hot breath of the Southern night; they could hear the long sweep of the pirogue through the glistening moonlit water, the beating of birds' wings, rising startled from among the reeds in the salt-water pools; they could see the faces of the lovers, pale, close together, rapt in oblivious forgetfulness, drifting into the unknown.

The champagne was cold, and its subtle fumes played fantastic tricks with Edna's memory that night.

Outside, away from the glow of the fire and the soft lamplight, the night was chill and murky. The Doctor doubled his old-fashioned cloak across his breast as he strode home through the darkness. He knew his fellow creatures better than most men;

knew that inner life which so seldom unfolds itself to unanointed eyes. He was sorry he had accepted Pontellier's invitation. He was growing old, and beginning to need rest and an imperturbed spirit. He did not want the secrets of other lives thrust upon him.

"I hope it isn't Arobin," he muttered to himself as he walked. "I hope to heaven it isn't Alcée Arobin."

XXIV

Edna and her father had a warm, and almost violent dispute upon the subject of her refusal to attend her sister's wedding. Mr. Pontellier declined to interfere, to interpose either his influence or his authority. He was following Doctor Mandelet's advice, and letting her do as she liked. The Colonel reproached his daughter for her lack of filial kindness and respect, her want of sisterly affection and womanly consideration. His arguments were labored and unconvincing. He doubted if Janet would accept any excuse— forgetting that Edna had offered none. He doubted if Janet would ever speak to her again, and he was sure Margaret would not.

Edna was glad to be rid of her father when he finally took himself off with his wedding garments and his bridal gifts, with his padded shoulders, his Bible reading, his "toddies" and ponderous oaths.

Mr. Pontellier followed him closely. He meant to stop at the wedding on his way to New York and endeavor by every means which money and love could devise to atone somewhat for Edna's incomprehensible action.

"You are too lenient, too lenient by far, Léonce," asserted the Colonel. "Authority, coercion are what is needed. Put your foot down good and hard; the only way to manage a wife. Take my word for it."

The Colonel was perhaps unaware that he had coerced his own wife into her grave. Mr. Pontellier had a vague suspicion of it which he thought it needless to mention at that late day.

Edna was not so consciously gratified at her husband's leaving home as she had been over the departure of her father. As the day approached when he was to leave her for a comparatively long stay, she grew melting and affectionate, remembering his many acts of consideration and his repeated expressions of an ardent attachment. She was solicitous about his health and his welfare. She bustled around, looking after his clothing, thinking about heavy underwear, quite as Madame Ratignolle would have done under similar circumstances. She cried when he went away, calling him her dear, good friend, and she was quite certain she would grow lonely before very long and go to join him in New York. But after all, a radiant peace settled upon her when she at last found herself alone. Even the children were gone. Old Madame Pontellier had come herself and carried them off to Iberville with their quadroon. The old madame did not venture to say she was afraid they would be neglected during Léonce's absence; she hardly ventured to think so. She was hungry for them—even a little fierce in her attachment. She did not want them to be wholly "children of the pavement," she always said when begging to have them for a space. She wished them to know the country, with its streams, its fields, its woods, its freedom, so delicious to the young. She wished them to taste something of the life their father had lived and known and loved when he, too, was a little child.

When Edna was at last alone, she breathed a big, genuine sigh of relief. A feeling that was unfamiliar but very delicious came over her. She walked all through the house, from one room to another, as if inspecting it for the first time. She tried the various chairs and lounges, as if she had never sat and reclined upon them before. And she perambulated around the outside of the house, investigating, looking to see if windows and shutters were secure and in order. The flowers were like new acquaintances; she approached them in a familiar spirit, and made herself at home among them. The garden walks were damp, and Edna called to the maid to bring out her rubber sandals. And there she stayed, and stooped, digging around the plants, trimming, picking dead, dry leaves. The children's little dog came out, interfering, getting in her way. She scolded him, laughed at him, played with him. The garden smelled so good and looked so pretty in the afternoon sunlight. Edna plucked all the bright flowers she could find, and went into the house with them, she and the little dog.

Even the kitchen assumed a sudden interesting character which she had never before perceived. She went in to give directions to the cook, to say that the butcher would have to bring much less meat, that they would require only half their usual quantity of bread, of milk and groceries. She told the cook that she herself would be greatly occupied during Mr. Pontellier's absence, and she begged her to take all thought and responsibility of the larder upon her own shoulders.

That night Edna dined alone. The candelabra, with a few candles in the center of the table, gave all the light she needed. Outside the circle of light in which she sat, the large dining-room looked solemn and shadowy. The cook, placed upon her mettle, served a delicious repast—a luscious tenderloin broiled *à point*. The wine tasted good; the *marron glacé* seemed to be just what she wanted. It was so pleasant, too, to dine in a comfortable *peignoir*.

She thought a little sentimentally about Léonce and the children, and wondered what they were doing. As she gave a dainty scrap or two to the doggie, she talked intimately to him about Etienne and Raoul. He was beside himself with astonishment and delight over these companionable advances, and showed his appreciation by his little quick, snappy barks and a lively agitation.

Then Edna sat in the library after dinner and read Emerson until she grew sleepy. She realized that she had neglected her reading, and determined to start anew upon a course of improving studies, now that her time was completely her own to do with as she liked.

After a refreshing bath, Edna went to bed. And as she snuggled comfortably beneath the eiderdown a sense of restfulness invaded her, such as she had not known before.

XXV

When the weather was dark and cloudy Edna could not work. She needed the sun to mellow and temper her mood to the sticking point. She had reached a stage when she seemed to be no longer feeling her way, working, when in the humor, with sureness and ease. And being devoid of ambition, and striving not toward accomplishment, she drew satisfaction from the work in itself.

On rainy or melancholy days Edna went out and sought the society of the friends she had made at Grand Isle. Or else she stayed indoors and nursed a mood with which she was becoming too familiar for her own comfort and peace of mind. It was not despair;

but it seemed to her as if life were passing by, leaving its promise broken and unfulfilled. Yet there were other days when she listened, was led on and deceived by fresh promises which her youth held out to her.

She went again to the races, and again. Alcée Arobin and Mrs. Highcamp called for her one bright afternoon in Arobin's drag. Mrs. Highcamp was a worldly but unaffected, intelligent, slim, tall blonde woman in the forties, with an indifferent manner and blue eyes that stared. She had a daughter who served her as a pretext for cultivating the society of young men of fashion. Alcée Arobin was one of them. He was a familiar figure at the race course, the opera, the fashionable clubs. There was a perpetual smile in his eyes, which seldom failed to awaken a corresponding cheerfulness in any one who looked into them and listened to his good-humored voice. His manner was quiet, and at times a little insolent. He possessed a good figure, a pleasing face, not overburdened with depth of thought or feeling; and his dress was that of the conventional man of fashion.

He admired Edna extravagantly, after meeting her at the races with her father. He had met her before on other occasions, but she had seemed to him unapproachable until that day. It was at his instigation that Mrs. Highcamp called to ask her to go with them to the Jockey Club to witness the turf event of the season.

There were possibly a few track men out there who knew the race horse as well as Edna, but there was certainly none who knew it better. She sat between her two companions as one having authority to speak. She laughed at Arobin's pretensions, and deplored Mrs. Highcamp's ignorance. The race horse was a friend and intimate associate of her childhood. The atmosphere of the stables and the breath or the blue grass paddock revived in her memory and lingered in her nose. She did not perceive that she was talking like her father as the sleek geldings ambled in review before them. She played for very high stakes, and fortune favored her. The fever of the game flamed in her cheeks and eyes, and it got into her blood and into her brain like an intoxicant. People turned their heads to look at her, and more than one lent an attentive ear to her utterances, hoping thereby to secure the elusive but ever-desired "tip." Arobin caught the contagion of excitement which drew him to Edna like a magnet. Mrs. Highcamp remained, as usual, unmoved, with her indifferent stare and uplifted eyebrows.

Edna stayed and dined with Mrs. Highcamp upon being urged to do so. Arobin also remained and sent away his drag.

The dinner was quiet and uninteresting, save for the cheerful efforts of Arobin to enliven things. Mrs. Highcamp deplored the absence of her daughter from the races, and tried to convey to her what she had missed by going to the "Dante reading" instead of joining them. The girl held a geranium leaf up to her nose and said nothing, but looked knowing and noncommittal. Mr. Highcamp was a plain, bald-headed man, who only talked under compulsion. He was unresponsive. Mrs. Highcamp was full of delicate courtesy and consideration toward her. She addressed most of her conversation to him at table. They sat in the library after dinner and read the evening papers together under the droplight; while the younger people went into the drawing-room nearby and talked. Miss Highcamp played some selections from Greig upon the piano. She seemed to have apprehended all of the composer's coldness and none of his poetry. While Edna listened she could not help wondering if she had lost her taste for music.

When the time came for her to go home, Mr. Highcamp grunted a lame offer to escort her, looking down at his slippered feet with tactless concern. It was Arobin who took her home. The car ride was long, and it was late when they reached Esplanade Street. Arobin asked permission to enter for a second to light his cigarette—his match safe was empty. He filled his match safe, but did not light his cigarette until he left her, after she had expressed her willingness to go to the races with him again.

Edna was neither tired nor sleepy. She was hungry again, for the Highcamp dinner, though of excellent quality, had lacked abundance. She rummaged in the larder and brought forth a slice of Gruyère and some crackers. She opened a bottle of beer which she found in the icebox. Edna felt extremely restless and excited. She vacantly hummed a fantastic tune as she poked at the wood embers on the hearth and munched a cracker.

She wanted something to happen—something, anything; she did not know what. She regretted that she had not made Arobin stay a half hour to talk over the horses with her. She counted the money she had won. But there was nothing else to do, so she went to bed, and tossed there for hours in a sort of monotonous agitation.

In the middle of the night she remembered that she had forgotten to write her regular letter to her husband; and she decided to do so next day and tell him about her afternoon at the Jockey Club. She lay wide awake composing a letter which was nothing like the one which she wrote next day. When the maid awoke her in the morning Edna was dreaming of Mr. Highcamp playing the piano at the entrance of a music store on Canal Street, while his wife was saying to Alcée Arobin, as they boarded an Esplanade Street car:

"What a pity that so much talent has been neglected! but I must go."

When, a few days later, Alcée Arobin again called for Edna in his drag, Mrs. Highcamp was not with him. He said they would pick her up. But as that lady had not been apprised of his intention of picking her up, she was not at home. The daughter was just leaving the house to attend the meeting of a branch Folk Lore Society, and regretted that she could not accompany them. Arobin appeared nonplused, and asked Edna if there were any one else she cared to ask.

She did not deem it worth while to go in search of any of the fashionable acquaintances from whom she had withdrawn herself. She thought of Madame Ratignolle, but knew that her fair friend did not leave the house, except to take a languid walk around the block with her husband after nightfall. Mademoiselle Reisz would have laughed at such a request from Edna. Madame Lebrun might have enjoyed the outing, but for some reason Edna did not want her. So they went alone, she and Arobin.

The afternoon was intensely interesting to her. The excitement came back upon her like a remittent fever. Her talk grew familiar and confidential. It was no labor to become intimate with Arobin. His manner invited easy confidence. The preliminary stage of becoming acquainted was one which he always endeavored to ignore when a pretty and engaging woman was concerned.

He stayed and dined with Edna. He stayed and sat beside the wood fire. They laughed and talked; and before it was time to go he was telling her how different life might have been if he had known her years before. With ingenuous frankness he spoke of what a wicked, ill-disciplined boy he had been, and impulsively drew up his cuff to exhibit upon his wrist the scar from a saber cut which he had received in a duel outside of Paris when he was nineteen. She touched his hand as she scanned the red cicatrice on the inside of his white wrist. A quick impulse that was somewhat spasmodic impelled her fingers to close in a sort of clutch upon his hand. He felt the pressure of her pointed nails in the flesh of his palm.

She arose hastily and walked toward the mantel.

"The sight of a wound or scar always agitates and sickens me," she said. "I shouldn't have looked at it."

"I beg your pardon," he entreated, following her; "it never occurred to me that it might be repulsive."

He stood close to her, and the effrontery in his eyes repelled the old, vanishing self in her, yet drew all her awakening sensuousness. He saw enough in her face to impel him to take her hand and hold it while he said his lingering good night.

"Will you go to the races again?" he asked.

"No," she said. "I've had enough of the races. I don't want to lose all the money I've won, and I've got to work when the weather is bright, instead of—"

"Yes; work; to be sure. You promised to show me your work. What morning may I come up to your atelier? To-morrow?"

"No!"

"Day after?"

"No, no."

"Oh, please don't refuse me! I know something of such things. I might help you with a stray suggestion or two."

"No. Good night. Why don't you go after you have said good night? I don't like you," she went on in a high, excited pitch, attempting to draw away her hand. She felt that her words lacked dignity and sincerity, and she knew that he felt it.

"I'm sorry you don't like me. I'm sorry I offended you. How have I offended you? What have I done? Can't you forgive me?" And he bent and pressed his lips upon her hand as if he wished never more to withdraw them.

"Mr. Arobin," she complained, "I'm greatly upset by the excitement of the afternoon; I'm not myself. My manner must have misled you in some way. I wish you to go, please." She spoke in a monotonous, dull tone. He took his hat from the table, and stood with eyes turned from her, looking into the dying fire. For a moment or two he kept an impressive silence.

"Your manner has not misled me, Mrs. Pontellier," he said finally. "My own emotions have done that. I couldn't help it. When I'm near you, how could I help it? Don't think anything of it, don't bother, please. You see, I go when you command me. If you wish me to stay away, I shall do so. If you let me come back, I—oh! you will let me come back?"

He cast one appealing glance at her, to which she made no response. Alcée Arobin's manner was so genuine that it often deceived even himself.

Edna did not care or think whether it were genuine or not. When she was alone she looked mechanically at the back of her hand which he had kissed so warmly. Then she leaned her head down on the mantelpiece. She felt somewhat like a woman who in a moment of passion is betrayed into an act of infidelity, and realizes the significance of the act without being wholly awakened from its glamour. The thought was passing vaguely through her mind, "What would he think?"

She did not mean her husband; she was thinking of Robert Lebrun. Her husband seemed to her now like a person whom she had married without love as an excuse.

She lit a candle and went up to her room. Alcée Arobin was absolutely nothing to her. Yet his presence, his manners, the warmth of his glances, and above all the touch of his lips upon her hand had acted like a narcotic upon her.

She slept a languorous sleep, interwoven with vanishing dreams.

XXVI

Alcée Arobin wrote Edna an elaborate note of apology, palpitant with sincerity. It embarrassed her; for in a cooler, quieter moment it appeared to her absurd that she should have taken his action so seriously, so dramatically. She felt sure that the significance of the whole occurrence had lain in her own self-consciousness. If she ignored his note it would give undue importance to a trivial affair. If she replied to it in a serious spirit it would still leave in his mind the impression that she had in a susceptible moment yielded to his influence. After all, it was no great matter to have one's hand kissed. She was provoked at his having written the apology. She answered in as light and bantering a spirit as she fancied it deserved, and said she would be glad to have him look in upon her at work whenever he felt the inclination and his business gave him the opportunity.

He responded at once by presenting himself at her home with all his disarming naïveté. And then there was scarcely a day which followed that she did not see him or was not reminded of him. He was prolific in pretexts. His attitude became one of good-humored subservience and tacit adoration. He was ready at all times to submit to her moods, which were as often kind as they were cold. She grew accustomed to him. They became intimate and friendly by imperceptible degrees, and then by leaps. He sometimes talked in a way that astonished her at first and brought the crimson into her face; in a way that pleased her at last, appealing to the animalism that stirred impatiently within her.

There was nothing which so quieted the turmoil of Edna's senses as a visit to Mademoiselle Reisz. It was then, in the presence of that personality which was offensive to her, that the woman, by her divine art, seemed to reach Edna's spirit and set it free.

It was misty, with heavy, lowering atmosphere, one afternoon, when Edna climbed the stairs to the pianist's apartments under the roof. Her clothes were dripping with moisture. She felt chilled and pinched as she entered the room. Mademoiselle was poking at a rusty stove that smoked a little and warmed the room indifferently. She was endeavoring to heat a pot of chocolate on the stove. The room looked cheerless and dingy to Edna as she entered. A bust of Beethoven, covered with a hood of dust, scowled at her from the mantelpiece.

"Ah! here comes the sunlight!" exclaimed Mademoiselle, rising from her knees before the stove. "Now it will be warm and bright enough; I can let the fire alone."

She closed the stove door with a bang, and approaching, assisted in removing Edna's dripping mackintosh.

"You are cold; you look miserable. The chocolate will soon be hot. But would you rather have a taste of brandy? I have scarcely touched the bottle which you brought me for my cold." A piece of red flannel was wrapped around Mademoiselle's throat; a stiff neck compelled her to hold her head on one side.

"I will take some brandy," said Edna, shivering as she removed her gloves and overshoes. She drank the liquor from the glass as a man would have done. Then flinging herself upon the uncomfortable sofa she said, "Mademoiselle, I am going to move away from my house on Esplanade Street."

"Ah!" ejaculated the musician, neither surprised nor especially interested. Nothing ever seemed to astonish her very much. She was endeavoring to adjust the bunch of violets which had become loose from its fastening in her hair. Edna drew her down upon the sofa, and taking a pin from her own hair, secured the shabby artificial flowers in their accustomed place.

"Aren't you astonished?"

"Passably. Where are you going? to New York? to Iberville? to your father in Mississippi? where?"

"Just two steps away," laughed Edna, "in a little four-room house around the corner. It looks so cozy, so inviting and restful, whenever I pass by; and it's for rent. I'm tired looking after that big house. It never seemed like mine, anyway—like home. It's too much trouble. I have to keep too many servants. I am tired bothering with them."

"That is not your true reason, *ma belle*. There is no use in telling me lies. I don't know your reason, but you have not told me the truth." Edna did not protest or endeavor to justify herself.

"The house, the money that provides for it, are not mine. Isn't that enough reason?"

"They are your husband's," returned Mademoiselle, with a shrug and a malicious elevation of the eyebrows.

"Oh! I see there is no deceiving you. Then let me tell you: It is a caprice. I have a little money of my own from my mother's estate, which my father sends me by driblets. I won a large sum this winter on the races, and I am beginning to sell my sketches. Laidpore is more and more pleased with my work; he says it grows in force and individuality. I cannot judge of that myself, but I feel that I have gained in ease and confidence. However, as I said, I have sold a good many through Laidpore. I can live in the tiny house for little or nothing, with one servant. Old Celestine, who works occasionally for me, says she will come stay with me and do my work. I know I shall like it, like the feeling of freedom and independence."

"What does your husband say?"

"I have not told him yet. I only thought of it this morning. He will think I am demented, no doubt. Perhaps you think so."

Mademoiselle shook her head slowly. "Your reason is not yet clear to me," she said.

Neither was it quite clear to Edna herself; but it unfolded itself as she sat for a while in silence. Instinct had prompted her to put away her husband's bounty in casting off her allegiance. She did not know how it would be when he returned. There would have to be an understanding, an explanation. Conditions would some way adjust themselves, she felt; but whatever came, she had resolved never again to belong to another than herself.

"I shall give a grand dinner before I leave the old house!" Edna exclaimed. "You will have to come to it, Mademoiselle. I will give you everything that you like to eat and to drink. We shall sing and laugh and be merry for once." And she uttered a sigh that came from the very depths of her being.

If Mademoiselle happened to have received a letter from Robert during the interval of Edna's visits, she would give her the letter unsolicited. And she would seat herself at the piano and play as her humor prompted her while the young woman read the letter.

The little stove was roaring; it was red-hot, and the chocolate in the tin sizzled and sputtered. Edna went forward and opened the stove door, and Mademoiselle rising, took a letter from under the bust of Beethoven and handed it to Edna.

"Another! so soon!" she exclaimed, her eyes filled with delight. "Tell me, Mademoiselle, does he know that I see his letters?"

"Never in the world! He would be angry and would never write to me again if he thought so. Does he write to you? Never a line. Does he send you a message? Never a word. It is because he loves you, poor fool, and is trying to forget you, since you are not free to listen to him or to belong to him."

"Why do you show me his letters, then?"

"Haven't you begged for them? Can I refuse you anything? Oh! you cannot deceive me," and Mademoiselle approached her beloved instrument and began to play. Edna did not at once read the letter. She sat holding it in her hand, while the music penetrated her whole being like an effulgence, warming and brightening the dark places of her soul. It prepared her for joy and exultation.

"Oh!" she exclaimed, letting the letter fall to the floor. "Why did you not tell me?" She went and grasped Mademoiselle's hands up from the keys. "Oh! unkind! malicious! Why did you not tell me?"

"That he was coming back? No great news, *ma foi.* I wonder he did not come long ago."

"But when, when?" cried Edna, impatiently.

"He does not say when."

"He says 'very soon.' You know as much about it as I do; it is all in the letter."

"But why? Why is he coming? Oh, if I thought—" and she snatched the letter from the floor and turned the pages this way and that way, looking for the reason, which was left untold.

"If I were young and in love with a man," said Mademoiselle, turning on the stool and pressing her wiry hands between her knees as she looked down at Edna, who sat on the floor holding the letter, "it seems to me he would have to be some *grand esprit;* a man with lofty aims and ability to reach them; one who stood high enough to attract the notice of his fellow-men. It seems to me if I were young and in love I should never deem a man of ordinary caliber worthy of my devotion."

"Now it is you who are telling lies and seeking to deceive me, Mademoiselle; or else you have never been in love, and know nothing about it. Why," went on Edna, clasping her knees and looking up into Mademoiselle's twisted face, "do you suppose a woman knows why she loves? Does she select? Does she say to herself: 'Go to! Here is a distinguished statesman with presidential possibilities; I shall proceed to fall in love with him.' Or, 'I shall set my heart upon this musician, whose fame is on every tongue?' Or, 'This financier, who controls the world's money markets?'"

"You are purposely misunderstanding me, *ma reine.* Are you in love with Robert?"

"Yes," said Edna. It was the first time she had admitted it, and a glow overspread her face, blotching it with red spots.

"Why?" asked her companion. "Why do you love him when you ought not to?"

Edna, with a motion or two, dragged herself on her knees before Mademoiselle Reisz, who took the glowing face between her two hands.

"Why? Because his hair is brown and grows away from his temples; because he opens and shuts his eyes, and his nose is a little out of drawing; because he has two lips and a square chin, and a little finger he can't straighten from having played baseball too energetically in his youth. Because—"

"Because you do, in short," laughed Mademoiselle.

"What will you do when he comes back?" she asked.

"Do? Nothing, except feel glad and happy to be alive."

She was already glad and happy to be alive at the mere thought of his return. The murky, lowering sky, which had depressed her a few hours before, seemed bracing and invigorating as she splashed through the streets on her way home.

She stopped at a confectioner's and ordered a huge box of bonbons for the children in Iberville. She slipped a card in the box, on which she scribbled a tender message and sent an abundance of kisses. Before dinner in the evening Edna wrote a charming letter to her husband, telling him of her intention to move for a while into the little house around the block, and to give a farewell dinner before leaving, regretting that he was not there to share it, to help her out with the menu and assist her in entertaining the guests. Her letter was brimming with cheerfulness.

XXVII

"What is the matter with you?" asked Arobin that evening. "I never found you in such a happy mood." Edna was tired by that time, and was reclining on the lounge before the fire.

"Don't you know the weather prophet has told us we shall see the sun pretty soon?"

"Well, that ought to be reason enough," he acquiesced. "You wouldn't give me another if I sat here all night imploring you." He sat close to her on a low tabouret, and as he spoke his fingers lightly touched the hair that fell a little over her forehead. She liked the touch of his fingers through her hair, and closed her eyes sensitively.

"One of these days," she said, "I'm going to pull myself together for a while and think—try to determine what character of a woman I am; for, candidly, I don't know. By all the codes which I am acquainted with, I am a devilishly wicked specimen of the sex. But some way I can't convince myself that I am. I must think about it."

"Don't. What's the use? Why should you bother thinking about it when I can tell you what manner of woman you are." His fingers strayed occasionally down to her warm, smooth cheeks and firm chin, which was growing a little full and double.

"Oh, yes! You will tell me that I am adorable; everything that is captivating. Spare yourself the effort."

"No; I shan't tell you anything of the sort, though I shouldn't be lying if I did."

"Do you know Mademoiselle Reisz?" she asked irrelevantly.

"The pianist? I know her by sight. I've heard her play."

"She says queer things sometimes in a bantering way that you don't notice at the time and you find yourself thinking about afterward."

"For instance?"

"Well, for instance, when I left her to-day, she put her arms around me and felt my shoulder blades, to see if my wings were strong, she said. 'The bird that would soar above the level plain of tradition and prejudice must have strong wings. It is a sad spectacle to see the weaklings bruised, exhausted, fluttering back to earth.' "

"Whither would you soar?"

"I'm not thinking of any extraordinary flights. I only half comprehend her."

"I've heard she's partially demented," said Arobin.

"She seems to me wonderfully sane," Edna replied.

"I'm told she's extremely disagreeable and unpleasant. Why have you introduced her at a moment when I desired to talk of you?"

"Oh! talk of me if you like," cried Edna, clasping her hands beneath her head; "but let me think of something else while you do."

"I'm jealous of your thoughts to-night. They're making you a little kinder than usual; but some way I feel as if they were wandering, as if they were not here with me." She only looked at him and smiled. His eyes were very near. He leaned upon the lounge with an arm extended across her, while the other hand still rested upon her hair. They continued silently to look into each other's eyes. When he leaned forward and kissed her, she clasped his head, holding his lips to hers.

It was the first kiss of her life to which her nature had really responded. It was a flaming torch that kindled desire.

XXVIII

Edna cried a little that night after Arobin left her. It was only one phase of the multitudinous emotions which had assailed her. There was with her an overwhelming feeling of irresponsibility. There was the shock of the unexpected and the unaccustomed. There was her husband's reproach looking at her from the external things around her which he had provided for her external existence. There was Robert's reproach making itself felt by a quicker, fiercer, more overpowering love, which had awakened within her toward him. Above all, there was understanding. She felt as if a mist had been lifted from her eyes, enabling her to look upon and comprehend the significance of life, that monster made up of beauty and brutality. But among the conflicting sensations which assailed her, there was neither shame nor remorse. There was a dull pang of regret because it was not the kiss of love which had inflamed her, because it was not love which had held this cup of life to her lips.

XXIX

Without even waiting for an answer from her husband regarding his opinion or wishes in the matter, Edna hastened her preparations for quitting her home on Esplanade Street and moving into the little house around the block. A feverish anxiety attended her every action in that direction. There was no moment of deliberation, no interval of repose between the thought and its fulfillment. Early upon the morning following those hours passed in Arobin's society, Edna set about securing her new abode and hurrying her arrangements for occupying it. Within the precincts of her home she felt like one who has entered and lingered within the portals of some forbidden temple in which a thousand muffled voices bade her begone.

Whatever was her own in the house, everything which she had acquired aside from her husband's bounty, she caused to be transported to the other house, supplying simple and meager deficiencies from her own resources.

Arobin found her with rolled sleeves, working in company with the house-maid when he looked in during the afternoon. She was splendid and robust, and had never appeared handsomer than in the old blue gown, with a red silk handkerchief knotted at random around her head to protect her hair from the dust. She was mounted upon a high stepladder, unhooking a picture from the wall when he entered. He had found the front door open, and had followed his ring by walking in unceremoniously.

"Come down!" he said. "Do you want to kill yourself?" She greeted him with affected carelessness, and appeared absorbed in her occupation.

If he had expected to find her languishing, reproachful, or indulging in sentimental tears, he must have been greatly surprised.

He was no doubt prepared for any emergency, ready for any one of the foregoing attitudes, just as he bent himself easily and naturally to the situation which confronted him.

"Please come down," he insisted, holding the ladder and looking up at her.

"No," she answered; "Ellen is afraid to mount the ladder. Joe is working over at the 'pigeon house'—that's the name Ellen gives it, because it's so small and looks like a pigeon house—and some one has to do this."

Arobin pulled off his coat, and expressed himself ready and willing to tempt fate in her place. Ellen brought him one of her dust-caps, and went into contortions of mirth, which she found it impossible to control, when she saw him put it on before the mirror as grotesquely as he could. Edna herself could not refrain from smiling when she fastened it at his request. So it was he who in turn mounted the ladder, unhooking pictures and curtains, and dislodging ornaments as Edna directed. When he had finished he took off his dust-cap and went out to wash his hands.

Edna was sitting on the tabouret, idly brushing the tips of a feather duster along the carpet when he came in again.

"Is there anything more you will let me do?" he asked.

"That is all," she answered. "Ellen can manage the rest." She kept the young woman occupied in the drawing-room, unwilling to be left alone with Arobin.

"What about the dinner?" he asked; "the grand event, the *coup d'état?*"

"It will be day after to-morrow. Why do you call it the *coup d'état?*' Oh! it will be very fine; all my best of everything—crystal, silver and gold, Sèvres, flowers, music, and champagne to swim in. I'll let Léonce pay the bills. I wonder what he'll say when he sees the bills."

"And you ask me why I call it a *coup d'état?*" Arobin had put on his coat, and he stood before her and asked if his cravat was plumb. She told him it was, looking no higher than the tip of his collar.

"When do you go to the 'pigeon house?'—with all due acknowledgment to Ellen."

"Day after to-morrow, after the dinner. I shall sleep there."

"Ellen, will you very kindly get me a glass of water?" asked Arobin. "The dust in the curtains, if you will pardon me for hinting such a thing, has parched my throat to a crisp."

"While Ellen gets the water," said Edna, rising, "I will say good-by and let you go. I must get rid of this grime, and I have a million things to do and think of."

"When shall I see you?" asked Arobin, seeking to detain her, the maid having left the room.

"At the dinner, of course. You are invited."

"Not before?—not to-night or to-morrow morning or to-morrow noon or night? or the day after morning or noon? Can't you see yourself, without my telling you, what an eternity it is?"

He had followed her into the hall and to the foot of the stairway, looking up at her as she mounted with her face half turned to him.

"Not an instant sooner," she said. But she laughed and looked at him with eyes that at once gave him courage to wait and made it torture to wait.

XXX

Though Edna had spoken of the dinner as a very grand affair, it was in truth a very small affair and very select, in so much as the guests invited were few and were selected with discrimination. She had counted upon an even dozen seating themselves at her round mahogany board, forgetting for the moment that Madame Ratignolle was to the last degree *souffrante* and unpresentable, and not foreseeing that Madame Lebrun would sent a thousand regrets at the last moment. So there were only ten, after all, which made a cozy, comfortable number.

There were Mr. and Mrs. Merriman, a pretty, vivacious little woman in the thirties; her husband, a jovial fellow, something of a shallow-pate, who laughed a good deal at other people's witticisms, and had thereby made himself extremely popular. Mrs. Highcamp had accompanied them. Of course, there was Alcée Arobin; and Mademoiselle Reisz had consented to come. Edna had sent her a fresh bunch of violets with black lace trimmings for her hair. Monsieur Ratignolle brought himself and his wife's excuses. Victor Lebrun, who happened to be in the city, bent upon relaxation, had accepted with alacrity. There was a Miss Mayblunt, no longer in her teens, who looked at the world through lorgnettes and with the keenest interest. It was thought and said that she was intellectual; it was suspected of her that she wrote under a *nom de guerre*. She had come with a gentleman by the name of Gouvernail, connected with one of the daily papers, of whom nothing special could be said, except that he was observant and seemed quiet and inoffensive. Edna herself made the tenth, and at half-past eight they seated themselves at table, Arobin and Monsieur Ratignolle on either side of their hostess.

Mrs. Highcamp sat between Arobin and Victor Lebrun. Then came Mrs. Merriman, Mr. Gouvernail, Miss Mayblunt, Mr. Merriman, and Mademoiselle Reisz next to Monsieur Ratignolle.

There was something extremely gorgeous about the appearance of the table, an effect of splendor conveyed by a cover of pale yellow satin under strips of lace-work. There were wax candles in massive brass candelabra, burning softly under yellow silk shades; full, fragrant roses, yellow and red, abounded. There were silver and gold, as she had said there would be, and crystal which glittered like the gems which the women wore. The ordinary stiff dining chairs had been discarded for the occasion and replaced by the most commodious and luxurious which could be collected throughout the house. Mademoiselle Reisz, being exceedingly diminutive, was elevated upon cushions, as small children are sometimes hoisted at table upon bulky volumes. "Something new, Edna?" exclaimed Miss Mayblunt, with lorgnette directed toward a magnificent cluster of diamonds that sparkled, that almost sputtered, in Edna's hair, just over the center of her forehead.

"Quite new; 'brand' new, in fact; a present from my husband. It arrived this morning from New York. I may as well admit that this is my birthday, and that I am twenty-nine. In good time I expect you to drink my health. Meanwhile, I shall ask you to begin with this cocktail, composed—would you say 'composed?'" with an appeal to Miss Mayblunt—"composed by my father in honor of Sister Janet's wedding."

Before each guest stood a tiny glass that looked and sparkled like a garnet gem.

"Then, all things considered," spoke Arobin, "it might not be amiss to start out by drinking the Colonel's health in the cocktail which he composed, on the birthday of the most charming of women—the daughter whom he invented."

Mr. Merriman's laugh at this sally was such a genuine outburst and so contagious that it started the dinner with an agreeable swing that never slackened.

Miss Mayblunt begged to be allowed to keep her cocktail untouched before her, just to look at. The color was marvelous! She could compare it to nothing she had ever seen, and the garnet lights which it emitted were unspeakably rare. She pronounced the Colonel an artist, and stuck to it.

Monsieur Ratignolle was prepared to take things seriously: the *mets*, the *entre-mets*, the service, the decorations, even the people. He looked up from his pompono and inquired of Arobin if he were related to the gentleman of that name who formed one of the firm of Laitner and Arobin, lawyers. The young man admitted that Laitner was a warm personal friend, who permitted Arobin's name to decorate the firm's letterheads and to appear upon a shingle that graced Perdido Street.

"There are so many inquisitive people and institutions abounding," said Arobin, "that one is really forced as a matter of convenience these days to assume the virtue of an occupation if he has it not."

Monsieur Ratignolle stared a little, and turned to ask Mademoiselle Reisz if she considered the symphony concerts up to the standard which had been set the previous winter. Mademoiselle Reisz answered Monsieur Ratignolle in French, which Edna thought a little rude, under the circumstances, but characteristic. Mademoiselle had only disagreeable things to say of the symphony concerts, and insulting remarks to make of all the musicians of New Orleans, singly and collectively. All her interest seemed to be centered upon the delicacies placed before her.

Mr. Merriman said that Mr. Arobin's remark about inquisitive people reminded him of a man from Waco the other day at the St. Charles Hotel—but as Mr. Merriman's stories were always lame and lacking point, his wife seldom permitted him to complete them. She interrupted him to ask if he remembered the name of the author whose book she had bought the week before to send to a friend in Geneva. She was talking "books" with Mr. Gouvernail and trying to draw from him his opinion upon current literary topics. Her husband told the story of the Waco man privately to Miss Mayblunt, who pretended to be greatly amused and to think it extremely clever.

Mrs. Highcamp hung with languid but unaffected interest upon the warm and impetuous volubility of her left-hand neighbor, Victor Lebrun. Her attention was never for a moment withdrawn from him after seating herself at table; and when he turned to Mrs. Merriman, who was prettier and more vivacious than Mrs. Highcamp, she waited with easy indifference for an opportunity to reclaim his attention. There was the occasional sound of music, of mandolins, sufficiently removed to be an agreeable accompaniment rather than an interruption to the conversation. Outside the soft, monotonous splash of a fountain could be heard; the sound penetrated into the room with the heavy odor of jessamine that came through the open windows.

The golden shimmer of Edna's satin gown spread in rich folds on either side of her. There was a soft fall of lace encircling her shoulders. It was the color of her skin, without the glow, the myriad living tints that one may sometimes discover in vibrant flesh. There was something in her attitude, in her whole appearance when she leaned her head against the high-backed chair and spread her arms, which suggested the regal woman, the one who rules, who looks on, who stands alone.

But as she sat there amid her guests, she felt the old ennui overtaking her; the hopelessness which so often assailed her, which came upon her like an obsession, like something extraneous, independent of volition. It was something which announced itself; a chill breath that seemed to issue from some vast cavern wherein discords wailed. There came over her the acute longing which always summoned into her spiritual vision the presence of the beloved one, overpowering her at once with a sense of the unattainable.

The moments glided on, while a feeling of good fellowship passed around the circle like a mystic cord, holding and binding these people together with jest and laughter. Monsieur Ratignolle was the first to break the pleasant charm. At ten o'clock he excused himself. Madame Ratignolle was waiting for him at home. She was *bien souffrante,* and she was filled with vague dread, which only her husband's presence could allay.

Mademoiselle Reisz arose with Monsieur Ratignolle, who offered to escort her to the car. She had eaten well; she had tasted the good, rich wines, and they must have turned her head, for she bowed pleasantly to all as she withdrew from table. She kissed Edna upon the shoulder, and whispered: *"Bonne nuit, ma reine; soyez sage."* She had been a little bewildered upon rising, or rather, descending from her cushions, and Monsieur Ratignolle gallantly took her arm and led her away.

Mrs. Highcamp was weaving a garland of roses, yellow and red. When she had finished the garland, she laid it lightly upon Victor's black curls. He was reclining far back in the luxurious chair, holding a glass of champagne to the light.

As if a magician's wand had touched him, the garland of roses transformed him into a vision of Oriental beauty. His cheeks were the color of crushed grapes, and his dusky eyes glowed with a languishing fire. *"Sapristi!"* exclaimed Arobin. But Mrs. Highcamp had one more touch to add to the picture. She took from the back of her chair a white silken scarf, with which she had covered her shoulders in the early part of the evening. She draped it across the boy in graceful folds, and in a way to conceal his black, conventional evening dress. He did not seem to mind what she did to him, only smiled, showing a faint gleam of white teeth, while he continued to gaze with narrowing eyes at the light through his glass of champagne. "Oh! to be able to paint in color rather than in words!" exclaimed Miss Mayblunt, losing herself in a rhapsodic dream as she looked at him.

> "'There was a graven image of Desire
> Painted with red blood on a ground of gold.'"

murmured Gouvernail, under his breath.

The effect of the wine upon Victor was to change his accustomed volubility into silence. He seemed to have abandoned himself to a reverie, and to be seeing pleasing visions in the amber bead.

"Sing," entreated Mrs. Highcamp. "Won't you sing to us?"

"Let him alone," said Arobin.

"He's posing," offered Mr. Merriman; "let him have it out."

"I believe he's paralyzed," laughed Mrs. Merriman. And leaning over the youth's chair, she took the glass from his hand and held it to his lips. He sipped the wine slowly, and when he had drained the glass she laid it upon the table and wiped his lips with her little filmy handkerchief.

"Yes, I'll sing for you," he said, turning in his chair toward Mrs. Highcamp. He clasped his hands behind his head, and looking up at the ceiling began to hum a little, trying his voice like a musician tuning an instrument. Then, looking at Edna, he began to sing:

> "Ah! si tu savais!"

"Stop!" she cried, "don't sing that. I don't want you to sing it," and she laid her glass so impetuously and blindly upon the table as to shatter it against a caraffe. The wine spilled over Arobin's legs and some of it trickled down upon Mrs. Highcamp's black gauze gown. Victor had lost all idea of courtesy, or else he thought his hostess was not in earnest, for he laughed and went on:

> "Ah! si tu savais
> Ce que tes yeux me disent"—

"Oh! you mustn't! you mustn't," exclaimed Edna, and pushing back her chair she got up, and going behind him placed her hand over his mouth. He kissed the soft palm that pressed upon his lips.

"No, no, I won't, Mrs. Pontellier. I didn't know you meant it," looking up at her with caressing eyes. The touch of his lips was like a pleasing sting to her hand. She lifted the garland of roses from his head and flung it across the room.

"Come, Victor; you've posed long enough. Give Mrs. Highcamp her scarf."

Mrs. Highcamp undraped the scarf from about him with her own hands. Miss Mayblunt and Mr. Gouvernail suddenly conceived the notion that it was time to say good night. And Mr. and Mrs. Merriman wondered how it could be so late.

Before parting from Victor, Mrs. Highcamp invited him to call upon her daughter, who she knew would be charmed to meet him and talk French and sing French songs with him. Victor expressed his desire and intention to call upon Miss Highcamp at the first opportunity which presented itself. He asked if Arobin were going his way. Arobin was not.

The mandolin players had long since stolen away. A profound stillness had fallen upon the broad, beautiful street. The voices of Edna's disbanding guests jarred like a discordant note upon the quiet harmony of the night.

XXXI

"Well?" questioned Arobin, who had remained with Edna after the others had departed.

"Well," she reiterated, and stood up, stretching her arms, and feeling the need to relax her muscles after having been so long seated.

"What next?" he asked.

"The servants are all gone. They left when the musicians did. I have dismissed them. The house has to be closed and locked, and I shall trot around to the pigeon house, and shall send Celestine over in the morning to straighten things up."

He looked around, and began to turn out some of the lights.

"What about upstairs?" he inquired.

"I think it is all right; but there may be a window or two unlatched. We had better look; you might take a candle and see. And bring me my wrap and hat on the foot of the bed in the middle room."

He went up with the light, and Edna began closing doors and windows. She hated to shut in the smoke and the fumes of the wine. Arobin found her cape and hat, which he brought down and helped her to put on.

When everything was secured and the lights put out, they left through the front door, Arobin locking it and taking the key, which he carried for Edna. He helped her down the steps.

"Will you have a spray of jessamine?" he asked, breaking off a few blossoms as he passed.

"No; I don't want anything."

She seemed disheartened, and had nothing to say. She took his arm, which he offered her, holding up the weight of her satin train with the other hand. She looked down, noticing the black line of his leg moving in and out so close to her against the yellow shimmer of her gown. There was the whistle of a railway train somewhere in the distance, and the midnight bells were ringing. They met no one in their short walk.

The "pigeon-house" stood behind a locked gate, and a shallow *parterre* that had been somewhat neglected. There was a small front porch, upon which a long window and the front door opened. The door opened directly into the parlor; there was no side entry. Back in the yard was a room for servants, in which old Celestine had been ensconced.

Edna had left a lamp burning low upon the table. She had succeeded in making the room look habitable and homelike. There were some books on the table and a lounge near at hand. On the floor was a fresh matting, covered with a rug or two; and on the walls hung a few tasteful pictures. But the room was filled with flowers. These were a surprise to her. Arobin had sent them, and had had Celestine distribute them during Edna's absence. Her bedroom was adjoining, and across a small passage were the dining-room and kitchen.

Edna seated herself with every appearance of discomfort.

"Are you tired?" he asked.

"Yes, and chilled, and miserable. I feel as if I had been wound up to a certain pitch—too tight—and something inside of me had snapped." She rested her head against the table upon her bare arm.

"You want to rest," he said, "and to be quiet. I'll go; I'll leave you and let you rest."

"Yes," she replied.

He stood up beside her and smoothed her hair with his soft, magnetic hand. His touch conveyed to her a certain physical comfort. She could have fallen quietly asleep there if he had continued to pass his hand over her hair. He brushed the hair upward from the nape of her neck.

"I hope you will feel better and happier in the morning," he said. "You have tried to do too much in the past few days. The dinner was the last straw; you might have dispensed with it."

"Yes," she admitted; "it was stupid."

"No, it was delightful; but it has worn you out." His hand had strayed to her beautiful shoulders, and he could feel the response of her flesh to his touch. He seated himself beside her and kissed her lightly upon the shoulder.

"I thought you were going away," she said, in an uneven voice.

"I am, after I have said good night."

"Good night," she murmured.

He did not answer, except to continue to caress her. He did not say good night until she had become supple to his gentle, seductive entreaties.

XXXII

When Mr. Pontellier learned of his wife's intention to abandon her home and take up her residence elsewhere, he immediately wrote her a letter of unqualified disapproval and remonstrance. She had given reasons which he was unwilling to acknowledge as adequate. He hoped she had not acted upon her rash impulse; and he begged her to consider first, foremost, and above all else, what people would say. He was not dreaming of scandal when he uttered this warning; that was a thing which would never have entered into his mind to consider in connection with his wife's name or his own. He was simply thinking of his financial integrity. It might get noised about that the Pontelliers had met with reverses, and were forced to conduct their *ménage* on a humbler scale than heretofore. It might do incalculable mischief to his business prospects.

But remembering Edna's whimsical turn of mind of late, and foreseeing that she had immediately acted upon her impetuous determination, he grasped the situation with his usual promptness and handled it with his well-known business tact and cleverness.

The same mail which brought to Edna his letter of disapproval carried instructions—the most minute instructions—to a well-known architect concerning the remodeling of his home, changes which he had long contemplated, and which he desired carried forward during his temporary absence.

Expert and reliable packers and movers were engaged to convey the furniture, carpets, pictures—everything movable, in short—to places of security. And in an incredibly short time the Pontellier house was turned over to the artisans. There was to be an addition—a small snuggery; there was to be frescoing, and hardwood flooring was to be put into such rooms as had not yet been subjected to this improvement.

Furthermore, in one of the daily papers appeared a brief notice to the effect that Mr. and Mrs. Pontellier were contemplating a summer sojourn abroad, and that their handsome residence on Esplanade Street was undergoing sumptuous alterations, and would not be ready for occupancy until their return. Mr. Pontellier had saved appearances!

Edna admired the skill of his maneuver, and avoided any occasion to balk his intentions. When the situation as set forth by Mr. Pontellier was accepted and taken for granted, she was apparently satisfied that it should be so.

The pigeon-house pleased her. It at once assumed the intimate character of a home, while she herself invested it with a charm which it reflected like a warm glow. There was with her a feeling of having descended in the social scale, with a corresponding sense of having risen in the spiritual. Every step which she took toward relieving herself from obligations added to her strength and expansion as an individual. She began to look with her own eyes; to see and to apprehend the deeper undercurrents of life. No longer was she content to "feed upon opinion" when her own soul had invited her.

After a little while, a few days, in fact, Edna went up and spent a week with her children in Iberville. They were delicious February days, with all the summer's promise hovering in the air.

How glad she was to see the children! She wept for very pleasure when she felt their little arms clasping her; their hard, ruddy cheeks pressed against her own glowing cheeks. She looked into their faces with hungry eyes that could not be satisfied with looking. And what stories they had to tell their mother! About the pigs, the cows, the mules! About riding to the mill behind Gluglu; fishing back in the lake with their Uncle Jasper; picking pecans with Lidie's little black brood, and hauling chips in their express wagon. It was a thousand times more fun to haul real chips for old lame Susie's real fire than to drag painted blocks along the banquette on Esplanade Street!

She went with them herself to see the pigs and the cows, to look at the darkies laying the cane, to thrash the pecan trees, and catch fish in the back lake. She lived with them a whole week long, giving them all of herself, and gathering and filling herself with their young existence. They listened, breathless, when she told them the house in Esplanade Street was crowded with workmen, hammering, nailing, sawing, and filling the place with clatter. They wanted to know where their bed was; what had been done with their rocking-horse; and where did Joe sleep, and where had Ellen gone, and the cook ? But, above all, they were fired with a desire to see the little house around the block. Was there any place to play? Were there any boys next door? Raoul, with pessimistic foreboding, was convinced that there were only girls next door. Where would they sleep, and where would papa sleep? She told them the fairies would fix it all right.

The old Madame was charmed with Edna's visit, and showered all manner of delicate attentions upon her. She was delighted to know that the Esplanade Street house was in a dismantled condition. It gave her the promise and pretext to keep the children indefinitely.

It was with a wrench and a pang that Edna left her children. She carried away with her the sound of their voices and the touch of their cheeks. All along the journey homeward their presence lingered with her like the memory of a delicious song. But by the time she had regained the city the song no longer echoed in her soul. She was again alone.

XXXIII

It happened sometimes when Edna went to see Mademoiselle Reisz that the little musician was absent, giving a lesson or making some small necessary household purchase. The key was always left in a secret hiding place in the entry, which Edna knew. If Mademoiselle happened to be away, Edna would usually enter and wait for her return.

When she knocked at Mademoiselle Reisz's door one afternoon there was no response; so unlocking the door, as usual, she entered and found the apartment deserted, as she had expected. Her day had been quite filled up, and it was for a rest, for a refuge, and to talk about Robert, that she sought out her friend.

She had worked at her canvas—a young Italian character study—all the morning, completing the work without the model; but there had been many interruptions, some incident to her modest housekeeping, and others of a social nature.

Madame Ratignolle had dragged herself over, avoiding the too public thoroughfares, she said. She complained that Edna had neglected her much of late. Besides, she was consumed with curiosity to see the little house and the manner in which it was conducted. She wanted to hear all about the dinner party; Monsieur Ratignolle had left *so* early. What had happened after he left? The champagne and grapes which Edna sent over were *too* delicious. She had so little appetite; they had refreshed and toned her stomach. Where on earth was she going to put Mr. Pontellier in that little house, and the boys? And then she made Edna promise to go to her when her hour of trial overtook her.

"At any time—any time of the day or night, dear," Edna assured her. Before leaving Madame Ratignolle said:

"In some way you seem to me like a child, Edna. You seem to act without a certain amount of reflection which is necessary in this life. That is the reason I want to say you mustn't mind if I advise you to be a little careful while you are living here alone. Why don't you have some one come and stay with you? Wouldn't Mademoiselle Reisz come?"

"No; she wouldn't wish to come, and I shouldn't want her always with me."

"Well, the reason—you know how evil-minded the world is—some one was talking of Alcée Arobin visiting you. Of course, it wouldn't matter if Mr. Arobin had not such a dreadful reputation. Monsieur Ratignolle was telling me that his attentions alone are considered enough to ruin a woman's name."

"Does he boast of his successes?" asked Edna, indifferently, squinting at her picture.

"No, I think not. I believe he is a decent fellow as far as that goes. But his character is so well known among the men. I shan't be able to come back and see you; it was very, very imprudent to-day."

"Mind the step!" cried Edna.

"Don't neglect me," entreated Madame Ratignolle; "and don't mind what I said about Arobin, or having some one to stay with you."

"Of course not," Edna laughed. "You may say anything you like to me." They kissed each other good-by. Madame Ratignolle had not far to go, and Edna stood on the porch a while watching her walk down the street.

Then in the afternoon Mrs. Merriman and Mrs. Highcamp had made their "party call." Edna felt that they might have dispensed with the formality. They had also come to invite her to play *vingt-et-un* one evening at Mrs. Merriman's. She was asked to go early, to dinner, and Mr. Merriman or Mr. Arobin would take her home. Edna accepted in a half-hearted way. She sometimes felt very tired of Mrs. Highcamp and Mrs. Merriman.

Late in the afternoon she sought refuge with Mademoiselle Reisz, and stayed there alone, waiting for her, feeling a kind of repose invade her with the very atmosphere of the shabby, unpretentious little room.

Edna sat at the window, which looked out over the house-tops and across the river. The window frame was filled with pots of flowers, and she sat and picked the dry leaves from a rose geranium. The day was warm, and the breeze which blew from the river was very pleasant. She removed her hat and laid it on the piano. She went on picking the leaves and digging around the plants with her hat pin. Once she thought she heard Mademoiselle Reisz approaching. But it was a young black girl, who came in, bringing a small bundle of laundry, which she deposited in the adjoining room, and went away.

Edna seated herself at the piano, and softly picked out with one hand the bars of a piece of music which lay open before her. A half-hour went by. There was the occasional sound of people going and coming in the lower hall. She was growing interested in her occupation of picking out the aria, when there was a second rap at the door. She vaguely wondered what these people did when they found Mademoiselle's door locked.

"Come in," she called, turning her face toward the door. And this time it was Robert Lebrun who presented himself. She attempted to rise; she could not have done so without betraying the agitation which mastered her at sight of him, so she fell back upon the stool, only exclaiming, "Why, Robert!"

He came and clasped her hand, seemingly without knowing what he was saying or doing.

"Mrs. Pontellier! How do you happen—oh! how well you look! Is Mademoiselle Reisz not here? I never expected to see you."

"When did you come back?" asked Edna in an unsteady voice, wiping her face with her handkerchief. She seemed ill at ease on the piano stool, and he begged her to take the chair by the window. She did so, mechanically, while he seated himself on the stool.

"I returned day before yesterday," he answered, while he leaned his arm on the keys, bringing forth a crash of discordant sound.

"Day before yesterday!" she repeated, aloud; and went on thinking to herself, "day before yesterday," in a sort of an uncomprehending way. She had pictured him seeking her at the very first hour, and he had lived under the same sky since day before yesterday; while only by accident had he stumbled upon her. Mademoiselle must have lied when she said, "Poor fool, he loves you."

"Day before yesterday," she repeated, breaking off a spray of Mademoiselle's geranium; "then if you had not met me here to-day you wouldn't—when—that is, didn't you mean to come and see me?"

"Of course, I should have gone to see you. There have been so many things—" he turned the leaves of Mademoiselle's music nervously. "I started in at once yesterday with the old firm. After all there is as much chance for me here as there was there—that is,

I might find it profitable some day. The Mexicans were not very congenial."

So he had come back because the Mexicans were not congenial; because business was as profitable here as there; because of any reason, and not because he cared to be near her. She remembered the day she sat on the floor, turning the pages of his letter, seeking the reason which was left untold.

She had not noticed how he looked—only feeling his presence; but she turned deliberately and observed him. After all, he had been absent but a few months, and was not changed. His hair—the color of hers—waved back from his temples in the same way as before. His skin was not more burned than it had been at Grand Isle. She found in his eyes, when he looked at her for one silent moment, the same tender caress, with an added warmth and entreaty which had not been there before—the same glance which had penetrated to the sleeping places of her soul and awakened them.

A hundred times Edna had pictured Robert's return, and imagined their first meeting. It was usually at her home, whither he had sought her out at once. She always fancied him expressing or betraying in some way his love for her. And here, the reality was that they sat ten feet apart, she at the window, crushing geranium leaves in her hand and smelling them, he twirling around on the piano stool, saying:

"I was very much surprised to hear of Mr. Pontellier's absence; it's a wonder Mademoiselle Reisz did not tell me; and your moving—mother told me yesterday. I should think you would have gone to New York with him, or to Iberville with the children, rather than be bothered here with housekeeping. And you are going abroad, too, I hear. We shan't have you at Grand Isle next summer; it won't seem—do you see much of Mademoiselle Reisz? She often spoke of you in the few letters she wrote."

"Do you remember that you promised to write to me when you went away?" A flush overspread his whole face.

"I couldn't believe that my letters would be of any interest to you."

"That is an excuse; it isn't the truth." Edna reached for her hat on the piano. She adjusted it, sticking the hat pin through the heavy coil of hair with some deliberation.

"Are you not going to wait for Mademoiselle Reisz?" asked Robert.

"No; I have found when she is absent this long, she is liable not to come back till late." She drew on her gloves, and Robert picked up his hat.

"Won't you wait for her?" asked Edna.

"Not if you think she will not be back till late," adding, as if suddenly aware of some discourtesy in his speech, "and I should miss the pleasure of walking home with you." Edna locked the door and put the key back in its hiding-place.

They went together, picking their way across muddy streets and sidewalks encumbered with the cheap display of small tradesmen. Part of the distance they rode in the car, and after disembarking, passed the Pontellier mansion, which looked broken and half torn asunder. Robert had never known the house, and looked at it with interest.

"I never knew you in your home," he remarked.

"I am glad you did not."

"Why?" She did not answer. They went on around the corner, and it seemed as if her dreams were coming true after all, when he followed her into the little house.

"You must stay and dine with me, Robert. You see I am all alone, and it is so long since I have seen you. There is so much I want to ask you."

She took off her hat and gloves. He stood irresolute, making some excuse about his mother who expected him; he even muttered something about an engagement. She struck a match and lit the lamp on the table; it was growing dusk. When he saw her face in the lamp-light, looking pained, with all the soft lines gone out of it, he threw his hat aside and seated himself.

"Oh! you know I want to stay if you will let me!" he exclaimed. All the softness came back. She laughed, and went and put her hand on his shoulder.

"This is the first moment you have seemed like the old Robert. I'll go tell Celestine." She hurried away to tell Celestine to set an extra place. She even sent her off in search of some added delicacy which she had not thought of for herself. And she recommended great care in dripping the coffee and having the omelet done to a proper turn.

When she reëntered, Robert was turning over magazines, sketches, and things that lay upon the table in great disorder. He picked up a photograph, and exclaimed:

"Alcée Arobin! What on earth is his picture doing here?"

"I tried to make a sketch of his head one day," answered Edna, "and he thought the photograph might help me. It was at the other house. I thought it had been left there. I must have packed it up with my drawing materials."

"I should think you would give it back to him if you have finished with it."

"Oh! I have a great many such photographs. I never think of returning them. They don't amount to anything." Robert kept on looking at the picture.

"It seems to me—do you think his head worth drawing? Is he a friend of Mr. Pontellier's? You never said you knew him."

"He isn't a friend of Mr. Pontellier's; he's a friend of mine. I always knew him—that is, it is only of late that I know him pretty well. But I'd rather talk about you, and know what you have been seeing and doing and feeling out there in Mexico." Robert threw aside the picture.

"I've been seeing the waves and the white beach of Grand Isle; the quiet, grassy street of the *Chênière;* the old fort at Grande Terre. I've been working like a machine, and feeling like a lost soul. There was nothing interesting."

She leaned her head upon her hand to shade her eyes from the light.

"And what have you been seeing and doing and feeling all these days?" he asked.

"I've been seeing the waves and the white beach of Grand Isle; the quiet, grassy street of the *Chenière* Caminada; the old sunny fort at Grande Terre. I've been working with a little more comprehension than a machine, and still feeling like a lost soul. There was nothing interesting."

"Mrs. Pontellier, you are cruel," he said, with feeling, closing his eyes and resting his head back in his chair. They remained in silence till old Celestine announced dinner.

XXXIV

The dining-room was very small. Edna's round mahogany would have almost filled it. As it was there was but a step or two from the little table to the kitchen, to the mantel, the small buffet, and the side door that opened out on the narrow brick-paved yard.

A certain degree of ceremony settled upon them with the announcement of dinner. There was no return to personalities. Robert related incidents of his sojourn in Mexico, and Edna talked of events likely to interest him, which had occurred during his absence. The dinner was of ordinary quality, except for the few delicacies which she had sent out to purchase. Old Celestine, with a bandana *tignon* twisted about her head, hobbled in and out, taking a personal interest in everything; and she lingered occasionally to talk patois with Robert, whom she had known as a boy.

He went out to a neighboring cigar stand to purchase cigarette papers, and when he came back he found that Celestine had served the black coffee in the parlor.

"Perhaps I shouldn't have come back," he said. "When you are tired of me, tell me to go."

"You never tire me. You must have forgotten the hours and hours at Grand Isle in which we grew accustomed to each other and used to being together."

"I have forgotten nothing at Grand Isle," he said, not looking at her, but rolling a cigarette. His tobacco pouch, which he laid upon the table, was a fantastic embroidered silk affair, evidently the handiwork of a woman.

"You used to carry your tobacco in a rubber pouch," said Edna, picking up the pouch and examining the needlework.

"Yes; it was lost."

"Where did you buy this one? In Mexico?"

"It was given to me by a Vera Cruz girl; they are very generous," he replied, striking a match and lighting his cigarette.

"They are very handsome, I suppose, those Mexican women; very picturesque, with their black eyes and their lace scarfs."

"Some are; others are hideous. Just as you find women everywhere."

"What was she like—the one who gave you the pouch? You must have known her very well."

"She was very ordinary. She wasn't of the slightest importance. I knew her well enough."

"Did you visit at her house? Was it interesting? I should like to know and hear about the people you met, and the impressions they made on you."

"There are some people who leave impressions not so lasting as the imprint of an oar upon the water."

"Was she such a one?"

"It would be ungenerous for me to admit that she was of that order and kind." He thrust the pouch back in his pocket, as if to put away the subject with the trifle which had brought it up.

Arobin dropped in with a message from Mrs. Merriman, to say that the card party was postponed on account of the illness of one of her children.

"How do you do, Arobin?" said Robert, rising from the obscurity.

"Oh! Lebrun. To be sure! I heard yesterday you were back. How did they treat you down in Mexique?"

"Fairly well."

"But not well enough to keep you there. Stunning girls, though, in Mexico. I thought I should never get away from Vera Cruz when I was down there a couple of years ago."

"Did they embroider slippers and tobacco pouches and hat-bands and things for you?" asked Edna.

"Oh! my! no! I didn't get so deep in their regard. I fear they made more impression on me than I made on them."

"You were less fortunate than Robert, then."

"I am always less fortunate than Robert. Has he been imparting tender confidences?"

"I've been imposing myself long enough," said Robert, rising, and shaking hands with Edna. "Please convey my regards to Mr. Pontellier when you write."

He shook hands with Arobin and went away.

"Fine fellow, that Lebrun," said Arobin when Robert had gone. "I never heard you speak of him."

"I knew him last summer at Grand Isle," she replied. "Here is that photograph of yours. Don't you want it?"

"What do I want with it? Throw it away." She threw it back on the table.

"I'm not going to Mrs. Merriman's," she said. "If you see her, tell her so. But perhaps I had better write. I think I shall write now, and say that I am sorry her child is sick, and tell her not to count on me."

"It would be a good scheme," acquiesced Arobin. "I don't blame you; stupid lot!"

Edna opened the blotter, and having procured paper and pen, began to write the note. Arobin lit a cigar and read the evening paper, which he had in his pocket.

"What is the date?" she asked. He told her.

"Will you mail this for me when you go out?"

"Certainly." He read to her little bits out of the newspaper, while she straightened things on the table.

"What do you want to do?" he asked, throwing aside the paper. "Do you want to go out for a walk or a drive or anything? It would be a fine night to drive."

"No; I don't want to do anything but just be quiet. You go away and amuse yourself. Don't stay."

"I'll go away if I must; but I shan't amuse myself. You know that I only live when I am near you."

He stood up to bid her good night.

"Is that one of the things you always say to women?"

"I have said it before, but I don't think I ever came so near meaning it," he answered with a smile. There were no warm lights in her eyes; only a dreamy, absent look.

"Good night. I adore you. Sleep well," he said, and he kissed her hand and went away.

She stayed alone in a kind of reverie—a sort of stupor. Step by step she lived over every instant of the time she had been with Robert after he had entered Mademoiselle Reisz's door. She recalled his words, his looks. How few and meager they had been for her hungry heart! A vision —a transcendently seductive vision of a Mexican girl arose before her. She writhed with a jealous pang. She wondered when he would come back. He had not said he would come back. She had been with him, had heard his voice and touched his hand. But some way he had seemed nearer to her off there in Mexico.

XXXV

The morning was full of sunlight and hope. Edna could see before her no denial—only the promise of excessive joy. She lay in bed awake, with bright eyes full of speculation. "He loves you, poor fool." If she could but get that conviction firmly fixed in her mind, what mattered about the rest? She felt she had been childish and unwise the night before in giving herself over to despondency. She recapitulated the motives which no doubt explained Robert's reserve. They were not insurmountable; they would not hold if he really loved her; they could not hold against her own passion, which he must come to realize in time. She pictured him going to his business that morning. She even saw how he was dressed; how he walked down one street, and turned the corner of another; saw him bending over his desk, talking to people who entered the office, going to his lunch, and perhaps watching for her on the street. He would come to her in the afternoon or evening, sit and roll his cigarette, talk a little, and go away as he had done the night before. But how delicious it would be to have him there with her! She would have no regrets, nor seek to penetrate his reserve if he still chose to wear it.

Edna ate her breakfast only half dressed. The maid brought her a delicious printed scrawl from Raoul, expressing his love, asking her to send him some bonbons, and telling her they had found that morning ten tiny white pigs all lying in a row beside Lidie's big white pig.

A letter also came from her husband, saying he hoped to be back early in March, and then they would get ready for that journey abroad which he had promised her so long, which he felt now fully able to afford; he felt able to travel as people should, without any thought of small economies—thanks to his recent speculations in Wall Street.

Much to her surprise she received a note from Arobin, written at midnight from the club. It was to say good morning to her, to hope she had slept well, to assure her of his devotion, which he trusted she in some faintest manner returned.

All these letters were pleasing to her. She answered the children in a cheerful frame of mind, promising them bonbons, and congratulating them upon their happy find of the little pigs.

She answered her husband with friendly evasiveness,—not with any fixed design to mislead him, only because all sense of reality had gone out of her life; she had abandoned herself to Fate, and awaited the consequences with indifference.

To Arobin's note she made no reply. She put it under Celestine's stove-lid.

Edna worked several hours with much spirit. She saw no one but a picture dealer, who asked her if it were true that she was going abroad to study in Paris.

She said possibly she might, and he negotiated with her for some Parisian studies to reach him in time for the holiday trade in December.

Robert did not come that day. She was keenly disappointed. He did not come the following day, nor the next. Each morning she awoke with hope, and each night she was a prey to despondency. She was tempted to seek him out. But far from yielding to the impulse, she avoided any occasion which might throw her in his way. She did not go to Mademoiselle Reisz's nor pass by Madame Lebrun's, as she might have done if he had still been in Mexico.

When Arobin, one night, urged her to drive with him, she went—out to the lake, on the Shell Road. His horses were full of mettle, and even a little unmanageable. She liked the rapid gait at which they spun along, and the quick, sharp sound of the horses' hoofs on the hard road. They did not stop anywhere to eat or to drink. Arobin was not needlessly imprudent. But they ate and they drank when they regained Edna's little dining-room—which was comparatively early in the evening.

It was late when he left her. It was getting to be more than a passing whim with Arobin to see her and be with her. He had detected the latent sensuality, which unfolded under his delicate sense of her nature's requirements like a torpid, torrid, sensitive blossom.

There was no despondency when she fell asleep that night; nor was there hope when she awoke in the morning.

XXXVI

There was a garden out in the suburbs; a small, leafy corner, with a few green tables under the orange trees. An old cat slept all day on the stone step in the sun, and an old *mulatresse* slept her idle hours away in her chair at the open window, till some one happened to knock on one of the green tables. She had milk and cream cheese to sell, and bread and butter. There was no one who could make such excellent coffee or fry a chicken so golden brown as she.

The place was too modest to attract the attention of people of fashion, and so quiet as to have escaped the notice of those in search of pleasure and dissipation. Edna had discovered it accidentally one day when the high-board gate stood ajar. She caught sight of a little green table, blotched with the checkered sunlight that filtered through the quivering leaves overhead. Within she had found the slumbering *mulatresse*, the drowsy cat, and a glass of milk which reminded her of the milk she had tasted in Iberville.

She often stopped there during her perambulations; sometimes taking a book with her, and sitting an hour or two under the trees when she found the place deserted. Once or twice she took a quiet dinner there alone, having instructed Celestine beforehand to prepare no dinner at home. It was the last place in the city where she would have expected to meet any one she knew. Still she was not astonished when, as she was partaking of a modest dinner late in the afternoon, looking into an open book, stroking the cat, which had made friends with her—she was not greatly astonished to see Robert come in at the tall garden gate. "I am destined to see you only by accident," she said, shoving the cat off the chair beside her. He was surprised, ill at ease, almost embarrassed at meeting her thus so unexpectedly. "Do you come here often?" he asked. "I almost live here," she said.

"I used to drop in very often for a cup of Catiche's good coffee. This is the first time since I came back."

"She'll bring you a plate, and you will share my dinner. There's always enough for two—even three." Edna had intended to be indifferent and as reserved as he when she met him; she had reached the determination by a laborious train of reasoning, incident to one of her despondent moods. But her resolve melted when she saw him before her, seated there beside her in the little garden, as if a designing Providence had led him into her path.

"Why have you kept away from me, Robert?" she asked, closing the book that lay open upon the table.

"Why are you so personal, Mrs. Pontellier? Why do you force me to idiotic subterfuges?" he exclaimed with sudden warmth. "I suppose there's no use telling you I've been very busy, or that I've been sick, or that I've been to see you and not found you at home. Please let me off with any one of these excuses."

"You are the embodiment of selfishness," she said. "You save yourself something—I don't know what—but there is some selfish motive, and in sparing yourself you never consider for a moment what I think, or how I feel your neglect and indifference. I suppose this is what you would call unwomanly; but I have got into the habit of expressing myself. It doesn't matter to me, and you may think me unwomanly if you like."

"No; I only think you cruel, as I said the other day. Maybe not intentionally cruel; but you seem to be forcing me into disclosures which can result in nothing; as if you would have me bare a wound for the pleasure of looking at it, without the intention or power of healing it."

"I'm spoiling your dinner, Robert; never mind what I say. You haven't eaten a morsel."

"I only came in for a cup of coffee." His sensitive face was all disfigured with excitement.

"Isn't this a delightful place?" she remarked. "I am so glad it has never actually been discovered. It is so quiet, so sweet, here. Do you notice there is scarcely a sound to be heard? It's so out of the way; and a good walk from the car. However, I don't mind walking. I always feel so sorry for women who don't like to walk; they miss so much—so many rare little glimpses of life; and we women learn so little of life on the whole.

"Catiche's coffee is always hot. I don't know how she manages it, here in the open air. Celestine's coffee gets cold bringing it from the kitchen to the dining-room. Three lumps! How can you drink it so sweet? Take some of the cress with your chop; it's so biting and crisp. Then there's the advantage of being able to smoke with your coffee out here. Now, in the city—aren't you going to smoke?"

"After a while," he said, laying a cigar on the table.

"Who gave it to you?" she laughed.

"I bought it. I suppose I'm getting reckless; I bought a whole box." She was determined not to be personal again and make him uncomfortable.

The cat made friends with him, and climbed into his lap when he smoked his cigar. He stroked her silky fur, and talked a little about her. He looked at Edna's book, which he had read; and he told her the end, to save her the trouble of wading through it, he said.

Again he accompanied her back to her home; and it was after dusk when they reached the little "pigeon-house." She did not ask him to remain, which he was grateful for, as it permitted him to stay without the discomfort of blundering through an excuse which he had no intention of considering. He helped her to light the lamp; then she went into her room to take off her hat and to bathe her face and hands.

When she came back Robert was not examining the pictures and magazines as before; he sat off in the shadow, leaning his head back on the chair as if in a reverie. Edna lingered a moment beside the table, arranging the books there. Then she went across the room to where he sat. She bent over the arm of his chair and called his name.

"Robert," she said, "are you asleep?"

"No," he answered, looking up at her.

She leaned over and kissed him—a soft, cool, delicate kiss, whose voluptuous sting penetrated his whole being—then she moved away from him. He followed, and took her in his arms, just holding her close to him. She put her hand up to his face and pressed his cheek against her own. The action was full of love and tenderness. He sought her lips again. Then he drew her down upon the sofa beside him and held her hand in both of his.

"Now you know," he said, "now you know what I have been fighting against since last summer at Grand Isle; what drove me away and drove me back again."

"Why have you been fighting against it?" she asked. Her race glowed with soft lights.

"Why? Because you were not free; you were Léonce Pontellier's wife. I couldn't help loving you if you were ten times his wife; but so long as I went away from you and kept away I could help telling you so." She put her free hand up to his shoulder, and then against his cheek, rubbing it softly. He kissed her again. His face was warm and flushed.

"There in Mexico I was thinking of you all the time, and longing for you."

"But not writing to me," she interrupted.

"Something put into my head that you cared for me; and I lost my senses. I forgot everything but a wild dream of your some way becoming my wife."

"Your wife!"

"Religion, loyalty, everything would give way if only you cared."

"Then you must have forgotten that I was Léonce Pontellier's wife."

"Oh! I was demented, dreaming of wild, impossible things, recalling men who had set their wives free, we have heard of such things."

"Yes, we have heard of such things."

"I came back full of vague, mad intentions. And when I got here—"

"When you got here you never came near me!" She was still caressing his cheek.

"I realized what a cur I was to dream of such a thing, even if you had been willing."

She took his face between her hands and looked into it as if she would never withdraw her eyes more. She kissed him on the forehead, the eyes, the cheeks, and the lips.

"You have been a very, very foolish boy, wasting your time dreaming of impossible things when you speak of Mr. Pontellier setting me free! I am no longer one of Mr. Pontellier's possessions to dispose of or not. I give myself where I choose. If he were to say, 'Here, Robert, take her and be happy; she is yours,' I should laugh at you both."

His face grew a little white. "What do you mean?" he asked.

There was a knock at the door. Old Celestine came in to say that Madame Ratignolle's servant had come around the back way with a message that Madame had been taken sick and begged Mrs. Pontellier to go to her immediately.

"Yes, yes," said Edna, rising; "I promised. Tell her yes—to wait for me. I'll go back with her."

"Let me walk over with you," offered Robert.

"No," she said; "I will go with the servant." She went into her room to put on her hat, and when she came in again she sat once more upon the sofa beside him. He had not stirred. She put her arms about his neck.

"Good-by, my sweet Robert. Tell me good-by." He kissed her with a degree of passion which had not before entered into his caress, and strained her to him.

"I love you," she whispered, "only you; no one but you. It was you who awoke me last summer out of a life-long, stupid dream. Oh! you have made me so unhappy with your indifference. Oh! I have suffered, suffered! Now you are here we shall love each other, my Robert. We shall be everything to each other. Nothing else in the world is of any consequence. I must go to my friend; but you will wait for me? No matter how late; you will wait for me, Robert?"

"Don't go; don't go! Oh! Edna, stay with me," he pleaded. "Why should you go? Stay with me, stay with me."

"I shall come back as soon as I can; I shall find you here." She buried her face in his neck, and said good-by again. Her seductive voice, together with his great love for her, had enthralled his senses, had deprived him of every impulse but the longing to hold her and keep her.

XXXVII

Edna looked in at the drug store. Monsieur Ratignolle was putting up a mixture himself, very carefully, dropping a red liquid into a tiny glass. He was grateful to Edna for having come; her presence would be a comfort to his wife. Madame Ratignolle's sister, who had always been with her at such trying times, had not been able to come up from the plantation, and Adèle had been inconsolable until Mrs. Pontellier so kindly promised to come to her. The nurse had been with them at night for the past week, as she lived a great distance away. And Dr. Mandelet had been coming and going all the afternoon. They were then looking for him any moment.

Edna hastened upstairs by a private stairway that led from the rear of the store to the apartments above. The children were all sleeping in a back room. Madame Ratignolle was in the salon, whither she had strayed in her suffering impatience. She sat on the sofa, clad in an ample white *peignoir*, holding a handkerchief tight in her hand with a nervous clutch. Her face was drawn and pinched, her sweet blue eyes haggard and unnatural. All her beautiful hair had been drawn back and plaited.

It lay in a long braid on the sofa pillow, coiled like a golden serpent. The nurse, a comfortable looking *Griffe woman* in white apron and cap, was urging her to return to her bedroom.

"There is no use, there is-no use," she said at once to Edna. "We must get rid of Mandelet; he is getting too old and careless. He said he would be here at half-past seven; now it must be eight. See what time it is, Joséphine."

The woman was possessed of a cheerful nature, and refused to take any situation too seriously, especially a situation with which she was so familiar. She urged Madame to have courage and patience. But Madame only set her teeth hard into her under lip, and Edna saw the sweat gather in beads on her white forehead. After a moment or two she uttered a profound sigh and wiped her face with the handkerchief rolled in a ball.   She appeared exhausted. The nurse gave her a fresh handkerchief, sprinkled with cologne water.

"This is too much!" she cried. "Mandelet ought to be killed! Where is Alphonse? Is it possible I am to be abandoned like this— neglected by everyone?"

"Neglected, indeed!" exclaimed the nurse. Wasn't she there? And here was Mrs. Pontellier leaving, no doubt, a pleasant evening at home to devote to her? And wasn't Monsieur Ratignolle coming that very instant through the hall? And Joséphine was quite sure she had heard Doctor Mandelet's coupé. Yes, there it was, down at the door.

Adèle consented to go back to her room. She sat on the edge of a little low couch next to her bed.

Doctor Mandelet paid no attention to Madame Ratignolle's upbraidings. He was accustomed to them at such times, and was too well convinced of her loyalty to doubt it.

He was glad to see Edna, and wanted her to go with him into the salon and entertain him. But Madame Ratignolle would not consent that Edna should leave her for an instant. Between agonizing moments, she chatted a little, and said it took her mind off her sufferings.

Edna began to feel uneasy. She was seized with a vague dread. Her own like experiences seemed far away, unreal, and only half remembered. She recalled faintly an ecstasy of pain, the heavy odor of chloroform, a stupor which had deadened sensation, and an awakening to find a little new life to which she had given being, added to the great unnumbered multitude of souls that come and go.

She began to wish she had not come; her presence was not necessary. She might have invented a pretext for staying away; she might even invent a pretext now for going. But Edna did not go. With an inward agony, with a flaming, outspoken revolt against the ways of Nature, she witnessed the scene of torture.

She was still stunned and speechless with emotion when later she leaned over her friend to kiss her and softly say good-by. Adèle, pressing her cheek, whispered in an exhausted voice: "Think of the children, Edna. Oh think of the children! Remember them!"

XXXVIII

Edna still felt dazed when she got outside in the open air. The Doctor's coupé had returned for him and stood before the *porte cochère*. She did not wish to enter the coupé, and told Doctor Mandelet she would walk; she was not afraid, and would go alone. He directed his carriage to meet him at Mrs. Pontellier's, and he started to walk home with her.

Up—away up, over the narrow street between the tall houses, the stars were blazing. The air was mild and caressing, but cool with the breath of spring and the night. They walked slowly, the Doctor with a heavy, measured tread and his hands behind him; Edna, in an absent-minded way, as she had walked one night at Grand Isle, as if her thoughts had gone ahead of her and she was striving to overtake them.

"You shouldn't have been there, Mrs. Pontellier," he said. "That was no place for you. Adèle is full of whims at such times. There were a dozen women she might have had with her, unimpressionable women. I felt that it was cruel, cruel. You shouldn't have gone."

"Oh, well!" she answered, indifferently. "I don't know that it matters after all. One has to think of the children some time or other; the sooner the better."

"When is Léonce coming back?"

"Quite soon. Some time in March."

"And you are going abroad?"

"Perhaps—no, I am not going. I'm not going to be forced into doing things. I don't want to go abroad. I want to be let alone. Nobody has any right—except children, perhaps—and even then, it seems to me—or it did seem—" She felt that her speech was voicing the incoherency of her thoughts, and stopped abruptly.

"The trouble is," sighed the Doctor, grasping her meaning intuitively, "that youth is given up to illusions. It seems to be a provision of Nature; a decoy to secure mothers for the race. And Nature takes no account of moral consequences, of arbitrary conditions which we create, and which we feel obliged to maintain at any cost."

"Yes," she said. "The years that are gone seem like dreams—if one might go on sleeping and dreaming—but to wake up and find— oh! well! perhaps it is better to wake up after all, even to suffer, rather than to remain a dupe to illusions all one's life."

"It seems to me, my dear child," said the Doctor at parting, holding her hand, "you seem to me to be in trouble. I am not going to ask for your confidence. I will only say that if ever you feel moved to give it to me, perhaps I might help you. I know I would understand, and I tell you there are not many who would—not many, my dear."

"Some way I don't feel moved to speak of things that trouble me. Don't think I am ungrateful or that I don't appreciate your sympathy. There are periods of despondency and suffering which take possession of me. But I don't want anything but my own way. That is wanting a good deal, of course, when you have to trample upon the lives, the hearts, the prejudices of others—but no matter— still, I shouldn't want to trample upon the little lives. Oh! I don't know what I'm saying, Doctor. Good night. Don't blame me for anything."

"Yes, I will blame you if you don't come and see me soon. We will talk of things you never have dreamt of talking about before.

It will do us both good. I don't want you to blame yourself, whatever comes. Good night, my child."

She let herself in at the gate, but instead of entering she sat upon the step of the porch. The night was quiet and soothing. All the tearing emotion of the last few hours seemed to fall away from her like a somber, uncomfortable garment, which she had but to loosen to be rid of. She went back to that hour before Adèle had sent for her; and her senses kindled afresh in thinking of Robert's words, the pressure of his arms, and the feeling of his lips upon her own. She could picture at that moment no greater bliss on earth than possession of the beloved one. His expression of love had already given him to her in part. When she thought that he was there at hand, waiting for her, she grew numb with the intoxication of expectancy. It was so late; he would be asleep perhaps. She would awaken him with a kiss. She hoped he would be asleep that she might arouse him with her caresses.

Still, she remembered Adèle's voice whispering, "Think of the children; think of them." She meant to think of them; that determination had driven into her soul like a death wound—but not to-night. To-morrow would be time to think of everything.

Robert was not waiting for her in the little parlor. He was nowhere at hand. The house was empty. But he had scrawled on a piece of paper that lay in the lamplight:

"I love you. Good-by—because I love you."

Edna grew faint when she read the words. She went and sat on the sofa. Then she stretched herself out there, never uttering a sound. She did not sleep. She did not go to bed. The lamp sputtered and went out. She was still awake in the morning, when Celestine unlocked the kitchen door and came in to light the fire.

XXXIX

Victor, with hammer and nails and scraps of scantling, was patching a corner of one of the galleries. Mariequita sat near by, dangling her legs, watching him work, and handing him nails from the tool-box. The sun was beating down upon them. The girl had covered her head with her apron folded into a square pad. They had been talking for an hour or more. She was never tired of hearing Victor describe the dinner at Mrs. Pontellier's. He exaggerated every detail, making it appear a veritable Lucullean feast. The flowers were in tubs, he said. The champagne was quaffed from huge golden goblets. Venus rising from the foam could have presented no more entrancing a spectacle than Mrs. Pontellier, blazing with beauty and diamonds at the head of the board, while the other women were all of them youthful hours, possessed of incomparable charms.

She got it into her head that Victor was in love with Mrs. Pontellier, and he gave her evasive answers, framed so as to confirm her belief. She grew sullen and cried a little, threatening to go off and leave him to his fine ladies. There were a dozen men crazy about her at the *Chênière;* and since it was the fashion to be in love with married people, why, she could run away any time she liked to New Orleans with Célina's husband.

Célina's husband was a fool, a coward, and a pig, and to prove it to her, Victor intended to hammer his head into a jelly the next time he encountered him. This assurance was very consoling to Mariequita. She dried her eyes, and grew cheerful at the prospect.

They were still talking of the dinner and the allurements of city life when Mrs. Pontellier herself slipped around the corner of the house. The two youngsters stayed dumb with amazement before what they considered to be an apparition. But it was really she in flesh and blood, looking tired and a little travel-stained.

"I walked up from the wharf," she said, "and heard the hammering. I supposed it was you, mending the porch. It's a good thing. I was always tripping over those loose planks last summer. How dreary and deserted everything looks!"

It took Victor some little time to comprehend that she had come in Beaudelet's lugger, that she had come alone, and for no purpose but to rest.

"There's nothing fixed up yet, you see. I'll give you my room; it's the only place."

"Any corner will do," she assured him.

"And if you can stand Philomel's cooking," he went on, "though I might try to get her mother while you are here. Do you think she would come?" turning to Mariequita.

Mariequita thought that perhaps Philomel's mother might come for a few days, and money enough.

Beholding Mrs. Pontellier make her appearance, the girl had at once suspected a lovers' rendezvous. But Victor's astonishment was so genuine, and Mrs. Pontellier's indifference so apparent, that the disturbing notion did not lodge long in her brain. She contemplated with the greatest interest this woman who gave the most sumptuous dinners in America, and who had all the men in New Orleans at her feet.

"What time will you have dinner?" asked Edna. "I'm very hungry; but don't get anything extra."

"I'll have it ready in little or no time," he said, bustling and packing away his tools. "You may go to my room to brush up and rest yourself. Mariequita will show you."

"Thank you," said Edna. "But, do you know, I have a notion to go down to the beach and take a good wash and even a little swim, before dinner?"

"The water is too cold!" they both exclaimed. "Don't think of it."

"Well, I might go down and try—dip my toes in. Why, it seems to me the sun is hot enough to have warmed the very depths of the ocean. Could you get me a couple of towels? I'd better go right away, so as to be back in time. It would be a little too chilly if I waited till this afternoon."

Mariequita ran over to Victor's room, and returned with some towels, which she gave to Edna.

"I hope you have fish for dinner," said Edna, as she started to walk away; "but don't do anything extra if you haven't."

"Run and find Philomel's mother," Victor instructed the girl. "I'll go to the kitchen and see what I can do. By Gimminy! Women have no consideration! She might have sent me word."

Edna walked on down to the beach rather mechanically, not noticing anything special except that the sun was hot. She was not dwelling upon any particular train of thought. She had done all the thinking which was necessary after Robert went away, when she lay awake upon the sofa till morning.

She had said over and over to herself: "To-day it is Arobin; to-morrow it will be some one else. It makes no difference to me, it doesn't matter about Léonce Pontellier—but Raoul and Etienne!" She understood now clearly what she had meant long ago when she said to Adèle Ratignolle that she would give up the unessential, but she would never sacrifice herself for her children.

Despondency had come upon her there in the wakeful night, and had never lifted. There was no one thing in the world that she desired. There was no human being whom she wanted near her except Robert; and she even realized that the day would come when he, too, and the thought of him would melt out of her existence, leaving her alone. The children appeared before her like antagonists who had overcome her; who had overpowered and sought to drag her into the soul's slavery for the rest of her days. But she knew a way to elude them. She was not thinking of these things when she walked down to the beach.

The water of the Gulf stretched out before her, gleaming with the million lights of the sun. The voice of the sea is seductive, never ceasing, whispering, clamoring, murmuring, inviting the soul to wander in abysses of solitude. All along the white beach, up and down, there was no living thing in sight. A bird with a broken wing was beating the air above, reeling, fluttering, circling disabled down, down to the water.

Edna had found her old bathing suit still hanging, faded, upon its accustomed peg.

She put it on, leaving her clothing in the bath-house. But when she was there beside the sea, absolutely alone, she cast the unpleasant, pricking garments from her, and for the first time in her life she stood naked in the open air, at the mercy of the sun, the breeze that beat upon her, and the waves that invited her.

How strange and awful it seemed to stand naked under the sky! how delicious! She felt like some new-born creature, opening its eyes in a familiar world that it had never known.

The foamy wavelets curled up to her white feet, and coiled like serpents about her ankles. She walked out. The water was chill, but she walked on. The water was deep, but she lifted her white body and reached out with a long, sweeping stroke. The touch of the sea is sensuous, enfolding the body in its soft, close embrace.

She went on and on. She remembered the night she swam far out, and recalled the terror that seized her at the fear of being unable to regain the shore. She did not look back now, but went on and on, thinking of the blue-grass meadow that she had traversed when a little child, believing that it had no beginning and no end.

Her arms and legs were growing tired.

She thought of Léonce and the children. They were a part of her life. But they need not have thought that they could possess her, body and soul. How Mademoiselle Reisz would have laughed, perhaps sneered, if she knew!"And you call yourself an artist! What pretensions, Madame! The artist must possess the courageous soul that dares and defies."

Exhaustion was pressing upon and overpowering her.

"Good-by—because I love you." He did not know; he did not understand. He would never understand. Perhaps Doctor Mandelet would have understood if she had seen him—but it was too late; the shore was far behind her, and her strength was gone.

She looked into the distance, and the old terror flamed up for an instant, then sank again. Edna heard her father's voice and her sister Margaret's. She heard the barking of an old dog that was chained to the sycamore tree. The spurs of the cavalry officer clanged as he walked across the porch. There was the hum of bees, and the musky odor of pinks filled the air.

THE AWAKENING

This story is carefully structured to give meaning to the action. Contrasting scenes of island/water and home/city are juxtaposed to illuminate each other: the former represents for Edna Pontellier a world free of restrictions; the latter, a stultifying world of personal and social obligations. The key to understanding the tension suggested in the structure is found in the title which signals the resolution.

Edna is the archetypal Sleeping Beauty: twenty-eight years old, married, and the mother of two, she experiences an awakening of her sensual self while vacationing on Grande Isle, a fashionable resort off the coast of New Orleans. Her new growth in self-awareness creates a need for independence and sexual freedom outside of marriage; and opening herself to new experiences, she falls in love with a young Creole, Robert Lebrun. However, Lebrun's strong regard for marriage bonds prevents an adulterous affair; and at the summer's end, he goes off to Mexico to forget Edna, and she returns to New Orleans to dream of him and assert her independence by completely throwing off the shackles of her Presbyterian upbringing as well as defying the rubrics of Creole society. Refusing to accompany her husband to New York, she sends the children to their grandmother's; moves out of their fine Esplanade Street house into a very small house nearby; and indulges herself in flaunting social obligations, taking painting lessons, smoking, wandering around the city unescorted, and having an extramarital fling. She sees her children, as well as her husband, as impediments to her freedom: she regards "mother-women"—those who watch over their flocks like hens—as humorous. Although Edna loves her children and respects her husband, she wants to be free of them: "I would give my life for my children, but I would not give myself," she tells her friend; and in the final scene she thinks that "they need not have thought they could possess her, body and soul."

This story is unusual for its time in its frank treatment of the sexuality of women. Edna, a wealthy upper-class woman, is a free spirit, such as had not appeared before in American literature. Her closest analogue is French naturalist Flaubert's Emma Bovary, but unlike Flaubert, Chopin makes no moral judgment about her woman protagonist. Chopin's predecessors in American fiction, even realists like Ellen Glasgow and Willa Cather, while protesting woman's plight in a man's world, espoused the old values and depicted woman as the guardian of those values. Kate Chopin's Edna not only throws away old values; she feels that the only value worthwhile for a woman is her freedom to express herself.

Although Chopin is avante garde in her treatment of women, her writing has some affinities with the local color tradition of Louisiana in both subject matter and landscape. She writes of Creoles; however, many of her Creoles do not fit the Creole stereotype. Léonce Pontellier's attitudes toward and expectations of his wife are no more typical of Creole husbands than of husbands in general of that time. He considers her his property and expects her to be satisfied in her role as wife, mother, homemaker and above all to observe the conventions of society, which include proper entertaining. Robert Lebrun is depicted very favorably and Adèle Ratignolle, Edna's best friend, is set in direct contrast to Edna. She is a "mother-woman" and she and her husband have an ideal marriage. Only Alcée Arobin, the womanizer with whom Edna has an affair, behaves like the stereotypical Creole.

The warm tropical waters of the Gulf, much used by local colorists purely for atmosphere, are given a new dimension in their seductive quality. The dominant imagery and symbol is the water which represents freedom; it is set against the city which represents repression. It is the water which caresses Edna into an awakening; it is the water that releases her from social inhibitions; and it is the water that finally provides a means of escape for her after Robert leaves her again (because he loves her), and she realizes that her life will be a succession of unsatisfying affairs. Chopin's use of the water as a universal symbol plus her heavy emphasis on the feminine sensibility broadens the story's appeal beyond local color.

A Night in Acadie

Kate Chopin

There was nothing to do on the plantation so Télesphore, having a few dollars in his pocket, thought he would go down and spend Sunday in the vicinity of Marksville.

There was really nothing more to do in the vicinity of Marksville than in the neighborhood of his own small farm; but Elvina would not be down there, nor Amaranthe, nor any of Ma'me Valtour's daughters to harass him with doubt, to torture him with indecision, to turn his very soul into a weathercock for love's fair winds to play with.

Télesphore at twenty-eight had long felt the need of a wife. His home without one was like an empty temple in which there is no altar, no offering. So keenly did he realize the necessity that a dozen times at least during the past year he had been on the point of proposing marriage to almost as many different young women of the neighborhood. Therein lay the difficulty, the trouble which Télesphore experienced in making up his mind. Elvina's eyes were beautiful and had often tempted him to the verge of a declaration. But her skin was over swarthy for a wife; and her movements were slow and heavy; he doubted she had Indian blood, and we all know what Indian blood is for treachery. Amaranthe presented in her person none of these obstacles to matrimony. If her eyes were not so handsome as Elvina's, her skin was fine, and being slender to a fault, she moved swiftly about her household affairs, or when she walked the country lanes in going to church or to the store. Télesphore had once reached the point of believing that Amaranthe would make him an excellent wife. He had even started out one day with the intention of declaring himself, when, as the god of chance would have it, Ma'me Valtour espied him passing in the road and enticed him to enter and partake of coffee and "baignés." He would have been a man of stone to have resisted, or to have remained insensible to the charms and accomplishments of the Valtour girls. Finally there was Ganache's widow, seductive rather than handsome, with a good bit of property in her own right. While Télesphore was considering his chances of happiness or even success with Ganache's widow, she married a young man.

164

From these embarrassing conditions, Télesphore sometimes felt himself forced to escape; to chance his environment for a day or two and thereby pin a few new insights by shifting his point of view.

It was Saturday morning that he decided to spend Sunday in the vicinity of Marksville, and the same afternoon found him waiting at the country station for the south-bound train.

He was a robust young fellow with good, strong features and a somewhat determined expression—despite his vacillations in the choice of a wife. He was dressed rather carefully in navy-blue "store clothes" that fitted well because anything would have fitted Télesphore. He had been freshly shaved and trimmed and carried an umbrella. He wore—a little tilted over one eye—straw hat in preference to the conventional gray felt; for no reason than that his uncle Télesphore would have worn a felt, and a battered one at that. His whole conduct of life had been planned on lines in direct contradistinction to those of his uncle Télesphore, whom he was thought in early youth to greatly resemble. The elder Télesphore could not read nor write, therefore the younger had made it the object of his existence to acquire these accomplishments. The uncle pursued the avocations of hunting, fishing and moss-picking; employments which the nephew held in detestation. And as for carrying an umbrella, Nonc Télesphore would have walked the length of the parish in a deluge before he would have so much as thought of one. In short, Télesphore, by advisedly shaping his course in direct opposition to that of his uncle, managed to lead a rather orderly, industrious, and respectable existence.

It was a little warm for April but the car was not uncomfortably crowded and Télesphore was fortunate enough to secure the last available window-seat on the shady side. He was not too familiar with railway travel, his expeditions usually made on horse-back or in a buggy, and the short trip promised to interest him. There was no one present whom he knew well enough to speak to: the district attorney, whom he knew by sight, a French priest from Natchitoches and a few faces that were familiar only because they were native.

But he did not greatly care to speak to anyone. There was a fair stand of cotton and corn in the fields and Télesphore gathered satisfaction in silent contemplation of the crops, comparing them with his own.

It was toward the close of his journey that a young girl boarded the train. There had been girls getting on and off at intervals and it was perhaps because of the bustle attending her arrival that this one attracted Télesphore's attention.

She called good-bye to her father from the platform and waved goodbye to him through the dusty, sun-lit window pane after entering, for she was compelled to seat herself on the sunny side. She seemed inwardly excited and preoccupied save for the attention which she lavished upon a large parcel that she carried religiously and laid reverentially down upon the seat before her.

She was neither tall nor short, nor stout nor slender; nor was she beautiful, nor was she plain. She wore a figured lawn, cut a little low in the back, that exposed a round, soft nuque with a few little clinging circlets of soft, brown hair. Her hat was of white straw, cocked up on the side with a bunch of pansies, and she wore gray lisle-thread gloves. The girl seemed very warm and kept mopping her face. She vainly sought her fan, then she fanned herself with her handkerchief, and finally made an attempt to open the window. She might as well have tried to move the banks of Red river.

Télesphore had been unconsciously watching her the whole time and perceiving her straight he arose and went to her assistance. But the window could not be opened. When he had grown red in the face and wasted an amount of energy that would have driven the plow for a day, he offered her his seat on the shady side. She demurred—there would be no room for the bundle. He suggested that the bundle be left where it was and agreed to assist her in keeping an eye upon it. She accepted Télesphore's place at the shady window and he seated himself beside her.

He wondered if she would speak to him. He feared she might have mistaken him for a Western drummer, in which event he knew that she would not; for the women of the country caution their daughters against speaking to strangers on the trains. But the girl was not one to mistake an Acadian farmer for a Western traveling man. She was not born in Avoyelles parish for nothing.

"I wouldn't want anything to happen to it," she said.

"It's all right w'ere it is," he assured her, following the direction of her glance, that was fastened upon the bundle.

"The las' time I came over to Foché's ball I got caught in the rain on my way up to my cousin's house, an' my dress! J'vous réponds! it was a sight Li'le mo', I would miss the ball. As it was, the dress looked like I'd wo' it weeks without doin'-up."

"No fear of rain to-day,' he reassured her, glancing out at the sky, "but you can have my umbrella if it does rain; you jus' as well take it as not."

"Oh, no! I wrap' the dress round' in toile-cirée this time. You goin' to Foché's ball? Didn I meet you once yonda on Bayou Derbanne? Looks like 1 know yo' face. You mus' come f'om Natchitoches pa'ish."

"My cousins, the Fédeau family, live yonda. Me, I live on my own place in Rapides since '92."

He wondered if she would follow up her inquiry relative to Foché's bail. If she did, he was ready with an answer, for he had decided to go to the ball. But her thoughts evidently wandered from the subject and were occupied with matters that did not concern him, for she turned away and gazed silently out of the window.

It was not a village; it was not even a hamlet at which they descended. The station was set down upon the edge of a cotton field. Near at hand was the post office and store; there was a section house; there were a few cabins at wide intervals, and one in the distance the girl informed him was the home of her cousin, Jules Trodon. There lay a good bit of road before them and she did not hesitate to accept Télesphore's offer to bear her bundle on the way.

She carried herself boldly and stepped out freely and easily, like a negress. There was an absence of reserve in her manner; yet there was no lack of womanliness. She had the air of a young person accustomed to decide for herself and for those about her.

"You said yo' name was Fédeau?" she asked, looking squarely at Télesphore. Her eyes were penetrating—not sharply penetrating, but earnest and dark, and a little searching. He noticed that they were handsome eyes; not so large as Elvina's, but finer in their expression. They started to walk down the track before turning into the lane leading to Trodon's house. The sun was sinking and the air was fresh and invigorating by contrast with the stifling atmosphere of the train.

"You said yo' name was Fédeau?" she asked.

"No," he returned. "My name is Télesphore Bacquette."

"An' my name; it's Zaïda Trodon. It looks like you ought to know me; I don' know w'y."

"It looks that way to me, somehow," he replied. They were satisfied to recognize this feeling—almost conviction—of pre-acquaintance, without trying to penetrate its cause.

By the time they reached Trodon's house he knew that she lived over on Bayou de Glaize with her parents and a number of younger brothers and sisters. It was rather dull where they lived and she often came to lend a hand when her cousin's wife got tangled in domestic complications; or, as she was doing now, when Foché's Saturday ball promised to be unusually important and brilliant. There would be people there even from Marksville, she thought; there were often gentlemen from Alexandria. Télesphore was as unreserved as she, and they appeared like old acquaintances when they reached Trodon's gate.

Trodon's wife was standing on the gallery with a baby in her arms, watching for Zaïda; and four little bare-footed children were sitting in a row on the step, also waiting; but terrified and struck motionless and dumb at sight of a stranger. He opened the gate for the girl but stayed outside himself. Zaïda presented him formally to her cousin's wife, who insisted upon his entering.

"Ah, b'en, pour ça! you got to come in. It's any sense you goin' to walk yonda to Foché's! Ti Jules, run call yo' pa." As if Ti Jules could have run or walked even, or moved a muscle!

But Télesphore was firm. He drew forth his silver watch and looked at it in a business-like fashion. He always carried a watch; his uncle Télesphore always told the time by the sun, or by instinct, like an animal. He was quite determined to walk on to Foché's, a couple of miles away, where he expected to secure supper and a lodging, as well as the pleasing distraction of the ball.

"Well, I reckon I see you all to-night," he uttered in cheerful anticipation as he moved away.

"You'll see Zaïda; yes, an' Jules," called out Trodon's wife good-humoredly. "Me, I got no time to fool with balls, J'vous réponds! with all them chil'ren."

"He's good-lookin'; yes," she exclaimed, when Télesphore was out of ear-shot. "An' dressed! it's like a prince. I didn' know you knew any Baquettes, you, Zaïda."

"It's strange you don' know 'em yo' se'f, cousine." Well, there had been no question from Ma'me Trodon, so why should there be an answer from Zaïda?

Télesphore wondered as he walked why he had not accepted the invitation to enter. He was not regretting it; he was simply wondering what could have induced him to decline. For it surely would have been agreeable to sit there on the gallery waiting while Zaïda prepared herself for the dance; to have partaken of supper with the family and afterward accompanied them to Foché's. The whole situation was so novel, and had presented itself so unexpectedly that Télesphore wished in reality to become acquainted with it, accustomed to it. He wanted to view it from this side and that in comparison with other, familiar situations. The girl had impressed him—affected him in some way; but in some new, unusual way, not as the others always had. He could not recall details of her personality as he could recall such details of Amaranthe or the Valtours, of any of them. When Télesphore tried to think of her he could not think at all. He seemed to have absorbed her in some way and his brain was not so occupied with her as his senses were. At that moment he was looking forward to the ball; there was no doubt about that. Afterwards, he did not know what he would look forward to; he did not care; afterward made no difference. If he had expected the crash of doom to come after the dance at Foché's, he would only have smiled in his thankfulness that it was not to come before.

There was the same scene every Saturday at Foché's! A scene to have aroused the guardians of the peace in a locality where such commodities abound. And all on account of the mammoth pot of gumbo that bubbled, bubbled, bubbled out in the open air. Foché in shirt-sleeves, fat, red and enraged, swore and reviled, and stormed at old black Douté for her extravagance. He called her every kind of name of every kind of animal that suggested itself to his lurid imagination. And every fresh invective that he fired at her she hurled it back at him while into the pot went the chickens and the pans-full of minced ham, and the fists-full of onion and sage and piment rouge and piment vert. If he wanted her to cook for pigs he had only to say so. She knew how to cook for pigs and she knew how to cook for people of les Avoyelles.

The gumbo smelled good, and Télesphore would have liked a taste of it. Douté was dragging from the fire a stick of wood that Foché had officiously thrust beneath the simmering pot, and she muttered as she hurled it smouldering to one side:

"Vaux mieux y s'méle ces affairs, lui; si non!" But she was all courtesy as she dipped a steaming plate for Télesphore; though she assured him it would not be fit for a Christian or a gentleman to taste till midnight.

Télesphore having brushed, "spruced" and refreshed himself, strolled about, taking a view of the surroundings. The house, big, bulky and weatherbeaten, consisted chiefly of galleries in every state of decrepitude and dilapidation. There were a few chinaberry trees and a spreading live oak in the yard. Along the edge of the fence, a good distance away, was a line of gnarled and distorted mulberry trees; and it was there, out in the road, that the people who came to the ball tied their ponies, their wagons and carts.

Dusk was beginning to fall and Télesphore, looking out across the prairie, could see them coming from all directions. The little Creole ponies galloping in a line looked like hobby horses in the faint distance, the mule-carts were like toy wagons. Zaïda might be among those people approaching, flying, crawling ahead of the darkness that was creeping out of the far wood. He hoped so, but he did not believe so; she would hardly have had time to dress.

Foché was noisily lighting lamps, with the assistance of an inoffensive mulatto boy whom he intended in the morning to butcher, to cut into sections, to pack and salt down in a barrel, like the Colfax woman did to her old husband—a fitting destiny for so stupid a pig as the mulatto boy. The negro musicians had arrived: two fiddlers and an accordion Player, and they were drinking whiskey from a black quart bottle which was passed socially from one to the other. The musicians were really never at their best till the quart bottle had been consumed.

The girls who came in wagons and on ponies from a distance wore, for the most part, calico dresses and sun-bonnets. Their finery they brought along in pillow-slips or pinned up in sheets and towels. With these they at once retired to an upper room; later to appear be-ribboned and be-furbelowed: their faces masked with starch powder, but never a touch of rouge.

Most of the guests had assembled when Zaïda arrived—"dashed up" would better express her coming—in an open, two-seated buckboard, with her cousin Jules driving. He reined the pony suddenly and viciously before the time-eaten front steps, in order to produce an impression upon those who were gathered around. Most of the men had halted their vehicles outside and permitted their women folk to walk up from the mulberry trees.

But the real, the stunning effect was produced when Zaïda stepped upon the gallery and threw aside her light shawl in the full glare of half a dozen kerosene lamps. She was white from head to foot—literally, for her slippers even were white. No one would have believed, let alone suspected that they were a pair of old black ones which she had covered with pieces of her first communion sash. There is no describing her dress, it was fluffy, like a fresh powder-puff, and stood out. No wonder she had handled it so reverentially! Her white fan was covered with spangles that she herself had sewed all over it; and in her belt and in her brown hair was thrust small sprays of orange blossom.

Two men leaning against the railing uttered long whistles expressive equally of wonder and admiration.

"Tiens! t'es pareille comme ain mariée, Zaïda," cried out a lady with a baby in her arms. Some young women tittered and Zaïda fanned herself. The women's voices were almost without exception shrill and piercing; the men's, soft and low-pitched.

The girl turned to Télesphore, as to an old and valued friend:

"Tiens! c'est vous?" He had hesitated at first to approach, but at this friendly sign of recognition he drew eagerly forward and held out his hand. The men looked at him suspiciously, inwardly resenting his stylish appearance, which they considered intrusive, offensive and demoralizing.

How Zaïda's eyes sparkled now! What very pretty teeth Zaïda had when she laughed, and what a mouth! Her lips were a revelation, a promise: something to carry away and remember in the night and grow hungry thinking of the next day. Strictly speaking, they may not have been quite all that; but in any event, that is the way Télesphore thought about them. He began to take account of her appearance; her nose, her eyes, her hair. And when she left him to go in and dance her first dance with cousin Jules, he leaned up against a post and thought of them: nose, eyes, hair, ears, lips and round, soft throat.

Later it was like Bedlam.

The musicians had warmed up and were scraping away indoors and calling the figures. Feet were pounding through the dance; dust was flying. The women's voices were piped high and mingled discordantly, like the confused, shrill clatter of waking birds, while the men laughed boisterously. But if some one had only thought of gagging Foché, there would have been less noise. His good humor permeated everywhere, like an atmosphere. He was louder than all the noise; he was more visible than the dust. He called the young mulatto (destined for the knife) "my boy" and sent him flying hither and thither. He beamed upon Douté as he tasted gumbo and congratulated her: "C'est toi qui s'y connais, ma fille! 'cré tonnere!"

Télesphore danced with Zaïda and then he leaned out against the post; then he danced with Zalda, and then he leaned against the post. The mothers of the other girls decided that he had the manners of a pig.

It was time to dance again with Zaïda and he went in search of her. He was carrying her shawl, which she had given to him hold.

"W'at time is it?" she asked him when he had found and secured her. They were under one of the kerosene lamps on the front gallery and he drew forth his silver watch. She seemed to be still laboring under some suppressed excitement that he had noticed before.

"It's fo'teen minutes pas' twelve," he told her exactly.

"I wish you'd find out w'ere Jules is. Go look yonda in the card-room if he's there, an' come tell me." Jules had danced with all the prettiest girls. She knew it was his custom after accomplishing this agreeable feat, to retire to the card-room.

"You'll wait yere till I come back?" he asked.

"I'll wait yere; you go on." She waited but drew back a little into the shadow. Télesphore lost no time.

"Yes, he's yonda playin' cards with Foché an some others I don' know," he reported when he had discovered her in the shadow. There had been a spasm of alarm when he did not at once see her where he had left her under the lamp.

"Does he look—look like he's fixed yonda fo' good?"

"He's got his coat off. Looks like he's fixed pretty comf'table fo' the next hour or two."

"Gi' me my shawl."

"You cole?" offering to put it around her.

"No, I ain't cole." She drew the shawl about her shoulders and turned as if to leave him. But a sudden generous impulse seemed to move her, and she added:

"Come along yonda with me."

They descended the few rickety steps that led down to the yard. He followed rather than accompanied her across the beaten and trampled sward. Those who saw them thought they had gone to take the air. The beams of light that slanted out from the house were fitful and uncertain, deepening the shadows. The embers under the empty gumbo-pot glared red in the darkness. There was a sound of quiet voices coming from under the trees.

Zaïda, closely accompanied by Télesphore, went out where the vehicles and horses were fastened to the fence. She stepped carefully and held up her skirts as if dreading the least speck of dew or of dust.

"Unhitch Jules' ho'se an' buggy there an' turn 'em 'roun' this way, please." He did as instructed, first backing the pony, then leading it out to where she stood in the half-made road.

"You goin' home?" he asked her, "better let me water the pony."

"Neva mine." She mounted and seated herself grasped the reins. "No, I ain't goin' home," she added. He, too, was holding the reins gathered in one hand across the pony's back.

"W'ere you goin'?" he demanded.

"Neva you mine w'ere I'm goin'."

"You ain't goin' anyw'ere this time o' night by yo'se'f?"

"W'at you reckon I'm 'fraid of?" she laughed. "Turn loose that ho'se," at the same time urging the animal forward. The little brute started away with a bound and Télesphore, also with a bound, sprang into the buckboard and seated himself beside Zaïda.

"You ain't goin' anyw'ere this time o' night by yo' se'f!" It was not a question now, but an assertion, and there was no denying it. There was even no disputing it, and Zaïda recognizing the fact drove on in silence.

There is no animal that moves so swiftly across a 'Cadian prairie as the little Creole pony. This one did not run nor trot; he seemed to reach out in galloping bounds. The buckboard creaked, bounced, jolted and swayed. Zaïda clutched at her shawl while Télesphore drew his straw hat further down over his right eye and offered to drive. But he did not know the road and she would not let him. They had soon reached the woods.

If there is any animal that can creep more slowlv through a wooded road than the little Creole pony, that animal has not yet been discovered in Acadie. This particular animal seemed to be appalled by the darkness of the forest and filled with dejection. His head drooped and he lifted his feet as if each hoof were weighted with a thousand pounds of lead. Any one unacquainted with the peculiarities of the breed would sometimes have fancied that he was standing still. But Zaïda and Télesphore knew better. Zaïda uttered a deep sigh as she slackened her hold on the reins and Télesphore, lifting his hat, let it swing from the back of his head.

"How you don' ask me w'ere I'm goin'?" she said finally. These were the first words she had spoken since refusing his offer to drive.

"Oh, it don' make any diff'ence w'ere I'm goin', I jus' as well tell you." She hesitated, however. He seemed to have no curiosity and did not urge her.

"I'm goin' to get married," she said.

He uttered some kind of an exclamation; it was nothing articulate—more like the tone of an animal that gets a sudden knife thrust. And now he felt how dark the forest was. An instant before it had seemed a sweet, black paradise; better than any heaven he had ever heard of.

"W'y can't you get married at home?" This was not the first thing that occured to him to say, but this was the first thing he said.

"Ah, b'en oui! with perfec' mules fo' a father an' mother! it's good enough to talk."

"W'y couldn' he come an' get you? W'at kine of a scound'el is that to let you go through the woods at night by yo'se'f?"

"You betta wait till you know who you talkin' about. He didn' come an' get me because he knows I ain't 'fraid; an' because he's got too much pride to ride in Jules Trodon's buckboard afta he done been put out o' Jules Trodon's house."

"W'at's his name an' w'ere you goin' to fine 'im?"

"Yonda on the other side the woods up at ole Wat Gibson's—a kine of justice of the peace or something. Anyhow he's goin' to marry us. An' afta we done married those tetes-de-mulets yonda on bayou de Glaize can say w'at they want."

"W'at's his name?"

"André Pascal."

The name meant nothing to Télesphore. For all he knew, André Pascal might be one of the shining lights of Avoyelles; but he doubted it.

"You betta turn 'roun'," he said. It was an unselfish impulse that prompted the suggestion. It was the thought of this girl married to a man whom even Jules Trodon would not suffer to enter his house.

"I done give my word," she answered.

"W'at's the matta with 'im? W'y don't yo' father and mother want you to marry 'im?"

"W'y? Because it's always the same tune! W'en a man's down eve'ybody's got stones to throw at 'im. They say he's lazy. A man that will walk from St. Landry plumb to Rapides lookin' fo' work; an' they call that lazy! Then, somebody's been spreadin' yonda on the Bayou that he drinks. I don' b'lieve it. I neva saw 'im drinkin', me. Anyway, he won't drink afta he's married to me; he's too fon' of me fo' that. He say he'll blow out his brains if I don' marry 'im."

"I reckon you betta turn roun'."

"No, I done give my word." And they went creeping on through the woods in silence.

"W'at time is it?" she asked after an interval. He lit a match and looked at his watch.

"It's quarta to one. W'at time did he say?"

"I tole 'im I'd come about one o'clock. I knew that was a good time to get away f'om the ball."

She would have hurried a little but the pony could not be induced to do so. He dragged himself, seemingly ready at any moment to give up the breath of life. But once out of the woods he made up for lost time. They were on the open prairie again, and he fairly ripped the air; some flying demon must have changed skins with him.

It was a few minutes of one o'clock when they drew up before Wat Gibson's house. It was not much more than a rude shelter, and in the dim starlight it seemed isolated, as if standing alone in the middle of the black, far reaching prairie. As they halted at the gate a dog within set up a furious barking; and an old negro who had been smoking his pipe at that ghostly hour, advanced toward them from the shelter of the gallery. Télesphore descended and helped his companion to alight.

"We want to see Mr. Gibson," spoke up Zaïda. The old fellow had already opened the gate. There was no light in the house.

"Marse Gibson, he yonda to ole Mr. Bodel's playin' kairds. But he neva' stay atter one o'clock. Come in, Ma'am; come in, suh; walk right 'long in." He had drawn his own conclusions to explain their appearance. They stood upon the narrow porch waiting while he went inside to light the lamp.

Although the house was small, as it comprised but one room, that room was comparatively a large one. It looked to Télesphore and Zaïda very large and gloomy when they entered it. The lamp was on a table that stood against the wall, and that held further a rusty looking ink bottle, a pen and an old blank book. A narrow bed was off in the corner. The brick chimney extended into the room and formed a ledge that served as mantel shelf. From the big low-hanging rafters swung an assortment of fishing tackle, a gun, some discarded articles of clothing and a string of red peppers. The boards of the floor were broad, rough and loosely joined together.

Télesphore and Zaïda seated themselves on opposite sides of the table and the negro went out to the wood pile to gather chips and pieces of boisgras with which to kindle a small fire.

It was a little chilly; he supposed the two would want coffee and he knew that Wat Gibson would ask for a cup the first thing on his arrival.

"I wonder w'at's keepin' 'im," muttered Zaïda impatiently. Télesphore looked at his watch. He had been looking at it at intervals of one minute straight along.

"It's ten minutes pas' one," he said. He offered no further comment.

At twelve minutes past one Zaïda's restlessness again broke into speech.

"I can't imagine, me, w'at's become of André! He said he'd be yere sho' at one." The old negro was kneeling before the fire that he had kindled, comtemplating the cheerful blaze. He rolled his eyes toward Zaïda.

"You talkin' 'bout Mr. André Pascal? No need to look fo' him. Mr. André he b'en down to de P'int all day raisin' Cain."

"That's a lie," said Zaïda. Télesphore said nothing.

"Tain't no lie, ma'am; he b'en sho' raisin' de ole Nick." She looked at him, too contemptuous to reply.

The negro told no lie so far as his bald statement was concerned. He was simply mistaken in his estimate of André Pascal's ability to "raise Cain" during an entire afternoon and evening and still keep a rendezvous with a lady at one o'clock in the moming. For André was even then at hand, as the loud and menacing howl of the dog testified. The negro hastened out to admit him.

André did not enter at once, he stayed a while outside abusing the dog and communicating to the negro his intention of coming out to shoot the animal after he had attended to more pressing business that was awaiting him within.

Zaïda arose, a little flurried and excited when he entered. Télesphore remained seated.

Pascal was partially sober. There had evidently been an attempt at dressing for the occasion at some early part of the previous day, but such evidences had almost wholly vanished. His linen was soiled and his whole appearance was that of a man who, by an effort, had aroused himself from a debauch. He was a little taller than Télesphore, and more loosely put together. Most women would have called him a handsomer man. It was easy to imagine that when sober, he might betray by some subtle grace of speech or manner, evidences of gentle blood.

"W'y did you keep me waitin', André? w'en you knew—" she got no further, but backed up against the table and stared at him with earnest startled eyes.

"Keep you waiting, Zaïda? my dear li'le Zaïdé, how can you say such a thing! I started up yere an hour ago an' that—w'ere's that damned ole Gibson?" He had approached Zaïda with the evident intention of embracing her, but she seized his wrist and held him at arm's length away. In casting his eyes about for old Gibson his glance alighted upon Télesphore.

The sight of the 'Cadian seemed to fill him with astonishment. He stood back and began to contemplate the young fellow and lose himself in speculation and conjecture before him, as if before some unlabeled wax figure. He turned for information to Zaïda.

"Say, Zaïda, w'at you call this? W'at kine of damn fool you got sitting yere? Who let him in? W'at you reckon he's lookin' fo'? trouble?"

Télesphore said nothing; he was waiting his cue from Zaïda.

"André Pascal," she said, "you jus' as well take the do' an' go. You might stan' yere till the day o' judgment on yo' knees befo' me; an' blow out yo' brains if you a mine to. I ain't neva goin' to marry you."

"The hell you ain't!"

He had hardly more than uttered the words when he lay prone on his back. Télesphore had knocked him down. The blow seemed to complete the process of sobering that had begun in him. He gathered himself together and rose to his feet; in doing so he reached back for his pistol. His hold was not yet steady, However, and the weapon slipped from his grasp and fell to the floor. Zaïda picked it up and laid it on the table behind her. She was going to see fair play.

The brute instinct that drives men at each other's throat was awake and stirring in these two. Each saw in the other a thing to be wiped out of his way—out of existence if need be. Passion and blind rage directed the blows which they dealt, and steeled the tension of muscles and clutch of fingers. They were not skillful blows, however.

The fire blazed cheerily; the kettle which the negro had placed upon the coals was steaming and singing. The man had gone in search of his master. Zaïda had placed the lamp out of harm's way on the high mantel ledge and she leaned back with her hands behind her upon the table.

She did not raise her voice or lift her finger to stay the combat that was acting before her. She was motionless, and white to the lips, only her eyes seemed to be alive and burning and blazing. At one moment she felt that André must have strangled Télesphore; but she said nothing. The next instant she could hardly doubt that the blow from Télesphore's doubled fist could be less than a killing one; but she did nothing.

How the loose boards swayed and creaked beneath the weight of the struggling men! the very old rafters seemed to groan; and she felt that the house shook.

The combat, if fierce, was short, and it ended out on the gallery whither they had staggered through the open door—or one had dragged the other—she could not tell. But she knew when it was over, for there was a long moment of utter stillness. Then she heard one of the men descend the steps and go away, for the gate slammed after him. The other went out to the cistern; the sound of the tin bucket splashing in the water reached her where she stood. He must have been endeavoring to remove traces of the encounter.

Presently Télesphore entered the room. The elegance of his apparel had been somewhat marred; the men over at the 'Cadian ball would hardly have taken exception now to his appearance.

"W'ere is André?" the girl asked.

"He's gone," said Télesphore'

She had never changed her position and now when she drew herself up her wrists ached and she rubbed them a little. She was no longer pale; the blood had come back into her cheeks and lips, staining them crimson. She held out her hand to him. He took it gratefully enough, but he did not know what to do with it; that is, he did not know what he might dare to do with it, so he let it drop gently away and went to the fire.

"I reckon we betta be goin', too," she said. He stooped and poured some of the bubbling water from the kettle upon the coffee which the negro had set upon the hearth.

"I'll make a li'le coffee firs'," he proposed, "an' anyhow we betta wait till ole man w'at's-his-name comes back. It wouldn't look well to leave his house that way without some kine of excuse or explanation."

She made no reply, but seated herself submissively beside the table.

Her will, which had been overmastering and aggressive, seemed to have grown numb under the disturbing spell of the past few hours. An illusion had gone from her, and had carried her love with it. The absence of regret revealed this to her. She realized, but could not comprehend it, not knowing that the love had been part of the illusion. She was tired in body and spirit, and it was with a sense of restfulness that she sat all drooping and relaxed and watched Télesphore make the coffee.

He made enough for them both and a cup for old Wat Gibson when he should come in, and also one for the negro. He supposed the cups, the sugar and spoons were in the safe over there in the corner, and that is where he found them.

When he finally said to Zaïda, "Come, I'm going to take you home now," and drew her shawl around her, pinning it under the chin, she was like a little child and followed whither he led in all confidence.

It was Télesphore who drove on the way back, and he let the pony cut no capers, but held him to a steady and tempered gait. The girl was still quiet and silent; she was thinking tenderly—a little tearfully of those two old têtes de-mulets yonder on Bayou de Glaize.

How they crept through the woods! and how dark it was and how still!

"W'at time it is?" whispered Zaïda. Alas! he could not tell her; his watch was broken. But almost for the first time in his life, Télesphore did not care what time it was.

A NIGHT IN ACADIE

As noted in the previous story, Chopin paints vivid pictures of her subjects. Offering a view of Acadian country and its people, this story abounds with sensory details that graphically portray these fun-loving independent-spirited people and their region. Although the emphasis is on the uniqueness of the culture and although the characters possess traits attributed to Acadians in general, the two main characters are sharply individualized through descriptive details, actions, and dialect.

The action centers around Télesphore, a robust young Acadian farmer who is looking for just the right wife, and Zaïda, who has already promised herself to André. The conflict is slight; it doesn't take long for Télesphore to overcome his rival. The contrasting scenes of heroic and commonplace in the struggle creates a humorous tone, almost mock-epic: "The brute instinct that drives men at each other's throat was awake and stirring . . . [and since] each saw in the other a thing to be wiped out of . . . existence . . . , passion and rage directed the blows . . . and steeled the tension of muscles and clutch of fingers." Meanwhile "the fire blazed cheerily; the kettle . . . was steaming and singing."

In Zaïda the reader sees the embryo of the independent free-thinking woman fully realized later in Edna Pontellier of *The Awakening:* "She carried herself boldly and stepped out freely and easily, like a negress. There was an absence of reserve in her manner; yet there was no lack of womanliness. She had the air of a young person accustomed to decide for herself." In antecedent action, she has already decided to elope with a man not even allowed in the family home, and she shows her mettle in a stand-off with Télesphore.

Télesphore, too, is independent, or perhaps stubborn. Although he had vacillated in choosing a wife, "his whole conduct of life had been planned on lines in direct contradistinction to those of his uncle . . . whom he was thought to greatly resemble. . . ." When Zaïda prepares to leave the dance, their wills clash:

"W'ere you goin'?"

"Neva you mine w'ere I'm goin'."

"You ain't goin' anyw'ere this time o' night by yo'sef!"

"W'at you reckon I'm 'fraid of? . . . Turn loose that ho'se!"

They both win: she goes and he accompanies her, not knowing she is hurrying to meet André.

Even the Creole pony has a will of its own: it "sails" across the prairie, but "creeps slowly" through the wooded road. No one, nothing, can alter its pace.

It is hard to imagine a scene more vividly depicted than the Saturday night dance at Foche's big, bulky, weatherbeaten house. "little Creole ponies galloping in a line looked like hobby horses in the faint distance; the mule carts were like toy wagons." In the air is the rich smell of gumbo as it bubbles in the pot, and the sound of musicians "scraping away," feet "pounding" the floor, and "women's voices piped high and mingling discordantly."

Throughout the story, Chopin keeps the tone light and humorous and merry. Although details of place and character are entirely within keeping of the Acadian stereotype, they have a freshness and liveliness that set the story apart from most local color.

CHARLES TENNEY JACKSON
(1874-   )

Charles Tenney Jackson was born in St. Louis to Colonel Charles Henry and Eliza Tenney Jackson. After graduation from high school, he attended the University of Wisconsin, but left to enter the army as a private in 1898. Later he served as a newspaper correspondent in the Spanish-American War. He was editor of *Modesto* [Wisconsin] *News* from 1905 to 1906 and staff writer for the *San Francisco Chronicle* and *Milwaukee Sentinel* from 1907 to 1908. In 1919 he married Carlotta Weir. A prolific writer, he is the author of *Loser's Luck* (1905), *Days of Souls* (1910), *My Brother's Keeper* (1911), *The Midlanders* (1912), *The Fountain of Youth* (1914), *John the Fool* (1915), *The Call to Colors* (1918), *Jimmy May in the Fighting Line* (1919), *Captain Sazarac* (1922), and many short stories. He spent several years in Louisiana and set several of his stories and novels there. The story printed below first appeared in *Short Stories* Magazine in 1921 and won an O. Henry Memorial Prize. The date of his death is not available.

183

The Man Who Cursed the Lilies

Charles Tenney Jackson

TEDGE looked from the pilot-house at the sweating deckhand who stood on the stubby bow of the *Marie Louise* heaving vainly on the pole thrust into the barrier of crushed water hyacinths across the channel.

Crump, the engineer, shot a sullen look at the master ere he turned back to the crude oil motor whose mad pounding rattled the old bayou stern-wheeler from keel to hogchains.

"She's full ahead now!" grunted Crump. And then, with a covert glance at the single passenger sitting on the foredeck cattle pens, the engineman repeated his warning, "Yeh'll lose the cows, Tedge, if you keep on fightin' the flowers. They're bad f'r feed and water-they can't stand another day o' sun!"

Tedge knew it. But he continued to shake his hairy fist at the deckhand and roar his anathemas upon the flower-choked bayou. He knew his crew was grinning evilly, for they remembered Bill Tedge's year-long feud with the lilies. Crump had bluntly told the skipper he was a fool for trying to push up this little-frequented bayou from Cote Blanche Bay to the higher land of the west Louisiana coast, where he had planned to unload his cattle.

Tedge had bought the cargo himself near Beaumont from a beggared ranchman whose stock had to go on the market, because, for seven months, there had been no rain in eastern Texas, and the short-grass range was gone.

Tedge knew where there was feed for the starving animals, and the *Marie Louise* was coming back light. By the Intercoastal Canal and the shallow string of bays along the Texas-Louisiana line, the bayou boat could crawl safely back to the grassy swamp lands that fringe the sugar plantations of Bayou Teche. Tedge had bought his living cargo so ridiculously cheap that if half of them stood the journey he would profit. And they would cost him nothing for winter ranging up in the swamp lands. In the spring he would round up what steers had lived and sell them, grass-fat, in New Orleans. He'd land them there with his flap-paddle bayou boat, too, for *the* Marie Louise ranged up and down the Intercoastal Canal and the

185

uncharted swamp lakes and bays adjoining, trading and thieving and serving the skipper's obscure ends.

Only now, when he turned up Cote Blanche Bay, some hundred miles west of the Mississippi passes, to make the last twenty miles of swamp channel to his landing, he faced his old problem. Summer-long the water-hyacinths were a pest to navigation on the coastal bayous, but this June they were worse than Tedge had ever seen. He knew the reason; the mighty Mississippi was at high flood, and as always then, a third of its yellow waters were sweeping down the Atchafalaya River on a "short cut" to the Mexican Gulf. And somewhere above, on its west bank, the Atchafalaya levees had broken and the flood waters were all through the coastal swamp channels.

Tedge grimly knew what it meant. He'd have to go farther inland to find his free range, but now, worst of all, the floating gardens of the coast swamps were corning out of the numberless channels on the *crevasse* water.

He expected to fight them as he had done for twenty years with his dirty bayou boat. He'd fight and curse and struggle through the *isles flotantes*, and denounce the Federal Government because it did not destroy the lilies in the obscure bayous where he traded, as it did on Bayou Teche and Terrebonne, with its pump-boats which sprayed the hyacinths with a mixture of oil and soda until the tops shriveled and the trailing roots then dragged the flowers to the bottom.

"Yeh'll not see open water till the river cleans the swamps of lilies," growled Crump. "I never seen the beat of 'em! The high water's liftin' 'em from ponds where they never been touched by a boat's wheel and they're out in the channels now. If yeh make the plantations yeh'll have to keep east'ard and then up the Atchafalaya and buck the main flood water, Tedge!"

Tedge knew that, too. But he suddenly broke into curses upon his engineer, his boat, the sea and sky and man. But mostly the lilies. He could see a mile up the bayou between cypress-grown banks, and not a foot of water showed. A solid field of green, waxy leaves and upright purple spikes, jammed tight and moving. That was what made the master rage. They were moving—a flower glacier slipping imperceptibly to the gulf bays. They were moving slowly but inexorably, and his dirty cattle boat, frantically driving into the blockade, was moving backward-stern first!

He hated them with the implacable fury of a man whose fists had lorded his world. A water-hyacinth-what was it? He could stamp one to a smear on his deck, but a river of them no man could fight. He swore the lilies had ruined his whisky-running years ago to the Atchafalaya lumber camps; they blocked Grand River when he went to log-towing; they had cost him thousands of dollars for repairs and lost time in his swamp ventures.

Bareheaded under the semi-tropic sun, he glowered at the lily-drift. Then he snarled at Crump to reverse the motor. Tedge would retreat again!

"I'll drive the boat clean around Southwest Pass to get shut of 'em! No feed, huh, for these cows? They'll feed sharks, they will! Huh, Mr. Cowman, the blisterin' lilies cost me five hundred dollars already!"

The lone passenger smoked idly and watched the gaunt cattle staggering, penned in the flat, dead heat of the foredeck. Tedge cursed him, too, under his breath. Milt Rogers had asked to make the coast run from Beaumont on Tedge's boat. Tedge remembered what Rogers said—he was going to see a girl who lived up Bayou Boeuf above Tedge's destination. Tedge remembered that girl—a Cajun girl whom he once heard *singing* in the floating gardens while Tedge was battling and cursing to pass the blockade.

He hated her for loving the lilies, and the man for loving her. He burst out again with his volcanic fury at the green and purple horde.

"They're a fine sight to see," mused the other, "after a man's eyes been burned out ridin' the dry range; no rain in nine months up there—nothin' green or pretty in—"

"Pretty!" Tedge seemed to menace with his little shifty eyes. "I wish all them lilies had one neck and I could twist it. Jest one head, and me stompin' it! Yeh!—and all the damned flowers in the world with it! Yeh! And me watchin' 'em die!"

The man from the dry lands smoked idly under the awning. His serenity evoked all the savagery of Tedge's feud with the lilies. Pretty! A man who dealt with cows seeing beauty in anything! Well, the girl did it—that swamp angel this Rogers was going to visit. That Aurelie Frenet who sang in the flower-starred river—

that was it! Tedge glowered on the Texan—he hated him, too, because this loveliness gave him peace, while the master of the *Marie Louise* must fume about his wheelhouse, a perspiring madman.

It took an hour for the *Marie* even to retreat and find steerageway easterly off across a shallow lake, mirroring the marsh shores in the sunset. Across the bayou boat wheezed and thumped drearily, drowning the bellowing of the dying steers. Once the deckhand stirred and pointed.

"Lilies, Cap'n—pourin' from all the swamps, and dead ahead there, now!"

Scowling, Tedge held to the starboard. Yes, there they were—a phalanx of flowers in the dusk. He broke into wild curses at them, his boat, the staggering cattle.

"I'll drive to the open gulf to get rid of 'em! Outside, to sea! Yeh! Stranger, yeh'll see salt water, and lilies drownin' in it! I'll show yeh 'em dead and dried on the sands like dead men's dried bones! Yeh'll see yer pretty flowers a-dyin'!"

The lone cowman ignored the sneer. "You better get the animals to feed and water. Another mornin' of heat and crowdin'—"

"Let 'em rot! Yer pretty flowers done it—pretty flowers—spit o' Hell! I knowed 'em—I fought 'em—I'll fight 'em to the death of 'em!"

His little red—rimmed eyes hardly veiled his contempt for Milt Rogers. A cowman, sailing this dusky, purple bay to see a girl! A girl who sang in the lily drift—asailing on this dirty, reeking bumboat, with cattle dying jammed in the pens! Suddenly Tedge realized a vast malevolent pleasure—he couldn't hope to gain from his perishing cargo; and he began to gloat at the agony spread below his wheelhouse window, and the cattleman's futile pity for them.

"They'll rot on Point Au Fer! We'll heave the stink of them, dead and alive, to the sharks of Au Fer Pass! Drownin' cows in dyin' lilies—"

And the small craft of his brain suddenly awakened coolly above his heat—Why, yes? Why hadn't he thought of it? He swung the stubby nose of the *Marie* more easterly in the hot, windless dusk. After a while the black deckhand looked questioningly up at the master.

"We're takin' round," Tedge grunted, "outside Au Fer!"

The black stretched on the cattle pen frame. Tedge was a master-hand among the reefs and shoals, even if the flappaddle *Marie* had no business outside. But the sea was nothing but a star—set, velvet ribbon on which she crawled like a dirty insect. And no man questioned Tedge's will.

Only, an hour later, the engineman came up and forward to stare into the faster—flowing water. Even now he pointed to a hyacinth clump.

"Yeh!" the master growled. "I'll show yeh, Rogers! Worlds o' flowers! Out o' the swamps and the tide'll send 'em back again on the reefs. I'll show yeh 'em—dead, dried white like men's bones." Then he began to whisper huskily to his engineer: "It's time fer it. Five hundred fer yeh, Crump—a hundred fer the nigger, or I knock his head in. She brushes the bar, and yer oil tank goes—yeh understand?" He watched a red star in the south.

Crump looked about. No sail or light or coast guard about Au Fer—at low tide not even a skiff could find the passages. He nodded cunningly:

"She's old and fire-fitten. Tedge, I knowed yer mind—I was always waitin' fer the word. It's a place fer it—and yeh say yeh carry seven hundred on them cows? Boat an' cargo three thousand seven hundred—"

"They'll be that singed and washed in the sands off Au Fer that nobody'll know what they died of!" retorted Tedge thickly. "Yeh, go down, Crump, and lay yer waste and oil right. I trust yeh, Crump—the nigger'll get his, too. She'll ride high and burn flat, hoggin' in the sand—"

"She's soaked with oil plumb for'ard to the pens now," grunted Crump. "She's fitten to go like a match all along when she bumps—"

He vanished, and the master cunningly watched the ember star southeasterly.

He was holding above it now, to port and landward. The white, hard sands must be shoaling fast under the cattle-freighted *Marie*. It little mattered about the course now; she would grind her nose in the quiet reef shortly.

Tedge merely stared, expectantly awaiting the blow. And when it came he was malevolently disappointed. A mere slithering along over the sand, a creak, a slight jar, and she lay dead in the flat, calm sea—it was ridiculous that that smooth beaching would break an oil tank, that the engine spark would flare the machine waste, leap to the greasy beams and floors.

The wheezy exhaust coughed on; the belt flapped as the paddle wheel kept on its dead shove of the *Marie's* keel into the sand. Hogjaw had shouted and run forward. He was staring into the phosphorescent water circling about the bow, when Crump raised his cry:

"Fire—amidships!"

Tedge ran down the after-stairs. Sulphurously he began cursing at the trickle of smoke under the motorframe. It was nothing—a child could have put it out with a bucket of sand. But upon it fell Tedge and the engineer, stamping, shouting, shoving oil—soaked waste upon it, and covertly blocking off the astounded black deckman when he rushed to aid.

"Water, Hogjaw!" roared the master. "She's gainin' on us—she's under the bilge floor now!" He hurled a bucket viciously at his helper. And as they pretended to fight the fire, Crump suddenly began laughing and stood up. The deck-man was grinning also. The master watched him narrowly.

"Kick the stuff into the waste under the stairs," he grunted. "Hogjaw, this here boat's goin'—yeh understand? We take the skiff and pull to the shrimp camps, and she hogs down and burns—"

The black man was laughing. Then he stopped curiously. "The cows—"

"Damn the cows! I'll git my money back on 'em! Yeh go lower away on the skiff davits. Yeh don't ask me nothin'—yeh don't know nothin'!"

"Sho', boss! I don't know nothin', or see nothin'!"

He swung out of the smoke already drifting greasily up from the foul waist of the *Marie Louise*. A little glare of red was beginning to reflect from the mirrored sea. The ripples of the beaching had vanished; obscurely, undramatically as she had lived, the *Marie Louise* sat on the bar to choke in her own fetid fumes.

Tedge clambered to the upper deck and hurried to his bunk in the wheelhouse. There were papers there he must save the master's license, the insurance policy, and a few other things. The smell of burning wood and grease was thickening; and suddenly now, through it, he saw the quiet, questioning face of the stranger.

He had forgotten him completely. Tedge's small brain had room but for one idea at a time: first his rage at the lilies, and then the wrecking of the *Marie*. And this man knew. He had been staring down the after-companionway. He had seen and heard. He had seen the master and crew laughing while the fire mounted.

Tedge came to him. "We're quittin' ship," he growled.

"Yes, but the cattle—" The other looked stupefiedly at him.

"We got to pull inside afore the sea comes up—"

"Well, break the pens, can't you? Give 'em a chance to swim for a bar. I'm a cowman myself—I cain't let dumb brutes burn and not lift a hand—"

The fire in the waist was beginning to roar. A plume of smoke streamed straight up in the starlight. The glare showed the younger man's startled eyes. He shifted them to look over the foredeck rail down to the cattle. Sparks were falling among them, the fire veered slightly forward; and the survivors were crowding uneasily over the fallen ones, catching that curious sense of danger which forewarns creatures of the wild before the Northers, a burning forest, or creeping flood, to move on.

"You cain't leave 'em so," muttered the stranger. "No; I seen you—"

He did not finish. Tedge had been setting himself for what he knew he should do. The smaller man had his jaw turned as he stared at the suffering brutes. And Tedge's mighty fist struck him full on the temple. The master leaned over the low rail to watch quietly.

The man who wished to save the cattle was there among them. A little flurry of sparks drove over the spot he fell upon, and then a maddened surge of gaunt steers. Tedge wondered if he should go finish the job. No; there was little use. He had crashed his fist into the face of a shrimp-seine hauler once, and the fellow's neck had shifted on his spine—and once he had maced a woman up-river in a shanty-boat drinking bout—Tedge had got away both times. Now and then, boasting about the shrimp camps, he hinted mysteriously at his two killings, and showed his freckled, hairy, right hand.

"If they find anything of him—he got hurt in the wreck," the master grinned. He couldn't see the body, for a black longhorn had fallen upon his victim, it appeared. Anyhow the cattle were milling desperately around in the pen; the stranger who said his name was Milt Rogers would be a lacerated lump of flesh in that mad stampede long ere the fire reached him. Tedge got his tin document box and went aft.

Crump and Hogjaw were already in the flat-bottomed bayou skiff, holding it off the *Marie Louise's* port runway, and the master stepped into it. The heat was singeing their faces by now.

"Pull off," grunted the skipper, "around east'ard. This bar sticks clean out o' water off there, and you lay around it, Hogjaw. They won't be no sea 'til the breeze lifts at sunup."

The big black heaved on the short oars. The skiff was a hundred yards out on the glassy sea, when Crump spoke cunningly, "I knowed something—"

"Yeh?" Tedge turned from his bow seat to look past the oarsman's head at the engineman. "Yeh knowed—"

"This Rogers, he was tryin' to get off the burnin' wreck and he fell, somehow or—"

"The oil tank blew, and a piece o' pipe took him," grunted Tedge. "I tried to drag him out o' the fire—Gawd knows I did, didn't I, Crump?"

Crump nodded scaredly. The black oarsman's eyes narrowed and he crouched dumbly as he rowed. Tedge was behind him—Tedge of the *Marie Louise* who could kill with his fists. No, Hogjaw knew nothing, he never would know anything.

"I jest took him on out o' kindness," mumbled Tedge. "I got no license fer passenger business. Jest a bum I took on to go and see his swamp girl up Des Amoureux. Well, it ain't no use sayin anything, is it, now?"

A mile away the wreck of the *Marie Louise* appeared as a yellow—red rent in the curtain of night. Red, too, was the flat, calm sea, save northerly where a sand ridge gleamed. Tedge turned to search for its outlying point. There was a pass here, beyond which the reefs began once more and stretched on, a barrier to the shoal inside waters. When the skiff had drawn about the sand spit, the reflecting waters around the *Marie* had vanished, and the fire appeared as a fallen meteor burning on the flat, black belt of encircling reef.

Tedge's murderous little eyes watched easterly. They must find the other side of the tidal pass and go up it to strike off for the distant shrimp camps with their story of the end of the *Marie Louise*—boat and cargo a total loss on Au Fer sands.

Upon the utter sea silence there came a sound—a faint bawling of dying cattle, of trampled, choked cattle in the fume and flames. It was very far off now; and tomorrow's tide and wind would find nothing but a blackened timber, a swollen, floating carcass or two—nothing more.

But the black man could see the funeral pyre; the distant glare of it was showing the whites of his eyes faintly to the master, when suddenly he stopped rowing. A drag, the soft sibilance of a moving thing, was on his oar blade. He jerked it free.

"Lilies, boss—makin' out dis pass, too, lilies."

"I see 'em—drop below 'em!" Tedge felt the glow of an unappeasable anger mount to his temples. "Damn 'em—I see 'em!"

There they were, upright, tranquil, immense hyacinths their spear-points three feet above the water, their feathery streamers drifting six feet below; the broad, waxy leaves floating above their bulbous surface mats—they came on silently under the stars; they vanished under the stars seaward to their death.

"Yeh!" roared Tedge. "Sun and sea tomorry—they'll be back on Au Fer like dried bones o' dead men in the sand I bear east'ard off of 'em!"

The oarsman struggled in the deeper pass water. The stiff bow suddenly plunged into a wall of green and purple bloom. The points brushed Tedge's cheek. He cursed and smote them, tore them from the low bow and flung them. But the engine—man stood up and peered into the starlight.

"Yeh'll not make it. Better keep up the port shore. I cain't see nothin' but lilies east'ard—worlds o' flowers comin' with the *crevasse* water behind 'em." He dipped a finger to the water, tasted of it, and grumbled on: "It ain't hardly salt, the big rivers are pourin' such a flood out o' the swamps. Worlds o' flowers comin' out the passes—"

"Damn the flowers!" Tedge arose, shaking his fist at them. "Back out o' 'em! Pull up the Au Fer side, and we'll break through 'em in the bay!"

Against the ebb-tide close along Au Fer reef, the oarsman toiled until Crump, the lookout, grumbled again.

"The shoal's blocked wi' 'em! They're stranded on the ebb. Tedge, yeh'll have to wait for more water to pass this bar inside 'em. Yeh try to cross the pass, and the lilies'll have us all to sea in this crazy skiff when the wind lifts wi' the sun.

"I'm clean wore out," the black man muttered. "Yeh can wait fer day and tide on the sand, boss."

"Well, drive her in, then!" raged the skipper. "The intide'll set before daylight. We'll take it up the bay."

He rolled over the bow, knee—deep in the warm inlet water, and dragged the skiff through the shoals. Crump jammed an oar in the sand, and warping the headline to this, the three trudged on to the white, dry ridge. Tedge flung himself by the first stubby grass clump.

"Clean beat—" he muttered. "By day we'll pass 'em. Damn 'em—and I'll see 'em dyin' in the sun—lilies like dried, dead weeds on the sand—that's what they'll be in a couple o' days—he said they was pretty, that fello' back there—" Lying with his head on his arm, he lifted a thumb to point over his shoulder. He couldn't see the distant blotch of fire against the low stars—he didn't want to. He couldn't mark the silent drift of the sea gardens 'n the pass, but he gloated in the thought that they were riding to their death. The pitiless sun, the salt tides drunk up to their spongy bulbs, and their glory passed—they would be matted refuse on the shores and a man could trample them. Yes, the sea was with Tedge, and the rivers, too, the flood waters were lifting the lilies from their immemorable strongholds and forcing them out to their last pageant of death.

The three castaways slept in the warm sand. It was an hour later that some other living thing stirred at the far end of Au Fer reef. A scorched and weakened steer came on through salt pools to stagger and fall. Presently another, and then a slow line of them. They crossed the higher ridge to huddle about a sink that might have made them remember the dry drinking holes of their arid home plains. Tired gaunt cattle mooing lonesomely, when the man came about them to dig with his bloody fingers in the sand.

He tried another place, and another—he didn't know—he was a man of the short—grass country, not a coaster; perhaps a sandy sink might mean fresh water. But after each effort the damp feeling on his hands was from his gashed and battered head and not life—giving water. He wiped the blood from his eyes and stood up in the starlight.

"Twenty-one of 'em—alive—and me," he muttered. "I got em off—they trampled me and beat me down, but I got their pens open. Twenty-one livin'—and me on the sands!"

He wondered stupidly how he had done it. The stern of the *Marie Louise* had burned off and sagged down in deepwater, but her bow hung to the reef, and in smoke and flame he had fought the cattle over it. They clustered now in the false water-hole, silent, listless, as if they knew the uselessness of the urge of life on Au Fer reef.

And after a while the man went on eastward. Where and how far the sand ridge stretched he did not know. Vaguely he knew of the tides and sun to-morrow. From the highest point he looked back. The wreck was a dull red glow, the stars above it cleared now of smoke. The sea, too, seemed to have gone back to its infinite peace, as if it had washed itself daintily after this greasy morsel it must hide in its depths.

A half hour the man walked wearily, and then before him stretched water again. He turned up past the tide flowing down the pass—perhaps that was all of Au Fer. A narrow spit of white sand at high tide, and even over that, the sea breeze freshening, the surf would curl?

"Ships never come in close, they said," he mused tiredly, and miles o' shoals to the land—and then just swamp for miles. Dumb brutes o' cows, and me on this—and no water nor feed, nor shade from the sun."

He stumbled on through the shallows, noticing apathetically that the water was running here. Nearly to his waist he waded, peering into the starlight. He was a cowman and he couldn't swim; he had never seen anything but the dry ranges until he said he would go find the girl he had met once on the upper Brazos—a girl who told him of sea and sunken forests, of islands of flowers drifting in lonely swamp lakes he had wanted to see that land, but mostly the Cajun girl of Bayou Des Amoureux.

He wouldn't see her now; he would die among dying cattle, but maybe it was fit for a cattleman to go that way—a Texas man and Texas cows.

Then he saw a moving thing. It rode out of the dark and brushed him. It touched him with soft fingers and he drew them to him. A water-hyacinth, and its purple spike topped his head as he stood waist-deep. So cool its leaves, and the dripping bulbs that he pressed them to his bloody cheek. He sank his teeth into them for the coolness on his parched tongue. The spongy bulb was sweet; it exhaled odorous moisture. He seized it ravenously. It carried sweet water, redolent of green forest swamps!

He dragged at another floating lily, sought under the leaves for the buoyant bulb. A drop or two of fresh water a man could press from each!

Like a starving animal he moved in the shoals, seeing more drifting garden clumps. And then a dark object that did not drift. He felt for it slowly, and then straightened up, staring about.

A flat-bottomed bayou skiff, and in it the oars, a riverman's blanket-roll of greasy clothes, and a tin box! He knew the box. On one end, in faded gilt, was the name, "B. Tedge." Rogers had seen it on the grimy shelf in the pilot-house of the *Marie Louise*. He felt for the rope; the skiff was barely, scraping bottom. Yes, they had moored it here—they must be camped on the sands of Au Fer, awaiting the dawn.

A boat? He didn't know what a Texas cowman could do with a boat on an alien and unknown shore, but he slipped into it, raised an oar and shoved back from the sandy spit. At least he could drift off Au Fer's waterless desolation. Tedge would kill him to-morrow when he found him there; because he knew Tedge had fired the *Marie* for the insurance.

So he poled slowly off. The skiff drifted now. Rogers tried to turn to the oar athwart, and awkwardly he stumbled. The oar seemed like a roll of thunder when it struck the gunwale.

And instantly a hoarse shout rose behind him. Tedge's voice— Tedge had not slept well. The gaunt cattle burning or choking in the salt tide, or perhaps the lilies of Bayou Bocuf—anyhow, he was up with a cry and dashing for the skiff. In a moment Rogers saw him.

The Texas man began driving desperately on the oars. He heard the heavy rush of the skipper's feet in the deepening water. Tedge's voice became a bull-like roar as the depth began to check him. To his waist, and the slow skiff was but ten yards away; to his great shoulders, and the clumsy oarsman was but five.

And with a yell of triumph Tedge lunged out swimming. Whoever the fugitive, he was hopeless with the oars. The skiff swung this way and that, and a strong man at its stern could hurl it and its occupant bottom—side up in Au Fer Pass. Tedge, swimming in Au Fer Pass, his fingers to the throat of this unknown marauder! There'd be another one go—and nothing but his hands—Bill Tedge's hands that the shrimp camps feared.

Just hold him under—that was all. Tread water, and hold the throat beneath until its throbbing ceased. Tedge could; he feared no man. Another overhand stroke, and he just missed the wobbling stern of the light skiff.

He saw the man start up and raise an oar as if to strike. Tedge laughed triumphantly. Another plunge and his fingers touched the gunwale. And then he dived; he would bring his back up against the flat bottom and twist his enemy's footing from under him. Then, in the deep water, Tedge lunged up for the flat keel, and slowly across his brow an invisible hand seemed to caress him.

He opened his eyes to see a necklace of opalescent jewels gathering about his neck; he tore at it and the phosphorescent water gleamed all about him with feathery pendants. And when his head thrust above water, the moment's respite had allowed the skiff to straggle beyond his reach.

Tedge shouted savagely and lunged again—and about his legs came the soft clasp of the drifting hyacinth roots. Higher, firmer, and he turned to kick free of them. He saw the man in the boat poling uncertainly in the tide not six feet beyond him. And now, in open water, Tedge plunged on in fierce exultance. One stroke—and the stars beyond the boatman became obscured; the swimmer struck the soft, yielding barrier of the floating islands. This time he did not lose time in drawing from them; he raised his mighty arms and strove to beat them down, flailing the broad leaves until the spiked blossoms fell about him. A circlet of them caressed his cheek. He lowered his head and swam bull-like into the drift; and when he knew the pressure ahead was tightening slowly to rubbery bands, forcing him gently from his victim, Tedge raised his voice in wild curses.

He fought and threshed the lilies, and they gave him cool, velvety kisses in return. He dived and came up through them; and then, staring upward, he saw the tall, purple spikes against the stars. And they were drifting—they were sailing seaward to their death. He couldn't see the boat now for the shadowy hosts; and for the first time fear glutted his heart. It came as a paroxysm of new sensation—Tedge of the *Marie Louise* who had never feared.

But this was different, this soft and moving web of silence. No, not quite silence, for past his ear the splendid hyacinths drifted with a musical creaking, leaf on leaf, the buoyant bulbs brushing each other. The islets joined and parted; once he saw open water and plunged for it—and over his shoulders there surged a soft coverlet. He turned and beat it, he churned his bed into a furious welter, and the silken curtain lowered.

He shrank from it now, staring. The feathery roots matted across his chest, the mass of them felt slimy like the hide of a drowned brute.

"Drownin' cows—" he muttered thickly—"comin' on a man driftin' and drownin'—no, no! Lilies, jest lilies—damn em!"

The tall spiked flowers seemed nodding—yes, just lilies, drifting and singing elfin music to the sea tide. Tedge roared once again his hatred of them; he raised and battered his huge fists into their beauty, and they seemed to smile in the stirlight. Then, with a howl, he dived.

He would beat them—deep water was here in the pass, and he would swim mightily far beneath the trailing roots—he would find the man with the boat yet and hurl him to die in the hyacinth bloom.

He opened his eyes in the deep, clear water and exulted. He, Tedge, had outwitted the bannered argosies. With bursting lungs he charged off across the current, thinking swiftly, coolly, now of the escape. And as he neared the surface he twisted to glance upward. It was light there a light brighter than the stars, but softer, evanescent. Mullet and squib were darting about or clinging to a feathery forest that hung straight down upon him. Far and near there came little darts of pale fire, gleaming and expiring with each stir in the phosphorescent water.

And he had to rise; a man could not hold the torturing air in his lungs forever. Yes, he would tear a path to the stars again and breathe. His arms flailed into the first tenuous streamers, which parted in pearly lace before his eyes. He breasted higher, and they were all about him now; his struggles evoked glowing bubble—jewels which drifted upward to expire. He grasped the soft roots and twisted and sought to raise himself. He had a hand to the surface bulbs, but a silken mesh seemed tightening about him.

And it was drifting—everything was drifting in the deep pass of Au Fer. He tried to howl in the hyancinth web, and choked—and then he merely fought in his close-pressing cocoon, thrusting one hard fist to grasp the broad leaves. He clung to them dumbly, his face so close to the surface that the tall spiked flowers smiled down—but they drifted inexorably with a faint, creaking music, leaf on leaf.

Tedge opened his eyes to a flicker of myriad lights. The sound was a roaring, now—like the surf on the reefs in the hurricane month; or the thunder of maddened steers above him across this flowery sea meadow. Perhaps the man he had killed rode with this stampede? Tedge shrank under the lilies—perhaps they could protect him now? Even the last stroke of his hands made luminous beauty of the underrunning tide.

An outward-bound shrimp lugger saw the figures on Au Fer reef and came to anchor beyond the shoals. The Cajun crew rode up to where Milt Rogers and Crump and the black deckhand were watching by a pool. The shrimpers listened to the cowman, who had tied the sleeve of his shirt about his bloody head.

"You can get a barge down from Morgan City and take the cows off before the sea comes high," said Rogers quietly. "They're eating the lilies—and they find sweet water in 'em. Worlds o' lilies driftin' to sea with sweet water in the bulbs!" And he added, watching Crump and the black man who seemed in terror of him: "I want to get off, too. I want to see the swamp country where worlds o' flowers come from!"

He said no more. He did not even look in the pool where Crump pointed. He was thinking of that girl of the swamps who had bid him come to her. But all along the white surf line he could see the green and purple plumes of the hyacinth warriors tossing in the

THE MAN WHO CURSED THE LILIES

Unlike Chopin's realistic portrayal of Acadian country, Jackson's picture is highly idealized. The conflict is man against nature, and the characters' attitudes toward the floating lilies function as an index to their spiritual state. Tench, as well as his associates, represents pure evil in man; and the lilies, the girl, and everything associated with them, represent external nature in all its beauty, beneficence, and innocence. Only in the romantic setting is there local color; the characters are allegorical.

Tedge, whose mercantile instincts overshadow morality, is carrying a boatload of cattle from the dried-up ranches of Texas through the intercoastal canal and bayous of southwestern Louisiana to the grassy prairies of Bayou Teche. Since he paid very little for the half-starved cows, he greedily plans to fatten them on free grazing and sell them at a huge profit in New Orleans. However, the hated lilies which clog the streams become his enemy; "he roars his anathemas at them" and struggles in a "volcanic fury" to defeat them. In his monomania, he personifies them: at first he imagines them "dead, dried white, like men's bones." In a fiendish attempt to recoup financially, he burns the boat without releasing the cattle or warning his passenger; and with his engineer he makes his way to Au Fer reef.

At this point the center of consciousness switches to the passenger who has somehow loosed the cattle and swum with them to the reef. He thinks of the Cajun girl who had told him of "sea and sunken forests, of islands of flowers drifting in lonely swamp lakes—he had wanted to see that land, but mostly the Cajun girl of Bayou Des Amoreux." As he stumbles and wades through the salty shallows, the lilies "touch him with soft fingers and he draws them to him. . . . A water hyacinth, and its purple spike topped his head as he stood waist-deep. So cool its leaves, and the dripping bulbs that he pressed them to his bloody cheek. He sank his teeth into them for the coolness on his parched tongue. The spongy bulb was sweet; it exhaled odorous moisture . . . it carried sweet water, redolent of green forest swamps!"

As the point of view switches back to Tench, he struggles in the water, perceiving the lilies as beautiful and seductive, but evil: "he raised his mighty arms and strove to beat them down. . . . A circlet of them caressed his cheek. . . . He fought and threshed the lilies, and they gave him cool velvety kisses in return. . . . The tall spiked flowers seemed nodding . . . drifting and singing elfin music to the sea tide . . . they seemed to smile in the starlight."

Jackson's view as represented in this story is thoroughly romantic: nature is the manifestation of a benign order of which Tench and his associates cannot partake. Tench projects the evil in his own heart onto nature. However, the passenger, who saves the cattle and is nourished by the lilies, and the girl "who sings of the lilies" belong to the realm of nature; they, along with the cattle (natural creatures), are saved while the evil Tench is destroyed. The floating islands and the grassy bayou country represent Edenic beauty and innocence; the man's search for the girl and her country is a spiritual journey.

Ruth McEnery Stuart
(1852-1917)

A native of Marksville in Avoyelles Parish, Louisiana, Ruth McEnery grew up in New Orleans. In 1879 she married Alfred Oden Stuart and went to Arkansas to live on his cotton plantation, but after his death four years later she returned to New Orleans where she began to write local color sketches. Life on both her father's and her husband's plantations provided material for her stories in which she depicted an idyllic relationship between contented black slaves and their beneficent white masters. She wrote also of the Arkansas hillbilly and the New Orleans Italian, but her best stories are of Louisiana plantations. A prolific writer, she published between 1891 and 1900 twelve volumes—short story collections and novelettes. After the turn of the century she tried verse as a means of portraying the history and beauty of her native region but continued to write short sketches. She died in 1917 in New York where she had lived after having established herself as a writer. The story printed below was first published in 1893 in *A Golden Wedding and Other Tales.*

Christmas Gifts[*]

Ruth McEnery Stuart

Christmas on Sucrier plantation, and the gardens are on fire with red flames of salvia, roses, geraniums, verbenas, rockets of Indian shot, brilliant blazes of coreopsis, marigold, and nasturtium, glowing coals of vivid portulaca.

Louisiana acknowledges a social obligation to respond to a Christmas freeze; but when a guest tarries, what is one to do?

She manufactures her ice, it is true. Why not produce an artificial winter? Simply because she does not care for it. If she did—? Such things are easily arranged.

Still, when he comes, a *guest*, she would not forget her manners and say him nay, any sooner than she would shrug her shoulders at a New England cousin or answer his questions in French.

She does the well-bred act to the death, summons her finest, fairest, most brilliant and tender of flower and leaf to await his coming: so today all her royal summer family are out in full court dress, ready to prostrate themselves at his feet.

This may be rash, but it is polite.

Her grandfather was both; and so the "Creole State," in touch with her antipodal brother in ancestor-worship, is satisfied.

But winter, the howling swell, forgetful of provincial engagements, does not come. Still, the edge of his promise is in the breeze to-day, and the flaring banana leaves of tender green look cold and half afraid along the garden wall.

The Yule log smoulders lazily and comfortably in the big fireplace, but windows and doors are open, and rocking chairs and hammocks swing on the broad galleries of the great house.

It is a rich Christmas of the olden time.

Breakfast and the interchange of presents are over.

Cautious approaches of wheels through the outer gates during the night, in the wee short hours when youth sleeps most heavily, have resulted in mysterious appearances: a new piano in the parlor; a carriage, a veritable antebellum chariot, and a pair of bays, in

[*]"Christmas Gifts" from *A Golden Wedding and Other Tales*. Reprinted by arrangement with Harper & Row Publishers, Inc.

the stable; guns, silver-mounted trappings, saddles, books, pictures, jewels, and dainty confections, within and piled about the stockings that hung around the broad dining-room chimney.

For there were sons and daughters on Sucrier plantation.

An easy-going, healthy, hearty, and happy man, of loose purse-strings and lax business habits, old Colonel Slack had grown wealthy simply because he lived on the shore where the tide always came in—the same shore where since '61 the waters move ever to the sea, and those who waited where he stood are stranded.

His highest ambitions in life were realized. His children, the elect by inheritance to luxurious ease, were growing up about him, tall, straight, and handsome, and happily free from disorganizing ambitions, loving the fleece-lined home-nest.

The marriage of an eldest daughter, Louise, to a wealthy next-door planter, five miles away, had seemed but to add a bit of broidery to the borders of his garment.

His pretty, dainty wife, in lieu of wrinkles, had taken on avoirdupois and white hair, and instead of shrivelling like a four-o'clock had bloomed into a regal evening-glory.

So distinctly conscious of all these blessings was the old colonel that his atmosphere seemed always charged with the electric quality which was happiness; but on occasions like to-day, when the depths of his tendernesses were stirred within him by the ecstasy of giving and of receiving thanks and smiles and thanks again from "my handsome wife," "my fine children," "my *loyal* slaves"—ah, this was the electric *flash!* It was joy! It was delight and exuberance of spirit! It was youth returned! It was Christmas!

In his heart were peace and good-will all the year round, and on Christmas—hallelujahs.

He had often been heard to say that if he ever professed religion it would be on Christmas; and, by the way, so it was, but not *this* Christmas.

A tender-souled, good old man was he, yet thoughtless, withal, as a growing boy.

Down in the quarters, this morning, the negroes, gaudily arrayed in their Sunday best, were congregated in squads about the benches in front of their cabins, awaiting the ringing of the plantation bell which should summon them to "the house" to receive their Christmas packages.

In the grove of China-trees around which the cabins were ranged, a crowd of young men and maidens flirted and chaffed one another on the probable gifts awaiting them.

One picked snatches of tunes on a banjo, another drew a bow across an old fiddle, but the greater number were giddily spending themselves in plantation repartee, a clever answer always provoking a loud, unanimous laugh, usually followed by a reckless duet by the two "musicianers."

Sometimes, when the jokes were too utterly delicious, the young "bucks" would ecstatically hug the China-trees or tumble down upon the grass and bellow aloud.

"What yer reck'n ole marster gwine give you, Unc' Tom?" said one, addressing an old man who had just joined the group and sat sunning his shiny bald head.

"'Spec' he gwine give Unc' Tom some hair-ile, ur a co'se comb," suggested a pert youth.

"Look like he better give you a wagon-tongue ur a bell-tongue, one, 'caze yo' tongue ain't long 'nough," replied Uncle Tom quietly, and so the joke was turned.

"I trus' he gwine give Bow-laigged Joe a new pair o' breeches!"

"Ef he do, I hope dey'll be cut out wid a circular saw!" came a quick response, which brought a scream of laughter.

"Wonder what Lucindy an' Dave gwine git?"

Lucinda and Dave were bride and groom of a month.

In a minute two big fellows were screaming and holding their sides over a whispered suggestion, when the word "cradle" escaped and set girls and all to giggling.

"Pity somebody wouldn't drap some o' you smart boys on a *corn-cradle* an' chop you up," protested the bride, with a toss of her head.

"De whole passel ob 'em wouldn't make nothin' but rotten-stone, ef dee was *grine* up," suggested Uncle Tom, with an intolerant smile.

"Den you ought use us fur tooth-powder," responded the wit again, and the bald-headed old man, confessing himself vanquished, good-naturedly bared his toothless gums to join in the laughter at his own expense.

A sudden clang of the bell brought all to their feet presently, and, strutting, laughing, prancing, they proceeded up to the house, the musicians tuning up afresh *en route,* for in the regular order of exercises arranged for the day they were to play an important part.

The recipients were to be ranged in the yard in line, about fifty feet from the steps of the back veranda where the master should stand, and, as their names should be called, to dance forward, receive their gifts, courtesy, and dance back to their places.

At the calling of the names music would begin.

The pair who by vote should be declared the most graceful should receive from the master's hand a gift of five dollars each, with the understanding that it should supply the eggnog for the evening's festivities, where the winners should preside as king and queen.

An interested audience of the master's family, seated on the veranda back of him, was a further stimulant to best effort.

The packages, all marked with names, were piled on two tables, those for men on one and the women's on the other, and the couples resulting from a random selection from each caused no little merriment.

All had agreed to the conditions, and when Lame Phoebe was called out with Jake Daniels, a famous dancer, they were greeted with shouts of applause.

Phoebe, enthused by her reception, and in no wise embarrassed by a short leg, made a virtue of necessity, advancing and retreating in a series of graceful bows, manipulating her sinewy body so dextrously that the inclination towards the left foot was more than concealed, and for the first time in his life Jake Daniels came in second best, as, amid deafening applause, Lame Phoebe bowed and wheeled herself back among the people.

Then came Joe Scott, an ebony swell, with Fat Sarey, a portly dame of something like three hundred avoirdupois—a difficult combination again.

That Sarey had not danced for twenty years was not through reluctance of the flesh more than of the spirit, for she was "a chile o' de kingdom," both by her own profession and universal consent. Laughing good-naturedly, with shaking sides she stepped forward, bowed first to her master and then to her partner, and, raising her right hand, began, in a wavering, soft voice, keeping-time to the vibrating melody by easy undulations of her pliable body, to sing:

"Dey's a star in de eas' on a Chris'mus morn.
    Rise up, shepherd, an' foller!
Hit'll lead ter de place whar de Saviour's born.
    Rise up, shepherd, an' foller!
Ef yer take good heed ter de angels' words,
You'll forgit yo flocks an' forgit yo' herds,
    An' rise up, shepherd, an' foller!
    Leave yo' sheep an'
    Leave yo' lamb an'
    Leave yo' ewe an'
    Leave yo' ram, an'
Rise up, shepherd, an' foller!"

Joe took his cue from the first note, and accommodating his movements to hers, elaborating them profusely with graceful gestures, he fell in with a rich, high tenor, making a melody so tender and true that the audience were hushed in reverential silence.

The first verse finished, Sarey turned slowly, and by an uplifted finger invited all hands to join in the chorus.

Rich and loud, in all four parts, came the effective refrain:

"Foller, foller, foller, foller,
Rise up, shepherd, rise an' foller,
    Foller de Star o' Bethlehem!"

Still taking the initiative, Sarey now bent easily and deeply forward in a most effusive parlor salutation as she received her gift; while Joe, as ever quick of intuition, also dispensed with the traditional dipping courtesy, while he surrendered himself to a profound bow which involved the entire length of his willowy person.

Turning now, without losing for a moment the rhythmic movement, they proceeded to sing a second verse:

"Oh, dat star's Stin shinin' dis Chris'mus day.
    Rise, O sinner, an' foller!
Wid an eye o' faith you c'n see its ray.
    Rise, o sinner, an' foller!

Hit'll hght yo' way thoo de fiel's o' fros',
While it leads thoo de stable ter de shinin' cross.
    Rise, o sinner, an' foller
    Leave yo' father.
    Leave yo' mother,
    Leave yo' sister,
    Leave yo' brother,
    rise, O sinner, an' foller!"

A slightly accelerated movement had now brought the performers back to their places, when the welkin rang with a full all-round chorus:

"Foller, foller, foller, foller,
Rise, O sinner, rise an' foller,
    Foller de Star o' Bethlehem!"

A few fervid high-noted "Amens!" pathetically suggestive of pious senility, were succeeded now by a silence more eloquent than applause.

Other dancers by youthful antics soon restored hilarity, however, and for quite an hour the festivities kept up with unabated interest.

Finally a last parcel was held up—only one—and when the master called, "Judy Collins!" adding, "Judy, you'll have to dance by yourself, my girl!" the excitement was so great that for several minutes nothing could be done.

Judy Collins, by a strange coincidence, was the only "old maid" on the plantation, and, as she was a dashing, handsome woman, she had given the mitten at one time or another to nearly every man present.

That she should have to dance alone was too much for their self-control.

The women, convulsed with laughter, held on to one another, while the men shrieked aloud.

Judy was the only self-possessed person present.

Before any one realized her intention, she had seized a new broom from the kitchen porch near, and stepped out into the arena with it in her hand.

Judy was grace itself. Tall, willowy, and lithe, stately as a pine, supple as a mountain-trout, she glided forward with her broom.

Holding it now at arm's-length, now balancing it on end and now on its wisps, tilting it at hazardous angels, but always catching it ere it fell, poising it on her finger-tips, her chin, her forehead, the back of her neck, keeping perfect time the while with the music, she advanced to receive her parcel, which, with a quick movement, she deftly attached to the broom-handle, and, throwing it over her shoulder, danced back to her place.

The performance entire had proven a brilliant success, and Judy's dance a fitting climax.

Needless to say, Judy insisted on keeping the broom.

The awarding of the prizes by acclamation to Joe Scott and Fat Sarey was the work of a moment, prettily illustrating the religious susceptibility of the voters.

Then followed a "few remarks" from the speaker of the occasion, and a short and playful response from the master, when the crowd dispersed, opening their bundles *en route* as they returned merrily to their cabins.

The parcels had been affectionately prepared. Besides the dresses, wraps, and shoes given to all, there were attractive trinkets, bottles of cologne, ribbons, gilt ear-rings or pins for the young women, cravats, white collars, shirtstuds, for the beaux, and for the old such luxuries as tobacco, walking-canes, spectacles, and the like, with small coins for pocket-money.

This year, in addition to the extra and expected "gift," each young woman received, to her delight, a flaring hoop-skirt; and such a lot of balloons as were flying about the plantation that morning it would be hard to find again.

Happy and care-free as little children were they, and as easily pleased.

Having retired for the moment necessary for their inflation and adornment, the younger element, balloons and beaux, soon returned to their popular holiday resort under the China-trees.

Though the branches were bare, the benches beneath them commanded a perennial fair-weather patronage; for where a bench and a tree are, there will young men and maidens be gathered together.

Lame Mose was there, with his new cushioned crutch, and Phil Thomas the preacher, looking ultraclerical and important in a polished beaver; while Lucinda and Dave, triumphant in the cumulative dignity of new bride-and-groomship, hoop-skirt and standing collar, actually strutted about arm in arm in broad daylight, to the intense amusement of the young folk, who nudged one another and giggled as they passed.

Such was the merry spirit of the group when Si, a young mulatto household servant, suddenly appeared upon the scene.

"'Cindy," said he, "master say come up ter de house—dat is, ef you an' Dave kin part company fur 'bout ten minutes."

"I don' keer nothin' 'bout no black ogly-lookin' some'h'n-'nother like Dave, nohow!" exclaimed Lucinda flirtatiously, as she playfully grasped Si's arm and proceeded with him to the house, leaving Dave laughing with the rest at her antics.

The truth was that, confidently expecting the descent of some further gift upon her brideship, Lucinda was delighted at the summons, and her face beamed with expectancy as she presented herself before her master.

"Lucindy," said he, as she entered, "I want you to mount Lady Gay and ride down to Beechwood this morning, to take some Christmas things to Louise and her chicks."

Lucinda's smile broadened in a delighted grin.

A visit to Beechwood to-day would be sure to elicit a present from her young mistress, "Miss Louise," besides affording an opportunity to compare presents and indulge in a little harmless gossip with the Beechwood negroes.

Lady Gay stood, ready saddled, waiting at the door. After a little delay in adjusting the assertive springs of her hoop-skirt to the pommel of the saddle, Lucinda started off in a gallop.

When she entered the broad hall at Beechwood, the family, children and all, recognizing her as an ambassador of Santa Claus, gathered eagerly about her, and as boxes and parcels were opened in her presence her eyes fairly shone with pleasure. Nor was she disappointed in her hope of a gift herself.

"I allus did love you de mos' o' ole Miss's chillen, Miss Lou," she exclaimed presently, opening and closing with infantile delight a gay feather-edged fan which Louise gave her.

"I does nachelly love red. Red seem like hit's got mo' color in it 'n any color."

"Dis heah's a reg'lar courtin'-fan," she added to herself, as she followed the children out into the nursery to inspect their new toys, fanning, posing, and flirting as she went. "Umph! ef I'd 'a' des had dis fan las' summer I'd 'a' had Dave all but crazy."

After enjoying it for an hour or more, she finally wrapped it carefully in her handkerchief and put it for safe keeping into her pocket. In doing so, her hand came in contact with a letter which she had forgotten to deliver.

"Law, Miss Lou!" she exclaimed, hurrying back, "I mos' done clair forgittin' ter gi' you yo' letter what' ole marster tol' me ter han' you de fus' thing."

"I wondered that father and mother had sent no message," replied Louise, opening the note. Her face softened into a smile, however, as she proceeded to read it.

"Why, you wretch, Lucindy!" she exclaimed, laughing, "you've kept me out of my two best Christmas gifts for an hour. I always wanted to own Lady Gay, and father writes that you are a fine, capable girl."

Lucinda cast a quick, frightened look at Louise and caught her breath.

"And I am so glad to know that you are pleased. Why didn't you tell me that you were a Christmas gift when you came?"

There was no longer any doubt. Lucinda could not have answered to save her life. The happy-hearted child of a moment ago was transformed into a desperate, grief-stricken woman.

"Why, Lucindy!" Louise was really grieved to discern the tragic look in the girl's face. "I am disappointed. I thought you loved me. I thought you would be delighted to belong to me—to be my maid—and not to work in the field any more and to have a nicer cabin in my yard—and a sewing-machine—and to learn to embroider—and to dress my hair—and to—."

The growing darkness in Lucinda's face warned Louise that this conciliatory policy was futile, and yet, feeling only kindily towards her, she continued.

"Tell me, Lucindy, why you are distressed. Don't you really wish to belong to me? Why did you say that you loved me the best?"

Words were useless. Louise was almost frightened as she looked again into the girl's face. Her eyes shone like a caged lion's, and her bosom rose and fell tumultuously.

After many fruitless efforts to elicit a response, Louise called her husband, and together they tried by kind assurances to pacify her; but it was vain. She stood before them a mute impersonation of despair and rage.

"You'd better go out into the kitchen for a while, Lucindy," said Louise finally, "and when I send for you I shall expect you to have composed yourself." Looking neither to right nor left, Lucinda strode out of the hall, across the gallery, down the steps, through the yard to the kitchen, gazed at by the assembled crowd of children both black and white.

"Cindy ain't but des on'y a little while ago married," said Tildy, a black girl who stood in the group as she passed out.

"Married, is she?" exclaimed Louise, eagerly grasping at a solution of the difficulty. "That explains. But why didn't she tell me? There must be some explanation. This is so unlike father. We are to dine at Sucrier this afternoon. Go, Tildy and tell Lucindy that we will see what can be done."

"Fo' laws-o'-mussy sakes, Miss Lou, please, ma'am, don't sen' me ter 'Cindy now. 'Cindy look like she gwine hurt somebody."

If she could have seen Lucinda at this moment, she might indeed have feared to approach her. When she had entered the kitchen a little negro who had followed at her heels had announced to the cook and her retinue,

"Cindy mad caze ole marster done sont 'er fur a Chris'mus-gif' ter Miss Lou." Whereupon there were varied exclamations:

"Umph!"

"You is a sorry-lookin' Chris'mus gift, sho!"

"I don't blame 'er!"

"What you frettin' 'bout, chile? You in heab'n here!"

"De gal's married," whispered some one in stage fashion, finally.

"Married!" shrieked old Silvy Ann from her corner where she sat peeling potatoes. "Married! Eh, Lord! Time you ole as I is, you won't fret 'bout no sech. Turn 'im out ter grass, honey, an' start out fur a grass-widder. I got five I done turned out in de pasture now, an' ef dee sell me out ag'in, Ole Abe'll be a-grazin' wid de res'!"

"Life is too short ter fret, honey! But ef yer *boun'* ter fret, fret 'bout *somet'n'!* Don't fret 'bout one o' deze heah long-laigged, good-fur-nothin' sca'crows name' Mister Man! Who you married ter, gal?"

"She married ter cross-eyed Dave," some one answered.

"Cross-eyed! De Lord! Let 'im go fur what he'll fetch, honey! De woods roun' heah is full o' straight-eyed ones, let 'lone game-eyes!" And the vulgar old creature encored her own wit with an outburst of cracked laughter.

"Ain't you 'shame' o' yo'se'f, Aunt Silvy Ann! 'Cindy ain't like you; she *married—wid a preacher.*"

"Yas, an' *un*married *'dout* no *preacher!* What's de good o' lockin' de do' on de inside wid a key, ef you c'n open it f'om de outside 'dout no key? I done kep' clair o' locks an' keys all my life, an' nobody's feelin's was hurt."

While old Silvy Ann was running on in this fashion, Texas, the cook, had begun to address Lucinda:

"Don't grieve yo' heart, baby. My ole man stay mo' fur 'n ole marster's f'om heah—'way down ter de cross-roads t'other side de bayou. How fur do daddy stay, chillen?" she added, as she broke red pepper into her turkey-stuffing.

"Leb'n mile," answered four voices from as many little black pickaninnies who tumbled over one another on the floor.

"You heah dat! *Leb'n mile,* an' ev'y blessed night he come home ter Texas! Yas, Ma'am, an' 'is lone star keep a lookout fur 'im too—a candle in de winder an' a tin pan o' membrance on de hyearth."

Seeing that her words produced no effect, Texas changed her tactics.

Approaching Lucinda, she regarded her with admiration: "Dat's a quality collar you got on, 'Cindy. An', law bless my soul, ef de gal 'ain't got on hoops! You gwine lead de style on dis planta—"

Texas never finished her sentence.

Trembling with fury, Lucinda snatched the collar from her neck and tore it into bits; then, making a dive at her skirts, she ripped them into shreds in her frantic efforts to destroy the hoop-skirt. Dragging the gilt pendants from her ears, tearing the flesh as she did so, she threw them upon the floor, and, stamping upon them, ground them to atoms.

Attracted next by her new brogans, she kicked them from her feet and hurled them, one after another, into the open fire. No vestige of a gift from the hand that had betrayed her would she spare.

While all this was occurring in the kitchen, a reverse side of the tragedy was enacting in the house.

A few moments after Lucinda's departure, while Louise and her husband were yet discussing the situation, another messenger came from Sucrier, this time a man, and again a gift, the "note" which he promptly delivered proving to be a deed of conveyance of "two adult negroes, by name Lucinda and David."

Then followed descriptions of each, which it was unnecessary to read.

The bearer seemed in fine spirits.

"Ole marster des sont me wid de note, missy," said he, courtesying respectfully, "an' ef yer please, ma'am, I'll go right back ef dey ain' no answer. We havin' a big time up our way ter-day."

"Why, don't you know what this is, Dave?"

"Yas, 'm, co'se I knows. Hit's—hit's a letter. Law, Miss Lou, yer reck'n I don' know a letter when I see it?"

"Yes, but this letter says that you are not to go back. Father has sent you as a Christmas gift to us."

"Wh—wh—h—how you say dat, missy?"

"Please don't look so frightened, Dave. From the way you all are acting to-day, I begin to be afraid of myself. Don't you want to belong to me?"

"Y—y—yas, 'm, but yer see, missy, I-I-I's married."

The hat in his hand was trembling as he spoke.

"And where is your wife?" Could it be possible that he did not know?

"She—sh—she—" The boy was actually crying. "She stay wid me. B—but marster des sont 'er on a arrant dis mornin'. Gord knows whar he sont 'er. I 'lowed maybe he sont 'er heah, tell 'e sont me."

The situation, which was plain now, had grown so interesting that Louise could not resist the temptation to bring the unconscious actors in the little drama together, that she might witness the happy catastrophe.

She whispered to Tildy to call Lucinda.

That Lucinda should have been summoned just at the crisis of her passion was most inopportune.

Tildy stood at a distance as she timidly delivered the message. Indeed, all the occupants of the kitchen had moved off apace and stood aghast and silent.

As soon as Lucinda heard the command, however, without even looking down at herself, with head still high in air and her fury unabated, she followed Tildy into the presence of her mistress.

Louise was frightened when she looked upon her; indeed it was some moments before she could command herself enough to speak.

The girl's appearance was indeed tragic.

In tearing the ribbon from her hair she had loosened the ends of the short braids, which stood in all directions. Her ears were dripping with blood, and her torn sleeve revealed her black arm, scratched with her nails, also bleeding.

Below her tattered skirt trailed long, detached springs, the dilapidated remains of the glorious structure of the morning.

Her tearless eyes gave no sign of weakening, and the veins about her neck and temples, pulsating with passion, were swollen and knotted like ropes.

She seemed to have grown taller, and the black circles beneath her eyes and about her swelling lips imparted by contrast an ashen hue grimly akin to pallor to the rest of her face.

As her mistress contemplated her, she was moved to pity.

"Lucindy"—she spoke with marked gentleness—"I showed you all our Christmas gifts this morning; but after you went out we received another, and I've sent for you to show you this too."

She hesitated, but not even by a quivering muscle did Lucinda give a sign of hearing.

"Look over there towards the library door, Lucindy, and see the nice carriage-driver father sent me."

Ah! now she looked.

For a moment only young husband and wife regarded each other, and them, oblivious to all eyes, the two Christmas gifts rushed into each other's arms.

The fountains of her wrath were broken up now, and Lucinda's tears came like rain. Crying and sobbing aloud, she threw her long arms around little Dave, and, dragging him out into the floor, began to dance.

Dave, more sensitive than she, abashed after the first surprise, became conscious and ashamed.

"Stop, 'Cindy! I 'clare, gal, stop! Stop, I say!" he cried, trying in vain to wrest himself from her grasp.

"You 'Cindy! You makes me 'shame'! Law, gal! Miss Lou, come here to 'Cindy!"

But the half-savage creature, mad with joy, gave no heed to his resistance as she whirled him round and round up and down the hall.

"Hallelujah! Glory! Amen! Glory be ter Gord, fur givin' me back dis heah little black, cross-eyed, bandy-legged nigger! Glory, I say!"

The scene was not without pathos. And yet—how small a thing will sometimes turn the tide of emotion! By how trifling a by-play does a tragedy become comedy!

In her first whirl, the trailing steels of Lucinda's broken hoop-skirt flew over the head of the cat, who sat in the door, entrapping her securely.

Round and round went poor puss, terror-stricken and wildly glaring, utterly unable to extricate herself, until finally a reversed movement freeing her, she sprang with a desperate plunge and an ear-spliting *"Miaou!"* by a single bound out of the back door.

This served to bring Lucinda to a consciousness of her surroundings.

Screaming with laughter, she threw herself down and rolled on the floor.

In rising, her eyes fell for the first time, with a sense of perception, upon herself.

Suddenly conscience-stricken, she threw herself again before her mistress.

"Fur Gord sake, whup me, Miss Lou!" she began; "whup me, ur put me in de stocks, one! I ain't no mo' fitt'n fur a Chris'mus gif' 'n one o' deze heah tiger-cats in de show-tent. Des look heah how I done ripped up all my purties, an' bus' my ears open, an' broken up all my hoop-granjer, all on 'count o' dat little black, cross-eyed nigger! I tell yer de trufe, missy, I ain't no bad-hearted nigger! You des try me! I'll hoe fur yer, I'll plough fur yer, I'll split rails fur yer, I'll be yo' hair-dresser, I'll run de sew'-machine fur yer, I'll walk on my head fur year, ef yer des leave me dat one little black scrooched-up some'h'n-'nother stan'in' over yonner 'g'inst de do', grinnin' like a chessy-cat. He ain't much, but, sech as 'e is an' what dey is of 'im, fur Gord sake, spare 'im ter me! Somehow, de place whar he done settled in my heart is des nachelly my *wil'-cat spot.*"

Sitting in her rags at her mistress's feet, in this fashion she approached the formal apology which she felt that her conduct demanded.

Somehow the conventional formula, "I ax yo' pardon," seemed inadequate to the present requirement.

She hardly knew how to proceed.

After hesitating a moment in some embarrassment, she began again, in a lower tone:

"Miss Lou, dis heah's Chris'mus, ain't it?"

"Yes; you know it is."

"An' hit's de day de Lord cas' orf all 'is glory an' come down ter de yearth, des a po' little baby a-layin' in a stable 'longside o' de cows an' calves, ain't it?"

"Yes."

"An' hit's de day de angels come a-singin' 'peace an' good-will,' ain't it?"

"Yes." "Miss Lou—"

"Well?"

"On de 'count o' all dat, honey, won't yer please, ma'am, pass over my wil'-cat doin's dis time, mistus?"

She waited a moment, and, not understanding how a rising lump in her throat kept her mistress silent, continued to plead:

"Fur Gord sake, mistus, I done said all de scripchur' I knows. What mo' kin I say?"

"What—what—what—what—what's all this?"

It was old Colonel Slack, standing in the front hall door.

At the sound of his voice, the three grandchildren ran to meet him, Louise following.

"You dear old father!" she exclaimed, kissing him. "You've grown impatient and come after us!"

"Certainly I have. What sort of spending the day do you call this? It's two o'clock now. But what's all this?" he repeated, approaching Lucinda, who had risen to her feet.

Dave had gradually backed nearly out of the door.

"Why, Lucindy, my girl! you look as if you'd had a tiff with a panther."

"Tell de trufe, marster, I done been down an' had a han'-ter-han' wrastle wid Satan ter-day, an' he all but whupped me out."

"How did you happen to send these poor children to us separately, father?" said Louise. "They had been almost broken-hearted, each thinking the other was to stay at Sucrier."

"Well, well, well! I am the clumsiest old blunderer! It's from Scylla to Charybdis every time. I didn't want my people to suspect they were going, just because it's Christmas, you know, and saying good-bye will cast a sort of shadow over things. Dave and Lucindy are immensely popular among the darkies. I knew they'd be glad to come; it's promotion, you see. Never thought of a misunderstanding. And so you poor children thought I wanted to divorce you, did you? And you, Lucindy, flew into a tantrum and tore the clothes off your back? I don't blame you. I'd tear mine off too. Rig her up again somehow, daughter, and let her go up to the dance tonight."

Opening his pocket-book, he took out two crisp five-dollar bills.

Handing one of them to Lucinda, he said:

"Here, girl, take this, and—don't you tell 'em I said so, but I thought you beat the whole crowd dancing this morning anyhow. And Dave, you little cross-eyed rascal you, step up here and get your money. Here's five dollars to pay for spoiling your Christmas. Now, off with you!"

As they passed out, Lucinda seized Dave's arm, and when last seen as they crossed the yard she was dragging the little fellow from side to side, dancing in her rags and flirting high in air the red fan, which by some chance had escaped destruction in her pocket.

Magnificent in a discarded ball-dress of her new mistress, Lucinda was the centre of attraction at the Sucrier festival that evening, and when questioned in regard to her toilet of the morning, she answered, with a playful toss of the head:

"What y'all talkin' 'bout, niggers? I wushes you ter on'erstan' dat I's a house-gal now! Yer reck'n I gwine wear common ornamints, same as you fiel'-hand's?"

CHRISTMAS GIFTS

In treating the Negro, most local color writers before the 1950s wrote about blacks in a sentimental, patronizing tone, picturing a benificent master with contented, happy-go-lucky slaves. The view was from the "big house," not the quarters. This story is no exception.

Virtually all the local color elements are present in this sentimental tale of Christmas on an antebellum Creole plantation. The setting, tone, and characters are all stereotypes; that is, they are slightly modified versions of fictional elements already established in Southern literature.

The story opens with a description of the beauty, the luxury, and the felicity of the Sucrier Plantation. Colorful flowers bloom in profusion; the Yule log smolders lazily and comfortably; extravagant presents are exchanged: a piano, a carriage, a pair of bays, guns, saddles, books, pictures, and other expensive items. The atmosphere is idyllic: the "tender-souled" master speaks of his "handsome wife," "fine children," and "loyal slaves." Down in the quarters, the Negroes, gaudily arrayed in their Sunday best, anxiously await their Christmas packages. Overcome by the humor in a joke, "the young 'bucks' ecstatically hug the China tree or tumble upon the grass and bellow aloud." Except for Lucinda and Dave, the newly married couple, the characters have no individuality; their names are often indicative of some physical deformity or feature: Bow-laiged Joe, Lame Phoebe, Fat Sarey, and Lame Mose. Lucinda (Cindy) emerges as a character only after she is given to the "Marster's" married daughter as a Christmas present. Upset by the separation from her husband "preacher Dave," she becomes "half-savage," ripping away her clothes and tearing her hair and flesh. Her actions, a source of entertainment for the Negroes around her, are narrated in a tone of amusement. After Cindy is reunited with Dave through the benevolence of the master, her actions are as extreme and as much a source of amusement as her earlier ones: she dances crazily with her "little black, cross-eyed, bandy-legged nigger," screams with laughter, and rolls on the floor."

The value of this story lies not in its originality but in its contribution to literary as well as social history. It is classic in its

221

depiction of the sensibility of writers of the period who viewed the master-slave relationship as idyllic; it is also classic in its ironic (innocent-eye) depiction of the heartache that the whims of owners brought upon their chattel property.

NOTE: The events of the story had to have occurred before the Civil War (in "olden times") because of slavery; however, the author in enumerating the Christmas presents, speaks of "a veritable ante-bellum chariot" thus indicating a post-war setting. Her reference to the master as "colonel" also suggests post-war.

Lyle Saxon

(1891 -1946)

Lyle Saxon was born September 4, 1891, in Baton Rouge. After graduating from Louisiana State University there, he worked as a journalist on the Chicago *Daily News* and later on the New Orleans *Item* and *Picayune*. From 1924 to 1932 he resided intermittently in New York and at Melrose Plantation near Natchitoches. Life on Melrose provided the material for his only novel *Children of Strangers* which deals with the descendants of mulattoes who once owned both land and slaves on Cane River, as well as for his most successful short story "Cane River," which won an O. Henry Memorial Prize in 1926. An authority on the history, customs, and folklore of Louisiana, Saxon channeled most of his energies into non-fiction. While serving as director of the W. P. A. Writers' Project in Louisiana, he edited *Gumbo Ya-Ya: A Collection of Folk Tales*, published in 1946 shortly before he died. "Cane River," printed below, first appeared in *Dial* in 1926.

Cane River

Lyle Saxon

Susie was not a native of Cane River country. She came here with an old woman called Aunt Dicey, from somewhere down Bayou Lafourche way, from southwest Louisiana. She was a bad one, always—a wild nigger girl with short hair that she combed straight out; and she wore nutmegs on a string around her neck, to ward off evil spirits. She was skinny and ugly; perhaps it was her very ugliness that filled the black men with unrest, as she went flaunting by. An untamed savage, that's what she was. "Trick-nigger" they called her—little old Susie with her scrawny arms, her rolling eyes, and her barbarous ways. Why, you could hear her laughing as she went traipsing through the fields, half a mile away. "Dat's dat Susie," folks would say, as they heard the shrill scream of her laughter coming across Cane River at night, "Dat's a crazy chile!"

She and Aunt Dicey lived in a tumble-down cabin, not far from the African Baptist Church, and Aunt Dicey washed clothes two days of each week, for the white folks at Yucca Plantation. She made a little garden, too, and kept chickens. She got along with everybody.

But that Susie! Oh, she was a bad one. First one boy, and then another: that long black boy of Papa Chawlie's, and the mulatto son of Ambrose Jenks—and even Babe Johnson, bandy-legged and under-sized. But Susie favoured Big Brown. He was six feet tall, and his profile was like that of Ethiopians in Egyptian carvings. And Big Brown had a way with women. Not that he was the marrying kind. He wasn't. He had learned city ways when he spent a year at Angola, the State Penitentiary, for shooting another negro one Christmas night . . . just shooting for nothing, being drunk and in a good humour.

Well, there's no stigma attached to the penitentiary, on Cane River. Many of the black boys have been in for a year or two, for bigamy, or a shooting scrape, or for some other minor offence like that—and it is rather like sending a boy off to college. Lord! Some of them are proud of it when they come back to the plantation again. Or, at least, Big Brown was that way. He came back to Cane

River when Susie was fourteen, when her popularity was at its height. There was little Babe Johnson, for instance. She flouted him with her wild antics and her monkey-shines. But Babe followed her, and used to slip up to Aunt Dicey's cabin on summer nights, carrying a big watermelon for her, on his shoulder. And Susie would eat it, there on the gallery, spitting out the seeds at him and making fun of him.

Then Big Brown came slouching up. He would take her to church, or to picnics, or fish-fries. She would come running. Aunt Dicey hated Brown, and tried to make Susie behave herself. But Lord! That Susie! Might as well try to make the sun stand still.

When trouble began to brew, well—Big Brown went off somewhere into the hills, and Susie was left alone with Aunt Dicey in the cabin on the river bank.

"I tol' yer so! I tol' yer so!" Aunt Dicey said over and over, as she sat rocking her ample body back and forth. But Susie, mis-shapen and ugly, would stand looking out of the door, to where the big red moon hung low in the sky over Cane River. Sometimes she would be racked with great sobs that shook her thin body. At other times she would laugh shrilly and say: "I don' keer! I don' keer!"

A month before the baby was born she married Babe Johnson. For Babe loved her, and that was the only way he could get her. Susie didn't love him, and didn't want to marry him; but Aunt Dicey begged and argued, and talked of the disgrace, and of "gettin' read out in chu'ch"—a terrible punishment in the old woman's eyes—and Susie gave in.

That sort of thing happens oftener than one would suppose, on Cane River where we plantation negroes know less of white folks' conventions than other negroes do. Here, you do what you want to do—and usually, that's the end of it. Babe had his dreams doubtless. This bad start—well, they would get past it and Susie would make him a good wife. And he would have her all to himself then—Susie, who turned the heads of all the nigger men, ugly old Susie, with her woolly hair, that she disdained to straighten with "ointment" as the other girls did, but which she wore standing on end, like a savage woman—Susie, with her skinny, mis-shapen body, and her big bare black feet, with charms dangling on dirty strings around her ankles. So they were married, the baby was born, and they lived in a new cabin that Mr. Guy built for them not far from Aunt Dicey's. For Babe was a favourite with Mr. Guy, who considered him the best field-hand that he had. Oh yes, Babe stood well with the white folks at Yucca Plantation, and they thought that Susie ought to thank her lucky stars that she had found a man who was willing to provide for her, who would buy her sleazy pink dresses, and plenty of cheap white lace to sew on them, or would let her buy red bandanna handkerchiefs to sew together into dresses, Cane River style.

Now Mr. Guy was not entirely pleased with Babe's marriage, because he liked Babe and considered him a fine boy. Even if he was slow in his work, his slowness was methodical; if Babe set out to do a thing he finished it. But Susie! Just one step from actual madness, with her monkey-motions and her apelike chatterings. The mentality of a child of five. And who would have guessed that quiet, stolid Babe would be taken in by one these trick-niggers! But the white man could never realize that the girl's very savagery was more provocative than the charms of those negresses who had taken on a veneer of civilization from the white folks. Just one bold side glance from Susie would send the black boys nudging and guffawing, as she swaggered barefoot down the dusty lane, a watermelon balanced on her head, singing as she went.

Mr. Guy's hard and fast code was: "Make your negroes work; make them respectful; try to treat them fair—but hands off in affairs among themselves, for these private things do not concern you." Mr. Guy felt that he did not understand his own race any too well, and there were things about negroes that were beyond him— although he had been born on a plantation, and there had been negroes around him all his life. The black folks liked Mr. Guy. He didn't "meddle them," as so many of the white planters did. That was the reason Mr. Guy never had labour troubles, and why there was never a vacant cabin on Yucca Plantation. And, as he always tried to play fair with them, he made no comment when Babe threw himself away on Susie. He told Babe that he could take that new cabin on the river bank, next door to Aunt Dicey's, near the lane that led to the church—a cabin built under a big Chinaberry tree, just across the river from the plantation store.

Babe and Susie got along fine for a while. The loiterers could hear her laughing in the evenings. For it was upon the store gallery that the black men gathered at night, loafing and "visitin'" together; the deserted building, tight-barred and dark, was their nightly meeting place; it was their club, their refuge from hot cabins full of squalling black children.

"Susie done quiet down," said Papa Chawlie, one night as they sat looking across the placid water to the light that glimmered in Babe's cabin.

"Babe's done bought him a 'cawdeen," commented a shapeless black shadow at his elbow.

An accordion, he meant. That was nice, too, because Susie could play upon the mouth-organ, and they heard her often, playing "blues" through the summer night. It was wrong, of course, because folks that belong to the church have no business playing the blues. It's ungodly. After you are baptized, you must give up your sinful ways, and play and sing hymn-tunes, or spirituals, or "ballots," or "jump-up" songs about folks in the Bible. Some of them are lively enough. There's that one beginning:

"Delilah wuz a woman, fine an' fair,
Pleasant-lookin' wid her coal-black hair . . ."

That was a grand one, with its surging refrain:

"Oh, if I wuz Sampson, I'd pull dat buildin' down!"

Law! But that Susie! No ballot-tunes and jump-up songs for her.

"I got a gal, so lean an' so tall,
Her big mouf flops open like a red parasol!"

Susie would shout shrilly, all thirty verses, some of them filthy, and Babe's accordion would accompany her, with its irresponsible whine. Sometimes, Babe would sing, too, tunes he had learned in lumber camps long ago:

"Oh, I got fifty dollars, an' I got it fo' to spen',
If the wimmin don' wan' it, gonna give it to de men!"

That was all of it, two lilting lines, ending in a wail. Susie liked that one and would join in with a wild shriek on the mouth-organ.

But the happiness was after all only transient, for Big Brown came back. He came slouching up to the store gallery one night, just as though he had never been away at all, and had never heard of Susie or the other girls.

"Who's dat singin' de blues, ovah de rivah?" he asked Papa Chawlie, and the old man answered: "Yo' know widdout my tellin' yo', Big Brown, dat's Susie singin'."

Brown said "Huh!" That was all, but the men on the gallery knew that his return meant unhappiness for Babe, and they were sorry, for they liked him.

And so it turned out, for Susie welcomed Big Brown with open arms. Not before Babe, of course, for Brown chose times when Babe was absent in the cotton fields; but he came to the cabin, and Aunt Dicey saw him go. She went down, herself, later, to remonstrate with Susie. But Susie just laughed and rolled her eyes. Oh, she was a bad one; no mistaking that.

It wasn't long before Babe knew, for gossip spreads rapidly.

Well, on Cane River the proper thing to do, if you can no longer ignore your wife's misdemeanors with another man, is to pick a quarrel with him on some pretext, beat him, or kill him, as you can, then the affair is settled. And pretexts are always easy to find. So Babe brushed against Big Brown, a little too roughly, one noon on the store gallery, and the fight ensued. But, of course, Big Brown had it all his own way. He beat Babe as one would beat a mad dog, and finally grabbed him by the shoulders and pounded his head against a roll of barbed wire that lay there by the cotton scales. Mr. Guy, hearing the scuffling, came out to see what it was all about, and he was so angry to see such brutality, that he picked up a club and gave Brown a crack over the head that would have killed a man whose skull was thinner.

But Brown bore Mr. Guy no grudge. Mr. Guy had his conventions, too, and both Babe and Brown knew that it was not the thing to fight on the store gallery. After a time, some men took Babe home in a rowboat, and Susie tied up his head with a white cloth, soaked in turpentine, the only antiseptic that was handy. Brown got his senses back, after a while, and staggered off to the cabin where he lived, down the lane that led to the gin.

The fight was over, and after that, when Babe and Brown passed in the road, they spoke as before:

"Howdy, Big Brown!"

"How 'bout yo', Babe?"

That was all. And not long after, Brown began slipping to Babe's cabin again, in the day-time, when Babe was plowing out in Mr. Guy's field. And Babe knew it, and, before long, Susie knew that Babe knew it.

But Susie didn't care. She was a bad one. Reckless, too, and laughing out in her sleep at night, like a crazy woman, until the sound waked Babe, and he would lie there in the moonlight that came in through the open door, and curse his weak body. . . . Oh, yes, Susie was a bad one, right enough, but Babe loved her. That was what hurt. For Babe knew that Big Brown didn't love her. He would lie awake until the moon set, and the grey mists hung low over the water; and he could hear the first roosters crowing, as they came fluttering down from the fig-trees by Aunt Dicey's cabin. Then, sleepless, he would rise, and wake Susie to make the coffee before he put on his overalls and hat, and went out to his day of plowing.

It was hard to find a way to get at Brown. For he wasn't employed on Yucca Plantation. He just lived there, as a good many others did. He was a trapper, that was why he went away into the hills and remained for days at a time. Sometimes, though, he made shorter trips, into the swamps a few miles back from the river bank. Bad places, those swamps, with their snakes and fevers; but Brown trapped 'possums and coons and skunks and even foxes there; and he sold the pelts. Sometimes he would be gone for a week, and would come back with a pile of hides that he sold to a man who came from New Orleans, once a month or so, to Mr. Guy's store. The man always paid in cash for the pelts, and so Brown had, nearly always, some money in hand—not commissary cheques, like the rest of us, to carry us over the periods of depression between the times when we sell our cotton, and, for a few weeks, have money to throw away with both hands.

Once Brown gave a string of beads to Susie, red beads unlike anything ever seen on Cane River before. The man who bought the pelts, brought them from New Orleans to Big Brown, in exchange for a particularly fine skin. And Susie flaunted those beads, although half a dozen negroes had seen Brown get them from the white man. Oh yes, Susie was a bad one. In spite of Aunt Dicey's prominence in the African Baptist Church, the members took a stand and had Susie "read out."

That is supreme disgrace—and on Cane River, it means that you are barred, not only from the church itself, but from all church activities and festivities—and these festivities of church folks are the only entertainments we have. But Susie just flounced, and said she didn't care. One Sunday, she sat on the gallery before her cabin, wearing the red beads, and with the baby on her knee—Big Brown's baby—and played on her mouth-organ. Played the blues, mind you, over and over, while people were passing on the way to church. Aunt Dicey shuddered, and thought of the red hell Susie was going to.

And Babe brooded. Day by day, he grew more morose, more silent. Finally, even Susie, old foolish Susie, noticed it.

"W-what yo' studyin' bout, Babe?" she asked him, once with something like fear in her voice.

"I'm studyin' bout Sunday," he answered. Only that. It might mean anything, but Susie asked no more. He had never asked her why she had stopped attending church, and why she had suddenly lost her old passion for shouting and singing hymns on Sunday morning.

It was just at this time that Big Brown ordered the bear trap from Mr. Guy—a brutal-looking steel trap, a trap so large that it came in a crate all by itself. For, back in the hills, miles away, where Big Brown rode, beyond the scarey woods that were full of malaria mosquitoes and bullfrogs and cottonmouthed moccasins, he had come across bear tracks. And a bearskin, nowadays, was not to be despised. There were cubs, too. Brown had seen their tracks in the soft mud by a spring. Yes, God only knows what lies in those remote hills beyond the swamp, where no one lives and few go, and where buzzards breed in caves on barren hillsides. "Carenco Roost" one hill is called—and from the Cane River valley, on clear days, you can see the buzzards circling high in the air, above its summit. But the buzzard hill seems as remote as the moon, although it is hardly more than ten miles away, through the swamp. On Cane River we do not wander too far away from the watercourse. The barren hills and swamps are not for us. We prefer to gather together in groups, where we can have our churches, and our social life, and where our work is waiting for us. No, the hills and swamps are not for plantation negroes, except of course for those bold and reckless spirits like Big Brown. It was along the dimly-marked trail to Carencro Roost that Brown toted the bear trap, slung over the back of a white pack mule he had borrowed from Papa Chawlie.

From the field, Babe saw him go, and bowed his head over the plow: "Git up, Mule!" he said to the beast that stood with drooping head in the simmering sun of August.

That night Babe asked Mr. Guy's permission to get Papa Chawlie to substitute for him in the field, while he went to town, twenty miles away.

"Business?" Mr. Guy smiled quizically, and almost asked a question, but, remembering the Cane River code, merely nodded assent. Better let him go now, and get it over with—whatever it was—for next month would be cotton-picking time, and Babe couldn't be spared then, as he was a valuable man at the gin. However, Mr. Guy did say that he hoped Babe wouldn't be gone long. The code permitted so much at least. Babe couldn't promise, exactly. It might be a week before he got back—he had important business to attend to.

Now everybody knew that Babe had no business in town, unless it was legal business—and that meant only one thing. So, in the evening speculation was rife, there on the store gallery; language was guarded, but the word "divo'ce" was bandied about. It was after nine o'clock, almost time to go, when Papa Chawlie said, suddenly:

"Fo' Gawd. Look at 'er, an' lissen at 'er!"

For Susie, brazen-faced Susie, was sitting on the gallery of her cabin, sitting there in plain view, with Big Brown lolling on the floor beside her; and she was playing for him upon the mouth-organ, playing the blues. Across the narrow river, the wailing strains came, whining with slow, suggestive undulation.

The watchers in the dark said no more than "ump!" or "Aie Yie!" those two expressions into which the negro can pack all human emotions, scorn, love, or mere lazy comment. After a time, they saw the two forms silhouetted in the cabin doorway, against the light of the smoky oil lamp. And presently, the light went out.

Then, the men on the store gallery yawned, and said goodnight to each other; and mounting their sleepy horses, rode slowly down the moonlit road, toward their cabins, dotted along the river bank. Yes, surely, Babe was justified in getting a divorce from that woman. She was just a low-down trick-nigger. No mistaking that.

But Babe was not, as they thought, riding toward town. As soon as he was out of sight of the store, he stopped the old calico pony and looked to the right and to the left. Then he turned the animal's head into the cotton rows, and kept on through the field. Nobody was plowing to-day, and there was no cabin from which the spying eyes of a woman could see him. Presently, he drew rein at the place where the cotton rows met the woodland. And again he looked about. Only the field, simmering in the sun, and the cool shadows of the moss-covered trees before him. He sighed. Then he clucked his tongue, and the thin pony began to go forward into the woods: "Git up, Hoss!" he said.

For hours he rode, the horse picking its way through the brush, avoiding depressions and fallen logs. By looking at the westering sun, Babe was able to make the wide circle he intended. At twilight, he had reached a point some eight miles back of his own cabin, and in the heart of the swamp. It was too late to go further, so he dismounted and unsaddled his horse, tying him with a rope so the animal could graze. From a sack tied to the saddle, Babe took a can of sausage, which he opened. He ate slowly. Then he lay down under a tree, watching the rising moon, and slapping at mosquitoes that whined over him—great black swamp mosquitoes, that settled on his face and hands like a veil and remained there until brushed off dead. Finally, he put his bandanna handkerchief over his face, slipped his hands into his pockets, and lay on his back, looking at the moon through the red cloth. At last he slept.

At the first streaks of dawn, he was on horseback again. This time he rode forward, into the swamp, looking carefully to right and left. Twice he changed his course. Finally, he found the trail for which he was looking—the tracks of two horses. This was the way that Big Brown had taken the afternoon before. Yes, surely, for further along, in a marshy place, Babe found both trails, one going into the hills, one returning. Babe rode carefully now, watching the ground intently, looking for something. It was nearly ten o'clock before he found the place where Brown had dismounted and left his horses.

Before him rose a steep hill, thickly wooded, and full of little ravines, depressions which had washed out in the tropical storms of bygones years, and which were now full of a dense undergrowth. Half an hour later, he found the trap, buried in leaves and soft earth, near the mouth of a cave in the hillside. It lay in a gully, a narrow place, approachable from only one side. The bait had been partially eaten by a 'possum or a skunk, or some other small animal, too light to spring the heavy trap.

Babe examined it carefully. Certainly, it was strong enough to break the leg of a horse-or man. He worked there for an hour before he succeeded in accomplishing his purpose; but, when he had finished, the trap was covered with a light layer of earth and rotting leaves, and was fully ten yards nearer the outer end of the gully, directly in the path.

Then he went back to his horse, tethered in the woods, and rode off. He hid the old pony in a thicket, a mile away—no use to be betrayed by the whinnying of an animal—and crept back on foot, to a point not far from the trail which he knew Big Brown would follow. There Babe waited, listening, and watching the sun which shone straight down.

Hours passed. The sun drew in and heavy clouds banked up in the south. Big raindrops came pattering down on the leaves. In the thicket, Babe smiled. All the better; no chance, now, for any one to see the tracks he had made. It seemed as though nature were working with him, for if this downpour had come yesterday, it would have been impossible for him to find the trap. He was wet through, as he sat there under the leaves. Toward twilight, the sky cleared and swarms of mosquitoes whined about him.

He began to wonder why Big Brown didn't come—and then, as his slow mind turned to possible reasons, he hung his head with shame. And the night closed around him. Sometimes he dozed; sometimes he sat motionless for hours, staring straight into the darkness; sometimes he swayed back and forth, as Aunt Dicey had done in the cabin. He slept a little, too, lightly, like an animal; waking at the slightest noise, only to stretch his body and doze again. By sun-up, he was alert, lying motionless in the wet brush, looking out through a tangle of wild grape-vines.

It was nearly nine o'clock, he reckoned by the sun, when Big Brown passed on horseback, singing as he rode, singing Babe's own song:

"Oh, I got forty dollars an' I got it fo' to spen',
If the wimmin don' wan' it, gonna give it to de men!"

Babe heard it die away, and, peering out, saw Brown get down from his horse, and tie the animal to a branch. Then the big fellow disappeared into the woods, going toward the ravine.

A minute later Babe heard a sharp snap, and a wild cry. After a time—a great while, it seemed—he heard calls for help. At first they were sharp and frantic, then slower; finally they ceased.

It was a long way back to his horse, but Babe reached him after nightfall. From the bundle tied to the saddle, he brought out another can of sausage, ate hungrily, and when he had finished, drank from a spring, like an animal, lying flat on the ground. He brought his horse to the water and saw him drink, then tethered him where there was green, tender grass. That night Babe slept.

Shortly after daylight he crawled back to the hilltop. Brown's horse, tied to a branch, was whinnying and pawing the ground.

Hum! He'd have to do something about that old white horse. Couldn't let it stay tied there. The poor thing would starve. Must be mighty thirsty right now, too. Another thing. Suppose someone should happen to come riding by and see that horse, and investigate.

Babe took the bridle from its head, and gave the beast a smart rap with a stick. He stood watching as the horse went blundering into the brush, stopping half a hundred yards away to grasp greedily at the dewy grass. Babe followed it for half a mile or more, driving it further and further into the woods. He threw clods of earth at it, and the horse began to run, jingling the iron rings fastened to the saddle.

That afternoon Babe dozed by the spring, near his calico pony as it munched the grass. It was pleasant by the spring. Little birds came down to drink, and if you lay quiet, they came quite close.

When he crept to the gully next morning, he saw long streams of red ants in the grass, going towards the trap.

The day was unbearably hot. Babe fanned himself with a bunch of dried grass, and dozed, and woke again to fight the mosquitoes and gnats. In the afternoon, he followed the stream that ran from the spring, until he reached a place where there was a bed of white sand. Here, he undressed and lay in the water that did not cover him. However, the sand was soft, and with a little labour, he was able to scoop out a depression big enough to fit his body; and he lay there for more than an hour, watching the leaves that drifted by in the slow-moving current: long green leaves, that were like little snakes; round red berries, like Susie's red beads.

That day was hot on Cane River, too. Mr. Guy had given notice that two full hours' rest be given the men and mules at midday, instead of one, as usual, and it was nearly three o'clock in the afternoon before the plantation bell rang for the hands to go back to the fields. Aunt Dicey, having come home in a flat-bottomed rowboat from the store, carrying a piece of salt meat in an old meal sack, turned in at the gate of Babe's cabin, deciding suddenly that she would stop and talk to Susie. Lately, she had given the girl a wide berth. But to-day, curiosity overcame distaste. She found Susie sitting listlessly beside the table, the baby in her lap. She looked—as the old woman said afterward—as though she were listening to some sound from a distance.

"What ails yo', Susie?" said Aunt Dicey, helping herself to a gourdful of water, from the pail on a shelf inside the door; "Is yo' worried becuz Babe ain't come back?"

The black girl shook her head, and the red beads clicked against a blue dish. The old woman bridled:

"It's scan'lous an' a shame," she said, "de way yo' wears dem beads, Susie. Gawd gonna strike yo' down. Yo' jus' watch!"

Instead of answering scornfully as usual, Susie raised one lanky arm and pointed to the China tree outside the door: "Look at dat leaf, Auntie!" she whispered tensely, "Oh my Gawd, jus' look at it!"

The day was airless, no breeze stirred, but in the China berry tree, one leaf was waving rapidly back and forth in the mounting heat-waves.

Aunt Dicey sniffed, as she saw Susie's shaking hands: "Ef yo's lookin' for sperrits, I speck yo' gwine to see sperrits," she said. But, sensing suddenly the realness of Susie's fear, she temporized: "Ah sho did heah a squinch owl in de tree, las' night. An' I heerd de dawg howl, too!"

Susie nodded. She looked long into the older woman's face, and then she said, in a hoarse whisper: "Auntie, sump'n done happen to 'im!"

"Babe's done gone to town to get a divo'ce f'um yo', dat's wat happen to 'im!" retorted Aunt Dicey. But Susie shook her head.

"Ah don' keer, ef he do . . . I don' keer!" . . . She gulped. "Auntie, sump'n done kotch Big Brown. All las' night, an' all de night befo', seems I heah 'im callin'. . . . He say: 'Susie . . . Oh, Susie!' ovah, an' ovah. It wuz like a dyin' man, Auntie. . . . It wuz like a dyin' man!"

Dicey rose. "So dat's whut's wurrying yo'!" she said.

"Fo' Gawd's sake, Susie! Don' yo' know whut dey's sayin' bout yo' at de sto'? Dey say, Big Brown done foun' out dat Babe's gone off to divo'ce yo', and he's lit out again. . . . Jus' like 'e done de fust time! Ha! Dat man don' wan' yo', Susie. He's jus' bewitch yo', dat's all!" And she moved toward the door. "Fo' Gawd's sake, don' go an' leave me, Aunt Dicey. . . ." Susie had taken the mouth-organ from the pocket of her apron, and was twisting it over and over in her fingers. But a voice from outside interrupted the words. Papa Chawlie was passing, and seeing Aunt Dicey emerging from the door of Susie's cabin, he hailed her:

"Hey, Dicey! Stump'n done happen to Big Brown! His ol' w'ite hoss is come home widdout 'im!" There was in his voice that joy which only evil tidings can evoke, "Yonder 'e is, grazin' in de lane by de gin. Good riddance to bad rubbish, ef yo' ax me!" And he shouted the last sentence, knowing that Susie would hear.

Suddenly, despite the stifling day, Aunt Dicey shivered, and turned back into the cabin. Susie was cowering against the chimney, the mouth-organ still clenched in her hand, her eyes rolling wildly. A hoarse scream broke from her lips, and she put her arms over her face, as though to ward off a nightmare.

"W-Whut yo' seein', Susie?" Aunt Dicey asked in a whisper, clutching the table's edge.

But the young black woman wheeled sharply about, and with the spring of an animal, was gone through the back door. Aunt Dicey could see her running, between the cotton rows, toward the swamp.

It stormed that night. Babe, crouched in a hollow tree, watched the blinding flashes of lightning, remembering how Susie feared it. Well, to-night, he would be back at Cane River, back with Susie, and master of his own cabin; in the morning that followed, he could return to his mules again, a peaceful man.

He dozed at intervals, despite the storm. Once, just at daylight he thought he heard screams in the woods, and lay listening, his hair tingling on his scalp, but heard no more; only the soughing of the wind, and the distant thunder.

By sunrise it was clear again; the rain had washed the air clean, and the sky was blue; the first rays of sunlight turned the dark tree-trunks to copper. Birds began calling in the thickets, and the soft moan of the wood-dove came with melancholy regularity, faint and sweet.

Shortly after the rising of the sun, Babe began his journey toward the gully. He went slowly, this morning, creeping along, keeping a sharp lookout, walking carefully in order to leave no trace. As he came near he saw a buzzard perched in a dead tree; and high in the air, another buzzard circling lower.

As his eyes descended from the tree to the path before him, he shivered and drew in his breath. For there was the print of a bare foot. Someone had walked with unerring step, directly to the trap, down into the gully.

Crouching in the bushes, he listened. Only the humming of insects came to him, and distant bird notes; the great song of the day was beginning as the sun rose. There was no other sound. Stillness, ominous silence. . . . Over in the gully, someone was lying in wait, spying upon him from behind the vines, for there were no returning footprints.

On hands and knees, Babe crouched, every nerve tense. Long minutes passed.

And then a thin, ghastly sound came to him—an incredible ripple, blown through reeds—music—a tuneless and discordant strain from a mouth-organ. It whined on the morning air, just one broken bar, then stopped.

A moment later, there was the rustling of leaves, and Susie appeared. She came staggering, slowly, her bare feet dragging.

She was quite close to him before she looked up, the mouth-organ against her lips, her woolly hair full of dew drops which glittered in the sunlight. She seemed incapable of controlling her eyes. He was not sure that she had seen him.

"Susie!" He moved toward her, his hand outstretched.

She started back, her eyes fixed upon him for a moment, an uncertain smile upon her face. Then, distressed and confused, she turned away from him.

"Come heah, Susie . . . I ain't gwine to hu't yo'. . . ."

He advanced upon her, cautiously, as one approaches a frightened dog:

"Susie . . . Susie . . . !" But she avoided him, running, floundering through the brush. Pursuing, he caught up with her in a little clearing, and came close.

"Susie, I ain't . . ." He grasped at her arm.

She jerked free and was off, under the trees, with a burst of loud, witless laughter. As soon as she had run a little way, she stopped and looked back at him, then raised the mouth-organ to her lips again; but as he came up, ran deeper into the woods.

In the clearing, Babe stood stupidly. From far off, an imperfect thread of melody was carried back to him—fainter and fainter— the same whimpering strain, over and over and over. . . .

Susie, "a wild nigger girl . . . with rolling eyes" is the center of interest in this local color story. The plot is simple. Susie, pregnant by Brown who deserts her, marries Babe Johnson, a steady hardworking man, but she continues her relationship with Big Brown on his sporadic returns. Babe, shamed by his wife's open infidelity, devises an ingenious scheme to save his marriage. The carefully prepared-for ending is ironic.

Point of view is crucial in analyzing this story since the white author adopts the persona of a black field hand to narrate the events. The narrator seems to have no character of his own distinct from that of the community, which has sharply defined standards of behavior. Relating the events in the vernacular of the plantation, he explains that because of their insular position, Cane River Plantation "negroes know less of white folks' conventions than other negroes do." He speaks of three levels of behavior, thus setting a norm for judging the aberrant Susie. Mr. Guy, who owns the plantation, follows a *laissez faire* policy regarding the plantation Negroes: he doesn't "meddle them;" his "'code" permits both beneficence and punishment but never intervention into their affairs. The Black community, aside from Susie and Brown, is homogeneous; they work hard, gather at the store at night to escape the tensions and heat of small cabins, attend the African Baptist Church, and believe "squinch owls" and howling dogs are death omens. Above all they are discreet in their marital infidelities to avoid being "read out of the church." Therefore they are scandalized by Susie's openness in her love affair.

Susie is a skinny ugly untamed savage who "is just one step from actual madness." Her primal sexuality lies in her ugliness, walk, and shrill screams of laughter which fill black men with unrest as she traipses the fields. Both Babe and Brown are enamored by her animal magnetism, but she loves only Brown, an ex-convict who is not the marrying kind. Their character traits are seen only in relation to Susie.

This is local color at its purest—an outside view imposed on the cultural peculiarities of a geographical enclave and its very special people—Cane River plantation Negroes. The action could not meaningfully take place in another setting.

Roark Bradford

(1896-1948)

Roark Bradford was born on August 21, 1896, on a cotton plantation in Tennessee, where during his formative years he was attracted to a plantation Negro minister's embellishment of biblical stories. In the early twenties, his career as a journalist took him to New Orleans, and except for a period of service during World War II he lived the rest of his life there, working on the New Orleans *Times-Picayune* and doing freelance writing. His interest in Negro storytelling came to fruition in Louisiana where his boyhood memories merged with adult experiences to produce accounts of Negro life in the South. Although his Negro characters are stereotypes and his tone somewhat patronizing, his feeling for Negroes was genuine. He was awarded an O. Henry Prize for "A Child of God" in 1927 and a Pulitzer Prize, jointly with Marc Connelly, in 1929 for the latter's stage adaptation of *Ole Man Adam and His Chillun* (1928) from which the story printed below is taken.

Green Pastures*

Roark Bradford

After old King Solonon died de kings got to comin' and goin' so
fast to hit made de Lawd dizzy tryin' to keep up wid who was de
king and who wa'n't de king. So he say, "Dis ain't gittin' nowheres.
Ef my people can't keep a king long enough for me to git acquainted
wid him, well, I'm gonter see what gonter happen."

So hit was a king over in de next town name Nebuchadnezzar
which yared de news, so he say, "Well, when de Lawd was sidin'
wid de Hebrew boys they was doin' some mighty struttin'. But now
wid de Lawd layin' back and watchin', I'll jest drap over and raise
me some sand." And so he did.

So ole King Nebuchadnezzar lined up his army and lit out.

"Halt, who comin' yar?" say de Hebrew sentry.

"Sad news is comin' yar," say King Nebuchadnezzar.

"Ain't yo' name King Nebuchadnezzar?" say de sentry.

"Dat's what dey calls me," he say. "What's yo' name?"

"Daniel," say de sentry.

"Well, Daniel," say Nebuchadnezzar, "I'm bringin' you some
sad news. I'm bringin' you de news which say I'm gonter raise me
some sand in dis town."

"You better let dis town alone," say Daniel. "When you raise a
ruckus in dis town you's raisin' a ruckus in de Lawd's town."

"I kotched de Lawd away f'm home, dis time," say
Nebuchadnezzar.

"You didn't kotch me away f'm home," say Daniel.

"Naw," say Nebuchadnezzar, "and I'm gonter use you. I'm
gonter feed my pet lines on you."

So de soldiers captured Daniel and de army marched into town
and raised a ruckus. They got drunk and they shot up de place. Den
when de sheriff tried to arrest 'em, dey locked de sheriff up in his
own jail and den burned de jail down wid him in hit. So they busted
out de window lights and they torn down de gyarden fences. So they
driv off de men and women and scared all de chillun.

"King Nebuchadnezzar," say Queen Nebuchadnezzar when he got back home, "did you spile dat town?"

"Did I spile hit?" say de king. "Queen Nebuchadnezzar, I didn't spile hit, I jest natchally ruint hit."

"Well, did you bring me somethin' back?" say de queen.

"I brang back some solid-gold drinkin' cups, and I brang back a few Hebrew boys to feed my lines on," he say.

"You's always bringin' back somethin' to drink out of, and somethin' to feed yo' lines on," say de queen, "but you ain't brang back nothin' to build me no fire wid. And yar poor me, settin' round de house queenin' all day long and 'bout to freeze to death."

"Well, queen," sayd de king. "I'm goodhearted. You kin have a few of my Hebrew boys to pitch on de fire."

So dey brought out a few of de Hebrew boys and pitch 'em on de fire. But when dey got to doin' de Hebrew boys like dat, de Lawd tuck a hand. "Jest go on and git pitched in de fire," say de Lawd, "'cause I ain't gonter let you git burnt." So when dey put de Hebrews in de fire hit jest sputtered a couple er times and went out.

"No wonder they won't burn," say King Nebuchadnezzar; "you ain't got no kindlin' in yar." So dey brang a armful of pine knots and toch off. And de pine knots burned and blazed and de Hebrew chillin jest sot round on de coals. "Bring my overcoat, King Nebuchadnezzar," say one of de Hebrew boys. "Hit's a draft in yar and I'm cold, and I don't want to git tuck down wid de phthisic."

"Well, dat whups me," say King Nebuchadnezzar. "I b'lieve I'll go on out and feed my lines. Bring dat boy Daniel out yar so I kin feed him to my lines."

So dey brang Daniel out, but Daniel wa'n't skeered. He been tawkin' wid de Lawd 'bout dem lines.

"Dem lines ain't hongry," say Daniel.

"Well, you kin stay among 'em to dey gits hongry," say de king.

"Well," say Daniel, "I wish you'd fix me up a bed and bring me some vittles, 'cause I'm gonter git mighty tired sleeping' on de ground wid nothin' but a line for my pillow to dem scound'els gits hongry enough to eat me."

"Dat's jest you and de lines about dat," say Nebuchadnezzar. "I'm goin' and put on my robes and wash my face and hands and git ready for de big doin's tonight."

So dat night ole King Nebuchadnezzar had a mighty feast. All de big folks and de quality folks in de town came, and hit kept de handmaidens busy dancin' and singin' and makin' music, and hit kept de handmen busy rollin' out de licker and knockin' out de bungs.

"When I invites y'all to come to a mighty feast," say Nebuchadnezzar, "do y'all have a mighty feast or don't you?"

"Yo' Majesty," say all de people, "we does."

"Well, den, is ev'ybody happy?" say Nebuchadnezzar.

"Don't we look happy?" say de people.

"Well, jest make yo' own fun," say Nebuchadnezzar. So some er de menfolks got to drinkin' de licker outer de bungholes, and some er de women got to passin' out and fallin' to sleep under de tables, and ev'ybody got to carryin' on scandalous.

"Whar all dem solid-gold cups which I tuck f'm de Hebrew boys?" say ole King Nebuchadnezzar.

"Put away," say de haid waiter.

"Well, bring 'em out so My Majesty kin drink some licker outer dem solid-gold drinkin'-cups," say ole King Nebuchadnezzar. And right dar was whar he made a big mistake, 'Cause dem cups wa'n't de Hebrew boys' cups. Dem was de Lawd's cups. So 'bout de time ole King Nebuchadnezzar drunk out of a solid-gold cup, de Lawd stepped right through de wall and wrote somethin' on hit, and den stepped right back again.

"I seen a ha'nt," say King Nebuchadnezzar.

"Hit's de licker," say de gal which is settin' in his lap. "Hit'll make you see mighty nigh anything." "Naw, hit ain't de licker," say Nebuchadnezzar. "Licker makes me see snakes. You can't fool me 'bout licker. I know when I sees snakes. I tell you I seen a ha'nt."

"Well," say de gal, "le's call him over and give him a drink."

"Ain't no time to git funny wid me now, gal," say Nebuchadnezzar. "I sees some writin' on de wall. Dat's what I sees."

"What do hit say?" say de gal.

"I didn't brought my glasses," say Nebuchadnezzar.

"I'm too drunk to read hit, too," say de gal. "Whyn't you call dat boy Daniel which is sleepin' wid de lines? He ain't drunk."

So dey sont for Daniel out in de lines' den.

"Read hit to me, Daniel," say Nebuchadnezzar, "and I'll give you de best job in my kingdom."

So Daniel look at de writin' and den he look at de king. "Ole King Nebuchadnezzar," he say, "you can't give me no job in yo' kingdom, 'cause f'm what I reads yonder on de wall, you ain't got no kingdom no more."

"Is dat a fack?" say Nebuchadnezzar. "What do hit say?"

"It's de Lawd's own handwritin'," say Daniel.

"Lawd writin' me a letter, is he?" say Nebuchadnezzar. "What he writin' to me, Daniel?"

"'Dear King Nebuchadnezzar', hit say," say Daniel, "'Heavy, heavy hangs over yo' haid. Yours truly, Lawd.'"

"Sounds like he's writin' me a riddle instid of a letter," say de king. "Well, riddle or letter," say Daniel, "dat's what hit say. And hit means dat de Lawd is done got tired er yo' foolishness and is done quit playin' wid you. Hit means dat befo' sunup you ain't gonter be no king no more. Dat is what hit means."

"So de Lawd don't like my style er bein' king?" say Nebuchadnezzar. "Well, I be doggone!" "De Lawd don't like yo' style and he ain't gonter try to change hit," say Daniel.

"What he gonter do?" say Nebuchadnezzar.

"He gonter change kings," say Daniel.

"Well," say Nebuchadnezzar, "bein' king ain't much fun, anyway. Ya'll boys and gals go right on wid de party as long as de licker holds out. I b'lieve I'm gonter go out and eat me a little grass."

GREEN PASTURES

Although by today's standards, this humorous depiction of Blacks is not politically correct and might be offensive to some, it was not meant to be. Bradford was genuinely interested in Negro storytelling—he considered it an art—and far from being a racial slur, the story was intended to show that Blacks possess a unique ability in storytelling. He had heard such tales told by Blacks.

The simplistic little tale needs no critical commentary.

'Tite Poulette

George Washington Cable

Kristian Koppig was a rosy-faced, beardless young Dutchman. He was one of that army of gentlemen who, after the purchase of Louisiana, swarmed from all parts of the cornmercial world, over the mountains of Franco-Spanish exclusiveness, like the Goths over the Pyrenees, and settled down in New Orleans to pick up their fortunes, with the diligence of hungry pigeons. He may have been a German; the distinction was too fine for Creole haste and disrelish.

He made his home in a room with one dormer window looking out, and somewhat down, upon a building opposite, which still stands, flush with the street, a century old. Its big, round-arched windows in a long, second-story row, are walled up, and two or three from time to tirne have had smaller windows let into them again, with odd little latticed peep-holes in their batten shutters. This had already been done when Kristian Koppig first began to look at them from his solitary dormer window.

All the features of the building lead me to guess that it is a remnant of the old Spanish Barracks, whose extensive structure fell by government sale into private hands a long time ago. At the end toward the swamp a great, oriental-looking passage is left, with an arched entrance, and a pair of ponderous wooden doors. You look at it, and almost see Count O'Reilly's artillery come bumping and trundling out, and dash around into the ancient Plaza to bang away at King St. Charles's birthday.

I do not know who lives there now. You might stand about on the opposite *banquette* for weeks and never find out. I suppose it is a residence, for it does not look like one. That is the rule in that region.

In the good old times of duels, and bagatelle-clubs, and theatre-balls, and Cayetano's circus, Kristian Koppig rooming as described, there lived in the portion of this house, partly overhanging the archway, a palish handsome woman, by the name—or going by the name—of Madame John. You would hardly have thought of her being "colored." Though fading, she was still of very attractive countenance, fine, rather severe features, nearly straight hair carefully kept, and that vivid black eye so peculiar to her kind.

249

Her smile, which came and went with her talk, was sweet and exceedingly intelligent; and something told you, as you looked at her, that she was one who had had to learn a great deal in this troublesome life.

"But!"—the Creole lads in the street would say—her daughter!" and there would be lifting of arms, wringing of fingers, rolling of eyes, rounding of mouths, gaspings and clasping of hands. "So beautiful, beautiful, beautiful! White?—white like a water lily! White—like a magnolia!"

Applause would follow, and invocation of all the saints to witness.

And she could sing. "Sing?" (disdainfully)—"if a moching-bird can *sing!* Ha!"

They could not tell just how old she was; they "would give her about seventeen."

Mother and daughter were very fond. The neighbors could hear them call each other pet names, and see them sitting together, sewing, talking happily to each other in the unceasing French way, and see them go out and come in together on their little tasks and errands. "'Tite Poulette," the daughter was called; she never went out alone.

And who was this Madame John?

"Why, you know!—she was"—said the wigmaker at the corner to Kristian Koppig—"I'll tell you. You know?—she was"—and the rest atomized off in a rasping whisper. She was the best yellow-fever nurse in a thousand yards round; but that is not what the wig-maker said.

A block nearer the river stands a house altogether different from the remnant of old barracks. It is of frame, with a deep front gallery over which the roof extends. It has become a den of Italians, who sell fuel by daylight, and by night are up to no telling what extent of deviltry. This was once the home of a gay gentleman, whose first name happened to be lohn. He was a member of the Good Children Social Club. As his parents lived with him, his wife would, according to custom, have been called Madame John; but he had no wife. His father died, then his mother; last of all, himself. As he is about to be off, in comes Madame John, with 'Tite Poulette, then an infant, on her arm.

"Zalli," said he, "I am going."

She bowed her head, and wept.

"You have been very faithful to me, Zalli."

She wept on.

"Nobody to take care of you now, Zalli."

Zalli only went on weeping.

"I want to give you this house, Zalli; it is for you and the little one."

An hour after, amid the sobs of Madame John, she and the "little one" inherited the house, such as it was. With the fatal caution which characterizes ignorance, she sold the property and placed the proceeds in a bank, which made haste to fail. She put on widow's weeds, and wore them still when 'Tite Poulette "had seventeen," as the frantic lads would say.

How they did chatter over her. Quiet Kristian Koppig had never seen the like. He wrote to his mother, and told her so. A pretty fellow at the corner would suddenly double himself up with beckoning to a knot of chums; these would hasten up; recruits would come in from two or three other directions; as they reached the corner their countenances would quickly assume a genteel severity, and presently, with her mother, 'Tite Poulette would pass—tall, straight, lithe, her great black eyes made tender by their sweeping lashes, the faintest tint of color in her Southern cheek, her form all grace, her carriage a wonder of simple dignity.

(The instant she was gone every tongue was let slip on the marvel of her beauty); but, though theirs were only the loose New Orleans morals of over fifty years ago, their unleashed tongues never had attempted any greater liberty than to take up the pet name, 'Tite Poulette. And yet the mother was soon to be, as we shall discover, a paid dancer at the *Salle de Condé*.

To Zalli, of course, as to all "quadroon ladies," the festivities of the Condestreet ball-room were familiar of old. There, in the happy days when dear Monsieur John was young, and the eighteenth century old, she had often repaired under guard of her mother—dead now, alas!—and Monsieur John would slip away from the dull play and dry society of Théâtre d'Orléans, and come around with his crowd of elegant friends; and through the long sweet hours of the ball she had danced, and laughed, and coquetted under her satin mask, even to the baffling and tormenting of that prince of gentlemen, dear Monsieur John himself. No man of questionable blood dare set his foot within the door. Many noble gentlemen were pleased to dance with her. Colonel De—and General La—: city councilmen and officers from the Government House. There were no paid dancers then. Every thing was decorously conducted indeed! Every girl's mother was there, and the more discreet always left before there was too much drinking. Yes, it was gay, gay!—but sometimes dangerous. Ha! more times than a few had Monsieur John knocked down some long-haired and long-knifed rowdy, and kicked the breath out of him for looking saucily at her; but that was like him, he was so brave and kind,—and he is gone!

There was no room for widow's weeds there. So when she put these on, her glittering eyes never again looked through her pink and white mask, and she was glad of it; for never, never in her life had they so looked for anybody but her dear Monsieur John, and now he was in heaven—so the priest said—and she was a sick-nurse.

Living was hard work; and, as Madame John had been brought up tenderly, and had done what she could to rear her daughter in the same mistaken way, with, of course, no more education than the ladies in society got, they knew nothing beyond a little music and embroidery. They struggled as they could, faintly; now giving a few private dancing lessons, now dressing hair, but ever beat back by the steady detestation of their imperious patronesses; and, by and by, for want of that priceless worldly grace known among the flippant as "money-sense," these two poor children, born of misfortune and the complacent badness of the times, began to be in want.

Kristian Koppig noticed from his dormer window one day a man standing at the big archway opposite, and clanking the brass knocker on the wicket that was in one of the doors. He was a smooth man, with his hair parted in the middle, and his cigarette poised on a tiny gold holder. He waited a moment, politely cursed the dust, knocked again, threw his slender sword-cane under his arm, and wiped the inside of his hat with his handkerchief.

Madame John held a parley with him at the wicket. 'Tite Poulette was nowhere seen. He stood at the gate while Madame John went up-stairs. Kristian Koppig knew him. He knew him as one knows a snake. He was the manager of the *Salle de Condé*.

Presently Madame John returned with a little bundle, and they hurried off together.

And now what did this mean? Why, by any one of ordinary acuteness the matter was easily understood, but, to tell the truth, Kristian Koppig was a trifle dull, and got the idea at once that some damage was being planned against 'Tite Poulette. It made the gentle Dutchman miserable not to be minding his own business, and yet—

"But the woman certainly will not attempt"—said he to himself—"no, no! she cannot." Not being able to guess what he meant, I cannot say whether she could or not. I know that next day Kristian Koppig, glancing eagerly over the "Ami *des Lois*," read an advertisement which he had always before skipped with a frown. It was headed, "*Salle de Condé*," and, being interpreted, signified that a new dance was to be introduced, the *Danse de Chinois*, and that a *young lady* would follow it with the famous "*Danse du Shawl.*"

It was the Sabbath. The young man watched the opposite window steadily and painfully from early in the afternoon until the moon shone bright; and from the time the moon shone bright until Madame John!—joy!—Madame John! and not 'Tite Poulette, stepped through the wicket, much dressed and well muffled, and hurried off toward the *Rue Condé*. Madame John was the "young lady;" and the young man's mind, glad to return to its own unimpassioned affairs, relapsed into quietude.

Madame John danced beautifully. It had to be done. It brought some pay, and pay was bread; and every Sunday evening, with a touch here and there of paint and powder, the mother danced the dance of the shawl, the daughter remaining at home alone.

Kristian Koppig, simple, slow-thinking young Dutchman, never noticing that he staid at home with his window darkened for the very purpose, would see her come to her window and look out with a little wild, alarmed look in her magnificent eyes, and go and come again, and again, until the mother, like a storm-driven bird, came panting home.

Two or three months went by.

One night, on the mother's return, Kristian Koppig coming to his room nearly at the same moment, there was much earnest conversation, which he could see, but not hear.

"'Tite Poulette," said Madame John, "you are seventeen."

"True, Maman."

"Ah! my child, I see not how you are to meet the future." The voice trembled plaintively.

"But how, Maman?"

"Ah! you are not like others; no fortune, no pleasure, no friend."

"Maman!"

"No, no,—I thank God for it; I am glad you are not; but you will be lonely, lonely, all your poor life long. There is no place in this world for us poor women. I wish that we were either white or black!"—and the tears, two "shining ones," stood in the poor quadroon's eyes.

The daughter stood up, her eyes flashing.

"God made us, Maman," she said with a gentle, but stately smile.

"Ha!" said the mother, her keen glance darting through her tears, "Sin made *me*, yes."

"No," said 'Tite Poulette, "God made us. He made us just as we are; not more white, not more black."

"He made you, truly!" said Zalli. "You are so beautiful; I believe it well." She reached and drew the fair form to a kneeling posture. "My sweet, white daughter!"

Now the tears were in the girl's eyes."And could I be whiter than I am?" she asked. "Oh, no, no! 'Tite Poulette," cried the other; "but if we were only *real* whites!—both of us; so that some gentleman might come to see me and say 'Madame John, I want your pretty little chick. She is so beautiful. I want to take her home. She is so good—I want her to be my wife.' Oh, my child, my child, to see that I would give my life—I would give my soul! Only you should take me along to be your servant. I walked behind two young men to-night; they were coming home from their office; presently they began to talk about you."

'Tite Poulette's eyes flashed fire.

"No, my child, they spoke only the best things. One laughed a little at times and kept saying 'Beware!' but the other—I prayed the Virgin to bless him, he spoke such kind and noble words. Such gentle pity; such a holy heart! 'May God defend her,' he said, *cherie*; he said, 'May God defend her, for I see no help for her.' The other one laughed and left him. He stopped in the door right across the street. Ah, my child, do you blush? Is that something to bring the rose to your cheek? Many fine gentlemen at the ball ask me often, 'How is your daughter, Madame John?'"

The daughter's face was thrown into the mother's lap, not so well satisfied, now with God's handiwork. Ah, how she wept! Sob, sob, sob; gasps and sighs and stifled ejaculations, her small right hand clinched and beating on her mother's knee; and the mother weeping over her.

Kristian Koppig shut his window. Nothing but a generous heart and a Dutchman's phlegm could have done so at that moment. And even thou, Kristian Koppig!—for the window closed very slowly.

He wrote to his mother, thus:

"In this wicked city, I see none so fair as the poor girl who lives opposite me, and who, alas! though so fair, is one of those whom the taint of caste has cursed. She lives a lonely, innocent life in the midst of corruption, like the lilies I find here in the marshes, and I have great pity for her. 'God defend her,' I said to-night to a fellow clerk, 'I see no help for her.' I know there is a natural, and I think proper, horror of mixed blood (excuse the mention, sweet mother), and I feel it, too; and yet if she were in Holland today, not one of a hundred suitors would detect the hidden blemish."

In such strain this young man wrote on trying to demonstrate the utter impossibility of his ever loving the lovable unfortunate, until the midnight tolling of the cathedral clock sent him to bed.

About the same hour Zalli and 'Tite Poulette were kissing good-night.

"'Tite Poulette, I want you to promise me one thing."

"Well, Maman?"

"If any gentleman should ever love you and ask you to marry,—not knowing, you know,—promise me you will not tell him you are not white."

"It can never be," said 'Tite Poulette. "But if it should," said Madame John pleadingly. "And break the law?" asked 'Tite Poulette, impatiently.

"But the law is unjust," said the mother.

"But it is the law!" "But you will not, dearie, will you?"

"I would surely tell him!" said the daughter. When Zalli, for some cause, went next morning to the window, she started.

"'Tite Poulette!"—she called softly without moving. The daughter came. The young man, whose idea of propriety had actuated him to this display, was sitting in the dormer window, reading. Mother and daughter bent a steady gaze at each other. It meant in French, "If he saw us last night!"—

"Ah! dear," said the mother, her face beaming with fun—

"What can it be, Maman?" "He speaks—oh! ha, ha!—he speaks—such miserable French!"

It came to pass one morning at early dawn that Zalli and 'Tite Poulette, going to mass, passed a cafe, just as—who should be coming out but Monsieur, the manager of the *Salle de Condé.* He had not yet gone to bed. Monsieur was astonished. He had a Frenchman's eye for the beautiful, and certainly there the beautiful was. He had heard of Madame John's daughter, and had hoped once to see her, but did not; but could this be she?

They disappeared within the cathedral. A sudden pang of piety moved him; he followed. Tite Poulette was already kneeling in the aisle. Zalli, still in the vestibule, was just taking her hand from the font of holy-water.

"Madame John," whispered the manager.

She courtesied. "Madame John, that young lady—is she your daughter?"

"She—she—is my daughter," said Zalli, with somewhat of alarm in her face, which the manager misinterpreted.

"I think not, Madame John." He shook his head, smiling as one too wise to be fooled.

"Yes, Monsieur, she is my daughter."

"O no, Madame John, it is only make-believe, I think."

"I swear she is, Monsieur de la Rue."

"Is that possible?" pretending to waver, but convinced in his heart of hearts, by Zalli's alarm, that she was lying. "But how? Why does she not come to our ball-room with you?"

Zalli, trying to get away from him, shrugged and smiled. "Each to his taste, Monsieur; it pleases her not."

She was escaping, but he followed one step more.

"I shall come to see you, Madame John."

She whirled and attacked him with her eyes. "Monsieur must not give himself the trouble!" she said, the eyes at the same time adding, "Dare to come!" She turned again, and knelt to her devotions. The manager dipped in the font, crossed himself, and departed.

Several weeks went by, and M. de la Rue had not accepted the fierce challenge of Madame John's eyes. One or two Sunday nights she had succeeded in avoiding him, though fulfilling her engagement in the Salle; but by and by pay-day,—a Saturday,— came round, and though the pay was ready, she was loath to go up to Monsieur's little office.

It was an afternoon in May. Madame John came to her own room, and, with a sigh, sank into a chair. Her eyes were wet.

"Did you go to his office, dear mother?" asked 'Tite Poulette.

"I could not," she answered, dropping her face in her hands.

"Maman, he has seen me at the window!"

"While I was gone?" cried the mother.

"He passed on the other side of the street. He looked up purposely, and saw me." The speaker's cheeks were burning red.

Zalli wrung her hands.

"It is nothing, mother; do not go near him."

"But the pay, my child."

"The pay matters not."

"But he will bring it here; he wants the chance."

That was the trouble, sure enough.

About this time Kristian Koppig lost his position in the German importing house where, he had fondly told his mother, he was indispensable.

"Summer was coming on," the senior said, "and you see our young men are almost idle. Yes, our engagement *was* for a year, but ah— we could not foresee"—etc., etc., "besides" (attempting a parting flattery), "your father is a rich gentleman, and you can afford to take the summer easy. If we can ever be of any service to you," etc., etc.

So the young Dutchman spent the afternoons at his dormer window reading and glancing down at the little casement opposite, where a small, rude shelf had lately been put out, holding a row of cigar-boxes with wretched little botanical specimens in them trying to die. 'Tite Poulette was their gardener; and it was odd to see,—dry weather or wet,—how many waterings per day those plants could take. She never looked up from her task; but I know she performed it with that unacknowledged pleasure which all girls love and deny, that of being looked upon by noble eyes.

On this peculiar Saturday afternoon in May, Kristian Koppig had been witness of the distressful scene over the way. It occurred to 'Tite Poulette that such might be the case, and she stepped to the casement to shut it. As she did so, the marvellous delicacy of Kristian Koppig moved him to draw in one of his shutters. Both young heads came out at one moment, while at the same instant—

"Rap, rap, rap, rap, rap!" clanked the knocker on the wicket. The black eyes of the maiden and the blue over the way, from looking into each other for the first time in life, glanced down to the arched doorway upon Monsieur the manager. Then the black eyes disappeared within, and Kristian Koppig thought again, and re-opening his shutter, stood up at the window prepared to become a bold spectator of what might follow.

But for a moment nothing followed.

"Trouble over there," thought the rosy Dutchman, and waited. The manager waited too, rubbing his hat and brushing his clothes with the tips of his kidded fingers.

"They do not wish to see him," slowly concluded the spectator.

"Rap, rap, rap, rap, rap!" quoth the knocker, and M. de la Rue looked up around at the windows opposite and noticed the handsome young Dutchman looking at him.

"Dutch!" said the manager softly, between his teeth.

"He is staring at me," said Kristian Koppig to himself;—"but then I am staring at him, which accounts for it."

A long pause, and then another long rapping. "They want him to go away," thought Koppig.

"Knock hard!" suggested a street youngster, standing by.

"Rap, rap"— The manager had no sooner recommenced than several neighbors looked out of doors and windows.

"Very bad," thought our Dutchman; "somebody should make him go off. I wonder what they will do."

The manager stepped into the street, looked up at the closed window, returned to the knocker, and stood wlth it in his hand.

"They are all gone out, Monsieur," said the street-youngster.

"You lie!" said the cynosure of neighboring eyes.

"Ah!" thought Kristian Koppig; "I will go down and ask him"— Here his thoughts lost outline; he was only convinced that he had somewhat to say to him, and turned to go down stairs. In going he became a little vexed with himself because he could not help hurrying. He noticed, too, that his arms holding the stair-rail trembled in a silly way, whereas he was prefectly calm. Precisely as he reached the street-door the manager raised the knocker; but the latch clicked and the wicket was drawn slightly ajar.

Inside could just be descried Madame John. The manager bowed, smiled, talked, talked, talked on, held money in his hand, bowed, smiled, talked on, flourished the money, smiled, bowed, talked on and plainly persisted in some intention to which Madame John was steadfastly opposed.

The window above, too,—it was Kristian Koppig who noticed that,—opened a wee bit, like the shell of a terrapin. Presently the manager lifted his foot and put forward an arm, as though he would enter the gate by pushing, but as quick as gunpowder it clapped—in his face!

You could hear the fleeing feet of Zalli pounding up the staircase.

As the panting mother re-entered her room, "See Maman," said 'Tite Poulette, peeping at the window, "the young gentleman from the way has crossed!"

"Holy Mary bless him!" said the mother.

"I will go over," thought Kristian Koppig, "and ask him kindly if he is not making a mistake."

"What are they doing, dear?" asked the mother, with clasped hands.

"They are talking; the young man is tranquil, but 'Sieur de la Rue is very angry," whispered the daughter; and just then—pang! came a sharp, keen sound rattling up the walls on either side of the narrow way, and "Aha!" and laughter and clapping of female hands from two or three windows.

"Oh! what a slap!" cried the girl, half in fright, half in glee, jerking herself back from the casement simultaneously with the report. But the "ahas" and laughter, and clapping of feminine hands, which still continued, came from another cause. 'Tite Poulette's rapid action had struck the slender cord that held up an end of her hanging garden, and the whole rank of cigar-boxes slid from their place, turned gracefully over as they shot through the air, and emptied themselves plump upon the head of the slapped manager. Breathless, dirty, pale as whitewash, he gasped a threat to be heard from again, and, getting round the corner as quick as he could walk, left Kristian Koppig, standing motionless, the most astonished man in that street.

"Kristian Koppig, Kristian Koppig," said Greatheart to himself, slowly dragging up-stairs, "what a mischief you have done. One poor woman certainly to be robbed of her bitter wages, and another—so lovely!—put to the burning shame of being the subject of a street brawl! What will this silly neighborhood say? 'Has the gentleman a heart as well as a hand?' 'Is it jealousy?'" There he paused, afraid himself to answer the supposed query; and then—"Oh! Kristian Koppig, you have been such a dunce!" "And I cannot apologize to them. Who in this street would carry my note, and not wink and grin over it with low surmises? I cannot even make restitution. Money? They would not dare receive it. Oh! Kristian Koppig, why *did you not mind your own business?* Is she any thing to you? Do you love her? *Of course not!* Oh!—such a dunce!"

The reader will eagerly admit that however faulty this young man's course of reasoning, his conclusion was correct. For mark what he did.

He went to his room which was already growing dark, shut his window, lighted his big Dutch lamp, and sat down to write. "Something *must* be done," said he aloud, taking up his pen; "I will be calm and cool; I will be distant and brief; but—I shall have to be kind or I may offend. Ah! I shall have to write in French; I forgot that; I write it so poorly, dunce that I am, when all my brothers and sisters speak it so well." He got out his French dictionary.

Two hours slipped by. He made a new pen, washed and refilled his inkstand, mended his "abominable!" chair, and after two hours more made another attempt, and another failure. "My head aches," said he, and lay down on his couch, the better to frame his phrases.

He was awakened by the Sabbath sunlight. The bells of the Cathedral and the Ursulines' chapel were ringing for high mass, and a mocking-bird, perching on a chimney-top above Madame John's rooms, was carolling, whistling, mewing, chirping, screaming, and trilling with the ecstasy of a whole May in his throat. "Oh! sleepy Kristian Koppig," was the young man's first thought, "—such a dunce!"

Madame John and daughter did not go to mass. The morning wore away, and their casement remained closed. "They are offended," said Kristian Koppig, leaving the house, and wandering up to the little Protestant affair known as Christ Church.

"No, possibly they are not," he said, returning and finding the shutters thrown back.

By a sad accident, which mortified him extremely, he happened to see, late in the afternoon,—hardly conscious that he was looking across the street, —that Madame John was—dressing. Could it be that she was going to the *Salle de Condé*? He rushed to his table, and began to write.

He had guessed aright. The wages were too precious to be lost. The manager had written her a note. He begged to assure her that he was a gentleman of the clearest cut. If he had made a mistake the previous afternoon, he was glad no unfortunate result had followed except his having been assaulted by a ruffian; that the *Danse du Shawl* was promised in his advertisement, and he hoped Madame John (whose wages were in hand waiting for her) would not fail to assist as usual. Lastly, and delicately put, he expressed his conviction that Mademoiselle was wise and discreet in declining to entertain gentleman at her home.

So, against much beseeching on the part of 'Tite Poulette, Madame John was going to the ball-room. "Maybe I can discover what 'Sieur de la Rue is planning against Monsieur over the way," she said, knowing certainly the slap would not be forgiven; and the daughter, though tremblingly, at once withdrew her objections.

The heavy young Dutchman, now thoroughly electrified, was writing like mad. He wrote and tore up, wrote and tore up, lighted his lamp, started again, and at last signed his name. A letter by a Dutchman in French!—what can be made of it in English? We will see:

MADAME AND MADEMOISELLE:

A stranger, seeking not to be acguainted, but seeing and admiring all days the goodness and high honor, begs to be pardoned of them for the mistakes, alas! of yesterday, and to make reparation and satisfaction in destroying the ornaments of the window, as well as the loss of compensation from Monsieur the manager, with the enclosed bill of the *Banque de la Louisiane* for fifty dollars ($50). And, hoping they will seeing what he is meaning, remains, respectfully, Kristian Koppig. P.S.—Madame must not go to the ball.

He must bear the missive himself. He must speak in French. What should the words be? A moment of study—he has it, and is off down the long threestory stairway. At the same moment Madame John stepped from the wicket, and glided off to the *Salle de Condé*, a trifle late.

"I shall see Madame John, of course," thought the young man, crushing a hope, and rattled the knocker. 'Tite Poulette sprang up from praying for her mother's safety. "What has she forgotten?" she asked herself, and hastened down. The wicket opened. The two innocents were stunned.

"Aw—aw"—said the pretty Dutchman, "aw,"—blurted out something in virgin Dutch, . . . handed her the letter, and hurried down street.

"Alas! what have I done?" said the poor girl, bending over her candle, and bursting into tears that fell on the unopened letter. "And what shall I do? It may be wrong to open it—and worse not to." Like her sex, she took the benefit of the doubt, and intensified her perplexity and misery by reading and misconstruing the all but unintelligible contents. What then? Not only sobs and sighs, but moaning and beating of little fits together, and outcries of soul-felt agony stifled against the bedside, and temples pressed into knitted palms, because of one who "sought *not to be* acquainted," but offered money—money!—in pity to a poor—shame on her for saying that!—a poor *nigresse*.

And now our self-confessed dolt turned back from a half-hour's walk, concluding there might be an answer to his note. "Surely Madame John will appear this time." He knocked. The shutter stirred above, and something white came fluttering wildly down like a shot dove. It was his own letter containing the fifty-dollar bill. He bounded to the wicket, and softly but eagerly knocked again.

"Go away," said a trembling voice from above.

"Madame John?" said he; but the window closed, and heard a step, the same step on the stair. Step, step, every step one step deeper into his heart. 'Tite Poulette came to the closed door.

"What will you?" said the voice within.

"I—I—don't wish to see you. I wish to see Madame John."

"I must pray Monsieur to go away. My mother is at the *Salle de Condé*."

"At the ball!" Kristian Koppig strayed off, repeating the words for want of definite thought. All at once it occurred to him that at the ball he could make Madame John's acquaintance with impunity. "Was it courting sin to go?" By no means; he should most likely, save a woman from trouble, and help the poor in their distress.

Behold Kristian Koppig standing on the floor of the *Salle de Condé*. A large hall, a blaze of lamps, a bewildering flutter of fans and floating robes, strains of music, columns of gay promenaders, a long row of turbaned mothers lining either wall, gentlemen of the portlier sort filling the recesses of the windows, whirling waltzers gliding here and there—smiles and grace, smiles and grace; all fair, orderly, elegant, bewitching. A young Creole's laugh mayhap a little loud, and—truly there were many sword-canes. But neither grace nor foulness satisfied the eye of the zealous young Dutchman.

Suddenly a muffled woman passed him, leaning on a gentleman's arm. It looked like—it must be, Madame John. Speak quick, Kristian Koppig; do not stop to notice the man!

"Madame John"—bowing—"I am your neighbor, Kristian Koppig."

Madame John bows low, and smiles—a ball-room smile, but is frightened, and her escort,—the manager,—drops her hand and slips away.

"Ah! Monsieur," she whispers excitedly, "you will be killed if you stay here a moment. Are you armed? No. Take this." She tried to slip a dirk into his hands, but he would not have it.

"Oh, my dear young man, go! Go quickly!" she plead, glancing furtively down the hall.

"I wish you not to dance," said the young man.

"I have danced already; I am going home. Come; be quick! we will go together." She thrust her arm through his, and they hastened into the street. When a square had been passed there came a sound of men running behind them. "Run, Monsieur, run!" she cried, trying to drag him; but Monsieur Dutchman would not.

"*Run*, Monsieur! Oh, my God! it is 'Sieur"—

"*That* for yesterday!" cried the manager, striking fiercely with his cane. Kristian Koppig's fist rolled him in the dirt.

"*That* for 'Tite Poulette!" cried another man dealing the Dutchman a terrible blow from behind.

"And *that* for me!" hissed a third, thrusting at him with something bright.

"*That* for yesterday!" screamed the manager, bounding like a tiger; "That!" "That!" "Ha!"

Then Kristian Koppig knew that he was stabbed.

"That!" and "That!" and "That!" and the poor Dutchman struck wildly here and there, grasped the air, shut his eyes, staggered, reeled, fell, rose half up, fell again for good, and they were kicking him and jumping on him. All at once they scampered. Zalli had found the night-watch.

"Buz-z z-z!" went a rattle. "Buz-z-z-!" went another.

"Pick him up."

"Is he alive?"

"Can't tell; hold him steady; lead the way, misses."

"He's bleeding all over my breeches."

"This way—here—around this corner."

"This way now—only two squares more."

"Here we are."

"Rap-rap-rap!" on the old brass knocker. Curses on the narrow wicket, more on the dark archway, more still on the twisting stairs.

Up at last and into the room.

"Easy, easy, push this under his head! never mind his boots!" So he lies—on 'Tite Poulette's own bed.

The watch are gone. They pause under the corner lamp to count profits;—a single bill—*Banque de la Louisiane,* fifty dollars. Providence is kind—tolerably so. Break it at the "Guillaume Tell." "But did you ever hear any one scream like that girl did?"

And there lies the young Dutch neighbor. His money will not flutter back to him this time; nor will any voice behind a gate "beg Monsieur to go away." 0, Woman!—that knows no enemy so terrible as man! Come nigh, poor Woman, you have nothing to fear. Lay your strange, electric touch upon the chilly flesh; it strikes no eager mischief along the fainting veins. Look your sweet looks upon the grimy face, and tenderly lay back the locks from the congested brows; no wicked misinterpretation lurks to bite your kindness.

Be motherly, be sisterly, fear nought. Go, watch him by night; you may sleep at his feet and he will not stir Yet he lives, and shall live—may live to forget you, who knows? But for all that, be gentle and watchful; be womanlike, we ask no more; and God reward you!

Even while it was taking all the two women's strength to hold the door against Death, the sick man himself laid a grief upon them.

"Mother," he said to Madame John, quite a master of French in his delirium, "dear mother, fear not; trust your boy; fear nothing. I will not marry 'Tite Polette; I cannot. She is fair, dear mother, but ah! she is not—don't you know, mother? don't you know? The race! the race! Don't you know that she is jet black. Isn't it?"

The poor nurse nodded "Yes," and gave a sleeping draught; but before the patient quite slept he started once and stared.

"Take her away,"—waving his hand—"take your beauty away. She is jet white. Who could take a jet white wife? 0, no, no, no, no!"

Next morning his brain was right.

"Madame," he weakly whispered, "I was delirious last night?" Zalli shrugged. "Only a very, very, wee, wee, trifle of a bit." "And did I say something wrong or—foolish?"

"O, no, no," she replied; "you only clasped your hands, so, and prayed, prayed all the time to the dear Virgin."

"To the virgin?" asked the Dutchman, smiling incredulously.

"And St. Joseph—yes, indeed," she insisted; "you may strike me dead."

And so, for politeness' sake, he tried to credit the invention, but grew suspicious instead.

Hard was the battle against death. Nurses are sometimes amazons, and such were these. Through the long, enervating summer, the contest lasted; but when at last the cool airs of October came stealing in at the bedside like long-banished little children, Kristian Koppig rose upon his elbow and smiled them a welcome.

The physician, blessed man, was kind beyond measure; but said some inexplicable things, which Zalli tried in vain to make him speak in an undertone. "If I knew Monsieur John?" he said, "certainly! Why, we were chums at school. And he left you so much as that, Madame John? Ah! my old friend John, always noble! And you had it all in that naughty bank? Ah, well, Madame John, it matters little. No, I shall not tell 'Tite Poulette. Adieu."

And another time:—"If I will let you tell me something? With pleasure, Madame John. No, and not tell anybody, Madame John. No, Madame, not even 'Tite Poulette. What?"—a long whistle—"is that pos-si-ble?—and Monsieur John knew it?—encouraged it?—eh, well, eh, well!—But—can I believe you, Madame John? Oh! you have Monsieur John's sworn statement. Ah! very good, truly, but— you say you have it; but where is it? Ah! to-morrow!" a sceptical shrug. "Pardon me, Madame John, I think perhaps, *perhaps you* are telling the truth."

"If I think you did right? Certainly! What nature keeps back, accident sometimes gives, Madame John; either is God's will. Don't cry. 'Stealing from the dead?' No! It was giving, yes! They are thanking you in heaven, Madame John."

Kristian Koppig, lying awake, but motionless and with closed eyes, hears in part, and, fancying he understands, rejoices with silent intensity. When the doctor is gone he calls Zalli.

"I give you a great deal of trouble, eh, Madame John?"

"No, no; you are no trouble at all. Had you the yellow fever— Ah! then."

She rolled her eyes to signify the superlative character of the tribulations attending yellow fever.

"I had a lady and gentleman once—a Spanish lady and gentleman, just off the ship; both sick at once with the fever— delirious—could not tell their names. Nobody to help me but sometimes Monsieur John! I never had such a time,—never before, never since,—as that time. Four days and nights this head touched not a pillow."

"And they died!" said Kristian Koppig.

"The third night the gentleman went. Poor Señor! 'Sieur John,— he did not know the harm,—gave him some coffee and toast! The fourth night it rained and turned cool, and just before day the poor lady"—

"Died!" said Koppig.

Zalli dropped her arms listlessly into her lap and her eyes ran brimful.

"And left an infant!" said the Dutchman, ready to shout with exultation.

"Ah! no, Monsieur," said Zalli. The invalid's heart sank like a stone.

"Madame John,"—his voice was all in a tremor,—"tell me the truth. Is 'Tite Poulette your own child?"

"Ah-h-h, ha! ha! what foolishness! Of course she is my child!" And Madame gave vent to a true Frenchwoman's laugh.

It was too much for the sick man. In the pitiful weakness of his shattered nerves he turned his face into his pillow and wept like a child. Zalli passed into the next room to hide her emotion.

"Maman, dear Maman," said 'Tite Poulette, who had overheard nothing, but only saw the tears.

"Ah! my child, my child, my task—my task is too great—too great for me. Le me go now—another time. Go and watch at his bedside."

"But, Maman,'—for Tite Poulette was frightened,—"he needs no care now."

"Nay, but go, my child; I wish to be alone."

The maiden stole in with averted eyes and tiptoed to the window—that *window*. The patient, already a man again, gazed at her till she could feel the gaze. He turned his eyes from her a moment to gather resolution. And now, stout heart, farewell; a word or two of friendly parting—nothing more.

"'Tite Poulette."

The slender figure at the window turned and came to the bedside.

"I believe I owe my life to you," he said.

She looked down meekly, the color rising in her cheek.

"I must arrange to be moved across the street, tomorrow, on a litter."

She did not stir or speak.

"And I must now thank you, sweet nurse, for your care. Sweet nurse! Sweet nurse!"

She shook her head in protestation.

"Heaven bless you,'Tite Poulette!"

Her face sank lower.

"God had made you very beautiful, 'Tite Poulette!"

She stirred not. He reached, and gently took her little hand, and as he drew her one step nearer, a tear fell from her long lashes. From the next room, Zalli, with a face of agonized suspense, gazed upon the pair, undiscovered. The young man lifted the hand to lay it upon his lips, when, with a mild, firm force, it was drawn away, yet still rested in his own upon the bedside, like some weak thing snared, that could only not get free.

"Thou wilt not have my love, 'Tite Poulette?"

No answer. "Thou wilt not, beautiful?"

"Cannot!" was all that she could utter, and upon their clasped hands the tears ran down.

"Thou wrong'st me, 'Tite Poulette. Thou dost not trust me; thou fearest the kiss may loosen the hands. But I tell thee nay. I have struggled hard, even to this hour, against Love, but I yield me now; I yield; I am his unconditioned prisoner forever. God forbid that I ask aught but that you will be wife."

Still the maiden moved not, looked not up, only rained down tears.

"Shall it not be, 'Tite Poulette?" He tried in vain to draw her.

"'Tite Poulette?" So tenderly he called! And then she spoke. "It is against the law."

"It is not!" cried Zalli, seizing her round the waist and dragging her forward. "Take her! she is thine. I have robbed God long enough. Here are the sworn papers—here! Take her; she is as white as snow—so! Take her, kiss her; Mary be praised! I never had a child—she is the Spaniard's daughter!"

'TITE POULETTE

This story concerns the injustices suffered in Creole society by quadroons—descendants of wealthy Creole planters and their Black mistresses. As they are presented in the late 1700s, they are almost white, but according to law must be classified as Black.

At the center of the story are Madam John, a quadroon, and her beautiful daughter 'Tite Poulette who move against a backdrop of Creole conventions. Kristian Koppig, a naive Dutchman, observes the action and it is through his eyes that most of the story unfolds. There is little character development. Like many of Cable's characters, they are exaggerated to make a point. Madam John and 'Tite Poulette are all good and all innocence respectively; Koppig is a caricature of ineptness and dullness, and Monsieur de la Rue, spoken of as "the snake," is pure evil.

Through antecedent action, given in flashbacks, the reader learns that Madam John was a "quadroon lady" who attended balls at the Salle de Condé where Creole gentlemen came to choose their mistresses and where "no man of questionable blood dared to set foot." Such ballrooms were elegant, and the young quadroon daughters, escorted and guarded zealously by their mothers, would come lavishly dressed to laugh and dance and coquette the evening away. Duels were a common occurrence, for the tempers of the young Creole gentlemen ran high.

After the death of her lover, Madam John lived a secluded life with her daughter who had been born shortly before her gentleman's death, leaving her house only to earn a meagre livelihood by nursing yellow fever patients and performing other menial chores "under the steady detestation of imperious patronesses."

The conflict is Madam John's struggle to protect her daughter, whom she keeps secluded from the evil Creole manager of Salle de Condé who has the right to take any young quadroon he desires. She laments "There is no place in the world for us poor [quadroon] women; I wish we were either black or white" and tells Poulette "if any gentleman should ask to marry you, promise me you will not tell him you are not white. Poulette reminds her of the law against intermarriage. Meanwhile Koppig, having fallen in love with Poulette from observing her through his dormer window and

269

misunderstanding most of what he sees, clashes with the villain in an almost-fatal encounter.

After Cable has made his point about the injustices of this society, he rights it all for Poulette by revealing that she is white after all, the daughter of yellow fever patients who died while Madam John was nursing them. Koppig, who had grieved because he couldn't marry one with black blood, now rejoices that she can become his wife. The story is sentimental and often resorts to bathos in describing the pathetic situation of these mixed breeds, but like many of Cable's other works that expose social injustice, it tells a good story.

Ada Jack Carver

(1890-1972)

Born in Natchitoches on April 7, 1890, Ada Jack Carver lived there until shortly after World War I when she settled with her husband John Snell in Minden. Her fictional world is a recreation of the exotic Cane River area around Natchitoches, which is populated largely by mixed-breed descendants of Creoles and Negroes. Like many Romantic writers with a love for the idyllic, she focuses on the picturesqueness of both scenery and people, but ultimately the conflicts of these people rise above geographic region and ethnic group. Carver's output was small but impressive. She published in the most prestigious magazines of her day and won the most distinctive short story awards in America—Harper's Prize, O. Henry Memorial Award, and O'Brien's Roll of Honor. "The Old One," printed below, first appeared in *Harper's*, 1926, and is included in *The Collected Works of Ada Jack Carver*, ed. Mary Dell Fletcher, 1980.

The Old One

Ada Jack Carver

Up to the time old Nicolette's grandson married, life was sweet, serene on Isle Brevelle. The free-mulattoes of French descent owned their land and raised cotton and corn and sugar cane. They maintained a convent for their children and a priest who shrived their souls in the little white church on the river. All day long the pigeons cooed from the low-hanging eaves of the houses. All day long the white geese waddled by on the roadside. It was true of course that Nicolette and Balthazar, her grandson, had only a strip of river front left— "shoestring land" it was called. But they made a good living. Balthazar was industrious, a quiet, likely boy with no inclination to gad about and waste his time philandering. "Hee! Hee!" old Nicolette would cackle. "Balthazar, he love his old granny. He ain't got time for no gal."

Every morning Balthazar arose at five, an unearthly hour along Cane River, where life is lazy and time means nothing. All day he worked in the fields, planting and hoeing the cotton. And at night he was well content to sit on the gallery and listen to Nicolette talk. The things that she told him! All about how, one time long ago, she was a girl in New Orleans; all about the quadroon balls down on the *de Rue Royale;* all about the soirées and the carryings-on. "In them days folks they knew how to take pleasure." All about the War, and the dark years of Reconstruction, and the little white graves of her daughters in the Isle Brevelle churchyard—five of them, all of a size. Five little graves, with names like flowers: Alcise, Delicia, Helen, Ozele, Francelette. ... She told Balthazar of his father, her only son; of how he ran away and was drowned, way down on Bayou Lafourche. "Look like I ain't got nobody left, only just you. They done all gone off and left me."

And then one day in spring when Balthazar was twenty-three he went and got married.

The girl was a blowsy, shrewish creature, pleasure-loving without being gay. She was French, but she was not a native of Isle Brevelle. She was not even a Catholic—a common girl, with no raising. She came from a town in North Louisiana, and her short skirts and ready laughter bewildered Nicolette and troubled her—

273

old Nicolette, with the ache of countless harrowing years in her strange mixed blood. Rose had a thousand ways of being vixenish, woman-ways; and in her hands poor Balthazar was as wax.

"Listen, Granny," Balthazar had said the day he brought Rose home a bride, all dressed up in yellow satin, "how 'bout you take one half the house and leave us the other half? *Hein?* That a good idea, ain't it? That suit both you women?"

Balthazar knew his old grandmother. He knew that she liked a place for things, and her things just *so.* And Balthazar knew his wife, or he thought he did. He had watched her fling her clothes about. Her stockings were always under the bed; her yellow satin dress flung over a chair. "The old un, she got to have place for thing," he told Rose. "Somewhere to put thing away."

And so Balthazar divided the house between the two women. Rose he installed on the southern side, where magnolias pushed in at the windows, milky with bloom. And Nicolette had the other half, on the north side of the dog-run; the front-room and the cuddy-hole room and the lean-to next to the kitchen. It seemed to Balthazar as he sat and smoked on the gallery that he had been wise beyond his years. But Balthazar did not know his wife. And it was not very long before Rose was saying, "They is two of us, Balthazar, you and me. You ask your Granny to give us the front-room. What do a old woman want with a front-room, I like to know!" But Balthazar demurred at this.

Much might be written, and much might be said, concerning the front-room of Isle Brevelle dwellings. It is not as other rooms. It is sacred; and in the front-room the head of the house resides. . . . Rose was sly and persistent.

"Let's move my bed in the front-room," she said, "for old Granny to sleep in. Huh! That tacky old thing she got ain't no good. I'm 'shame for my friends come and see it."

And so, before very long, Nicolette, whimpering, watched them move her big four-poster into the little cuddy-hole room, off on the "ell." Nicolette's bed was a big square bed with carved headboard and tapering posts. It has lost all its sheen and polish; it was ashy with age, and was mottled and scratched. But Nicolette loved it. It mattered little to her that it sagged and creaked, that the silk tester hung in shreds. In the front-room Rose's bed, with the shiny brass knobs, looked alien and disturbing. Granny stared at it resentfully and blinked.

"Me, I go where my bed go," she declared. "I was born in that bed, and my children they was born in that bed. My old man he die in that bed. And me, some day I die in him too."

Therefore, it came about that Rose took over the front-room, and moved her Victrola into it; and old Nicolette, bag and baggage, followed her four-poster bed into the cuddy-hole room. With her she took her marble-top bureau, her "press," and her Virgin Mary. But even here she was not safe from Rose's intrusion. Of a Sunday, when Balthazar and Rose came home from church, Rose always took off her clothes in Nicolette's room. And old Nicolette, hobbling in from her chair under the umbrella-china, would find Rose's things all over the place—queer garments like nothing old Nicolette's eyes had ever encountered. "Nobody ever come back here," Rose would explain. "It don't matter if things is upset." And it would seem to Nicolette that Rose's slinky petticoats were crawling about like snakes, and all her long silk stockings, so full of holes. . . . Sometimes Nicolette, grumbling, her little eyes red and malignant, would sweep Rose's clothes off of the bed to the floor. "That gal! Her and her shiftless way!"

And Rose was meddlesome too, like a child. She would stand and pick at Granny's keepsakes on top of the marble-top bureau. "What this thing here, Granny?" she would ask, with her insolent laugh. "This little white lady all dress up in blue—"

And Granny would quiver and tremble with rage. "Put that down, gal! Stop meddle them thing! Bah, I shake you, Rose . . . that thing is *saint*. That is little St. Joseph."

Old Nicolette's treasures were beautiful in her sight: two or three colored post cards showing views of New Orleans, a picture of the church in Natchitoches, a faded paper rose, a valentine, photographs of her children, and chromos of all the saints. When Rose's plump unhallowed fingers touched them Nicolette's flesh would crawl on her bones. "That gal! That Rose!" she would mutter.

When Nicolette's grandson had been married a year hard times came to Isle Brevelle. First one thing and then another, as if a curse had been laid on the land. An overflow in April and a drouth in July and August, when the hot earth drank up the river and it shrank to a silver trickle. And then came the funny green grasshoppers, and the ants and the bugs and the scorpions. The distant hills grew lean, forlorn; and in the curious beauty and apathy of the land the people hungered, and many were sick. But Rose, who was used to town ways, was unaware of it all. They meant nothing to her, the seared yellow fields and the cracking clay banks of the river. Rose still painted her amber cheeks and went about like a loose woman.

"Rose, *chère*," Balthazar begged, "don't go and buy nothing no more honey, down at Poleon's store. We ain't got no money."

Poleon owned the commissary on Isle Brevelle. He kept everything; dry-goods and notions; rosaries and coffins; groceries and false-faces; silk stockings and coco-cola; prayer-books and knick-knacks; and lip-sticks and white altar candles. Poleon's store was paradise for Rose and, despite Balthazar's pleading, she went and charged what she wanted. . . . It was that year, too, in August, that Rose took it into her head that she and Balthazar must have a car, a secondhand car. It was all so easy. "You go to town and you pay fifty dollar, and the car is yours," she said to Balthazar, rolling her big, lustrous eyes. Of course, afterward, you had to plank down so much a month; but once the initial payment was made, it was easy sailing. Everyone had a Ford, Rose insisted; and a few persons on Isle Brevelle possessed big cars. Rose became obsessed with the subject of automobiles. "Look like I'll go crazy, honey," she told Balthazar, "if we don't get us a car . . . stuck here all day long with old Granny. Look like I'll go crazy, way down here on this sleepy old river. You must think I'm old too, like Granny, *hein?*"

Poor Balthazar sighed and shook his head. Balthazar was slow-witted—he was not quick like his grandmama—and in summer his brain wouldn't work because of the chills and the fever. He already owed much to Poleon; he was up to his neck in debt. And he owed the merchants in town, too, for seed and for fertilizer. But he was in love with Rose. Her smooth golden skin enchanted him, and her drowsy insolent voice. Her fingers, full of cheap imitation rubies and pearls, moved over his hair. . . . "Balthazar, honey, let's get us a car. Let's ride up and down on the river-road these nice moonlight nights."

The nights were lovely that August; as if under the spell of the moon, the stricken land forgot all its trouble. Up and down the river-roads the people drove, all night until nearly sunrise.

One morning Rose said to old Nicolette, "Granny, you is always a-praying. Pray to your little blue saint over there that we get us a car." She laughed her shrill, ready laughter, and Nicolette was offended. The old woman's starchy, black, spread-out skirts flowed over the floor.

"Saint ain't got no ear for such sinful pray," Nicolette crackled, blinking. She glared at Rose who was wearing three strands of beads around her smooth yellow throat. "You better go pray your own self, for your sin," Granny admonished. "You turn them bead into prayer-bead. Bead, they is made for pray, and not for look pretty. And you go turn your heart into prayer heart. "

In September, although it had rained a little, everyone knew there would be no cotton, no corn, and no sugar cane. How calm and deceptive the blue land looked, how sulky with beauty along the fresh flow of the river! It was hard to believe that people would starve. . . . One morning Nicolette sat in her chair under the umbrella-china. The river shone in the sunshine. White geese swam under the bank, and a crane stepped gingerly along the shore with his slim coral legs. The lilies were thick in the little bays, shining against the dark banks. A paper-mulberry tree dripped its yellow leaves into the water. "Hey-law!" old Granny grunted. . . . Along the banks, each with its strip of riverfront, squatted the low adobe houses of the people, the free-mulattoes. The houses had blue batten-shutters and wide, leaning clay chimneys. Time was, before the War, when the people had lived in clover, and had even owned slaves. Now the negroes looked down upon them, with hatred and bitter scorn. "Dem stuck-up yaller folkses—"

Nowadays the priest on Isle Brevelle was concerned for them. Where did they come from? Whither were they going? And what would be the measure of their end? The land was old; the river was old; even the children were old, the poor little babies. Once a man from a distant state had come and had lectured to them. "What can you expect?" he had said. "You live too much to yourselves. Your blood is thin, petered out. You need new blood, new life." Well, Balthazar had brought new blood to the river, to Isle Brevelle. He had gone up in North Louisiana and had brought home a wife. But

Rose didn't fit, that silly Rose—always talking about the way they lived up there where she had come from—Rose who had worked for white-folks and had strange city ways. She was common, a girl with no raising. And she wasn't a Catholic, either. Rose wasn't anything. She had no respect for her elders.

Presently, as Granny dozed, Rose came around the corner of the house. Her face was flushed and eager, her eyes bright. "I hear some one coming," she said. "I hear a car." Rose loved company. She had the gift of gab. She went down the path and leaned on the gate, between the tall twin cedars. Old Nicolette had not heard the car. She strained her deafened ears. She could see it now, coming across the bridge. It turned and nosed into the lane, a big shining car; and Rose spoke over her shoulder, "Granny, it's white folks," she said, beginning to pull at her hair. "It's white folks from down at Natchitoches-town." Rose stooped and pulled up her stockings, which were hanging about her thick ankles.

The car drew up in front of the gate. There were two men in the car and three women, and a child, a little girl. The women stared at Rose expectantly and with friendly smiles. "We are looking for antiques, for old furniture," one of them said. "And Poleon told us down at the store that you might have something to show us." The young women began to get out of the car, but the little girl stayed with the men. "You stay with Daddy, right in the car," one of the young women said. Old Nicolette was disappointed. The child was so pretty, so clean-looking. Granny would have loved to talk to the child, to take her into the front-room where the fluted pink sea-shells lay on the hearth.

Rose, wearing the craven painted smile that she saved for Natchitoches people, invited the women in. And something inside of old Nicolette began to hurt, deep down. She hobbled into the house behind the white women, making little noises in her throat. A fear and a sadness came into her eyes. "They . . . what they after, them white lady?" Nicolette asked herself. "Look funny to me, them rich lady . . . wanting us old, wore-out thing." The voices of the young women filled the house, bounced on the low-beamed ceiling. "How quaint it all is!" one of them said. "Imagine living like this."

They talked with their pretty gay voices and looked about. They stared at Rose's iron bed with the big brass knobs. And then one of the young women said, "Surely you must have an old bed, out in the shed or somewhere. You see, we want *old* things."

Nicolette leaned against the doorway, catching at it with her hands. The women were swarming into her room, into her cuddy-hole. They stood within the door, and stared . . . stared at Nicolette's bed. There was a little hollow place in the bed, just Nicolette's shape and size; and the old woman thrust out a long bony hand. She was ashamed of her "josie" spread out on the bed, of her old alpaca skirt, of some odds and ends of quilt scraps. She began to cackle, deep in her throat "That the bed I was born in," old Nicolette said, "and my children was born in that bed."

But no one paid any attention to what Nicolette said. They were staring at the bed. One of the young women caressed the posts, laid her white fingers upon them. "Beautiful!" she whispered. . . . *Her* bed, old Nicolette's bed. The only thing on God's green earth she possessed.

And now Rose was saying, "Yes ma'am. I think he will sell you the bed, provide his Granny is willing. He sell for fifty dollar, yes. I ask him come twelve o'clock." Nicolette clutched out with her clawlike hands. Her voice quavered, stuck in her throat. But nobody heard her. "Yes, Ma'am," Rose was saying, "I think Balthazar he will sell." Something greedy, avaricious, shone in Rose's eyes. She laughed loud and shrill. "We rather have us a car," she said, "than a four-poster bed."

Nicolette heard like one in a dream. Once, as she stood looking on from the door, she reached out and timidly touched the skirt of one of the young white women, felt of it, and smoothed it with her long bony hand. It was exquisite and soft to her groping old fingers. Silk! One time she too had worn silk, before this young woman was born. She knew how it felt, next to your skin. She thought of New Orleans, of the quadroon balls down on the old *Rue Royale*. . . . In those days life went round and round, like a young girl dancing. Granny began to talk to herself, in low mutters, "Rose, she want to sell my bed. From under me, yes. I was born in that bed, and I die in him." Nicolette listened; and now Rose was saying, "This here is Tuesday. Well, you come back on Friday—you get it then. You wait, I'll manage. Come back on Friday." Rose winked at the young white women, and laughed; and the white women turned and smiled at Nicolette indulgently, as people smile at a child.

When the big car had gone there remained a hardness and brightness all over the little old house. And the voices of the young white women echoed against the ceiling. Rose of a sudden was gentle, nice to old Nicolette. "Granny," she said, "how you like us to buy you a nice iron bed, just like mine? From down at Poleon's store."

Nicolette began to puff on her corncob pipe, very fast. But Granny said nothing. No use trying to out-talk Rose. She went and sat under the china tree, and tried to plan what to do. There was Balthazar, her grandson now. Which one would Balthazar listen to, at noon when he came from the fields? She watched Rose silently out of malignant old eyes. Rose went about singing, her steps light and free. She was thinking about that car she was going to buy. Already, Nicolette knew, she could feel herself at the wheel, going to visit her relatives way up in North Louisiana, riding out of a Sunday all dressed up in yellow satin. No telling what that Rose would do, once she got hold of a car. She already talked too sweet-mouth with the boys down at Poleon's store. Rose had better stay home and behave herself, and try to get some religion.

At noon a blue haze lay over the river, and the chickens were cackling sleepily all puffed up under the house. Nicolette dozed in her chair, she could scarcely keep her eyes open. And Rose moved about in the kitchen, lifting potlids and rattling dishes. She was knowing and sly, that Rose; and Granny knew what she was up to. She was making gumbo for Balthazar. Rose could be sweet when she wanted to. Well, Granny would see him first. She'd sit here and wait for his coming. "Balthazar, son," she would say, "I won't sell my bed. I was born in that bed, and I die there."

When Granny opened her eyes it was long past noon, and Balthazar had gone back to the fields. Something hurt deep in old Nicolette's breast. What had happened? . . . Then she remembered. She saw Rose stepping about in the house, with a ribbon the color of pomegranate blossoms stuck in her hair "Granny!" Rose called, "is you ready to eat? You sho' is take a long nap."

Granny got to her feet. "Rose!" she cried shrilly, and her voice was hard and vehement. "Rose! I won't sell my bed. I was born in that bed, and I die there."

Rose, laughing, slouched into the yard, and the red ribbon shone in the sun. "Ah, now, Granny—you wait. Balthazar he say he won't sell, only unless you is willing. You wait, you see what a nice, fine bed we buy you down at the store."

That evening, when Balthazar came home, they had it nip and tuck, Rose and old Nicolette. Balthazar was distressed. "Now, Rose, honey. Now, Granny—" But he might as well have tried to stop two coffee-mills. Rose talked, her red tongue flashing; and old Nicolette threw out her hands. "Oh, yi! Yi! Yi! I won't sell my bed!" . . . One minute Balthazar's arms would be around Rose, his cheek hot against her hair. Then he would steal compassionate looks at his grandmother. "Rose," Balthazar cautioned, "fifty dollar—that just the beginning, honey."

A day or two later, on Thursday, Rose assumed an air of triumph, of secrecy. She smiled to herself as she went about getting breakfast and Granny was troubled. What could Rose be up to now? By and by when Balthazar had gone and the pots were washed and beds made Rose came and sat with old Granny, under the china tree. "What you think?" she began, her voice held a drowsy laugh; "what you think Granny, hein? Me and Balthazar . . . we is going to have lil' baby. Maybe a sweet lil' son."

Nicolette blinked very fast. This she had waited for, more than a year. A great-grandson! A lil' baby! Something warm welled up in her heart, her old fingers twitched. It would be nice to have a child about, something to love and cuddle. A child who would play in the front-room with the pretty shells on the hearth. She took her pipe out of her mouth and began to cackle. "A lil' baby! Well, I bet, me, Balthazar he is proud." And then, quick on the heels of her gladness, a fear caught at her heart. Balthazar now would give in to Rose. Granny knew men, she knew Balthazar. Rose would have her way with him, and she'd sell Granny's bed.

When Balthazar came in from the fields he walked blithely, his head very high. He stooped and kissed his old grandmother. "Granny, we must humor Rose. We must let Rose sell that old bed." Nicolette heard him and swallowed hard, and she could not find any words to express the things that she wanted to say. She followed Balthazar into the house, making wistful, futile movements with her hands.

The next morning, on Friday, Granny awakened very early. "To-day they come get my bed. Them white lady come tote my bed off to town—" Granny lay and smiled to herself. In the night she had thought of a plan. She was wise; she had lived a long time, and she knew. "Me, I been watch that Rose last night, and I know," Granny said to herself. "I know that Rose she is tell one big story. She ain't go' have no baby. That Rose, she just lying to get her own way. Me, I know."

And so at six o'clock when Balthazar came in with the morning coffee old Nicolette lay very still. "Rose . . . she ain't the only one what can lie," old Nicolette said to herself. She began to moan under her covers. "Balthazar, son, I been take by the foot. I can't move. And I ache in my bone. Look like I done have a stroke in the night."

Balthazar stared at his grandmother. She lay very tiny and yellow in the big square old bed. There were shadows on her face, in her wrinkled cheeks, and her eyes were sunken like dead eyes. Balthazar patted the worn quilt that was spread over her. "Granny," he said, "what you say I pick you up, and move you into our room? . . . into our bed? To-day them white lady come—"

But Nicolette closed her eyes. She appeared not to have heard him. "Oh yi! Yi!" she moaned, softly, under her breath. She watched Balthazar out of one eye, saw he was worried and anxious. And she smiled to herself. "They won't get my bed. Not from under me, no!"

Balthazar tiptoed out of the room, and Nicolette lay very still in her sweet, warm place. The big bed embraced her. Lying there so safe and high, she felt like a princess. Above her the ragged tester hung in long crimson ribbons. The four posts of the bed were solid and lovely yet in their grime. They pointed straight up to heaven. They were pointing her right up to God. . . .

By and by Balthazar returned, bringing Rose with him. In vain Rose argued, cajoled. "We move you into our bed, if you sick. And send get a doctor. Look, Granny, Balthazar he can lift you, so it won't hurt." But Nicolette shook her head. "I got misery down in my leg," she said. "If you touch me it hurt very bad." Rose gave her a look, a woman's look, and stuck out her tongue. And Balthazar saw and was troubled. Poor Balthazar! He tried to reason with Granny. "A young woman, they is peculiar, Granny, in this kind of condition. A young woman, they is made different." He tried to reason with Rose, his wife, "A old woman, they is peculiar, Rose. They is childish and set in their ways. A old un, they is made different." But it did no good. Rose flounced out of the room, red and angry, and banged the pans and pots about. At last, shrugging his shoulders, Balthazar went out to the fields.

When he had gone Rose came back into Nicolette's room. "I know you, Granny," Rose said. "You ain't sick. You *is mean*, that the thing what ail you. You is mean and wicked old woman."

"I—I *sick*," old Granny insisted. "I been took with sick in my bone." She lay and blinked very fast. "You is lie your own self, Rose. When you say you is going to have lil' child. You too is tell lie. And the good Lord, he go' punish you yet."

That afternoon the white ladies came for Nicolette's bed. The old woman, lying taut and scared, heard the big car at the gate, heard the confusion, the soft gay voices. The white ladies came up on the gallery, into old Nicolette's room. Rose was nice to them, full of blandishment. She knew how to treat white ladies. She smiled at them, and then at old Granny. "Granny, they done come brought a truck for your bed. But me, I tell 'em you sick. You been took with your bone." Rose sighed, and her heavy cheeks hung. She looked sleepy, voluptuous, full of trouble, and one of the white ladies said, "I should like very much to paint you, Rose. You're a type. Have you Spanish blood in your veins?" Rose lied and said yes, she was Spanish. Rose claimed all the various bloods in her veins save her negro blood. That she ignored. She gave the ladies her painted smile, and shook her head, tapping her forehead. The young white women were sympathetic. They stared at old Granny and talked above her as if she were deaf or a child. "Poor old thing! Yes, we quite understand. Old people are full of such notions."

Rose smiled and looked wise and winked at them. "You wait, I manage. Soon I go down to Poleon's store and telephone you to come get the bed. You wait I know how to manage old Granny. I'll let you know soon, when to come.

Three days, four days, a week went by, and still old Granny refused to get up. "Well," Rose had declared that first day, "she can lay there and starve. I ain't go' wait on old Granny, and her just as hardy as I is." And so it fell upon Balthazar to bring fresh flowers every day to put in front of the Virgin, to shoo the chickens and cats from the room so Granny could sleep, to fetch water for her and coffee, and mush and sweet milk and clabber. The things Rose cooked in the kitchen smelled very good, very appetizing. But Rose decreed that if Granny were sick she couldn't eat like well folks. She must eat only sick folks' vittles: soft tasteless food that Granny detested: old Granny, with the rich gnawing memories of New Orleans deep in her heart. Sometimes Nicolette thought she would give her eyeballs for some collards and file-gumbo. She lay sometimes for hours and thought of garlic and onions. But she knew she could not demand these things. A sick person couldn't eat, Rose had said. And Granny was sick. If she so much as put her feet to the floor, Rose would snatch up her bed. Rose would take it from under her and send it away to town. Sometimes when Balthazar came in to see her old Nicolette lapsed into French, as if she were out of her head: all about the quadroon balls down on the old *Rue Royale,* all about the soirées and the carryings-on. Jabber, jabber, jabber, jabber! until Rose would clap her hands to her ears and shriek with impatience, "Balthazar! She give me the jimmie! How long is Granny go' stay in that bed?"

Another week passed, and the time was October. The land still lay with the drouth at its throat. But now little rags and wisps of smoke went up from the chimneys. For the days were cool, the sky very blue. All day Rose gazed at the shining roads, stretching away in the sunlight. "Balthazar," she would coax fretfully, "if we had us a car! If only Granny would sell that bed . . . How long you think Granny'll lay there?"

One bright October morning when Balthazar was out in the fields Rose came into Nicolette's room. "I'm tired of this foolishness, Granny," she said. "To-day after dinner I'm going down to Poleon's store. And I'll telephone them women come get the bed on *to-morrow.*" Granny protested feebly, and grunted. But Rose's voice was hard and cold. "Balthazar's going to town in the morning," she said. "He'll be gone all day. Now, Granny, you listen to me—" Rose came and stood threateningly over old Nicolette's bed. She glared and her black eyes flashed. "You been in this bed long enough, Granny. Now, you listen to me, what I say. To-morrow we here by our own self, just you and me. Nobody out in the field to hear if you call. Now, to-morrow you crawl out that bed, or I pull you out. You see these two strong arm? Well, you get out that bed to-morrow, or I lock you up in the woodshed."

Old Granny shrank, put her hands to her ears. Time was when Granny could talk, could have out-talked even Rose. Now her throat felt tight and dry; no words would come. Could it be that she really was sick? . . . Perhaps God the Father had punished her for telling a lie. A terror came upon her, and her hands shook under the covers.

"You *mean*, that's what," Rose was saying. "What is a old bed to you, and we promise to buy you a new one?"

Granny whimpered and plucked at her covers. "You mean, too," she said. "You is mean, wicked gal—"

That afternoon, true to her threat, Rose dressed and went down to Poleon's store. Through her little window Granny watched her, watched her red ribbons gleam in the sun. . . . By and by Granny pulled herself up, and sat propped against her pillows. The house was quiet, with the yellow sunshine warm at the doors and windows. Slowly, cautiously, grunting a little, Granny put her feet to the floor. "I believe, me, I go eat some collards. I believe I'd feel better," she told herself, "if I go eat while Rose is away. They smelled good at dinnertime, them greens. Maybe to-night I have strength for tell Balthazar, tell him what that Rose say to me."

Granny began her long and hazardous trip to the kitchen. The floor rocked under her stealthy old feet, and objects blurred and receded. But once in the kitchen Granny dipped into the greasy pot on the back of the stove. She ate, smacking her lips. Then, fearfully, she stuffed some greens into a brownpaper bag and hobbled back to her room. Safe once more in the cuddy-hole room, Granny hid the bag in a chink of the moldering wall. "I eat him when I get hungry again," she thought. "To-night I get up and eat him."

Before Rose came back from the store the sun had gone down under the river, and out of the yellow adobe walls a pink spider crawled and was gone. Old Nicolette lay in bed and dozed. In the front-room she heard Balthazar, heard him whistle, moving about. She tried to call his name, but her voice sounded futile and weak. There was something she wanted to tell him. What was it? She could not remember. . . . The long hours crawled, and then, like the spider, they scuttled away and were gone. Once Balthazar came to the door. "Is you all right, Granny?" he asked. And once Nicolette heard an owl, out in her umbrella-china. She lay and listened and pulled her quilt. . . . Across the window, in the north, a star fell and died like a spark, and in her dim old brain pictures of far-away places passed and faded, and passed yet again. She saw her five little daughters—how pretty they were! She saw herself a girl again, down on the old *Rue Royale. Tick, tock* went the clock on the mantel. Then slower and slower . . . *tick!* She could scarcely hear it. Had it stopped? It is bad luck for your clock to run down in the night. Balthazar must have forgotten to wind it. Poor Baithazar, poor little grandson! There was something she wanted to tell him. What was it?

Once Granny prayed to the Virgin: "Mary, Sister, Mother, Child." But the prayer seemed to stick in her throat. Well, Mary had had no daughter-in-law! How could *she* know, understand? A faint wind stirred through the room, and the dried magnolia leaves on the wall rustled and fell to the floor. Granny dozed and dozed again. And then she awoke with a start. The moon was flooding the room, just like day. It must be long after midnight. Slowly, cautiously, Granny pulled herself up in bed. She would get up and eat, some collards and nice salt meat. Then she'd feel better.

She reached in the chink of the wall for the brown-paper bag and sat down in her old creaking rocker. She began to eat hungrily, with her fingers. She sat and dozed in her chair. . . . When she awakened she was stiff, and her body was racked with pain. A strange terror seized her, a fear of the day that was coming. . . . And her bed! Where was her four-poster bed? She had lost it. She couldn't see it. It was gone, in the little dim room. Rose, that Rose, had taken her bed.

Granny stretched out her arms, in the darkness closing about her. If she could but reach the haven of her four-poster bed again! . . . Ah! She could feel it now. Her fingers caught and clutched at the posts. Weak, her throat thick with breathing, Granny crawled under her covers. She talked to herself brokenly, pulling at the quilt. . . . If only God would let her take her four-poster bed up to heaven.

In the cold dawn Balthazar got up and made morning coffee. He dreaded the trip into town, dreaded to stop at Poleon's store to try and stave off his debts. In the lot through the fog he could see the dark gaunt bulk of the mules. A fog makes a place so still: it swallows and eats up the world; only the sound of a heron crying, across the dim river. The fire in the kitchen stove felt good, warmed his bones.

Balthazar took a cup of coffee in to Rose. He found her sitting on the side of the bed, preparing to dress. She yawned and her heavy hair hung in her eyes. "What time you get back from town?" she asked. "It'll be good dark, *hein*, Balthazar?" Balthazar grunted. "Yeah, good dark. Rose, honey, be good to the old un." Rose sipped the hot fragrant coffee, and a sly little smile curved her lips. Suddenly she got up, stepped out on the bare cold floor. Her black eyes were furtive. "Balthazar, give me old Granny's cup," she said. "Let me take the coffee in to her."

Balthazar, pleased, poured a cup for Nicolette and patted Rose's shoulder. "I wish you two would make up," he said. "You and old Granny."

Rose opened the door of the cuddy-hole room and stepped inside. "Granny!" she called. "Granny!" . . . The place was so still; the curtains hung straight and limp at the window. Rose peered at the bed. Then she put a hand to her mouth, palm outward, and drew it over her face. She began to back out of the room, the hot coffee splashing over her nightgown. "Balthazar!" She gave a little cry. "Balthazar, come quick! It's the old un! Old Granny—"

As soon as some of the neighbors had come Balthazar left to get Poleon to see to the funeral arrangements. Rose watched him go. She must hurry and clean up the house. Soon the relatives from town would be coming, and so much to do! She had to get dressed too. In the front-room, away from the dead woman, Rose made up the bed, picked up her clothes. "Poor old Granny," she said. "Poor old Granny." She felt nervous, excited. But she could not help thinking, deep in her heart, "Now we can sell the bed, and no trouble. After the funeral . . . them lady can come here and get it— and maybe—maybe to-morrow, we buy us a car."

It was nine o'clock when Balthazar returned, bringing with him Poleon to see to the funeral arrangements. Poleon was a big man on Isle Brevelle, wealthy and much respected. No one could die without Poleon; no one could die or be buried. He looked about the house and shook his head dubiously. And he stared at Rose—Rose all hung with beads and buckles and cheap, flashy rubies and pearls. Look here, Balthazar," Poleon said, and his mouth turned down at the corners, "you owe me much money already. How you go' pay for the funeral, *hein?* For your old granny' coffin." Poleon was crafty and shrewd, a good business man. He stood in the little cuddy-hole room and gazed down at old Granny, where she lay in the four-poster bed. She lay very tiny and still, her eyes closed, her little hands crossed on her bosom.

"Well, Balthazar," Poleon said, "this sho' is a nice bed you got, all hid away." Poleon trailed his fingers along the tapering posts. "Yes, a fine antique bed, as them white lady say. This is the bed I hear your wife try to bargain about, to them rich white lady in town." Poleon's little eyes gleamed; he looked furtive, thoughtful. "Well, I'll tell you what I'll do for you, Balthazar. You give me the bed. I'll take the bed off your hand. It'll pay for the old lady's funeral, huh . . . and a nice fine coffin to boot. That suit you, my friend? That all right? Well—?

Rose heard him and came and stood in the door. Her heavy cheeks hung, and she pushed back her dark hair.

And it seemed to her that old Nicolette lay there and smiled.

THE OLD ONE

Since Carver's mulattoes live in a society very unlike Cable's, her treatment of them is quite different. She avoids the stereotypes and the sentimentality often seen in portrayals of mulattoes, perhaps because they are not seen in relation to whites. This story concerns the descendants of Creoles *de couleur*, free-mulattoes, of Isle Brevelle in Natchitoches Parish—proud people who "before the war . . . lived in clover and even owned slaves." But times have changed, we learn from old Nicolette's reminiscing. Even the Negroes look down upon them with hatred and scorn, calling them "dem stuck-up yaller folkses." Although their fortunes are reduced and they have only a "shoestring" of river front left, life is sweet and serene and filled with the past. And Nicolette's grandson Balthazar, a quiet industrious boy with no inclination to philander, is content to sit surrounded by relics of the past and listen to Nicolette recall her girlhood—the quadroon balls in New Orleans, the soirees, the Civil War and dark years of Reconstruction, and the deaths of family members. This story sets tradition against modernity; old age against youth; and wisdom—the defense of age, against sexuality—the weapon of youth.

Balthazar's marriage to an outsider (not even a Catholic, a common girl with no raising, from a town in north Louisiana) provides the conflict, which is illuminated by the contrast in setting. Nicolette's house, to which Balthazar brings his bride, is divided by a hall, a dog run. Rose, whose name, as well as location in the house, suggests youth, is installed on the southern side, where "the magnolias pushed in at the window, milky with bloom." The old mistress lives in the north side which includes the front room, the cubby-hole room and the lean-to room next to the kitchen. When the inevitable battle begins, it is between these two worlds that Balthazar stands, his head telling him that his grandmother is right, his glands insisting that Rose is. In a clever *coup d'etat* Rose usurps the old woman's position by appropriating the front room, which is in Isle Brevelle society a special place reserved for the head of the house.

Tradition broken and Rose provided with a power base, the old order begins to crumble. Nicolette's move to the back room foreshadows her defeat, and the final life-death struggle centers

289

on her old four-poster bed which has always been a part of her life: "I was born in that bed, and my children they was born in that bed. My old man he die in that bed. And some day I die in him too."

Rose, bored with the stillness of Isle Brevelle, insists that they sell the bed for $50.00 to antique hunters, so that Rose can have a car. "Look like I'll go crazy, honey, if we don't get us a car . . . stuck here all day long with Granny." In order to prevent the sale of the bed (Balthazar has now succumbed to the charms of the lovely golden-skinned Rose), Nicolette takes to the bed, feigning illness. Rose counterattacks by feigning pregnancy. The two deadlock, with Granny growing physically weaker every day and Rose growing more assured as she looks at the dying woman. But old age cannot survive against youth any more than tradition can survive against change, and in her death the frail old woman loses, or seems to lose, the battle. Defeat turns into a kind of victory, however, when Poleon, a crass money grubber who runs the nearby general store, claims the bed for funeral expenses, thus thwarting Rose in her plans. The story ends ironically, but not affirmatively: the past (Granny and the bed) is gone, replaced by a vulgar materialism (Rose and Poleon fighting over the spoils).

Arna Bontemps

(1902-1973)

Arna Bontemps was born in Alexandria, but at an early age he moved to California where he was graduated in 1923 from Pacific Union College. Because of his interest in writing, he moved to New York in 1924 and was associated with prominent figures in the Harlem Renaissance. After writing, teaching, and attending graduate school in New York, he moved to Alabama where he taught and wrote while seeking his cultural heritage, and later to Chicago where he acquired a Master's degree. Accepting a job at Fisk University, he moved to Nashville, and except for brief teaching assignments at Yale and the University of Chicago and lecture tours, he remained there until his death in 1973. He wrote in "Why I Returned" that for him "a break with the past and the shedding of his Negro-ness were not only impossible but unthinkable." Therefore, much of his fiction is woven from early remembrances and family tales of life in Louisiana. He depicts with restraint and detachment the dignity and courage of the Negro. The story printed below first appeared in 1933 in *Opportunity: A Journal of Negro Life;* it was later collected in *Old South: A Summer Tragedy and Other Stories,* 1973.

A Summer Tragedy*

Arna Bontemps

Old Jeff Patton, the black share farmer, fumbled with his bow tie. His fingers trembled, and the high, stiff collar pinched his throat. A fellow loses his hand for such vanities after thirty or forty years of simple life. Once a year, or maybe twice if there's a wedding among his kin-folks, he may spruce up; but generally fancy clothes do nothing but adorn the wall of the big room and feed the moths. That had been Jeff Patton's experience. He had not worn his stiff-bosomed shirt more than a dozen times in all his married life. His swallow-tailed coat lay on the bed beside him, freshly brushed and pressed, but it was as full of holes as the overalls in which he worked on week days. The moths had used it badly. Jeff twisted his mouth into a hideous toothless grimace as he contended with the obstinate bow. He stamped his good foot and decided to give up the struggle.

"Jennie," he called.

"What's that, Jeff?" His wife's shrunken voice came out of the adjoining room like an echo. It was hardly bigger than a whisper.

"I reckon you'll have to he'p me wid this heah bow tie, baby," he said meekly. "Dog if I can hitch it up."

Her answer was not strong enough to reach him, but presently the old woman came to the door, feeling her way with a stick. She had a wasted, dead-leaf appearance. Her body, as scrawny and gnarled as a stringbean, seemed less than nothing in the ocean of frayed and faded petticoats that surrounded her. These hung an inch or two above the tops of her heavy, unlaced shoes and showed little grotesque piles where the stockings had fallen down from her negligible legs.

"You oughta could do a heap mo' wid a thing like that 'n me—beingst as you got yo' good sight."

"Looks like I *oughta* could," he admitted. "But ma fingers is gone democrat on me. I get all mixed up in the looking glass an' can't tell whicha way to twist the devilish thing."

*Reprinted by permission of Dodd, Mead & Co. from *The Old South* by Arna Bontemps. Copyright 1933 by Arna Bontemps. Copyright renewed 1961 by Arna Bontemps. Copyright © 1973 by Alberta Bontemps. Executrix.

Jennie sat on the side of the bed and old Jeff Patton got down on one knee while she tied the bow knot. It was a slow and painful ordeal for each of them in this position. Jeff's bones cracked, his knee ached, and it was only after a half dozen attempts that Jennie worked a semblance of a bow into the tie.

"I got to dress maself now," the old woman whispered. "These is ma old shoes an' stockings, and I ain't so much as unwrapped ma dress."

"Well, don't worry 'bout me no mo', baby," Jeff said. "That 'bout finishes me. All I gotta do now is slip on that old coat 'n ves' and I'll be fixed to leave."

Jennie disappeared again through the dim passage into the shed room. Being blind was no handicap to her in that black hole. Jeff heard the cane placed against the wall beside the door and knew that his wife was on easy ground. He put on his coat, took a battered top hat from the bed post, and hobbled to the front door. He was ready to travel. As soon as Jennie could get on her Sunday shoes and her old black silk dress, they would start.

Outside the tiny log house the day was warm and mellow with sunshine. A host of wasps was humming with busy excitement in the trunk of a dead sycamore. Grey squirrels were searching through the grass for hickory nuts and blue jays were in the trees, hopping from branch to branch. Pine woods stretched away to the left like a black sea. Among them were scattered scores of log houses like Jeff's, houses of black share farmers. Cows and pigs wandered freely among the trees. There was no danger of loss. Each farmer knew his own stock and knew his neighbor's as well as he knew his neighbor's children.

Down the slope to the right were the cultivated acres on which the colored folks worked. They extended to the river, more than two miles away, and they were today green with the unmade cotton crop. A tiny thread of a road, which passed directly in front of Jeff's place, ran through these green fields like a pencil mark.

Jeff, standing outside the door with his absurd hat in his left hand, surveyed the wide scene tenderly. He had been forty-five years on these acres. He loved them with the unexplained affection that others have for the countries to which they belong.

The sun was hot on his head, his collar still pinched his throat, and the Sunday clothes were intolerably hot. Jeff transferred the hat to his right hand and began fanning with it. Suddenly the whisper that was Jennie's voice came out of the shed room.

"You can bring the car round front whilst you's waitin'," it said feebly. There was a tired pause; then it added, "I'll soon be fixed to go."

"A'right, baby," Jeff answered. "I'll get it in a minute."

But he didn't move. A thought stuck him that made his mouth fall open. The mention of the car brought to his mind, with new intensity, the trip he and Jennie were about to take. Fear came into his eyes: excitement took his breath. Lord, Jesus!

"Jeff . . . Oh Jeff," the old woman's whisper called.

He awakened with a jolt. "Hunh, baby?"

"What you doin?"

"Nuthin. Jes studyin'. I jes been turning' things round 'n round in ma mind."

"You could be gettin' the car," she said.

"Oh yes, right away, baby."

He started round to the shed, limping heavily on his bad leg. There were three frizzly chickens in the yard. All his other chickens had been killed or stolen recently. But the frizzly chickens had been saved somehow. That was fortunate indeed, for these curious creatures had a way of devouring "poison" from the yard and in that way protecting against conjure and bad luck and spells. But even the frizzly chickens seemed now to be in a stupor. Jeff thought they had some ailment; he expected all three of them to die shortly.

The shed in which the old model-T Ford stood was only a grass roof held up by four corner poles. It had been built by tremulous hands at a time when the little rattletrap car had been regarded as a peculiar treasure. And, miraculously, despite wind and downpour, it still stood.

Jeff adjusted the crank and put his weight on it. The engine came to life with a sputter and bang that rattled the old car from radiator to tail light. Jeff hopped into the seat and put his foot on the accelerator. The sputtering and banging increased. The rattling became more violent. That was good. It was good banging, good sputtering and rattling, and it meant that the aged car was still in running condition. She could be depended on for this trip.

Again Jeff's thought halted as if paralyzed. The suggestion of the trip fell into the machinery of his mind like a wrench. He felt dazed and weak. He swung the car out into the yard, made a half turn, and drove around to the front door. When he took his hands off the wheel, he noticed that he was trembling violently. He cut off the motor and climbed to the ground to wait for Jennie.

A few moments later she was at the window, her voice rattling against the pane like a broken shutter.

"I'm ready, Jeff."

He did not answer, but limped into the house and took her by the arm. He led her slowly through the big room, down the step, and across the yard.

"You reckon I'd oughta lock the do'?" he asked softly.

They stopped and Jennie weighed the question. Finally she shook her head.

"Ne' mind the do'," she said. "I don't see no cause to lock up things."

"You right," Jeff agreed. "No cause to lock up."

Jeff opened the door and helped his wife into the car. A quick shudder passed over him. Jesus! Again he trembled.

"How come you shaking so?" Jennie whispered.

"I don't know," he said.

"You mus' be scairt, Jeff."

"No, baby, I ain't scairt."

He slammed the door after her and went around to crank up again. The motor started easily. Jeff wished that it had not been so responsive. He would have liked a few more minutes in which to turn things around in his head. As it was, with Jennie chiding him about being afraid, he had to keep going. He swung the car into the little pencil-mark road and started off toward the river, driving very slowly, very cautiously.

Chugging across the green countryside, the small, battered Ford seemed tiny indeed. Jeff felt a familiar excitement, a thrill, as they came down the first slope to the immense levels on which the cotton was growing. He could not help reflecting that the crops were good. He knew what that meant, too; he had made forty-five of them with his own hands. It was true that he had worn out nearly a dozen mules, but that was the fault of old man Stevenson, the owner of the land: Major Stevenson had the odd notion that one mule was all a share farmer needed to work a thirty-acre plot. It was an expensive notion, the way it killed mules from overwork, but the old man held to it. Jeff thought it killed a good many share farmers as well as mules, but he had no sympathy for them. He had always been strong, and he had been taught to have no patience with weakness in men. Women or children might be tolerated if they were puny, but a weak man was a curse. Of course, his own children—

Jeff's thought halted there. He and Jennie never mentioned their dead children any more. And naturally he did not wish to dwell upon them in his mind. Before he knew it, some remark would slip out of his mouth and that would make Jennie feel blue. Perhaps she would cry. A woman like Jennie could not easily throw off the grief that comes from losing five grown children within two years. Even Jeff was still staggered by the blow. His memory had not been much good recently. He frequently talked to himself. And, although he had kept it a secret, he knew that his courage had left him. He was terrified by the least unfamiliar sound at night. He was reluctant to venture far from home in the daytime. And that habit of trembling when he felt fearful was now far beyond his control. Sometimes he became afraid and trembled without knowing what had frightened him. The feeling would just come over him like a chill.

The car rattled slowly over the dusty road. Jennie sat erect and silent, with a little absurd hat pinned to her hair. Her useless eyes seemed very large and very white in their deep sockets. Suddenly Jeff heard her voice, and he inclined his head to catch the words.

"Is we passed Delia Moore's house yet?" she asked.

"Not yet," he said.

"You must be drivin' mighty slow, Jeff."

"We jes as well take our time, baby."

There was a pause. A little puff of steam was coming out of the radiator of the car. Heat wavered above the hood. Delia Moore's house was nearly half a mile away. After a moment Jennie spoke again.

"You ain't really scairt, is you, Jeff?"

"Nah, baby, I ain't scairt."

"You know how we agreed—we gotta keep on goin'."

Jewels of perspiration appeared on Jeff's forehead. His eyes rounded, blinked, became fixed on the road.

"I don't know," he said with a shiver. "I reckon it's the only thing to do."

"Hm."

A flock of guinea fowls, pecking in the road, were scattered by the passing car. Some of them took to their wings; others hid under bushes. A blue jay, swaying on a leafy twig, was annoying a roadside squirrel. Jeff held an even speed till he came near Delia's place. Then he slowed down noticeably.

Delia's house was really no house at all, but an abandoned store building converted into a dwelling. It sat near a crossroads, beneath a single black cedar tree. There Delia, a catlike old creature of Jennie's age, lived alone. She had been there more years than anybody could remember, and long ago had won the disfavor of such women as Jennie. For in her young days Delia had been gayer, yellower, and saucier than seemed proper in those parts. Her ways with menfolks had been dark and suspicious. And the fact that she had had as many husbands as children did not help her reputation.

"Yonder's old Delia," Jeff said as they passed.

"What she doin'?"

"Jes sittin' in the do'," he said.

"She see us?"

"Hm," Jeff said. "Musta did."

That relieved Jennie. It strengthened her to know that her old enemy had seen her pass in her best clothes. That would give the old she-devil something to chew her gums and fret about, Jennie thought. Wouldn't she have a fit if she didn't find out? Old evil Delia! This would be just the thing for her. It would pay her back for being so evil. It would also pay her, Jennie thought, for the way she used to grin at Jeff—long ago when her teeth were good.

The road became smooth and red, and Jeff could tell by the smell of the air that they were nearing the river. He could see the rise where the road turned and ran along parallel to the stream. The car chugged on monotonously. After a long silent spell, Jennie leaned against Jeff and spoke.

"How many bale o' cotton you think we got standin'?" she said.

Jeff wrinkled his forehead as he calculated.

"'Bout twenty-five, I reckon."

"How many you make las' year?"

"Twenty-eight," he said. "How come you ask that?"

"I's jest thinkin'," Jennie said quietly.

"It don't make a speck o' diff'ence though," Jeff reflected. "If we got much or if we get little, we still gonna be in debt to old man Stevenson when he gets through counting up agin us. It's took us a long time to learn that."

Jennie was not listening to these words. She had fallen into a trance-like meditation. Her lips twitched. She chewed her gums and rubbed her old gnarled hands nervously. Suddenly, she leaned forward, buried her face in the nervous hands, and burst into tears. She cried aloud in a dry, cracked voice that suggested the rattle of fodder on dead stalks. She cried aloud like a child, for she had never learned to suppress a genuine sob. Her slight old frame shook heavily and seemed hardly able to sustain such violent grief.

"What's the matter, baby?" Jeff asked awkwardly. "Why you cryin' like all that?"

"I's jes thinkin'" she said.

"So you the one what's scairt now, hunh?"

"I ain't scairt, Jeff I's jes thinkin' 'bout leavin' eve'thing like this—eve'thing we been used to. It's right sad-like."

Jeff did not answer, and presently Jennie buried her face again and continued crying.

The sun was almost overhead. It beat down furiously on the dusty wagon path road, on the parched roadside grass, and the tiny battered car. Jeff's hands, gripping the wheel, became wet with perspiration; his forehead sparkled. Jeff's lips parted and his mouth shaped a hideous grimace. His face suggested the face of a man being burned. But the torture passed and his expression softened again.

"You mustn't cry baby," he said to his wife. "We gotta be strong. We can't break down."

Jennie waited a few seconds, then said, "You reckon we oughta do it, Jeff? You reckon we oughta go 'head an' do it really?"

Jeff's voice choked; his eyes blurred. He was terrified to hear Jennie say the thing that had been in his mind all morning. She had egged him on when he had wanted more than anything in the world to wait, to reconsider, to think things over a little longer.

Now *she* was getting cold feet. Actually, there was no need of thinking the question through again. It would only end in making the same painful decision once more. Jeff knew that. There was no need of fooling around longer.

"We jest as well to do like we planned," he said. "They ain't nuthin else for us now—it's the bes' thing."

Jeff thought of the handicaps, the near impossibility, of making another crop with his leg bothering him more and more each week. Then there was always the chance that he would have another stroke, like the one that had made him lame. Another one might kill him. The least it could do would be to leave him helpless. Jeff gasped . . . Lord, Jesus! He could not bear to think of being helpless, like a baby, on Jennie's hands. Frail, blind Jennie.

The little pounding motor of the car worked harder and harder. The puff of steam from the cracked radiator became larger. Jeff realized that they were climbing a little rise. A moment later the road turned abruptly and he looked down upon the face of the river.

"Jeff."

"Hunh?"

"Is that the water I hear?"

"Hm. Tha's it."

"Well, which way you goin' now?"

"Down this-a way," he answered. "The road runs 'longside o' the water a lil piece."

She waited a while calmly. Then she said, "Drive faster."

"A'right, baby," Jeff said.

The water roared in the bed of the river. It was fifty or sixty feet below the level of the road. Between the road and the water there was a long smooth slope, sharply inclined. The slope was dry; the clay had been hardened by prolonged summer heat. The water below, roaring in a narrow channel, was noisy and wild.

"Jeff."

"Hunh?"

"How far you goin?"

"Jes a lil piece down the road."

"You ain't scairt is you, Jeff?"

"Nah, baby," he said trembling.   "I ain't scairt."

"Remember how we planned it, Jeff. We gotta do it like we said. Brave-like."

"Hm."

Jeff's brain darkened. Things suddenly seemed unreal, like figures in a dream. Thoughts swam in his mind foolishly, hysterically, like little blind fish in a pool within a dense cave. They rushed, crossed one another, jostled, collided, retreated, and rushed again. Jeff soon became dizzy. He shuddered violently and turned to his wife.

"Jennie, I can't do it. I can't." His voice broke pitifully.

She did not appear to be listening. All the grief had gone from her face. She sat erect, her unseeing eyes wide open, strained and frightful. Her glossy black skin had become dull. She seemed as thin and as sharp and bony as a starved bird. Now, having suffered and endured the sadness of tearing herself away from beloved things, she showed no anguish. She was absorbed with her own thoughts, and she didn't even hear Jeff's voice shouting in her ear.

Jeff said nothing more. For an instant there was light in his cavernous brain. That chamber was, for less than a second, peopled by characters he knew and loved. They were simple, healthy creatures, and they behaved in a manner that he could understand. They had quality. But since he had already taken leave of them long ago, the remembrance did not break his heart again. Young Jeff Patton was among them, the Jeff Patton of fifty years ago who went down to New Orleans with a crowd of country boys to the Mardi Gras doings. The gay young crowd—boys with candy-striped shirts and rouged brown girls in noisy silks—was like a picture in his head. Yet it did not make him sad. On that very trip Slim Bums had killed Joe Beasley—the crowd had been broken up. Since then Jeff Patton's world had been the Greenbrier Plantation. If there had been other Mardi Gras carnivals, he had not heard of them. Since then there had been no time; the years had fallen on him like waves. Now he was old, worn out. Another paralytic stroke like the one he had already suffered would put him on his back for keeps. In that condition, with a frail blind woman to look after him, he would be worse off than if he were dead.

Suddenly Jeff's hands became steady. He actually felt brave. He slowed down the motor of the car and carefully pulled off the road. Below, the water of the stream boomed, a soft thunder in the deep channel. Jeff ran the car onto the clay slope, pointed it directly toward the stream, and put his foot heavily on the accelerator. The little car leaped furiously down the steep incline toward the water. The movement was nearly as swift and direct as a fall. The two old black folks, sitting quietly side by side, showed no excitement. In another instant the car hit the water and dropped immediately out of sight.

A little later it lodged in the mud of a shallow place. One wheel of the crushed and upturned little Ford became visible above the rushing water.

A SUMMER TRAGEDY

Written by a Negro about his own people, this story is one of the first attempts to portray the human emotions of the Negro. Typically a white narrator depicted the Negro interacting with whites and recorded only external behavior—his good nature, his penchant for comedy, and his gratitude toward his white benefactor. This story takes the reader into the Negro cabin and into the Negro consciousness, thus offering a far different viewpoint from other local color stories of the period.

There is a great deal of fine craftsmanship in this story of an aged couple preparing for a trip. Although there is pathos in the plight of the old couple, the author maintains a consistent tone of restraint. The pride and dignity of both Jeff and Jennie are suggested in the opening paragraphs as they dress for the trip in their Sunday best: old Jeff's arthritic hands struggle to put on his freshly pressed moth-eaten swallow-tailed coat and master the bow tie and buttons; blind Jennie taps her way around the cabin, dressing in her Sunday best silk dress and shoes. As the line of action moves, the reader gradually realizes that this is not a trip to church or some festive occasion; it's an awesome trip: "fear came into his eyes; excitement took his breath." Through other references to "fear" and "trembling" interspersed in the details of preparation and journey, the action continues to rise until the purpose of the trip is revealed. Although the final scene is shocking, it is not surprising; it has been skillfully prepared for.

Pervading the entire story is an atmosphere of dryness and deadness created through imagery. Jennie has a "dead-leaf appearance;" she is "as thin and sharp and bony as a starved bird;" her "cracked voice suggests the rattle of fodder on dead stalks." The frizzly chickens are in a death "stupor," and the grass beside the dusty road is "parched." There is an implicit comparison between old Jeff's creaking body and the old Model-T Ford that "sputters," "rattles," and "bangs" as he cranks it for the trip.

Set in contrast to the imagery of deadness is imagery of life that surrounds the cabin: wasps humming, squirrels scampering, blue jays hopping, pine trees stretching. These images of life not only counterpoint the death imagery, they also serve to remind Jeff of what he is leaving; immediately afterward he feels fear.

The river, like the car, is noisy. The "little pounding motor worked harder and harder" to get to the river where the "water ..., roaring in a narrow channel, was noisy and wild." As the car plunges into the river, a subtle fusion of images occurs: the physical mode of travel blends with the symbolic as the old couple embark on their spiritual journey.

Elma Godchaux

(1893-1941)

Elma Godchaux was born on a Louisiana plantation near New Orleans, the daughter of Edward Godchaux and the granddaughter of Leon Godchaux, founder of the Godchaux sugar empire. After spending several years in the East where she attended Radcliffe College and later resided in New York, she returned to New Orleans and began her writing career. She was the author of many short stories, several of which were included in Edward J. O'Brien's *Best Short Stories*, as well as in the O. Henry Prize Stories. *Stubborn Roots*, a novel, was published in 1936, and at the time of her death Miss Godchaux was working on her second novel. All of her writing concerns the Louisiana scene—the people of the swamplands and sugarcane plantations. The story printed below was published in *Southern Review* in 1936.

The Horn That Called Bambine

Elma Godchaux

When I was a child, I used to hear Shoolie blow his horn. I used to feel sorry for Shoolie. When I grew to be a woman, I could still hear that horn sounding, and felt the same old sadness filling me up and choking me. It was always at sunset time that I heard the horn, when I was coming home from the field, dead-tired, feeling my heavy head and arms and the straight line of pain at the back of my neck as I dragged along. I heard Shoolie's horn and raised my head and looked over the cotton field and a green patch of cane, hunting for Shoolie, though I knew he wasn't there; I knew his horn was blowing in my head. I sighed, thinking of the things Shoolie had saved me from and the things he had brought me. Shoolie always liked me. But I never did nothing for Shoolie. I kept on down the road, thinking, and took the rise, thinking and hearing Shoolie's horn. The Lowell-sack full of cotton was awful heavy on my shoulder. I pulled it along and coughed, trying to get the dry cotton dust out of my throat. I felt my skirt sticking to my legs when I bent my knees, working up the rise. I couldn't never get used to the hill between my house and the cotton field, though I didn't know how many times I had climbed it from the field. Dan didn't think nothing of my climbing it. Dan didn't think much. He never thought why I couldn't get used to working in the field and lugging an old Lowell-sack. Mamma and Papa never believed in sending their girls to the fields. They said field work wasn't for white girls; if you were a nigger, it was different. Oh God, I thought, nobody couldn't tell what he might come to. Mamma and Papa would turn over in their graves, seeing me dragging the cotton. I kept on going, thinking if it hadn't been for Shoolie, maybe I wouldn't be harnessed to a Lowell-sack like a nigger.

I heard his horn. But the blasts didn't sound full no more, though, as if he was moving off or getting tired blowing. He used to get awful tired. He used to say he got tired enough to drop dead and his mouth hurt him. I used to wish he would stop, because I knew there wasn't no use in his blowing like that. But he wouldn't listen.

The blasts I heard were faint, faint. Then one of Fred Turner's fat white roosters hopped on the fence rail and crowed and killed Shoolie's horn; it was blotted out as if it had never been. Everything was quiet. Fred Turner's house looked bare and lonesome. It was a two-story house stuck on top of the hill. The whole world was beneath it. Far below it, the Turner pear trees and some bamboo made a blurry darkness; nothing grew near it. I could make out Mrs. Turner sitting on the gallery in one of the two rocking-chairs, rocking. I lowered my head and hurried on and got into the darkness of the big black oak and let out my breath. She was perched up there like she was sitting in a tower. She was rocking and rocking, nervous. I could hear her heels clicking. I coughed. Seemed to me, I could see her red eyes from where I was. They were always as red as blood. I wished I didn't have to see her or Fred or the house of theirs neither. I wondered were Mrs. Turner's eyes red from crying or because she ate morphine. She measured out her morphine on her long black fingernails. Everybody knew how she did it as good as if they seen her do it. Me and Dan often talked about her. He'd talk and talk until I got up and went about my business because I couldn't stand so much talk. I'd talk about Shoolie too. Talk about Miss Maime and Fred always led to talk about Shoolie. I wished I could forget them. But some things nobody forgot, things that marked lives the way trees and bushes marked roads and made them different from other roads. Shoolie and Fred had marked my life. I wondered if all the folks I knew had markers in their lives that I couldn't see. I stole another glance at Miss Maime. My sweat felt cold. None of us could see Miss Maime without a tremble. Miss Maime, we all called her since as far back as I could remember. She was some older than Fred Turner and looked a lot older. She had it easy too. But I didn't want it like she had it. I didn't want to be her.

My Lowell bumped against the tree roots and jogged over the ruts and hustled me along. The road was dropping down the hill and narrowing into the lane, following the bayou. Dead Bayou had been choked for a long time by matted hyacinths. I never did see any water in it. It looked under its flowers like the covered coffin I saw once in an old newspaper, and enormous long coffin lying there between the trees. Every summer and long into the fall, it was purple with flowers. That summer me and Dan got married, I used to pick big bunches of the hyacinths. But they died in no time and we stopped picking them. We never picked the blackeyed Susans that came later to the edges of the bayou. We soon found out we didn't have the time for flowers. The big coffin under the blanket of hyacinths stretched past my gate. Night was closing on it, sucking it in. I turned away and pushed on the gate. Dan never remembered to oil the hinges. I told myself I had to remind him again. I got tired reminding him about things. The iron pot I boiled my wash in swelled up, enormous, almost blocking the path to the house. We had put it in the shade of the sycamore tree, so I could work without the sun hitting me. I liked the pot. Dan said I was foolish liking an old pot. But it used to belong to Mamma and stood in her yard. It reminded me of when I was a child. It made me think how rested and strong I felt when I was a child. A couple of days after Mamma died, me and Dan borrowed Turner's team and went out and fetched the pot and some of Mamma's other things. I didn't like Dan asking young Fred Turner for the team; but there was nothing else we could have done. I wanted the pot. I always remembered Mamma when I saw it and Bambine too, Bambine stirring the clothes with a wooden stick. When all of us children were small, Bambine used to come over on Mondays and help Mamma with the wash. Papa never minded getting help. He didn't expect us girls to wash heavy clothes no more than Mamma did. We had it easy. The boys had it hard, but not us girls. After I was married to Dan, I could see how easy I'd had it.

We helped Mamma in the house and had to keep ourselves clean; and in the fall of the year we went to Turner's sugar mill after syrup. Sometimes old man Turner used to let us ride the mule that turned the crusher. I could ride the mule round and round longer than anybody else could. I could ride until old man Turner's nigger had to change the mule, because the mule got dizzy. Young Fred Turner used to watch me. Sometimes he laughed and called something to me. "You can't stand no more than a mule." Or something like that. I knew he was joking me. His words'd be all but smothered by giggles. When I got off the mule, I wouldn't be able to stand up and him and me would laugh together. Sometimes he'd follow me home; but most often he wouldn't; he'd have business to do at the mill; to have heard him talk, anybody would have thought he was running the mill instead of his old man. He'd stand and watch me. I'd feel his eyes on me as I climbed the stile and turned up the road. I passed my hand over the back of my dress to see if my skirt was down all right. I knew I looked ugly with the heavy bucket dragging one side of me down. Old man Turner gave me a big bucket for a nickel. Bees used to follow me home. Sometimes they bumped against the hand that toted the bucket; but they didn't sting me. When I got home, Bambine maybe would be in the yard, washing, and maybe Shoolie would be hanging over the fence, staring at her. They wouldn't be talking. Shoolie'd be staring at her like he couldn't see her enough, or hadn't ever seen her before and didn't live with her day in and day out in the cabin up Snake Lane. She would keep stirring the clothes, her heavy lips hanging down, still, like lips cut out of wood, and her breasts moving the least bit as she moved the stick; her breasts weren't loose like Mamma's; they looked hard, but full and heavy. I didn't blame Shoolie for hanging round looking at her. A silky flag of steam rose and floated over her head. She didn't pay any mind to Shoolie or little Toog playing near her or the clothes foaming over the top of the pot; she stirred and stirred like she was wound up to stir. I got the gate and Shoolie jumped off it and held it open and looked at me. Then he leaned close to me and blurted out, "Don't you tell your Mamma I is here," talking fast and holding his breath. "Don't you tell her nothing. You hear, Miss Florie? Please, Miss Florie." Mamma didn't like him hanging round, staring at Bambine like he was crazy. But I knew Shoolie didn't mean no harm. And he never kept Bambine from working. She raised her head and looked at me. Her hair stuck out. Her black face was shining with sweat, so was her neck; she looked polished all over like the fine piano the Turners had in their house. She stretched her flat nose. "Florie," talking, slow, in a deep voice, "give me a lick of your syrup." I held the bucket for her and she dug the handle of her stick into the syrup and lifted it out, dripping. Toog cried out and she leaned down and fed him. When she stood up again, her full height looked awful tall. She licked her hand and the stick.

It seemed to me now as I walked up the path round the fat pot that I could see Bambine standing up stirring, her heavy lips hanging, gleaming, painted with syrup. I could see Toog with his shift hardly covering his belly and Shoolie staring, green eyes clear as glass; I never saw a clear-eyed nigger until I saw Shoolie. I thought I could hear Mamma's chickens scuttling out of my path; she used to keep a lot of chickens; and the pigs raising themselves out of the mire and the old cow, Bottle, coming after me, nuzzling the bucket. Dan and me never had enough chickens to make a noise scuttling and we never bothered with pigs; we could buy pork at the store when we had money. And we could drive the cow out of the yard to live on the woods. We didn't milk her more than every other day in cotton-picking time. It was a good thing her feed was poor, I thought, or she'd have suffered not being milked. I knew I wasn't walking to Mamma's door, but my own. My baby came running to me. She was whimpering. I wiped her nose with my hand. Toog was stuffing some sticks into the stove.

"Toog," I fussed, "why you ain't started the fire before now? What you been doing? The baby's hongry. Why you didn't give her a cold sweet potato?"

Toog didn't answer. He went on shoving in the sticks. He never spoke much, like his mamma, and his lips hung down like hers. But his eyes were like Shoolie's, strange, light, not nigger eyes. The baby leaned against me, munching the potato. I took her in my arms.

"Toog," sitting down and talking to his back, "keep stirring the grits so it ain't going to be lumpy." I was too tired to move. "God, I wish I could learn you." The baby smelled hot. I held her close to me. She was awful hungry. I kept fussing at Toog, "Dish out the food. Make haste. I don't know how come you let the baby get so hongry." He piled the food on the plate and set it on the table and didn't talk back to me. He wasn't a sassy nigger. He was a lot like Shoolie. I coughed. "Dish out your supper, Toog," I said. "I reckon you're hongry enough to eat."

He took his plate to the shed room and sat down on the bench under the low roof. His back looked like a pencil line scratched on the darkness, awful thin. I kept watching the little thin line that was him. He helped me a lot and I always let my sharp temper lash out at him. But I knew Toog didn't mind as long as I kept him and fed him, and I was going to keep him as long as I kept myself, the same as if he was my own. Darkness was covering the yard and reaching into the room where I sat. I couldn't see hardly anything but the sycamore tree raising its white trunk high into the darkness. The locusts were singing. Dan ought to've been coming home. I always had to worry about Dan. The baby nestled down in my lap. But I wanted her to eat some more. I want you to grow up fine. "Come on," I begged. "Eat some more I want you to grow up fine. I don't want you picking cotton. I don't want you having it hard. You ain't going to neither, not if me and Dan can help it." I knew I was a fool sitting up talking to the baby and her sleeping. I went on talking like a fool, "God, I'm glad you're a girl." I sniffled and coughed and hugged her and she was sleeping and the darkness made me feel bad. It made me feel like I wanted to see my boys. They were the same as dead. Night was like death, I thought, foolish, as black and secret. Dan was hard on the boys. He was too hard. But I knew he didn't mean no harm to them. But he beat them awful. The boys ran away because they hated him. He beat them so awful. Oh God, thanks for making my baby a girl. Girls didn't get beat and girls didn't leave home. Bambine had left. But she was a nigger. Folks said she went clear to New Orleans. After that, Shoolie took to blowing his horn every day at sunset.

We children used to go down the lane to watch him. He'd step out of his cabin and turn right up the lane and puff his cheeks, blowing hard on the cow horn a good number of times; then he'd turn left and blow. I'd call to him when I couldn't stand to watch him no more, "Shoolie." And he'd lower the horn. He was always a polite nigger. "Bambine's in New Orleans," I'd say. "She ain't going to hear you no matter how hard you blow." He'd answer, stubborn, "She going to hear. Listen. Don't you hear that sound traveling away?" Nobody could tell that nigger nothing about blowing for Bambine. But he was a good nigger. I kept at him, "You oughtn't to wear yourself out blowing like that. Bambine's having a good time in New Orleans. Folks say that yellow nigger that took her has got some money." He panted, "Just let me tell her I'm waiting." Little Toog stood in back of his papa, watching. Shoolie went on, "She coming back. You going to see." Then he leaned forward and whispered, breathless, "You better be watching out for yourself, Miss Florie. Something tells me maybe I'm going to be blowing for you some day like I'm blowing for Bambine now. You better be watching out some yellow man don't tote you off. He ain't no nigger, but he's yellow as some niggers. You better watch out, Miss Florie. You is too pretty for your own good." I laughed and pretended I didn't know what he was talking about. I said, "Shoolie. Don't talk crazy." Everybody laughed because they all thought he wasn't all there. He didn't pay any mind to them. "I'm telling you for your own good," he whispered. "Mind out for yourself." I stopped laughing. His face looked awful sad; I couldn't laugh; and his eyes kept watching me as though his eyes were going to tell me things his mouth couldn't. I knew he liked me. Maybe because I never told Mamma when I caught him hanging on the fence behind Bambine.

I thought a lot about Shoolie, mostly at sunset time. He made me feel all choked up and bad. I hoped he knew I was keeping Toog. I could hear one of my scrawny hens that was too hungry to roost pecking round Toog's feet. Toog dropped her some sweet potato. Toog was always good to dumb beasts. I knew he was good to the baby too.

I called out, "Toog. Don't you give that old hen all your sweet potato."

Then I heard Dan in the yard. I knew it was him by the way his feet dragged. I got up and lit the lamp and put his food on to heat. His body made a black smear in the doorway. I looked at him. He looked strange, so black and heavy.

He came close to me and stooped over the baby. "What she's doing, asleep already?" he fussed. Ain't she asleep early?" He put his hand over her face.

"Don't you wake her up," I cried. "She's all wore out and she just ate."

He kept looking at her and blurted all of a sudden, "They got a new schoolteacher over at Cotton Port. Old Babe Landry just tole me. I bet this kid is going to be smart, smarter than the boys." He stopped and wet his lips. He sat down at the table, quick, and I put his food in front of him. I didn't know what had come over him because we never talked about the boys.

"Eat your supper," I said, trying to cover up his words. I sat facing him. "Did you get the wagon loaded?" I asked, natural.

"Sho'. It's loaded." And dropped his fork.

"Well, why you don't eat?" I asked.

"I been studying about Fred Turner's crop," he said, slow, like he was choosing his words. "He's got a nice crop on the land he works with the niggers, plenty nicer than ours. I reckon you know what that means."

"No," I said, biting my lip. "No. What it means?"

"Well, maybe he ain't going to let us go halves with him next year. He ain't the one to let us go halves if we don't make much. He's got to keep Miss Maime in morphine, don't he?" He kind of laughed.

"Don't start that talk," I cried. "For God sake. What we going to do if he don't let us go halves?"

"Don't ask me. How do I know?"

My lip hurt. "He'll let us go halves," I cried. "You see if he don't. It ain't so much work for him. We have all the worry," I hurried on, "and he gets half our crop no matter what."

"We ain't going to make eight bales this year," Dan said, pushing my words aside.

"We ain't going to make five."

"This is a bad year for everybody," I reminded him. "We ain't had no rain in the growing time."

"Turner did good on the land he worked himself," he said again. "It held the wet good. He worked it a lot."

"Well, eat your supper," I said, tired. I knew there wasn't no use trying to tell Dan something. "It's seven o'clock right now," I went on. "We got to get to bed. We got to be up at three if you got the wagon loaded. It's loaded, ain't it, Dan?" keeping at him. "It's ready to drive to the gin? Ain't it? Ain't it?"

The baby moved and fussed.

"Stop yelling," Dan cried. "You're waking up the baby yourself."

"Hush, hush, dearie. She ain't awake," I whispered. "You got it loaded? Ain't you? It's loaded?" It wasn't that he was lazy. But I had to keep after him.

"I said it was," he growled. "I reckon you heard me."

"Well, make haste now," I said, "and come to bed."

I went to the next room and put the baby on the bed. I didn't wash her because she was sleeping.

I called out, "Dan. Come on to bed." I didn't want him sitting fretting.

For once, he got right up and came into the dark room. I could make him out, standing near me, fiddling with his clothes. I began working with mine. My body felt heavy and big. Dan unbuttoned his clothes, slow. I could smell the sweat on him and me. I went to the shed and washed. But Dan was too tired.

I climbed in the bed after him and pulled down on the baby's nightgown. Dan touched her once and turned away from her and me. I could hear the locusts singing and singing. I couldn't sleep. It was hot in the bed. I smelled cotton.

Me and Dan left the baby sleeping on the bed.

Outside, everything was still. No wind moved the leaves. Only a white mist was moving, rising from the bayou. I could hear the horse thudding in the deep dust. Dan was leading him by a loose rein. I wasn't thinking a thing about Fred Turner. I was just walking along, and there he was. He was coming down the hill, a couple of niggers with him. The sight of him knocked out my breath. It always did, no matter how often I saw him. I wasn't scared of him exactly. I just didn't like seeing him. I prayed God he wasn't going to stop us. He came, walking a little ahead of the niggers, big, his hip-pocket bulging with the gun he always toted, his chest sticking out, tearing through the mist. Fred Turner was always like that, always seemed to be tackling something with all his strength. I couldn't catch my breath. He was just across the bayou from me, right close, looking at me. His eyes were two points. I waited like a fool instead of walking on.

He shouted at me, "You all sho' you got enough cotton to tote to the gin?" and laughed. "You all are some farmers," laughing.

His laughs prickled up my back like icy fingers. Me and Dan didn't say nothing. Fred Turner's eyes were gone; all of a sudden as if they had been rubbed out. I heard Dan and the old horse thudding on. I knew I had to move.

I could see our wagon-load of cotton by the side of the road. It needed packing down. I got my shoes off, quick, and climbed on the load and stamped. I stamped, fierce. I wished I was stamping Turner. Then I felt like I was stamping him. My face burned. I was mashing him out of my life. I wasn't talking to him. I was just mashing him. He wasn't going to be a marker no more. I was paying him for what he did to Shoolie.

Dan called to me, "For God sakes, that's enough. What you reckon you packing down?"

I stopped and looked at Dan and jumped off the wagon. I watched it rumble into the darkness and get swallowed.

The milky mist was moving off over the fields, slow. It made them look sad and kind of scary. I walked on down the road through the stillness, stretching my legs wide. They were as strong as a man's legs. My heart was big and strong too. I could feel it beating. I ought to have talked up to Turner, I thought, mad with myself. He wasn't no better than me and Dan. I ought to have talked right back to him. I stood still, hearing wagon-chains rattling, knowing they were Turner's. I waited and saw him coming, riding above the mist. I made myself stand there and look straight at him. I had bold eyes and I made them hold Turner. They seemed to drag his wagon to a stop. He looked down at me. His eyes got under my clothes. Fred Turner's eyes always did that.

He laughed that laugh of his as if he wasn't having any fun. "Well, if it ain't Miss Florie again. Hello, Florie." His hard voice smashed the silence. I looked down at my feet. So did the nigger beside him look down. "You ain't lost your tongue, have you?" he yelled. "You can say good morning, I reckon, without dying from it."

I worked my tongue. But I didn't make a sound. I nodded, and that seemed to satisfy him. I was sweating. My body felt awful hot.

He took his eyes off me at last and looked over the field. "I might get that white nigger down the road named Lamson to go halves with me," he said and spit over the side of the wagon. "This is good land. I'm going to make a good crop off it. Now what you going to say to that? What you going to say?" he kept on. "You better speak up."

I coughed and swallowed. "There ain't been no rain," I panted. "You can't do nothing without rain."

"You can work the ground good," he threw back. "The fellow you married is too lazy." He never had no use for Dan. "You work the ground good," he went on, "and the crop'll be good. I ain't going to have no scraggly cotton with no bolls, throwing away the land. I ain't going to have it. Damn it."

I didn't move and neither did the nigger. Turner took his eyes off me and put them on the nigger and on me again. He was watching how dead-quiet he made me and the nigger.

He raised his whip and touched me with it, squirming it over my shoulder, and I didn't flinch so much as an eye lash. "Yes ma'am," he whined, "you better watch out. You might find

yourselves chased off here and that nigger, Lamson, going halves."
He watched me a long minute and I didn't move. One of his horses
blew some air through its nose and that roused him and he gave the
horse a lick with the whip. I knew he wanted to make the beast as
quiet as he did us humans, me and the nigger. "Giddap," he cried,
giving the horse another lick. The wagon rattled. The nigger jolted
by me like a rag doll, so still and spineless.

I stood there. Oh God, I thought, I was a fool; I couldn't open my
mouth to Turner. I was a fool believing I could mash him out of my
life. He wasn't no dead marker neither. He was a cat with busy
claws. He had caught me and Dan and the baby too. We were the
mice. I couldn't do nothing. I wished Dan was the man to stand up to
Turner. But I knew there wasn't no use wishing. Dan couldn't do
nothing, no more than Shoolie could. I raised my heavy feet and
moved. I was tired trying to do something against Fred Turner. I was
tired thinking too. Poor Shoolie. His horn was still now.

Fred had been dead-set against his blowing. Everybody felt
sorry for Shoolie; but not Fred Turner, he didn't feel sorry. He said
Shoolie didn't have no right blowing and sending the sound out over
the Turners' field. Fred always made it a point to make the nigger
stop blowing. No matter where Fred was when he heard the horn,
he would quit what he was doing and go off down Shoolie's lane
and stop before Shoolie and holler and, if Shoolie didn't stop quick
enough, he'd grab the nigger's arm. I saw him many a time. The
nigger would turn his scared eyes to Fred and lower the horn. Fred'd
laugh and spit. "The nigger's crazy," he'd say to me after he
finished spitting. "I ain't going to have that horn blowing in my
ears. He ain't going to make me crazy or deaf neither." And Shoolie
looked at me. He never looked long at Fred. "I hate good-for-
nothing niggers like Shoolie," Fred went on.

I walked, slow, lugging my heavy thoughts. The mist was gone.
The hyacinths looked faded and old. The sky was red; it made a
wall in front of me. The air was heavy. I couldn't hardly breathe.
Miss Maime was sitting on the gallery. I watched her rocking and
the sound she made rode across the bayou to me. She had a white
shawl round her head. She looked like a ghost. Her heels kept
clicking, sharp, rocking and never stopping. Seemed like her heels
were following me.

I half ran down the hill, thanking God I wasn't her. I kept thinking I wasn't her and thanking God for it and for Dan and my baby who was a girl. Dan wasn't quick and smart like Fred Turner was or nothing like that and I knew it. But I didn't care. I wouldn't have been Miss Maime married to Fred Turner for nothing on earth. I wiped my face.

I shoved open my gate, and my baby was sitting on the ground. I grabbed her, quick, and hugged her. She squirmed. She didn't like to be grabbed and hugged like that. I sat her down and laughed; but I didn't feel like laughing. Toog had a fire going on the bricks under the wash pot. He was limping round the yard, hunting sticks. I watched him and all of a sudden I was wondering if he remembered me when I was a kid stopping in his daddy's cabin. If I went to the woods in back of the cabin to pick blackberries, I always stopped to see Shoolie. I'd always give Shoolie a big helping out of my bucket. I never asked Toog if he remembered something, and he never said.

Toog and me used to watch Shoolie stuff the berries down his throat. Shoolie'd laugh. "You all are having as much fun as if you all was eating," he'd say. Then he'd stand up and wipe his hands on his pants and say, "Me and Toog is much obliged for the berries. Since Bambine is gone, we ain't got no time for picking." He'd break off and open his eyes and go on in a changed voice, "I swear to God, Miss Florie, you sho' is pretty, too pretty for your own good. You is like Bambine, I always said it, too fine for your own self." I didn't laugh. I kept staring back at him. I knew he hated Fred. All the niggers hated Fred Turner. They were scared of him. I used to feel kind of proud of the way the niggers all hated Fred and were scared of him. I used to look at Fred's cold gray eyes and his heavy hands and his strong neck and the way it sat in the middle of his square shoulders and I used to think Fred Turner couldn't help being fine and strong and making folks scared of him. And he wasn't scared of nothing.

Me and Fred used to go walk at the end of the long summer days. Mamma and Papa never cared, because Fred was a Big Dog and I was doing good for myself getting Fred Turner. We always went to the Scary Woods. The path there was hidden and dark and me and Fred could press close together. The cypress trees and oaks and sycamores, reaching above us, looked like tall haunts. Fred would squeeze my arm and I'd feel his touch run through me. "You ain't scared?" he'd whisper. I giggled, "I am and I ain't." And wouldn't know if it was fear or love that made my skin creep. He twisted my arm close to him, and I didn't cry out; I didn't mind being hurt; I knew his strong love made him hurt me. I didn't want to leave the woods. I wanted to be hidden with Fred. We walked along, slow, squeezing each other and stopping sometimes and following the path that was like a hole through the trees and coming out at last into the open where the pale light of dusk was lying. "You wasn't scared?" Fred asked. His eyes made my face hot. "You don't have to be scared of nothing when you're with me," he went on, spitting the way he did when he said something he meant real hard. "I got a gun," he explained. "Look here. Nobody can't afford to go nowheres without a gun." I said, "Put it up. For goodness sake." And grinned. "I didn't know a gun was good for haunts." His rough voice pushed against my face. You knew the kind of man Fred was the minute he opened his mouth. "I don't give that for a man that don't tote a gun," snapping his fingers. I said again, "Put it up." Shoolie's horn swallowed my words. He was blowing it, hard. Fred's face got fiery and there was a white line round his mouth. He cried out, "There's that fool nigger. I'm going to make him stop that blowing if it's the last thing I do. He's got his nerve blowing like he owned the world." I was scared, I didn't know why, of something in Fred's red and white face. I argued, "He ain't hurting you. Why you don't let him alone?" He turned on me, yelling, "I don't like that blowing. I ain't never liked it. If you like a nigger making a racket, I don't. And I been telling Shoolie." He grabbed my wrist and started down Shoolie's lane. The blowing swelled out and sounded awful mournful. I tried to pull away, crying, "I don't want to go yonder. I ain't going." His voice was hard, strong, like iron. "Come on," he cried. "And look here," turning me to face him, "when we're married, you ain't going to be saying what you going to do and what you ain't." He gave me a funny look like he was seeing me for the first time. And pulled me on. His grip on my arm felt like an iron grip. The horn sound was opening like a funnel and we were walking into the middle of it. Shoolie was standing in the lane with Toog near; little Toog was pouting and picking his nose. Fred yelled out, "Stop that blowing." Shoolie took the horn out of his mouth. The sound broke off like it was stepped on. Shoolie began begging, "I got to be blowing. Excuse me, Mr. Fred. It's time." Fred hollered, "You quit." But the nigger raised the horn and blew. Fred grabbed the nigger's arm and yelled, "You goddamn sassy nigger." Shoolie pulled away. I never knew what got into Shoolie that day. He yanked his arm away from Fred. He was little and thin; but he was strong. He was panting, "It ain't nothing to you, white man. I'm got to blow. Bambine might be waiting. I got to blow for her to come home." He blew, stubborn. Fred yelled, "Quit. Quit, you black son of a—" The blowing was going off over Fred's head when his shot smashed it. The awful loud shot knocked the horn out of Shoolie's mouth, broke against the trees. A thin ribbon of smoke moved away. Shoolie screamed. He was holding his stomach and screaming. Blood slid between his fingers. He looked at it. Then looked at Fred and babbled out, "You killed me. You killed me." He said it over and over. "You killed me. For nothing. I wasn't doing you nothing. I was blowing for Bambine. She was listening for me to blow. You killed me." He rocked and turned his eyes to me; they were clear as clear mirrors. "Miss Florie," he cried and toppled down, slow, and hit the ground and his eyes kept hold of me and didn't change as though they didn't feel that fall. "Miss Florie, you seen him," he went on, "you seen him. I didn't do him nothing. He did it for nothing. You seen him. You better go on away from him. You better go on," in a new strong voice, "go on. Run." He rolled a little like a log finding a place on a pile. His mouth was open. One big blood bubble ballooned between his fingers. I screamed and ran. My throat felt tight. Fred called me. I couldn't hardly breathe. He kept yelling. But he wasn't chasing me. I ran past my house. I knew Dan would be at the store, wishing I had let him come over home.

There was a lot of men on the store gallery. They were talking and yawning and chewing and spitting like always. I didn't hardly see them. I ran to Dan and threw my arms around his neck and hugged him and cried. Dan's arms covered me and I felt safe. But that day was a long time ago. I never felt that safe again.

I wiped my face, wishing Shoolie was back again. I stirred the clothes in the pot, slow, like I used to see Bambine stir them, wishing the old days were back with Bambine in Mamma's yard and Shoolie hanging over the gate. I blew my nose on my apron and stirred and stirred. Steam kept blowing up from the pot and covering me. I stirred. I didn't stop when I heard Dan fumbling with the gate. He came on in the yard, touching the baby's head when he passed her.

I called to him, "Dan. How much'd the load make?"

"A bale," he said, "four hundred and eighty pounds."

"That ain't much."

"It ain't bad," he gave back, pulling off the horse's bridle.

"Well," I said, and stopped stirring. I could feel my heart hanging in me, heavy. "You saw Turner?"

"Sho'. He was yonder. Getting ginned." I waited. And Dan saw me wait. "He didn't say much," Dan said. "But we're going halves another year. He let that out." I didn't move. Dan watched me. "Well," he asked me, "ain't you satisfied?"

"Sho'," I said and stirred. The smell and the mist from the steaming clothes rose up between me and Dan. The gray mist was as good as walls around me. I was in the world alone, but only for a minute and Shoolie's horn was sounding breaking down my walls. I never had heard his horn before in the broad daylight. The sound was close to me, covering me and moaning, moaning words about me and Dan. Me and Dan, we were mice in the same cat's paws, the paws that had killed Shoolie. We couldn't do nothing. Me and Dan kept staring at each other. And Shoolie was tired. The blowing faded. It spread out, thin, over the fields and dropped down into the hollow where the bayou was. I pulled my eyes away from Dan's and lowered my head and stirred; he moved across the yard; and I kept stirring.

THE HORN THAT CALLED BAMBINE

This story has minimal plot. The conflict is slight; it involves the question of whether Fred Turner, owner of the farm, will allow Florie, the narrator, and her husband, Dan, to continue as sharecroppers since their crop has failed. The chronology is softly blurred as Florie's memory moves back and forth to retrieve pieces of the pattern of the tale and fit them into her present predicament.

The sound of the horn, which pervades the story, fills it with a sadness associated with loss. Shoolie, a black farmhand, had lost his wife Bambine to another man; and he tried each evening at sunset to call her back by blowing on a homemade cow horn. The sound has remained in Florie's mind through the years, and as she hears the horn, she reflects, as she has done countless times, on the sound and events of a particular day. A sensitive, compassionate woman who obviously related to Shoolie as a person rather than as a Negro, she understood his feelings—his love for Bambine, his sadness, his loneliness, and his compulsion to blow the horn. It expressed both his sense of loss and his hope that she would hear it and return. But because the sound of it irritated Fred Turner, the mill owner's brash pistol-toting son who planned to marry Florie, he killed him. Horrified as Shoolie falls at her feet, Florie runs away and rushes into the arms of Dan, an irresponsible man whom she soon marries.

Unable to rid herself of the sound of the horn or the image of Shoolie, Florie reflects constantly on his impact on her life. On the one hand, Shoolie's blowing and his brutal death "saved" her from marrying Fred, the prosperous bully; on the other hand, it propelled her into a loveless marriage with one of Fred's sharecroppers, which doomed her to a life of field work that she has been taught is beneath her. Then there is also her inability to come to terms with her deep feeling for Shoolie: as a fellow human he is her close friend, and she has taken his child Toog to rear; but the Southern code is still operative—Toog works for his room and board and eats in the side shed.

Unlike local color stories, this story does not exploit peculiarities of either the area or the people. It does, however, establish a strong sense of place in the easily visualized details of

322

the cotton and cane fields, the syrup mill, and the hyacinth-choked bayous as a backdrop for deep and ambiguous emotions.

James Aswell

(1906-1955)

James Aswell was born in Baton Rouge, but as the son of a U.S. Representative, he spent much of his childhood in Washington, D.C., where he became a cub reporter at the age of fifteen. After attending the University of Virginia for three years, he began working for King Features Syndicate in New York. In 1947 he returned with his wife to Natchitoches where he had lived during his father's tenure as president of Louisiana State Normal School (now Northwestern State University). There he remained until his death in 1955 farming, writing, and taking an active stand in anti-Longism politics. His first major novel was *The Midsummer Fires,* described by Erskine Caldwell as the "only novel in American literature that successfully tells the tragic and ageless story of the defeat and despair of man's estate in middle life." Other novels include *There's One in Every Town* (1951), *Birds and Bees* (1953), and *Young and Hungry-Hearted* (1955). He also wrote a number of short stories, published in leading magazines of the day but as yet uncollected. The story printed below first appeared in *Woman's Magazine* in 1949.

The Shadow of Evil*

James Aswell

The dawn was cool and full of promise, but the promise was false. By ten o'clock even dogs and children and the bloodless old would be gasping under the obscenities of the sun.

Clari thought, There should be no dilemma—this should be the happiest day of our marriage so far. Yet she had begun to feel nervous from the very moment they started loading the car for the trip to the Capital City.

"This is it, Babe." Steve grinned proudly. "Ten to one this is it."

"Yes." Clari smiled brightly.

She was a small girl, a bright Baltic blonde with an uptilted nose, frailly made, not beautiful, but freshly cute against Steve's massive maleness. Sometimes, lying beside his great bulk in bed at night, she had reflected wryly, "How huge this boy, and yet how weak. How little I am beside him. And yet how strong." But then she would be possessed of doubt that she was strong at all or, if she were, in what places. She knew the places Steve was weak in, though; yes, she knew every one of them, knew them well.

He asked, "You lock the door?"

"Yes, Governor."

Steve got in beside her, grinning, happy. He swept his hat off, put his foot on the starter.

"Here we go."

Clari's face softened as she watched him, and the sheer physical attraction he had for her liquidated every doubt for a grateful moment.

They drove away from the green clapboard cottage, through the sleepy-eyed town, and down the straight highway. Ahead, two hundred miles of suffocating, glare-flashed miles led straight to the Capital City; to glory, no less; to the almost certain fruition of Steve's great, obsessive hope. For the governor wouldn't have summoned them unless he had a real political plum to offer Steve when they got there.

Yes, and at the end of this trip she must come face to face with her own incorrigible apprehension. Apprehension of what? There

*Reprinted by permission of Gregory Hesselberg.

was Hugh; she would meet him again this night. She was miserable at the prospect (and around the misery crawled a twinkling, mocking ring of delight). But Hugh was not the whole reason for her vast disquiet. She could handle him, if that were all there was to worry over. Hugh was the past, rationalized and forsworn. It was the future that so ominously waited down the empty road.

At Le Feu the sun was up, and they crossed the bayou and kept on through the short business street to the cotton fields beyond. In front of Bayonville's general store four Negroes grinned and waved, recognizing Steve.

He waved back and chuckled. "Wave to them. Governor Kanger says by next election fifty thousand of 'em will be voting in the state."

She was silent. He went on, "We'll knock 'em off with that pension, just like we knocked off the country po' whites. Governor Kanger's pretty smart about those things, almost as smart as his cousin was. He saw the nigger thing coming and he'll take 'em over solid—when I run."

"Steve, do me a favor, please. Don't use that word."

He glanced at her, quizzical, grinning. "Still a Yankee, huh, baby? They don't mind what they're called. They're used to it."

"I'm not thinking of them. I'm thinking of you. That word makes you lose dignity. It cheapens you."

He made a face at the road. "All right. Colored ladies and gentlemen."

She took breath in. She felt that she was sinking into odious glue. And it wasn't Steve's fault. He was caught too.

When men chose a path to power, their wives went too, unquestioning, so what was eating her? Social conscience? Bunk. Women fell in love with mankind only when they couldn't contrive a satisfactory love affair with a man. But the facetiousness of that thought did not ring entirely true with her.

Let Steve have his hour! It would be her hour too, wouldn't it? The governor's wife. The First Lady. The Mansion. And they were still so young, they could savor it all to the full. Steve had come so very near to utter smashup after he got back from the war. A trickle of terror sent her limp just to remember those awful days and weeks during that period—when Steve, starting with a cocktail at home or even a glass of beer, would progress through brawls at the Elks Club, disappearances for days at a time, until owners of near or far honky-tonks telephoned. Then came the days around the house after that, when he would alternately swear off and beg for a drink, and the inevitable finale in the sanitarium in a neighboring state.

It was an ache that went right through you, watching your lover melt and decompose before your eyes into a lump of pink dough. The two psychiatrists at the sanitarium told her it was just a sickness like any other, and outside moral judgment. But she was sure that the two psychiatrists did judge—that they gloated over the spectacle of this splendid animal brought low, made lesser than they were, trembling and dependent.

Steve seemed to tune in her thought.

"Do you realize I haven't had a drink in eight months?"

"Yes, darling. I think it's wonderful."

"All that crazy stuff's behind me. You don't have to worry any more. I just have an allergy or something to alcohol, and now that I know it I can cope with it." He chuckled. "Governor Kanger's been checking up—don't you worry. He knows all that bunk is finished, else he wouldn't have called."

The broad, handsome face was tranquil with confidence. He said, "Do you also realize you and I have a good chance of living in the Governor's Mansion for four years after the next election?"

She nodded slightly.

"Doesn't it give you a bang?"

She stared at the road, thinking back to something, wondering whether she ought to mention it.

"Good Lord, honey, doesn't the prospect thrill you?"

"Oh, sure, Steve. But do you remember? You remember when we were at Central State, when we first knew each other, eight years ago? Lord, eight years!"

Steve squinted at the road ahead. "Remember? Sure. Lots of things. What, for instance?"

"Well, about your band. How you were going to play your way around the world. With me as the vocalist." She sighed. "You know—that has always seemed a good idea to me."

"Shucks. That was kid stuff, Ree." He seemed to want to close the subject, to get on with his driving or another discussion.

"I know."

Hot. Not unbearable smotheration yet, but a slowly rising, brassy glare. She eyed the fine coppery hair on Steve's left wrist; it was a big wrist, competent, virile on the steering wheel in sunlight, marked by a neat, three-inch scar.

"I guess politics runs in the blood," Steve said. "I got elected to the House of Representatives easily enough didn't I?"

He meant his father, of course, when he said politics ran in the blood—and he *had* been elected easily to the state House of Representatives. But that was because of his father. She remembered Stephen Lenihan, Sr., in the final year of his life.

Yes, Senator Lenihan's son could be elected to almost anything he wanted, because the old man had been respected and loved all over the state—even nationally. Most astounding to Clari was the fact that he had been respected and loved for his enormous integrity. That this was a paradox in politics she knew from what she had seen of politicians since. She would always be proud, even grateful, to remember that the Senator had approved of her. His pride was so solid, so unpurchasable; she wished that Steve could be like the old man.

In a way, she had repaid the old Senator's approval of her—and in the same act betrayed Steve. It was a trivial thing, but recollection of it still flicked her with guilt. Steve was campaigning for Carl Kanger, after Kanger's first cousin—the fabulous governor, the despot—had died from a marksman's gun during a parade.

Steve had said, "Politics is a business in this state. Sure, some of the Kanger's friends have been crooked and got caught. Most of it was exaggerated by the high-hat, sissy do-gooders who want the jobs. Dad doesn't understand. He's too high-principled to be practical. My future, now—"

Yes. Old Man Lenihan hadn't understood. He had considered all the Kangers vermin, but he hadn't been violent about it, just shrugged and twisted his face into an expression of scorn. "Let Steve find out. He's young. He's not for politics—I know. But you're good for him. Pick him up when he's bumped by that Camorra of heels—he'll be bumped and he'll need you."

It had been said gently, with love. So she had gone into the privacy of the voting booth and marked her ballot for the grave little anti-Kanger man, whom Steve opposed. But the man represented what Steve's father had wanted for himself and his son; he spoke with such high earnestness and clearly read books and bathed regularly—frailties the Kangers ostentatiously disdained the deeper they got in the country. She had voted against Carl Kanger, against Steve's candidate, perhaps against Steve's political future. She had voted, really, for the illusion of public office she had held before she felt herself swallowed up in

Kanger politics. She had voted even for Hugh, in a way. Hugh had been responsible for so much of her thinking. She wished he hadn't. She wished she had never met him, for more than one reason. She could see him now, the young instructor in social studies, angular and ugly and magnetic as a lodestone.

Damn Hugh forever. Not only for the months of their terrible, doomed love affair, but for the way he had taught her to think. Except for Hugh, she might be without a worry, humming this moment down the slowly cooking ribbon of flat highway, going with her husband into fulfillment and high adventure. Why had she come to this land of heat and subtle, stalking, unnameable terror, anyway? There had never been any politics talked in her home. Her father, a quiet Lett cabinetmaker, had brought her mother and herself down for a season to get away from the Wisconsin winter—and they had stayed. Then she had found herself suddenly married to Steve, with the episode of Hugh over and finished, and a steel-trap world of heat, implacable heat and politics and vituperation and snide maneuver closing around her.

Steve turned off beside a pair of red gas pumps in front of a low, rawpine structure plastered with beer and snuff signs. On the dirty window a sign read HURD MASTOCK: GEN'L MERCHANDISE. Clari could smell stock feed, and the paint on the car cooking. A pearl of perspiration crawled down one small breast; she shuddered.

A fat, dirty man with a stubble of gray beard waddled out into the sun.

"Hi, Mr. Steve," he said without warmth, unsmiling. "Brother wants to see you. Did you git my post card?"

Steve got out of the car, hearty and beaming. He gripped the other man's hand. "You bet I did. That's why I'm here. How's Hurd?"

"Ain't no better. An' he's sick with worryin'." The man's blue eyes were slitted, bitter.

"We'll fix that. Come on, Clari, I want you to meet my good friend Pete Mastock. You never met my wife, did you, Pete?"

Pete's expression did not change. He watched Clari come around the front of the car into the horror of the hot, white gravel.

Clari stuck out her hand and tried to smile.

Pete touched it limply with a dirty paw. He looked down quickly, almost servilely.

Pete opened the screen and they moved ahead of him into the odd, rancid darkness typical of little lost general stores in the Deep South. Then Clari's pupils expanded and she could see.

The room was unbelievably cluttered with a sad, vagarious stock. It always came joltingly to Clari to remember that these things were necessities of life—buttons, slightly tarnished knives, loaves of bread, cheap candy, a bunch of bananas, the stack of flyspecked shoe boxes over the counter, on which new clothing with a vague, used air was carelessly piled. There was the glass case with the candies, the tired brown and pink and white cakes.

In the spicy, hushed dimness were three people. A little girl in a filthy dun dress, sucking on a popsicle and viewing the newcomers from the tops of her eyes. She seemed no more than eight, although she had startling little breasts like crab apples. A blowsy white woman slumped on a stool behind the main counter. A young man in faded overalls sat on the counter near her, lazily chewing tobacco. It was an alien, hostile, still life.

They moved through a back door into a bedroom.

For an instant Clari thought she was going to faint as the gagging sourness of the close quarters smote her. The room was disordered, the iron bed unmade. A bureau held a litter of medicine bottles, glasses, spoons and a pair of men's suspenders. A large wardrobe of incongruous pink wood stood open in a corner, displaying a jumble of dirty clothes. In a rocker sat a man in his undershirt with a striped bathrobe thrown carelessly across his lap. His huge head sat crookedly on a withered body. He was any age beyond fifty. A week's stubble of white whiskers fuzzed his face. His eyes were blue, quick-blinking and shrewd.

Steve smiled at Clari. "This is my good friend Hurd Mastock, Clari. He just about runs politics in this neck of the woods. Darling, these are our kind of people—the salt of the earth."

The repellent man in the chair nodded complacently. "We only lost seventeen votes for Carl the last election. That was out of a hunnerd an' eighty. You gonna see Carl?"

"Yes. Today."

"You tell him that. You tell him we only lost seventeen votes in this district out of a hunnered an' eighty. I want him to know."

"He knows you're a great friend of his," Steve said.

The room pressed downward on Clari. She was panting, smothering, but she clenched her fists and resolved not to allow it.

"I been sick," Hurd Mastock complained, settling in the chair. "'Scuse me for not gittin' up. I been sick as a dog."

"That ain't no lie," Pete Mastock said, near animation.

Hurd rolled his lips against his gums. "You know I'm a Kanger man. Always was. But I supported yore dad, too, and you. I supported yore dad every time he run. He was the greatest senator this state ever had. If you're half as good a man you'll be all right. You know that?"

Steve nodded, swallowing hard.

And now, suddenly, Clari watched her husband with sharp awareness.

Steve was moistening his lips and shifting his weight uneasily, trying to smile. The mention of his father seemed to embarrass him, make him tense. He massaged the long, pale scar on his left hand. It was one of his common nervous mannerisms, particularly under strain. She had never paid it much mind. But now she remembered the training camp injury—the knife slash in close combat drill—and excitedly she bestowed upon it a new significance. Could that have been what was eating on him ever since the war? Was that why he had never touched a piano since his return—why he always brushed the subject aside and said, "No more of that stuff. The voters look down on piano players. All they'll take is a guitar." It was always said lightly, with a grin. But it was the wound, it was his injured wrist, that had kept him from going back to the piano, as he'd planned, when they left school and he went into the army. And not having the dream—the piano—he had catapulted into the twin poppylands of politics and heavy drink.

Lord, but that sounded too easy. The psychiatrists at the sanitarium surely had drilled too deep to miss such an obvious surface pool. Still, she felt nearer to a clue during this racing moment than she ever had felt before. At least, for the first time she knew that the constant eulogies of his father apparently assaulted Steve's ego, put him through some sort of interior agony. He might not even know, consciously, that he suffered—or why. But he did suffer, of that she was sure.

"You can win for guvna—on your father's name. We'll back you. You gonna have a fight, though, son. The Charley Lake crowd's talkin' big about indictments and stuff like that. Carl oughta be more careful. You tell him Hurd Mastock said to watch his step— the po' folks expect him to get his, long as he divides with them. He's gotta do it careful, though. And you—you watch that booze. Otherwise you'll be out, too."

A flame of anger flared through Clari. The presumption, the sneering patronage of this creature!

"Steve hasn't had a drink in a year!" she cried in a strange, fierce voice.

Hurd Mastock looked at her, rubbing the white stubble of his chin. He addressed Steve then.

"Take the wife with you when you speak. Make her get out amongst the po' people and not be afraid of sweat, boy. She dresses too fancy. Get her some clothes like po' folks wear."

Steve laughed.

With a sigh Hurd Mastock then got down to business.

"I got a boy, Willie, they're trying to take in this new peacetime draft. I want you to fix it with Carl and get him loose."

Steve shifted stance uneasily. "You know I'd like to help, but I don't know—"

The man in the chair shrugged impatiently. "You can get him off, all right. I know that. Carl Kanger can get him off in five minutes. I done a lot for Carl and I want him to do me this favor in return."

"I'll see—"

"Don't see. You tell Carl Kanger to put the heat on that draft board in town. I want Willie here with me. I'm sick. I'm sick as a dog." He shifted in the chair and, involuntarily or by design, his face showed pain."Those rich men on the draft board in town tried to take my two other boys in the war. And both farmers, too! Carl's got new men on that board now. C. K. Fanner is chairman, you know how Carl kept him out of jail in that truck deal. I want the heat turned on—And I want on the pension, too."

His voice, petulant now and almost snarling, paused.

"Don't worry, Hurd. Those are the first things I'll take up with the governor."

In a quick, searing vision Clari could see Hugh addressing his class, hear his harsh, ardent voice saying, *"Beware of the Little Greed" as well as of the Big Greed." It's always with us and it's just as ugly."*

That was the year Hugh shifted from teaching to newspaper work.

Hugh saw so much so clearly. Yet there remained a paradox in his remark about the Little Greed—there were thousands with ignoble little greeds who voted for Senator Lenihan only because he *was* strong and incorruptible—the kind of man who wouldn't cater to petty greed. She surrendered the problem, knowing only that all this about Steve and the governorship was wrong and ominous. Steve, amiable and easygoing, worrying a piano at Blanding Ford or on the pier at Inlet City or for a school prom—yes, that was good and as it should be. But not Steve as governor, nor herself as the governor's wife. It was a distortion of manifest destiny. Some people were meant to be simply obscure and merry—and Steve was one of those persons.

In the car once more, heading south, Clari asked timidly, "Steve, suppose you're defeated for governor. What would you do? Couldn't you go into something else besides politics? This state— these people—kind of scare me."

He reached down and squeezed her hand.

"Don't worry. I'm not going to be defeated. You'll get used to the people. Kid 'em along. That's politics. I feel it in my bones—this is our big break. I can't lose."

"But suppose you did?" Clari asked.

Steve lifted his hand back to the wheel.

"In that case I don't know anything I could do. It would be pretty rugged." He wet his lips. "In the army I spent a winter in Okinawa learning hot drums. I might get up a small band."

"Oh, Steve, that wouldn't be bad! You could get up a band and we could work together traveling around like we planned once—"

He cut her off. "Clari, you talk like a fool! Don't you realize I'm set up to be governor of this state? Don't you realize what that means to you and me both? Quit fighting me all the time!"

She nodded slowly. They drove on across the sizzling land. It was too hot to quarrel, too hot to think, too hot to worry about the closing future.

They rolled on in silence. Unconsciously Steve ran his right hand along the thin white scar, up and back, up and back, steering with his left hand, Clari noticed idly. Through thin layers of the cloth the plastic seat cover burned her flanks.

The sundown shower did no good; it simply filled the leafy streets of the Capital City with a choking purple steam. Not even the air-conditioning unit in the small office off the foyer of the governor's mansion brought relief. It seemed to be exhausted, now, after its day-long battle with the fiery air. Clari sat on a hard chair along the wall and toyed listlessly with a magazine she had read through twice. At a desk bristling with colored buttons and telephone switches a dark man in a state policeman's uniform pored over a crossword puzzle.

She had been in here an hour and a half. She felt useless and worried. She had not seen the governor. Steve had been taken off by a dog-faced little man, "to wait till the boss can see you," right after they arrived.

She'd heard about the Kangers for years; she knew that Carl was a coarse, snarling, vindictive man. His radio speeches had told her that in the campaigns—although his friends said he was "human" and "earthy." She knew that he had lived for years in the shadow of his equally vituperative cousin, who had possessed also wit and sharp intelligence, in addition to the lack of scruple that was a family trait. Steve did not deny any of this; instead he explained it. "That's politics. That's what the people want—they don't want sweet-smelling reformers in this state any more. They want a tough horse who'll bring them fodder. Carl Kanger is one of those. And he keeps his word."

Now the night was imminent. Through the small, barred windows, she could see movement on the lawn and the wink of lights—flares, it seemed.

"What's that?" she asked finally. "Are they having fireworks out there?"

The trooper looked at her. His white teeth gleamed.

"No ma'am. That's the old-age pension crowd. They going to give the guvna a torchlight parade to the capitol tonight and thank him for what he done for them."

She peered at the shadows, the lights moving against the windows in milky splashes. From afar came a thin murmur of voices.

The trooper chuckled.

"We brought them in from all over. Sent school busses. It's gonna be some crowd.

"They must be crazy about the governor."

The policeman looked puzzled. He put his pencil behind his ear. "Yes, ma'am." And then he added, "Shucks, they knew better than not to come. They were rounded up and told. They wanna keep gettin' those checks, don't they?" He laughed.

Clari stared at her crossed knees. A curious sense of heartbreak, of pity for the futile gathering of old people lighting their torches on the lawn oppressed her.

Where was Hugh?

She flushed to think that her gay postcard to him in care of the paper, announcing their visit to the Capital City, probably had merely given him warning. "Good. Now I can keep out of the way of that dame. I certainly don't want to get involved in complications at this late date." No, that wasn't like Hugh. Wasn't it? It was like a man.

After all, could she blame him? Why should he rejoice at the only possible implication of a communication from her—the proffer of old, cold food for warming over?

Somewhere in a pink and gold twilight of mirrors and smoke and rich, closed doors, Steve hung hypnotized in the web. Did she love Steve?

She was frightened for him. That much she knew. This was like no other anxiety she had known. Not like the nights of insecurity, with Steve ticketed for the sanitarium and the sly patronage of the psychiatrists for them both; that was bad, but it was ponderable and could be met.

If she could only talk over with Hugh this new problem. He had had so many quick, bright solutions—or at least he could put them slickly into words. He could name the evil. She tried to remember Hugh, his look, the sound of his voice. But he came in blurred.

Why shouldn't she rejoice that Steve had a chance for security as governor—that *she* had a chance for security? Heaven knew they had experienced precious little of it. There was the tiny income, the gradual erosion of their small home under successive mortgages which would have crashed down on them long ago except that Steve's name was on the lips of bankers as the probable gubernatorial heir. Why, this would mean permanent security! Governors didn't retire in this state to the poor farm—not Kanger governors, at least.

Now she glanced at the barred window and cringed.

A face was there, a white, old face, grinning and Hogarthian, contorted by a sort of snide ecstasy.

The cop saw it too, and with a gesture of annoyance rose from his desk, pulling his revolver from a shoulder holster. He waved the gun urgently at the face and it disappeared into the darkness with a surprised, hurt look.

"Those—" The cop glanced at Clari and deleted the profanity. "Those jugheads," he said. He replaced the gun in its holster.

Steve came into the room, hurried and flushed.

"Sorry I was held-up, darling." He strode up close to her and said softly, "Things look good."

And then he stiffened, shushing her with a finger.

Carl Kanger stood in the doorway. He was a large, loose-jointed man with a fleshy nose and a prominent, mobile mouth. His eyes were red-flecked, unsteady, haunted. He wore creased slacks and a shirt open wide at the throat. He had an air about him of aggressive, surly purpose, and also of perpetual readiness for flight.

"This your wife, Steve?"

The voice had gravel in it and abstraction. His eyes were focused inside the little room and somehow also looking backward, furtively, behind him.

"Darling, I want you to meet Governor Kanger," Steve said, proud and nervous.

"I'm very honored," Clari said, straining a smile.

The governor did not offer to shake hands. He stood loosely in the doorway, flicking his gaze over her. He ordered the trooper out of the room with a motion of his thumb.

"I'm gonna make your husband governor," the hoarse voice rasped. "You watch yourself, girl. Don't get no scandal on you. And keep him off that booze. You hear that?"

Anger stabbed her again. But she knew that this was a crisis and she managed to nod demurely.

"And don't get the idea that you've moved in here yet. You ain't." Then, amazingly, his lips worked into a grisly smile. "Don't worry, cutie-pie. You two just do what you're told and you'll be all right." He spit lustily against the baseboard.

Then he eyed Steve. "You come out here again, boy. I want you to meet Pietro. He just come in. You never met him, did you?"

For the first time Steve looked scared.

"He won't bite you." The governor chuckled. "You been readin' them lyin' newspapers."

He turned to Clari, narrowing his eyes. "We'll only be gone a minute. Then we'll all ride up to the capitol for the ceremonies and the big dinner. After that a caucus of my leaders is gonna talk with Steve to make sure he'll go along on everything. That'll be at ten, you hear, girl? You get him there. Sober, huh?" His eyes glowed sardonically.

Steve said, "Don't worry, Governor, I'll be there."

"Damn right you will, if you want to be governor of this state. Far as I'm concerned the deal's set, but you gotta convince my leaders and Pietro that you'll go along like they want and that you're gonna stay off that booze." He suddenly turned back toward the door, shouting into the corridor, "Keep them bloodsucking reporters outa here."

"Be right back," Steve said to Clari, handling his wrist. He followed his master.

Clari felt a great surge of pity for him as he left to meet Pietro Bell, who was reported to be the multi-millionaire owner of night clubs in New York and Chicago and, it was whispered, a dealer in marijuana and numbers, a contributor to campaigns.

She relaxed with effort. In her mind the words "Trapped, trapped, trapped," sang monotonously.

Then she heard Hugh's voice.

"I tell you I don't want to see the governor. I want to see a friend of mine who's around here."

"And I told you I'd lose my job if you come in here. Didn't you hear what the governor told you last time? You can't—"

They shared the doorway then, a short, bald trooper and the lanky figure of Hugh.

The other trooper reached for his gun.

Clari cried in alarm, "Don't—he's all right. I know him."

Grinning, Hugh elbowed his way into the small room. "Hello, Tom." He waved to the trooper with the nervous revolver. "You better quit waving that thing around. The governor's going to be shot some day and people may wonder whether you did it."

The trooper replaced his gun, his face worried. But surprise kept him from halting Hugh's stride across the room and over to Clari.

"Hello, Clari. You look swell."

He was the same as ever, lean, angular, owlish behind his horn-rimmed glasses and graying now over the ears—but he seemed to her in this moment no less than an angel of rescue. Her heart whipped against its walls.

"Hugh—"

But the trooper at the desk had got over his surprise and was angry now—and frightened.

"You get out of here. Now." He put a foot forward in Hugh's direction.

"Okay, okay." Hugh gave Clari his gnome's smile.

"Where can I call you?" He backed toward the door.

"Wait," she said. "I'll walk outside with you, Hugh."

"Now, ma'am," the trooper interposed, "the governor said—"

"You shut up!" she blazed at him, releasing the tension of the hours with him as a cellmate. "I'll do what I please!"

She preceded Hugh under the seal of the state and the initials of Riley Kanger which he had ordered carved over the front door when he was governor.

Outside, the hot night rose up around them. For a space she reeled back. Then she sucked the heavy air into her lungs delightedly. She was glad to be out of the sinister house and its ersatz cool; glad to have her fingers on Hugh's sleeve. The sensible grayness of his suit seemed to her to symbolize the soberness, the unvarying strength of Hugh that always had given her a sense of security while she was with him.

They walked along the flagstone porch of the house, not speaking. On the lawn, the old-age pensioners were being herded into ranks before the mansion. The march would begin from here.

"From what I hear, this will soon be your front porch," Hugh said uneasily, when they stopped and inspected each other.

She shook her head, trying to untangle a knot in her throat.

"Hugh—I'm glad to see you." That was all she managed.

And she was. She watched his long, homely face as he thumbed a lighter and the tiny flame licked up. Once she had petted an Afghan puppy with a face much like Hugh's.

"Hugh, I've thought about you so much!"

That wasn't entirely true. She hadn't really thought about him very much until today. But she wanted him aware of her again— enough to help her now. A hope was forming in her mind, and she knew that she might even have to be brazen to carry it out. But pride was very little to risk to escape the trap that was settling about her. Alone, she couldn't make a move against what Steve wanted; his hold on her was too strong for that. But with Hugh to drain strength from, perhaps she could find a solution.

"I've thought about you too." Hugh's tone was not comfortable. "I'm leaving here, you know. I'm going with Associated Press in Washington. Tomorrow. I'm so glad I got to see you one more time."

"You're leaving for good?"

"Yes, Clari. There's nothing more here for me." He hesitated and went on fast, "You're going to be in the middle of big doings, though. Steve probably will be elected, from all I hear."

"Oh, isn't it horrible, Hugh! What can I do about it?"

The masses of overheated air were in movement now. There was lightning, constant and increasing, and behind it the low growling of new storm. Hugh's hand tightened on her arm.

She bit her lip.

"All these political people, Hugh—they're horrible."

"Do you know them? Do you know the real country people?"

"Yes. All day—Why, the more I see of them the more horrible they get. And that Carl Kanger. And Bell. The people of this state love crooks. Hugh. They want crooks. I wonder where this democracy business we used to talk about has gone to. Hugh, is it this bad all over?"

"It's good and bad everywhere. It dips and rises. The alternatives are so bad they keep it going."

She was irritated. "Don't talk like a professor, Hugh. Tell me what's going to happen to us—to me!" She wanted all answers quick and lucid, even when she knew there were no quick and lucid answers. Hugh was leaving, wasn't he? Hugh was running too.

He moved a millimeter closer to her. "Steve has an opportunity in this state."

She was near to tears. She touched Hugh, clung to him a little. "They're running Steve because they know he's weak and they can control him."

"No, Clari. Listen. Had you thought of it this way? They're running Steve because his name is Lenihan. They need a man that's clean and recalls Senator Lenihan's self-respect and decency. This gang knows that the things they've been doing are going to blow wide open. It's a tribute to the people, for all their ignorance and petty self-interest, that a fine name can still pull their votes. That's why this crowd is running Steve. They smell jail—but with the magic of the Lenihan name they hope to prolong the stealing. Steve could balk them if he'd try."

"Just words," she murmured. "Take me with you, Hugh, out of this. You still want me, Hugh?"

He put both arms around her and drew her close. What am I saying, doing? she thought.

"I never wanted anybody else. I never loved anybody else."

"Take me away from here."

He held her tight. Then he said clearly, "No."

Clari knew that this time was a decisive moment in her life, and she wondered why she was so relieved to be rejected.

"No," he repeated solidly. "You see, I love you, always have, and you never loved me. I knew. You're a strange little girl. You thought you could have a romance with a point of view, an I.Q. It wasn't very good for you, was it? You love Steve the only way a man wants to be loved." His voice was faint at the end.

A band began to play in the dark street. A wind was blowing with rain drops in it. The lightning streaks flashed close before the thunder now. Hugh stepped away from her, a foot, a final league. He smelled faintly of old manuscripts, she thought; it was a thought from the past.

"You'll get used to politics."

"Don't patronize me!" she cried in sudden anger. "You know as well as I do Steve has got no business being governor. It'll kill him. It'll kill me."

"Running off with me would kill him too. And you. And me."

Abruptly, lights went on high up on the ceiling of the gallery. The screen doors opened and three men emerged, two policemen with the governor hunched and walking fast between them.

"Look." Hugh chuckled. "He's afraid of lightning. The finger of God."

A long, black limousine appeared suddenly and silently at the mansion stoop. The door opened and the governor got in, with an apprehensive glance at the sky. Then a tall, overdressed woman came out of the mansion at a near run and got into the car with the governor. The door clucked shut and the limousine slunk away, two motorcycles following.

Now the screen door opened again and Steve came out and looked about frantically.

"Clari! Where have you been?" He strode toward them nervously. "You're holding up the works, you know that?"

Then he recognized Hugh. They'd only met twice and Steve thought of him vaguely as "that professor Clari used to have a crush on."

"Hello, sir." Steve's tone had the mingled respect and patronage of the young for the mature. "You're with a paper here, aren't you?" They shook hands.

"I was. I'm leaving tomorrow. I wanted to say good-by to Clari—and you. Hope I didn't mess up your schedule."

"No. Clari, we're in the second car. Here it comes now." He was excited.

He had no time for small talk.

She was in the dark, soft cradle of the limousine beside Steve before she could even tell Hugh good-by. But as they moved off she saw him, lean and owlish and slightly stooped, arguing with the trooper. Obviously he was being told to get away from there.

Steve rubbed his wrist in the fragrant, new-car gloom.

"Everything's fixed. Bell says okay." He laughed boyishly. "I rang the Bell. All I've got to do now is hand a line to that bunch of Kanger leaders at ten tonight and we're in." He sighed. "Clari, you just don't realize what this means."

"Maybe I don't." She tried to squeeze the hopefulness out of her voice when she asked, "If the leaders decide against it tonight, that would mean you couldn't run, wouldn't it?"

"Don't worry about that. They've heard a lot of rumors and things. But as soon as they see I'm sober and ready to deal with them from here out it'll be in the bag. It isn't just the rumors they've heard. They want to be sure I'm no panty-waist—trying to reform the world, like Charley Lake and his crowd."

"I hope it all works out," she said tiredly.

But as their big car was maneuvered behind the preceding limousine, and followed by the popeyes of other headlights lining up for the parade to the capitol, Clari felt only utter entrapment. No energy for rebellion remained. Now she was committed, carried forward willy-nilly on the dark lane. She wondered about the stooped, owlish, gentle man back on the mansion porch. How could she possibly have conceived of him as a knight of deliverance, or even as a source of clarification for her confusion and fear? Fear of what? Why, there was the smell of conspiracy and fear over this parade. It started with the hoarse, bitter man in the car ahead who surely was afraid.

Yet Steve wasn't feeling fear at all, apparently. He sat upright, hands on his knees, communing with his star. What a baby he was, and what a bruising he would get from—Senator Lenihan's phrase came back—this Camorra of heels. And she was supposed to be on hand to pick him up when he was smashed down. But she wouldn't be able to. He would be smashed down too far for any saving.

An odd thought crossed her mind. They were in this car, moving toward an honor as sinister as a guillotine, because Steve had a scar on his wrist. All this was a flare-up of that old wound. Otherwise, Steve probably wouldn't even have gone into the Legislature. He might well have been on the road tonight—they might have been on the road together—with a small band, obscure and merry and capable of small laughters and small tears, wedded to a simple but sure destiny. If only, if only. . . .

They rolled along, the nervous lightning still jittering overhead. A ragged crowd lined the streets, staring without enthusiasm. Behind, the band played softly and the old-age pensioners sang in a ragged falsetto as they marched. The procession slowed as the leaders reached the capitol building. Floodlights bathed the steps and the wide stone plaza before the main entrance, where the ceremony would be held. Clari could see chairs set out there and a microphone and many figures moving.

Lord, would she have to sit up there, in full view?

But this was just the beginning.

If she had the words, if she could find the eloquence, even now she might pour out to Steve the full force of her apprehension, her certainty that he had no business in politics, that he was being used and would be destroyed, that they must turn quickly at this final moment when escape was still possible and go another way.

But Steve was past all argument. He'd only get furiously angry and think she was a liability to him in the moment of his great opportunity.

Over the chauffeur's shoulder, through the glass partition, she saw the parade leaders turn and start up the capitol steps in a double file.

That was when it happened—as their limousine came to a halt in a pool of shadow under a live-oak tree, half a block from the square.

She did not see the man approach the car. The door was flung open suddenly and a lean, drawn face confronted them. It was a young man's face, with eyes in it of unforgettable, malevolent hatred.

Steve said, "Hey!" in alarm, and made a protective movement out of his seat, for the intruder was on Clari's side. In that split second of awareness, as the baleful eyes glittered through the yellow light, Clari was sure that the thing the man was raising in his hand was a gun and that Steve, or both of them, would be assassinated.

But nothing exploded.

Instead, a soft object fell on the floor of the car and a fierce young voice screeched at them, "Run this for governor, you Kanger bum!"

The next moments were confused and would always be unclear in detail to her.

The head disappeared. There were shouts, a shot, running feet. Clari saw the culprit overtaken as he reached the curb. Half a dozen troopers seemed to materialize out of the darkness and converge on the running figure at once. They became a blur of bodies, with something down under the blur. She saw hands with clubbed pistols in them and feet being swung back to kick. And she heard a shrill moan that faded.

The chauffeur was peering anxiously into the tonneau. He, too, had a drawn gun.

"You folks all right? You all right?"

"We're all right," Steve said. His voice was shaken.

"Don't let them kill him," Clari said, as she stared at the object the man had tossed to the floor of the car.

At first she thought it was a fur neckpiece.

Then she understood.

"Why, that guy threw a skunk at us!" Steve cried in a startled tone. "Take that thing out of here, will you, chauffeur?"

"A skunk!" he repeated as they began to move again slowly. "You smell it? It's really not as bad as you'd think being thrown right in here."

Steve relaxed in the seat. "Why, that man could have shot me, you know that?"

Clari sat still and tense, trying to understand the scorn and hatred in the man's eyes. How many were there like him?

But, oddly, the incident did not increase her sense of fear of the crowd, the men around Kanger, or Kanger himself and the floodlighted space where she would have to sit for an hour, listening to the governor's hoarse bombast. She felt better. All through the travestied ceremonies, she could not put down a new impression that there was courage and self-respect here and there in the dark, faceless throng. And when Steve was introduced and stood up to take his bow, the volume of the applause lifted her spirits. The ovation was not for Steve, she knew; it was for Senator Lenihan and for the principles which had not quite died with him.

It never rained hard. The storm wheeled and veered off from the Capital City; the lightning flickered out and Governor Kanger did not have to worry about the finger of God through the closing moments of the affair. Cool air came into the city on the flank of the storm.

There was a convivial melee after the speaking. The crowd surged up around them, there was much handshaking, and they were swept and eddied off in the flow of humanity until they were blessedly anonymous again in a capitol corridor.

"Let's find the eats," Steve said, linking her arm through his. And he added, "You hear that crowd? When I stood up? They want me, honey; they want me for governor."

They went down on a packed elevator to the basement, where in the cafeteria a large group of political workers was scheduled for a buffet supper of barbecue and potato salad. They encountered a solid wall of people.

All order had collapsed and men, women and children were pushing and clawing their way toward the food.

"No politician is worth this to my feet," a woman moaned.

Steve shook his head, peering on tiptoe over the heads of the crowd. "I guess they sold tickets to everybody in the state. That's the way it always is. If I can find a policeman."

But Clari tugged on his arm, dragged his ear down lower. "They won't miss us, Steve. Let's go out and get a quiet dinner. Just the two of us."

"No, they'll expect—" He sighed and shrugged. "Oh, well, why not?"

The street they took toward the little restaurant called Pete's Garden—a favorite of theirs—was surprisingly quiet and unfrequented. Under the heavy foliage of the old trees the street was cool and fresh. They held hands as they walked.

And Clari was suddenly, illogically, happy and relieved. She felt that somewhere under the cloak of this abruptly friendly night was a solution and a benevolent rearrangement of destiny, a clue to the right road out. It was on the tip of her tongue if she could, with a burst of perception, articulate it, if she could say, "I've just thought, Steve. This is what we'll do—"

Their heels rang on the pavement. Far up ahead the neon name of the Pete's Garden sign twinkled.

She tightened her hand on his and knew that she wanted this big, confused boy with a wonderful simplicity of physical desire she had never felt for Hugh. He was hers, after all.

"Stop a minute," she demanded. "Kiss me, Steve. Kiss me hard."

And then she said, "Is that the best you can do?"

He did better, and as they continued on toward Pete's Garden he chuckled happily, seeming to catch her own strange elation and content.

"Say, I feel all different tonight. That drinking business, for instance. I feel absolutely confident I can handle it now. I won't, of course, but I could take a drink with you tonight to celebrate and stop right there."

The carefully worded protest which rose automatically to her lips—and which he wanted from her, and expected, to get him over this vulnerable moment—died before it was uttered.

They both were thinking of the ten o'clock date with Kanger's leaders.

Clari said, "Yes, Steve, I feel you've got that whipped too. All these months! Maybe it would do your morale good to have a drink tonight and prove to yourself you can handle it. I'll have one with you!"

They began to hurry again toward the blooming sign.

Dear Lord, forgive me, Clari thought for what I'm doing to him.

But it was a solution. With all its inevitable cycle of horror, it was still a road out. The only road she had. What was it Hugh had said about alternatives? Maybe all life was a matter of picking lesser evils. And despite the known trauma, the risk she was choosing for them both, somewhere up ahead, beyond the inevitable spree, she could see light. She knew Steve better now; she knew what had caused the canker on his soul, now, and she could help him cure it. On the route they would travel otherwise, she couldn't help him at all.

Steve let go of her hand and massaged the scar on his wrist.

"This has been a wonderful day for us, hasn't it?"

Somehow she was sure why he had made it a question. Somehow she was sure he, too, knew what was going to happen.

THE SHADOW OF EVIL

Politics—its powerful machine and its capacity to corrupt—is the subject of this story. Steve, son of the highly respected late Senator Lenihan, is being considered for the machine's gubernatorial candidate. Although he is artistically inclined and had aspired to a career in music, those plans have been put away; and he is elated, flattered, and scared when the incumbent governor, who by law cannot succeed himself, asks him to come down to the capital for an "examination" by the controlling politicians. His name is important since his late father was known for his integrity; but it is not integrity they want from him: it is Steve's weakness and willingness to let them continue in their populist rule. A recovering alcoholic, naive and inexperienced in politics, he is attracted to the power offered him and envisions himself doing good for the poor people.

The limited omniscient viewpoint, centered in the consciousness of Clari, his midwestern wife, brings a fresh interpretation to the Machiavellian policies. She is both shocked and disgusted at the petty political dictators with whom they come into contact and understands very clearly the moral degradation her husband would suffer as a puppet for the out-going governor. Steve, on the other hand, lacks the insight to interpret words and actions of the politicians and is caught up in the promises of power.

Election to the governor's office would allow Steve a second chance at success, his musical career having failed because of a slight wound to the wrist. The scar that he nervously touches suggests that his fragile artistic sensibility lies buried beneath it; it serves as a barrier between his real self and the mask he is putting on to enter politics.

Clari's act at the end is irony in its purest form—she destroys him to save him. Alcohol is his nemesis; yet after weighing the destruction of alcohol abuse against the moral corruption that sleazy politics brings on, she chooses alcoholism.

Although the setting is not named, there are several historical and geographical clues to indicate that the story is set in Louisiana and is partly autobiographical. The author was the son of a highly respected Louisiana congressman. The geographical features—sleepy-eyed town two hundred miles north of the capital, the stop at a grocery store-cafe just before entering bayou country, the capital and the governor's mansion—suggest Natchitoches, Lebeau, and Baton Rouge, respectively. The steamy heat which grows more intense as they penetrate bayou country reflects Louisiana's climate, and the Populist governor is surely a composite of Earl and Huey Long. Finally, Aswell's wife, like Steve's, was from the Midwest.

Truman Capote

(1924-1984)

Born in New Orleans, Truman Streckfus Persons (later named Capote after his stepfather Joseph Garcia Capote) lived there until his parents were divorced when he was four. The rest of his childhood was unstable as he passed back and forth among relatives, chiefly elderly spinster cousins in Alabama. When he was thirteen he began his education in the East, and the brilliant but introvert child was praised highly by his teachers. The publication of "Miriam" launched him on his literary career in 1945 (it was awarded an O. Henry Memorial Prize in 1946). Capote is not Southern in the sense of Faulkner and others whose interest in time and place dominates their works, but his interest in the abnormal aspects of human psychology ties him to the Southern Gothic tradition. Interested especially in the dream world and the subconscious, Capote conveys in many of his works a sense of other-worldness, entirely divorced from realism. For that reason many of his works lack a strong sense of place. The landscape in his Southern stories is definitely Southern, although not necessarily identifiable with any specific place. Physical details and customs usually blend to present a composite of Louisiana and Alabama. *In Cold Blood*, his ninth book, represents the culmination of the author's desire to establish a new literary form: the nonfiction novel. The story printed below was first published in *Mademoiselle*, December 1956, and was later reprinted in *Breakfast at Tiffany's: A Short Novel and Three Stories* in 1958.

A Christmas Memory[*]

Truman Capote

Imagine a morning in late November. A coming of winter morning more than twenty years ago. Consider the kitchen of a spreading old house in a country town. A great black stove is its main feature; but there is also a big round table and a fireplace with two rocking chairs placed in front of it. Just today the fireplace commenced its seasonal roar.

A woman with shorn white hair is standing at the kitchen window. She is wearing tennis shoes and a shapeless gray sweater over a summery calico dress. She is small and sprightly, like a bantam hen; but, due to a long youthful illness, her shoulders are pitifully hunched. Her face is remarkable—not unlike Lincoln's, craggy like that, and tinted by sun and wind; but it is delicate too, finely boned, and her eyes are sherry-colored and timid. "Oh my," she exclaims, her breath smoking the windowpane, "it's fruitcake weather!"

The person to whom she is speaking is myself. I am seven; she is sixty-something. We are cousins, very distant ones, and we have lived together—well, as long as I can remember. Other people inhabit the house, relatives; and though they have power over us, and frequently make us cry, we are not, on the whole, too much aware of them. We are each other's best friend. She calls me Buddy, in memory of a boy who was formerly her best friend. The other Buddy died in the 1880's, when she was still a child. She is still a child.

"I knew it before I got out of bed," she says, turning away from the window with a purposeful excitement in her eyes. "The courthouse bell sounded so cold and clear. And there were no birds singing; they've gone to warmer country, yes indeed. Oh, Buddy, stop stuffing biscuit and fetch our buggy. Help me find my hat. We've thirty cakes to bake."

It's always the same: a morning arrives in November, and my friend, as though officially inaugurating the Christmas time of year that exhilarates her imagination and fuels the blaze of her heart, announces: "It's fruitcake weather! Fetch our buggy. Help me find my hat."

The hat is found, a straw cartwheel corsaged with velvet roses out-of-doors has faded: it once belonged to a more fashionable relative. Together we guide our buggy, a dilapidated baby carriage, out to the garden and into a grove of pecan trees. The buggy is mine; that is, it was bought for me when I was born. It is made of wicker, rather unraveled, and the wheels wobble like a drunkard's legs. But it is a faithful object; springtimes, we take it to the woods and fill it with flowers, herbs, wild fern for our porch pots; in the summer, we pile it with picnic paraphernalia and sugar-cane fishing poles and roll it down to the edge of a creek; it has its winter uses, too: as a truck for hauling firewood from the yard to the kitchen, as a warm bed for Queenie, our tough little orange and white rat terrier who has survived distemper and two rattlesnake bites. Queenie is trotting beside it now.

Three hours later we are back in the kitchen hulling a heaping buggyload of windfall pecans. Our backs hurt from gathering them: how hard they were to find (the main crop having been shaken off the trees and sold by the orchard's owners, who are not us) among the concealing leaves, the frosted, deceiving grass. Caarackle! A cherry crunch, scraps of miniature thunder sound as the shells collapse and the golden mound of sweet oily ivory meat mounts in the milk-glass bowl. Queenie begs to taste, and now and again my friend sneaks her a mite, though insisting we deprive ourselves. "We mustn't, Buddy. If we start, we won't stop. And there's scarcely enough as there is. For thirty cakes." The kitchen is growing dark. Dusk turns the window into a mirror: our reflections mingle with the rising moon as we work by the fireside in the firelight. As last, when the moon is quite high, we toss the final hull into the fire and with joined sighs, watch it catch flame. The buggy is empty, the bowl is brimful.

We eat our supper (cold biscuits, bacon, blackberry jam) and discuss tomorrow. Tomorrow the kind of work I like best begins: buying. Cherries and citron, ginger and vanilla and canned Hawaiian pineapple, rinds and raisins and walnuts and whiskey and oh, so much flour, butter, so many eggs, spices, flavorings: why, we'll need a pony to pull the buggy home.

But before these purchases can be made, there is the question of money. Neither of us has any. Except for skinflint sums persons in the house occasionally provide (a dime is considered very big money); or what we earn ourselves from various activities: holding rummage sales, selling buckets of hand-picked blackberries, jars of homemade jam and apple jelly and peach preserves, rounding up flowers for funerals and weddings. Once we won seventy-ninth prize, five dollars, in a national football contest. Not that we know a fool thing about football. It's just that we enter any contest we hear about: at the moment our hopes are centered on the fifty-thousand-dollar Grand Prize being offered to name a new brand of coffee (we suggested "A.M."; and, after some hesitation, for my friend thought it perhaps sacrilegious, the slogan "A.M.! Amen!"). To tell the truth, our only *really* profitable enterprise was the Fun and Freak Museum we conducted in a back-yard woodshed two summers ago. The Fun was a stereopticon with slide views of Washington and New York lent us by a relative who had been to those places (she was furious when she discovered why we'd borrowed it); the Freak was a three-legged biddy chicken hatched by one of our own hens. Everybody hereabouts wanted to see that biddy: we charged grownups a nickel, kids two cents. And took in a good twenty dollars before the museum shut down due to the decease of the main attraction.

But one way and another we do each year accumulate Christmas savings, a Fruitcake Fund. These moneys we keep hidden in an ancient bead purse under a loose board under the floor under a chamber pot under my friend's bed. The purse is seldom removed from this safe location except to make a deposit, or, as happens every Saturday, a withdrawal; for on Saturdays I am allowed ten cents to go to the picture show. My friend has never been to a picture show, nor does she intend to: "I'd rather hear you tell the story, Buddy. That way I can imagine it more. Besides, a person my age shouldn't squander their eyes. When the Lord comes, let me see him clear." In addition to never having seen a movie, she has never: eaten in a restaurant, traveled more than five miles from home, received or sent a telegram, read anything except funny papers and the Bible, worn cosmetics, cursed, wished someone harm, told a lie on purpose, let a hungry dog go hungry. Here are a few things she has done, does do: killed with a hoe the biggest rattlesnake ever seen in this county (sixteen rattles), dip snuff (secretly), tame hummingbirds (just try it) till they balance on her finger, tell ghost stories (we both believe in ghosts) so tingling they chill you in July, talk to herself, take walks in the rain, grow the prettiest japonicas in town, know the recipe for every sort of old-time Indian cure, including a magical wart-remover.

Now, with supper finished, we retire to the room in a faraway part of the house where my friend sleeps in a scrap-quilt covered iron bed painted rose pink, her favorite color. Silently, wallowing in the pleasures of conspiracy, we take the bead purse from its secret place and spill its contents on the scrap quilt. Dollar bills, tightly rolled and green as May buds. Somber fifty-cent pieces, heavy enough to weight a dead man's eyes. Lovely dimes, the liveliest coin, the one that really jingles. Nickels and quarters, worn smooth as creek pebbles. But mostly a hateful heap of bitter-odored pennies. Last summer others in the house contracted to pay us a penny for every twenty-five flies we killed. Oh, the carnage of August: the flies that flew to heaven! Yet it was not work in which we took pride. And, as we sit counting pennies, it is as though we were back tabulating dead flies. Neither of us has a head for figures; we count slowly, lose track, start again. According to her calculations, we have $12.73. According to mine, exactly $13. "I do hope you're wrong, Buddy. We can't mess around with thirteen. The cakes will fall. Or put somebody in the cemetery. Why, I wouldn't dream of getting out of bed on the thirteenth." This is true: she always spends thirteenths in bed. So, to be on the safe side, we subtract a penny and toss it out the window. Of the ingredients that go into our fruitcakes, whiskey is the most expensive, as well as the hardest to obtain: State laws forbid its sale. But everybody knows you can buy a bottle from Mr. Haha Jones. And the next day, having completed our more prosaic shopping, we set out for Mr. Haha's business address, a "sinful" (to quote public opinion) fish-fry and dancing cafe down by the river. We've been there before, and on the same errand: but in previous years our dealings have been with Haha's wife, an iodine-dark Indian woman with brassy peroxided hair and a dead-tired disposition. Actually, we've never laid eyes on her husband, though we've heard that he's an Indian too. A giant with razor scars across his cheeks. They call him Haha because he's so gloomy, a man who never laughs. As we approach his café (a large log cabin festooned inside and out with chains of garish-gay naked light bulbs and standing by the river's muddy edge under the shade of river trees where moss drifts through the branches like gray mist) our steps slow down. Even Queenie stops prancing and sticks close by. People have been murdered in Haha's cafe. Cut to pieces. Hit on the head. There's a case coming up in court next month. Naturally these goings-on happen at night when the colored lights cast crazy patterns and the victrola wails. In the daytime Haha's is shabby and deserted. I knock at the door, Queenie barks, my friend calls: "Mrs. Haha, ma'am? Anyone to home?"

Footsteps. The door opens. Our hearts overturn. It's Mr. Haha Jones himself! And he is a giant; he *does* have scars; he *doesn't* smile. No, he glowers at us through Satan-tilted eyes and demands to know: "What you want with Haha?"

For a moment we are too paralyzed to tell. Presently my friend half-finds her voice, a whispery voice at best: "If you please, Mr. Haha, we'd like a quart of your finest whiskey."

His eyes tilt more. Would you believe it? Haha is smiling! Laughing too. "Which one of you is a drinkin' man?"

"It's for making fruitcakes, Mr. Haha. Cooking."

This sobers him. He frowns. "That's no way to waste good whiskey." Nevertheless, he retreats into the shadowed café and seconds later appears carrying a bottle of daisy yellow unlabeled liquor. He demonstrates its sparkle in the sunlight and says: "Two dollars."

We pay him with nickels and dimes and pennies. Suddenly, jangling the coins in his hand like a fistful of dice, his face softens. "Tell you what," he proposes, pouring the money back into our bead purse, "just send me one of them fruitcakes instead."

"Well," my friend remarks on our way home, "there's a lovely man. We'll put an extra cup of raisins in *his* cake."

The black stove, stoked with coal and firewood, glows like a lighted pumpkin. Eggbeaters whirl, spoons spin round in bowls of butter and sugar, vanilla sweetens the air, ginger spices it; melting, nose-tingling odors saturate the kitchen, suffuse the house, drift out to the world on puffs of chimney smoke. In four days our work is done. Thirty-one cakes, dampened with whiskey, bask on window sills and shelves.

Who are they for?

Friends. Not necessarily neighbor friends: indeed, the larger share are intended for persons we've met maybe once, perhaps not at all. People who've struck our fancy. Like President Roosevelt. Like the Reverend and Mrs. J. C. Lucey, Baptist missionaries to Borneo who lectured here last winter. Or the little knife grinder who comes through town twice a year. Or Abner Packer, the driver of the six o'clock bus from Mobile, who exchanges waves with us every day as he passes in a dust cloud whoosh. Or the young Wistons, a California couple whose car one afternoon broke down outside the house and who spent a pleasant hour chatting with us on the porch (young Mr. Wiston snapped our picture, the only one we've ever had taken). Is it because my friend is shy with everyone *except* strangers that these strangers, and merest acquaintances, seem to us our truest friends? I think yes. Also, the scrapbooks we keep of thank-you's on White House stationery, time-to-time communications from California and Borneo, the knife grinder's penny post cards, make us feel connected to eventful worlds beyond the kitchen with its view of a sky that stops.

Now a nude December fig branch grates against the window. The kitchen is empty, the cakes are gone; yesterday we carted the last of them to the post office, where the cost of stamps turned our purse inside out. We're broke. That rather depresses me, but my friend insists on celebrating—with two inches of whiskey left in Haha's bottle. Queenie has a spoonful in a bowl of coffee (she likes her coffee chicory-flavored and strong). The rest we divide between a pair of jelly glasses. We're both quite awed at the prospect of drinking straight whiskey; the taste of it brings screwed-up expressions and sour shudders. But by and by we begin to sing, the two of us singing different songs simultaneously. I don't know the words to mine, just: *Come on along, come on along, to the dark-town strutters' ball.* But I can dance: that's what I mean to be, a tap dancer in the movies. My dancing shadow rollicks on the walls; our voices rock the chinaware; we giggle: as if unseen hands were tickling us. Queenie rolls on her back, her paws plow the air, something like a grin stretches her black lips. Inside myself, I feel warm and sparky as those crumbling logs, carefree as the wind in the chimney. My friend waltzes round the stove, the hem of her poor calico skirt pinched between her fingers as though it were a party dress: *Show me the way to go home,* she sings, her tennis shoes squeaking on the floor. *Show me the way to go home.*

Enter: two relatives. Very angry. Potent with eyes that scold, tongues that scald. Listen to what they have to say, the words tumbling together into a wrathful tune: "A child of seven! whiskey on his breath! are you out of your mind? feeding a child of seven! must be loony! road to ruination! remember Cousin Kate? Uncle Charlie? Uncle Charlie's brother-in-law? shame! scandal! humiliation! kneel, pray, beg the Lord!"

Queenie sneaks under the stove. My friend gazes at her shoes, her chin quivers, she lifts her skirt and blows her nose and runs to her room. Long after the town has gone to sleep and the house is silent except for the chimings of clocks and the sputter of fading fires, she is weeping into a pillow already as wet as a widow's handkerchief.

"Don't cry," I say, sitting at the bottom of her bed and shivering despite my flannel nightgown that smells of last winter's cough syrup, "don't cry," I beg, teasing her toes, tickling her feet, "you're too old for that."

"It's because," she hiccups, "I am too old. Old and funny."

"Not funny. Fun. More fun than anybody. Listen. If you don't stop crying you'll be so tired tomorrow we can't go cut a tree."

She straightens up. Queenie jumps on the bed (where Queenie is not allowed) to lick her cheeks. "I know where we'll find real pretty trees, Buddy. And holly too. With berries big as your eyes. It's way *off* in the woods. Farther than we've ever been. Papa used to bring us Christmas trees from there: carry them on his shoulder. That's fifty years ago. Well, now: I can't wait for morning."

Morning. Frozen rime lusters the grass; the sun, round as an orange and orange as hot-weather moons, balances on the horizon, burnishes the silvered winter woods. A wild turkey calls. A renegade hog grunts in the undergrowth. Soon, by the edge of knee-deep, rapid-running water, we have to abandon the buggy. Queenie wades the stream first, paddles across barking complaints at the swiftness of the current, the pneumonia-making coldness of it. We follow, holding our shoes and equipment (a hatchet, a burlap sack) above our heads. A mile more: of chastising thorns, burs and briers that catch at our clothes; of rusty pine needles brilliant with gaudy fungus and molted feathers. Here, there, a flash, a flutter, an ecstasy of shrillings remind us that not all the birds have flown south. Always, the path unwinds through lemony sun pools and pitch vine tunnels. Another creek to cross: a disturbed armada of speckled trout froths the water round us, and frogs the size of plates practice belly flops; beaver workmen are building a dam. On the farther shore, Queenie shakes herself and trembles. My friend shivers, too: not with cold but enthusiasm. One of her hat's ragged roses sheds a petal as she lifts her head and inhales the pine-heavy air. "We're almost there; can you smell it, Buddy?" she says, as though we were approaching an ocean.

And, indeed, it is a kind of ocean. Scented acres of holiday trees, prickly-leafed holly. Red berries shiny as Chinese bells: black crows swoop upon them screaming. Having stuffed our burlap sacks with enough greenery and crimson to garland a dozen windows, we set about choosing a tree. "It should be," muses my friend, "twice as tall as a boy. So a boy can't steal the star." The one we pick is twice as tall as me. A brave handsome brute that survives thirty hatchet strokes before it keels with a creaking rending cry. Lugging it like a kill, we commence the long trek out. Every few yards we abandon the struggle, sit down and pant. But we have the strength of triumphant huntsmen; that and the tree's virile, icy perfume revive us, goad us on. Many compliments accompany our sunset return along the red clay road to town; but my friend is sly and noncommittal when passers-by praise the treasure perched in our buggy: what a fine tree and where did it come from? "Yonderways," she murmurs vaguely. Once a car stops and the rich mill owner's lazy wife leans out and whines: "Give ya two-bits cash for that ol tree." Ordinarily my friend is afraid of saying no; but on this occasion she promptly shakes her head: "We wouldn't take a dollar." The mill owner's wife persists. "A dollar, my foot! Fifty cents. That's my last offer. Goodness, woman, you can get another one." In answer, my friend gently reflects: "I doubt it. There's never two of anything."

Home: Queenie slumps by the fire and sleeps till tomorrow, snoring loud as a human.

A trunk in the attic contains: a shoebox of ermine tails (off the opera cape of a curious lady who once rented a room in the house), coils of frazzled tinsel gone gold with age, one silver star, a brief rope of dilapidated, undoubtedly dangerous candy-like light bulbs. Excellent decorations, as far as they go, which isn't far enough: my friend wants our tree to blaze "like a Baptist window," droop with weighty snows of ornament. But we can't afford the made-in-Japan splendors at the five-and-dime. So we do what we've always done: sit for days at the kitchen table with scissors and crayons and stacks of colored paper. I make sketches and my friend cuts them out: lot of cats, fish too (because they're easy to draw), some apples, some watermelons, a few winged angels devised from saved-up sheets of Hershey-bar tin foil. We use safety pins to attach these creations to the tree; as a final touch, we sprinkle the branches with shredded cotton (picked in August for this purpose). My friend, surveying the effect, clasps her hands together. "Now honest, Buddy. Doesn't it look good enough to eat?" Queenie tried to eat an angel.

After weaving and ribboning holly wreaths for all the front windows, our next project is the fashioning of family gifts. Tie-dye scarves for the ladies, for the men a home-brewed lemon and licorice and aspirin syrup to be taken "at the first Symptoms of a Cold and after Hunting." But when it comes time for making each other's gift, my friend and I separate to work secretly. I would like to buy her a pearl-handled knife, a radio, a whole pound of chocolate-covered cherries (we tasted some once, and she always swears: "I could live on them, Buddy, Lord yes I could—and that's not taking His name in vain"). Instead, I am building her a kite. She would like to give me a bicycle (she's said so on several million occasions: "If only I could Buddy. It's bad enough in life to do without something you want; but confound it, what gets my goat is not being able to give somebody something you want *them* to have. Only one of these days I will, Buddy. Locate you a bike. Don't ask how. Steal it, maybe"). Instead, I'm fairly certain that she is building me a kite —the same as last year, and the year before: the year before that we exchanged slingshots. All of which is fine by me. For we are champion kite-fliers who study the wind like sailors; my friend, more accomplished than I, can get a kite aloft when there isn't enough breeze to carry clouds.

Christmas Eve afternoon we scrape together a nickel and go to the butcher's to buy Queenie's traditional gift, a good gnawable beef bone. The bone, wrapped in funny paper, is placed high in the tree near the silver star. Queenie knows it's there. She squats at the foot of the tree staring up in a trance of greed: when bedtime arrives she refuses to budge. Her excitement is equaled by my own. I kick the covers and turn my pillow as though it were a scorching summer's night. Somewhere a rooster crows: falsely, for the sun is still on the other side of the world.

"Buddy, are you awake?" It is my friend, calling from her room, which is next to mine; and an instant later she is sitting on my bed holding a candle. "Well, I can't sleep a hoot," she declares. "My mind's jumping like a jack rabbit. Buddy, do you think Mrs. Roosevelt will serve our cake at dinner?" We huddle in the bed, and she squeezes my hand I-love-you. "Seems like your hand used to be so much smaller. I guess I hate to see you grow up. When you're grown up, will we still be friends?" I say always. "But I feel so bad, Buddy. I wanted so bad to give you a bike. I tried to sell my cameo Papa gave me. Buddy—" she hesitates, as though embarrassed—"I made you another kite." Then I confess that I made her one, too; and we laugh. The candle burns too short to hold. Out it goes, exposing the starlight, the stars spinning at the window like a visible caroling that slowly, slowly daybreak silences. Possibly we doze; but the beginnings of dawn splash us like cold water: we're up, wide-eyed and wandering while we wait for others to waken. Quite deliberately my friend drops a kettle on the kitchen floor. I tap-dance in front of closed doors. One by one the household emerges, looking as though they'd like to kill us both; but its Christmas, so they can't. First, a gorgeous breakfast: just everything you can imagine—from flapjacks and fried squirrel to hominy grits and honey-in-the-comb. Which puts everyone in good humor except my friend and I. Frankly, we're so impatient to get at the presents we can't eat a mouthful.

Well, I'm disappointed. Who wouldn't be? With socks, a Sunday school shirt, some handkerchiefs, a hand-me-down sweater and a year's subscription to a religious magazine for children. *The Little Shepherd*. It makes me boil. It really does.

My friend has a better haul. A sack of Satsumas, that's her best present. She is proudest, however, of a white wool shawl knitted by her married sister. But she says her favorite gift is the kite I built her. And it is very beautiful; though not as beautiful as the one she made me, which is blue and scattered with gold and green Good Conduct stars; moreover, my name is painted on it, "Buddy."

"Buddy, the wind is blowing."

The wind is blowing, and nothing will do till we've run to a pasture below the house where Queenie has scooted to bury her bone (and where, a winter hence, Queenie will be buried, too). There, plunging through the healthy waist-high grass, we unreel our kites, feel them twitching at the string like sky fish as they swim into the wind. Satisfied, sun-warmed, we sprawl in the grass and peel Satsumas and watch our kites cavort. Soon I forget the socks and hand-me-down sweater. I'm as happy as if we'd already won the fifty-thousand-dollar Grand Prize in that coffee-naming contest.

"My, how foolish I am!" my friend cries, suddenly alert, like a woman remembering too late she has biscuits in the oven. "You know what I've always thought?" she asks in a tone of discovery, and not smiling at me but a point beyond. "I've always thought a body would have to be sick and dying before they saw the Lord. And I imagined that when He came it would be like looking at the Baptist window: pretty as colored glass with the sun pouring through, such a shine you don't know it's getting dark. And it's been a comfort: to think of that shine taking away all the spooky feeling. But I'll wager it never happens. I'll wager at the very end a body realizes the Lord has already shown Himself. That things as they are"—her hand circles in a gesture that gathers clouds and kites and grass and Queenie pawing earth over her bone—"just what they've always seen, was seeing Him. As for me, I could leave the world with today in my eyes."

This is our last Christmas together.

Life separates us. Those who Know Best decide that I belong in a military school. And so follows a miserable succession of bugle-blowing prisons, grim reveille-ridden summer camps. I have a new home too. But it doesn't count. Home is where my friend is, and there I never go.

And there she remains, puttering around the kitchen. Alone with Queenie. Then alone. ("Buddy dear," she writes in her wild hard-to-read script, "yesterday Jim Macy's horse kicked Queenie bad. Be thankful she didn't feel much. I wrapped her in a Fine

Linen sheet and rode her in the buggy down to Simpson's pasture where she can be with all her Bones . . .").

For a few Novembers she continues to bake her fruitcakes single-handed; not as many, but some: and, of course, she always sends me "the best of the batch." Also, in every letter she encloses a dime wadded in toilet paper: "See a picture show and write me the story." But gradually in her letters she tends to confuse me with her other friend, the Buddy who died in the 1880's; more and more thirteenths are not the only days she stays in bed: a morning arrives in November, a leafless birdless coming of winter morning, when she cannot rouse herself to exclaim: "Oh my, it's fruitcake weather!"

And when that happens, I know it. A message saying so merely confirms a piece of news some secret vein had already received, severing from me an irreplaceable part of myself, letting it loose like a kite on a broken string. That is why, walking across a school campus on this particular December morning, I keep searching the sky. As if I expected to see, rather like hearts, a lost pair of kites hurrying toward heaven.

This story vividly and succintly describes the childhood world of the narrator growing up in the care of an aging female cousin who is herself "still a child." Other adults in the house have power over them, he explains, but they rarely impinge on the closed world of the boy and his "special friend," both of whom find great pleasure in the simplest things in life. Although the setting is indefinite, it is clearly the rural South where the pace of living is very slow in the thirties.

The loose plot focuses on the activities of a particular Christmas, but it conveys a sense of continuity with the past. Each act is unconsciously ritualistic, exciting and meaningful, not because it is new, but rather because it is a part of the past and evokes memories. First of all, when the courthouse bell sounds clear and cold and the birds no longer sing, then it is fruit cake time—thirty cakes to bake. Excitement abounds in the preparations—dragging out the old baby buggy to haul the "windfall pecans," searching for and cracking the nuts, scraping up hoarded money for the ingredients, and most daring of all, buying illegal alcohol for mellowing the cake. Then comes the baking of the cakes— "eggbeaters whirl, spoons spin . . . vanilla sweetens the air, and ginger spices it." Finally it is time to ship the cakes to "people who struck our fancy"—people like President Roosevelt, the bus driver who waves every day through the dust, and a Baptist missionary—thirty people, all strangers, because "my friend is shy with everyone but strangers." After the cakes go out, they observe the traditions of searching for and cutting the tree, scrapping up decorations, and finally the exchanging of homemade presents.

In his seemingly effortless characterization of his friend, the boy also characterizes himself. He comments lovingly and admiringly in a few childish statements on what his friend *has* and *has not* done: she *has not* ever seen a picture show (nor does she ever intend to), eaten in a restaurant, traveled over five miles from home, read anything except the funny paper and the Bible, worn cosmetics, or wished anyone harm. Just as these are positive features so are what she *has* done: killed the biggest rattlesnake ever seen in the country, tamed humming birds, dipped snuff (secretly), talked to herself, walked in the rain, and cured warts.

She is simple-minded and natural—her feelings are spontaneous, not measured by social conventions; her activities are off-color and disapproved of by the "powers in the house" whose unseen presence provides the only tension in their otherwise ideal world.

This story, like others by Capote, shows his love for the unusual and his understanding and appreciation of the loneliness suffered by the psychologically different. It is memorable for its integration of stylistic elements—child's point of view, sensory imagery, and nostalgic tone—with subject matter graphically portraying a world gone forever.

Junius Edwards

(1929-)

Junius Edwards was born in Alexandria in 1929 and educated at the University of Oslo, Norway. His works, like those of many of his contemporaries, concern white racism, focusing on the naive young black who in his ignorance does not realize that he is a second-class citizen and therefore brings trouble upon himself. Although the tone of his works is polemic and his message social, his stories have created interest. His works include one novel, *If We Must Die,* and several short stories which have been widely anthologized. The story printed below first appeared in *Urbanite* in 1961 .

Liars Don't Qualify

Junius Edwards

Will Harris sat on the bench in the waiting room for another hour. His pride was not the only thing that hurt. He wanted them to call him in and get him registered so he could get out of there. Twice, he started to go into the inner office and tell them, but he thought better of it. He had counted ninety-six cigarette butts on the floor when a fat man came out of the office and spoke to him.

"What you want, boy?"

Will Harris got to his feet.

"I came to register."

"Oh, you did, did you?"

"Yes sir."

The fat man stared at Will for a second, then turned his back to him.

As he turned his back, he said, "Come on in here."

Will went in.

It was a little office and dirty, but not so dirty as the waiting room. There were no cigarette butts on the floor here. Instead, there was paper. They looked like candy wrappers to Will. There were two desks jammed in there and a bony little man sat at one of them, his head down, his fingers fumbling with some papers. The fat man went around the empty desk and pulled up a chair. The bony man did not look up.

Will stood in front of the empty desk and watched the fat man sit down behind it. The fat man swung his chair around until he faced the little man.

"Charlie," he said.

"Yeah, Sam," Charlie said, not looking up from his work.

"Charlie. This boy here says he come to register."

"You sure? You sure that's what he said, Sam?" Still not looking up. "You sure? You better ask him again, Sam."

"I'm sure, Charlie."

"You better be sure, Sam."

"All right, Charlie. All right. I'll ask him again," the fat man said. He looked up at Will. "Boy. What you come here for?"

"I came to register."

369

The fat man stared up at him. He didn't say anything. He just stared, his lips a thin line, his eyes wide open. His left hand searched behind him and came up with a handkerchief. He raised his left arm and mopped his face with the handkerchief, his eyes still on Will.

The odor from under his sweat-soaked arm made Will step back. Will held his breath until the fat man finished mopping his face. The fat man put his handkerchief away. He pulled a desk drawer open, and then he took his eyes off Will. He reached in the desk drawer and took out a bar of candy. He took the wrapper off the candy and threw the wrapper on the floor at Will's feet. He looked at Will and ate the candy.

Will stood there and tried to keep his face straight. He kept telling himself: I'll take anything. I'll take anything to get it done.

The fat man kept his eyes on Will and finished the candy. He took out his handkerchief and wiped his mouth. He grinned, then he put his handkerchief away.

"Charlie." The fat man turned to the little man.

"Yeah, Sam."

"He says he come to register."

"Sam, are you sure?"

"Pretty sure, Charlie."

"Well, explain to him what it's about." The bony man still had not looked up.

"All right, Charlie," Sam said, and looked up at Will. "Boy, when folks come here, they intend to vote, so they register first."

"That's what I want to do," Will said.

"What's that? Say that again."

"That's what I want to do. Register and vote." The fat man turned his head to the bony man.

"Charlie."

"Yeah, Sam."

"He says . . . Charlie, this boy says that he wants to register and vote."

The bony man looked up from his desk for the first time. He looked at Sam, then both looked at Will.

Will looked from one of them to the other, one to the other. It was hot and he wanted to sit down. *Anything. I'll take anything.*

The man called Charlie turned back to his work, and Sam swung his chair around until he faced Will.

"You got a job?" he asked.

"Yes, sir."

"Boy, you know what you're doing?"

"Yes, sir."

"All right," Sam said. "All right."

Just then, Will heard the door open behind him, and someone came in. It was a man.

"How you all? How about registering?"

Sam smiled. Charlie looked up and smiled.

"Take care of you right away," Sam said, and then to Will. "Boy. Wait outside."

As Will went out, he heard Sam's voice: "Take a seat, please. Take a seat. Have you fixed up in a little bit. Now, what's your name?"

"Thanks," the man said, and Will heard the scrape of a chair.

Will closed the door and went back to his bench.

Anything. Anything. Anything. I'll take it all.

Pretty soon the man came out smiling. Sam came out behind him, and he called Will and told him to come in. Will went in and stood before the desk. Sam told him he wanted to see his papers: Discharge, High School diploma, Birth Certificate, Social Security Card, and some other papers. Will had them all. He felt good when he handed them to Sam.

"You belong to any organization?"

"No, sir."

"Pretty sure about that?"

"Yes, sir."

"You ever heard of the 15th Amendment?"

"Yes, sir."

"What does that one say?"

"It's the one that says all citizens can vote."

"You like that, don't you boy? Don't you?"

"Yes, sir. I like them all."

Sam's eyes got big. He slammed his right fist down on his desk top. "I didn't ask you that. I asked you if you liked the 15th Amendment. Now, if you can't answer my questions . . ."

"I like it," Will put in, and watched Sam catch his breath.

Sam sat there looking up at Will. He opened and closed his desk-pounding fist. His mouth hung open.

"Charlie."

"Yeah, Sam." Not looking up.

"You hear that?" looking wide-eyed at Will. "You hear that?"

"I heard it, Sam."

Will had to work to keep his face straight.

"Boy," Sam said. "You born in this town?"

"You got my birth certificate right there in front of you. Yes, sir."

"You happy here?"

"Yes, sir."

"You got nothing against the way things go around here?"

"No, sir."

"Can you read?"

"Yes, sir."

"Are you smart?"

"No, sir."

"Where did you get that suit?"

"New York."

"New York?" Sam asked, and looked over at Charlie. Charlie's head was still down. Sam looked back to Will.

"Yes, sir," said Will.

"Boy, what you doing there?"

"I got out of the Army there."

"You believe in what them folks do in New York?"

"I don't know what you mean."

"You know what I mean. Boy, you know good and well what I mean. You know how folks carry on in New York. You believe in that?"

"No, sir," Will said, slowly.

"You pretty sure about that?"

"Yes, sir."

"What year did they make the 15th Amendment?"

". . . 18 . . . 70," said Will.

"Name a signer of the Declaration of Independence who became President."

". . . John Adams."

"Boy, what did you say?" Sam's eyes were wide again.

Will thought for a second. Then he said, "John Adams."

Sam's eyes got wider. He looked to Charlie and spoke to a bowed head. "Now, too much is too much." Then he turned back to Will.

He didn't say anything to Will. He narrowed his eyes first, then spoke.

"Did you say *just* John Adams?"

"*Mister* John Adams," Will said, realizing his mistake.

"That's more like it," Sam smiled. "Now, why do you want to vote?"

"I want to vote because it is my duty as an American citizen to vote."

"Hah," Sam said, real loud. "Hah," again, and pushed back from his desk and turned to the bony man.

"Charlie."

"Yeah, Sam."

"Hear that?"

"I heard, Sam."

Sam leaned back in his chair, keeping his eyes on Charlie. He locked his hands across his round stomach and sat there.

"Charlie."

"Yeah, Sam."

"Think you and Elnora be coming over tonight?"

"Don't know, Sam," said the bony man, not looking up. "You know Elnora."

"Well, you welcome if you can."

"Don't know, Sam."

"You ought to, if you can. Drop in, if you can. Come on over and we'll split a corn whisky."

The bony man looked up.

"Now, that's different, Sam."

"Thought it would be."

"Can't turn down corn if it's good."

"You know my corn."

"Sure do. I'll drag Elnora. I'll drag her by the hair if I have to."

The bony man went back to work.

Sam turned his chair around to his desk. He opened a desk drawer and took out a package of cigarettes. He tore it open and put a cigarette in his mouth. He looked up at Will, then he lit the cigarette and took a long drag, and then he blew the smoke, very slowly, up toward Will's face.

The smoke floated up toward Will's face. It came up in front of his eyes and nose and hung there, then it danced and played around his face, and disappeared.

Will didn't move, but he was glad he hadn't been asked to sit down.

"You have a car?"

"No, sir."

"Don't you have a job?"

"Yes, sir."

"You like that job?"

"Yes, sir."

"You like it, but you don't want it."

"What do you mean?" Will asked.

"Don't get smart, boy," Sam said, wide-eyed. "I'm asking the questions here. You understand that?"

"Yes, sir."

"All right. All right. Be sure you do."

"I understand it."

"You a Communist?"

"No, sir."

"What party do you want to vote for?"

"I wouldn't go by parties. I'd read about the men and vote for a man, not a party."

"Hah," Sam said, and looked over at Charlie's bowed head. "Hah," he said again, and turned back to Will.

"Boy, you pretty sure you can read?"

"Yes, sir."

"All right. All right. We'll see about that." Sam took a book out of his desk and flipped some pages. He gave the book to Will.

"Read that loud," he said.

"Yes, sir," Will said, and began: "'When in the course of human events, it becomes necessary for one people to dissolve the political bands which have connected them with another, and to assume among the powers of the earth the separate and equal station to which the Laws of Nature and of Nature's God entitle them, a decent respect to the opinions of mankind requires that they should declare the causes which impel them to the separation."

Will cleared his throat and read on. He tried to be distinct with each syllable. He didn't need the book. He could have recited the whole thing without the book.

"'We hold these truths to be self-evident, that all men are created equal, that they . . .'"

"Wait a minute, boy," Sam said. "Wait a minute. You believe that? You believe that about 'created equal'?"

"Yes, sir," Will said, knowing that was the wrong answer.

"You really believe that?"

"Yes, sir." Will couldn't make himself say the answer Sam wanted to hear.

Sam stuck out his right hand, and Will put the book in it. Then Sam turned to the other man.

"Charlie."

"Yeah, Sam."

"Charlie, did you hear that?"

"What was it, Sam?"

"This boy, here, Charlie. He says he really believes it."

"Believes what, Sam? What you talking about?"

"This boy, here . . . believes that all men are equal, like it says in The Declaration."

"Now, Sam. Now you know that's not right. You know good and well that's not right. You heard him wrong. Ask him again, Sam. Ask him again, will you?"

"I didn't hear him wrong, Charlie," said Sam, and turned to Will. "Did I, boy? Did I hear you wrong?"

"No, sir."

"I didn't hear you wrong?"

"No, sir."

Sam turned to Charlie.

"Charlie."

"Yeah, Sam."

"Charlie. You think this boy trying to be smart?"

"Sam. I think he might be. Just might be. He looks like one of them that don't know his place."

Sam narrowed his eyes.

"Boy," he said. "You know your place?"

"I don't know what you mean."

"Boy, you know good and well what I mean."

"What do you mean?"

"Boy, who's . . ." Sam leaned forward, on his desk. "Just who's asking questions, here?"

"You are, sir."

"Charlie. You think he really is trying to be smart?"

"Sam, I think you better ask him."

"Boy."

"Yes, sir."

"Boy. You trying to be smart with me?"

"No, sir."

"Sam."

"Yeah, Charlie."

"Sam. Ask him if he thinks he's good as you and me."

"Now, Charlie. Now, you heard what he said about The Declaration."

"Ask, anyway, Sam."

"All right," Sam said. "Boy. You think you good as me and Mister Charlie? "

"No, sir," Will said.

They smiled, and Charlie turned away.

Will wanted to take off his jacket. It was hot, and he felt a drop of sweat roll down his right side. He pressed his right arm against his side to wipe out the sweat. He thought he had it, but it rolled again, and he felt another drop come behind that one. He pressed his arm in again. It was no use. He gave it up.

"How many stars did the first flag have?"

". . . Thirteen."

"What's the name of the mayor of this town?"

". . . Mister Roger Philip Thornedyke Jones."

"Spell Thornedyke."

". . . Capital T-h-o-r-n-d-y-k-e, Thornedyke."

"How long has he been mayor? "

". . . Seventeen years."

"Who was the biggest hero in the War Between the States?"

". . . General Robert E. Lee."

"What does that 'E' stand for?"

". . . Edward."

"Think you pretty smart, don't you?"

"No, sir."

"Well, boy, you have been giving these answers too slow. I want them fast. Understand? Fast."

"Yes, sir."

"What's your favorite song?"

"Dixie," Will said, and prayed Sam would not ask him to sing it.

"Do you like your job?"

"Yes, sir."

"What year did Arizona come into the States?"

"1912."

"There was another state in 1912."

"New Mexico, it came in January and Arizona in February."

"You think you smart, don't you?"

"No, sir."

"Don't you think you smart? Don't you?"

"No, sir."

"Oh, yes, you do, boy."

Will said nothing.

"Boy, you make good money on your job?"

"I make enough."

"Oh. Oh, you not satisfied with it?"

"Yes, sir. I am."

"You don't act like it, boy. You know that? You don't act like it."

"What do you mean?"

"You getting smart again, boy. Just who's asking questions here?"

"You are, sir."

"That's right. That's right."

The bony man made a noise with his lips and slammed his pencil down on his desk. He looked at Will, then at Sam.

"Sam," he said. "Sam, you having trouble with that boy? Don't you let that boy give you no trouble, now, Sam. Don't you do it."

"Charlie," Sam said. "Now, Charlie, you know better than that. You know better. This boy here knows better than that, too."

"You sure about that, Sam? You sure?"

"I better be sure if this boy here knows what's good for him."

"Does he know, Sam?"

"Do you know, boy?" Sam asked Will.

"Yes, sir."

Charlie turned back to his work.

"Boy," Sam said. "You sure you're not a member of any organization?"

"Yes, sir. I'm sure."

Sam gathered up all Will's papers, and he stacked them very neatly and placed them in the center of his desk. He took the cigarette out of his mouth and put it out in the full ash tray. He picked up Will's papers and gave them to him.

"You've been in the Army. That right?"

"Yes, sir."

"You served two years. That right?"

"Yes, sir."

"You have to do six years in the Reserve. That right?"

"Yes, sir."

"You're in the Reserve now. That right?"

"Yes, sir."

"You lied to me here, today. That right?"

"No, sir."

"Boy, I said you lied to me here today. That right?"

"No, sir."

"Oh, yes, you did, boy. Oh, yes, you did. You told me you wasn't in any organization. That right?"

"Yes, sir."

"Then you lied, boy. You lied to me because you're in the Army Reserve. That right?"

"Yes, sir. I'm in the Reserve, but I didn't think you meant that. I'm just in it, and don't have to go to meetings or anything like that. I thought you meant some kind of civilian organization."

"When you said you wasn't in an organization, that was a lie. Now, wasn't it, boy?"

He had Will there. When Sam had asked him about organizations, the first thing to pop in Will's mind had been the communists, or something like them.

"Now, wasn't it a lie?"

"No, sir."

Sam narrowed his eyes.

Will went on.

"No, sir, it wasn't a lie. There's nothing wrong with the Army Reserve. Everybody has to be in it. I'm not in it because I want to be in it."

"I know there's nothing wrong with it," Sam said. "Point is, you lied to me here, today."

"I didn't lie. I just didn't understand the question," Will said.

"You understood the question, boy. You understood good and well, and you lied to me. Now, wasn't it a lie?"

"No, sir."

"Boy. You going to stand right there in front of me big as anything and tell me it wasn't a lie?" Sam almost shouted. "Now, wasn't it a lie?"

"Yes, sir," Will said, and put his papers in his jacket pocket.

"You right, it was," Sam said. Sam pushed back from his desk.

"That's it, boy. You can't register. You don't qualify. Liars don't qualify."

"But . . ."

"That's it." Sam spat the words out and looked at Will hard for a second, and then he swung his chair around until he faced Charlie.

"Charlie."

"Yeah, Sam."

"Charlie. You want to go out to eat first today?"

Will opened the door and went out. As he walked down the stairs, he took off his jacket and his tie and opened his collar and rolled up his shirt sleeves. He stood on the courthouse steps and took a deep breath and heard a noise come from his throat as he breathed out and looked at the flag in the court yard. The flag hung from its staff, still and quiet, the way he hated to see it; but it was there, waiting, and he hoped that a little push from the right breeze would lift it and send it flying and waving and whipping from its staff, proud, the way he liked to see it.

He took out a cigarette and lit it and took a slow deep drag. He blew the smoke out. He saw the cigarette burning in his right hand, turned it between his thumb and forefinger, made a face, and let the cigarette drop to the court-house steps.

He threw his jacket over his left shoulder and walked on down to the bus stop, swinging his arms.

LIARS DON'T QUALIFY

This story of the early sixties is set in the midst of civil rights protests and is typical of propagandistic writing of the era. Largely dramatic, it pits a young black veteran's patience against the insults of two white voter registrars who have obviously designed questions to trip him up. The dramatic form works well since the encounter is brief and no exposition is necessary. Neither is there need for character development; the flat characters represent liberal and conservative ideology of the time, each determined to win. In spite of the young black's resolve (he thinks "I'll take anything to get it done"), he is defeated. The story achieves its effect through its Hemingway-like terse dialog form.

Shirley Ann Grau

(1929-)

Shirley Ann Grau was born in New Orleans, but later moved to Alabama where she was graduated from Booth School in Montgomery. Returning to New Orleans, she took a baccalaureate degree from Tulane University in 1950 and later attended graduate school there while she was writing her first book, published in 1955. Shortly afterward she married James K. Feibleman, a Tulane philosophy professor, by whom she has three children. The bayous of Louisiana and the Gulf Coast of Alabama provide the setting for most of her stories, which are filled with natural detail. Her insight into a variety of characters, particularly Negroes, as well as her natural ease in dealing with Negro-white relationships has won the praise of critics. Her first book, *The Black Prince and Other Stories*, is felt by many to be her best work; however, it is her third novel, *The Keepers of the House*, that received the most attention. For it she received a Pulitzer Prize in 1964. The story below is from *The Black Prince and Other Stories* published in 1963.

The Way of a Man[*]

Shirley Ann Grau

For five years the boy lived with his old father in the house on Bayou St. Philippe.

It was a good house, snug and tight against the brief cold winds of the tumbled gray January sky and the hard quick squalls of August. The house was built on good solid ground, a high bank of shells, that stuck up out of the marsh like the back of an alligator: a great alligator extending nearly two miles from the state highway, winding and twisting out into the Gulf marsh where the tides were salty and sea fish came up into the bayou mouths. The house stood at the end of the winding shell ridge, farthest away from the highway, the end where Bayou St. Philippe made a circle in from the east and let its slow yellow-green waters into the Gulf.

It was a comfortable clapboard house with one room and a lean-to kitchen. Inside was a double bed; a cylinder-shaped oil stove for winter; and a chest that the man had brought from New Orleans once when he was young and had gone into the city for a spree: a low chest and of some light wood—cedar or maple, it was hard to tell after so many years. And tacked carefully to the wall over the chest was a colored lithograph of the Virgin, tall and serene in a bright blue gown; from the same nail dangled a black-bead rosary, its cross missing.

None of the walls were painted—inside or out—but time had given the boards a uniform black stain. Outside also blacked by time and weather, were racks for drying nets, the small kind that a single man could handle, for he always fished alone; and racks for drying the muskrat pelts when he trapped during the season.

The boy, whose name was William, had been born in this house and until he was five years old had played among the racks and breathed the smell of nets and of drying pelts and watched wind shadows roll over the marsh grass.

He had been born in the house—one hot September afternoon. The sky was a still high arch of bright blue: the sun slid down it like a silver dime. In the south a mass of thunderclouds sat low on the horizon; the waters of the Gulf moved with the peculiar nervous tremor of a storm on them somewhere.

He was not long being born. His mother cried quietly and briefly in the hot afternoon, saw that her child was a man, and fell asleep. No one seemed particularly concerned. When the work was done, his grandmother rolled down the sleeves of her long-sleeved cotton print dress, nodded to her daughter, and began the walk back across the marsh. As she went she saw the old man who was her daughter's husband coming back from a day's fishing.

When the boy was two, his mother left. She was a young woman, not more than twenty then, with a long lithe body and quick darting eyes. She had married the old man because of two mistakes. She thought he was too old to give her a child and she thought that he was rich. Within a year she had a child growing in her body. And she never saw his money.

A government pension check came regularly each month on the third. They held it for him at the post office over in Port Allen; he walked in to fetch it. He had done this for so many years that the two men who sorted the mail looked specially for his envelope—light brown with the blue check showing through the strip of cellophane—and put it up on a little shelf beside the general-delivery window to wait for him.

"Say, Uncle," one of them asked him once, "how come the government's sending you money?"

The old man took the check in his knotted black fingers. "Account I was in the war."

"Which war?" the man said. "There's been a lot of them."

The old man blinked his eyes slowly.

"It couldn't a been the Civil War," the white man said. He had hold of one end of the envelope. "You ain't that old."

His partner came and leaned on the counter beside him. "I bet it was the Spanish War, wasn't it, Uncle?"

"You in the fighting, Uncle?" the other one asked.

"I done press the pants and shine the shoes for them that's done the fighting," the old man said with dignity and pulled his envelope from the white man's hand.

Holding his check carefully in two fingers, he always went directly across the street to the bank to cash it. When he had the bills in his hand, he would buy food for the month and fishing gear or some new traps, and on his way home he'd pick up a jug of corn likker.

That was it. His young wife never saw his money. She was convinced he had hidden it somewhere; she spent days searching and found nothing. But she was certain he was rich.

It wasn't any life for a young woman, a pretty woman. One day she was gone. When the old man came home, there was only his son in the house, a fuzzy-headed black boy with bright brown eyes and a constant smile. The old man called for his wife once and walked once around the house, looking over the marsh on all sides. Then he went in and began supper himself. The boy followed him inside, climbed on the edge of the table, and waited for food.

The next morning the old man sat in the sun and mended his nets. The boy crouched on the edge of the bayou and tried to catch the little water lizards with his hands.

William was young and agile as a black monkey and noisy. And his father was very old and slow. And so one day the man took down the boy's cap from the nail where it had been hanging and put it on the nervous kinky head, and folded the boy's clothes in a brown paper bag. Then he took his son by the hand and walked into town to give him back to his mother. He stopped only once—in the grocery to ask where she was living—and then went directly to the house. There he knocked on the door and she herself came to answer it—a young woman wearing a pink print dress stretched tight across full hips and heavy breasts. The old man pointed down to the boy and dropped his hand and turned around without a word and walked away. The woman looked down at her son—at his thin long black limbs and his thin quick monkey face—and then up at the broad heavy stooped back of the man as he walked away. And she asked her son: "Don't he feed you none, the old man?"

The boy nodded and grinned. The upper row of his front teeth was missing.

"He can afford to, him," the woman said. "He can sure afford to, him." Then she turned and walked back into the house, leaving the door open behind her. He son followed her, stopping to pick up the brown paper parcel of clothes that his father had dropped on the steps.

That was how he came to his mother, after his father had shown that he would have no more to do with him. And he lived with her until he was fourteen and the police caught him stealing tires. Then he was sent up to the north part of the state to the reform school.

Three years later he was back knocking on his mother's door. And she opened it and stood leaning against the doorjamb studying him. "You a man grown," she said. "I used to could look down at you and you was a boy. But now I got to look up because you a man."

"Reckon so," he said.

He was a man grown. Not tall but broad: his father's build. There were such muscles across his back that he almost seemed to be stooping. He had the same quick nervous face of his childhood, the same nervous uptwitching of the left corner of the mouth.

Because he was a man, he did not live in his mother's house. She fixed him a bed in the kitchen (her house had only two rooms), a pillow and a blanket rolled up to be out of the way; and she kept it there in case the officer who was in charge of his parole should come around looking. He did come occasionally—a slight dark Negro, whose dark-blue police uniform did not fit him, whose name was Matthew Pettis. The first time he came she met him at the door and asked him in and offered him some coffee and said that her son was working on the oyster boats because he was so strong— for all that he was just seventeen, he was a man grown. She showed him the bed. And Pettis nodded and rubbed his black kinky hair, and his little shiny black eyes danced all over the room.

The next time Pettis came, William happened to be there and he and his mother sat side by side on the bed in the front room and answered yes sir and no sir to the questions and looked with quiet brown eyes into Pettis's restless quick ones.

When the policeman had gone, William stood up and stretched and pulled on his cap and sauntered slowly out of the house. His mother did not notice he was gone until she called to ask him if he wanted anything to eat. She opened the front door and called for him out into the street. Then she went back and began to eat herself. She did not think of him again. She did not know where he had gone or where he was living. She did not wonder about it. A man could make his own way.

He was living in Bucktown, a double line of colored houses strung out along a dirt road and only a couple of miles from the oyster docks. He had a girl there, short, plump, and high-brown colored. Her name was Cynthia Lee. She was always laughing, always showing her short square teeth and her dull red gums. She worked at the shrimp plant that was a little farther down the shore. He'd worked there too, once, when he'd first come back.

He'd quit because the work was too light, for a man. And he went to the oyster boats, where the pay was better and the work was enough to try the muscles of a strong back. He'd been saying hello to her for over a week before he got the nerve to ask her to have a beer with him on Saturday night. She said, "I reckon so," with her quick bright grin and a little jerk of her head.

They went to the Smile Inn, which was the closest bar for Negroes, and they had three beers each, and then, because it was Saturday and the place got very crowded and men kept bumping into her round little body and saying: "Excuse me," with a grin, he pointed to the door.

"It too crowded," he said. "I don't study getting all mashed up by people none."

She just laughed and pushed her way to the door.

He walked her home. It was night and there weren't any lights along the dirt road. They stumbled in ruts and held on to each other, laughing. The moon came up finally over the straggling thin pines and they could see the road in front of them.

"I ain't used to coming home this late," she said.

"Ain't you?"

"No," she said. "Ma'll give me hell."

"Seems like you could handle her with no trouble." He rubbed his chin with the back of his hand. "Seems like you'd better be worrying about your pa."

She grinned; in the uncertain moon glow her little square teeth flashed white in the darkness of her face. "He done picked up and gone a long time ago."

"That right?" William said.

"Ma don't miss him none." She laughed again and stumbled in a deep rut. He caught her around the waist.

"Cynthia Lee," he said, "seems like you can't even walk none. You sure must be drunk."

"Me?" Her laugh went up and down the dark. "I can't even hold no likker."

He tightened his arm "I reckon I know one kind you could." He kissed her. Her square white teeth clamped on his lower lip. He hissed with pain and slapped her away from him. She stumbled backwards and sat down. Her body made a soft sound against the ground. He rubbed his lip for a few moments and then bent over her. He had thought she was crying; but she was only laughing softly.

It was settled after that. He lived with her in her mother's house in Bucktown. And since her mother was a big jolly woman who worked as a cook in one of the white houses on the beach, and who thought William was a fine handsome man, things went well.

One evening after work he went out to see his father. He had not been there since he was a little boy and he wondered if he remembered the way. He began to walk down the highway, the highway that led into the city. It was a dry time. The wheels of the cars on the asphalt strip stirred up dust and he coughed and covered his nose and mouth with one hand. He rubbed the other hand across his face and felt the grit of the dust on it. He pulled a handkerchief out of his pocket and wiped his face carefully, for he knew that his skin was black and that the light dust would streak it. And he did not want to appear before his father with a face streaked up like the clowns he had seen in a circus once. (At the reform school once for good behavior they had given him a pass to the circus and had let him go alone. He had been so fascinated and dazed by all that he had seen that he had returned to the school, forgetting his plan to break parole and run away. When it was too late, he remembered with a sick feeling in his stomach. He was calling himself all the names he could think of, whispering them clearly to himself, when the chaplain, a fat little man with a bald pink head, came and shook his hand and told him that he was proud of him, that he had behaved like a man.)

When William saw the white shell road leading off the highway, he knew that he would remember the way, even if it had been years since his father had taken him by the hand and, walking so fast that he had to run and stumble after, had brought him over to his mother.

The shell road ran south and ended with a small wharf where some white fisherman kept their boats dragged up above the tides on slips of rough wood. Just before the road's end a footpath went off straight eastward through the waist-high grasses that moved in any wind. At the end was Bayou St. Philippe and his father's house. Long before he got close, he could see the house on the ridge of high ground, a square little weathered building with a slanting lean-to for a kitchen and a slanting little pile of firewood. Though it was warm spring weather, his father had built a little fire outside on the grass-free stretch of ground. He was sitting alongside it now on a straight-back cane chair he had brought from inside.

William remembered the chair; he was sure it was the same one that had been there when he was a boy. He remembered trying to climb the ladder back and stumbling to the floor with the chair over him like a tent. And his father had pulled him free with one hand and with the other had given him a slap across the head that made his eyes blur and his ears sing. William stopped and stared at the old man and wondered how he had been able to hit so hard.

He wore tennis shoes; the old man had not heard him come up. He had not lifted his head from the redfish he was cleaning. Very slowly, eyes squinting with the effort, he was removing the fish scales.

"Hi," said William.

The old man looked at him slowly over the smoke and haze of the fire. Slowly he put the fish back in the wicker basket at his side.

"You remember me?" William asked, and stepped closer, his hands jammed down in his pockets, wondering if he had got all the road dust off his face, for he did not want his father to laugh at him.

The old man looked at him slowly, up and down, without answering. His face in the firelight in the dusk was very old and very lined. Even the blackness of his skin was beginning to gray—like a film of dust was gathering over it.

"You remember me?" William repeated.

The old man nodded slowly, very slowly. "You a man grown now. A man grown."

"I past seventeen," William said, and squared his shoulders.

He stepped up to the fire and took the fish out of the basket and held out his hand for the scaling knife, and when the old man gave it to him he finished the cleaning in a few quick movements. "I been working on the oyster boats," he said.

"I worked the boats," his father said, and folded his hands together and rested his chin on them.

"You did?" William studied his father. He was a big man, big as his son, or he had been once. He was stooped now so that he always seemed to be huddling into himself.

The old man took the cleaned fish and went inside. William picked up the chair and followed him.

"You want I should put it on to cook?" William asked.

The old man shook his head.

"You ain't changed nothing," William said. The room was just as he remembered it. He opened the wood shutter on the side that looked out on the bayou and, beyond that, a quarter mile away, the Gulf. "It's rough out there," he said. "It's gonna be a rough night."

It began to rain while they were eating. "First come in over a month." His father did not stop chewing, his jaws moved slowly up and down.

"Lay the dust a little," William said.

In one comer the roof leaked; water ran down the wall. But neither of them noticed. The old man went and lay on his bed and almost immediately fell asleep. William stretched on the floor, pillowed his head on a pile of nets, listened to the rain, and thought about his girl until he fell asleep too.

The water that had leaked in through the roof ran down the smooth boards of the floor and touched his cheek. He lifted his head, rubbing at his face, and saw that it was morning.

The door was open. William rolled over and peered out of it. His father was standing there right on the edge of the bayou, looking down toward its mouth and the Gulf.

When William stood up he saw the skiff too: overturned, half awash, caught just inside the bayou. He jammed hands in his pockets and looked around. The squalls of the past night had not changed the appearance of the marsh; but then the grasses never changed from summer to winter. Even after a hurricane had whipped through them they rose fresh and untouched.

"I plain don't see nobody," he told his father.

The old man swung his head slowly back and forth as if he were looking for somebody.

"Look," William said, "iffen you don't want that boat, I sure enough do."

The old man kept his skiff pulled up alongside the house. William shoved it down into the water. Then quickly he got the oars, which were leaning against the wall; and when he turned he found that his father was sitting in the boat waiting.

"That all right with me," William said. "You just plain remember that my boat."

"Who done seen it?" his father said. "I plain ask you."

"That don't matter." William picked up the oars and fitted them into the locks. "I the one to get it in, and it mine."

"I plain ask you: who done seen it first?"

"Jesus," William said. "I plain telling you: that mine."

His father did not answer. He did not seem to hear.

"I plain telling you," William said. "I done spoke out first."

He began to row down to the overturned skiff. The water was rough and occasionally he felt a wet slap in his face—cool for all the warmth of the day. As he rowed he stared up at the sky, which was low and hazy, and thought about the things he could do with a boat of his own. After a coat of paint nobody would recognize it.

"Look," his father said. "They got a net out."

He lifted his oars and rested them and turned his head. Strands of net were caught across the skiff and a few feet out were five colored cork floats.

"That net ain't gonna be worth nothing," his father said.

"Jesus," William told him, "I ain't wanting that net. I plain wanting the boat."

His father stared at him. His old face was lined with determination. "Who seen it first?"

"I ain't arguing," William said. "I telling you. That mine."

They came alongside the skiff. Their own prow nosed into the reeds. The old man reached out and touched the other hull, tapping it softly with his fingers. Using one of the oars for a pole, William pushed against it. "Jesus," he said. "She's fast. She caught up fast."

"She ain't gonna come loose that way," his father said.

"I know that, man." William felt his ears get hot with anger. "I plain know that."

"There ain't no way but get out and push her off."

William stood up and walked down to the prow of the skiff. With the oar he tested the depth of the water. "Jesus," he said when he lifted the oar, "that near waist deep."

He took the pack of cigarettes out of his shirt pocket and put it carefully in a dry place under the seat. Then he swung himself over the side. "I only doing this," he told his father, "account of it my boat. I gonna get it and it mine."

His father did not answer.

"I don't want no trouble with you," William said.

His father did not appear to hear.

William looked at him and knew that he would have trouble and did not care.

The water came to his waist, and it was cold. He felt his clothes hamper his movements and he wished he could have taken them off. But there might be jellyfish about, and even though he knew that their red stinging marks were harmless he was afraid of them.

And because he was afraid and did not want to be, he splashed noisily and quickly around to the other skiff. The bayou floor was a tangled mass of seaweed; he stumbled and his face touched the water. He spluttered and wiped the green weed taste away with the back of his hand. He saw that the stem of the boat was caught on a mound of sand; he climbed up beside it, pushing down the reeds. The water scarcely came to his ankles here.

He stopped and looked at his father, who was sitting without moving and watching him.

"I the one who pushed this loose," William said, "you remember."

The old man blinked his eyes slowly.

William said: "You ain't strong enough to push this off."

The eyes kept blinking at him.

"I got this, so it mine. Man's got a right to what he can get."

His father still did not answer. William felt his ears sing with anger. He bent and hooked his fingers under the stern handles, lifting and pushing. The muscles across his shoulders and back tensed against his shirt. He heard the wet cloth tear as the boat floated free.

They towed the skiff back up the bayou. "There's net all over her," the old man said.

"She pulls heavy," William said.

On the shore William sat down and began to take off his shoes. He shook them and stood them carefully aside to dry out. His father could pull up the skiff, he thought.

He noticed something strange. For a minute he wasn't sure what it was. Then he realized: the quiet. Before, up to a minute before, there had been the sounds of his father moving about the skiff. Then suddenly everything stopped. He lifted his head abruptly and saw his father standing there, his back to him, and looking down at the skiff. And William sat where he was, wiping his face slowly with one hand, and stared at the skiff they had found.

It was right side up now. And he saw that there were more nets tangled around it than he had thought. And through their black crisscross he saw a yellow dress and white skin.

He got to his feet slowly and walked over and stood beside his father and looked down at the snarl of black net—and the girl tangled in it, caught in it, lying there, face down on the shells, one arm pulled up, twisted and broken over her head.

"Sweet Jesus," William said. His heart was beating so fast he could hardly talk. "Sweet Jesus Christ."

"She caught up under the seats," his father said.

"She been to a party,"

William said very slowly. She was wearing an evening dress, bright yellow, with a full skirt that the water had shredded and wrapped around her legs. William looked down at her and rubbed his chin and fought down the sickness in his throat. "Maybe she done took too much to drink and went out fishing for a joke."

"That might could be," his father said.

She had red hair, short red hair, bright in the sun. The yellow dress had fallen to her waist, and her back and shoulders shone white and slender. He had never seen such white skin.

There was a quivering in his stomach, but he said calmly, the way a man should: "I done reckon she went out cause she got a little too much, and the storm caught her up and killed her."

"That might could be," his father said.

There was one thing a man had to do. William pulled his heavy knife from his pocket and went to work cutting through the nets, slowly. The tips of his fingers rubbed against the yellow taffeta underskirt. He stared at the white curve of her back and saw that the skin was not so perfect. It had been torn in some places, but the water had washed all the blood away.

He cut through the last of the nets and folded up the knife and put it away and sat back on his heels and tried to get courage to turn her over. He had seen the face of the drowned before.

His father's black old hand took her shoulder and turned her. She was not quite stiff yet; he let her fall on her back. William jerked his head aside and closed his eyes so that he should not see. He got to his feet, stumbling, and walked away.

He heard his father say: "Ain't you a man grown?" But he kept walking until he got to the house and sat down on the steps.

"A man's got a call not to look at some things," he said aloud. His breath was coming short and quick. When he'd been little and breathed like that, he'd been crying. But he was not crying now.

A man didn't have to look at some things just to prove he was a man. "A man's got no call like that," he said aloud.

He could imagine what her body would look like. The picture had flashed in his mind when he saw his father turn her over, even though he shut his eyes so that he would not see. The picture came into his mind and stayed there—her body shining white and perfect, shining wet and dead.

He felt dizzy suddenly. His head kept going in wide swinging circles, circles that left streaks of color behind them. He reached down both hands and held tightly to the steps. But that did not help any. He lifted both hands and took hold of his head. He held the outside of his head steady, but the inside behind his eyes kept turning.

He was almost afraid . . . he did not know what was happening to him. Then his head was all right. He opened his eyes. And lifted his head and even looked over at the shore where his father had stood. He saw that the girl's boat was still there, but his father's boat was gone. He stood up and saw his father out at the bayou's mouth. He saw the yellow of the dress too, and then his father changed the course of the boat and began to row southward, paralleling the shoreline. William sat down again and listened.

And although he knew better, he felt that if he listened hard enough he could hear the splash when his father found a spot that was far enough away and pushed the girl's body over.

"A man's got no call to do some things," he said aloud. "Iffen he don't want to." He straightened up, folded his arms and felt the muscles of his back stiffen. A man had muscles like that.

He sat and stared at the ground that was bare of grass and that last night's rain had crisscrossed with thin little lines. He sat and thought about the things a man could do. And gradually he lifted his eyes until he was staring across the uncertain ground, the marsh, and the straight grasses that moved in the slightest wind.

Finally he heard his father come back. When he turned around, the old man had his skiff up on the bank and was standing looking at the other one. He held his chin in one wrinkled black hand as he studied the boat.

William got up slowly and walked over to him. "It done take you a long while."

"I done went quite a ways." The hand kept rubbing the chin, the thin black chin with the irregular tufts of white whiskers.

William felt in his shirt pocket for the cigarettes, remembered where they were, and walked over to the boat to look for them.

He had put the pack under the bow seat. He remembered very distinctly. He remembered the smooth slick feel of the cellophane on his fingers when he put it there.

"I plain see what happened," he said to the bottom of the skiff. "I plain see what happened." He straightened up and turned to his father. And held out his hand.

The old man did not move.

William hunched his shoulders slightly. "I ain't no kid," he said, "to get things taken from me. I a man grown that can take what his."

Slowly the old man took the pack of cigarettes out of his trouser pocket and handed it to his son. Slowly William lit one.

The old man put a foot up on the gunwale of the second skiff. "I got me a mighty pretty skiff here."

William looked at him from under his brows. "I wouldn't have a dead skiff for no amount of money."

The old man reached down and scratched his ankle. "Yes, sir, a real pretty skiff."

"Listen," William said. Always when he was angry his ears began to hurt and bum. "Iffen I wanted that boat there . . ."

"Yes, sir," the old man said, and rubbed his foot up and down the gunwale. "A sweet boat. This here is plain my lucky day."

"I a man can take what he wants," William said. "And I plain wouldn't have nothing to do with that there boat."

The old man reached down and pulled off a strip of grass that had caught inside the boat. "Got myself a new boat."

"You damn keep it," William said. Holding the cigarette between his lips, he began to walk away. "I ain't arguing with you."

From behind him the old man spoke. "And you supposed to be a man grown."

"A man don't have to do every single thing. Some things he don't do."

He went to his mother's house. He was very angry. And he was hungry. The door of the icebox stuck. He jerked at it so savagely that it crashed open against the wall. He heard his mother come and stand in the doorway behind him.

"I looking for something to eat," he said, and glanced at her over his shoulder. She had just got up; she still wore a red flower-printed housecoat.

"There ain't nothing there. Stan come in and I fix him a real supper last night." Stan was her husband, a railroad waiter with a lean, hungry black face, who always drew long runs and was very seldom in town.

William slammed shut the door. "I reckon I better go find something."

"You been fishing?" his mother asked. She was staring at his trousers, which were still wet at the seams.

"I been to see the old man." He began to walk toward the door.

She caught his arm, stopping him. "He ain't give you no breakfast?"

"I ain't one to ask," he said.

She hooked both thumbs in the belt of her housecoat and spread her palms downward against her hips. "With all that money he got—"

Stan called sleepily: "That William you talking to, honey?"

"Nobody else," she said. "Don't you go getting jealous." She turned back to her son, but all she saw was the screen door closing behind him.

She called after him: "Why ain't you got him to give you something?"

"I ain't wanted nothing from him," he said.

William did not see his father again for nearly four months. At night sometimes the old black face, its cheeks and jaw studded with tufts of white hair, floated through his dreams. During the day he did not think of him. He had his job on the oyster boats (it was a good season and a heavy one) and he had his girl, whose name was Cynthia Lee.

One Friday evening in November he stood drinking his beer in Jack's Café with some of the other fellows from his boat. Cynthia Lee came up to him and pulled at his arm. Her mouth was open, but this time not smiling. She told him that Matthew Pettis and another policeman were asking for him at his mother's.

He put the glass down on the bar and turned it around and around slowly. He could guess what had happened. Something had gone wrong in the deal he had with Clarence Anderson and Mickey Lane. He thought briefly of the newspaper-wrapped package hidden in his room and the brown dry weeds inside. He wondered if the police had found that. They did not know where he lived; he was supposed to stay with his mother. But there were always people who would tell them.

Maybe he could get to the package before they did. . . . He wondered how much the police knew; maybe they had the package already. They would find it soon if he didn't get back to it. But maybe they were waiting for him there. . . . Maybe . . .

Cynthia jiggled his arm. "What you aiming to do? What you studying to do?"

"I getting out," he said.

She called after him as he left—"William!"—but he did not bother to answer. He did not have time.

He turned away from the houses and the lights in the windows and, running, twisted and turned down back alleys until he found himself in the open country. He stopped for a moment and caught his breath and listened. There were nothing but pines, thin straggling pines growing in the sandy ground, there wasn't even a wind to rustle their needles. But he saw Matthew Pettis's quick black face behind every tree and every hackberry bush. A quivering began deep down in his stomach. "A man got no call to be afraid," he said.

He left the pine ridge and made his way through the swampy grounds. He was tired from a day's work on the oyster boat, but he made himself move at a trot. The close damp night odor was beginning to come up from all around him.

He did not know exactly where he was going until he saw the square boards of his father's house right in front of him over the reeds. Then he stopped and thought for a minute. "There's things a man can ask for," he said. And he knew he would ask the old man for money, for enough money to get him to the city, to New Orleans.

He walked closer. The sun was down, but the light was still good enough for him to see the second boat, the girl's boat, pulled up high against the north side of the house. The old man had painted it dark green, but William still recognized it, and from four months past the memory of the girl flashed into his mind. He shook his head to be rid of it. Death frightened him.

As he had done before, he ate with the old man—fish and canned beans. And because it was near to the time the pension check came (on the third of every month),

William began to wonder if the old man would have any money at all. William sat very still, thinking, rubbing his underlip with his tongue and wondering how he should ask. Finally he said: "I done got myself in trouble."

The old man dunked the two plates up and down in a bucket of water and wiped them on the sleeve of his shirt. "That right?"

"You might could sound more interested," William said. "You might could."

"Ain't no interest to me," his father said. His thick nubby black fingers reached for the package of cigarettes on the shelf beside the door, the shelf that was nothing but a board resting on two wood blocks fastened to the wall with tenpenny nails.

"I gonna need some money."

The old man lit his cigarette slowly and did not answer.

"I gonna need just enough money to get me to New Orleans."

The old man tipped his chair back against the wall and smoked slowly.

"I shoulda been paid tomorrow. So I ain't got any money."

"I ain't got none either."

"Sure you got it," William said. "Everybody know you got it."

"Everybody but me," the old man said.

"I got to get to New Orleans," William said, and rubbed his fingers up and down the edge of the table, bending them and pressing on them hard as he could.

"You can walk."

"It eighty-odd miles," William said.

The ashes from the old man's cigarette dropped to the floor.

"A man's got a right to ask some things," William said.

The old man did not answer.

"Iffen I stay around here the police catch me sure."

"That right?" his father said, and closed wrinkled lids over his eyes.

William got up and stood in the door, looking across the grasses. All he could see was Pettis's thin face under the blue cap. He closed his eyes and shook his head, but the image followed him. His jaw began to tremble and he held it with his hand.

"And you supposed to be a man," his father said softly; his lips scarcely moved. "You supposed to be a man and you afraid. You plain afraid."

William spun around. The rubber soles of his tennis shoes squeaked on the boards. "I ain't afraid." He felt quick tears spurt down his cheeks. "I got a right to ask."

His father laughed, soundlessly as old people always do, and doubled up on his chair. His father opened his mouth and laughed at him. "And you a man . . ."

The tears filmed his eyes and wet his mouth as he stumbled across the room. His hip stuck something that must have been the edge of the table; his head was filled with the echo of his own sobbing as he went stumbling toward his father. "A man got a right to some things."

He felt his arm go up, but it was not his arm moving. He could not see when his fist came down, but he felt something crumble. "A man got a right . . ."

He stood there crying until the tears were all used up.

His father was dead. He had gone down like an old wall that had been dry and toppling for years, waiting for someone to push it over. He had fallen from his chair and lay on his side, one arm stretched out gently.

William shook his head slowly, back and forth. Unbelieving. He had forgot that old bones were brittle from wear. He had forgot that the bigness of a man meant nothing against age, that old men die easily.

William held up his hand and looked at it. There was no blood on it. He looked down at his father. In the dusk he could see no marks on the black old face. The boy rubbed his knuckles slowly with the fingers of his left hand. He had not meant to: the old man had died so easily.

After a while William lifted his head and listened, sniffling back the last of the tears. He walked over to the window, pushed open the shutter a bit, and looked out. The night was going to be foggy. You could see it beginning already in the reeds at the edge of the bayou, white fog lying along the ground like a strip of bandage. It would be thick, come night—even thicker when the smoke came down from the cypress stumps they were burning to the north.

He stood looking out the window, squinting his eyes, thinking. He wondered where he should go. There was his mother's; he would trust her. But the police would be sure to watch there. There was Cynthia Lee and the house in Bucktown. But they would have found out about that by now. He had friends, but he did not want to trust them. Not now.

William looked down at the old man lying on the boards of the floor with the chair fallen over him and he shook his head. He had not meant to kill him. He lifted his arm and held it in the same position. He felt the muscles in his shoulder and along the arm. They had killed the old man. He had not done it. Not with his mind. He had lifted his arm, and his muscles and his strength and his youth had done it. He swung his arm outward, repeating the blow. Then he rubbed his head and turned from his father to the window and the stretch of bayou and Gulf and the fog that was coming up slowly.

He would have to sleep out. There were plenty of places of high ground near the road. Most nights he would not have minded that. But tonight with the fog, the fog that was mixed with cypress smoke, with sweet fleshy cypress smoke . . .

There was no help for it. He pulled closed the shutter and turned back to the room. Like a man should, he straightened his shoulders and looked down at his father. Already it was so dark that he could not see the face at all, only the vague outline of the body. It might have been anyone lying there. It might have been— but he knew it wasn't. He knew that it was his father lying dead with the side of his skull crushed in. Maybe even the mark of a fist along the side of his head. There was no help for that either. He had not intended to, but he had done it, and now there was no use standing shivering like a baby. A man did what he did and didn't study about it afterwards.

If he were to sleep out, William knew that he would need a blanket. The fog would be cold and the night was going to be long. He stepped over his father and reached for the blanket on the bed. It was tucked in tightly, and when he jerked at it the light mattress came loose. Something hit the floor with the quick sound of metal and rolled toward him and struck his foot. He jumped, then bent down and felt around on the dark floor with his fingers to see what it was that had come jumping out toward him, as if it had been meant for him. His fingers touched and recognized it and lifted it up: a silver dollar.

Then William remembered what he had come for. And what he had nearly forgotten. He reached into his pocket for a lighter. The first two tries the flint did not spark. He shook it, saying softly: "Damn!" Then he was holding a small yellow flame in his hand. He checked the coin in his fingers: a dollar. And he bent down over the bed to see what else was hidden under the mattress.

The light caught the sheen of the round silver pieces lined up on one of the slats of the bed. He held the light down and counted them slowly, using his finger as a pointer. There were six of them, and the one he held in his hand made seven.

One by one he picked them up and dropped them in his pocket. That was all: seven of them.

There was a kerosene lamp by the window. He lit it and searched carefully around the bed. And found nothing. He began to get angry. He jerked the bed from the wall and looked behind it. He yanked open the drawers of the chest and went through them, tossing the stuff on the bed. He felt behind the window frame and found nothing. His anger increased, anger at the old man lying on the floor, the old man who kept only seven silver dollars.

William went out to the lean-to kitchen. There was only a single rough shelf holding four cans; he knocked that over too. He noticed a loose floor board. Using the handle of the pot, he pried it open; there was only ground underneath. He put his hand through the opening and pulled up a handful of dry musty earth. He threw it against the wall with disgust.

"God damn, God damn, God damn," he whispered softly to himself. He looked out, this time on the side away from the bayou. Fog was thicker there over the marsh, making the grasses silvery, translucent almost, floating. It was like the fog sucked away all color.

Fog was always sucking away, William thought. When you walked through it you could feel it sucking at your skin, sucking away at your skin, trying to wither you up. When he slept he could cover himself all up with the blanket, head and all, so that it could not reach him.

There were two other loose floor boards. He pried them up and found only ground under them. He broke the boards across his knee and tossed them into a corner.

He went through his father's pockets carefully: three nickels and two pennies and a smooth brown rabbit's foot on a key chain with a single heavy key. William held the key up to the lamp and turned it slowly in the light. Then he looped the chain around his fingers, snapped it, and let the key roll to the floor. The rabbit's foot he put in his pocket with the nickels.

He picked up the chair that had been knocked over and put it against the wall and sat down. He sat and thought what he should do and where he should go. He began to wish he could stay right where he was; but already he thought he could begin to smell the dead. There was always a smell; the girl had had it too, young as she was and as washed clean with salt water.

He would have to go. He stood up, held the chair by the back, and smashed it to pieces against the wall. The wood splintered and cut his hand. He sucked at the palm until there was no longer any blood taste.

If he could only stay where he was—he would be safe. He glanced out at the fog that was thickening by the moment. The road from town would be almost blocked up by now; a police car couldn't get through.

He could stay where he was and be safe . . . but he couldn't stay. He looked down at his father. The lamp wasn't bright enough to show his face. It might have been anybody lying there. Anybody who was dead.

William leaned against the wall and rubbed his head slowly with both hands. Then he picked up the quilt and folded it around his shoulders to keep the fog away from him. And he opened the door.

The fog was very heavy now, but low: a white strip that covered the grass and the ground and cut the trees in half. William hunched the quilt high over his head.

A man did what he had to do. . . .

Sometimes he did not intend to, but things came to him and he did them.

He did not mean to kill the old man. He looked back into the room. The lamp was running out of oil; the wick was burning with a sputtering blue flame. The light did not reach down to the floor. There mightn't have been anyone lying there at all.

William stared at the dark floor and tried to remember how the old man had looked. And could not.

The police would remember; Matthew Pettis would remember. William saw the smooth black face under the peaked visor of the blue cap, the short slim body, the nervous fingers, and the quick black eyes, shiny as oil in the sunlight. Pettis would remember, and he would follow him; it would be his job to follow him.

William pulled closed the door behind him and hugged the quilt tighter around his body. He would find a place to sleep tonight near the highway. In the morning he would flag down the first bus; there would be enough money for the fare. And even Pettis would have a hard time finding him in a city as big as New Orleans.

He turned around slowly. In another hour the fog would be too heavy to walk in, even. He would have to be near the road before it got that thick, so thick that he could not move. He fingered the quilt: a good heavy one. He would need it, sitting by the road waiting for the sun to come with morning. It was a big quilt too, wide and long; he would wrap himself up in it so that the fog could not reach him, the sucking fog that was heavy with the sweet smoke of cypress.

He leaned back against the wall for a minute, shivered, and was afraid, the way a boy is afraid playing a game in the dark. Then he remembered and stood up straight and walked off as quickly as he could with the quilt hunched around his shoulders: the things a man has done he must abide with.

Manhood is the subject of this story. Born into a loveless home, abandoned by his mother and merely tolerated by his father, William lives in the isolated coastal marsh world of his fisherman father for whom human communication is unnecessary. Only his basic physical needs are met. When "the upper row of his front teeth were missing," his father leads him to his mother's door, points down at him, and leaves him. No words are spoken. He lives there until he is fourteen when he is sent to a reform school for stealing tires. On his release three years later, he is tall, broad, and muscled; and "after studying him" his mother announces "You a man grown." This statement and variants of it become a refrain, repeated twenty-two times in the course of sixteen pages, always in the context of decision making. The story pivots on the meaning of becoming a man.

Emphasis on William's manhood is ironical: it implies a rite of passage (not necessarily formal), a transition from one state to another, an accomplishment or achievement, the gaining of insight, or at the least some emotional development. But for William, manhood is purely a physical attainment. There is no indication that reform school affects him. He is incarcerated for breaking the law, and he continues to break it after his release. (He had planned to escape, but his childhood enthusiasm over the wonders of the circus causes him to forget his plans).

The young man spends his entire life adrift in a sea of silence and apathy, disconnected from human emotions—love, compassion, understanding. He therefore lacks the capacity to feel. No value system operates in his life, only the echo of "a man got a right to what he can get." When he returns to his father's lean-to and discovers a fishing boat containing a dead girl's body, he attempts to assert his manhood in a struggle with his father over possession of the boat. Forced to back down and then taunted about his lack of manhood, he merely replies "A man don't have to do every single thing." When he later returns to the old man's shack and kills him, manhood again is foremost in his mind: "a man did what he did and didn't study about it afterwards." By the end of the story, it is clear that he uses his physical "manhood" to fend for himself and the term "man" to justify his actions after the fact.

The economy of style with which his life is sketched and the detachment in tone emphasize his emptiness and isolation.   The remote setting is also functional in conveying his aloneness; in the end the fog which envelops him is analagous to the metaphorical cocoon that existentialists use in depicting man's disconnection.

Ernest Gaines

(1933-)

Ernest Gaines was born in Oscar, Louisiana, on February 15, 1933, and as a boy worked in sugarcane fields there. In 1948 he moved to Vallejo, California, to live with his mother and stepfather. Gaines's extensive reading about the rural South and Negroes convinced him that neither was portrayed correctly and motivated him to write a novel at the age of sixteen. The novel was a failure, but after extensive study and experimentation he reworked it and published it fifteen years later as *Catherine Carmier*. Gaines's fiction is drawn from his boyhood home in Louisiana, and although he admits being influenced by both Faulkner and Hemingway, his style is his own, deriving from his subject matter. His sympathy with the problems of the Negro does not affect his artistic commitment; always maintaining distance he presents racial struggles not in doctrinal but in universal terms. His most successful novel *The Autobiography of Miss Jane Pittman* was televised by CBS in January of 1974. The story below first appeared in *Sewanee Review* in 1963 and is included in *Bloodline*, 1968.

Just Like a Tree*

Ernest Gaines

I shall not;
   I shall not be moved.
I shall not;
   I shall not be moved.
Just like a tree that's
planted side the water.
   Oh, I shall not be removed.

I made my home in glory;
   I shall not be moved.
Made my home in glory;
   I shall not be moved.
Just like a tree that's
planted side the water.
   Oh, I shall not be removed.

(from an old Negro spiritual)

CHUCKKIE

PA HIT HIM on the back and he jeck in the chains like he pulling, but ever'body in the wagon know he ain't, and Pa hit him on the back again. He jeck again like he pulling, but even Big Red knew he ain't doing a thing.

"That's why I'm go'n get a horse," Pa say. "He'll kill that other mule. Get up there, Mr. Bascom."

"Oh, let him alone," Grandmon say. "How would you like it if you was pulling a wagon in all that mud?"

Pa don't answer Grandmon; he just hit Mr. Bascom on the back again.

"That's right, kill him," Grandmon say. "See where you get mo' money to buy another one."

"Get up there, Mr. Bascom," Pa say.

"You hear me talking to you, Emile?" Grandmon say. "You want me to hit you with something?"

"Ma, he ain't pulling," Pa say.

"Leave him alone," Grandmon say.

Pa shake the lines little bit, but Mr. Bascom don't even feel it, and you can see he letting Big Red do all the pulling again. Pa say something kind o' low to hisself, and I can't make out what it is.

I low' my head little bit, 'cause that wind and fine rain was hitting me in the face, and I can feel Mama pressing close to me to keep me warm. She sitting on one side o' me and Pa sitting on the other side o' me, and Grandmon in the back o' me in her setting chair. Pa didn't want to bring the setting chair, telling Grandmon there was two boards in that wagon already and she could sit on one of 'em all by herself if she wanted to, but Grandmon say she was taking her setting chair with her if Pa liked it or not. She say she didn't ride in no wagon on nobody board, and if Pa liked it or not that setting chair was going.

"Let her take her setting chair," Mama say. "What's wrong with taking her setting chair."

"Ehhh, Lord," Pa say, and picked up the setting chair and took it out to the wagon. "I guess I'll have to bring it back in the house, too, when we come back from there."

Grandmon went and clambed in the wagon and moved her setting chair back little bit and sat down and folded her arms, waiting for us to get in, too. I got in and knelt down side her, but Mama told me to come up there and sit on the board side her and Pa so I could stay warm. Soon 's I sat down, Pa hit Mr. Bascom on the back, saying what a trifling thing Mr. Bascom was, and soon 's he got some mo' money he was getting rid o' him and getting him a horse.

I raise my head to look see how far we is.

"That's it, yonder," I say.

"Stop pointing," Mama say, "and keep your hand in your pocket."

"Where?" Grandmon say, back there in her setting chair.

"Cross the ditch, yonder," I say.

"Can't see a thing for this rain," Grandmon say.

"Can't hardly see it," I say. "But you can see the light little bit. That chinaball tree standing in the way."

"Poor soul," Grandmon say. "Poor soul."

I know Grandmon was go'n say poor soul, poor soul, 'cause she had been saying poor soul, poor soul ever since she heard Aunt Fe was go'n leave from back there.

EMILE

Darn cane crop to finish getting in and only a mule and a half to do it. If I had my way I'd take that shotgun and a load o' buckshots and—but what's the use.

"Get up, Mr. Bascom—please," I say to that little dried-up, long-eared, tobacco-color thing. "Please, come up. Do your share for God sake—if you don't mind. I know it's hard pulling in all that mud, but if you don't do your share, then Big Red'll have to do his and yours, too. Please—"

"Oh, Emile, shut up," Leola say.

"I can't hit him," I say, "or Mama back there'll hit me. So I'll talk to him. Please, Mr. Bascom, if you don't mind it. For my sake. No, not for mine; for God sake. No, not even for His'n; for Big Red sake. A fellow mule just like yourself is. Please, come up."

"Now, you hear that boy blaspheming God in front o' me there," Mama say. "Ehhh, Lord. Keep it up. All this bad weather there like this whole world coming apart—a clap o' thunder come there and knock the fool out you. Just keep it up."

Maybe she right, and I stop. I look at Mr. Bascom there doing nothing, and I just drove up. That mule know long 's Ma's alive he go'n do just what he want to do. He know when Pa was dying he told Ma to look at him, and he know no matter what he do, no matter what he don't do, Ma ain't go'n never let me do him anything. Sometimes I even feel Ma care mo' for Mr. Bascom 'an she care for me her own son.

We come up to the gate and I pull back on the lines.

"Whoa up, Big Red," I say. "You don't have to stop, Mr. Bascom. You never started."

I can feel Ma looking at me back there in that setting chair, but she don't say nothing.

"Here," I say to Chuckkie.

He take the lines and I jump down on the ground to open the old beatup gate. I see Etienne's horse in the yard, and I see Chris new red tractor side the house, shining in the rain. When Ma die, I say to myself, Mr. Bascom you going. Ever'body getting tractors and horses and I'm still stuck with you. You going, brother.

"Can you make it through?" I ask Chuckkie. "That gate ain't too wide."

"I can do it," he say.

"Be sure to make Mr. Bascom pull," I say.

"Emile, you better get back up here and drive 'em through," Leola say. "Chuckkie might break up that wagon."

"No, let him stay down there and give orders," Mama say, back there in that setting chair.

"He can do it," I say. "Come on, Chuckkie Boy."

"Come up, here, mule," Chuckkie say.

And soon 's he say that, Big Red make a lunge for the yard, and Mr. Bascom don't even move, and 'fore I can bat my eyes I hear "pow-wow; sagg-sagg; pow-wow." But above all the other noise, Leola up there screaming her head off. And Mama—not a word; just sitting there looking at me with her arms still folded.

"Pull Big Red," I say. "Pull Big Red, Chuckkie."

Poor little Chuckkie up there pulling so hard till one of his little arms straight out in back; and Big Red throwing his shoulders and ever'thing else in it, and Mr. Bascom just walking there just 's loose and free like he's suppose to be there just for his good looks. I move out the way just in time to let the wagon go by me, pulling half o' the fence in the yard behind it. I glance up again, and there's Leola still hollering and trying to jump out, but Mama not saying a word-just sitting there in that setting chair with her arms still folded.

"Whoa," I hear little Chuckkie saying. "Whoa up, now."

Somebody open the door and a bunch of people come out on the gallery.

"What the world—?" Etienne say. "Thought the whole place was coming to pieces there."

"Chuckkie had a little trouble coming in the yard," I say.

"Goodness," Etienne say. "Anybody hurt?"

Mama just sit there 'bout ten seconds, then she say something to herself and start clambing out the wagon.

"Let me help you there, Aunt Lou," Etienne say, coming down the steps.

"I can make it," Mama say. When she get on the ground she look at Chuckkie. "Hand me my chair there, boy."

Poor little Chuckkie up there with the lines in one hand, get the chair and hold it to the side, and Etienne catch it just 'fore it fall. Mama start looking at me again, and it look like for at least a hour she stand there looking at nobody but me. Then she say, "Ehhh, Lord," like that again, and go inside with Leola and the rest o' the people.

I look back at half o' the fence laying there in the yard, and I jump back on the wagon and guide the mules to the side o' the house. After unhitching 'em and tying 'em to the wheels, I look at Chris pretty red tractor again, and me and Chuckkie go inside. I make sure he kick all the mud off his shoes 'fore he go in the house.

LEOLA

Sitting over there by that firehalf, trying to look joyful when ever'body there know she ain't. But she trying, you know; smiling and bowing when people say something to her. How can she be joyful, I ask myself; how can she be? Poor thing, she been here all her life—or the most of it, let's say. 'Fore they moved in this house, they lived in one back in the woods 'bout a mile from here. But for the past twenty-five or thirty years, she been right in this one house. I know ever since I been big enough to know people I been seeing her right here.

Aunt Fe, Aunt Fe, Aunt Fe, Aunt Fe; the name's been 'mongst us just like us own family name. Just like the name o' God. Like the name of town—the city. Aunt Fe, Aunt Fe, Aunt Fe, Aunt Fe.

Poor old thing; how many times I done come here and washed her clothes for her when she couldn't do it herself. How many times I done hoed in that garden, ironed her clothes, wrung a chicken neck for her. You count the days in the year and you'll be pretty close. And I didn't mind it a bit. No, I didn't mind it a bit. She there trying to pay me. Proud—Lord, talking 'bout pride. "Here." "No, Aunt Fe; no." "Here; here." "No, Aunt Fe. No. No. What would Mama think if she knowed I took money from you? Aunt Fe, Mama would never forgive me. No. I love doing these things for you. I just wish I could do more." "You so sweet," she would say.

And there, trying to make 'tend she don't mind leaving. Ehhh, Lord.

I hear a bunch o' rattling 'round in the kitchen and I go back there. I see Louise stirring this big pot o' eggnog.

"Louise," I say.

"Leola," she say.

We look at each other and she stir the eggnog again. She know what I'm go'n say next, and she can't even look in my face.

"Louise, I wish there was some other way."

"There's no other way," she say.

"Louise, moving her from here 's like moving a tree you been used to in your front yard all your life."

"What else can I do?"

"Oh, Louise, Louise."

"Nothing else, but that."

"Louise, what people go'n do without her here?"

She stir the eggnog and don't answer.

"Louise, us'll take her in with us."

"You all no kin to Auntie. She go with me."

"And us'll never see her again."

She stir the eggnog. Her husband come back in the kitchen and kiss her on the back o' the neck and then look at me and grin. Right from the start I can see I ain't go'n like that nigger.

"Almost ready, Honey?" he say.

"Almost."

He go to the safe and get one o' them bottles of whiskey he got in there and come back to the stove.

"No," Louise say. "Everybody don't like whiskey in it. Add the whiskey after you've poured it up."

"Okay, Hon."

He kiss her on the back o' the neck again. Still don't like the nigger. Something 'bout him ain't right.

"You one o' the family?" he say.

"Same as one o' the family," I say. "And you?"

He don't like the way I say it, and I don't care if he like it or not. He look at me there a second, and then he kiss her on the ear.

"Un-unnn," she say, stirring the pot.

"I love your ear, Baby," he say.

"Go in the front room and talk with the people," she say.

He kiss her on the other ear. A nigger do all that front o' public got something to hide. He leave the kitchen. I look at Louise.

"Ain't nothing else I can do," she say.

"You sure? You positive?"

"I'm sure. I'm positive," she say.

The front door open and Emile and Chuckkie come in. A minute later Washington and Adrieu come in, too. Adrieu come back in the kitchen there, and I can see she been crying. Aunt Fe is her Godmother, you know.

"How you feel, Adrieu?"

"That weather out there," she say.

"Y'all walked?"

"Yes."

"Us here in the wagon. Y'all can go back with us."

"Y'all the one tore the fence down?" she ask.

"Yes, I guess so. That brother-in-law o' yours in there letting Chuckkie drive that wagon."

"Well, I don't guess it'll matter too much. Nobody go'n be here, anyhow."

And she start crying again. I take her in my arms and pat her on the shoulder, and I look at Louise stirring the eggnog.

"What I'm go'n do and my nan-nane gone? I love her so much."

"Ever'body love her."

"Since my mama died, she been like my mama."

"Shh," I say. "Don't let her hear you. Make her grieve. You don't want her to grieve, now, do you?"

She sniffs there 'gainst my dress few times.

"Oh, Lord," she say. "Lord, have mercy."

"Shhh," I say. "Shh. That's what life's 'bout."

"That ain't what life's 'bout," she say. "It ain't fair. This been her home all her life. These the people she know. She don't know them people she going to. It ain't fair."

"Shhh, Adrieu," I say. "Now, you saying things that ain't your business."

She cry there some mo'.

"Oh, Lord, Lord," she say.

Louise turn from the stove.

"'Bout ready now," she say, going to the middle door. "James, tell everybody to come back and get some."

JAMES

Let me go on back there and show these country niggers how to have a good time. All they know is talk, talk, talk. Talk so much they make me buggy 'round here. Damn this weather—wind, rain. Must be a million cracks in this old house.

I go to that beat-up safe in that corner and get that fifth of Mr. Harper (in the South now; got to say Mister), give the seal one swipe, the stopper one jerk, and head back to that old wood stove. (Man, like, these cats are primitive—goodness. You know what I mean? I mean like wood stoves. Don't mention TV, man, these cats here never heard of that.) I start to dump Mr. Harper in the pot and Baby catches my hand again and say not all of them like it. You ever heard of anything like that? I mean a stud's going to drink eggnog, and he's not going to put whiskey in it. I mean he's going to drink it straight. I mean, you ever heard anything like that? Well, I wasn't pressing none of them on Mr. Harper. I mean me and Mr. Harper get along too well together for me to go around there pressing. I hold my cup there and let Baby put a few drops of this egg stuff in it, then I jerk my cup back and let Mr. Harper run. Couple of these cats come over (some of them aren't too lame) and set their cups, and I let Mr. Harper run again. Then this cat says he got 'nough. I let Mr. Harper run for this other stud, and pretty soon he says, "Hold it. Good." Country cat, you know. "Hold it. Good." Real country cat. So I raise the cup to see what Mr. Harper's doing. He's just right. I raise the cup again. Just right. Mr. Harper; just right.

I go to the door with Mr. Harper under my arm and the cup in my hand and I look into the front room where they all are. I mean there's about ninety-nine of them in there. Old ones, young ones, little ones, big ones, yellow ones, black ones, brown ones—you name them brother, and they were there. And what for? Brother, I'll tell you what for. Just because me and Baby was taking this old chick out of these sticks. You ever seen anything like it before? There they are looking sad just because me and Baby was taking this one old chick out of these sticks. Well, I'll tell you where I'd be at this moment if I was one of them. With that weather out there like it is, I'd be under about five blankets with some little warm belly pressing against mine. Brother, you can bet your hat I wouldn't be here. Man, listen to that thing out there. You can hear that rain beating on that old house like grains of rice; and that wind coming through them cracks like it does in those Charlie Chaplin movies. Man, like you know—like whooo-ee; whooo-ee. Man, you talking about some weird cats.

I can feel Mr. Harper starting to massage my wig and I bat my eyes twice and look at the old girl over there. She's still sitting in that funny-looking little old rocking-chair, and not saying a word to anybody. Just sitting there looking in the fireplace at them two pieces of wood that isn't giving out enough heat to warm a baby, let alone ninety-nine grown people. I mean, you know, like that sleet's falling out there like all get-up-and-go, and them two pieces of wood are lying there just as dead as the rest of these way-out cats.

One of the old cats—I don't know which one he is—Mose, Sam, or something like that—leans over and pokes in the fire a minute, then a little blaze shoots up, and he raises up, too, looking as satisfied as if he'd just sent a rocket into orbit. I mean these cats are like that. They do these little bitty things, and they feel like they've really done something. Well, back in these sticks, I guess there just isn't nothing big to do.

I feel Mr. Harper touching my skull now—and I notice this little chick passing by me with these two cups of eggnog. She goes over to the fireplace and gives one to each of these old chicks. The one sitting in that setting chair she brought with her from God knows where, and the other cup to the old chick that me and Baby are going to haul from here sometime tomorrow morning. Wait, man, I mean like, you ever heard of anybody going to somebody else house with a chair? I mean wouldn't you call that an insult at the basest point? I mean, now, like tell me what you think of that? I mean, here I am at my pad, and here you come bringing your own stool. I mean, now, like man, you know. I mean that's an insult at the basest point. I mean, you know . . . you know, like way out . . .

Mr. Harper, what you doing, boy?—I mean Sir. (Got to watch myself, I'm in the South. Got to keep watching myself.)

This stud touches me on the shoulder and raise his cup and say, "How 'bout a taste?" I know what the stud's talking about, so I let Mr. Harper run for him. But soon 's I let a drop get in, the stud say, "'Nough." I mean I let about two drops get in, and the stud's got enough. Man, I mean, like you know. I mean these studs are way out. I mean like way back there. This stud takes a swig of his eggnog and say, "Ahhh." I mean this real down home way of saying "Ahhhh." I mean, man, like these studs—I notice this little chick passing by me again, and this time she's crying. I mean weeping, you know. And just because this old ninety-nine-year-old chick's packing up and leaving. I mean, you ever heard of anything like that? I mean, here she is as pretty as the day is long and crying because me and Baby are hauling this old chick away. Well, I'd like to make her cry. And I can assure you, brother, it wouldn't be from leaving her. I turn and look at Baby over there by the stove, pouring eggnog in all these cups. I mean, there're about twenty of these cats lined up there. And I bet you not half of them will take Mr. Harper along. Some way-out cats, man. Some way-out cats. I go up to Baby and kiss her on the back of her neck and give her a little pat where she likes for me to pat her when we're in the bed. She say "Uh-uh," but I know she likes it anyhow.

BEN O

I back under the bed and touch the slop jar, and I pull back my leg and back somewhere else, and then I get me a good sight on it. I spin my aggie couple times and sight again and then I shoot. I hit it right squarely in the center and it go flying over the firehalf. I crawl over there to get it and I see 'em all over there drinking they eggnog and they didn't even offer me and Chuckkie none. I find my marble on the bricks, and I go back and tell Chuckkie they over there drinking eggnog.

"You want some?" I say.

"I want shoot marble," Chuckkie say. "Yo' shot."

"I want some eggnog," I say.

"Shoot up, Ben O," he say.

"I'm getting cold staying in one place so long. You feel that draft?"

"Coming from the crack under that bed," I say.

"Where?" Chuckkie say, looking for the crack.

"Over by that bed post over there," I say.

"This sure 's a beat-up old house," Chuckkie say.

"I want me some eggnog," I say.

"Well, you ain't getting none," Grandmon say, from the firehalf. "It ain't good for you."

"I can drink eggnog," I say. "How come it ain't good for me? It ain't nothing but eggs and milk. I eat chicken, don't I? I eat beef, don't I?"

Grandmon don't say nothing.

"I want me some eggnog," I say.

Grandmon still don't say no more. Nobody else don't say nothing, neither.

"I want me some eggnog," I say.

"You go'n get a eggnog," Grandmon say. "Just keep that noise up."

"I want me some eggnog," I say; "and I 'tend to get me some eggnog tonight."

Next thing I know, Grandmon done picked up a chip out o' that corner and done sailed it back there where me and Chuckkie is. I duck just in time, and the chip catch old Chuckkie side the head.

"Hey, who that hitting me?" Chuckkie say.

"Move, and you won't get hit," Grandmon say.

I laugh at old Chuckkie over there holding his head, and next thing I know here's Chuckkie done haul back there and hit me in my side. I jump up from there and give him two just to show him how it feel, and he jump up and hit me again. Then we grab each other and start tussling on the floor.

"You, Ben O," I hear Grandmon saying. "You, Ben O, cut that out. Y'all cut that out."

But we don't stop, 'cause neither one o' us want be first. Then I feel somebody pulling us apart.

"What I ought to do is whip both o' you," Mrs. Leola say. "Is that what y'all want?"

"No'm," I say.

"Then shake hand."

Me and Chuckkie shake hand.

"Kiss," Mrs. Leola say.

"No'm," I say. "I ain't kissing no boy."

"Kiss him, Chuckkie," she say.

Old Chuckkie kiss me on the jaw.

"Now, kiss him, Ben O. "

"I ain't kissing no Chuckkie," I say. "No'm. Uh-uh."

And the next thing I know, Mama done tipped up back o' me and done whop me on the leg with Daddy belt.

"Now, kiss him," she say.

Chuckkie turn his jaw to me and I kiss him. I almost want wipe my mouth. Kissing a boy.

"Now, come back here and get you some eggnog," Mama say.

"That's right, spoil 'em," Grandmon say. "Next thing you know they be drinking from bottles."

"Little eggnog won't hurt 'em, Mama," Mama say. "That's right," Grandmon say. "Never listen. It's you go'n suffer for it. I be dead and gone, me."

AUNT CLO

Be just like wrapping a chain round a tree and jecking and jecking, and then shifting the chain little bit and jecking and jecking some in that direction, and then shifting it some mo' and jecking and jecking in that direction. Jecking and jecking till you get it loose, and then pulling with all your might. Still it might not be loose enough and you have to back the tractor up some and fix the chain round the tree again and start jecking all over. Jeck, jeck, jeck. Then you hear the roots crying, and then you keep on jecking, and then it give, and you jeck some mo', and then it falls. And not till then that you see what you done done. Not till then you see the big hole in the ground and piece of the taproot still way down in it—a piece you won't never get out no matter if you dig till doomsday. Yeah, you got the tree—least got it down on the ground, but did you get the taproot? No. No, sir, you didn't get the taproot. You stand there and look down in this hole at it and you grab yo' axe and jump down in it and start chopping at the taproot, but do you get the taproot? No. You don't get the taproot, sir. You never get the taproot. But, sir, I tell you what you do get. You get a big hole in the ground, sir; and you get another big hole in the air where the lovely branches been all these years. Yes, sir, that's what you get. The holes, sir, the holes. Two holes, sir, you can't never fill no matter how you try.

So you wrap yo' chain round yo' tree again, sir, and you start dragging it. But the dragging ain't so easy, sir, 'cause she's a heavy old tree—been there a long time, you know—heavy. And you make yo' tractor strain, sir, and the elements work 'gainst you, too, sir, 'cause the elements, they on her side, too, 'cause she part o' the elements, and the elements, they part o' her. So the elements, they do they little share to discourage you—yes, sir, they does. But you will not let the elements stop you. No, sir, you show the elements that they just elements, and man is stronger than elements, and you jeck and jeck on the chain, and soon she start to moving with you, sir, but if you looked over yo' shoulder one second you see her leaving a trail—a trail, sir, that can be seen from miles and miles away. You see her trying to hook her little fine branches in different little cracks, in between pickets, round hills o' grass, round anything they might brush 'gainst. But you is a determined man, sir, and you jeck and you jeck, and she keep on grabbing and trying to hold, but you stronger, sir—course you the strongest—and you finally get her out on the pave road. But what you don't notice, sir, is just 'fore she get on the pave road she leave couple her little branches to remind the people that it ain't her that want leave, but you, sir, that think she ought to. So you just drag her and drag her, sir, and the folks that live in the house side the pave road, they come out on they gallery and look at her go by, and then they go back in they house and sit by the fire and forget her. So you just go on, sir, and you just go and you go, and for how many days? I don't know. I don't have the least idea. The North to me, sir, is like the elements. It mystify me. But never mind, you finally get there, and then you try to find a place to set her. You look in this corner and you look in that corner, but no corner is good. She kinda stand in the way no matter where you set her. So finally, sir, you say, I just stand her up here a little while and see, and if it don't work out, if she keep getting in the way, I guess we'll just have to take her to the dump.

CHRIS

Just like him, though, standing up there telling them lies when ever'body else feeling sad. I don't know what you do 'thout people like him. And, yet, you see him there, he sad just like the rest. But he just got to be funny. Crying in the inside, but still got to be funny.

He didn't steal it though. Didn't steal it a bit. His grandpa was just like him. Mat? Mat Jefferson? Just like that. Mat could make you die laughing. 'Member once at a wake. Pa Bully wake. Pa Bully laying up in the coffin dead as a door nail. Ever'body sad and drooping 'round the place. Mat look at that and start his lying. Soon half o' the place laughing. Funniest wake I ever went to, and yet—

Just like now. Look at 'em. Look at 'em laughing. Ten minutes ago you would 'a' thought you was at a funeral. But look at 'em now. Look at her there in that little old chair. How long she had it? Fifty years—a hundred? It ain't a chair no mo'. It's little bit o' her. Just like her arm, just like her leg.

You know I couldn't believe it. I couldn't. Emile passed the house there the other day, right after the bombing, and I was in my yard digging a water drain to let the water out in the road. Emile, he stopped the wagon there 'fore the door. Little Chuckkie, he in there with him with that little rain cap buckled up over his head. I go out to the gate and I say, "Emile, it's the truth?"

"The truth," he say. And just like that he say it. "The truth."

I look at him there, and he looking up the road to keep from looking at me. You know they been pretty close to Aunt Fe ever since they been children. His own mama and Aunt Fe, they been like sisters there together.

Me and him, we talk there little while 'bout the cane cutting, then he say he got to get on to the back. He shake them lines and drive on.

Inside me, my heart feel like it done swole up ten times the size it ought to be. Water come in my eyes, and I got to 'mit I cried right there. Yes, sir, I cried right there by my gate.

Louise come in the room and whisper something to Leola, and they go back in the kitchen. I can hear 'em moving things 'round back there, still getting things together they go'n be taking. If offer me anything, I'd like that big iron pot out there in the yard. Good for boiling water when you killing hog, you know.

You can feel the sadness in the room again. Louise brought it in when she come in and whispered to Leola. Only she didn't take it out when her and Leola left. Ever' pan they move, ever' pot they unhook keep telling you she leaving, she leaving.

Etienne turn over one o' them logs to make the fire pick up some, and I see the boy, Lionel, spreading out his hand over the fire.

Watch out, I think to myself, here come another lie. People, he just getting started.

ANNE-MARIE DUVALL

"You're not going?"

"I'm not going," he says, turning over the log with the poker. "And if you were in your right mind, you wouldn't go either."

"You just don't understand."

"Oh, I understand. She cooked for your pa. She nursed you when your mama died."

"And I'm trying to pay her back with a seventy-nine cents scarf. Is that too much?"

He is silent, leaning against the mantel, looking down at the fire. The fire throws strange shadows across the big old room. Father looks down at me from against the wall. His eyes do not say go nor stay. But I know what he would do.

"Please go with me, Edward."

"You're wasting your breath."

I look at him a long time, then I get the small package from the coffee table.

"You're still going?"

"I am going."

"Don't call for me if you get bogged down anywhere back there."

I look at him and go out to the garage. The sky is black. The clouds are moving fast and low. A fine drizzle is falling, and the wind coming from the swamps blows in my face. I cannot recall a worse night in all my life.

I hurry into the car and drive out of the yard. The house stands big and black in back of me. Am I angry with Edward? No, I'm not angry with Edward. He's right. I should not go out into this kind of weather. But what he does not understand is I must. Father definitely would have gone if he was alive. Grandfather definitely would have gone also. And therefore, I must. Why? I cannot answer why. Only I must go.

As soon as I turn down that old muddy road I begin to pray. Don't let me go into that ditch, I pray. Don't let me go into that ditch. Please don't let me go into that ditch.

The lights play on the big old trees along the road. Here and there the lights hit a sagging picket fence. But I know I haven't even started yet. She lives far back into the fields. Why? God, why does she have to live so far back? Why couldn't she have lived closer to the front? But the answer to that is as hard for me as is the answer to everything else. It was ordained before I—before father—was born—that she should live back there. So why should I try to understand it now?

The car slides towards the ditch, and I stop it dead and turn the wheel, and then come back into the road again. Thanks, father. I know you're with me. Because it was you who said that I must look after her, didn't you? No, you did not say it directly, father. You said it only with a glance. As grandfather must have said it to you, and as his father must have said it to him.

But now that she's gone, father, now what? I know. I know. Aunt Lou and Aunt Clo.

The lights shine on the dead, wet grass along the road. There's an old pecan tree, looking dead and all alone. I wish I was a little nigger gal so I could pick pecans and eat them under the big old dead tree.

The car hits a rut, but bounces right out of it. I am frightened for a moment, but then I feel better. The windshield wipers are working well, slapping the water away as fast as it hits the glass. If I make the next half mile all right, the rest of the way will be as good. It's not much over a mile now.

That was too bad about that bombing—killing that woman and her two children. That poor woman; poor children. What is the answer? What will happen? What do they want? Do they know what they want? Do they really know what they want? Are they positively sure? Have they any idea? Money to buy a car, is that it? If that is all, I pity them. Oh, how I pity them.

Not much farther. Just around that bend and—there's a water hole. Now what?

I stop the car and just look out at the water a minute, then I get out to see how deep it is. The cold wind shoots through my body like needles. Lightning comes from towards the swamps and lights up the place. For a split second the night is as bright as the day. The next second it is blacker than it has ever been.

I look at the water, and I can see that it's too deep for the car. I must turn back or I must walk the rest of the way. I stand there a while wondering what to do. Is it worth it all? Can't I simply send the gift by someone tomorrow morning? Suppose she leaves without getting it, then what? What then? Father would never forgive me. Neither would grandfather or great-grandfather either. No, they wouldn't—

The lightning flashes again and I look across the field, and I can see the tree in the yard a quarter of a mile away. I have only one choice. I must walk. I get the package out of the car and stuff it in my coat and start out.

I don't make any progress at first, but then I become a little warmer and I find I like walking. The lightning flashes just in time to show up a puddle of water, and I go around it. But there's no light to show up the second puddle, and I fall flat on my face. For a moment I'm completely blind, then I get slowly to my feet and check the package. It's dry, not harmed. I wash the mud off my raincoat, wash my hands, and start out again.

The house appears in front of me, and as I come into the yard, I can hear the people laughing and talking. Sometimes I think niggers can laugh and joke even if they see somebody beaten to death. I go up on the porch and knock and an old one opens the door for me. I swear, when he sees me he look as if he's seen a ghost. His mouth drops open, his eyes bulge—I swear.

I go into the old crowded and smelly room, and every one of them looks at me the same way the first one did. All the joking and laughing has stopped. You would think I was the devil in person.

"Done, Lord," I hear her saying over by the fireplace. They move to the side and I can see her sitting in that little rocking chair I bet you she's had since the beginning of time. "Done, Master," she says. "Child, what you doing in weather like this? Y'all move; let her get to that fire. Y'all move. Move, now. Let her warm herself."

They start scattering everywhere.

"I'm not cold, Aunt Fe," I say. "I just brought you something— something small—because you're leaving us. I'm going right back."

"Done, Master," she says. Fussing over me just like she's done all her life. "Done, Master, child, you ain't got no business in a place like this. Get close to this fire. Get here. Done, Master."

I move closer, and the fire does feel warm and good.

"Done, Lord," she says.

I take out the package and pass it to her. The other niggers gather around with all kinds of smiles on their faces. Just think of it—a white lady coming through all of this for one old darky.

She starts to unwrap the package, her bony little fingers working slowly and deliberately. When she sees the scarf—the seventy-nine cents scarf—she brings it to her mouth and kisses it.

"Y'all look," she says. "Y'all look. Ain't it the prettiest little scarf y'all ever did see? Y'all look."

They move around her and look at the scarf. Some of them touch it.

"I go'n put it on right now," she says. "I go'n put it on right now."

She unfolds it and ties it round her head and looks up at everybody and smiles.

"Thank you, ma'am," she says. "Thank you, ma'am, from the bottom my heart."

"Oh, Aunt Fe," I say, kneeling down beside her. "Oh, Aunt Fe."

But I think about the other niggers there looking down at me, and I get up. But I look into that face again, and I must go back down again. And I lay my head in that bony old lap, and I cry and I cry, and I don't know how long. And I feel those old fingers, like death itself, passing over my hair and my neck. I don't know how long I kneel there crying, and when I stop, I get out of there as fast as I can.

ETIENNE

The boy come in, and soon right off they get quiet, blaming the boy. If people could look little farther then the tip of they nose— No, they blame the boy. Not that they ain't behind the boy what he doing, but they blame him for what she must do. What they don't know is that boy didn't start it, and the people that bombed the house didn't start it, neither. It started a million years ago. It started when one man envied another man for having a penny mo' 'an he had, and then the man married a woman to help him work the field so he could get much 's the other man, but when the other man saw the man had married a woman to get much 's him, he, himself, he married a woman, too, so he could still have mo'. Then they start having children—not from love; but so the children could help 'em work so they can have mo'. But even with the children one man still had a penny mo' 'an the other so the other man went and bought him a ox, and the other man did the same—to keep ahead of the other man. And soon the other man had bought him a slave to work the ox so he could get ahead of the other man. But the other man went out and bought him two slaves so he could stay ahead of the other man, and the other man went out and bought him three slaves. And soon they had a thousand slaves apiece, but they still wasn't satisfied. And one day the slaves all rose and kill the masters, but the masters had organized theyself a good police force, and the police force, they come out and kill the two thousand slaves.

So it's not this boy you see standing here 'fore you, 'cause it happened a million years ago. And this boy here 's just doing something the slaves done a million years ago. Just that this boy here ain't doing it they way. 'Stead of raising arms 'gainst the masters, he bow his head.

No, I say; don't blame the boy 'cause she must go. 'Cause when she's dead, and that won't be long after they get her up there, this boy's work will still be going on. She's not the only one that's go'n die from this boy's work. Many mo' of 'em go'n die 'fore it over with. The whole place—ever'thing. A big wind is rising, and when a big wind rise, the sea stirs, and the drop o' water you see laying on top the sea this day won't be there tomorrow, 'cause that's what wind do, and that's what life is. She ain't nothing but one o' these drops o' water laying on top the sea, and what this boy 's doing is called the wind . . . and she must be moved. No, don't blame the boy. Go out and blame the wind. No, don't blame him, 'cause tomorrow what he doing today somebody go'n say he ain't done a thing. 'Cause tomorrow will be his time to be turned over just like it's hers today. And after that be somebody else to turn over. And it go'n go like that till it ain't nobody left to turn over.

"Sure, they bombed the house," he say; "because they want us to stop. But if we stopped today, then what good would we have done? What good? They would have just died in vain."

"Maybe if they had bombed your house you wouldn't be so set on keeping this up."

"If they had killed my mother and brothers and sisters, I'd press just that much harder. I can see you all point. I can see everyone's point. But I can't agree with you. You blame me for their being bombed. You blame me for Aunt Fe's leaving. They died for you and for your children. And I love Aunt Fe as much as anybody in here. Nobody in here love her more than I do. Not one of you." He looks at her. "Don't you believe me, Aunt Fe?"

She nods—that little white scarf still tied round her head.

"How many times have I eaten in your kitchen, Aunt Fe? A thousand times? How many times have I eaten tea cakes and drank milk on your steps, Aunt Fe? A thousand times? How many times have I sat at this same firehalf with you, just the two of us, Aunt Fe? Another thousand times, two thousand times? How many times have I chopped wood for you, chopped grass for you, ran to the store for you? Five thousand? How many times we've walked to church together, Aunt Fe? Gone fishing at the river together—how many thousands of times? I've spent as much time in this house as I've spent in my own. I know every crack in the wall. I know every corner. With my eyes closed, I can go anywhere in here without bumping into anything. How many of you can do that? Not many of you." He looks at her. "Aunt Fe?"

She looks at him.

"Do you think I love you, Aunt Fe?"

She nods.

"I love you, Aunt Fe, as much as I do my own parents. I'm going to miss you as much as I'd miss my own mother if she was to leave me. I'm going to miss you, Aunt Fe, but I'm not going to stop what I've started. You told me a story once, Aunt Fe, about my great-grandpa. Remember? Remember how he died?" She looked in the fire and nod.

"Remember how they lynched him? chopped him to pieces?"

She nods.

"Just the two of us were sitting here beside the fire when you told me that. I was so angry. I felt like killing. But it was you who told me to get killing out of my head. It was you who told me I would only bring harm to myself and sadness to the others if I killed. Do you remember that, Aunt Fe?"

She nods, still looking in the fire.

"You were right. We cannot raise our arms. Because it would mean death for ourselves, as well as for the others. But we will do something else. And that's what we will do." He look at the other people. "And if they were to bomb my own mother's house tomorrow, I still wouldn't stop."

"I'm not saying stop," Louise says. "That's up to you. I'm just taking Auntie from here before hers is the next house they get to."

The boy look at Louise, and then at Aunt Fe again. He go to the chair where she sitting.

"Good bye, Aunt Fe," he say, picking up her hand. The hand done shriveled up to almost nothing. Look like nothing but loose skin's covering the bones. "I'll miss you," he say.

"Good bye, Emmanuel," she say. She look at him a long time. "God be with you."

He stand there holding the hand a while longer, then he nod his head and leave the house. The people stir around little bit, but nobody say anything.

AUNT LOU

They tell her good bye, and half of 'em leave the house crying, or want to cry, but she just sit there side the firehalf like she don't mind going at all. When Leola ask me if I'm ready to go, I tell her I'm staying right there till Fe leave that house. I tell her I ain't moving one step till she go out that door. I been knowing her for the past fifty some years now, and I ain't 'bout to leave her on her last night here.

That boy, Chuckkie, want stay with me, but I make him go. He follow his mon and pa out the house and soon I hear that wagon turning round. I hear Emile saying something to Mr. Bascom even 'fore that wagon get out the yard. I tell myself, Well, Mr. Bascom, you sure go'n catch it, and me not there to take up for you—and I get up from my chair and go to the door.

"Emile?" I call.

"Whoa," he say.

"You leave that mule 'lone, you hear me?"

"I ain't doing him nothing, Mama," he say.

"Well, you just mind you don't," I say. "I'll sure find out."

"Yes'm," he say. "Come up here, Mr. Bascom."

"Now, you hear that boy. Emile?" I say.

"I'm sorry, Mama," he say. "I didn't mean no harm."

They go out in the road, and I go back to the firehalf and sit down again. Louise stir round in the kitchen a few minutes, then she come in the front where we at. Ever'body else, they gone. That husband o' hers there got drunk long 'fore mid-night, and they had to put him to bed in the other room.

She come there and stand by the fire.

"I'm dead on my feet," she says.

"Why 'on't you go to bed," I say. "I'm go'n be here."

"You all won't need anything?"

"They got wood in that corner?"

"Plenty."

"Then we won't need a thing."

She stand there and warm, and then she say good night and go round the other side.

"Well, Fe?" I say.

"I ain't leaving tomorrow, Lou," she say.

"Course you is," I say. "Up there ain't that bad."

She shake her head. "No, I ain't going nowhere."

I look at her over in her chair, but I don't say nothing. The fire pops in the firehalf, and I look at the fire again. It's a good little fire—not too big, not too little. Just 'nough there to keep the place warm.

"You want sing, Lou?" she say, after a while. "I feel like singing my 'termination song."

"Sure," I say. She start singing in that little light voice she got there, and I join with her. We sing two choruses, and then she stop.

"My 'termination for Heaven," she say. "Now—now—"

"What the matter, Fe?" I say.

"Nothing," she say. "I want get in my bed. My gown hanging over there."

I get the gown for her and bring it back to the firehalf. She get out of her dress slowly, like she don't even have 'nough strength to do it. I help her on with her gown, and she kneel down there side the bed and say her prayers. I sit in my chair and look at the fire again.

She pray there a long time—half out loud, half to herself. I look at her there, kneeling down there, little like a little old girl. I see her making some kind o' jecking motion there, but I feel she crying 'cause this her last night here, and 'cause she got to go and leave ever'thing behind. I look at the fire.

She pray there ever so long, and then she start to get up. But she can't make it by herself. I go to help her, and when I put my hand on her shoulder, she say, "Lou; Lou."

I say, "What's the matter, Fe?"

She say, "Lou; Lou."

I feel her shaking in my hand with all her might. Shaking like a person with the chill. Then I hear her taking a long breath—long—longest I ever heard anybody take before. Then she calm down—calm, calm.

"Sleep on, Fe," I say. "When you get up there, tell 'em all I ain't far behind."

The title of this story takes its name from an old hymn and refers to Aunt Fe, a ninety-nine-year-old black woman whose relatives are planning to move her to the North in order to protect her from civil rights activism in the area. Aunt Fe insists that she is too old to be uprooted and planted elsewhere.

The story's success lies largely in the author's use of multiple points of view. Ten stream-of-consciousness narrators move the action across the last few hours in Aunt Fe's life. They skillfully represent a range of emotions, attitudes, and interests while reflecting on her life and participating in the solemn farewell family gathering that comprises the time frame of the story. They also represent a cross section of a large cohesive family: young and old; male and female, blood relatives and close friends, black and white, and finally a black outsider.

Through the minds of the various characters the sequence of events unfolds. Although the action pivots on a bombing that has killed three members of a black family, that action appears only in the background; in the foreground is the immediate concern of each. For Emile it is getting Mr. Bascomb, the privileged mule, to help Big Red pull the wagon and deliver them to the family gathering; for Chuckkie and Ben O, the youngsters, it is seeing cousins again— playing marbles and begging for a sip of eggnog; for the women young and old, it is making Aunt Fe comfortable and preparing her for the trip North.

Etienne's view is significant: he is probably speaking for the author himself when he places the bombing in a cosmic context. His concern is for "the boy" (the community activist)—since everyone is blaming him for the immediate crisis: "not that they ain't behind . . . what he is doing, but they blame him for what she must do." Etienne sees the strife as a local manifestation of a universal problem: "it started a million years ago . . . when one man envied another for having a penny mo' 'an he had" and it has continued. Man's desire to trample on his fellow man has its roots in human greed—not race.

James's view is that of an outsider and it impinges sharply upon the feelings of love, admiration, and sorrow that fill the house. An in-law from the North, he shows both scorn and amusement at the simple ways of his wife's relatives ("these country niggers"); his main concern is spiking his eggnog with "Mr. Harper." Both his superior attitude and his "hep cat" language set him apart: "Wait, man, I mean like, you ever heard of anybody going to somebody else house with a chair? I mean wouldn't you call that an insult . . . I mean, now like tell me what you think of that? I mean here I am at my pad, and here you come bringing your own stool. I mean, you know. . . you know, like way out . . . ."

The ways and simple goodness of these people are familiar to Anne-Marie Duvall, the daughter of the white plantation owner, whose thoughts and words are revealed as she stumbles along through the dark and rain on that final night, thinking how she had bonded with the old black woman when at the death of her mother, Aunt Fe had nursed her and loved her. Anne-Marie feels a sense of guilt for letting the years slip between them and is ashamed of the seventy-nine-cent scarf she is taking as a farewell gift. Rain, cold, and mud impede her journey, but memories of her father give her not only a sense of duty but also the strength to pay her final respects.

Details of the landscape and setting, casually revealed in the idiom of poor uneducated black people, build effectively to the climax and resolution—the dead grass and pecan tree, the cold winter rain, the run-down cabin, the dying fire on the hearth, and the darkness that comes at the end of the story. Aunt Fe's self-willed death prevents her "just like a tree" from being moved.

John H. Wildman

(1911-1992)

John Hazard Wildman was born in Mobile, Alabama, where he spent his early years, but lived in Louisiana over half of his life. After receiving the bachelor's, master's, and Ph. D. degrees at Brown University and teaching there for three years, he joined the English faculty at Louisiana State University in Baton Rouge where he remained until his retirement in 1980. In addition to short stories, he published scholarly articles, novels, and poetry. He died in his native city in 1992. The story printed below first appeared in *The Sewanee Review* in 1977.

A House in Arabia*

John H. Wildman

Mr. Moreau's fingers awoke with his brain. They moved quickly from the dark underside of the sheet, night, and came over to the top, and moved a short distance, and stopped on daylight bare.

The fingers rested; but his brain, his imagination, moved on, for it was restless. It was restless all the time now, but most of all when he had abruptly awakened. He had always possessed something in his head that would not stay still. When he had been young, his greatest joys and achievements had come from this. Small joys, titanic in essence, angels dancing on the head of a pin, innumerable angels, bright, adding colors to the rainbow, dancing, dancing, being angels, not cramped by space, to whose laws they were not subject. From a priest's sermon Mr. Moreau had been able to open his imagination and let this segment of suggestion shove itself in. He had not understood, understanding not applying here anyhow. He had been suffered by something grand; that was it.

His apprehension had been true, especially when he had built his small house not far from the levee, his wife dead and children and grandchildren specking the countryside in little mounds of lazy ants who got along best by doing the least, and so he was able to have taught those obnoxious insects something of value. His children had let him go from them because he had wanted to go and because they were tolerant of themselves and others. Strong young male Moreaus and Landrys and Schexnayders and Boudreaus, his grandsons, had helped in building the little house; for the family, with the great wisdom of lazy people, could be very energetic and efficient in emergencies. Mr. Moreau had settled in this house. He had put together his small garden in the back—very good turnip greens in November; he had a garden of flowers in the front. He treated flowers in a friendly way but took no nonsense from them. They eagerly responded and bore blooms the way that his female

*"A House in Arabia" by John Hazard Wildman was first published in the *Sewanee Review*, 85, No. 2 (Spring 1977). Copyright © 1977 by the University of the South. Reprinted with the permission of the editor of the *Sewanee Review*.

descendants bore children. They were good orthodox Catholic flowers.

He did almost nothing except drink very black coffee all day; watch the levee exhibit its moods, especially herald spring early, always turning green before it should and being remarkably impervious to cold spells; hoe a little in his garden; walk a goodly distance to mass on Sundays and holy days of obligation; but mainly sit in a rocking-chair and feel good. It had never occurred to him or to the civilization in which he lived that serving God consisted of getting richer to the day of his death or forgetting himself in purposeful endeavor. They also serve who only sit and rock and let their minds go this way and that, amiably. God is accessible in all places: on the head of a pin, within the sphere of influence of a chair slowly and endlessly rocking, nine months on the front porch or the back porch, three months in the winter inside the house, mainly near a window.

Across the gravel road that ended at the River Road, which stuck to the levee like the just-discarded skin of a snake, there were large sugarcane fields. He used to like to watch the progress of the cane from the time of its first-raised light-green sharp blades in November through the thrusting of spring and the thicknesses of summer, as mysterious as a decade of his rosary, and the fall cutting, sending over to him the friendly smells, to the ultimate fields of bagasse, stubble, and earth held together in a dark richness and in mellow neutral tones.

He might some time see over the levee the tops of funnels of tankers, going up or down the Mississippi, blanketing the land with sounds, hungry sounds because their insides needed oil or bellowing sounds because they were full of oil.

An Arab from the university had come to the nearest village once, East come West for science's sake. He and Mr. Moreau had struck up a friendship at the corner grocery. The Arab had visited Mr. Moreau once or twice and had drunk coffee before taking some science and the shallow side of the United States back to wherever he came from; and one Christmas he had given Mr. Moreau a handsome card, with a passage from the Koran saying good things about Christ and Mary. But the picture on the outside was what hit Mr. Moreau hard. Not actually hard. *Focusingly.* It was a reproduction of a nineteenth-century romantic watercolor of Jaffa, in bright colors, with a carefully defined idealized background of minarets, little windows in high stone houses that mixed themselves up with hills and made Mr. Moreau yearn to live for the rest of his life in a room in one of them, cozily contemplating vastness. The picture brought to a point all that was insinuated by the sugarcane: his small garden; his little house that he wrapped around himself; his rocking chair, which had learned to accommodate itself completely to his bottom; the ease of an accomplished rock one way, the counterease of a rock in the other direction; the mellow blast of the ships across the fields; comfort that was vast; peace uncloseted; littleness in which to know that which was large and suggestive; angels dancing on the head of a pin.

Mr. Moreau kept the picture on a small table by his bed so that he could see it just before he turned off that luxury, which was new to small country places, the electric light, and also watch the day, like to like, come with increasing strength upon it in the morning.

He was very happy. Like happy aging people, he did not count the years. He only knew—not really being conscious of the fact, simply suffused by it—that his physical freedom and the world in which his larger being dwelt were intimately tied together, that one could not exist without the other.

This he felt, not theorizing about it. He showed most positive realization of the fact when, as he sat on his porch, he tightened his fingers self-satisfying around the arms of his chair, breathing deeply, and laid placid eyes down upon all he saw, especially that which lay in the softened distance. For this he needed cozy personally arranged comfort, opening out onto splendid stretches of space.

One day while Mr. Moreau was rocking on his front porch and watching his heavy-blooming petunias sag under a summer sun so that they would have plenty of strength to rise up in the late-afternoon shadows, he stopped rocking his chair and slouched over its side.

He stayed that way until one of his children happened to come by an hour later. This was a rich grown-up child; oil wells had come in on his land.

He had his wife put Mr. Moreau in a hospital. Only the best for Puh-père.

Most of the family cried. Most of them wanted to take care of him at their own places. But the son and also his wife had studied much psychology and especially the more pious forms of sociology at the state university. They knew what was best. They also had firm moral chins. They could not be answered. The doctor was sensibly neutral on their side.

So Mr. Moreau had been taken first to the hospital, his dead eyes alive with fear.

Physically he got much, much better, for all the best had been done for him: geriatrics reached new peaks in his case, the nurses' smiles were irremovable, and the doctors stank of earnestness, breakthroughs, cleanliness, sex, health, know-how, cheerful obtuseness, and youth.

They let him have his Arabian Christmas card brought and put where he could see Jaffa, romanticized, on the metal dresser beyond the foot of his bed.

Mr. Moreau's recovery was miraculous. He became himself again. He could use all of his limbs and his insides. His imagination they left untouched, so even it came back.

All he needed now was a sense of happiness. That, though, remained elusive.

"It's out of the question for you ever to live alone again," his son told him. "The rest of the family just don't have what you need. You could stay with us, if you want to. But wouldn't you be happier if you were with people your own age and you could talk about the old days?"

Who wanted to talk to old people their own age? He had fallen in love with speaking silences and crickets that did not demand an answer.

"Yes," Mr. Moreau said. It was the quickest way to get rid of his son. He hoped that the coffee was better there than it was here. Here he took dark, which seemed to him unusually light and nasty. "Light is for senior citizens from the North," a nurse had told him through joyful capped teeth. Mr. Moreau wondered what goings-on took place in the North, where his imagination had never wished to go. But people have their ways; and the good God made bitterweed too.

Mr. Moreau had his plans.

So from the hospital they moved him to this place, Care-Away. Jaffa came along. The coffee was just as bad. That became minor however. He was feeling other needs, also. Good coffee was merely part of them.

This morning, the fingers of his mind crept to Jaffa. He had only the haziest notion of where Jaffa was; but he called the vast enclosing space around it Arabia. A place in Arabia. A small room in Jaffa from which to look out. A house in Arabia. His own home, really.

This clean kept-up institution, even though it was close to the ground, was alien to him as Arabia was not. The grounds were too neat, the flowers in the beds too disciplined. Only the woods on the edge of the estate brought him a little peace when he looked at them. On the other side of them Miss Larner, one of the nurses, the dominant one, said to him, was the River Road. The levee was beyond it. "I saw it once," she had said. "But what's there to see? Just a mound running along. The road isn't even paved yet. But they'll get to that pretty soon. Let's have our bath now."

"How far is it to Rocheville?" he had asked.

"Oh," she had said, "you'd turn to your left on the River Road and go for miles and miles. Want to go to the bathroom and bathe yourself?"

"Yes, ma'am," he had said.

Today his eyes rested long on Jaffa. His hand moved on the day laid on the white sheet that stretched over the hills and valleys of his body. He was used to flat land. It was flat around Jaffa in the foreground of the picture. There was a dominant hill in the background, chopped into smaller units—but really one hill. It was flat around his house, except for the levee.

That day, firming up his plan, he walked without permission to the shopping center, about three-blocks' distance from Care-Away. He was on a small allowance from his son, so that he could buy candy and insipid paperbacks from the little place in the lobby.

Consequently, when he set off, he had money in his pocket.

Mr. Moreau stopped at a china store that sold mixed goods, and he bought a knife, a sharp one with a blade that was not too long, but long enough. He wanted to eat sugarcane again. It was fall, a beautiful fall; all around him now was October, days that were clear and warm but not hot, nights that were cool but not cold. He wanted to chew on a joint of sugarcane. This was part of his plan. In his imagination sugarcane had become almost a sacrament. The thought of its growing vastly but eventually contained before his small front porch gave him large comfort. Even more the thought of peeling off its shiny hard covering and chewing the fiber and tasting, *feeling,* the flow of sweet juice onto his tongue, down his throat, was to experience the transubstantiation of the juice into all moments of his life when smallness had been the conveyor of the splendor and the ultimate. The touch of the stringy pulp and the taste of the juice were not merely facts. They were conductors to something beyond themselves; and this something was the strength of his boyhood, which he had never regretted leaving behind him. No, he had not left it behind him: he had moulded it into his manhood and into his old age. Even when his sense of smell had become dimmed, he could still smell a cool March wind coming down on him from the levee; he could feel mud, deliciously cool, ooze up between his toes in a shaded swampy place in July. He would think of faraway places then. It was unthinkable to go to them. How could he? It was enough to think of them.

And so on through his circumscribed expanding days all the way to the small house and to Jaffa, water-colored.

But not to Care-Away.

He had bought the knife and stowed it away and was nearly back to the sterile comforts of the home when the Care-Away stationwagon caught him.

"It's that drawing of Arabs," Miss Larner said. Her whole face was stone. It was a horrible spectacle to see stone. Especially stone that was put there to brighten the landscape. To beautify it, even. But he could see that she was being helpful.

When they walked into the dazzlingly clean entrance of Care-Away, she called out in panic-quenching joyousness: "Here he is. Safe and sound." The ladies at the concession gave Mr. Moreau smiles that tried to understand and worked mightily in that direction. This was truly good, and he tried back; but there was no real connection either way.

"You don't *look* tired," one of the ladies said. This was closer. It really touched. It was true.

"He needs a brief nap now," said Miss Larner. "Just a little lying down with his clothes on."

Mr. Moreau didn't feel tired at all. But this was the final touch. *With his clothes on.* No finding of the knife.

When they had got to his room, Miss Larner showed mild panic. "Why did you do this to us?" she asked. She was hurt, but she snapped back. "You have a slight cough," she said. "I'll get some syrup." Both going and coming, her rubber-soled shoes made emphatically, steadily paced sucking sounds on the floor, not at all like mud coming up through toes. She held the bottle over the bedside table and poured. Mr. Moreau reached up manfully to take the spoon from Miss Larner. His arm jerked convulsively; and syrup poured from both spoon and bottle onto the table and all over the watercolor of Jaffa.

"Never mind," said Miss Larner. "We'll have this cleaned up in a jiffy." She was soon back with another bottle and a clean spoon. This time Mr. Moreau swallowed the sticky stuff.

Miss Larner even brought back Jaffa—washed. But it was faded and limp and bent. "I'm going to bring you a cheerful picture," she said. "One that will make you happy right here and now."

What bothered Mr. Moreau was Miss Larner's evident sincerity. She was not a bad woman. She simply belonged to a world that he did not like to touch. She softened. The stone of her face turned into albino mud. Her smile flew in and landed. It was just as if she had reached up, caught, and put false teeth in again. "Would you like a little clear broth?" she asked.

"No," said Mr. Moreau. "I'll just sleep. Call me when we're supposed to eat. I'm hungry."

Miss Larner glowed in the splendor of tremendous achievement. "Now that's the spirit," she said. "I'll call when it's time."

When she had left, Mr. Moreau looked at the picture which she had brought, spit on it, tore it up, and then threw it into the wastepaper basket. He had his plan.

He stood on the edge of expectation. Things were working out just as they should. He did not feel at all bad from having walked. He felt good. He could have walked much, much farther. He was not sleepy. He was proud of his teeth. They were all there and sound: unusual for his age. He would have to cut the sugarcane very thin.

He looked down at the torn-up remains of Miss Larner's picture. It had depicted three old people with different expressions indicating joyful hysterics. A middle-aged doctor was telling them a joke. He was leaning jovially forward in his chair. You could tell he was a doctor because there was a stethoscope hanging loosely around his neck. The old people were lolling back comfortably in their chairs.

This picture had exactly indicated the non-negotiable distance between Mr. Moreau's and Miss Larner's worlds.

Four days later—for she had been off for a while—Miss Larner brought in a very cold, very wide, very deep smile. It got down to the roots of her lower teeth. "Friends again?" she asked.

"Good friends," said Mr. Moreau, who was scared of her, but also happy. Scared, though. She looked into him so. And yet, he could see, she was trying. But she could not touch him. She belonged too much to another universe. It contained neither Arabia nor his own Louisiana.

She started to take his pulse. He was always more afraid of this than of her eyes. He felt that she could *name* his pulse and everything that caused it to do what it did. She could name it even before she took it—at the moment when she first touched her fingers to his wrist. She came down upon him and told him what to be. At least tried, getting near to success. Only God had the right to do that—and He wouldn't. Not until you asked Him of your own free will, the priest had said. Mr. Moreau never asked Miss Larner. He never intended to.

"Why, you're excited," she said.

"Maybe I'm happy," questioned Mr. Moreau. This way seemed to make it less of a lie.

"You're learning to be more at home here," Miss Larner told him. Her eyes were proud of achievement and greedy for more. "You're learning to face reality. You've accepted Care-Away as your permanent home. I can see a happy future for you."

"Yes," agreed Mr. Moreau.

"*If* you'll behave."

"Yes," he agreed again.

"That's the ticket." Her hard management of his happiness was so distant from the house in Arabia as to be unascertainable. As far away as the smell of the sweet disinfectant that pervaded Care-Away from the March wind over clover on the levee.

"You look nappy," said Miss Larner.

"I'm sleepy," said Mr. Moreau.

"Then dream of bees and butterflies," said Miss Larner, blundering briefly into his life, unaware.

It was very early, just when dawn was breaking, long before even that nasty cup of coffee was brought around.

His room was midway down a corridor. The nurse who sat up on this shift had a chair which let her look down all four corridors, but sometimes she went to a sofa which was more comfortable than the chair. He had caught her there once when he had come to ask for an aspirin, something to do.

He did not trouble to shave. He simply put his clothes on. He did not even urinate, for fear of making noise. He could urinate in the woods. He took nothing except his knife and the faded, wrinkled, washed-out watercolor of Jaffa. They went into different pockets.

He stood at his door for a few minutes, afraid to look out. Then he took courage and slyly peered down the corridor. No nurse in the chair. He thought he heard snores from around the corner.

He went quickly out of his room, holding his shoes, and down the corridor in the opposite direction. He turned the little knob on the door that led to outside and slowly pulled the bolt until he had got it free. He drew it to the utmost reach of its chain and let it dangle. It scratched against the door once. He stood very still. Miss Mary Langdale, whose bedroom was near to his, was apt to wake up in the night and say "Who's there?" for no reason at all. The nurse would always come to quiet her. He was fearful of this happening now. But he had great success. She was quiet, not even giving little whistling sounds in her sleep.

He opened the door and went out quickly, shutting it quietly behind him. It would click. The crisp air accentuated this. He put his shoes on and urinated—as a concession to delicacy—behind a tree. Then he hurried along and the air hugged him all over. He was home already. Clean air, clean earth, both friendly, without rules. Air and earth, close around him, suggesting extension. He was home already; space was annihilated. He would walk through home until he came to the place where home said: "Rest and rock." That would be his house.

Turn left on the River Road when you come out of the woods.

He did not do exactly that. He crossed the pebbly road and went up on the levee and to its slanting other side and down. He was amazed at how little his heart beat, how fresh he felt when he had climbed.

The base of the riverside of the levee had a trail beside it. He turned left into it. He walked that path for long, long distances. He had to stop and rest a while. He went to sleep. When he had been a boy, he used to sleep on the levee for a while in the afternoon, and his back would itch and he would sometimes get redbugs, but he liked all of it, especially the smells and the earth-curves and grass-pokings under him.

He woke and walked some more. He felt tired, but he didn't feel dizzy.

He saw a hunter, who probably shouldn't have been there. Maybe that was why he waved cordially. Or maybe he just waved cordially. Mr. Moreau waved back.

He rested some more. There was a pecan tree growing here. That was funny. Pecans did not like ground so low. There were not any nuts on the ground, though. It was too early.

He sat down and leaned against the pecan and slept.

When he awoke, he was hungry and very tired, and the sun was getting low. From where he was sitting, it would soon slip down over the edge of the trees beyond the wide river.

Mr. Moreau decided to be bold. Boldness had worked lots of times in his life. It had built his house for him.

He walked up the levee and down the other side. This time he did pant quite a bit and feel wavery. But also happy. He went down into a ditch and up its other side to the River Road, which was still pebbly. All of this stretch, all the way to his home, would be unpaved. He would ask for a ride. That was the boldest action of all. It would succeed. He willed it. He felt that he was stronger than Miss Larner, pulse-inspectingly cunning. He had got beyond her and all of her effects. This might get her in trouble. He did not want that. She was a well-meaning nuisance. Like his rich son and daughter-in-law. Let her lead her life and let him lead his.

He stood and waited, feeling very, very tired. Something was clamped around his heart. There was a dizziness in his head. But all this fitted in. There was a deliriously happy union between him and all the parts of his home.

A car came along. He could tell, as it neared him, that it was an old car.

He began waving his arm.

There was a young fellow in the car. He stopped.

"Going up towards Rocheville?" Mr. Moreau asked.

The young guy was the rare sort that do not ask questions or call you Pops. He treated Mr. Moreau and his situation as perfectly understandable.

"Just on the other side of it," he said. "Hop in. I got time, so I came this way."

"I'm getting out at a house on the road, this way from Rocheville," Mr. Moreau said.

"That's fine with me," the young man said.

They talked about this and that, and eventually the young man said, "You look tired. You hungry?"

"Yes," Mr. Moreau answered.

So they stopped at a little grocery store and had cokes and sandwiches wrapped in waxed paper and hard cookies with pink icing on them.

"The radio says they're looking for some old guy who got out of a rest home," the grocer said, taking Mr. Moreau in very carefully.

"Well, it isn't this one," the young man said. "He's my grandfather."

"Oh, sure," the grocer answered. "Sure."

Mr. Moreau felt a lot better when they were on their way again.

The young guy let him out at his place.

"Thanks," Mr. Moreau said. The young guy seemed like a part of his home too. He felt warm toward him. He confused him a little with one of his grandsons.

"Bye, now," the young man said, and he was off.

The yard in the darkness was a tangle, but it smelled sweet. He could get at it tomorrow. Familiarness hugged him all around. He felt in his pocket for the knife. It was there. So was the crumpled picture. He could smell cut sugarcane across the other road. The whole field had probably not been cut. Anyway he could find a stalk or two in the morning, a joint to cut and then peel and then slice into small slivers.

His gate was slantingly open. He went through and managed to pull it up enough to close it and let the latch fall.

He did not have a key, and his door was locked. He had never locked it himself.

He found that his rocker and another chair had been left outside. It was cool with night when he eased himself into it. He rocked two or three rockings and then fell asleep.

The sun was in his eyes when he woke up. There was also an addition to the sun.

It was Miss Larner. Her car was out front, looking as clean and imprisoning as the wings at Care-Away.

"This is naughty of you," she was saying. She smiled. This was human of her, but not comforting.

Mr. Moreau came awake all at once.

"You can't take me," he said. "I'm at home."

"Aw, come on," Miss Larner said. "Your son will be along soon. Don't you want to see him? And have some coffee in your own comfortable room at Care-Away?"

She softened. "You'll be seeing him tonight. Now come along. We must get you back to food and bed. Think how long you might have been here if the grocer hadn't told me. You might have caught the sniffles. You don't want to catch the sniffles, do you? Come along now."

Mr. Moreau slyly put one hand on the arm of the chair. She leaned over to help him. He put his right hand in his pocket.

Miss Larner did not smell sweet. She merely smelled clean. The sun did not do anything beautiful for her uniform. She had very big breasts, but she did not seem like a woman. He let the breasts plow against him, dough attempting to make fertile a hard resisting soil.

He was too tired to rise. He *used* his tiredness until she was almost sprawling on him.

Then he pulled his right hand out of his pocket. The knife was not the kind that opens and shuts. It was rigid. It had uncomfortably scraped a little against him as he walked. He hadn't minded.

With pretended feebleness he let Miss Larner grab his right elbow; her pull was most helpful when he shoved in the knife as far as he could just under her left breast. For so strong a woman she gave an oddly light gasp and curled her hand in toward his. But this was hard for her to do. He managed to get the knife out quickly and push it in again. It was a very sharp knife. When he had bought it he had explained what he wanted it for; and the clerk had told him just the right thing. "It's good for anything *tough*," the man had said.

Miss Larner went backward. She hadn't said anything except the little gasp. Her eyes, though, were points of bewilderment set in her own brand of mud. She made a terrific thump on the floor, and the porch railing held her there, sitting upright, for a moment. Then she went sideways; and Mr. Moreau went to her. It had been a little difficult, getting up.

"Even if you have to kill," the priest had said, "self-defense is not murder."

Mr. Moreau went back to his rocker. First, he pulled out his wrinkled picture and held Jaffa fragmented, yet unified, too. He felt good, but he also felt bad—bad enough to die. This was just the right little place to think of vastness, to get the hang of it.

For a while he remained in blank elation. Then, much more willingly than Miss Larner, he died.

Set in the heart of Acadian country, this story focuses on the problems of old age and failing health. Through the consciousness of old Mr. Moreau, the reader sees the quiet desperation of old age and the inherent callousness of institutionalization. On the surface the conflict between the old man and Miss Larner, a nurse, is slight; for each treats the other with respect. This, then, is not a clash of two people but rather what each stands for. She is the system— the cold clinical institution—that must impose rules for the general welfare of old people who have lost their identity. He is the spirit of independence, of self-reliance, of individualism.

As the story opens, Mr. Moreau has settled peacefully and happily into old age, accepting its physical limitations and enjoying the expanding of imagination that sedentary life affords him. His mind has always been "restless," able to create visions of the infinite and "small joys titanic in essence." He enjoys his house, his small flower garden, and the view from his front porch—the cane fields and beyond them the Mississippi River. He enjoys thinking of the sweet juice of sugarcane; to him it represents all of the sweetness of life, even the experience of transubstantiation. Most of all, however, he enjoys imagining that he lives in a strange looking house in Arabia, pictured on a post card he once received.

The old man's life changes after a brief illness sends him to a nursing home. Relatives plus psychology and sociology and geriatrics, the author suggests ironically, have all the answers for the welfare of old people—a rigid routine; a sterile, clinical atmosphere; three meals a day; and other old people. Mr. Moreau is somewhat successful in using his imagination to block out his surroundings and Nurse Larner's constant patronizing, but she is a strong-willed person intent on doing her duty. As he dreams of once again eating sugarcane, he can savor its sweetness in his mouth and feel its miraculous powers as it becomes the sacramental wine. The picture post card becomes a larger part of his existence: he gazes at the romantic house so far away, the hill in the background, the many rooms—"his own home really." After Nurse Larner inadvertently blurs his picture and then throws it away, the house dream is gone. He then conceives and executes a plan to realize the sugarcane dream. The plan involves acquiring a knife (for cutting the cane) before slipping out of the nursing home; the execution of it involves many hours of walking and hiding.

Final confrontation between the two forces is inevitable; the strength of wills suggest no compromise. When Miss Larner attempts to take him back to the nursing home, Mr. Moreau plunges the knife into her side, doing so without malice. He is simply defending himself against a system that has robbed him of his humanity. He then dies peacefully in his own rocking chair on his own porch, totally devoid of guilt.

Looking at the story in the context of Louisiana literary tradition points up change in treatment of both minority groups and the landscape. There is no suggestion that Mr. Moreau's independent spirit is an ethnic trait; he is seen, not as a Cajun but as a person—a lonely old man caught in the upheaval of family traditions. Not only are cultural peculiarities absent, the exotic landscape often used for atmosphere is missing. Both the sugarcane, which is integral to the plot, and the oil freighters on the river function as symbols: the sugarcane is associated with the old way of life—the agrarian way—as well with life itself; the oil tankers suggest an industrial economy and are linked with the loss of tradition.

John William Corrington

(1932- 1988)

Born in Tennessee and reared in Shreveport, Louisiana, John William Corrington was graduated from Centenary College there in 1956. His graduate degrees include an M. A. from Rice (1960), a Ph. D. from the University of Sussex (1964), and a J. D. from Tulane Law School (1976). After teaching at Louisiana State University and Loyola University of the South, he entered law practice in New Orleans. His first volume of poetry, *Where We Are* (1962), won the Charioteer Poetry Prize; and his short stories have won several prizes, including the O. Henry Memorial Award in 1976. In addition he has published three novels. Corrington's view is historical and when his works are set in the present, they generally use the past as a means of interpreting and measuring the present. The story printed below first appeared in *Southern Review* in 1978 and was included in *The Actes and Monuments* published in 1980.

Every Act Whatever of Man*

John William Corrington

I

IT WAS HIS HABIT to come to the courthouse early when he had business there. He would nod to the janitor as the large ancient doors opened, and then, the rising sun behind him, he would walk up and down the silent shadowed corridor, a dog run with offices, chambers, and courtrooms off to either side.

When he had a trial, he would do the last-minute acts of mental construction at this time, search out the questions to be asked that he had not discovered yet. On those days, he would pace rapidly through the shadows, hardly noticing the dark obscure portraits of long-dead judges that adorned the walls along the corridor, or even noticing later the growing number of lawyers and functionaries as they came in to begin their day. Not until his opponent, or the clerk of the court where he was to try, came up to him would he cease his pacing and look up, distracted, to see that the sun was high and it was time to work.

Other times, when there was no trial, he would go to five o'clock mass in the tiny church of the Holy Redeemer, and then, Christ upon him, would pace the courthouse corridor, rosary in hand, his thoughts not religious in the common sense, but pieced together out of almost seventy-five years of life, fifty at the law. His study was Christendom, that long wave of meaning which had reached from Jerusalem to Byzantium, from Aachen to St. Stephanie, Louisiana. He would remember his father, a sorrowful mystery, blurred by forty years gone. He would remember the town when vegetable carts and a butcher shop had done his family and friends for a supermarket. There had been a time when young people stayed in St. Stephanie, or, leaving, spent a year or two or three in New Orleans, then came back to marry and begin a family, telling no one anything of that Carthage to the East where, in the Quarter, souls were lost, and sin lapped at the steps of St. Louis

*"Every Act Whatever of Man" from *The Actes and Monuments* by John William Corrington. Copyright © by the University of Illinois Press 1978. Reprinted by arrangement with the author and publisher.

Cathedral, like water from the Mississippi, against levees which often did not hold.

He would consider what it meant to serve the law, to bring a poor man's suit, and walk away afterward, some small piece of justice done. He would think of what he had seen on the late news: terror, assassination, acts of vengeance, things so foul that their like had never been seen in this courthouse, and, God willing, never would be.

It was as if he were forging a new rosary, one other than that handed to St. Dominic. One no less mysterious or laden with grace, but one in which the great hierophantic events in the life of the Savior were replaced with the happenings of the day. He would consider the little girl raped, killed, her body dismembered and thrown into the river there at New Orleans. And as he considered, he would recite a decade of the rosary for the repose of that small soul, but more for her family and loved ones who even then must be suffering an agony which the child in her innocence was far beyond.

Or he would reflect on the priests who deserted their calls—a decade to bring them faith and return of grace again. Or he would remember his very special intention: those children destroyed by abortion, whose half-formed bodies and slumbering souls had been, by the millions, given over to a holocaust as violent, vicious—and legal—as that of the Nazis against God's Chosen Ones.

Sometimes a groan would escape him as he paced.

—Sir, the janitor might say. —Mr. Journé, is something wrong?

He would come to himself then, smile, shake his head, slip his rosary into his pocket, still keeping hold of the bead he was telling, and go on pacing as the sun rose on another day in the courts.

That morning, as he paced, a young clerk came up to him quietly.

Mr. Journé, Judge Soniat would like to see you. . . .

He looked up. Michael Soniat here at this hour? He glanced at his watch. It was barely seven-thirty, two and a half hours before court. He walked behind the young clerk whose name he did not know—there were so many nowadays, they came and went so quickly. It was just before he reached the oaken door of the judge's chamber that he lost count of his beads.

II

Miss Lefebre put down her copy of *Screen Stars* with the picture of Jack Nicholson on the cover. The old man had moved—or was it that the rhythm of his breathing had changed perceptibly? Or was it simply that they had the monitor set absurdly high again. Anyhow, that shrill high keening hurt her head, and she reached over and pushed the button that silenced it. Then she looked at the old man.

He was large. Not fat, but wide and fleshy. Even lying there, he gave the illusion of strength, each of his hands as large as both of hers put together. His face was flushed with that appearance of bogus health you come to recognize, even expect, in the terminally ill. His eyes were open. Not staring, as is so often the case with patients in coma, simply looking out at the far wall where some pious old lady had insisted they hang a crucifix. It was as if he were giving minute and indefatigable scrutiny to that image of wood and plaster, seeking its meaning, trying to penetrate its accidents, that he might discover the essence within or beyond, wherever essences reside.

Miss Lefebre smoothed the bedclothes out of habit, though the old man, paralyzed and motionless, had not disturbed them. There was, beyond the facade of professionalism which LSU Nursing School had given her, some feeling for old people like him. Alone, dying inch by inch, kept alive by the virtuoso technics and electronics of the doctors. It was, she thought, following the old man's eyes, always the young doctors who ordered the machine hookups in cases like this. And she thought she knew why. The old doctors had made their peace with death. They had seen worse than death. Perhaps, beyond that, they believed that death was, for all its horror, a gateway, an ending in which a new beginning was implicit. The young doctors believed in nothing whatever but their own skill and their capacity to develop new machines, new techniques to press death back farther and farther. The old man's lips moved, and Miss Lefebre was mildly surprised. Then she heard a deep grating sound so harsh and elemental that it seemed to be coming from the very walls of the hospital room. It took her several seconds to realize that it was a human voice.

—Ah, Mrs. Baxter, the voice said, —must not hate, and surely must not study on revenge. Time is short, and the Lord . . . put that girl out of your mind . . . make a good act of contrition . . .

III

George Slack was sitting on the back porch eating a cantaloupe. It was chilled, tangy and sweet. He looked out over the yard past the swimming pool, down toward the somnolent river where his power boat was moored. He was in a state of unthinkingness, simply appreciating what there was, and what he had of it. He tried not to think of Amy, because he would not see her until Wednesday. He could never see her on weekends, of course, and even during the week it wasn't smart to simply plan meeting at a bar—much less a local motel.

Now he *was* thinking of her, thinking of her eyes, her casual laughter. The way she responded to him. She was the girl he should have met thirty years before. If he had stayed in New Orleans, taken the job with the wholesale coffee distributors there on Decatur Street . . . by now . . .

For some reason, as he set down his spoon, he looked at his hands. They were the hands of a man moving deep into the wrong end of middle age, liver-spotted, the flesh drying, showing veins and tendons clearly, as if the skin were becoming transparent, a palimpsest upon which each year etched additional lines.

My God, George Slack thought with a sudden shock. I'm dying inch by inch. Pieces of me are sloughing off, veins clouding up. It's really true. He closed his eyes, because it was embarrassing even to think silently that way. As if he had not been taught always that life was a passing shadow pointed toward eternity, toward that other life which would never end.

Even now, he could remember Father O'Malley hearing catechism in the parochial school, and he remembered, too, that of all his classmates, he was most attentive, most anxious to know his whole duty, and to hear the promises of God. Because, in those days, he had feared death very much. He had lost his father and mother in an automobile wreck, had been raised by his mother's sister, and he had believed somehow, for no certain reason, that the death which had claimed his parents that rain-swept evening in 1936, was awaiting him, too, a curse not to be put off, but to be completed at last by his own death.

So he had been devout for years. Perhaps it had been the beginning of the Second War that had convinced him of the commonness of death, that he had no special rendezvous with it, and that in fact the mystifications of the Church had little or nothing to do with a natural phenomenon which came in time to all things born on the earth.

He had tried to talk about it to Father O'Malley. The war was on then, and the regular baseball coach for the high school team had enlisted in the Marines (he would not be back. He would vanish like smoke while on a patrol deep into the jungles of Guadalcanal with the 2nd Marine Division, only to arise once more as a gold star, and a blue, white and red diamond-shaped patch dotted with stars in the trophy case of the St. Stephanie high school, that and a slightly blurred photo from years before, when he had been young and lean—his first year coaching—before the beer and crawfish, fried chicken and andouille had gotten to him) so Father O'Malley knocked out flies and grounders, squinted at the infield play, and explained to the boys how baseball was a figure of life itself, and that to win at either called for discipline, strength, skill and faith.

—Yeah, one of the older boys nodded cynically, —but in life, if they catch you far enough off base, they kill you.

Father O'Malley had fixed the boy with his large beautiful brown eyes, started to say something, and then let it go. It was the spring of 1943, and kids were talking differently. Especially if they were reaching draft age about graduation time.

After practice, he had walked back to the rectory of the church with the priest. It was that strange pause between daylight and twilight he had always called "the yellow moment," when, for perhaps five minutes, everything—trees, houses, cars, even people are touched by a tone of rich deep yellow, a tone from the pallet of some Flemish master.

When he had told Father O'Malley of his doubts, the priest had laughed. Not in a casual way to indicate unconcern, but a rich deep laughter as old and wise and affectionate as the priesthood itself. He had put his arm around George Slack's shoulders.

—How old are you now, boy?

—Seventeen, Father.

—Well, that's old enough. Old enough to be fighting for your country in a few months.

—Yes, Father.

—There's something I meant to tell you one day. Later, I thought. But the Lord picks his time for these things. How much do you recall about the accident . . . ?

—The . . . accident. I remember I was at home, waiting. It got late. A state trooper brought Aunt Grace . . . then I went to stay with . . .

—Ah, and you never saw them again?

—They . . . closed the coffins. I never . . .

—I was at the hospital that night. When they brought your mother and father from Madisonville . . .

—You saw . . . ?

Father O'Malley hunched his shoulders and they walked on. It was twilight now, and the edges of things had started to blur and run. Ahead, he could see the bulk of the church and the small rectory beside it. The cross on top of the church was outlined against the pink and gray clouds, the crimson and gold streaks of last light even then fading from the sky.

—Your mother was . . . they . . . she was gone. But your father . . .

—He was . . . alive . . . ? They always told me they were . . . both . . . instantly . . .

—Ah, well, what do you say to a ten-year-old boy, Georgie? Do you give an exact report on the terrible thing that . . .

—No. No. I guess you . . . make it easy . . .

—With no way to make it easy. But you don't add weight to the cross he has to bear . . .

They had reached the rectory. Old Mrs. Wise, long dead now, had fixed hot chocolate while they moved into Father O'Malley's study. It was dark and quiet there, only a single small lamp on the battered old desk. The walls were solid with bookcases filled with crumbling leather volumes whose titles were undecipherable. A window was open, and the chill spring breeze blew in, adding sharpness to the scent of old leather and incense that seemed part of the structure of the room. The chocolate came, and George Slack had put his fielder's glove down between his feet, sipped the hot brew, waiting for what Father O'Malley would say, dreading when he should begin.

Father O'Malley picked up a blackened pipe which was almost invisible in the soft light from the study lamp.

—Ah, he had only a few minutes. He was in much pain. He spoke of you, of your dear mother. Then, because we both knew he had somewhere to be, he made his confession. And I had hardly done with absolution, but he was gone. That easily, Georgie. It was a fine noble man's kind of death, you know?

The tears had come, but they did not flow, and he had hardly heard the homily the priest addressed to him on a Christian death, using as text that of his own father. After a while, he had risen, thanked Father O'Malley, and left. Only weeks later, he had graduated, joined the Army Air Corps, and spent a year of horror in the skies over Germany and central Europe.

George Slack came to himself, the emptied cantaloupe before him, his hands gripping the edge of the table. Something had called him back. It was a sound in the kitchen. Elizabeth came into the breakfast room, her arms loaded with flowers. It's spring again, he thought. Thirty-three years on. His wife smiled at him. She still possessed that dark almost Latin prettiness —what they used to call long ago a "languishing" quality—that had drawn him to her long ago. But now it required effort on her part. She worked at it, and still the patching showed. There were no liver-spots on her hands; her waist was still small, but her eyes seemed to have grown smaller, more deeply seated. There was a look of wornness, wisdom, about her. She looked . . . kindly, now. As one who would, whatever the circumstances, do her duty. Christ, he thought, it's happening to her, too. And I don't care. I don't give a goddamn. I just . . . want to see Amy.

—For Father O'Malley, Elizabeth said, almost brightly.

—He won't see them, George said, and felt a flush come to his cheeks. He wasn't that kind of person. He didn't *want* to be that kind of person. He wanted to be decent—with Elizabeth, with the old priest he had not spoken to in almost thirty years—with his daughter, Jill—with everyone but Amy. With her, he wanted to be indecent. Constantly.

Elizabeth looked away, and went on arranging the flowers.—It would be nice if you . . . wanted to visit . . .

—It would be pointless. I haven't seen him . . . I don't go to his church . . .

—He is . . . part of St. Stephanie. If he had tended your car for fifty years . . . if he were a gardener who saw to your yard for fifty years.

Her eyes were wide now, and he wondered if the anger was simply a respond to his impiety, his lack of decorum. He wondered if she could possibly know anything, feel anything. The waning of his emotion had not snapped the bond between them. She *could* know—without knowing that she knew.

—You'll have to appear decent, whether you want to or not. Jill took my car. She had some errands to run for Dr. Aronson. Then she's going to pick up Amy and bring her back for the weekend. Some young men are taking them to Baton Rouge . . . an auto race or . . .

He got up from the table, dropping his napkin.

—You'll have to drop me by the hospital . . . at least that.

He turned toward her, his face filled with an unfelt and unintended irony.

—I can do . . . at least that, he said.

IV

—Morning, Walter, Judge Soniat said, looking up from his desk.

—Mike, I never knew you to be an early riser, Walter Journé said, sitting down, looking about for Miss Althea, who always presided at pretrials and other meetings, presenting the lawyers with steaming mugs of the thickest, blackest coffee in South Louisiana.

—She's not here, Walt. She came real early, brewed it, and left. Fix your own. First time in thirty years. Won't kill you.

—Want a little freshening, he asked the judge, who nodded.

He poured the coffee, leaving Judge Soniat's black, considering some cream for his own.

From behind him, he could hear Soniat rustling through papers.

—You heard about the old man, Walt?

—What? Ah, Father O'Malley, of course.

—Like someone discovering the timbers they built this town on, and chopping one down.

—Yes. My God, do you know he's been here, had been seeing to people . . . how long?

—Nineteen-twenty-seven. In the spring. You aren't that much older than I am, son.

—. . . served in the Great War, didn't he . . . ?

—. . . from the Irish Channel. Told me once he came home with the stink of men's blood on him, and never got free of it or slept a night through until he . . .

—. . . entered the seminary. Said he'd lie or cheat, steal or blaspheme before he'd hurt another of God's creatures again . . .

They sat, the rising sun cutting a golden path between them on the judge's desk. The steam from their coffee rose in the sunlight, twisting, flattening as the breeze moved it here and there.

Judge Soniat pushed a blue and yellow box of cigars toward him. Journé reached in, took out a long slender stogie. Marsh-Wheeling. Since 1840. One of those things you come to expect. Part of the weather—like great Gulf clouds, magnolias and jasmine and gardenias in the spring. Things you count on.

—He's got no people, Walt. Nobody. His only heir will be the diocese.

—You have his will?

—Drew it up in 1940. Never wanted anything changed. Church gave him everything. Wants to give it back.

—Is there . . . any . . . chance?

—Not a goddamned one. Spoke to old Aronson last evening. Says the sooner the better. Stroke destroyed his brain. The cognitive and operative sections are gone. Just like an explosion in there . . .

—How long . . . ?

The judge shrugged. —Can't say. When he came in, one of the young residents put him on the machines, you know. Worked like a beaver to keep his breathing. Damned kids. They're so bright. Smart as hell . . .

Journé smiled. —But, you're thinking, maybe they could use some judgment?

—I don't know. What am I supposed to say? I'm just a country judge, Walt. Father O'Malley is . . . what?

—Eighty. Maybe a year or so more . . .

Soniat got up from his desk, scratched his uncombed gray hair. He laughed without humor. —You know, goddamnit, he married Mary Ann and me. And he was there when . . .

—I remember. . .

—Used to go up to the . . . house every two weeks with us until Michael junior died.

Journé remembered the small boy he had seen only twice, once as a newborn, once in his coffin. He had been an extreme mongoloid. He had died in the East Louisiana Hospital of an infection. It was not uncommon.

Soniat's voice was blurred. —He didn't have to go up there . . . said Mike was one of his parishioners, too. Said God never, never gave us a burden we couldn't bear. Proved it. Showed it to us. Made his own teaching flesh.

The judge sat down again. He was silent for a long time. Then he passed a legal-sized sheet of paper over to Journé.

—It's an order ready for my signature. I want you to take over as curator. I don't want to give this one to some kid out of LSU or Tulane . . .

Journé nodded. You give these small jobs to the youngsters, ordinarily. It gets them before the court, and they pick up seventy-five dollars here, a hundred there. It is what lawyers do. But sometimes even a simple task has overtones, becomes a ceremony. Judge Soniat would not hand over Father O'Malley to some young man who did not know him, had perhaps never seen his face.

—I called the chancery in New Orleans, told them what the situation was. Said they'd send someone over . . . his confession, if he can. Last rites, anyhow . . .

—And the church . . .

—Oh, they'll have visiting priests for a while . . . do you remember . . . ?

—Barely. It seems like he was always here.

—No, before him was an old German priest . . . had served with the Union army in the Confederate War . . . used to preach the evils of rebellion . . . old bastard . . .

—You can't remember that . . .

—Oh, I remember him. I most especially remember my father telling him one Sunday after mass that good Southern people didn't require political education from . . . a hun . . .

They both laughed.

—My God, in those days . . .

—My mother knew we were all in for excommunication . . . but they sent Father O'Malley instead. His first sermon . . .

—That I do remember, somehow. How he was the son of rebellious people himself, and understood those deep passions . . .

—. . . Spoke of the Easter rising, compared it with the War . . . people, rightly or wrongly, put upon too long . . .

—And then saying that, at last, only resurrection, not insurrection, could cure the anguish of proud people—a rising against sin, weakness, the flesh . . .

They were still again. —I'll be goddamned if I can figure remembering a sermon from . . . what . . . ?

—. . . Almost fifty years ago, Journé said smiling. Soniat smiled, too, as he signed the order. —And they say old men can't remember.

—Oh, Michael, Journé said, rising slowly. —We remember just fine. What we want to remember.

V

Dr. Amadeus Aronson had finished his breakfast in the hospital cafeteria. Now he would walk out on the grounds for fifteen minutes or so. Then it would be time for rounds. Sometimes he was tired, already irritable before any silly ass on the staff gave him reason. It had to do with certain pains he could not be rid of, and which would not kill him. Minor arthritic changes. Where they hurt.

He took one step onto the porch, surveyed the old oaks and magnolias that surrounded the hospital. He was proud of them. Twenty years ago, when the hospital board had obtained this plantation land from the Callais estate, the architects had wanted to clear out all the old trees—"a solidly modern appearance" was what was wanted. Dr. Aronson had pointed out that it was much easier to replace insensitive architects than hundred-year-old trees. He had made his point, and now there was hardly a window in the complex from which patients could not see trees which had been planted long before they were born, and which would outlive them. Perhaps that was the essence of what he had wanted to say through his practice: the continuity of generations. Birth eases death as death heals birth. If a man sees himself in perspective, life should be a joy. He is a partner in the festival of being, an invited guest along with his fellows, society, the cosmos. Under God.

It was then that Miss Lefebre found him.

—Doctor, the old . . . Father O'Malley . . .

Dr. Aronson turned quickly. —Is he . . . changed?

—He's . . . doctor, he's talking.

Dr. Aronson snorted. The help you get nowadays. —That, Miss . . . what's your name?

—Lefebre, doctor. Amy Lefebre.

—That, Miss Lefebre, is impossible. His speech centers were destroyed by the cerebral accident. He cannot move. He cannot talk. He is not conscious, despite his eyes remaining open. You heard someone in the hall.

The young nurse was very pretty. She was, in fact, exceptional. Dr. Aronson found it hard to believe he had not noticed her. But what was she saying?

—. . . made my report. I invite the doctor to come examine his patient who is not only talking, but who will not shut up, and who is even imitating other people's voices . . .

Dr. Aronson reached out for Miss Lefebre's arm, pulled her close, sniffed her breath—which was very sweet—glanced at her arms, stared into her eyes, and thumped her gingerly on the elbow with his fingers. She jumped. He studied for a further moment.— I'll come, he said.

VI

Miss Casey Lacour was president of the Ladies Altar Society of Holy Redeemer Church. As such, she was the acknowledged liaison between Father O'Malley and the ladies of the congregation. It was her task to carry back to the others his wishes regarding the decorations of the church, and such other ancillary matters as were the responsibilities of the Altar Society.

She had served for almost twenty years. Not so much because she was beloved as that she had the time and the willingness to see to details, while the other ladies simply offered an afternoon here or some money there.

Miss Lacour took her work seriously. She had virtually memorized the liturgical year, and as years drew on, she came to know what the priest wished on Easter, on Christmas, at Pentecost. She knew which feasts he regarded as significant, and which of less importance. Miss Lacour had spent numberless afternoons with Father O'Malley. Indeed, she had made the nine First Fridays each and every time they had been offered, so that the treasury of graces she had stored up was inestimable. She had been the solid center of support for every novena and vigil at Holy Redeemer for thirty years, and no morning mass had been celebrated without her presence in almost that long.

Now she was desolate. Since Monday, she had divided her waking hours between the silent church and the waiting room of the hospital. She had tried by prayer to maintain her closeness to Father O'Malley, who wandered now in a limbo between life and death, and to blot out from her memory the awful events that had suddenly torn asunder the fabric of her life. Somehow, she had not expected this. She had supposed that one day her life would end amidst the physical and spiritual furniture she had so carefully collected and lovingly arranged. At such cost. For so long.

She had envisioned the end of her life in many ways: as she placed, so early on Easter morning, a last perfect lily in a vase before the statue of Christ risen, there would be a moment of hazy forgetfulness, and she would find herself standing in fact before the Holy Redeemer she had so long served. All the sacrifice and grace that had been hers on earth now compacted into that symbolic lily she held out to Him. He would smile and receive it, and her eternity would begin.

Or it would be during confession. There in the darkness, she would be reciting to Father O'Malley the threshold sins of pride, anger, covetousness that were the curse of involvement with the Altar Society ladies who, individually, sowed so little and yet wished to reap all. Then she would reach the Great Sin once more. She would recite what had happened that spring day in 1944 still again, whispering it breathlessly from yet another vantage point, trying to explain to the distant and momentarily impersonal spirit of love and understanding on the other side of the grate that forgiveness was not, could not be perfected until the discovery was complete, until the confessing was done.

And Father O'Malley would say to her, sighing, —Casey, Casey, it is all done when the will moves forever away from its sinful object. When the heart turns around, it is forgiven. Now you must learn to give up that afternoon, all the wrongful ecstasy and the awful guilt of it. It will never be the twenty-first of April, 1944, again. Not in all eternity. The young man is dead; the child is dead, never lived, indeed. It is forgiven . . .

And she would die then, feel her soul drift out from her old unrealized indifferent body, feel the chill of time and space evaporating, the essence of herself, which was ageless and eyeless, longing for eternity and light. Then she would reach the downs, a field in Sussex in April while the invasion was preparing, and he would be there, and it would happen again, only untainted by flesh and the curse of earth, and she would be ashamed of nothing because sin, *that* sin, is of the flesh only, and whatever else, there would be no windblown dark November following, no sudden letter announcing the end of April dreams turned to blood and death in the hedgerows. But most of all, beyond all else, no rush of terror, no trip to London to the small hospital in Wigmore Street. No, not in death. Nor the boat trip home, the time in New York and New Jersey where in her desperation . . .

Miss Lacour opened her eyes. She had not been sure whether she would find herself in the small pew before the side altar of Holy Redeemer, or sitting in the quiet waiting room of the hospital. It was the hospital, and she saw Dr. Aronson moving rapidly down the hall toward Father O'Malley's room, his face dark and concerned. She rose and followed him quickly. She tried to speak to him, but he didn't even hear her soft voice. He entered the room, and almost without thought, she followed him. A young nurse was with him, and as she stood in the shadows at the back of the room, the doctor and the young nurse moved close to the bed where Father O'Malley lay. The doctor examined him closely, shining a small flashlight into his open eyes. He checked the vital signs, then read the chart quickly. For a moment, there was no sound in the room at all. Then Dr. Aronson spoke, his voice low, incredibly vicious.

—I want you to erase . . . this last entry. Do it now and initial it.

The young nurse stared back at him coldly. —I will not falsify that chart . . . not for . . .

—Ah, Casey, what in God's name can I say to you . . . ?

The voice was that of Father O'Malley. Or, it was almost his voice. But not quite. Not the tired gentle voice she had known during the last years. It was rather that voice rejuvenated, made stronger, younger.

—You can . . . tell me . . . it's all right, Father . . . tell me that . . .

Miss Lacour's eyes widened. It was her own voice that she heard now. Only not quite. Rather her voice as it had been. In 1955, perhaps. In 1960. But hers, down to the tremulous undertone, the inaudible gasp, holding back those hysterical tears that remained ever present even now. Then it was Father O'Malley's voice again.

—It *isn't* all right, girl. Not in this world or the next. It is forgiven, has been since I pronounced the words of absolution over you thirteen years ago . . . but . . . all right? My God, how can a thing that happened in the world, a thing done, ever be erased, made not to have occurred . . . ? Can you unring the bells of Holy Redeemer, Casey Lacour . . . ?

It had been 1958. Now she remembered. That very tone, those very words. In the confessional, in the secret August heat. He had told her that a thing done was eternal, because by its very happening in God's imperfect world, it subsisted in eternity, in His perfect Mind. She felt herself falling back against the wall as Dr. Aronson leaned down over the old priest, his face a mask of astonishment and something akin to fear. The young nurse stood close by, her eyes flaming with triumph, a cold smile on her lips.

—. . . oh, girl, I know your shame, your desperation, the loss of your young man . . . but in God's mercy, you could have spared the child . . . what kind of demon took you to that English hell where they . . .

And her voice cut in, almost strangled with sobs—even as it had eighteen years before.

—Not without him. He swore he'd come back. That we'd be one . . .

—And, damnit, Casey, so you were. You sinned with him, but don't you see? That new life, the one you threw away in Lond . . . it was his and yours . . . he tried to keep his promise . . .

Miss Lacour was sitting on the floor now. She was not unconscious, only transported, and her eyes were fixed on a lithograph of the Holy Family that hung above his bed. Where she had placed it the day after his attack. Father O'Malley's eyes still probed the room's shadows far above her head where Jesus Christ in plaster simulacrum lay against varnished wood.

Dr. Aronson stood by the bed, shaking his head as the old priest talked on. Miss Lefebre was checking the connections on the bank of glistening machines on the far side of his bed. Her eyes crossed those of Dr. Aronson time and again.

—I'm sorry, Miss . . . Lefebre. These things don't . . . happen. Never in the literature, never in my experience . . .

—Don't bother, doctor. It's just that I'm . . . a good nurse. I don't. . . hear things.

—Of course not.

His hand touched hers on the bed sheet where she was smoothing it.

—You're . . . a splendid nurse. Neither of them saw Miss Lacour struggle to her feet, and open the door and leave. Later, if asked, they could say with utter certainty that she had not been to see Father O'Malley that day.

VII

It was early evening now, and the sun was beginning to lose itself in the clouds that were coming up from the Gulf. A tall thunderhead stood over the town, and the TV weather man over in Houma had said there was a fifty percent chance of evening showers that night.

Walter Journé sat in his office which was, in fact, one of the two parlors of his home. He had finished writing up some small matters, and at the bottom of the papers he had come across the order signed by Judge Soniat by which he was made curator for Father O'Malley. He picked it up and stared at it as if he had never seen it. What a curious thing, he thought, and laughed silently at the pun. The curator had once stood for ancient Roman soldiers, to protect their interests when they fought outside Italy. It was the Republic's way of protecting those absentee in her service. And later, for those who, though at home, yet were absent—the *furiosi*, the mad, whose spirits sojourned elsewhere though their bodies lay with the jurisdiction of the state.

Mr. Journé loved the Civil law because there came to it no problem that men had not struggled with before. And not simply Englishmen whose law was as rough and recent as their ways, but Spaniards, Frenchmen, Germans—even Russians and Arabs. All had their civil codes. To be a civilian lawyer was like standing for a moment at the end of the law's long intricate web. This strand, two millennia old, still grew, was vital, and no man who served within it was left alone with his problem. If the code of Louisiana had no answer, then the *Code Napoleon*. If not that, then Justinian or Gaius, the *Corpus Juris Civillis*. What work could man undertake that had not been done before, by those of every tongue and hue, who had preceded, those brothers in the law?

He set the order out on his desk, clear now of the week's matters. How was it, he wondered, that he should be seeing to a man who had always seen to him? Father O'Malley was the only priest he had known as a grown man. When he had come back from Law School in New Orleans, they had become friends. They would go fishing. Sometimes, on a long weekend at a fishing camp Journé owned near Ville Platte, they would pass the evenings, after cleaning up the dishes, with a mason jar of good local liquor. Father O'Malley had always claimed that prohibition was against the law of Nature, and that no man was obliged to obey a law aimed at altering the very nature of man itself.

One night, after many drinks, he had told Journé about Ypres, the second battle, when the Germans had used poison gas for the first time. How incredible it was to see men drowning in their own fluids, how many of his friends farther toward the sea had perished.

He spoke of the Great War, of men drowning in mud, of trench rats as big as dogs, of men killing German prisoners, no more than boys, shooting them in retaliation for the ugliness and hatred of it all, while the boys cried,—*Bitte, bitte.*

They sat in the dusk there, watching the individual shadows of the cypress melt and blend into blocks of shadow. Father O'Malley drank another glassful of the whiskey. His voice was getting thick now, and Journé knew he was approaching his limit even though he could no longer make out his face.

—Years later, the curse of it on me, when I entered the seminary in Cork, can you guess how I disposed of it? Can you? Hell no, Walter Journé, you decent man, you. I said, bless me, father, for I have sinned. In the war, I killed . . . "Ah," but my confessor said back, "in a just war, killing is no sin." —Aha, I answered him back,—if that's so, how is it I'm as sure to be damned for it as the sun will rise, and our Jesus died to save? After a while, when I saw there'd be no reply, I left the good old man who would see me through to ordination with his own best thoughts, and I went outside, and I cried . . . bitter, bitter the tears . . . and all that twenty-five years ago, and more . . .

Later, Journé had helped him to bed, and the next day they had driven in Walter's 1935 Ford V-8 back to St. Stephanie. They had always been friends thereafter, but they did not fish or drink together any more, and Journé came to understand what the seal of the confessional meant. The ultimate privilege of the ultimate advocate with his ultimate client.

Journé put the paper aside. It was twilight now, and sure enough, rain had begun to fall. He walked out onto the front porch just in time to see a car pulling into his oyster-shell driveway, and to squint at the darts of rain falling through the headlights.

VIII

Jill Slack sat in the car till Amy Lefebre came out. It had started to rain, and she just didn't feel gracious. She was tired. Tired of her family. It seemed strange that all the time she had been growing up her family had been wonderful. Or at the least, covert. Now it was like a snake pit. Her father hardly ever spoke to her mother, and her mother seemed to have an inexhaustible catalogue of petty slights and annoyances that she wanted to work through with Jill. Over and over again. Second childhood, she considered. Both of them. Or what was that other thing? *Games People Play?* Mother's adult to father's child? Or the other way around? She had read a review. Or had she read the book? Anyhow, she felt dragged out. Which was a shame. Clay Moore was coming from Lafayette where he worked at Exxon. Clay was fun. They'd always made it real good together. She didn't know the other boy. Somebody from New Orleans, somebody Amy had known at school. Sometimes Jill wished she had finished school. Not that she wanted to nurse, but it was something. Something to tell people you were, something you did. Doing something was important. No, it wasn't—to her—but people seemed to *think* it was important. Nowadays, you had to *do* something. No one ever asked what her mother did. She was a mother, a housewife. That took care of that. But someone always wanted to know . . .

Amy pulled open the door, and almost fell into the car. Her hair was glistening with rain, and against the distant lights of the hospital, her profile was perfect. Jill loved Amy, really loved her. But you get tired of perfection. Thank God she had a simply miserable disposition to go with those looks.

—Christ, what a day, Amy said. She was looking in her purse for her cigarettes. She found one loose, and cursed when her wet hands soaked it through. She had not even looked at Jill yet.

—This one you'd never believe. Everything that could happen did. Miracles, encounters, goofs, confrontations, sudden reversals, attempted seductions, general screw ups . . .

—Sounds like an ordinary day at City General, Jill said as she started up the car.

—No, really. I almost got fired for writing the truth on a chart, and an hour later he . . .

—Who?

—Oh, you know. Aronson. King of the Jungle. An hour after he wanted to fire me, he was trying to put the make on me.

—Really? Dr. Aronson? God, I didn't know he even had one, much less gave it any consideration.

—Ummm . . . I'm not sure. I sort of think it . . . was my mind.

Jill laughed out loud. The rain was still hard, and the headlights of passing cars refracted into thousands of needles of light. It was hard to steer straight. —Come on, big lady. You've got a perfectly fine mind . . . but I never saw anyone pay it the slightest attention. Your . . . other things keep getting in the way.

Amy nibbled her lip and tried to comb her hair in the dark. It fell out like thick burnished silk to lie along her shoulders as if there were no rain at all. —No, really. It was . . . what happened with Father O'Malley . . .

—How is he? He baptized me, gave me First Communion . . .

—Ummm . . . he's different.

—Better . . . ? Worse . . . ?

—Different. I mean, he's supposed to be a vegetable, you know. Terrible hemorrhage in the brain. Some kind of aneurysm. Blew his brains out, according to Aronson. Just a matter of a few days . . . but today, this morning, he began to talk . . .

—That's a hopeful sign, Jill said, concentrating on the road.

—Dummy, you didn't *hear* what I said. His brain is gone. I mean, gone. Deep coma . . . you remember the lectures from second year . . .

—But you said . . . Amy blew a fat smoke ring. It broke up on the windshield, and turned to mist on the glass.

—He's talking, but not consciously. You won't *believe* what he's doing.

—?

—He's . . . he's repeating confessions . . .

—Oh, Amy, my God. That's gross. Really . . .

—Hon, I'm not being . . . blasphemous or whatever you call it . . . He's doing it. He started this morning. Something about a Mrs. Baxter. Something about Mrs. Baxter wanted revenge against some girl . . .

—I never heard of a Mrs. Baxter. Not ever. And I know everybody in town . . .

—That was just the start. And anyhow, it's not the *weirdest* . . . he does *both sides* . . .

—What? —I mean, he does the voice of the other person, too. He says what he said. But he says what they said, too. God, it's . . . it's weird.

—Amy, you're putting me on . . .

—No, there was a Mrs. Tohler . . . she lost a son in some war. She . . . couldn't stand to have her husband touch her. Something it wasn't clear. Anyhow, he died at Le Shima . . . somewhere in Viet Nam, I guess. She hated her husband . . . because he was alive, and her son Eddie was dead . . . so Father O'Malley told her he couldn't give her absolution until she worked it out. He was . . . really hard. Said she was a corrupt woman, loved her son too much, unnaturally, and then she broke down and told him what she had done when the boy was small . . .

Amy left off as the car pulled down the shell and gravel drive under the portico. She'd been at the house often, had visited since the days she'd been Jill's roommate in New Orleans. But she was not used to it. George T. Slack, oil and gas properties. This was what you could get with oil and gas properties. Twenty-six rooms, swimming pool, tennis courts, a cathedral ceiling in the living room, and a step-down nook near a walk-in fireplace. Hell, why didn't it snow? Or why hadn't she met George T. Slack when he was hustling his first well? Of course, that was probably before she was born. But it sounded like an exciting time. He'd been in the Air Corps. Bombing Germany. He'd been hit with flak, had lain in the waist of the ship near his gun watching his blood flow, then slowly freeze. Which saved him, he said. Over Frankfort, the cold had frozen his blood. And, he had gone on, staring at the small pitted scars in his legs and stomach, nothing unthawed me—until you. It had been very good, really. Elizabeth and Jill had been in Dallas for a week of shopping, and when her shift was over, she'd go to the house, sleep, swim, fix salad, and choose a wine. Then he'd come, and like a college boy, couldn't wait for it. Beside the pool, in bed, in the living room. Once in the kitchen, she'd astonished him with her own favorite kind of loving. Something Elizabeth couldn't even have imagined. Not with a blueprint and a book of instructions, he'd gasped.

As they got out of the car, Amy picked up her overnight case and started up the steps, thinking of the aftermath. Wednesday evenings. In a tiny place he'd rented outside Boutté. They'd have dinner at a small Cajun restaurant and then go play house for a few hours. It was a dingy place, but he was very good. She liked the feel of his body. Not just a good-looking carcass, but the body of a man who had flown three miles above the earth, sending down judgment.

Once she had grown glum about it. It could go nowhere. He'd never walk away, and Elizabeth would live to be eighty. Once, on a weekend, when he'd been in Kuwait or some impossible place, she'd gone . . . to confession.

The implication of that struck her just as she came into the kitchen where Elizabeth was pouring coffee. Elizabeth looked up and saw the expression on Amy's face. She smiled warmly. She had always liked Amy. Surely the most intelligent and sensible of Jill's friends.

—You look as if you'd seen a ghost, Amy.

For a moment, Amy was speechless. She was trying to recall what she had said, whether Father O'Malley had called her by name. Even if he hadn't, would it matter? Maybe he hadn't called Mrs. Baxter by name, either, the first time. How could anybody know, or be sure?

—Oh, no ma'am. It's just the rain, the storm, and I'm . . . I guess I'm beat.

Elizabeth Slack handed her a cup of coffee. —Then it won't break your heart that your young man and Jill's both called. Said the storm was awful North and East of us. Some of the roads are out . . .

—Oh, really? No, I'd rather sleep. It's a good night for sleeping.

She and Jill and Elizabeth drank their coffee and chatted awhile. Oddly, Jill never mentioned what Amy told her about the priest. Somehow, to Jill, it was not a central matter. She was still very young, and changes go almost unnoticed.

IX

In his hospital room, Father O'Malley was breathing steadily. It was late, now, and only the night lamp gave soft illumination to the room. His eyes were still open, but there was an expression almost of hilarity on his face. His lips were moving, but no sound came forth. The night nurse glanced in. When she had no other duties, she ordinarily sat with the old man. She was one of his parishioners, and it pleased her to attend this impromptu vigil. But earlier he had been talking, some of it peculiar, something about damned filthy fuckers, strafing the trenches . . . there they go, those damned fuckers . . . She would say nothing to anyone, of course, but she was astonished. Even in delirium, a priest . . . it tested her faith. She looked at the line of glowing instrument faces in the large bank beside his bed. The insane thought came to her, that it was the machines that made him talk so. She shook her head, and went to check the other intensive care rooms. But all the same, what kind of sense did it make to hook up an eighty-year-old man with his brain gone to that rank of superexpensive gadgets. Father O'Malley was gone, and had left behind the merely human remnant with its insufferably dirty mouth.

X

The young priest smiled, and Walter Journé smiled back at him. Father Veulon was from New Orleans. He was assigned to the archdiocese. He went where there was trouble, where decisions had to be made. He was of the new clergy. He had had a course in decision making at Harvard Business School while he was taking his Master of Sacred Theology at the seminary. He really felt more comfortable with professionals, he told Mr. Journé; there is an apostolate of lawyers, doctors, and businessmen. Mr. Journé said he had no doubt of it. Father Veulon asked if he anticipated any legal difficulties, such as with Father O'Malley's will being probated. Mr. Journé raised his eyebrows slightly, and allowed that, at least in the country parishes, there was one formality before probate would be possible.

—And what is that? Father Veulon asked.

—The testator must be dead, Mr. Journé told him.

XI

It was almost midnight, and the rain had softened. It fell gently, barely making a sound against the trees, the roof of George Slack's house. It had not stopped, but the thunder was distant now, moving eastward. She could hear it, sullen and inchoate, toward New Orleans. The rain fell quietly, its sound muffled, against the leaves, in the gutters of George Slack's house. She came to herself, awake suddenly and eyes open, looking out into the yard where certain lights illuminated the distant pool, where oaks and magnolias stood in sharp relief against the bulk of shadows behind.

She had tried to sleep, but it was impossible. In her half-consciousness, she heard Father O'Malley telling again the sins of his people, assigning to them penances, arguing the meaning of what had happened to them and because of them in a world they had not made, nor he accepted. She thought how small, condensed it all sounded. Had the world actually become larger?

Was it possible that Father O'Malley's world had been determined in its size by his consciousness? Or was her world an illusion, not nearly so large as she would like to imagine? Everything depended on this. She had to know. But there was no way to know. She was left on her own.

It was then that she heard the door open. She did not grow tense, because she knew who it must be. She heard his breathing. Then she heard his voice.

—Amy . . . ?

—Yes . . .

—Oh, my God, how I love you, he said, his voice as distant, hollow, and uncertain as a boy's.

—Oh Georgie, she said, and what she had been thinking vanished from her mind.

XII

The rain was hardly more than a soft tattoo on the leaves now. Even though the sky was still clouded over, one could walk without being soaked, and that was what Miss Casey Lacour was doing. She had put on her best suit, and now she was walking through the bare shower toward Holy Redeemer Church. She was smiling a smile no one had seen in thirty years. Her face, just for then, was that of a woman half her age.

Because, she thought, I am walking somewhere for the first time since I got off that train at King's Cross Station, heading toward a rendezvous with death. Now I am walking toward . . . Ah, God, please love me. He or she—would be thirty-two years old today, and walking in this small rain. Wouldn't he? Oh Christ, forgive me for waiting so long. And in your heavenly mercy, touch that good priest who so long ago gave me absolution and tried to give me understanding, and please Jesus, let them be waiting for me, my husband and my son . . . or my daughter, if it was so in your eternity . . .

The rain became heavier then, and Miss Lacour increased her pace almost to a run to reach the cover of Holy Redeemer Church before it became a downpour again.

XIII

It was almost morning, but Judge Soniat had had a restless night. He rose, the usual pain in his lower back, the usual bad taste in his mouth. He slipped into his bathrobe, and walked slowly through the darkened house which his ability and labor had purchased. Even his bare feet sounded hollowly in this house of no children. Oh Jesus, he thought, I should have left years ago. Why stay in a place where seeds cannot . . .

The morning paper awaited him there on the front steps. As if an engineer had placed it there. Precisely where it should have been. A blind man could have found it. He picked it up, threw away the rubber band and glanced at the headlines as he walked back toward the kitchen.

HUNDREDS DIE IN BEIRUT

the newspaper told him. He closed his eyes and walked the last few yards to the coffeepot without even seeing where he was going.

XIV

Early Monday morning, George Slack was awake. He called his lawyer and headed for his office. He was waiting for a phone call. All his nerves were alive, ready, prepared for action. Even beyond his horror, he had not felt so alive in thirty years. It was strange to be challenged at all. Much less from such a strange quarter. But George understood the way things are: a challenge is a challenge. Where it comes is secondary. Isn't it?

XV

Mr. Journé strode back and forth in the hall of the courthouse. He had a trial this morning. At ten o'clock. He had read the depositions, reread all the evidence. His lady had been injured by the act of another. This morning would see the truth told. As he paced, he reconstituted the testimony of the opposition in his mind. There was no doubt. He would win.

But down the hall, at Mike Soniat's door, he saw the young clerk beckoning to him. He frowned. Even the hall of the courthouse at 6:30 in the morning has no privacy. People will be . . . everywhere. With demands, with needs. Lord God.

Mike Soniat had already poured the coffee. He looked very tired.

—We've got a problem, he said.

—I reckoned that, Walter Journé said. —But I've already talked to the young man. The insurance company has decided to make a last stand here. Lord, they all remind me of Custer.

—No, Soniat said. —Father O'Malley.

—What?

—A petition for an injunction . . . to . . . end heroic measures . . .

Walter Journé squinted at his friend. He had never had any problem understanding Mike Soniat before. He might disagree with his decisions. But he understood him. —I don't think I'm . . .

Soniat's face was expressionless. He held a paper in his hand.

—I have here a petition which asks that I order all extraordinary measures ceased in the matter of Father Cornelius O'Malley, that I direct the hospital and its staff to allow him death with dignity, to end his suffering . . .

—I . . . don't understand, Mike. What the hell . . . ?

Mike Soniat leaned back in his chair, his face still revealing nothing. —Walt, haven't you heard? Where the hell do you live? In a vacuum-sealed box?

Journé took that as an insult. He put his coffee down. —I live, goddamnit, in my house. Where I have lived for fifty and more years. What's going on here, Mike . . . ?

But even before he answered, Walter Journé knew that the case was altered, that it was a lawyer talking to a judge. Not Walt talking to Mike.

—He's at the point of death, Judge Soniat said. —But somehow he's . . . talking. About people. About everything that ever happened in this town . . .

Journé was not sure he grasped what the judge was saying. —Talking, he said.

—It's something . . . that happens. He's repeating . . . all his confessions, everything. From God knows when . . . until now . . .

—My God, Journé said. —How is that possible . . . ?

The judge shrugged. —They found Miss Lacour this morning . . . in the church . . .

—What . . . ?

—. . . Dead. She had gone there . . . when? Saturday night or Sunday morning. She had cut her wrists. There was this note . . .

The judge handed a piece of paper to Mr. Journé. He took it gingerly, read it slowly, thinking of Casey Lacour, such a fine lady. Oh Lord, the cost of being a survivor.

> I go to meet those who have awaited me for thirty years. I go gladly, because Father O'Malley, even in his last days, had made me see that I should have paid long ago the small price of life for the great gift of love. God, his illness is my health. Thank you, God, and forgive me hurrying. Please. Please.

—Dr. Aronson called. Said the old man had been talking about what Miss Lacour had told him years ago. About a boy she met while she was in England. About a baby she . . . didn't have. Maybe a nurse's aide told her. It doesn't matter . . .

Mr. Journé stared at the judge. —That's right. It doesn't matter.

There was silence between them for a moment. The silence that comes between rivals in the law. After a moment, Journé came to himself.

—Who filed the petition . . . ?

—John Doe, Judge Soniat said.

—What the goddamned hell are you talking about?

—It's valid. We have an attorney of record from Baton Rouge . . .

—Who the hell's the plaintiff . . . ?

—He alleges irreparable damage, a proper interest . . . and that he cannot make himself known . . . because to do so would . . . amount to the same damage . . . He alleges the old man can't recover, can't even live more than a few days . . . but that many people will be hurt if he goes on . . .

Journé felt his face flush with anger. —That's not a petition . . . that's a bad joke . . .

Judge Soniat returned his glare. —We're going to have a hearing at 11:00. Is that convenient for your, Mr. Journé?

—I don't believe this . . .

—There's law on it. You've read that New Jersey case . . .

—This isn't son-of-a-bitching New Jersey, your honor . . . This is Louisiana. . . Who's a plaintiff that has any proper relationship to Father . . .

—. . . Father Veulon . . . from the archdiocese . . . he . . . joined with the John Doe plaintiff . . . to end Father O'Malley's . . . suffering . . .

—My God, Mr. Journé gasped. —Mike, is this a . . . set-up?

Judge Soniat's eyes did not waver. —I'll see you at eleven o'clock, counsellor, he said.

XVI

Elizabeth Slack was carrying her flowers into the hospital when Dr. Aronson met her.

—For Father O'Malley . . . ?

—Yes. How is he?

—He's terminal. A matter of hours or days.

—He can't . . . recover?

—No, Liz. I'm sorry . . .

She went onward, toward the corner room, pushed the door open, smiling, and before Miss Lefebre could say anything, Elizabeth had placed the vase full of daffodils on the table beside the bed.

—That much, at least, Amy, she said triumphantly.

Amy returned her stare without emotion. —Mrs. Slack, no one is admitted . . .

—And why not, Elizabeth asked, her voice rising. Dr. Aronson said . . . he said there was . . . no hope. How can we hurt one with no . . . hope?

Amy was about to answer, but she was too late. And she, like Elizabeth, was transfixed by that deep, strong, distant voice that brought back a past neither of them had known.

—Ah, my sweet Christ, Father O'Malley said, —What have you done, George? Do you know what you've done? In that car? It was an accident, wasn't it . . . ?

And another voice answered, a voice neither Elizabeth nor Amy had ever heard.

—Ye . . . yes, Father . . . killed . . . killed the whore, didn't I . . . didn't . . . I?

—You killed a woman you swore to love and honor till death, you damned fool . . .

—She . . . they . . . everybody . . . knew . . . everybody but . . . me
. . .

—What of the boy, George? What about your son?

—No. No . . . her . . . *his* son. Not mine. Blood tests. In Baton
Rouge. I . . . that . . . bastard . . . not mine, you understand . . . not
mine . . It's certain . . . not mine . . .

Father O'Malley was silent for a moment, his dry lips working.
His eyes closed, and it seemed that there were tears on his cheeks,
but it was impossible to be sure, because Miss Lefebre moved so
quickly, her small cloth mopping his expressionless face.

—Really, Mrs. Slack . . . Dr. Aronson . . .

—Shut up, Elizabeth said, her eyes wide, her ears perked. —
Just shut up, Amy . . .

—George, you're dying, do you know it? You're dying with her
blood on your hands . . . in the name of Jesus, make a good act of
contrition . . .

—My ass . . . I'd kill her a hundred times, do you hear? Do you
. . . do you . . .

—George, in God's name, think of the boy . . . think of your
immortal soul . . .

—. . . Ga . . . Goddamn the bastard, and my soul . . . is . . . is . . .

Father O'Malley fell silent, his eyes fixed on the distant
crucifix. Elizabeth watched him, hardly believing what she had
heard.

—Mrs. . . . Slack . . . you've got to leave, do you understand . . . ?

Elizabeth shook her head, closed her eyes for a moment, then
turned to Amy. Her voice was soft, composed, her smile serene.

—Of Course, Amy, I don't know what . . . I was thinking of . . .

XVII

Dr. Aronson was meeting the press. He had hardly gotten to the
hospital before the newspaper and television people began
demanding, on behalf of the public's right to know, that he clarify
certain stories which had already traveled as far as New Orleans
and Baton Rouge. It was said that a priest in St. Stephanie had
gone mad and begun blackmailing those who had gone to him for
the sacrament of penance. There had been one death, possibly as
many as three. Someone questioned whether, at the insistence of

certain church officials, the priest was being confined there at the hospital under deep sedation. Dr. Aronson shook his head and said, no comment. But it was not as simple as that.

—Is it true, a young woman from Channel 6 in New Orleans asked, that there is . . . something . . . abnormal about . . . Father O'Neill's ailment . . . something . . . beyond . . . medicine . . . ?

My God, Aronson thought. Demonism. Voodoo.

—No, he said. —Father O'Neill . . . I mean Father O'Malley suffered a severe cerebral accident last Wednesday. His brain was . . . virtually destroyed . . .

—Then how can he be doing these things, a reporter from the *Advocate* demanded.

—He isn't doing anything, Dr. Aronson shot back, angrily. — Except dying.

—Look, doctor, some of us saw that note. The one the old lady wrote. One of the deputies at the sheriff's office . . .

—. . . nothing to do with Father O'Malley. She was elderly, lonely . . .

—Some of your staff says the old man is talking, telling things that happened in the 1920s . . . that he was talking in foreign languages . . .

—A volunteer nurse's aide said she heard the living voice of her mother who died in 1941, making a confession . . . heard her mother confess an act against nature with her father . . . she says-she's considering suit . . . ruined her memory of her family . . .

XVIII

—George, Amy was saying. —George, is that you? Listen, honey . . . what? She is? Oh, my God. Don't pay any attention to anything she tells you . . . really, she's making it all up, she's a spiteful bitch. No? Believe me . . . she . . . what? I'm not. I never asked you for . . . oh, goddamn you . . . Go ahead. And every single word she says is true . . .

XIX

Mr. Journé had just put the finishing touches on an act of sale that would be passed the next day, when Father Veulon strode into his office with that ubiquitous, confident smile of his. It was as if he had an arsenal of expressions, each stamped out to grace an occasion but none which was not rehearsed, the result of considerable market research. He was not much like Father O'Malley.

—Yes, Father, what can I do for you? Father Veulon sat down unasked, raised the crease in his black trousers, glanced at his digital wrist watch and smiled.

—At . . . eleven, I think . . . the hearing . . .

—Yes?

—Judge Soniat tells me that . . . your representation in a case . . . like this is . . . *pro forma.*

Mr. Journé bristled. —About as *pro forma* as your consecration of the host, Father . . .

—But . . . you're court appointed . . . for legal purposes . . .

—Father, the nature of my representation is a legal matter. What's your interest . . . ?

—I . . . I've spoken with His Excellency . . .

—And who would that be . . . ?

—I mean the Archbishop, of course . . . He feels that any prolongation of Father O'Malley's life . . . under the circumstances . . . given the hopelessness of it . . . He would prefer . . . death with dignity . . .

Mr. Journé's eyes locked on those of the priest. —I never saw that kind, he said. —Ordinarily they puke and bleed and gasp. They give up very slowly, unwillingly . . . perhaps, though, you have a charm . . .

Father Veulon tried to look scandalized. —I thought . . . you were . . . a Catholic, Mr. Journé . . .

—So did I. But then Judas was a Catholic, wasn't he?

—So you mean to . . .

—Right to the Supreme Court, Mr. Journé said. —Good day, Father.

XX

He had gone now, and Elizabeth was relieved. Truly, there is an ecstasy in being free from a burden you can no longer justify. She giggled aloud as she poured herself a cup of freshly brewed coffee. —Bastard, she shouted into the empty house. —Bastard . . .

It was not freedom from him, from the Bastard. That was nothing. It didn't matter. One Bastard or another, or none at all. No, that didn't matter. It was the Other Thing. About what she had heard, she could feel compassion. He was a person who could not do well with that truth suddenly jutting out of the earth after forty years. As if it had never been buried in those two graves that he never visited on that rainy January day so long ago. As if, rather, it had only been placed in a time machine, sent off to return with full vigor and potency a little later.

Her face lost its hilarity. She was thinking of Father O'Malley. For some reason, she was remembering an afternoon in 1946. It was his last year with the baseball team. The young men were coming home now, somebody had said. It was possible to obtain the services of someone more suitable. The boys had resented it, but in 1946 boys did not strike or sit in. They only played their hearts out and somehow made the Class A semifinals. She had gone on the trip to Baton Rouge on the bus, with George. One of their first dates. The team had lost in the semifinals. But they had lifted Father O'Malley high on their shoulders, carrying him back to the bus when the game was over. She remembered him there, up high, flustered, tears in his eyes, a man of fifty who had never really learned to take love and admiration in stride, his hands touching the hands, the caps, the shoulders, and faces of the boys.

—Ah, God, she had heard him almost shout,—how the Lord loves good fighters, boys . . .

The tintype of that moment stayed fixed in her mind for a moment, and then began to fade, the background first, then the boys and the tumult, even the warmth of the June day until at last, like the smile of Alice's cat, there remained in frozen frame only the flushed face of Father O'Malley, a lock of gray hair over his eyes, unfading, sharp edged, as if his presence had been the only truth of that day so long ago.

She closed her eyes and opened them, and he was gone. He had not blurred and then slowly disappeared like the rest, like George, like that distant weather encircling the ephemeral game. He had only vanished.

I wonder, Elizabeth thought, if he is so sharply etched because I knew somehow what he bore, what every one of us put upon him, and what he could not put away, give over, share with anyone else. We had our births and deaths and agonies. He had his own, and all of ours. My God, how can all that die? How can he?

She drank down her coffee, and started for the car. Somehow it was changed now, changed utterly. She could hardly remember the pain or the hatred she had felt Saturday night when she had awakened to find the bed beside her empty. What she had come to know, she knew. But it no longer had meaning. It was changed. She saw that they were all Bastards, teasing, hurting, because they were alone. She had heard those last terrible moments of his father's life, and she had thought she was running from the room with her awful new weapon to scourge him, to twist away his pride and self-respect, to punish him. But she hadn't. She had fled, fearing another revelation, one meant for her from that dying oracle created by fifty years of silence amidst them and their ways.

She climbed into her car, started it quickly, and did not hear the uncharacteristic squeal of tires as she pulled out of the driveway.

—Ah, God, she said aloud over the music of the easy-listening station, —How the Lord loves a fighter.

XXI

—I'll see you in chambers, gentlemen, Judge Soniat told Walter Journé and the attorney from Baton Rouge. —You come along, too, Father Veulon. I'll recognize you as a friend of the court . . .

—Where's the principal, Mr. Journé asked harshly. —I want to see the plaintiff . . .

—He's represented, the judge said shortly. —This is Mr. Amacker from Price, Moses and Amacker in Baton Rouge.

They shook hands as they walked toward the judge's chambers. The courtroom was almost full now with newspaper people, TV reporters, and a gaggle of townspeople.

Mr. Journé stepped before Judge Soniat's desk. —I want the plaintiff, Mike. He's alleging irreparable harm, and I have the right to examine him on that allegation . . . under the act . . .

—This isn't a criminal trial . . .

—In Louisiana, the rules of evidence are identical . . . and there's a death involved . . .

Judge Soniat brushed him off. —Now gentlemen, I mean to settle this in chambers. Then we will go out there, I will read my decision in about two minutes, and these nasty sons of bitches from the city—sorry, Mr. Amacker, Father, I mean the newsmen—can go crawl back into the walls and under the rocks where they came from . . .

—I'm filing for supervisory writs just as soon as you get done, Mike, Mr. Journé said. —Unless they all go home with no story at all.

Judge Soniat looked across at Miss Althea, his secretary. She was crying, and the tears were dropping onto her stenographer's pad.

—Now, gentlemen, Mr. Journé is here to show cause why I should not grant a permanent injunction ordering the hospital to cease and desist from taking any extraordinary measures to preserve the life of Cornelius O'Malley, lately pastor of Holy Redeemer Church, now in the parish hospital, under the care of Dr. Amadeus Aronson. It is alleged that Father O'Malley is, in fact, clinically dead, but that he is being kept alive by mechanical means which are cruel and unnatural although he has no hope of recovery or of leading a meaningful life. It is alleged further that in his terminal condition, without his volition, he is and has been for several days, revealing the secrets of the confessional and things told him by hundreds of people in the most strict and holy confidence, and that these revelations have already caused pain, suffering, and death, and will cause much more, including to the John Doe who institutes this suit because of the irreparable damage that will be done him if certain things told by him to said Father O'Malley should be revealed . . .

The voice of Judge Soniat droned on. It appeared that there was no end to the petition. Mr. Journé almost smiled, imagining the terror of John Doe, one who confessed and assumed that that was the end of it—not only in the next world, but this one as well. Now, suddenly, he was faced with the horror which had plagued even Guido da Montefeltro, burning in hell: that his sins should be revealed on earth. Mr. Journé considered what might be the value of a confession when one was prepared to end a life rather than have his sins revealed. Surely the good Southern Baptists had found a better solution: open confession before the congregation; or none at all. Perhaps a secret confession was no confession, simply a deal. I will set my wickedness out before God, with the understanding that it shall never be known to man. But who had been most injured by the wickedness? Was the right of man to know and to forgive less than that of God?

—. . . be removed from any and all mechanical devices or support systems of whatever kind, and allowed to die a natural death with dignity.

Judge Soniat was done. He took off his glasses.

—This appears to be a case of first impression in Louisiana. Once the ways of death were . . . beyond our tampering. Now . . .

He stared out the window. They could hear the soft sound of Miss Althea's sobbing. The sun was high and hot, and through open windows the sweet, incredibly pure fragrance of magnolia and gardenia came.

The judge 's head snapped back around. Damnit, Althea, stop that sniveling . . .

The sound stopped abruptly, then began again, perhaps a little louder. —I'm going to get a tape recorder in a minute or two . . . I mean it.

Miss Althea was quiet. —Mr. Amacker, did you want to add anything to your petition?

The young lawyer cleared his throat. He was not ill at ease. Not civilized enough to be nervous, Mr. Journé considered. Another technician.

—Your honor, the situation we have here is unique. We have a wonderful old man who passed most of his life in this town, whose contribution . . . but now, in the closing hours of his life, he . . . he's jeopardizing the very community and people he served for fifty years. He is, according to Dr. Aronson, clinically unable to support his own life without the marvelous instruments and mechanisms at the hospital . . .

There was much more praise of the hospital, of the town, of the court, and especially of Father O'Malley. Mr. Journé considered it sounded more like a testimonial dinner speech than a demand for capital punishment. But Amacker was good. He knew how to go about it. He knew better than to play the prosecutor, knew that the judge had nerved himself up to consider this petition, was obviously nerved enough to issue the order. It would not take much to wreck that readiness. No, Journé, he's a smart young bastard. Not going to do my work for me.

Amacker was finishing. —Heavy with years, loaded down with memories of his people's anguish. If he could, he'd say, this shouldn't go on. I'm hurting people in my final delirium that I'd rather die for than hurt . . . better death with dignity. Now. Once for all . . .

Amacker smiled kindly at Mr. Journé. —After all, what does Father O'Malley have to fear from death? His whole life has been . . . a preparation for it . . . after this death, there is no other . . .

Amacker's voice almost broke as he concluded. Mr. Journé shook his head. This little bastard would be governor or senator in a couple of years. He was a lot better than good. He'd covered almost all the ground.

Judge Soniat looked over at Mr. Journé. —Well, Walter?

Mr. Journé looked around the room. —Does Father Veulon plan to have a say . . . ?

Soniat looked at him. —Father . . . ?

Father Veulon gave the judge one of his most organized smiles. —I had thought . . . after Mr. Journé was done . . .

—Oh, no, Father, Mr. Journé said. —If you're speaking for the writ, you can do it right now . . .

—But I . . . I have only Father O'Malley's interests . . .

—Crap, Mr. Journé heard himself say. —I'm his curator . . . you're his hangman . . .

—All right, Walter, Judge Soniat said. —Watch your mouth. If you want to talk, Father, it'll have to be now . . . I want this thing done right.

Father Veulon shrugged. Mr. Journé smiled almost imperceptably. Their orchestration was thrown off. Not an important thing, but something.

Father Veulon spoke of the sanctity of the confessional, the price in human suffering that had been paid through two millennia in order to assure the silence that Father O'Malley was now breaking, through no fault of his own. He pointed out how the priest's affliction was causing him to break his most sacred vows, and by doing so, to injure his people, his priesthood, and the church itself.

Nothing in church doctrine demanded this extraordinary treatment, Father Veulon said. Death is not the great terror, after all. When there could be no meaningful life, then wasn't it time to cease the almost demonic determination to keep the body alive at all cost . . . ?

—Death is the common end, Father Veulon said. —Why should it be resisted when such resistance is of no help to the dying, and a positive injury to those who must go on living . . . ?

The room was quiet for a moment. Then Mr. Journé got up stretched, and walked around the capacious chambers.

—I guess I must be missing something, he said, —because you all make killing seem so right, so inevitable. You make it sound like ending a life is the greatest favor you can render. What you all are setting forth for the judge to consider is that a lawyer and a priest say that justice and truth can best be served by getting this old priest underground as fast as it can be done . . . what can I say to that? I feel like somebody picked me up and took me back forty years and three thousand miles away. I feel like some poor devil of an *advocat* before a Nazi court arguing that you shouldn't kill or maim a feebleminded woman, that maybe even killing Jews for the sake of the state misses what the state is about . . .

Mr. Journé argued for a long time, but he couldn't break out of the Alice-in-Wonderland feeling, as if judge Soniat and Amacker and Father Veulon were no more than a pack of cards, and that this whole business was like Moot Court back in school, that, when it was done, everyone would laugh, and say "April fool," and go home, and Father O'Malley would either recover despite the diagnosis, or he would die in his own time, surrounded by people who loved him. Mr. Journé knew better, but that feeling still clung. So he decided to end it. How do you argue with a pack of cards?

—If it weren't for his talking, no one would be here. It's not death with dignity you want. It's silence and secrecy. If I could guarantee that, you'd all go home. But you and your miserable John Doe, you want him quiet, and it happens that the only way you see to manage that is by seeing him dead . . . It won't be the first time some guilty conspirators remembered that dead men tell no tales.

That last seemed to bother Father Veulon, but Mr. Amacker just continued to look concerned.

Then Mr. Journé's eyes narrowed. He looked at Judge Soniat for a long moment. —It's as if, seeing that it was a burden on society, a priest should refuse to baptize or give care to a helpless feeble-minded child . . .

Mr. Journé heard his own voice, but he could not believe the words. He would have supposed that he had never spoken them, that they had been no more than phantasmagoria of an old man lonely too long, words thought but never spoken. But Judge Soniat's face gave proof that he had spoken his thoughts. Michael Soniat stared at him, his face bleached by sudden emotion.

I shouldn't have done that, Mr. Journé thought in the pendulous silence which swung above them, both men speechless, but the very burden of soundlessness, passing from one to the other with the fierce urgency of terminal conversation. I shouldn't because the old man wouldn't have, not to save his life.

He said more, remembering none of it, able later only to conjure the recollection of a fabric of skewed language fluttering like torn curtains in the window of an empty house. He would remember feeling abstracted, removed from the small circle whose shadows, pinned to a distant book-lined wall, grew perceptibly shorter as he argued. He would be amazed that he could have gone on till one o'clock, Amacker and Veulon at first passive as funeral mutes, then restless, eyes wandering out to the sun-flamed street where the town's blood flowed, cell by cell in the people passing, incredibly unaware of the loss being compounded so near their ordinary ways, and finally paying no attention at all, looking at Judge Soniat with pleading expressions, almost as if they had decided to join with Journé in his struggle against death with dignity.

But it isn't compassion or understanding or the power of words that drives them, Mr. Journé remembered thinking. There's no turning-around in the bastards. They're just hungry. And they need to piss.

He paused, tried to remember what he had said, what he might have left unsaid. It was late. Finish it. Never just stop. Unworthy of the craft. There must always be a coda. To let them know you could go on all day.

—I didn't know that you demanded a man's death because he spoke the truth, because, as a matter of fact, you're dead certain he is speaking the truth, the whole truth, and nothing but the truth . . . what we demand of a man in court can get him killed nowadays . . . no, I didn't know that . . . it took a big-town lawyer and a hot-shot priest to let me know . . .

He stopped then. It was way past one o'clock and he was tired. He was trying to think ahead, to the Court of Appeal, to the Supreme Court, to what he would say there. There was talk between Mr. Amacker and the Judge, and then, almost before Mr. Journé could grasp what he was saying, Judge Soniat was giving them his decision.

—Of opinion that this writ should issue, since no medical purpose can be served by the mere extension of bodily functions where all sentient and meaningful life has ended irreversibly . . .

Mr. Journé's shoulders slumped. The pack of cards had assumed the status of reality.

—I'll be filing for an appeal, Mr. Journé said slowly, not comprehending the look of pity in Judge Soniat's eyes. The Judge turned to his secretary.

—Miss Althea, you dial up Judge Walker . . . He said he'd be standing by . . .

The Judge turned to Mr. Journé. —We'll step out, Walter, so you can speak to Justice Walker . . . I talked to him this morning . . . the Supreme Court is ready to take this case directly as *res nova* . . .

Mr. Journé could tell that Amacker and the priest had known. It came across his mind that he had lived too long, much too long. God knows what the world would be like in another twenty years. But, surely, he had lived too long.

Mr. Journé watched Miss Althea slowly dial the long-distance number of the Louisiana Supreme Court. He remembered her telling him not so long ago that it seemed unnatural, long distance with no operator. Then, suddenly, as he watched her head bent over the push-button telephone, he saw her for just a moment as she had been thirty-five years before. He had known her mother and father, her brother who sold used cars in Slidell and died in a fishing accident in Lake Borgne. Lord, how he knew the details of the lives he had lived out his own among. But not the inside, not the portion that Father O'Malley knew.

Could there be such a thing as a spiritual delict, Mr. Journé wondered. *Every act whatever of man that causes injury to another obliges him by whose fault it occurs to repair it.* That lovely convoluted prose of the *Code*. *Every* act. Of course, not that of a child of tender years, not that of *a furiosus*, one gone in his own visions, out beyond the reach of common reason. But Father O'Malley was neither a child nor a madman. Could his stroke absolve him? No, nothing could. Every act whatever. And what act had the old man not known? His act had been to reveal those other acts; his tort to bring up to light the shame and pain and evil of a whole community. Ah Lord, today we do not send the scapegoat forth. If he names the sins put upon his head, we simply pull him off the machine.

—I've, got Justice Walker . . .

Miss Althea was starting to cry again. She put down the phone and followed the others out of chambers.

Mr. Journé stared at the phone and picked it up. The voice at the other end was one he recognized. Leave it to Michael Soniat. He had chosen the one Supreme Court judge they both knew: Harold Walker. Short, jovial, a Santa Claus of a man. From their district. A fine legal scholar, an activist who used the *Code* like a canvas to sketch out his own ideas of the meaning of the law, and who always required that whatever formula you used, you got down to the rights and wrongs of a case. Mr. Journé's heart sunk within him. Harold Walker was a pragmatist.

He remembered arguing a case before the Circuit Court of Appeal before Harold went to the high court. Mr. Journé had had a fine case. He had had the law, the *Code*, even the precedents, for whatever they might matter. But Harold had interrupted his argument, and fixed him with that affectionate jovial smile of his, and asked.

—Well, well, Mr. Journé, you've laid it all out for us, and I see what you're saying. But is it right?

Lord God, is it right? What kind of a maniac judge asks that of a lawyer? The judge is supposed to answer that question, not the advocate. No, the lawyer, having taken a case, is supposed to have only one view, and to argue that view until a final decision cuts him short. No one has the right to ask the advocate to judge. He cannot. It is not his function.

—Hello, Harold, Mr. Journé said, and then he listened.

When he hung up, he sat down, drew out a white handkerchief, and wiped his forehead. Justice Walker had not asked him what was right this time.

XXII

It was late afternoon now, and Miss Lefebre was on duty next to Father O'Malley. He had been quiet for a long time. She had wet his lips with water. She was very high. Was it Percodan, Darvon? She couldn't remember. Something. Oh, Christ, she should have had courage, should have left her enameled pill box alone. Now her head was full of peculiar things raised up from her childhood. Was she moistening the lips of Christ, or was what seemed to be cotton really coals, and were those the lips of the prophet Isaiah, or was she out on the edge of something she couldn't handle? Christ, why don't people just lie down and die?

But if that was what she really felt, then why was she touching the old man's lips again so quickly? Why were her lips touching his dry pink forehead where the silver hair had been combed back so immaculately?

XXIII

George Slack was drunk and walking toward the hospital. He was not clear in his purpose. Perhaps he wanted to hear his father's voice through the lips of the old man. He could not remember his father's voice, and amidst the liquor, it had come to him that he would be willing to hear that voice say anything, admit to any crime, profess any horror. Just to be able to hear that voice again.

He stumbled once, and fell into some shrubbery, but after a few minutes, he got to his feet and started again. It began to rain. It was a soft rain, and he hardly noticed it, only the gradual wetting of his suit which grew heavier and heavier, until at last he threw away his jacket, pulled off his tie. But he kept walking.

XXIV

The raindrops fell on Elizabeth Slack's windshield and they made her feel very old. Make the small rain to fall, she thought, wondering where those words had come from, suddenly into her mind. Her anger had passed. Even the pain had begun to ebb. It was pride, after all, wasn't it? The notion that she could be all things to him, and no one, truly, is all things to anyone. Not even to themselves. People reach for what they need, most especially when they feel the slow inexorable pain of age, terminal and irreversible, coming upon them. They do not suppose that it can be altered. They only imagine that it can be put off, held at bay for an hour, a day, a week. One precious night? I think they are probably older afterward, she thought. They use up something of themselves in trying to hold off what is coming to be themselves.

She wondered where he was now. The rain fell harder. The radio, between easy-listening tunes, said that rain was general all over South Louisiana, from Lafayette up as far as McComb. It ran down her windshield like tears, and Elizabeth shivered, recreating in her mind that winter rain long ago, in 1936, and car out of control like the man within it, hurtling toward a concrete bridge abutment so recently completed by workers for the WPA. To end his agony, to defeat the woman who had hurt him already beyond defeat, thinking not at all of the child who was waiting, who would wait for forty years for word of what had befallen them.

—Oh my God, can you forgive me, Elizabeth said aloud, unsure of whether the forgiveness she asked was God's. Or his. Wherever he was. Now, tonight. In the rain.

XXV

Dr. Aronson was driving. In the seat beside him Judge Soniat and Mr. Journé sat silent. In the rear seat Father Veulon watched his breath fog the side window. He would try to get back to New Orleans tonight, rain or no rain. Even if he had to rent a car.

The car pulled up in front of the hospital. There were a number of cars there with the call letters of TV stations in New Orleans and Baton Rouge.

—Goddamn, Dr. Aronson said. —Excuse me, Father. Oh, the hell with excusing me. Those stinking vultures . . .

They sat wordless for a moment. —Vultures follow killers, Mr. Journé said.

—That's uncalled for, Judge Soniat said roughly.

—Don't push me, Michael, Mr. Journé said. —This isn't your courtroom . . .

Dr. Aronson shrugged. There was nothing to be done. He could see another clump of reporters around the side of the emergency entrance. —As well here as there, he said, and opened his door.

The rain was coming in gusts now, and the men ran clumsily under the portico of the hospital, pushing past reporters who shouted questions at them, and followed them into the reception area, and down the corridor until two sheriff's deputies sent ahead by the Judge pushed them back roughly and kept them there in the reception area, where visitors and families of patients looked at them with astonishment.

They brushed the rain from their garments as they walked, still silent, saying nothing to one another.

The room was dark after the brightly-lit corridor, and for a moment they could not penetrate the darkness with nothing but the night-light above the bed and the glow of the instruments for illumination. Then they came to themselves, and saw Amy Lefebre kneeling beside the bed, her hand intertwined with the unresisting hand of Father O'Malley, whose eyes remained fixed on the crucifix which must have seemed as distant as the moon, if indeed, he could see it at all.

Father Veulon hurried to assist Miss Lefebre to her feet. It was obvious that she was not herself. Somehow she had hurt her hands, and they were bleeding. A nurse's aide took her outside, and even within the room, it was possible to hear her voice, and the muted sounds of the reporters down the corridor.

—. . . killing a saint . . . God forgive . . . bless me, father . . .

Judge Soniat exchanged a glance with Dr. Aronson. —Did you want me to read the order, doctor . . . ?

Dr. Aronson stared back at him. —I really think we can . . . do without that, Judge.

Father Veulon went to the bed and began to give Father O'Malley the sacrament of Extreme Unction. He placed the holy oil on his head, his hands, his feet. Father O'Malley stirred, his lips moved, as if they were searching for a voice to give them meaning. His eyes seemed to follow Father Veulon . . .

—Ah, son, Father O'Malley said, his voice hoarse, coming from a vast distance. —No, no, you must give that up. What worse crime is there . . . ?

Another voice came from him. —But . . . it's . . . it's what I *am*, Father. Isn't it . . . isn't love what . . . we're supposed to have?

—Not love . . . a thing that kills the spirit . . . the ruin of all fleshly ruins. My God, better you be with a poor innocent girl . . .

—No, I don't *want* that . . .

Father Veulon reddened, did his work quickly.

—I'm . . . through now, he said, making a final unconvincing sign of the cross over Father O'Malley, who had fallen silent again.

—All right, Doctor, Judge Soniat said, and the doctor moved toward the machines.

Mr. Journé moved toward the bed. He took the old man's hand in his, some of the chrism rubbing onto his fingers. —Go in peace, Cornelius, Mr. Journé said, tears running down his face. —I tried to . . . never mind. I'll be along in no time at all . . .

Father O'Malley roused again, his eyes turning toward Mr. Journé for sure. He looked at him for a long moment.

—For your penance, he said, —say ten Our Fathers, ten Hail Marys . . . and a good act of contrition . . . now . . .

While Dr. Aronson snapped switches, Mr. Journé knelt beside the bed. Behind him, Judge Soniat found himself kneeling, too, saying

—Oh, my God . . .

XXVI

When they came out, the reporters had been pushed outside by the deputies, and some had left rather than stand in the rain. There was one car with the call letters of a TV station in New Orleans owned by the Jesuits, and Father Veulon, after making cursory farewells, hastened to it, spoke with the driver briefly, and got in as it drove away.

Just beyond the portico, George Slack lay in the rain, coatless, a rill of blood running down his mouth where a deputy had struck him, mistaking him for an exceptionally obstreperous reporter. Beside him, Elizabeth knelt, wiping away the blood, telling him in a voice so soft that it could hardly be heard above the rustle of the rain, that not a word she had told him earlier was true, and that he had to try to get up now, try to get to the car. They had to go home.

Then there was only Judge Soniat and Mr. Journé left standing under the portico. The rain had let up, but it had not stopped. They stood speechless beside one another, hearing above the soft sound of the rain yet falling the louder sound of it dripping from the eaves of the hospital, from the trees all around, scuttling downward to earth through the drains. In the distance, a pair of headlights lanced through the darkness for a moment, and then was lost again in the gloom.

Judge Soniat cleared his throat and started to walk down the driveway. He paused for a moment and, without quite turning, looked backward at Mr. Journé.

—See you in court, Counselor, he said, and then walked on.

EVERY ACT WHATEVER OF MAN

The salient stylistic feature of this story is the use of multiple viewpoints through which the story of a dying priest unfolds. As the story opens, the brain-dead priest is repeating conversations from the confessional that involve some of the most respected people in a small South Louisiana town. Each major character has some relationship to the priest and is presented through a section (or sections) which explore or comment on the value and sanctity of the confessional, the right to terminate life (euthanasia and abortion), and the past as a guide to the present. Morality, religion, medicine, and the law come into play in dealing with the crisis caused by the exposing of sins, confessed and atoned for years before. In both the legal and medical professions, there are two viewpoints—old and young, past and present.

The medical viewpoint is expressed succintly by a nurse as she watches the old man "dying inch by inch" and kept alive by electrcnics. She reflects that "It [is] always the young doctors who order machine hookups in cases like this. The old doctors [having seen worse than death] have made their peace with death." The young doctors, she thinks, believe in "nothing whatever but their own skill and their capacity to develop new machines, new techniques, new machines to press death back farther and farther."

Through the reminiscing of Mr. Journe, a very old lawyer, the old priest comes alive as a person—one who had come to God through atonement for his part in a war of carnage and who had served God faithfully in the community. Mr. Journe is a traditionalist who sees the past as a means of measuring the present: "His study was Christendom, that long wave of meaning which had reached from Jerusalem to Byzantium, from Aachen to St. Stephanie, Louisiana." He thinks of his calling as a lawyer, his one desire to see justice done; he thinks of all the suffering in the world—the "children destroyed by abortion, whose half-formed bodies and slumbering souls had been, by the millions, given over to a holocaust as violent, vicious—and legal—as that of the Nazis against God's Chosen Ones." And finally, having been appointed by the court as the advocate of the priest, he thinks of other legalized killing—that of the terminally ill, remembering a time when death came to everyone naturally. His first legal step brushed off by the judge, he speaks from his heart, as a human being. "I feel like some poor devil of an advocate before a Nazi court arguing that you shouldn't kill or maim a feeble-minded woman. . . ." He sums up his case with "It's not death with dignity you want. It's silence." But the modern view, represented by Judge Sonait and the young lawyer from Baton Rouge, prevails: "wonderful old man, in the closing hours of his life, jeopardizing the very community and people he served, unable to support his life without the . . . marvelous mechanisms at the hospital. . . . If he could he'd say, he'd say this shouldn't go on . . . better death with dignity."

This story captures the essence of both mind and place of this South Louisiana town without sacrificing universal for local concerns. Through the depiction of man as a creature in time wrestling with moral and ethical problems, the events transcend the people and problems of St. Stephanie, Louisiana.

Ellen Gilchrist

(1935-   )

Born February 20, 1935, in Vicksburg, Mississippi, Ellen Gilchrist was graduated in 1967 from Millsaps College and did graduate work at the University of Arkansas in 1976. Gilchrist lived for several years in New Orleans; out of that experience came her first volume of short stories *In the Land of Dreamy Dreams* (1981). Her only novel *The Annunciation* (1983) was a Book-of-the-Month selection in Sweden and an alternate in this country. *Victory Over Japan* (1984), another collection of short fiction, won the American Book Award in 1985.

The story printed below is taken from *In the Land of Dreamy Dreams*. In her ironical view of New Orleans life, Gilchrist is evocative of Pulitzer Prize winner John Kennedy Toole; in her penchant for shock, she is close to Flannery O'Connor but lacks her moral center.

Rich*

Ellen Gilchrist

Tom and Letty Wilson were rich in everything. They were rich in friends because Tom was a vice-president of the Whitney Bank of New Orleans and liked doing business with his friends, and because Letty was vice-president of the Junior League of New Orleans and had her picture in *Town and Country* every year at the Symphony Ball.

The Wilsons were rich in knowing exactly who they were because every year from Epiphany to Fat Tuesday they flew the beautiful green and gold and purple flag outside their house that meant that Letty had been queen of the Mardi Gras the year she was a debutante. Not that Letty was foolish enough to take the flag seriously.

Sometimes she was even embarrassed to call the yardman and ask him to come over and bring his high ladder.

"Preacher, can you come around on Tuesday and put up my flag?" she would ask.

"You know I can," the giant black man would answer. "I been saving time to put up your flag. I won't forget what a beautiful queen you made that year."

"Oh, hush, Preacher. I was a skinny little scared girl. It's a wonder I didn't fall off the balcony I was so scared. I'll see you on Monday." And Letty would think to herself what a big phony Preacher was and wonder when he was going to try to borrow some more money from them.

Tom Wilson considered himself a natural as a banker because he loved to gamble and wheel and deal. From the time he was a boy in a small Baptist town in Tennessee he had loved to play cards and match nickels and lay bets.

In high school he read *The Nashville Banner* avidly and kept an eye out for useful situations such as the lingering and suspenseful illnesses of Pope Pius.

"Let's get up a pool on the day the Pope will die," he would say to the football team, "I'll hold the bank." And because the Pope took a very long time to die with many close calls there were times when Tom was the richest left tackle in Franklin, Tennessee.

Tom had a favorite saying about money. He had read it in the *Reader's Digest* and attributed it to Andrew Carnegie. "Money," Tom would say, "is what you keep score with. Andrew Carnegie."

Another way Tom made money in high school was performing as an amateur magician at local birthday parties and civic events. He could pull a silver dollar or a Lucky Strike cigarette from an astonished six-year-old's ear or from his own left palm extract a seemingly endless stream of multicolored silk chiffon or cause an ordinary piece of clothesline to behave like an Indian cobra.

He got interested in magic during a convalescence from German measles in the sixth grade. He sent off for books of magic tricks and practiced for hours before his bedroom mirror, his quick clever smile flashing and his long fingers curling and uncurling from the sleeves of a black dinner jacket his mother had bought at a church bazaar and remade to fit him.

Tom's personality was too flamboyant for the conservative Whitney Bank, but he was cheerful and cooperative and when he made a mistake he had the ability to turn it into an anecdote.

"Hey, Fred," he would call to one of his bosses. "Come have lunch on me and I'll tell you a good one."

They would walk down St. Charles Avenue to where it crosses Canal and turns into Royal Street as it enters the French Quarter. They would walk into the crowded, humid excitement of the quarter, admiring the girls and watching the Yankee tourists sweat in their absurd spun-glass leisure suits, and turn into the side door of Antoine's or breeze past the maitre d' at Galatoire's or Brennan's.

When a red-faced waiter in funereal black had seated them at a choice table, Tom would loosen his Brooks Brothers' tie, turn his handsome brown eyes on his guest, and begin.

"That bunch of promoters from Dallas talked me into backing an idea to videotape all the historic sights in the quarter and rent the tapes to hotels to show on closed-circuit television. Goddamit, Fred, I could just see those fucking tourists sitting around their hotel rooms on rainy days ordering from room service and taking in the Cabildo and the Presbytere on T.V." Tom laughed delightedly and waved his glass of vermouth at an elegantly dressed couple walking by the table.

"Well, they're barely breaking even on that one, and now they want to buy up a lot of soft porn movies and sell them to motels in Jefferson Parish. What do you think? Can we stay with them for a few more months?"

Then the waiter would bring them cold oysters on the half shell and steaming pompano *en papillote* and a wine steward would serve them a fine Meursault or a Piesporter, and Tom would listen to whatever advice he was given as though it were the most intelligent thing he had ever heard in his life.

Of course he would be thinking, "You stupid, impotent son of a bitch. You scrawny little frog bastard, I'll buy and sell you before it's over. I've got more brains in my balls than the whole snotty bunch of you."

"Tom, you always throw me off my diet," his friend would say, "damned if you don't."

"I told Letty the other day," Tom replied, "that she could just go right ahead and spend her life worrying about being buried in her wedding dress, but I didn't hustle my way to New Orleans all the way from north Tennessee to eat salads and melba toast. Pass me the French bread."

Letty fell in love with Tom the first time she laid eyes on him. He came to Tulane on a football scholarship and charmed his way into a fraternity of wealthy New Orleans boys famed for its drunkenness and its wild practical jokes. It was the same old story. Even the second, third, and fourth generation blue bloods of New Orleans need an infusion of new genes now and then.

The afternoon after Tom was initiated he arrived at the fraternity house with two Negro porters and sat in the low-hanging branches of a live oak tree overlooking Henry Clay Avenue directing them in painting an official-looking yellow-and-white-striped pattern on the street in front of the property. "D-R-U-N-K," he yelled to his painters, holding on to the enormous limb with one hand and pushing his black hair out of his eyes with the other. "Paint it to say D-R-U-N-K   Z-O-N-E."

Letty stood near the tree with a group of friends watching him. He was wearing a blue shirt with the sleeves rolled up above his elbows, and a freshman beanie several sizes too small was perched on his head like a tipsy sparrow.

"I'm wearing this goddamn beanie forever," Tom yelled. "I'm wearing this beanie until someone brings me a beer," and Letty took the one she was holding and walked over to the tree and handed it to him.

One day a few weeks later, he commandeered a Bunny Bread truck while it was parked outside the fraternity house making a delivery. He picked up two friends and drove the truck madly around the Irish Channel, throwing fresh loaves of white and whole-wheat and rye bread to the astonished housewives.

"Steal from the rich, give to the poor," Tom yelled, and his companions gave up trying to reason with him and helped him yell.

"Free bread, free cake," they yelled, handing out powdered doughnuts and sweet rolls to a gang of kids playing baseball on a weed covered vacant lot.

They stopped off at Darby's, an Irish bar where Tom made bets on races and football games, and took on some beer and left off some cinnamon rolls.

"Tom, you better go turn that truck in before they catch you," Darby advised, and Tom's friends agreed, so they drove the truck to the second-precinct police headquarters and turned themselves in. Tom used up half a year's allowance paying the damages, but it made his reputation.

In Tom's last year at Tulane a freshman drowned during a hazing accident at the Southern Yacht Club, and the event frightened Tom. He had never liked the boy and had suspected him of being involved with the queers and nigger lovers who hung around the philosophy department and the school newspaper. The boy had gone to prep school in the East and brought weird-looking girls to rush parties. Tom had resisted the temptation to blackball him as he was well connected in uptown society.

After the accident, Tom spent less time at the fraternity house and more time with Letty, whose plain sweet looks and expensive clothes excited him.

"I can't go in the house without thinking about it," he said to Letty. "All we were doing was making them swim from pier to pier carrying martinis. I did it fifteen times the year I pledged."

"He should have told someone he couldn't swim very well," Letty answered. "It was an accident. Everyone knows it was an accident. It wasn't your fault." And Letty cuddled up close to him on the couch, breathing as softly as a cat.

Tom had long serious talks with Letty's mild, alcoholic father, who held a seat on the New Stock Exchange, and in the spring of the year Tom and Letty were married in the Cathedral of Saint Paul with twelve bridesmaids, four flower girls, and seven hundred guests. It was pronounced a marriage made in heaven, and Letty's mother ordered masses said in Rome for their happiness.

They flew to New York on the way to Bermuda and spent their wedding night at the Sherry Netherland Hotel on Fifth Avenue. At least half a dozen of Letty's friends had lost their virginity at the same address, but the trip didn't seem prosaic to Letty.

She stayed in the bathroom a long time gazing at her plain face in the oval mirror and tugging at the white lace nightgown from the Lylian Shop, arranging it now to cover, now to reveal her small breasts. She crossed herself in the mirror, suddenly giggled, then walked out into the blue and gold bedroom as though she been going to bed with men every night of her life. She had been up until three the night before reading a book on sexual intercourse. She offered her small unpainted mouth to Tom. Her pale hair smelled of Shalimar and carnations and candles. Now she was safe. Now life would begin .

"Oh, I love you, I love, I love, I love you," she whispered over and over. Tom's hands touching her seemed a strange and exciting passage that would carry her simple dreamy existence to a reality she had never encountered. She had never dreamed anyone so interesting would marry her.

Letty's enthusiasm and her frail body excited him, and he made love to her several times before he asked her to remove her gown.

The next day they breakfasted late and walked for a while along the avenue. In the afternoon Tom explained to his wife what her clitoris was and showed her some of the interesting things it was capable of generating, and before the day was out Letty became the first girl in her crowd to break the laws of God and the Napoleonic Code by indulging in oral intercourse.

Fourteen years went by and the Wilsons' luck held. Fourteen years is a long time to stay lucky even for rich people who don't cause trouble for anyone.

Of course, even among the rich there are endless challenges, unyielding limits, rivalry, envy, quirks of fortune. Letty's father grew increasingly incompetent and sold his seat on the exchange, and Letty's irresponsible brothers went to work throwing away the money in Las Vegas and L.A. and Zurich and Johannesburg and Paris and anywhere they could think of to fly to with their interminable strings of mistresses.

Tom envied them their careless, thoughtless lives and he was annoyed that they controlled their own money while Letty's was tied up in some mysterious trust, but he kept his thoughts to himself as he did his obsessive irritation over his growing obesity.

"Looks like you're putting on a little weight there," a friend would observe.

"Good, good," Tom would say, "makes me look like a man. I got a wife to look at if I want to see someone who's skinny."

He stayed busy gambling and hunting and fishing and being the life of the party at the endless round of dinners and cocktail parties and benefits and Mardi Gras functions that consume the lives of the Roman Catholic hierarchy that dominates the life of the city that care forgot.

Letty was preoccupied with the details of their domestic life and her work in the community. She took her committees seriously and actually believed that the work she did made a difference in the lives of other people.

The Wilsons grew rich in houses. They lived in a large Victorian house in the Garden District, and across Lake Pontchartrain they had another Victorian house to stay in on the weekends, with a private beach surrounded by old moss-hung oak trees. Tom bought a duck camp in Plaquemines Parish and kept an apartment in the French Quarter in case one of his business friends fell in love with his secretary and needed someplace to be alone with her. Tom almost never used the apartment himself. He was rich in being satisfied to sleep with his own wife.

The Wilsons were rich in common sense. When five years of a good Catholic marriage went by and Letty inexplicably never became pregnant, they threw away their thermometers and ovulation charts and litmus paper and went down to the Catholic adoption agency and adopted a baby girl with curly black hair and hazel eyes. Everyone declared she looked exactly like Tom. The Wilsons named the little girl Helen and, as the months went by, everyone swore she even walked and talked like Tom.

At about the same time Helen came to be the Wilsons' little girl, Tom grew interested in raising Labrador retrievers. He had large wire runs with concrete floors built in the side yard for the dogs to stay in when he wasn't training them on the levee or at the park lagoon. He used all the latest methods for training Labs, including an electric cattle prod given to him by Chalin Perez himself and live ducks supplied by a friend on the Audubon Park Zoo Association Committee.

"Watch this, Helen," he would call to the little girl in the stroller, "watch this." And he would throw a duck into the lagoon with its secondary feathers neatly clipped on the left side and its feet tied loosely together, and one of the Labs would swim out into the water and carry it safely back and lay flat his feet.

As so often happens when childless couples are rich in common sense, before long Letty gave birth to a little boy, and then to twin boys, and finally to another little Wilson girl. The Wilsons became so rich in children the neighbors all lost count.

"Tom," Letty said, curling up close to him in the big walnut bed, "Tom, I want to talk to you about something important." The new baby girl was three months old. "Tom I want to talk to Father Delahoussaye and ask him if we can use some birth control. I think we have all the children we need for now.

Tom put his arms around her and squeezed her until he wrinkled her new green linen B. H. Wragge, and she screamed for mercy.

"Stop it," she said, "be serious. Do you think it's all right to do that?"

Then Tom agreed with her that they had had all the luck with children they needed for the present, and Letty made up her mind to call the cathedral and make an appointment. All her friends were getting dispensations so they would have time to do their work at the Symphony League and the Thrift Shop and the

New Orleans Museum Association and the PTAs of the private schools.

All the Wilson children were in good health except Helen. The pediatricians and psychiatrists weren't certain what was wrong with Helen. Helen couldn't concentrate on anything. She didn't like to share and she went through stages of biting other children at the Academy of the Sacred Heart of Jesus.

Letty felt like she spent half her life sitting in offices talking to people about Helen. The office she sat in most often belonged to Dr. Zander. She sat there twisting her rings and avoiding looking at the box of Kleenex on Dr. Zander's desk. It made her feel like she was sleeping in a dirty bed even to think of plucking a Kleenex from Dr. Zander's container and crying in a place where strangers cried. She imagined his chair was filled all day with women weeping over terrible and sordid things like their husbands running off with their secretaries or their children not getting into the right clubs and colleges.

"I don't know what we're going to do with her next," Letty said, "if we let them hold her back a grade it's just going to make her more self-conscious than ever."

"I wish we knew about her genetic background. You people have pull with the sisters. Can't you find out?"

"Tom doesn't want to find out. He says we'll just be opening a can of worms. He gets embarrassed even talking about Helen's problem."

"Well," said Dr. Zander, crossing his short legs and settling his steel-rimmed glasses on his nose like a tiny bicycle stuck on a hill, "let's start her on Dexedrine."

So Letty and Dr. Zander and Dr. Mullins and Dr. Pickett and Dr. Smith decided to try an experiment. They decided to give Helen five milligrams of Dexedrine every day of twenty days each month, taking her off the drugs for ten days in between.

"Children with dyslexia react to drugs strangely," Dr. Zander said. "If you give them tranquilizers it peps them up, but if you give them Ritalin or Dexedrine it calms them down and makes them able to think straight."

"You may have to keep her home and have her tutored on the days she is off the drug," he continued, "but the rest of the time she should be easier to live with." And he reached over and patted

Letty on the leg and for a moment she thought it might all turn out all right after all.

Helen stood by herself on the playground of the beautiful old pink-brick convent with its drooping wrought-iron balconies covered with ficus. She was watching the girl she liked talking with some other girls who were playing jacks. All the little girls wore blue-and-red-plaid skirts and navy blazers or sweaters. They looked like a disorderly marching band. Helen was waiting for the girl, whose name was Lisa, to decide if she wanted to go home with her after school and spend the afternoon. Lisa's mother was divorced and worked downtown in a department store, so Lisa rode the streetcar back and forth from school and could go anywhere she liked until 5:30 in the afternoon. Sometimes she went home with Helen so she wouldn't have to ride the streetcar. Then Helen would be so excited the hours until school let out would seem to last forever.

Sometimes Lisa liked her and wanted to go home with her and other times she didn't, but she was always nice to Helen and let her stand next to her in lines.

Helen watched Lisa walking toward her. Lisa's skirt was two inches shorter than those of any of the other girls, and she wore high white socks that made her look like a skater. She wore a silver identification bracelet and Revlon nail polish.

"I'll go home with you if you get your mother to take us to get an Icee," Lisa said. "I was going last night but my mother's boyfriend didn't show up until after the place closed so I was going to walk to Manny's after school. Is that O.K.?"

"I think she will," Helen said, her eyes shining. "I'll go call her up and see."

"Naw, let's just go swing. We can ask her when she comes." Then Helen walked with her friend over to the swings and tried to be patient waiting for her turn.

The Dexedrine helped Helen concentrate and it helped her get along better with other people, but it seemed to have an unusual side effect. Helen was chubby and Dr. Zander had led the Wilsons to believe the drug would help her lose weight, but instead she grew ever fatter. The Wilsons were afraid to force her to stop eating for fear they would make her nervous, so they tried to reason with her.

"Why can't I have any ice cream?" she would say. "Daddy is fat and he eats all the ice cream he wants." She was leaning up against Letty, stroking her arm and petting the baby with her other hand. They were in an upstairs sitting room with the afternoon sun streaming in through the French windows. Everything in the room was decorated with different shades of blue, and the curtains were white with old-fashioned blue-and-white-checked ruffles.

"You can have ice cream this evening after dinner," Letty said, "I just want you to wait a few hours before you have it. Won't you do that for me?"

"Can I hold the baby for a while?" Helen asked, and Letty allowed her to sit in the rocker and hold the baby and rock it furiously back and forth crooning to it.

"Is Jennifer beautiful, Mother?" Helen asked.

"She's O.K., but she doesn't have curly black hair like you. She just has plain brown hair. Don't you see, Helen, that's why we want you to stop eating between meals, because you're so pretty and we don't want you to get too fat. Why don't you go outside and play with Tim and try not to think about ice cream so much?"

"I don't care," Helen said, "I'm only nine years old and I'm hungry. I want you to tell the maids to give me some ice cream now," and she handed the baby to her mother and ran out of the room.

The Wilsons were rich in maids, and that was a good thing because there were all those children to be taken care of and cooked for and cleaned up after. The maids didn't mind taking care of the Wilson children all day. The Wilsons' house was much more comfortable than the ones they lived in, and no one cared whether they worked very hard or not as long as they showed up on time so Letty could get to her meetings. The maids left their own children with relatives or at home watching television, and when they went home at night they liked them much better than if they had spent the whole day with them.

The Wilson house had a wide white porch across the front and down both sides. It was shaded by enormous oak trees and furnished with swings and wicker rockers. In the afternoons the maids would sit on the porch and other maids from around the neighborhood would come up pushing prams and strollers and the children would all play together on the porch and in the yard. Sometimes the maids fixed lemonade and the children would sell it to passersby from a little stand.

The maids hated Helen. They didn't care whether she had dyslexia or not. All they knew was that she was a lot of trouble to take care of. One minute she would be as sweet as pie and cuddle up to them and say she loved them and the next minute she wouldn't do anything they told her.

"You're a nigger, nigger, nigger, and my mother said I could cross St. Charles Avenue if I wanted to," Helen would say, and the maids would hold their lips together and look into each other's eyes.

One afternoon the Wilson children and their maids were sitting on the porch after school with some of the neighbors' children and maids. The baby was on the porch in a bassinet on wheels and a new maid was looking out for her. Helen was in the biggest swing and was swinging as high as she could go so that none of the other children could get in the swing with her.

"Helen," the new maid said, "it's Tim's turn in the swing. You been swinging for fifteen minutes while Tim's been waiting. You be a good girl now and let Tim have a turn. You too big to act like that."

"You're just a high yeller nigger," Helen called, "and you can't make me do anything." And she swung up higher and higher.

This maid had never had Helen call her names before and she had a quick temper and didn't put up with children calling her a nigger. She walked over to the swing and grabbed the chain and stopped it from moving.

"You say you're sorry for that, little fat honky white girl," she said, and made as if to grab Helen by the arms, but Helen got away and started running, calling over her shoulder, "nigger, can't make me do anything."

She was running and looking over her shoulders and she hit the bassinet and it went rolling down the brick stairs so fast none of the maids or children could stop it. It rolled down the stairs and threw the baby onto the sidewalk and the blood from the baby's head began to move all over the concrete like a little ruby lake.

The Wilsons' house was on Philip Street, a street so rich it even had its own drugstore. Not some tacky chain drugstore with everything on special all the time, but a cute drugstore made out of a frame bungalow with gingerbread trim. Everything inside cost twice as much as it did in a regular drugstore, and the grown people could order any kind of drugs they needed and a green Mazda pickup would bring them right over. The children had to get their drugs from a fourteen-year-old pusher in Audubon Park named Leroi, but they could get all the ice cream and candy and chewing gum they wanted from the drugstore and charge it to their parents.

No white adults were at home in the houses where the maids worked so they sent the children running to the drugstore to bring the druggist to help with the baby. They called the hospital and ordered an ambulance and they called several doctors and they called Tom's bank. All the children who were old enough ran to the drugstore except Helen. Helen sat on the porch steps staring down at the baby with the maids hovering over it like swans, and she was crying and screaming and beating her hands against her head. She was in one of the periods when she couldn't have Dexedrine. She screamed and screamed, but none of the maids had time to help her. They were too busy with the baby.

"Shut up, Helen," one of the maids called. "Shut up that goddamn screaming. This baby is about to die."

A police car and the local patrol service drove up. An ambulance arrived and the yard filled with people. The druggist and one of the maids rode off in the ambulance with the baby. The crowd in the yard swarmed and milled and swam before Helen's eyes like a parade.

Finally they stopped looking like people and just looked like spots of color on the yard. Helen ran up the stairs and climbed under her cherry four-poster bed and pulled her pillows and her eiderdown comforter under it with her. There were cereal boxes and an empty ice cream carton and half a tin of English cookies under the headboard. Helen was soaked with sweat and her little Lily playsuit was tight under the arms and cut into her flesh. Helen rolled up in the comforter and began to dream the dream of the heavy clouds. She dreamed she was praying, but the beads of the rosary slipped through her fingers so quickly she couldn't catch them and it was cold in the church and beautiful and fragrant, then dark, then light, and Helen was rolling in the heavy clouds that rolled her like biscuit dough. Just as she was about to suffocate they rolled her face up to the blue air above the clouds. Then Helen was a pink kite floating above the houses at evening. In the yards children were playing and fathers were driving up and baseball games were beginning and the sky turned gray and closed upon the city like a lid.

And now the baby is alone with Helen in her room and the door is locked and Helen ties the baby to the table so it won't fall off.

"Hold still, Baby, this will just be a little shot. This won't hurt much. This won't take a minute." And the baby is still and Helen begins to work on it.

Letty knelt down beside the bed. "Helen, please come out from under there. No one is mad at you. Please come out and help me, Helen. I need you to help me."

Helen held on tighter to the slats of the bed and squeezed her eyes shut and refused to look at Letty.

Letty climbed under the bed to touch the child. Letty was crying and her heart had an anchor in it that kept digging in and sinking deeper and deeper.

Dr. Zander came into the bedroom and knelt beside the bed and began to talk to Helen. Finally he gave up being reasonable and wiggled his small gray-suit body under the bed and Helen was lost in the area of arms that tried to hold her.

Tom was sitting in the bank president's office trying not to let Mr. Saunders know how much he despised him or how much it hurt and mattered to him to be listening to a lecture. Tom thought he was too old to have to listen to lectures. He was tired and he wanted a drink and he wanted to punch the bastard in the face.

"I know, I know," he answered, "I can take care of it. Just give me a month or two. You're right. I'll take care of it."

And he smoothed the pants of his cord suit and waited for the rest of the lecture.

A man came into the room without knocking. Tom's secretary was behind him.

"Tom, I think your baby has had an accident. I don't know any details. Look, I've called for a car. Let me go with you."

Tom ran up the steps of his house and into the hallway full of neighbors and relatives. A girl in a tennis dress touched him on the arm, someone handed him a drink. He ran up the winding stairs to Helen's room. He stood in the doorway. He could see Letty's shoes sticking out from under the bed. He could hear Dr. Zander talking. He couldn't go near them.

"Letty," he called, "Letty, come here, my god, come out from there."

No one came to the funeral but the family. Letty wore a plain dress she would wear any day and the children all wore their school clothes.

The funeral was terrible for the Wilsons, but afterward they went home and all the people from the Garden District and from all over town started coming over to cheer them up. It looked like the biggest cocktail party ever held in New Orleans. It took four rented butlers just to serve the drinks. Everyone wanted to get in on the Wilsons' tragedy.

In the months that followed the funeral Tom began to have sinus headaches for the first time in years. He was drinking a lot and smoking again. He was allergic to whiskey, and when he woke up in the morning his nose and head was so full of phlegm he had to vomit before he could think straight.

He began to have trouble with his vision.

One November day the high yellow windows of the Shell Oil Building all turned their eyes upon him as he stopped at the corner of Poydras and Carondelet to wait for a streetlight, and he had to pull the car over to a curb and talk to himself for several minutes before he could drive on.

He got back all the keys to his apartment so he could go there and be alone and think. One afternoon he left work at two o'clock and drove around Jefferson Parish all afternoon drinking Scotch and eating potato chips.

Not as many people at the bank wanted to go out to lunch with him anymore. They were sick and tired of pretending his expensive mistakes were jokes.

One night Tom was gambling at the Pickwick Club with a poker group and a man jokingly accused him of cheating. Tom jumped up from the table, grabbed the man and began hitting him with his fists. He hit the man in the mouth and knocked out his new gold inlays.

"You dirty little goddamn bond peddler, you son of a bitch! I'll kill you for that," Tom yelled, and it took four waiters to hold him while the terrified man made his escape. The next morning Tom resigned from the club.

He started riding the streetcar downtown to work so he wouldn't have to worry about driving his car home if he got drunk. He was worrying about money and he was worrying about his gambling debts, but most of the time he was thinking about Helen. She looked so much like him that he believed people would think she was his illegitimate child. The more he tried to talk himself into believing the baby's death was an accident, the more obstinate his mind became.

The Wilson children were forbidden to take the Labs out of the kennels without permission. One afternoon Tom came home earlier than usual and found Helen sitting in the open door of one of the kennels playing with a half-grown litter of puppies. She was holding one of the puppies and the others were climbing all around her and spilling out onto the grass. She held the puppy by its forelegs, making it dance in the air, then letting it drop. Then she would gather it in her arms and hold it tight and sing to it.

Tom walked over to the kennel and grabbed her by an arm and began to paddle her as hard as he could.

"Goddamn you, what are you trying to do? You know you aren't supposed to touch those dogs. What in the hell do you think you're doing?"

Helen was too terrified to scream. The Wilsons never spanked their children for anything.

"I didn't do anything to it. I was playing with it," she sobbed.

Letty and the twins came running out of the house and when Tom saw Letty he stopped hitting Helen and walked in through the kitchen door and up the stairs to the bedroom. Letty gave the children to the cook and followed him.

Tom stood by the bedroom window trying to think of something to say to Letty. He kept his back turned to her and he was making a nickel disappear with his left hand. He thought of himself at Tommie Keenen's birthday party wearing his black coat and hat and doing his famous rope trick. Mr. Keenen had given him fifteen dollars. He remembered sticking the money in his billfold.

"My god, Letty, I'm sorry. I don't know what the shit's going on. I thought she was hurting the dog. I know I shouldn't have hit her and there's something I need to tell you about the bank. Kennington is getting sacked. I may be part of the housecleaning."

"Why didn't you tell me before? Can't Daddy do anything?"

"I don't want him to do anything. Even if it happens it doesn't have anything to do with me. It's just bank politics. We'll say I quit. I want to get out of there anyway. That fucking place is driving me crazy."

Tom put the nickel in his pocket and closed the bedroom door. He could hear the maid down the hall comforting Helen. He didn't give a fuck if she cried all night. He walked over to Letty and put his arms around her. He smelled like he'd been drinking for a week. He reached under her dress and pulled down her pantyhose and her underpants and began kissing her face and hair while she stood awkwardly with the pants and hose around her feet like a halter. She was trying to cooperate.

She forgot that Tom smelled like sweat and whiskey. She was thinking about the night they were married. Every time they made love Letty pretended it was that night. She had spent thousands of nights in a bridal suite at the Sherry Netherland Hotel in New York City.

Letty lay on the walnut bed leaning into a pile of satin pillows and twisting a gold bracelet around her wrist. She could hear the children playing outside. She had a headache and her stomach was queasy, but she was afraid to take a Valium or an aspirin. She was waiting for the doctor to call her back and tell her if she was pregnant. She already knew what he was going to say.

Tom came into the room and sat by her on the bed.

"What's wrong?"

"Nothing's wrong. Please don't do that. I'm tired."

"Something's wrong."

"Nothing's wrong. Tom, please leave me alone."

Tom walked out through the French windows and onto a little balcony that overlooked the play yard and the dog runs. Sunshine flooded Philip Street, covering the houses and trees and dogs and children with a million volts a minute. It flowed down to hide in the roots of trees, glistening on the cars, baking the street, and lighting Helen's rumpled hair where she stooped over the puppy. She was singing a little song. She had made up the song she was singing.

"The baby's dead. The baby's dead. The baby's gone to heaven."

"Jesus God," Tom muttered. All up and down Philip Street fathers were returning home from work. A jeep filled with teenagers came tearing past and threw a beer can against the curb.

Six or seven pieces of Tom's mind sailed out across the street and stationed themselves along the power line that zigzagged back and forth along Philip Street between the live oak trees.

The pieces of his mind sat upon the power line like a row of black starlings. They looked him over.

Helen took the dog out of the buggy and dragged it over to the kennel.

"Jesus Christ," Tom said, and the pieces of his mind flew back to him as swiftly as they had flown away and entered his eyes and ears and nostrils and arranged themselves in their proper places like parts of a phrenological head.

Tom looked at his watch. It said 6:15. He stepped back into the bedroom and closed the French windows. A vase of huge roses from the garden hid Letty's reflection in the mirror.

"I'm going to the camp for the night. I need to get away. Besides, the season's almost over."

"All right," Letty answered. "Who are you going with?"

"I think I'll take Helen with me. I haven't paid any attention to her for weeks."

"That's good," Letty said, "I really think I'm getting a cold. I'll have a tray up for supper and try to get some sleep."

Tom moved around the room, opening drawers and closets and throwing some gear into a canvas duffel bag. He changed into his hunting clothes.

He removed the guns he needed from a shelf in the upstairs den and cleaned them neatly and thoroughly and zipped them into their carriers.

"Helen," he called from the downstairs porch. "Bring the dog in the house and come get on some play clothes. I'm going to take you to the duck camp with me. You can take the dog."

"Can we stop and get beignets?" Helen called back, coming running at the invitation.

"Sure we can, honey. Whatever you like. Go get packed. We'll leave as soon as dinner is over."

It was past 9:00 at night. They crossed the Mississippi River from the New Orleans side on the last ferry going to Algier's Point. There was an offshore breeze and a light rain fell on the old brown river. The Mississippi River smelled like the inside of a nigger cabin, powerful and fecund. The smell came in Tom's mouth until he felt he could chew it.

He leaned over the railing and vomited. He felt better and walked back to the red Chevrolet pickup he had given himself for a birthday present. He thought it was chic for a banker to own a pickup.

Helen was playing with the dog, pushing him off the seat and laughing when he climbed back on her lap. She had a paper bag of doughnuts from the French Market and was eating them and licking the powdered sugar from her fingers and knocking the dog off the seat.

She wasn't the least bit sleepy.

"I'm glad Tim didn't get to go. Tim was bad at school that's why he had to stay home, isn't it? The sisters called Momma. I don't like Tim. I'm glad I got to go by myself." She stuck her fat arms out the window and rubbed Tom's canvas hunting jacket. "This coat feels hard. It's all dirty. Can we go up in the cabin and talk to the pilot?"

"Sit still, Helen."

"Put the dog in the back, he's bothering me." She bounced up and down on the seat. "We're going to the duck camp. We're going to the duck camp."

The ferry docked. Tom drove the pickup onto the blacktop road past the city dump and on into Plaquemines Parish.

They drove into the brackish marshes that fringe the Gulf of Mexico where it extends in ragged fingers along the coast below and to the east of New Orleans. As they drove closer to the sea the hardwoods turned to palmetto and water oak and willow.

The marshes were silent. Tom could smell the glasswort and black mangrove, the oyster and shrimp boats.

He wondered if it were true that children and dogs could penetrate a man's concealment, could know him utterly.

Helen leaned against his coat and prattled on.

In the Wilson house on Philip Street Tim and the twins were cuddled up by Letty, hearing one last story before they went to bed.

A blue wicker tray held the remains of the children's hot chocolate. The china cups were a confirmation present sent to Letty from Limoges, France.

Now she was finishing reading a wonderful story by Ludwig Bemelmans about a little convent girl in Paris named Madeline who reforms the son of the Spanish ambassador, putting an end to his terrible habit of beheading chickens on a miniature guillotine.

Letty was feeling better. She had decided God was just trying to make up to her for Jennifer.

The camp was a three-room wooden shack built on pilings out over Bayou Lafourche, which runs through the middle of the parish.

The inside of the camp was casually furnished with old leather office furniture, hand-me-down tables and lamps, and a walnut poker table from Neiman-Marcus. Photographs of hunts and parties were tacked around the walls. Over the poker table were pictures of racehorses and their owners and an assortment of ribbons won in races.

Tom laid the guns down on the bar and opened a cabinet over the sink in the part of the room that served as a kitchen. The nigger hadn't come to clean up after the last party and the sink was piled with half-washed dishes. He found a clean glass and a bottle of Tanqueray gin and sat down behind the bar.

Helen was across the room on the floor finishing the beignets and trying to coax the dog to come closer. He was considering it. No one had remembered to feed him.

Tom pulled a new deck of cards out of a drawer, broke the seal, and began to shuffle them.

Helen came and stood by the bar. "Show me a trick, Daddy. Make the queen disappear. Show me how to do it."

"Do you promise not to tell anyone the secret? A magician never tells his secrets."

"I won't tell. Daddy, please show me, show me now."

Tom spread out the cards. He began to explain the trick.

"All right, you go here and here, then here. Then pick up these in just the right order, but look at the people while you do it, not at the cards."

"I'm going to do it for Lisa."

"She's going to beg you to tell the secret. What will you do then?"

"I'll tell her a magician never tells his secrets."

Tom drank the gin and poured some more.

"Now let me do it to you, Daddy."

"Not yet, Helen. Go sit over there with the dog and practice it where I can't see what you're doing. I'll pretend I'm Lisa and don't know what's going on."

Tom picked up the Kliengunther 7 mm. magnum rifle and shot the dog first, splattering its brains all over the door and walls. Without pausing, without giving her time to raise her eyes from the red and gray and black rainbow of the dog, he shot the little girl.

The bullet entered her head from the back. Her thick body rolled across the hardwood floor and lodged against a hat rack from Jody Mellon's old office in the Hibernia Bank Building. One of her arms landed on a pile of old *Penthouse* magazines and her disordered brain flung its roses north and east and south and west and rejoined the order from which it casually arose.

Tom put down the rifle, took a drink of the thick gin, and, carrying the pistol, walked out onto the pier through the kitchen door. Without removing his glasses or his hunting cap he stuck the .38 Smith and Wesson revolver against his palate and splattered his own head all over the new pier and the canvas covering of the Boston Whaler. His body struck the boat going down and landed in eight feet of water beside a broken crab trap left over from the summer.

A pair of deputies from the Plaquemines Parish sheriff's office found the bodies.

Everyone believed it was some terrible inexplicable mistake or accident.

No one believed that much bad luck could happen to a nice lady like Letty Dufrechou Wilson, who never hurt a flea or gave anyone a minute's trouble in her life.

No one believed that much bad luck could get together between the fifteenth week after Pentecost and the third week in Advent.

No one believed a man would kill his own little illegitimate dyslexic daughter just because she was crazy.

And no one, not even the district attorney of New Orleans, wanted to believe a man would shoot a $3,000 Labrador retriever sired by Super Chief out of Prestidigitation.

RICH

The narrator of this story comments satirically on the life style and values of a New Orleans Catholic society. Through deliberate word choices that bring out ironic contrast between narrator and author attitude (or words and meaning), she makes clear that this is a world with mixed-up values. Speaking as a detached observer, she draws a vivid picture of Tom and Letty Wilson and the world they epitomize. They are "rich"; they are "lucky"; they have "common sense."

Tom, a lucky Tennessee country boy who enters New Orleans society on a Tulane football scholarship, uses his "common sense" in joining a fraternity of wealthy New Orleans boys "famed for its drunkenness." His marriage to Letty, a rich socialite, is both common sensical and lucky: Letty's mother "ordered masses said in Rome" for their happiness, and he becomes a banker through her father's influence. When five years pass with no children, it is common sense to adopt a little girl (who looks almost exactly like Tom and later walks and talks like him), and "as so often happens when childless couples are rich in common sense," they soon become "rich" in children of their own. Agreeing that Letty is neglecting her club work because of all her "luck" in having babies, Tom encourages her to do as her friends have done—get permission from the Church to use birth control. When he acquires Labrador retrievers, he is sensible in using "all the latest methods for training Labs, including an electric cattle prod given him by Chalin Perez."

They continue to show common sense when the psychiatrist suggests examining the genetic background of their dyslexic adopted child: Letty innocently quotes Tom: " We'd just be opening a can of worms." Sitting in the doctor's office, she thinks of women weeping over "terrible and sordid things like husbands running off with secretaries or their children not getting into the right clubs."

Their "luck" holds fourteen years; then the adopted child in one of her temper tantrums accidentally kills the baby, and the parents being away, the maids run to the nice neighborhood drugstore for help. (In this drugstore "grown people could order any kind of drugs they needed, but the children had to get their drugs from a fourteen-year-old pusher in Audubon Park.") After the funeral, "all the people from all over the Garden District and from all over town came to cheer them up . . . [at] the biggest cocktail party ever held in New Orleans."

Finally when his common sense and luck are gone, Tom takes his gun, dog, and adopted daughter to his camp in Lafourche Parish. The unemotional narrator, with a terrible difference between her words and the effect they achieve, relates: he takes his gun and "splatter[s] the dog's brains all over the door and walls" and almost simultaneously shoots the child: "One of her arms landed on a pile of old *Penthouse* magazines and her disordered brain flung its roses north and east and south and west." Then he "spattered his own head all over the new pier."

Their friends are shocked, but not for the expected reasons. It is not unbelievable that such a "mistake or accident" could happen but rather that it could happen "between the fifteenth week after Pentecost and the third week in August." It is not unbelievable that he could "kill his own little illegitimate daughter" but that he could kill her "just because she was crazy." It is not shocking that he could kill himself but that he could "shoot a $3,000 Labrador retriever sired by Super Chief out of Prestidigitation." The final irony is that the "infusion of new genes" thought to strengthen the blue blood line actually has a disastrous effect.

By use of ironic contrast, the author obliquely comments on the shallowness of a glittering world. Although she does not present the characters as having basic character flaws, (they are, in fact, nice people), she does satirize their weakness in blindly conforming to the expectations of society.

The New Orleans of this story is not the enchanted city of romance and legend, of tourist literature. Beneath the glitter, people live, make terrible mistakes, and suffer.

David Madden

(1933-)

Born in Knoxville, Tennessee, to James Helvy and Emile Merritt Madden, David Madden started writing at a very early age and by age fourteen had a literary agent. After graduation in 1951 from Knoxville High School, he attended the University of Tennessee but left school to travel and perform odd jobs. He served briefly in the Merchant Marines and in the army from 1953 to 1955. He holds a B. S. degree from the University of Tennessee and an M. A. from San Francisco State College and studied at Yale on a John Golden Fellowship. In 1957 he married Margaret Roberta Young by whom he has one son, Blake.

He has served on the faculty of a number of colleges and universities, including Appalachian State, Centre College, University of Louisville, Kenyon College, Ohio State, and University of North Carolina. Since 1968 he has been a teacher and writer-in-residence at Louisiana State University. He has published literary criticism and plays and has edited several books. He is well known for his unusually effective dramatic readings from his fiction.

His novels include *The Beautiful Greed, Cassandra Singing, Brothers in Confidence, Bijou, The Suicide's Wife, Pleasure Dome,* and *On the Big Wind.* He has also published two collections of short stories—*The Shadow Knows,* and *The New Orleans of Possibilities,* from which this selection is taken.

The New Orleans of Possibilities

David Madden

Rind mist prickling his nostrils, he crushed the orange slice against his palate, constricted his gullet to keep from swallowing too much of the surging juice at once, enjoying even the sting where his new pipe had burnt the tip of his tongue.

"Where did you get this orange?" Kenneth asked the woman at the next table whose smile as she had offered him the fruit had enhanced the shockingly sudden deliciousness of the juice.

"At the produce market down the street," said the man, realizing the woman had not heard Kenneth, enrapt as she obviously was in the first hour of the Sunday morning of lovers.

"I haven't had a real orange in years," Kenneth said to the woman, who turned toward him, the breeze blowing her hair across her eyes. She smiled again, *for* him now.

Eating the orange, section by section, Kenneth glanced at the lovers, who, in their felicity, had chosen more strawberries, bananas, black cherries, peaches, and oranges than their stomachs could hold, whose overflow of felicity and fruit had touched him. So it was not only in balmy breeze and Sunday morning sunlight that they basked.

New Orleans, the most romantic city of his imagination, the city in which he had once expected to realize so many possibilities, had become so routine, he had awakened in the Royal Sonesta this morning to a palpable, almost urgent impulse to do something slightly unusual. Having supper alone at Begue's last night, on the occasion of his thirty-sixth birthday, he had realized that except for Charleston he had seen—though only as a salesman can see— every American city he had ever wanted to see. Doubting there would ever be a necessity to go to Charleston and failing to imagine it as a vacation attraction 'for Helen and John made him sad. But up in the room, looking down on Bourbon Street, where he no longer felt safe walking at night, he had realized too that New Orleans, his favorite city even over San Francisco, had in his routine become almost as bland as an airport layover. And when the morning light woke him, he knew he had not felt merely the blues of a man away from home on his mid-passage birthday. He had projected his life to live in cities, and the cities were gone. Sipping *café au lait* with fifty tourists outside the Café du Monde and eating beignets had not quite met his criterion for something slightly unusual. The gift of the orange, the woman's smile, had.

The lovers left their table littered with fruit peelings, seeds, rinds, pits. Unable to sustain the shared moment in the breeze and sunlight, Kenneth walked toward the produce market, his system so unused to juice straight from the rind that he felt nauseated.

The second time he had come to New Orleans the heat, humidity, and pollution had been so intense he had seen the market from an air-conditioned touring bus with Helen and John. The first time, he had come alone to handle a new account and had confined his walking to Bourbon Street.

The mingled odors of fruits and vegetables were so intense that he tasted the market before he smelled it.

Walking under the long open-sided shed, down the narrow aisle between the stalls, Kenneth felt as if the bodies, faces, hands, and the fruit and vegetables were a palpitating morass that excited and delighted him, reminding him of his childhood birthday parties in Indiana. He bought pears, apples, peaches, bananas, a pineapple, strawberries, oranges, and tomatoes, and wondered what he would do with them. Appointments in Houston and Dallas lay between New Orleans and home. I may never *see* stuff like this again in my lifetime, he thought, smiling condescendingly at his isolated gesture.

Entering the lower end of the shed, he saw that this section was given over to a flea market. He wished Helen, who loved garage sales, could be there. The intriguingly slummy atmosphere of this part of the French Quarter, of the market, drew him among the tables, some of which were set up in the parking spaces. Bright old clothes hung from the barred windows of a discarded streetcar with Desire as its destination. Inside a high iron fence, tourists were being guided through the vast Old Mint building, recently restored after decades as a prison.

His mood fluctuated between revulsion at the sleaziness and excitement at possibilities. Looking at objects that ranged from cheap new pseudocraft products to genuine antiques, from trash to bizarre oddities of some value to collectors, he forgot the queasiness that *café au lait*, powdered-sugar-sprinkled beignets, and orange juice had induced. Realizing that he had fully acted on impulse to break routine and open himself to possibilities made him feel a sense of adventure, and a little anxiety made him reach for objects he had never imagined he would ever want to look at, much less buy and use and enjoy.

"For the man who has everything," Helen had said, presenting the pipe three days before his birthday. Now he had twelve pipes, only one of which got the use and care a pipe demands. And here, too, among the disgorgings of New Orleans attics were discarded pipes that perhaps someone here would be glad to smoke.

That a buyer had been imagined for each likely and unlikely object on disarrayed display intrigued him as much as the objects themselves. The snaggle-toothed old woman, who looked like a caricature of a witch, had sat in a foul-smelling room somewhere in this sprawling city and imagined a buyer for those rusty iron pots. Kenneth paid her three-fifty for the cast-iron corn-stick mold, so heavy it almost balanced the load of fruit in his other hand.

And that bearded man, whose underarm stench, palpable as flesh, reached across the table, had stooped among those coils of barbed wire and anchors and canoe paddles, seeing buyers clearly enough to load it all into the back of his VW van and haul it down here at daybreak. Kenneth passed on by the barbed wire.

And this spaced-out girl, dark circles under her eyes, veinless smooth hands trembling more visibly than the old woman's, had squatted in some chairless, mattress-strewn, windowless slave quarters off a courtyard as sump-smelling as a Venice canal, convincing herself someone would buy one or two or three of the old photographs she had foraged out of attics and basements and rooms of abandoned houses, old houses torn down, and trash cans where she had hoped perhaps to find edibles. Too flummoxed by such incomprehensible assumptions to move on, Kenneth stopped, stared down into the lopsided cardboard box into which the girl had dumped thousands of photographs, mostly snapshots muted in time's sepia tone.

The moist fruit had dampened the bag. He lifted and hugged it, damp side against his coat, and walked on among the 78-rpm records, the fabrics and shirts and blouses and dresses, the rings and buttons, the glass insulators, the Mississippi driftwood and cypress knees, the old comic books, the tables of unfocusable clutter, the neater displays of antique toys, the moldy books and *National Geographics* dating from the twenties, that Kenneth was too burdened to leaf through.

He made the rounds, continuing long after fatigue and nausea and the increasing heat and humidity had made him sluggish, as if to miss even scanning sight of any of this stuff would wake him in the middle of the night in Houston or Dallas or home in Chicago, regretful, with that gnawing sense of unfinished business. The peculiarness of such a premonition making him feel a need to assert his own control over his behavior, he turned away from the flimsier tables lined up alongside the streetcar named Desire, and with the phrase, *he retraced his steps,* consciously in his mind, went back the way he came.

Kenneth waited for a young man in overalls and wide-brimmed leather hat to pay for the photographs he had stuffed into his pockets.

"May I set these down a moment?" Kenneth looked at the dark circles around the girl's eyes. She nodded rapidly, unblinking.

He reached into the bulging box, asking, "How much are these?" to make conversation, for the girl made him uneasy. He picked one of the photographs gently from the clutter, as if handling someone's personal effects.

"Fifty cents a handful."

"You don't sell them one by one?"

"Fifty cents a handful."

Imagining the young man in overalls grabbing two fistfuls, cramming his pockets, crushing some of the photos, shocked Kenneth.

"Get out the pictures, Granny." His grandmother used to imitate the way he had said that when he was a boy. Then she would honor his new request and take the hat box down off the shelf in her closet and sit beside him on the couch and gently pick them one by one from the loose pile. He felt an urge to tell this girl what his grandmother said, to imitate *her* voice imitating his own, but even had she not stared at him, seeing nothing, he knew he wouldn't have told anybody.

His fingers webbed together to cradle his head, a man leans back in a high-backed straight chair, his foot braced on a white railing that runs blurred out of the edge of the photograph toward the end of the porch, getting thinner as it reaches his foot, the toe of the other foot touching the floor almost delicately. Someone caught his semicandid pose at the turn of the century. The locale was possibly the Garden District. Smiling, imagining his grandmother's response Kenneth placed the photograph back on top, trying to put it where he found it.

He picked up a raw recruit of the forties, saluting, mock-serious, his billed cap resting on his ears. On V-J Day was he in Times Square or beneath a white headstone in France? He laid it down.

Propped up in a hospital bed, a young woman in a lace-trimmed nightgown holds her newborn baby. The kind of shot Kenneth had once snapped himself.

A plump man in suspenders sits in his favorite chair under a fringed lamp on a stand, his delicately smoking cigar held between the fingers of his up-raised hand, at the ready.

An old man changes a tire on a road in arid hills, a little boy sitting on the running board. The man's wife probably took this one. Out West, on vacation.

An elementary school class against a freshly washed blackboard, half of the children smiling, half tight-lipped. Losing their baby teeth?

A child sits on a table, a birthday cake with three candles between its legs, presents heaped on both sides. Kenneth had one of himself at four, a similar pose.

A young man in a jogging outfit, his arms full of old record albums, stopped to glance over Kenneth's shoulder at a family in their backyard under a mimosa tree, a man in hammock, a child in diapers wearing a sailor hat, lifting the long handle of a lawn mower, a woman taking a bite from a piece of cake, an old man reaching for an apple from a tree, smiling for the camera.

"You want that one, sir?"

"I'm just looking."

"Mind if I take it?"

"No, go ahead."

"Fifty cents a handful," the girl said, with no more response to the young man than to Kenneth, who was feeling older than thirty-six the longer he stood there.

The young man obediently grabbed "a handful" and carefully slipped them into the pocket where he had found the fifty-cent piece.

Kenneth wondered whether older people had bought any of the pictures. As he picked them up at an increasingly faster tempo, his assumption that they came from many sources was confirmed. The faces from picture to picture bore no resemblance to each other, although a few that turned up in succession were in a sequence. They seemed to span decades, with many settings beyond New Orleans. Kenneth looked at her. Maybe she wanders in a trance like a gypsy from city to city, rummaging in trash cans. A free romantic life, for which he felt a fleeting envy, irrational not only because she looked like death warmed over, but because "wandering from city to city" described his own life.

A young man and his date pose in formals at a prom. Kenneth wondered whether the slim young man now had a pot belly.

A telephone operator of the forties, surprised, ruins a candid shot, shouting no, her hand thrust out to blot the camera eye.

Children, perhaps a Sunday school class, at a picnic, one boy in a swimsuit, looking straight up into the sky. Kenneth imagined an airplane.

A grinning young man opens the door of his new, perhaps his first, car, early fifties model.

A man behind a soda fountain, his hand on the nozzle, two girls having turned from their sodas to smile at-good ol' George, Kenneth imagined. I can remember cool soda fountains, said Kenneth, almost aloud. Helen would get a kick out of this one. They were just going out when we came in.

"I'd like to buy this one."

"Fifty cents a handful."

"No, just this one. Glad to pay fifty cents for this one."

"Look, man, I'd like to dump all of this, save me the hassle of lugging it back to the room. Take a handful, will you?"

"Why not?" He pushed together, like strewn bridge cards, enough to stack on his right palm.

As he slipped the stack into his coat pocket, she said, still not looking at him, not seeing him, "Take two—no extra charge."

That would be greedy, he started to say, but the comment seemed inappropriate even for her benumbed ears. He started aligning another stack.

"Look, man, like they aren't going to bite you."

"No, I just . . ." He wondered how, in such situations, such marginal people manage to make one feel inept, inferior.

Digging down with a kind of venal abandon, Kenneth dredged up an overflowing handful, noticing that one of those that spilled was a snapshot of a young man sucking in his belly, flexing his muscles, letting his pants drop over his hips below his navel, clenching teeth and bugging eyes that were the spitting image of his own. He smiled self-consciously, as if the girl, her hand still held out for the fifty cents, had discerned the resemblance in the same instant of surprise.

Now what do you know about that? Amazing. He'd always heard that by the law of averages there must be somewhere on the earth someone who exactly resembles yourself, and in all time and all the universe, someone who is your exact duplicate, or your *doppelgänger*, a scary concept that had universal appeal. And once, he had picked up the newspaper, startled at the face of a bush pilot who had crashed in the Alaskan wilds, survived subzero weather for five weeks, and lay in the hospital. Even with a tube up the nose, the frost-bitten face against the white pillow was so obviously his own, he called Helen out of the shower, dripping, to look at it. "That's Kenneth Howard all right," she corroborated.

Picking it up, recalling the girl's assurance it wouldn't bite, Kenneth started to slide it beneath the deck as a novelty item to startle Helen and John and party guests. Within the magnifying range of his first pair of glasses, the face proved to be Kenneth's own.

The exhilarating moment of discovering a wild coincidence faded quickly into reasonable doubt. He put the second deck in his other coat pocket and looked closely at the face. Holding his breath, his teeth clenched in a jack-o-lantern grin, his eyes bulging like Peter Lorre. Who could—could even he?—say whether the face was his. When? When he was about seventeen. Where? Against the side of a garage, the white paint peeling badly. He remembered his severe sunburn peeling that summer. But that was not his father's garage. Perhaps a neighbor's. He tried to remember, and couldn't. He looked for a scar or some revealing mark on his naked chest. All his scars dated from college football. Was that black spot the size of a nickel his navel? How does one recognize one's own navel? He laughed. But it didn't seem as funny as on the surface it ought to have. Well, it's not me.

Imagining the girl scrutinizing him for his strange behavior, Kenneth looked up. Still, she saw nothing catatonic her palm open, not impatiently. Indifferently.

Not possible. Not possible? Hadn't he always thought of New Orleans as the city of possibilities? In New Orleans, what was not possible? Uneasily, he smiled, shrugged it off as a wild coincidence, the kind of experience you come to New Orleans for, even if you're coming anyway for routine reasons, and slipped the photo into his coat pocket with the others, wondering who had snapped this shot.

Idly, as he felt in his pocket for a fifty cent piece, he pushed his fingers through the box, stirring up images. He handed her two quarters and picked up the corn-stick mold. As he lifted it, the bag broke, and he had to chase the fruit down the aisle among shuffling feet. People helped him. It's the business suit. He remembered reading an article that answered the question, Who gets helped, where and when, if somebody drops something in a public place? Noticing that the oranges rolled the greater distance gave him a comforting sense of workaday reality. And there were the bananas lying where they had landed. None of the fruit was ruined except for several squashed peaches; rising imperceptibly, bruises would show hours later.

He eased his armload onto the table and walked briskly to the fruit and vegetable stalls and paid a dime for a paper bag. Walking back, the possibility struck him that if there was *one*, there could be another, perhaps others, in the bulging shapeless box, and he hurried to her table, afraid his fifty cents added to the day's take might have given her enough for a fix and she would be gone.

The girl, the box, the fruit were still there. He offered her an orange. She shook her head in revulsion.

The back of a man's head, severely barbered, as he leans away from the camera to kiss a woman, blotting out her face.

A woman smells a rose on a bush, wearing a flared hat of the forties.

A girl wearing a Keystone Cop hat and coat, a moustache pasted under her nose, thrusts herself toward a boy behind bars in a gag shot at an amusement park.

A formal gathering at an outdoor celebration of some sort—no, a funeral. Photographs *are* deceptive, Kenneth thought decisively.

Practicing, a majorette twirls her baton, fractioning her face.

A man washing his car. I think I know that guy. Kenneth set it aside.

A man working at his desk, looks up, smiles quizzically at the camera.

A sober-faced little girl pushes a toy, no, a regular baby carriage down a cracked sidewalk. Empty, or occupied?

His head turned, his eyes half-closed, his mouth oddly ajar, Kenneth, in an ambiguous setting, caught in a Polaroid shot, the surface poorly prepared by the chemical substance he almost smelled now. Cracking, scratched, perhaps by fingernails pawing over the contents of the box. Kenneth licked his lips. The eyes blurred, closing. Perhaps another—no, not another coincidence. He rejected the possibility that some submerged need in him was looking for resemblances. Letting the picture drop on the cast-iron corn-stick mold, he dug farther.

Firemen pose in front of a fire hall, standing, hanging all over a new engine, perhaps only freshly washed-yes, water sparkles, drips from the fenders.

A man, leering, pretends to sneak into an outhouse marked WOMEN.

A businessman, perhaps a government official, presents a check and a handshake to a well-dressed middle-aged woman.

A man strides down a crowded sidewalk, caught unaware in a shot obviously snapped by a sidewalk photographer.

A young man poses with his parents at a high-school graduation ceremony, the mother blurring herself as she moves toward her son, as if to kiss him.

A young woman sits in a swing, empty swings on each side, blowing cigarette smoke toward the camera.

If I find one more, just one more, then. . . . The third was clear, his face quite natural, the suit his first job suit, the setting unmistakably the front of the building, at the curb, beside the red, white, and blue mailbox and the *Keep Chicago Clean* courtesy trash receptable. What was the occasion? Probably not his first day because he stood there (waiting for the light to turn green) with such aplomb, one hand in his pocket, the other casually holding a cigarette at ease-obviously between puffs, not in a hurry, looking straight into Kenneth's New Orleans stare, but not into the camera's lens. Looking, like the girl, at nothing in particular, but unlike the girl, so young and vibrantly alive and receptive, he struck Kenneth as a charming, likable young man in his early twenties. He couldn't see the street sign but he knew it was Halstead and Grand. When was it taken? Who took it? The questions drew such total blanks, he didn't start going over the possibilities. He wanted to dig for more.

One impression held his attention on the picture already in his hand—he didn't seem to realize he was being photographed. He looked at the Polaroid. Obviously candid. He pulled out the muscleflexing shot—even around this classic exhibitionist pose hovered a sense of privacy violated. The show-off eyes were introspective. He set the three aside, neatly together.

A man driving a tractor looks up as if responding reluctantly to a request.

A stiffly posed, badly retouched color shot of a married couple.

An infant wearing a knitted tam manages a brilliant smile with only a single tooth. The brilliance in the eyes. Was it still there?

A teen-age boy strains to pose for a self-portrait as he presses the shutter release lever on the camera, seen in the lower right-hand corner of a bathroom mirror.

People in tennis togs crowd around as a man in a suit presents a trophy to a man dressed for tennis. Kenneth thought one of the spectators resembled a man he knew years ago.

Through glass from the rear, a shot of himself standing in an empty room, his back to the camera, looking out a call window in an old house, wearing his football jersey, number 8. The stance, one foot cocked back, his body leaning, his elbow propping it against the window frame, his arm bent back so he could palm the back of his head, the other hand in his pocket, was obviously not a conscious pose for a photograph. He seemed to have been shot through a side window at an angle that caught him looking out a front window.

The possibility that anyone he knew had taken these pictures without his knowledge as a joke—they were not, except for the muscle-flexing pose, gag pictures, and he remembered none of the situations or occasions—was so remote, he left himself open to a joking assumption the CIA had had him under surveillance since he was seventeen—or maybe younger. He looked for younger shots.

A teen-age girl in shorts strikes a pinup pose against sheets on a clothesline.

A man sets his face in a mindless expression for a passport or an ID photo that has turned yellow.

Kenneth looked for someone he might know, even vaguely, in a family-reunion grouping on steep front porch steps.

A woman and a boy pose in front of a monument, looking so intimately at the photographer, Kenneth lucidly imagined the photographer himself.

A woman has turned from the trunk of a car, a sandwich held up to her open mouth, four other people bent over, their backs toward Kenneth, who, unable to see their faces, feels uneasy.

A double-exposed shot of Kenneth reading a newspaper on a train, so intent upon a particular article he holds the paper and thus his body at an awkward angle, giving the photographer an opening. On the train window, as if it were a reflection, a child sits on a shetland pony. A Chicago train? Nothing showed to answer his question. He had ridden hundreds of trains, perhaps thousands.

He looked at the girl, wondering whether she might not suddenly recognize him as a recurrent image in her scavenged collection. She was still in a hypnotic world of her own making or of some chemical's conjuring. He took off his jacket, lapped it over the bag of fruit, picked his sweat-saturated polyester shirt away from his skin, wiped his hands along the sides of his pants, licked his lips again. His mouth was too dry.

Kenneth began to dig into the box, shuffling quickly past the little brown studio portraits of the 1860s whose edges crumbled, leaving his fingertips gritty, past the baby pictures—in his mother's collection, he had never recognized himself—past the group pictures that obviously excluded him, past the ones with Spanish-moss backgrounds, New Orleans settings, nothing specific to look for, his breathing fitful against the expectation that each movement of his hand would turn up out of this deep box his face. The savage's fear that cameras snatched, photographs held the soul captive made Kenneth laugh at his own fearfulness.

A young man of the seventies sits in the grass on the levee playing a guitar, a barge passing behind him.

The rim of a pale shadow in bright sunlight smokes on a stucco wall, the partial outline of a camera looking as if it is attached to the photographer's hip.

A couple sit on a New Orleans streetcar, having exchanged hats, exhibiting beer cans.

A company picnic. Kenneth looked anxiously for someone he may have known at some phase of his life.

A man sleeps, perhaps pretends to sleep, in a fishnet hammock.

Kenneth is having lunch with a man whose fork obscures his face. Kenneth sits before his own plate as if wondering whether he can eat it all. Between himself and the man—he tried to recognize the ornate cuff links—communication has visibly ceased or not yet really begun, perhaps was never resumed. What restaurant was that? His memory responded to nothing in the decor. *November 1972* printed in the white margin stimulated nothing. It did not appear to be one of those restaurants where girls come around taking pictures of moments to be treasured forever. No third party had said, "Hold it! Smile! That's terrific!"

"Say, miss. . . . Say, miss?"

"Fifty cents a handful."

"I know, but I just wanted to—I just wondered—could you tell me where you collected these photographs?"

"I don't remember."

He showed her one of the pictures. "Do you have any more of this fellow here?"

He showed her the one of his back in the empty room.

"I don't know."

He showed her the one on the street corner. "Him. Recognize him?"

"No."

"Him?"

"No."

"How about him?"

"No."

"They're me. They're all me." He looked into her lackluster eyes. "See? Each one of them resembles me to a T. I mean, they *are* of me. Somebody took. . . . Do they look like me?"

She nodded, expressionless.

"Then do you remember where you first found them?"

"No."

"Do you remember when?"

"No."

Pigeons perch on a woman's arm, tourists feeding pigeons behind her, a European cathedral in the background.

A boy stands at attention to show off his new scout uniform.

An elderly couple stands in front of a tour bus, the letters spelling its destination backwards.

A religious ceremony, ambiguous.

A man shows a string of fish, a river flowing in the background.

A young man and a young woman sit on a diving board, in profile, looking away from the camera, squinting into the sun.

A little boy sits on a plank placed across the arms of a barber chair, obviously captured on the occasion of his first haircut.

Kenneth stands in line at an airport, the destination on the board unclear. He is lighting his pipe, his lips pursed on the stem. Another Polaroid. Between himself and the woman in front of him, a fat boy in shorts takes snapshots with a mini-camera. In the picture the boy snapped—of his mother, his father, his sister, his aunt, his teacher, his friend, a stranger who caught his eye—one could see perhaps the person who had taken Kenneth's. The combination of images—in hand and imagined—made him aware of the nausea again. He had to make it to a bathroom quick.

He riffled through the box, thinking, I'm missing some, I must be missing some—there's no system to what I'm doing. The pictures, too quickly scanned, spilled from his hands back into the shifting clutter out of which he had fished them. The sun, the nausea, the eyestrain in the bright polluted air made him too weak for the task of sorting them all out on the cramped table.

"Will you be here all day?"

The girl shrugged her shoulders, "Man, how do I know?"

"Here, I'll pay for these—I'm—I'll come back right away—here, let me take some more handfuls." He shoved a handful into his right pants pocket, spilling, another into his left pants pocket, spilling, into both his back pockets, his inside breast pockets, his shirt, worrying about the effect of his sweat on them, stuffed some into the bag with the fruit, picked up the ones he had spilled, and gave her five dollars.

"Keep the change and try to stay around awhile, I'll come right back." He turned, hugging the bag of fruit, carrying the corn-stick mold out through the stalls, the parking spaces, and went back to her. "Well, did you get them all in the same place?"

"No, man."

"The same town? New Orleans?"

"Yeah. Maybe. Take another handful at a discount. Only a quarter."

"I just hope you're still here. I want to go through them one by one, systematically."

He made a final effort to see a glimmer of recognition in her eyes, and failing, turned away again, feeling distance increase between himself and the box hunched on the table.

In the dirty narrow street he flagged a taxi.

Lying stripped to his briefs, on his bed in the Royal Sonesta, the nausea ebbing, the photographs spread around him, he said over and over, Who took these pictures?

As he named his brother, his sister, his mother, his father, his other relatives, Helen, John, and a combination of them to account for the variety, each possibility struck him as so absurd, the rapidity with which he rejected them made him pant in exasperation with himself for even considering them.

He scanned the pictures slowly, hoping to stop short at the face of someone who might have become somehow obsessed, a creepy childhood friend, a spurned sweetheart, an oddball relative, or a deranged business associate.

Looking up at the ceiling, he saw himself in many places, at many periods in his life, all past his seventeenth year, but he saw no faces of likely secret photographers.

What happened to the people who had taken them, causing the pictures to end up in the New Orleans flea market?

Was this person or persons male or female? Young or old? A contemporary? Known to him? Known well? A mere acquaintance? A business rival? Or a stranger? Friend or stranger, loved one or enemy, his frustration, his helpless astonishment had a quality of zero that he felt in his bones.

In the batches he had snatched up at the last moment, he had found other shots of himself. He is gassing up the car at a self-service island. Sitting on the bench as a player. Having a drink, sitting on the patio. Waiting for his bags to show up at a carousel in an airport. Walking the dog. Looking at stills outside a movie theater. Sitting in a lobby, his face hidden by a newspaper, as if he were a private eye, but obviously himself. Caught taking trash down a driveway to the curb. Lighting a cigarette in a stadium with friends, their faces turned away from the camera. Doing what people in the other photographs did. Sometimes strangers in the frame with him, but most often alone. As if he were being contemplated.

Each of the snapshots declared at a glance that he had not posed the image he held in his hand. Several types of cameras had taken the pictures, a range of paper sizes, shapes, stocks had been used. The quality of the photography ranged from awful to professional. A few were dated by the processors, a few had been dated in pencil, perhaps by the same hand but not one he recognized. Age or neglect had yellowed some. The negatives of some had been scratched. Some soiled, damaged. A few had tabs of fuzzy black paper or smears of rubber cement on the backs as if they had been preserved in a scrapbook, then ripped out and put away or discarded.

Some of the places he recognized but couldn't fix in time. For some, he determined a time, but was at a loss to name the place. Perhaps he, she, they had kept a record of the dates and the places. Sometimes, he even remembered generally how he had felt, once specifically (melancholy), but not the context.

Lying on the double bed as if on a rubber raft at sea, he tried to go over every possibility again, imposing a kind of system. But each sequence to which he tried to adhere was besieged by so many unaccounted-for possibilities and sheer impossibilities, he abandoned them and gave himself up to chance. If a photo was worth a thousand words, he needed the words for these, because, as a neutral voice told him, "The camera never lies."

He scrutinized each picture of himself for the third time, straining his eyes to detect ghost images such as spiritualists and

UFO enthusiasts claim to see, or as religious fervor discerns Christ's visage in commonplace photographs. He remembered reading about a news photographer who happened upon a wreck on the highway and who shot the scene too fast to distinguish faces until his own seventeen-year-old son's face became more and more distinct in the developing tray.

The bounce of the springs as he jumped off the bed spilled some of the pictures onto the carpet. As he picked them up, he realized that the almost reverent care he used came not from narcissism but from respect for the feelings of the person or group who, he was inclined to conclude, had pursued through the years an obsession to chronicle his life.

Returning to the Market, he caught a glimpse of the Sunday morning lovers, hoped they would wave to him, but more than a hundred people milling about the flea-market tables distracted them.

The girl was gone, but behind the box a little black boy's head was visible from the eyes up, his hands clutching the top, as if he were guarding.

"Where's the lady?"

"You the man?"

"Yes, where did she go?"

"She split, man. Said, give me a dollar for this box of pictures and a man come in a business suit give you a million dollars for this ol' box of trash."

"Here's two tens. Okay?"

"Man, that trash belong to *you*." He took the two tens and shoved the box toward Kenneth.

Kenneth picked up the box, looked around for any strays, and turned, lifting his knee to balance, as he embraced the shifting bulky sides of the torn cardboard box, feeling mingled awe and anxiety, remembering the two men who had bought pictures, feeling an impulse to track them down, wondering whether and from what angle sudden light was for a fraction of an instant flooding a dark chamber, etching his struggle on sensitized paper.

THE NEW ORLEANS OF POSSIBILITIES

On a first reading, this story might seem a bit puzzling. Readers have grown to expect stories set in New Orleans to dwell on local color, certainly not on sleazy areas. Almost as if consciously rejecting the stereotypical romantic image, the author introduces a character already bored with standard tourist attractions. The third person narrator relates so matter-of-factly the strange experience of Kenneth, a prosaic middle-age traveling salesman, that most readers identify with him and expect a plausible explanation for an unbelievable event. A closer look, however, will reveal that his is a subjective experience and that the author has very skillfully developed his character as being not only open to a fantasy but ready to induce it.

Kenneth is bored with big cities, even "New Orleans, the most romantic city of his imagination, the city in which he had once expected to realize so many possibilities." It has become so "routine," so "bland" that he feels the impulse to do "something slightly unusual" to make the city become exciting again. Sitting among other tourists, sipping café au lait and eating beignets outside Café du Monde is a part of the routine, he thinks, as a woman nearby hands him an orange slice. Eating the fruit is a very sensuous experience for him: "the rind mist prickle[s] his nostrils," and the "the surging juice" stings his palate as he crushes the orange slice against it. Enlivened by the experience, he heads toward the French Market, where the odors of exotic fruit are "so intense that he tasted the market before he smelled it." The fruit seems to induce in him a heady almost-intoxicating feeling that releases him from his previous apathetic state and he acts on "impulse to break the routine and open himself to possibilities."

Having bought his fruit, he enters a flea market and becomes so fascinated by the array of junk that he feels the need to "assert control over his behavior"; nevertheless he is drawn to a sleazy stall where "a spaced-out girl" is selling old photographs she had foraged out of attics and basements and trash cans. As he rummages through the photographs, the strange adventurous feeling that has been building reaches a climax: he finds a candid shot of himself; then he finds others, dozens—all clearly pictures of himself in unfamiliar places. It is significant that the first is a picture of a boy roughly seventeen, and although the second is a bit blurred, the third reveals a young man in his twenties "vibrantly alive and receptive." He finds what amounts to a photographic chronicle of his adult life, all poses unconscious. His rational self rejects such coincidence while the unconscious aspect of his ego has sought all along to recapture a time of excitement and thrill that is given only to youth.   He asks himself over and over, "Who took these pictures?" and as he handles them "reverently," he assures himself that he does so not from narcissism but out of respect for the feelings of "the persons or group" who had taken them. The answer to his question is, of course, that he, himself, took them. These are stored images of himself in places and on occasions, most of which never existed.   Through introspection and fantasy and a touch of narcissism, he creates excitement in the city where anything is possible.

Because stories set in Louisiana, particularly New Orleans, often overplay local features to the detriment of universal, Madden wisely steers his protagonist away from strange and colorful to the commonplace—a flea market. But the romance of the city is present, nevertheless; its enchantment, which seems dormant, triggers "a suspension of disbelief" in Kenneth and works a kind of magic on him. In this way, Madden avoids the romantic trappings while letting them work for him.

ANDRE DUBUS
(1936-)

Andre Dubus was born in Lake Charles, the son of Andre Jules and Katherine Burke Dubus. A Roman Catholic of French heritage, he writes often of characters with backgrounds similar to his. After graduation from high school, he attended a local college, McNeese State, before entering the U. S. Marine Corps where he was commissioned a lieutenant in 1958 and promoted to captain in 1964. In 1966 he was awarded an MFA degree from the University of Iowa and since that time has been a teacher of modern fiction and creative writing at Bradford College in Massachusetts. He was married in 1958 to Particia Lowe with whom he has four children. Divorced in 1970, he married Tommie Cotter in 1975. In addition to the many short stories published in magazines and journals, he published a novel, *The Lieutenant* in 1967 and several collections of short stories: *Separate Flights, Adultery and Other Choices, Finding a Girl in America,* and *The Times Are Never So Bad.* The story printed here is from the latter collection.

Sorrowful Mysteries*

André Dubus

WHEN GERRY FONTENOT is five, six, and seven years old, he likes to ride in the car with his parents. It is a grey 1938 Chevrolet and it has a ration stamp on the windshield. Since the war started when Gerry was five, his father has gone to work on a bicycle, and rarely drives the car except to Sunday Mass, and to go hunting and fishing. Gerry fishes with him, from the bank of the bayou. They fish with bamboo poles, corks, sinkers, and worms, and catch perch and catfish. His father wears a .22 revolver at his side, for cottonmouths. In the fall Gerry goes hunting with him, crouches beside him in ditches bordering fields, and when the doves fly, his father stands and fires the twelve-gauge pump, and Gerry marks where the birds fall, then runs out into the field where they lie, and gathers them. They are soft and warm as he runs with them, back to his father. This is in southern Louisiana, and twice he and his father see an open truck filled with German prisoners, going to work in the sugar cane fields.

He goes on errands with his mother. He goes to grocery stores, dime stores, drugstores, and shopping for school clothes in the fall, and Easter clothes in the spring, and to the beauty parlor, where he likes to sit and watch the women. Twice a week he goes with her to the colored section, where they leave and pick up the week's washing and ironing. His mother washes at home too: the bedclothes, socks, underwear, towels, and whatever else does not have to be ironed. She washes these in a wringer washing machine; he likes watching her feed the clothes into the wringer, and the way they come out flattened and drop into the basket. She hangs them on the clothesline in the backyard, and Gerry stands at the basket and hands them to her so she will not have to stoop. On rainy days she dries them inside on racks, which in winter she places in front of space heaters. She listens to the weather forecasts on the radio, and most of the time is able to wash on clear days.

The Negro woman washes the clothes that must be ironed, or starched and ironed. In front of the woman's unpainted wooden house, Gerry's mother presses the horn, and the large woman comes out and takes the basket from the back seat. Next day, at the sound of the horn, she brings out the basket. It is filled with ironed, folded skirts and blouses, and across its top lie dresses and shirts on hangers. Gerry opens the window his mother has told him to close as they approached the colored section with its dusty roads. He smells the clean, ironed clothes, pastels and prints, and his father's white and pale blue, and he looks at the rutted dirt road, the unpainted wood and rusted screens of the houses, old cars in front of them and tire swings hanging from trees over the worn and packed dirt yards, dozens of barefoot, dusty children stopping their play to watch him and his mother in the car, and the old slippers and dress the Negro woman wears, and he breathes her smell of sweat, looks at her black and brown hand crossing him to take the dollar from his mother's fingers.

On Fridays in spring and summer, Leonard comes to mow the lawn. He is a Negro, and has eight children, and Gerry sees him only once between fall and spring, when he comes on Christmas Eve, and Gerry's father and mother give him toys and clothes that Gerry and his three older sisters have outgrown, a bottle of bourbon, one of the fruit cakes Gerry's mother makes at Christmas, and five dollars. Leonard receives these at the back door, where on Fridays, in spring and summer, he is paid and fed. The Fontenots eat dinner at noon, and Gerry's mother serves Leonard a plate and a glass of iced tea with leaves from the mint she grows under the faucet behind the house. She calls him from the back steps, and he comes, wiping his brow with a bandanna, and takes his dinner to the shade of a sycamore tree. From his place at the dining room table, Gerry watches him sit on the grass and take off his straw hat; he eats, then rolls a cigarette. When he has smoked, he brings his plate and glass to the back door, knocks, and hands them to whoever answers. His glass is a jelly glass, his plate blue china, and his knife and fork stainless steel. From Friday to Friday the knife and fork lie at one side of a drawer, beside the compartments that hold silver; the glass is nearly out of reach, at the back of the second shelf in the cupboard for glasses; the plate rests under serving bowls in the china cupboard. Gerry's mother has told him and his sisters not to use them, they are Leonard's, and from Friday to Friday, they sit, and from fall to spring, and finally forever when one year Gerry is strong enough to push the lawn mower for his allowance, and Leonard comes only when Gerry's father calls him every Christmas Eve.

Before that, when he is eight, Gerry has stopped going on errands with his mother. On Saturday afternoons he walks or, on rainy days, rides the bus to town with neighborhood boys, to the movie theater where they watch westerns and the weekly chapter of a serial. He stands in line on the sidewalk, holding his quarter that will buy a ticket, a bag of popcorn, and, on the way home, an ice-cream soda. Opposite his line, to the right of the theater as you face it, are the Negro boys. Gerry does not look at them. Or not directly: he glances, he listens, as a few years later he will do with girls when he goes to movies that draw them. The Negroes enter through the door marked *Colored*, where he supposes a Negro woman sells tickets, then climb the stairs to the balcony, and Gerry wonders whether someone sells them popcorn and candy and drinks up there, or imagines them smelling all the bags of popcorn in the dark beneath them. Then he watches the cartoon and previews of next Saturday's movie, and he likes them but is waiting for the chapter of the serial whose characters he and his friends have played in their yards all week; they have worked out several escapes for the trapped hero and, as always, they are wrong. He has eaten his popcorn when the credits for the movie appear, then a tall man rides a beautiful black or white or palomino horse across the screen. The movie is black and white, but a palomino looks as golden and lovely as the ones he has seen in parades. Sitting in the dark, he is aware of his friends on both sides of him only as feelings coincident with his own: the excitement of becoming the Cisco Kid, Durango Kid, Red Ryder, the strongest and best-looking, the most courageous and good, the fastest with horse and fists and gun. Then it is over, the lights are on, he turns to his friends, flesh again, stands to leave, then remembers the Negroes. He blinks up at them standing at the balcony wall, looking down at the white boys pressed together in the aisle, moving slowly out of the theater. Sometimes his eyes meet those of a Negro boy, and Gerry smiles; only one ever smiles back.

In summer he and his friends go to town on weekday afternoons to see war movies, or to buy toy guns or baseballs, and when he meets Negroes on the sidewalk, he averts his eyes; but he watches them in department stores, bending over water fountains marked *Colored*, and when they enter the city buses and walk past him to the rear, he watches them, and during the ride he glances, and listens to their talk and laughter. One hot afternoon when he is twelve, he goes with a friend to deliver the local newspaper in the colored section. He has not been there since riding with his mother, who has not gone for years either; now the city buses stop near his neighborhood, and a Negro woman comes on it and irons the family's clothes in their kitchen. He goes that afternoon because his friend has challenged him. They have argued: they both have paper routes, and when his friend complained about his, Gerry said it was easy work. Sure, his friend said, you don't have to hold your breath. You mean when you collect? No, man, when I just ride through. So Gerry finishes his route, then goes with his friend: a bicycle ride of several miles ending, or beginning, at a neighborhood of poor whites, their houses painted but peeling, their screened front porches facing lawns so narrow that only small children can play catch in them; the older boys and girls play tapeball on the blacktop street. Gerry and his friends play that, making a ball of tape around a sock, and hitting with a baseball bat, but they have lawns big enough to contain them. Gerry's father teaches history at the public high school, and in summer is a recreation director for children in the city park, and some nights in his bed Gerry hears his father and mother worry about money; their voices are weary, and frighten him. But riding down this street, he feels shamefully rich, wants the boys and girls pausing in their game to know he only has a new Schwinn because he saved his money to buy it.

He and his friend jolt over the railroad tracks, and the blacktop ends. Dust is deep in the road. They ride past fields of tall grass and decaying things: broken furniture, space heaters, stoves, cars. Negro children are in the fields. Then they come to the streets of houses, turn onto the first one, a rutted and dusty road, and breathe the smell. It is as tangible as the dust a car raises to Gerry's face as it bounces past him, its unmuffled exhaust pipe sounding like gunfire, and Gerry feels that he enters the smell, as you enter a cloud of dust; and a hard summer rain, with lightning and thunder, would settle it, and the air would smell of grass and trees. Its base is sour, as though in the heat of summer someone has half-filled a garbage can with milk, then dropped in citrus fruit and cooked rice and vegetables and meat and fish, mattress ticking and a pillow, covered it, and left it for a week in the July sun. In this smell children play in the street and on the lawns that are dirt too, dust, save for strips of crisp-looking yellowish grass in the narrow spaces between houses, and scattered patches near the porches. He remembers the roads and houses and yards from riding with his mother, but not the smell, for even in summer they had rolled up the windows. Or maybe her perfume and cigarettes had fortified the car against the moment the laundry woman would open the back door, or reach through the window for her dollar; but he wonders now if his mother wanted the windows closed only to keep out dust. Women and men sit on the front porches, as Gerry and his friend slowly ride up the road, and his friend throws triangular-folded papers onto the yards, where they skip in rising dust.

It is late afternoon, and he can smell cooking too: hot grease and meat, turnip or mustard greens, and he hears talk and laughter from the shaded porches. Everything seems to be dying: cars and houses and tar paper roofs in the weather, grass in the sun; sparse oaks and pines and weeping willows draw children and women with babies to their shade; beneath the hanging tent of a willow, an old man sits with two crawling children wearing diapers, and Gerry remembers Leonard eating in the shade of the sycamore. Gerry's father still phones Leonard on Christmas Eve, and last year he went home with the electric train Gerry has outgrown, along with toy soldiers and cap pistols and Saturday serials and westerns, a growth that sometimes troubles him: when he was nine and ten and saw that other neighborhood boys stopped going to the Saturday movies when they were twelve or thirteen, he could not understand why something so exciting was suddenly not, and he promised himself that he would always go on Saturdays, although he knew he would not, for the only teenaged boy who did was odd and frightening: he was about eighteen, and in his voice and eyes was the desperation of a boy lying to a teacher, and he tried to sit between Gerry and his friends, and once he did before they could close the gap, and all through the movie he tried to rub Gerry's thigh, and Gerry whispered *Stop it,* and pushed at the wrist, the fingers. So he knew a time would come when he would no longer love his heroes and their horses, and it saddened him to know that such love could not survive mere time. It did not, and that is what troubles him, when he wonders if his love of baseball and football and hunting and fishing and bicycles will die too, and wonders what he will love then.

He looks for Leonard as he rides down the road, where some yards are bordered with colored and clear bottles, half-buried with bottoms up to the sun. In others a small rectangle of flowers grows near the porch, and the smell seems to come from the flowers too, and the trees. He wants to enter one of those houses kept darkened with shades drawn against the heat, wants to trace and define that smell, press his nose to beds and sofas and floor and walls, the bosom of a woman, the chest of a man, the hair of a child. Breathing through his mouth, swallowing his nausea, he looks at his friend and sees what he knows is on his face as well: an expression of sustained and pallid horror.

On summer mornings the neighborhood boys play baseball. One of the fathers owns a field behind his house; he has mowed it with a tractor, and built a backstop of two-by-fours and screen, laid out all infield with a pitcher's mound, and put up foul poles at the edge of the tall weeds that surround the outfield. The boys play every rainless morning except Sunday, when all but the two Protestants go to Mass. They pitch slowly so they can hit the ball, and so the catcher, with only a mask, will not get hurt. But they pitch from a windup, and try to throw curves and knuckleballs, and sometimes they play other neighborhood teams who loan their catcher shin guards and chest protector, then the pitchers throw hard.

One morning a Negro boy rides his bicycle past the field, on the dirt road behind the backstop; he holds a fishing pole across the handlebars, and is going toward the woods beyond left field, and the bayou that runs wide and muddy through the trees. A few long innings later, he comes back without fish, and stops to watch the game. Standing, holding his bicycle, he watches two innings. Then, as Gerry's team is trotting in to bat, someone calls to the boy: Do you want to play? In the infield and outfield, and near home plate, voices stop. The boy looks at the pause, the silence, then nods, lowers his kickstand, and slowly walks onto the field.

'You're with us,' someone says. 'What do you play?'

'I like first.'

That summer, with eight dollars of his paper route money, Gerry has bought a first-baseman's glove: a Rawlings Trapper, because he liked the way it looked, and felt on his hand, but he is not a good first baseman: he turns his head away from throws that hit the dirt in front of his reaching glove and bounce toward his body, his face. He hands the glove to the boy.

'Use this. I ought to play second anyway.'

The boy puts his hand in the Trapper, thumps its pocket, turns his wrist back and forth, looking at the leather that is still a new reddish brown. Boys speak their names to him. His is Clay. They give him a place in the batting order, point to the boy he follows.

He is tall, and at the plate he takes a high stride and a long, hard swing. After his first hit, the outfield plays him deeply, at the edge of the weeds that are the boys' fence, and the infielders back up. At first base he is often clumsy, kneeling for ground balls, stretching before an infielder has thrown so that some balls nearly go past or above him; he is fearless, though, and none of the bouncing throws from third and deep short go past his body. He does not talk to any one boy, but from first he calls to the pitcher: *Come babe, come boy;* calls to infielders bent for ground balls: *Plenty time, plenty time, You got him;* and, to hitters when Gerry's team is at bat: *Good eye, good eye.* The game ends when the twelve o'clock whistle blows.'

'That it?' Clay says as the fielders run in while he is swinging two bats on deck.

'We have to go eat,' the catcher says, taking off his mask, and with a dirt-smeared forearm wiping sweat from his brow.

'Me too,' he says, and drops the bats, picks up the Trapper, and hands it to Gerry. Gerry looks at it, lying across Clay's palm, looks at Clay's thumb on the leather.

'I'm a crappy first baseman.' he says. 'Keep it.'

'You kidding?'

'No. Go on.'

'What you going to play with?'

'My fielder's glove.'

Some of the boys are watching now; others are mounting bicycles on the road, riding away with gloves hanging from the handlebars, bats held across them.

'You don't want to play first no more?'

'No. Really.'

'Man, that's some *glove*. What's your name again?'

'Gerry,' he says, and extends his right hand. Clay takes it, and Gerry squeezes the big, limp hand; releases it.

'Gerry,' Clay says, looking down at his face as though to memorize it, or discern its features from among the twenty white faces of his morning.

'Good man,' he says, and turning, and calling goodbyes, he goes to his bicycle, places his fishing pole across the handlebars, hangs the trapper from one, and rides quickly up the dirt road. Where the road turns to blacktop, boys are bicycling in a cluster, and Gerry watches Clay pass them with a wave. Then he is in the distance, among white houses with lawns and trees; is gone, leaving Gerry with the respectful voices of his friends, and peace and pride in his heart. He has attended a Catholic school since the first grade, so knows he must despise those feelings. He jokes about his play at first base, and goes with his Marty Marion glove and Ted Williams Louisville Slugger to his bicycle. But riding home, he nestles with his proud peace. At dinner he says nothing of Clay. The Christian Brothers have taught him that an act of charity can be canceled by the telling of it. Also, he suspects his family would think he is a fool.

A year later, a Negro man in a neighboring town is convicted of raping a young white woman, and is sentenced to die in the electric chair. His story is the front-page headline of the paper Gerry delivers, but at home, because the crime was rape, his mother tells the family she does not want any talk about it. Gerry's father mutters enough, from time to time, for Gerry to know he is angry and sad because if the woman had been a Negro, and the man white, there would have been neither execution nor conviction. But on his friends' lawns, while he plays catch or pepper or sits on the grass, whittling branches down to sticks, he listens to voluptuous voices from the porches, where men and women drink bourbon and talk of niggers and rape and the electric chair. The Negro's name is Sonny Broussard, and every night Gerry prays for his soul.

On the March night Sonny Broussard will die, Gerry lies in bed and says a rosary. It is a Thursday, a day for the Joyful Mysteries, but looking out past the mimosa, at the corner streetlight, he prays with the Sorrowful Mysteries, remembers the newspaper photographs of Sonny Broussard, tries to imagine his terror as midnight draws near—,why midnight? and how could he live that day in his cell?—and sees Sonny Broussard on his knees in the Garden of Olives; he wears khakis, his arms rest on a large stone, and his face is lifted to the sky. Tied to a pillar and shirtless, he is silent under the whip; thorns pierce his head, and the fathers of Gerry's friends strike his face, their wives watch as he climbs the long hill, cross on his shoulder, then he is lying on it, the men with hammers are carpenters in khakis, squatting above him, sweat running down their faces to drip on cigarettes between their lips, heads cocked away from smoke; they swing the hammers in unison, and drive nails through wrists and crossed feet. Then Calvary fades and Gerry sees instead a narrow corridor become cells with a door at the end; two guards are leading Sonny Broussard to it, and Gerry watches them from the rear. They open the door to a room filled with people, save for a space in the center of their circle, where the electric chair waits. They have been talking when the guard opens the door, and they do not stop. They are smoking and drinking and knitting; they watch Sonny Broussard between the guards, look from him to each other, and back to him, talking, clapping a hand on a neighbor's shoulder, a thigh. The guards buckle Sonny Broussard into the chair. Gerry shuts his eyes, and tries to feel the chair, the straps, Sonny Broussard's fear; to feel so hated that the people who surround him wait for the very throes and stench of his death. Then he feels it, he is in the electric chair, and he opens his eyes and holds his breath against the scream in his throat.

Gerry attends the state college in town, and lives at home. He majors in history, and is in the Naval ROTC, and is grateful that he will spend three years in the Navy after college. He does not want to do anything with history but learn it, and he believes the

Navy will give him time to know what he will do for the rest of his life.

He also wants to go to sea. He thinks more about the sea than history; by Christmas he is in love, and thinks more about the girl than either of them. Near the end of the year, the college president calls an assembly and tells the students that, in the fall, colored boys and girls will be coming to the school. The president is a politician, and will later be lieutenant-governor. There will be no trouble at this college, he says. I do not want troops or federal marshals on my campus. If any one of you starts trouble, or even joins in on it if one of them starts it, I will have you in my office, and you'd best bring your luggage with you.

The day after his last examinations, Gerry starts working with a construction crew. In the long heat he carries hundred-pound bags of cement, shovels gravel and sand, pushes wheelbarrows of wet concrete, digs trenches for foundations, holes for septic tanks, has more money than he has ever owned, spends most of it on his girl in restaurants and movies and night clubs and bars, and by late August has gained fifteen pounds, most of it above his waist, though beneath that is enough for his girl to pinch, and call his Budweiser belt. Then he hears of Emmett Till. He is a Negro boy, and in the night two white men have taken him from his great-uncle's house in Mississippi. Gerry and his girl wait. Three days later, while Gerry sits in the living room with his family before supper, the news comes over the radio: a search party has found Emmett Till at the bottom of the Tallahatchie River; a seventy-pound cotton gin fan was tied to his neck with barbed wire; he was beaten and shot in the head, and was decomposing. Gerry's father lowers his magazine, removes his glasses, rubs his eyes, and says: 'Oh my Lord, it's happening again.'

He goes to the kitchen and Gerry hears him mixing another bourbon and water, then the back screen door opens and shuts. His mother and the one sister still at home are talking about Mississippi and rednecks, and the poor boy, and what were they thinking of, what kind of men *are* they? He wants to follow his father, to ask what memory or hearsay he had meant, but he does not believe he is old enough, man enough, to move into his father's silence in the backyard.

He phones his girl, and after supper asks his father for the car, and drives to her house. She is waiting on the front porch, and walks quickly to the car. She is a petite, dark-skinned Cajun girl, with fast and accented speech, deep laughter, and a temper that is fierce when it reaches the end of its long tolerance. Through generations the Fontenots' speech has slowed and softened, so that Gerry sounds more southern than French; she teases him about it, and often, when he is with her, he finds that he is talking with her rhythms and inflections. She likes dancing, rhythm and blues, jazz, gin, beer, Pall Malls, peppery food, and passionate kissing, with no fondling. She receives Communion every morning, wears a gold Sacred Heart medal on a gold chain around her neck, and wants to teach history in college. Her name is Camille Theriot.

They go to a bar, where people are dancing to the jukebox. The couples in booths and boys at the bar are local students, some still in high school, for in this town parents and bartenders ignore the law about drinking, and bartenders only use it at clubs that do not want young people. Gerry has been drinking at this bar since he got his driver's license when he was sixteen. He leads Camille to a booth, and they drink gin and tonics, and repeat what they heard at college, in the classroom where they met: that it was economic, and all the hatred started with slavery, the Civil War leaving the poor white no one about whom he could say: *At least I ain't a slave like him*, leaving him only: *At least I ain't a nigger*. And after the war the Negro had to be contained to provide cheap labor in the fields. Camille says it might explain segregation, so long as you don't wonder about rich whites who don't have to create somebody to look down on, since they can do it from birth anyway.

'So it doesn't apply,' she says.

'They never seem to, do they?'

'What?'

'Theories. Do you think those sonsabitches—do you think they tied that fan on before or after they shot him? Why barbed wire if he was already dead? Why not baling wire, or—'

The waitress is there, and he watches her lower the drinks, put their empty glasses on her tray; he pays her, and looks at Camille. Her face is lowered, her eyes closed. Around midnight, when the crowd thins, they move to the bar. Three couples dance slowly to Sinatra; another kisses in a booth. Gerry knows they are in high school when the boy lights a cigarette and they share it: the girl draws on it, they kiss, and she exhales into his mouth; then the boy does it. Camille says: 'Maybe we should go north to college, and just stay there.'

'I hear the people are cold as the snow.'

'Me too. And they eat boiled food with some kind of white sauce. 'You want some oysters?'

'Can we get there before they close?'

'Let's try it,' he says. 'Did you French-smoke in high school?'

'Sure.'

A boy stands beside Gerry and loudly orders a beer. He is drunk, and when he sees Gerry looking at him, he says: 'Woo. They *did* it to him, didn't they? 'Course now, a little nigger boy like that, you can't tell'—as Gerry stands so he can reach into his pocket—'could be he'd go swimming with seventy pounds hanging on his neck, and a bullet in his head'—and Gerry opens the knife he keeps sharp for fish and game, looks at the blade, then turns toward the voice: 'Emmett *Till* rhymes with *kill*. Hoo. Hot*damn*. Kill *Till*—'

Gerry's hand bunches the boy's collar, turns him, and pushes his back against the bar. He touches the boy's throat with the point of the knife, and his voice comes yelling out of him; he seems to rise from the floor with it, can feel nothing of his flesh beneath it: 'You like *death? Feel* it!'

He presses the knife until skin dimples around its point. The boy is still, his mouth open, his eyes rolled to his left, where the knife is. Camille is screaming, and Gerry hears *Cut his tongue out! Cut his heart out!* Then she is standing in front of the boy, her arms waving, and Gerry hears *Bastard bastard bastard*, as he watches the boy's eyes and open mouth, then hears the bartender speaking softly: 'Take it easy now. You're Gerry, right?' He glances at the voice; the bartender is leaning over the bar. 'Easy, Gerry. You stick him there, he's gone. Why don't you go on home now, okay?'

Camille is quiet. Watching the point, Gerry pushes the knife, hardly a motion at all, for he is holding back too; the dimple, for an instant, deepens and he feels the boy's chest breathless and rigid beneath his left fist. 'Okay,' he says, and releases the boy's shirt, folds the knife, and takes Camille's arm. Boys at the bar and couples on the dance floor stand watching. There is music he cannot hear clearly enough to name. He and Camille walk between the couples to the door.

Two men, Roy Bryant and John William Milan, are arrested, and through hot September classes Gerry and Camille wait for the trial. Negroes sit together in classes, walk together in the corridors and across the campus, and surround juxtaposed tables in the student union, where they talk quietly, and do not play the jukebox. Gerry and Camille drink coffee and furtively watch them; in the classrooms and corridors, and on the grounds, they smile at Negroes, tell them hello, and get smiles and greetings. The Negro boys wear slacks and sport shirts, some of them with coats, some even with ties; the girls wear skirts or dresses; all of them wear polished shoes. There is no trouble. Gerry and Camille read the newspapers and listen to the radio, and at night after studying together they go to the bar and drink beer; the bartender is polite, even friendly, and does not mention the night of the knife. As they drink, then drive to Camille's house, they talk about Emmett Till, his story they have read and heard.

He was from Chicago, where he lived with his mother; his father died in France, in the Second World War. Emmett was visiting his great-uncle in Money, Mississippi. His mother said she told him to be respectful down there, because he didn't know about the South. One day he went to town and bought two cents' worth of bubble gum in Roy Bryant's store. Bryant's wife Carolyn, who is young and pretty, was working at the cash register. She said that when Emmett left the store and was on the sidewalk, he turned back to her and whistled. It was the wolf whistle, and that night Roy Bryant and his half-brother, John William Milan, went to the great-uncle's house with flashlights and a pistol, said *Where's that Chicago boy,* and took him.

The trial is in early fall. The defense lawyer's case is that the decomposed body was not Emmett Till; that the NAACP had put his father's ring on the finger of that body; and that the fathers of the jurors would turn in their graves if these twelve Anglo-Saxon men returned with a guilty verdict, which, after an hour and seven minutes of deliberation, they do not. That night, with Camille sitting so close that their bodies touch, Gerry drives on highways through farming country and cleared land with oil derricks and gas fires, and on bridges spanning dark bayous, on narrow blacktop roads twisting through lush woods, and gravel and dirt roads through rice fields whose canals shimmer in the moonlight. The windows are open to humid air whose rush cools his face.

When they want beer, he stops at a small country store; woods are behind it, and it is flanked by lighted houses separated by woods and fields. Oyster shells cover the parking area in front of the store. Camille will not leave the car. He crosses the wooden porch where bugs swarm at a yellow light, and enters: the store is lit by one ceiling light that casts shadows between shelves. A man and a woman stand at the counter, talking to a stout woman behind it. Gerry gets three six-packs and goes to the counter. They are only talking about people they know, and a barbecue where there was a whole steer on a spit, and he will tell this to Camille.

But in the dark outside the store, crunching on oyster shells, he forgets: he sees her face in the light from the porch, and wants to kiss her. In the car he does, kisses they hold long while their hands move on each others' backs. Then he is driving again. Twice he is lost, once on a blacktop road in woods that are mostly the conical silhouettes and lovely smell of pine, then on a gravel road through a swamp whose feral odor makes him pull the map too quickly from her hands. He stops once for gas, at an all-night station on a highway. Sweat soaks through his shirt, and it sticks to the seat, and he is warm and damp where his leg and Camille's sweat together. By twilight they are silent. She lights their cigarettes and opens their cans of beer; as the sun rises he is driving on asphalt between woods, the dark of their leaves fading to green, and through the insect-splattered windshield he gazes with burning eyes at the entrance to his town.

This is a story of a boy's growing up, with the focus on his increasing awareness of racial inequality in a southern Louisiana city. Although the action spans approximately fifteen years and takes Gerry into college, the narration centers on the boy's reaction to specific events involving black people. As he watches, absorbs, and experiences, his responses progress gradually and logically through four stages: sensation (smells and sights repel and attract), physical (he gives the glove), emotional (he suffers vicariously), and finally a combination of emotional, physical, and mental (he tries to kill a young man and formulates his ideology).

Sensory impressions, which both repel and attract him, are particularly important in his formative years. At six, they are predominately visual: "unpainted wood and rusted screens of the houses, old cars in front of them and tire swings"; at twelve, olfactory: "he enters the smell as you enter a cloud of dust"—the "sour smell of garbage," then the smell of "hot grease, meat, turnip or mustard greens." He wants to enter a house and "trace and define that smell, press his nose to the beds and sofas, . . . the bosom of a woman. . . ."

His first contact with blacks comes on the white boys' baseball diamond when a black boy stops to watch the game. When one of the boys asks him if he wants to play, he is confused, but he walks slowly onto the field; Gerry gives him his position as first-baseman, as well as his glove. Afterwards Gerry feels "peace and pride" in his heart, "but having been told by the Christian Brothers at his school that an act of charity should not be talked about, he tries to forget it. The children's welcoming the black boy to their game signifies that racial prejudice is not inherent but instilled; Gerry's act of giving goes beyond mere acceptance of the boy; it foreshadows his subsequent acts and feelings.

While he is still in high school, a black man is electrocuted for raping a white woman. All during the trial, Gerry prays for his soul, and on the night of his death, he transforms him into a Christ figure crowned with thorns and carrying the Cross. Then he forces himself into a vicarious experience of feeling the electrocution.

In college during the racial strife of the sixties, he smiles at the blacks on the campus and expresses his feelings to his girl friend, but does not overtly protest racial injustice. Then during the trial of the men charged with murdering Emmett Till, a young black visiting in Mississippi, he hears a drunk in a bar loudly hurling racial slurs about Till. His remarks serve to open the floodgates of Gerry's pent-up feelings; his identification with blacks is so complete that except for an intervener, he would have killed the young man. The final scene suggests for him a new beginning and complete separation from the town and its ideology: "as the sun rises . . . he gazes with burning eyes at the entrance to his town."

The author's strategy is to trace the constituents of motivation and show how they converge to a point of fusion in the bar scene and to total alienation in the final scene.

MARTHA LACY HALL
(1923-)

Martha Lacy Hall was born in Magnolia, Mississippi, the daughter of William Monroe and Elizabeth Goza Lacy. Educated at Whitworth College for Women, Brookhaven, Mississippi, she married Sherril Hall, Jr. (now deceased) in 1941 and had three children. She worked for the Memphis *Press-Scimitar* before moving to Baton Rouge where she served as an editor at LSU Press from 1968 to 1979 and managing editor from 1979 to 1984. Currently fiction editor for the Press, she continues to live in Baton Rouge. Her stories have appeared in *The Southern Review, Virginia Quarterly*, and other literary journals. She is the author of three collections of short stories: *Call It Living, Music Lesson,* and *The Apple-Green Triumph and Other Stories.* The latter was chosen for the 1991 edition of *Prize Stories: the O. Henry Awards.* Hall's works are all Southern in flavor; her comic sensibility has been compared to that of Eudora Welty. The story printed here is the title story in her latest collection.

The Apple-Green Triumph*

Martha Lacy Hall

BEFORE OPENING the car door, Lucia took a deep breath of the Louisiana night air. She was not unaware of its heaviness, its moistness, the smells of Lake Pontchartrain—salt, seaweed, water creatures, all mixed with the sounds produced by the wind slapping water against the seawall, soughing in the tops of tall pines against a black sky.

She pressed hard on the starter in the old Triumph. It ground, coughed, and was silent. "Oh, my God," she said, and hit the steering wheel with her fist. If it wouldn't start, she would just have to have Everett paged at the New Orleans airport. Tell him to get on a Greyhound bus for Mississippi. He should have done that in the first place or flown into Jackson. "Start!" she growled and pressed again, and it did. She floored the accelerator, in neutral, and the engine roared underfoot, confident and, as always, a little arrogant for so small a tiger. The beam of the headlights crawled across the wall and the screened porch as she slowly backed out of the carport and turned toward the street.

"I'm out of my mind," she said aloud. "I'm just out of my ever-loving mind." She had begun talking to herself after Chris died two years ago. They had had such a good time talking that when he was no longer there she just kept on talking. "I am my own best company," she sometimes said, picking figs or surveying herself at the full-length mirror, ready to go out. She slowed and looked at her watch under the corner streetlight. Ten o'clock.

"Seventy-five-year-old fool heading to New Orleans at ten o'clock at night." She braked, shifted the gear, and rounded the corner, leaving Lakeshore Drive. "A damn fool." The lights beamed across the spray-painted command on the wall of the high school gym: LADY OF MERCY STOMP HOLY GHOST FRIDAY NIGHT!

Scarcely aware of thunder to the south, she drove slowly, peering intently through her glasses and the flat little windshield.

*"The Apple-Green Triumph" was first published in *The Apple-Green Triumph* by Martha Lacy Hall. Copyright © 1990 by Martha Lacy Hall. Reprinted by permission of Louisiana State University Press.

She had decided not to drive at night over a year ago, and she felt that her dear old car might be better able to make it across the twenty-six-mile causeway than she was. "Old cars can be overhauled." As this one had been recently. A big car rushed up to an intersection and slammed to a stop. Startled, she swore.

"Just tell me one thing good about being old, just one thing!" She simply hadn't felt this way as long as she had Chris. Any woman who claimed she didn't need a strong man didn't know what she was talking about. She drove on toward the causeway, through a tunnel of night-darkened oaks between the streetlights of Ste. Marie, Louisiana. "I just have to do it," she said, tears in her voice. Everett hadn't changed a bit. She hadn't seen him for nearly ten years and never expected him to fly down for Ann's services. And what did he do but call her at nine o'clock tonight out of the blue, from the New Orleans airport.

"Can you pick me up?" he said, like he was down at the Ste. Marie bus depot and it was twenty years ago.

"Do you know how old I am?" she wanted to scream at him.

"Brat. Sixty-year-old brat." He hadn't come for the other funerals—Dora's, Tom's, Margaret's. Not since their parents'. Well, Ann was his twin. Maybe there still was something special there, dormant, come to life at the incident of death. And some burst of confidence and energy had made her say, "I'll pick you up. Just sit tight." The call had given her an illusion of vigor, the big sister again, always there, ready. She had to do it.

When she thought of Ann she began to cry and had to pull over to the curb and hold her face in a handful of tissues. "I thought I was through crying," she sobbed. "Ann, Ann! I could kill you for leaving me high and dry like this." Then she began to laugh at what she'd said. Ann would have laughed. She took another tissue from the box on the dash and cleaned her glasses and blew her nose. As she drove back onto the wide highway, wind gusts swept overland from the lake, bringing the first raindrops.

"Don't rain! Don't rain!"

By the time she approached the causeway she was in a downpour, windshield wipers working fast and noisily. She pulled up to the toll booth and handed the man a dollar. Reflected lights blurred on the choppy water of Lake Pontchartrain. Red lights and white lights nearby, and far ahead a smoldering luminescence in the low, heavy clouds over New Orleans.

"Bad night to be headin' for Sin City," the man said.

"Mission of mercy," said Lucia, and moved forward, chin high.

Chris's apple-green Triumph was in fine shape for its age. Duffy Peek had just been all over it, spent three days like he and Chris used to do together. She loosened her tight grip on the steering wheel, arthritis grinding out its pain in knobby knuckles, hurting like the devil. For that matter it hurt in her shoulders, neck, back. "Just a dilapidated old bag of bones."

But she could quickly call up one of those lovely healing memories of Chris's voice: "Cut that out, you beautiful babe. You're in great shape, and you look like a million dollars," and she saw that wide smile, white teeth, tanned face. Fine old face. The car seemed more cozy and safe while rain pounded the canvas top, windshield, and danced on the hood.

Then Ann pushed back into Lucia's thoughts. Ann and Everett had been her real-live dolls. She was fifteen when they were born, she was the eldest of six, the tallest, the child-lovingest, the chauffeur, Mother pro tem, Daddy called her. She adored the twins and simply took them over, rocked two cribs at once, changed diapers, warmed bottle's—old-fashioned bottles with rubber nipples that Everett learned to pull off in his crib. Lucia carried them around, baby legs straddling both her hips. She dressed them in their little matching clothes for Myrt to roll them down to the Methodist Church corner in their double stroller, where all the nurses gathered in the afternoons with their charges, little white children fresh from their bathtubs. Ann became her love, and they had remained close for the rest of Ann's life.

"I never could believe she grew up. How did she get to be sixty years old? She barely made that. Why did she have to die before me? Emphysema, like the others. And Daddy. Ann didn't even smoke." Lucia had spent the last months going back and forth between Ste. Marie and Sweet Bay, sitting with Ann at home or in the hospital, at whichever place Ann lay propped up, crowding words between breaths, oxygen tank nearby, plastic tubes in her nostrils. They reviewed their whole lives. "And I made you my executor!" Lucia said, accusingly, and they laughed like fools, as they always had, no matter how bad off Ann was. No matter how hard it was for Lucia. Almost to the end. They weren't together when she died in her sleep.

"I can't believe things are ending this way. I've buried all of them. All but Everett. God knows he'd better outlive me. I'm sick of sitting on the edges of graves in that plot." She would talk to Everett about that, about his place now. Thank God for him. A good dependable younger family member. "Perhaps he will come back home with me for a few days, and we can relax, visit, talk about the future. The wind and rain came on hard from the lake, almost blindingly. She couldn't possibly drive the minimum speed. Traffic was blessedly light.

An enormous white semi was overtaking the green Triumph, fast. "Slow down, idiot." How could he see to drive that fast? The white hulk rumbled past, rocking the small car fearsomely.

She remembered the day Chris drove it into her driveway, a tiny motor-roaring thing, the top down, unfolded his long legs, and rose from the brown leather seat. "Are you Mrs. Collins?" he asked, and his smile was as arresting as his apple-green car.

"I am," said Lucia, removing her gardening gloves and dropping the bamboo rake on the leaf pile. She took hasty note of his appearance, thatch of white hair, rumpled by the wind, plaid well-tailored shirt, good suitably faded jeans, and white deck shoes. He had a newspaper under his arm. He was the boater who had called in answer to her ad.

"My name is Neilson, Chris Neilson. I called about your ad. Let's see, you have a lantern, Coleman stove, rope, fishing tackle. Got an anchor?"

"That and more." She smiled politely.

"May, I see them?"

"Certainly. They're right back here in the storeroom. I'll, get the key." She fetched the key off the kitchen hook, and Chris Neilson followed her to the dark green door off the carport. She switched on the light. "I have a 50-horsepower motor, some seats, life preservers, quite a few things. Go in and look them over."

He stayed in the storeroom a while. She could tell what he was examining by the familiar sounds of wood, metal, canvas. When he stepped out he smiled again and said, "You all lost interest in boating?"

"My husband died several years ago, and I'm just now getting rid of some of his things."

"I know how that is. Been through it. I'm going to try living on my boat."

"I see. Well, do you see anything you need in there?"

"I surely do. Are those two new deck chairs for sale? I could use them. And the lantern I could use. How about the radio?"

"Any of it or all of it." She reached in her shirt pocket and handed him a typewritten list with prices.

"Good," he said. "Tell you what. I live in New Orleans, but I'll be back in a pickup this afternoon late if that's okay."

"That's fine. I'll be here."

He smiled again and slid into the car.

"You have a—an interesting car. I don't believe I ever saw a sportscar that color."

"Probably not. I had this one painted. Gaudy, isn't it?"

"It's bright . . . spring-like," she laughed like he wasn't a stranger. She was the stranger.

After he left she picked up her rake and poked it around in the leaves. What an interesting man. She hadn't noticed an "interesting man" since Henry died. She embarrassed herself.

Lucia realized she was handling the car well despite everything. She felt a ripple of pride in her spine. The Triumph was so small, not even comfortable, really, but she couldn't part with the crazy little thing. First she had sold Chris's pickup, then finally her sedan. Sentiment. What made men love their cars so? She had loved the man, and the car was the most tangible thing she had left of him. "Oh, Chris." She was married to Chris for eight years—a fling and a lark for an old couple. Old in birthdays. She couldn't remember either of them being sick for a day together. "It was more than a fling and a lark."

"You look like a smart woman. What do you do?" he said later when he dropped by with no excuse.

Confronted with such a question, she blurted, "I work like a dog in this house and yard. I make fig and mayhaw preserves and green-tomato pickles. I read a couple of books a week. I 'do' book reviews." She stopped, aghast at her ready biography to a stranger. That was the beginning. He was interested.

Lucia loosened her hurting hands. "What we did was laugh and talk." And live a little. A lot. Like she had not thought possible. For eight years. Sometimes she still found it hard to believe that they had had the good fortune to find each other. "Right there in your own backyard," he would say and put his arms around her.

One night eating their own catch on the deck of his boat, rocking ever so gently on the Tchefuncte River, he said, "Marry me and come live on my boat."

"Marry you! You want to get legally hitched to a sixty-five-year-old crone?" It was as good as "Yes."

"I want your money."

"My dowry consists of my medicare."

"I'll accept that." More seriously, "So, we're sixty-five years old. Let's see how much fun we can have."

So they were married. By a New Orleans judge they both knew. They lived in her house on the lake, but she became a boat person, too. It was an unruffled transition, becoming a married woman again. Chris was an affectionate man. To her naïve surprise, he was a tender and passionate lover, and to her greater surprise, her pleasure with him was more intense than she had ever known. "You're some woman," Chris would say. And "Back from the dead!" That was lagniappe.

They drove to New Orleans for Saints games at the Superdome and for shows at the Saenger. They dined with friends at home, in the city, and in restaurants around the lake. They cooked on the grill, and they played gin and sipped wine in the evening.

Occasionally Chris would have an extra evening drink or two, on the boat anchored a mile or so from the north shore. He would tell her ribald stories and sing noisily from an endless repertoire of war songs, using his glass for a baton.

Creeping along in the night through wind and rain over Lake Pontchartrain, Lucia shook her head remembering Chris singing one night, "Bless em all! Bless em all! The long, and the short and the tall! There'll be no promotions this side of the ocean. So cheer up, my lads, Fuckem all!"

"Hush up, Chris! Your voice carries across this water like you have a microphone." She was interrupted by a baritone from a winking light a quarter mile farther out. "Fuckem all! Fuckem all!

The long and the short . . ." And then they could all hear the laughter bounce over the light chop and under the sparkling stars in a blue-black sky.

Lucia pulled into a turnaround area and stopped the car. She rested her head on the steering wheel. "It won't be long, now. I'm doing fine. But thank the Lord Everett can take the wheel for the two hours to Mississippi." Their aged cousins, sisters, both in their late eighties, were putting them up. "What a treat! What a treat!" Cousin May had chirped over the phone, "Having you children with us again." Then she caught herself. "Oh my dear, I'm forgetting myself. We are all in grief for dear little Ann. She was like a sister to me." And Lucia knew Cousin May was getting Ann mixed up with their mother Ann.

Lucia lifted her head. The last day of his life Chris had said to her, "You're a youthful handsome woman, Lucia. I love that thick white hair and those gorgeous legs."

"You're crazy," Lucia had said, pinching his bottom as he walked past her toward the stern. A few moments later he had a heart attack and without a word fell overboard. She went down after him with life preservers, but he was dead, his white hair washing back and forth like anemones between his fishing line and the stern.

She put the Triumph in drive and moved out behind a state trooper. "Halleluja, I've got me an escort!" But the white car wove away at high speed and was lost to her. "Well. I'm on my own again." The rain had slowed to a drizzle when she turned toward the airport. The speeding cars and trucks in the six-lane interstate unnerved her, and she addressed her maker reverently each time she moved farther left, lane by lane. "Christ," she murmured when she spied the metal sign New Orleans International Airport that directed traffic to a new overpass she didn't know about. Her heart in her mouth, she managed to move back to the far-right lane. And the Triumph roared up the ramp and back over the traffic she had just left. Not daring to feel giddy, she found herself traveling parallel to jet runways. Strobe lights marked the airport drive.

"That keeps those huge things from thinking this is another runway." Then she saw the sign telling her how to get short-term parking directions, and she was able to park on the first level. "I made it on instruments," she gasped, as she took the keys from the car. She was extremely stiff and in pain when she stood beside her car. "I'm too old for this." Two teen-aged boys looked backward at the old car, its classic body glittering in a coat of raindrops under the endless rows of fluorescent tubes. They grinned but looked concerned as they saw her effort to straighten her back and walk toward the elevator.

"I've never been in here unescorted."

"I beg your pardon?" said a young woman.

"Nothing. Nothing. Just talking to myself. Do it all the time." She wanted to get to a rest room.

Inside she began walking and scanning the crowd, looking for her tall younger brother. She was surrounded by a shifting sea of people speaking Spanish, French, Indian, and no telling what else, all under the nasal drone of the PA speaker. Her eyes, tired, swept over young, old, babies, nuns, sailors, people in wheelchairs, obese men and women waddling to and from the concourses. One very fat gray-haired man was bearing down on her, looking into her eyes, smiling. The smile caught her eye. Only that—that crooked half-smile.

"Everett?"

"What's the matter, Lucia? Don't you know me?" He was carrying a dark blue suit bag.

"Everett! I didn't." She closed her mouth with effort. "Everett," she said again.

He leaned forward and laid his cheek against hers briefly. "I reckon I have put on a little weight since you saw me last."

"Yes. Yes. I'm glad to see you, Everett. It's good you could come."

"I hate to put you out. Hope you didn't have any trouble. Was the weather good? I've been in here so long, I don't know what it's doing outside."

"The weather? Oh yes, well, it rained a little. Nothing uh . . . let's go in here and order a cup of coffee or a Coke, maybe. I need to find a rest room. Are you hungry?"

"No. I just had a couple of hamburgers and a malt. I'm ready to roll. Ready to hit that interstate. Get on up to Cousin May and them's for some shuteye. I've been here over three hours."

"Well, I need something." And Lucia steered them into a coffeeshop. She went ahead and ordered coffee and a ham sandwich before going to a rest room.

"Oh, I guess I'll have one, too," said Everett. "And an order of fries. Traveling makes me hungry." Bulk made sitting difficult for him. "Have to fly first class. More room to spread out, you know."

"Excuse me, Everett," she murmured. "I'll be right back." She got up painfully.

"Why you're all crippled up!" He seemed surprised.

Lucia pressed her lips together and walked to the rest room. inside a booth she sat down and began to laugh and cry. "This is hysterics. What am I going to do? I'm too tired to drive on. My God, he won't fit into the car."

"Is anything wrong?" came a voice from the next booth. "Do you need help?"

"No. Oh, no. Thank you. I just talk to myself. Sometimes what I say is funny, so I laugh. . . ."

Silence.

The floodgates of Lucia's bladder opened, and for a moment she reveled in the greatest relief she had felt in days. She didn't say anything more aloud, but as she went out she patted her white bangs at the mirror and took a quick and satisfying look at her figure.

Everett was waiting for her. "I hate to see you so crippled up."

"Everett, what do you weigh, honey?"

"Three-twenty-five, right now." Then he gave one of his famous ha-ha-has. "Haven't you ever seen a fat man, Lucia?"

"It's just that I've never seen a 325-pound man in this family. You know, we all have tended to be slim. Slender." She wished she hadn't asked his weight.

"Well, you've seen one now," he said, steadying himself with the chair beside him. "These sure are little bitty old chairs."

Lucia laughed. They ate their sandwiches. "We may have a problem, Everett," she said, blotting the corners of her mouth with the stiff paper napkin.

"What's that?"

"Well, I drive a very small car. I'm just not perfectly sure you can get comfortable, completely comfortable . . . I was counting on you to drive us home . . ." She wanted to cry.

"You haven't gone and bought one of those little bitty old Jap cars have you?"

"No. No. Actually it's English. Belonged to my husband . . . it's small . . ." Her voice trailed off.

"Oh-oh." Everett's voice boomed, "I drive a Cadillac. Have to have a heavy car. Just kills my legs and back to ride in one of . . ."

"I really was counting on your driving. I'm not crazy about driving at night."

"Looks like you made it over here all right."

"Yes. Well, it wasn't easy."

"If I'd felt like driving, I'd have driven myself down in my Cadillac, We'll do okay. You got a pillow in it so I can stretch out?"

Chris's voice loomed in her ear. "Lucia, honey, you're being a fool. Tell that sonofabitch to get a taxi to a hotel."

Everett's face blanched when he saw the apple-green Triumph. "Lucia! Why in hell is an old lady like you driving this thing?"

Lucia was indignant. "Look, Everett, try to squeeze in. If you can't get in, we'll have to get you a room across the Airline at the Hilton. This happens to be the only car I have."

He put his bag in the small trunk, muttering, "Ruining my good clothes," and stuffed himself into the little bucket seat. "Goddamn, Lucia. You'll have to bury me too when we get home. I still say 'home' even though the house is gone. And everybody is gone. Everybody but us. I can't believe Ann is gone. I kept thinking I'd come down to see her. We were close. A long time ago. Did she suffer much?"

"She suffered plenty. But she died peacefully."

"I'm glad to hear she went out easy." Then Everett began to wheeze. "I've got it too. We got it from Daddy. I quit smoking two years ago. Don't drink a drop," he added.

Lucia turned toward Baton Rouge.

"Here now. We're not going to Baton Rouge, are we?"

"Of course not. We turn north on I-55." Lucia hurt all over. She was getting a headache, and her eyes were too tired to cry. "Lord give me strength. What a fool I am."

"How's that?" Everett shouted over the engine.

She shook her head.

Everett tried to shift his bulk, but it was like trying to move a grapefruit in a demitasse spoon. "My circulation is going. In my legs," he hollered. He didn't have to shout.

"Mercy, Everett. Let me get out of this heavy traffic, and I'll stop every little while and let you get out and walk a bit."

But he grunted negatively, and she knew it was because it wasn't worth it to him trying to get out and back in. She turned north off the spillway interstate and drove in silence all the way to Lake Maurepas. "Let's stop at Heidenreidt's and get another cup of coffee. You can walk around."

"Okay, Lucia."

She parked the car near the door of the seafood restaurant which had been there as long as she could remember. "Make you nostalgic?"

"Yeah," said Everett, managing to extricate himself from the passenger seat. Lucia felt a terrible sadness over this baby brother she had once carried about like a ragdoll, who came home tall and thin and hurt from the long battle for the hills of South Korea and began his own battles in civilian life. A succession of jobs, two failed marriages, the loss of a young child. Poor boy.

In the old restaurant on the shore of Maurepas, Everett sat on a stool and ordered a dozen raw oysters. "Don't you want some, Lucia? My treat."

"No thank you, Everett."

"Remember how Daddy used to stop here on his way home from New Orleans and pick up a gallon of oysters? He and Mama would get in the kitchen and meal 'em up and season 'em and fry 'em in that big black iron skillet? Drain 'em on brown paper? Remember that big old white platter of Mama's? Heaped up, hot and crisp. Whooee!" He began dipping crackers in catsup and horseradish while an old black man shucked the oysters. "Y'all got any boiled crawfish" he asked the sleepy waitress.

"Yeah. Want some?"

"Everett," said Lucia, "I'm afraid you'll be sick. And we need to be on our way pretty soon."

"Okay. Lord Jesus, I hate to think of stuffing myself back into that little bitty old car. How come you're driving that thing, hon,' Now tell me the truth. You having a hard time, Lucia?"

"I've got some problems, Everett, but they don't have anything to do with my car or money. It was my husband's car, and I chose to keep it. Ordinarily, I just use a car to go to the post office and the A & P."

"Well, you made a mistake. You ought to get yourself a good heavy sedan." ·

"I'm sorry you're uncomfortable."

"I'm not complaining. I just hate to see you in such reduced circumstances."

"My circumstances are not reduced."

Everett dispatched a baker's dozen large raw oysters, lifting each, dipped red in the catsup mixture, to his mouth, and uttering a sound of appreciation of the taste.

They drove a long time on I-55 without talking. As they passed the Tangipahoa exit he said, "Was Ann right with her maker?"

"I beg your pardon?"

"Was she saved? Was she born again?"

"What in the hell are you talking about, Everett?"

"Don't blaspheme. She never was religious, Lucia. I wasn't either. Way back there. I'm just asking if you think my sister got right with the Lord."

Lucia was livid. "Yes," she said calmly, "I'm sure she and the Lord were on good terms."

"Well, I'm glad to hear it. After my last divorce I turned myself over completely to Jesus Christ, and I faithfully support Him."

"What church are you a member of? I know your last wife was Catholic."

"Don't belong to any. That is churchhouse. I support the Lord's work through several television ministries. They're saving souls like all getout all over the world. Did you ever think about how many souls are in hell, went there before the television came along and took the gospel to the farthest corner of the planet? Some people are going to rot in hell for persecuting these dedicated servants of the Lord who pack food to all those starving little boogers in Africa and all."

Lucia took her eyes off the highway for a split second to look at her brother. "You wouldn't possibly be including Louisiana's own, would you?"

"Most particularly. The Lord has simply put that poor fellow through a baptism of fire with Satan. The man's coming back. Just listen to him on the TV."

"I ran across him one time looking for a Saints game." They crossed the state line. "You're back in Mississippi, Everett."

Lucia tried to help her backache by pressing harder against the back of her seat. Since they had turned onto I-55 they had both been aware consciously or unconsciously that they were back in the world they knew best, the marshland above New Orleans, that edge of Louisiana that slid toward the state line, into the slow gentle sweep of low hills that meant Mississippi. Oh, it was different. A few miles made all the difference in the world.

"Yeah," he said. "I do appreciate your holding Ann's body till I could get here for the funeral."

"Body? I don't think you understand, Everett."

"Don't understand what?"

"This is to be a memorial service at the church. Ann's remains were cremated."

"Cremated! Cremated! Who is responsible for that?"

Rain was falling again. Lucia turned on the wipers. "It was Ann's wish."

"So! She wasn't saved! Of all the unholy, pagan things to do to my sister. You mean she's already . . . already burnt up?"

"Her remains are ashes."

"Well, I'll be goddamned."

"Now, who's blaspheming?"

"Why have I gone to all this trouble and expense and discomfort coming all the way down here from West Virginia? Huh? Tell me that?"'

There just wasn't room in the little car for him to blow up. "I assumed you wanted to attend your twin sister's memorial service. We'll have an interment of the ashes in the plot. What's the difference?"

"Difference! I thought I was going to get to see her. See how she looked."

"I'm sorry you feel . . . cheated." Lucia's head was splitting. Her eyes were cloudy, and she cursed herself for where she was and wept inside for her baby sister and for Everett, who in no way resembled the boy or the man she remembered. She still had miles to travel. It must be nearly two o'clock. "What's a seventy-five-year-old fool doing on a highway this time of night? Morning."

"How's that?"

"Nothing, Everett. Just talking to myself."

"How long you been doing that?"

"Doing what?"

"Talking to yourself."

"A good while now. It was a deliberate decision. To talk to myself, I mean."

"For crying out loud. Are you bonkers?"

When Lucia saw Aunt May's porch light she moaned softly with relief.

"Listen, Lucia. I appreciate what you did—driving to New Orleans to get me. But I'll get a ride to Jackson and get a plane out of there to Charleston. Tomorrow afternoon, I guess. Late. Whenever this is all over—whatever it is we're having. Whatever you're having. Hell, I don't care. I mean . . ."

Lucia opened her door. The dome light cast a weak glow in the small space of the car. Her fingers held the cool metal of the handle as she searched Everett's profile, softened by age and shadow. Her only family, now. And she his. She smiled and laid her hand on his arm. "I understand. I know you'll be more comfortable in a big car. Wish I'd had a Cadillac just for tonight. Because I love you, Everett. I mean that."

"I know."

They walked through the fragrant, dewy grass toward Aunt May's porch.

In Aunt May's guest room, Lucia lay in the big four-poster she had first slept in and fallen out of before she could walk. Now, three quarters of a century later she did her deep-breathing exercise to relax. Deep, deep till her lower ribs bowed upward. The old house was quiet in the predawn darkness. Listening, remembering, as old houses do. Lucia let out a long breath. Such profound silence seemed to hold out a mystical beckoning. It wasn't the first time she had quite calmly thought she might die in her sleep. She inhaled.

The night after Chris died she had gone to bed in a friend's guest room, believing the enormous weight of sorrow would stop her heart as she slept. She had carefully arranged her arms on the covers so she would not be in disarray when they found her in the morning. But she had waked up in daylight, grateful to be alive and able to meet the day.

She exhaled and whispered to the dark room, "No. Twenty-four hours from now I'll be sound asleep in my own bed." The mattress pressed up against her as her body grew heavier, ever heavier, then moved weightlessly into the warm engulfing arms of sleep.

THE APPLE-GREEN TRIUMPH

A seventy-five-year-old arthritic woman driving a flashy green sportscar through a coastal storm at night to meet and cram into her car a three-hundred-twenty-five-pound brother and chauffeur him to a funeral in Mississippi provides the narrative line of this story. The skillfully modulated tension between the serious and the comic makes the tone of the story noteworthy.

Lucia, who talks to herself because she is her "own best company" explains her sudden laughter to a puzzled stranger: "I just talk to myself. Sometimes what I say is funny, so I laugh." Old age is serious business—death of loved ones, loneliness, aching arthritic joints—but Lucia's ability to see the comic aspects of life and particularly to laugh at her own actions provides the humor in her twenty-six-mile trip to the New Orleans airport and then on to Mississippi for her sister's funeral. "Seventy-five-year-old fool heading to New Orleans at ten o'clock at night," she mutters as she grinds and regrinds the starter of the aging Triumph, which she sees as a parallel to herself, "an old bag of bones." But "old cars can be fixed," she adds. Fitting Everett into the car is like "trying to move a grapefruit in a demitasse spoon." Her sense of the ridiculous is counterpointed by her brother's density, thoughtlessness, and seriousness; and the tone becomes satirical when he turns the conversation to religion: "Did you ever think about how many souls are in hell, went there before the television came along and took the gospel to the farthest corner of the planet?" As he praises "Louisiana's own," (evangelist), she offers wryly that she had run into him once "looking for a Saints game."

Another striking aspect of story is its diction. Lucia and Everett occasionally lapse into an idiom typical of rural Louisiana speech. She "work[s] like a dog . . . making fig and mayhaw preserves and green-tomato pickles." He voices his concern for "starving little boogers in Africa and all" as they drive toward "Cousin May and them's for some shuteye." Also notable are sensory details: Louisiana night air—"its heaviness, its moistness, the smells of Lake Ponchartrain—salt, seaweed, water creatures, all mixed with the sounds [of] wind slapping water against the seawall, soughing in the tops of tall pines against a black sky." These details produce a sense of place, and details of Lucia's confrontation with the storm produce a sense of conflict: "rain lashing the windshield" and "wind gusts sweeping overland from the lake." "I made it on instruments," she gasps as she parks the little car, aptly named Triumph.

There is a double journey in the story—Lucia's literal one to the airport and funeral, characterized by almost-zero visibility on the Lake Ponchartrain causeway, and the metaphorical trip, evoked by the use of her late husband's car and the death of her sister. Memory moves back and forth as "she calls up lovely healing memories of [her late husband's] voice"; then remembering herself at fifteen loving and taking care of the twins, Ann and Everett, she "weeps inside," feeling "a terrible sadness for this [obese] baby brother she had carried about like a ragdoll." This is a story of family relationships as death comes calling, but even death cannot obscure Lucia's comic vision of life.

SHORT FICTION FOR FURTHER READING

Augustin, George. *Romances of New Orleans*. New Orleans: L. Graham and Son, 1891.

Bartlett, Napier. *Stories of the Crescent City*. New Orleans: Steel and Co. 1869.

Beach, Rex Ellingwood. *Crimson Gardenia and Other Tales of Adventure*. New York: Burt, 1916.

Benefield, John Barry. *Short Turns*. New York: Century, 1926.

Bontemps, Arna. *Lonesome Boy*. Boston: Houghton Mifflin, 1955.

———. *Old South: A Summer Tragedy and Other Stories*. Dodd Meade, 1973.

Bradford, Roark. *Let the Band Play Dixie and Other Stories*. New York: Harper, 1934.

———. *Old Man Adam and His Chillun*. New York: Harper, 1928.

Cable, George Washington. *Madam Delphine*. New York: Scribner, 1896.

———. *Old Creole Days*. New York: Scribner, 1907.

———. *Strong Hearts*. New York: Scribner, 1889.

Capote, Truman. *Breakfast at Tiffany's and Other Stories*. New York: New American Library, 1958.

Carver, Ada Jack. *The Collected Works of Ada Jack Carver*. Ed. Mary Dell Fletcher. Natchitoches: Northwestern State University Press, 1979.

Cherry, Kelly. *Conversion*. New Paltz, N. Y.: Treacle Press, 1979.

Coquille, Walter. *Mayor of Bayou Pom Pom*. New Orleans: American Printing Co. 1929.

Corrington, John William. *The Collected Stories.* Columbia, Mo.: University of Missouri Press, 1989.

Crone, Moira. *The Winnebago Mysteries and Other Stories.* New York: Fiction Collective, 1982.

Davis, Mary Evelyn [Mollie Moore Davis]. *An Elephant's Track and Other Stories.* New York: Harper, 1897.

Dubus, André. *Adultery and Other Choices.* Boston: Godine, 1977.

——. *Finding a Girl in America.* Boston: Godine, 1980.

——. *Separate Flights.* Boston: Godine, 1975.

——. *The Times Are Never So Bad.* Boston: Godine, 1983.

Egan, Lavinia Hartwell. *A Bundle of Faggots: Short Stories of Louisiana and the South.* Franklin, La.: 1895.

Falls, Rose C. *Cheniere Caminade, or The Wind of Death.* New Orleans: Hopkins: 1893.

Gilchrist, Ellen. *Blue-Eyed Buddhist and Other Stories.* London: Faber, 1990.

——. *Drunk with Love.* Boston: Little Brown, 1986.

——. *In the Land of Dreamy Dreams.* Fayetteville: University of Arkansas Press, 1981.

——. *Light Can Be Both Wave and Particle.* Boston: Little Brown, 1989.

——. *Victory over Japan.* Boston: Little Brown, 1984.

Gaines, Ernest. *Bloodline.* New York: W. W. Norton, 1976.

——. *A Long Day in November.* New York: Dial, 1971.

Godchaux, Elma. "Wild Nigger," *The Best Short Stories of 1935.* Ed. Edward J. O'Brien. Boston: Houghton Mifflin, 1936.

————. "Chains," *O. Henry Memorial Prize Stories of 1936.* Ed. Harry Hanson. New York: Doubleday Doran, 1937.

Grau, Shirley. *The Black Prince and Other Stories.* New York: Knopf, 1958.

————. *The Wind Shifting West.* New York: Knopf, 1973.

Grosvenor, Johnston. *Strange Stories of the Great River.* New York: Harper, 1918.

Hall, Martha Lacy. *The Apple-Green Triumph and Other Stories.* Baton Rouge: Louisiana State University Press, 1990.

————. *Call It Living:* Three Stories. Athens, Ga.: Press of the Nightowl, 1981.

————. *Music Lesson.* Urbana: University of Illinois Press, 1984.

Haxton, Josephine Ayres [Ellen Douglas]. *Black Cloud, White Cloud.* Boston: Houghton Mifflin, 1963.

Harrison, Edith Ogden. *Gray Moss.* Chicago: Seymour, 1929.

Hay, Corrine. *Light and Shade 'round Gulf and Bayou.* Boston: Roxburgh, 1921.

Hearn, Lafcadio. *Chita, A Memory of Last Island.* New York: Harper, 1889.

Jackson, Charles Tenney. *Captain Sazarac.* Indianapolis, Bobbs, 1902.

————. *John, the Fool, An American Romance.* Indianapolis, Bobbs, 1915.

Jamison, Cecelia Viets Dakin. *Ropes of Sand.* Boston: J. R. Osgood, 1873.

Janvier, Margaret Thompson [Margaret Vandergrift]. *Little Belle and Other Stories.* Philadelphia: Henry T. Coats, n. d.

Jefferson, Sonia Wilmetta Johnson. *Short Stories.* Baton Rouge: Franklin Press, 1978.

King, Grace. *Balcony Stories.* New York: Macmillan, 1925.

——. *Tales of a Time and Place.* New York: Harper, 1892.

Lea, Fannie Heaslop. *Jaconette Stories.* New York: Sturgis and Walton, 1912

Lee, Addie McGrath. *Playing 'possum and Other Pine Woods Stories.* Baton Rouge: Truth and Job Office, 1895.

Louisiana in the Short Story, ed. Lizzie Carter McVoy. Baton Rouge: Louisiana State University Press, 1940.

Louisiana Stories, ed. Ben Forkner. Gretna, La.: Pelican, 1990.

Madden. David. *The New Orleans of Possibilities* [and Other Stories]. Baton Rouge: Louisiana State University Press, 1982.

——. *The Shadow Knows.* Louisiana State University Press, 1970.

Morgan, Berry. *The Mystic Adventures of Roxy Stoner.* Boston: Houghton Mifflin, 1974.

Nelson, Alice Ruth [Moore] Dunbar. *Goodness of St. Rocque and Other Stories.* New York: Dodd Meade, 1899.

——. *Violets and Other Tales.* Boston: Monthly Review Press, 1895.

New Orleans Stories, ed. John Miller and Genevieve Anderson, ed. San Francisco: Chronicle Books, 1991.

Peddie, Jon. *Crayfish Women and Other Stories.* New Orleans: Wetzel, Inc., 1930.

Porter, Katherine Anne. "Old Mortality," *The Old Order.* New York: Harcourt Brace, 1939.

Something in Common, ed. Anne Brewster Dobie. Baton Rouge: Louisiana State University Press, 1991.

Sparling, Edward Earl. *Under the Levee.* New York: Scribner, 1925.

Stockton, Francis Richard. *Afield and Afloat.* New York: Scribner, 1900.

Stories of the South. Addison Hibbard, ed. New York: Norton, 1931.

Stuart, Ruth McEnery. *Aunt Amity's Silver Wedding.* New York: Century, 1909.

———. *A Golden Wedding and Other Tales.* New York: Harper, 1899; rpt. New York: Garret Press, 1969.

———. *The Haunted Photograph and Other Stories.* New York: Century, 1911.

———. *Holly and Pizen and Other Stories.* New York: Century, 1899.

———. *In Simpkinville.* New York: Harper, 1897; rpt. Freeport, N. Y.: Books for Libraries.

———. *Moriah's Mourning and Other Half-Hour Sketches.* New York: Harper, 1898.

———. The Second Wooing of Salina Sue and Other Stories. New York: Harper, 1905.

———. *Solomon Crowe's Christmas Pocket and Other Tales.* New York: Harper, 1897; rpt. New York: Books for Libraries, 1969.

Welty, Eudora. "No Place for You, My Love," *The Bride of the Innisfallen.* New York: Harcourt Brace Jovanovich, 1955.

Williamson, Roland. *The Star Well and Other Stories.* New York: Knickerbocker, 1916.

Young, Stark. *Feliciana.* New York: Scribner, 1935.